ALSO BY PETER V. BRETT

The Warded Man
The Great Bazaar

THE
DESERT
SPEAR

Ballantine Books DEL REY New York

THE
DESERT
SPEAR

PETER V. BRETT

Copyright © 2010 by Peter V. Brett

Published in the United States by Del Rey, an imprint of The Random House Publishing Group, a division of Random House, Inc., New York.

DEL REY is a registered trademark and the Del Rey colophon is a trademark of Random House, Inc.

Published in the United Kingdom by HarperVoyager, an imprint of HarperCollins Publishers, London.

Library of Congress Cataloging-in-Publication Data

Brett, Peter V.
The desert spear / Peter V. Brett.
p. cm.
ISBN 978-0-345-50381-7
1. Demonology—Fiction. I. Title.
PS3602.R4583D47 2010
813'.6—dc22   2010001645

Printed in the United States of America on acid-free paper

www.delreybooks.com

2 4 6 8 9 7 5 3 1

First U.S. Edition

Book design by Liz Cosgrove

For Dani and Cassie

ACKNOWLEDGMENTS

The Desert Spear is by far the longest and most challenging work I've ever attempted. Weaving eight active POV characters into a cohesive story stretched my feeble mind quite thin, and I could not have managed it without the support of my friends and family and, most of all, my test readers, who took the time to read the book in its early stages and offer the criticism and advice that helped evolve it into the story you hold in your hands. Thank you to: Myke, Matt, Dani, Stacy, Amelia, Jay, Mom, Denise, Cobie, Jon, Nancy, Sue, my agent Joshua, my editors Anne & Emma, my copy editor Laura, my international publishers & translators, and all the fans of the first book who took the time to write to me and give me encouragement as I struggled to make *The Desert Spear* my best work even as the rest of my life was turning upside down with a new baby and career. Thank you, all. You mean the world to me.

CONTENTS

PROLOGUE

MIND DEMONS

:: 333 AR WINTER ::

IT WAS THE NIGHT before new moon, during the darkest hours when even that bare sliver had set. In a small patch of true darkness beneath the thick boughs of a cluster of trees, an evil essence seeped up from the Core.

The dark mist coalesced slowly into a pair of giant demons, their rough brown skin knobbed and gnarled like tree bark. Standing nine feet at the shoulder, their hooked claws dug at the frozen scrub and pine of the forest floor as they sniffed at the air. A low rumble sounded in their throats as black eyes scanned their surroundings.

Satisfied, they moved apart and squatted on their haunches, coiled and ready to spring. Behind them, the patch of true darkness deepened, corruption blackening the forest bed as another pair of ethereal shapes materialized.

These were slender, barely five feet tall, with soft charcoal flesh quite unlike the gnarled armor of their larger brethren. On the ends of delicate fingers and toes, their claws seemed fragile—thin and straight like a woman's manicured nail. Their sharp teeth were short, only a single row set in a snoutless mouth.

Their heads were bloated, with huge, lidless eyes and high, conical craniums. The flesh over their skulls was knobbed and textured, pulsing around the vestigial nubs of horns.

For long moments, the two newcomers stared at each other, foreheads throbbing, as a vibration passed in the air between them.

One of the larger demons caught movement in the brush and reached out with frightening quickness to snatch a rat from its cover. The coreling brought the rodent up close, studying it curiously. As it did, the demon's snout became ratlike, nose and whiskers twitching as it grew a pair of long incisors. The coreling's tongue slithered out to test their sharpness.

One of the slender demons turned to regard it, forehead pulsing. With a flick of its claw, the mimic demon eviscerated the rat and cast it aside. At the command of the coreling princes, the two mimics changed shape, becoming enormous wind demons.

The mind demons hissed as they left the patch of true darkness and starlight struck them. Their breath fogged with the cold, but they gave no sign of discomfort, leaving clawed footprints in the snow. The mimics bent low, and the coreling princes walked up their wings to take perch on their backs as they leapt into the sky.

They passed over many drones as they winged north. Big and small, these all cowered until the coreling princes passed, only to follow the call left vibrating in their wake.

The mimics landed on a high rise, and the mind demons slid down to the ground, taking in the sight below. A vast army spread out on the plain, white tents dotting the land where the snow had been trampled to mud and frozen solid. Great humped beasts of burden stood hobbled in circles of power, covered in blankets against the cold. The wards around the camp were strong, and sentries, their faces wrapped in black cloth, patrolled its perimeter. Even from this distance, the mind demons could sense the power of their warded weapons.

Beyond the camp's wards, the bodies of dozens of drones littered the field, waiting for the day star to burn them away.

Flame drones were the first to reach the rise where the princes waited. Keeping a respectful distance, they began to dance in worship, shrieking their devotion.

Another throb, and the drones quieted. The night grew deathly silent even as a great demon host gathered, drawn to the call of the coreling princes. Wood and flame drones stood side by side, their racial hatred forgotten, as wind drones circled in the sky above.

Ignoring the congregation, the mind demons kept their eyes on the plain below, their craniums pulsing. After a moment, one glanced to its mimic, imparting its desires, and the creature's flesh melted and swelled, taking the form of a massive rock demon. Silently, the gathered drones followed it down the hill.

On the rise, the two princes and the remaining mimic waited. And watched.

When they were close to the camp, still under the cover of darkness, the mimic slowed and waved the flame drones ahead.

The smallest and weakest of corelings, flame drones glowed about the eyes and mouth from the fires within them. The sentries spotted them immediately but the drones were quick, and before the sentries could raise an alarm they were upon the wards, spitting fire.

The firespit fizzled where it struck the wards, but at the mind demons' bidding, the drones focused instead on the piled snow outside the perimeter, their breath instantly turning it to scalding steam. Safe behind the wards, the sentries were unharmed, but a hot, thick fog arose, stinging their eyes and tainting the air even through their veils.

One of the sentries ran off through the camp, ringing a loud bell. As he did, the others darted fearlessly beyond the wards to skewer the nearest flame demons on their warded spears. Magic sparked as the weapons punched through their sharp, overlapping scales.

Other drones attacked from the sides, but the sentries worked in unison, their warded shields covering one another as they fought. Shouts could be heard inside the camp as other warriors rushed to join in the battle.

But under cover of fog and dark, the mimic's host advanced. One moment the sentries' cries were of victory, and the next they were of shock as the demons emerged from the haze.

The mimic took the first human it encountered easily, sweeping the man's feet away with its heavy tail and snatching a flailing leg as he fell. The hapless warrior was lifted aloft by the limb, his spine cracked like a whip. Those unlucky warriors who faced the mimic next were beaten down by the body of their fallen comrade.

The other drones followed suit, with mixed success. The few sentries were quickly overwhelmed, but many drones were slow to take advantage, wasting precious time rending the dead bodies rather than preparing for the next wave of warriors.

More and more of the veiled men flowed out of the camp, falling quickly into ranks and killing with smooth, brutal efficiency. The wards on their weapons and shields flared repeatedly in the darkness.

Up on the rise, the mind demons watched the battle impassively, showing no concern for the drones falling to the enemy spears. There was a throb in the cranium of one as it sent a command to its mimic on the field.

Immediately, the mimic hurled the corpse into one of the wardposts around the camp, smashing it and creating a breach. Up on the rise, there was another throb, and the other corelings broke off from engaging the warriors and poured through the gap into the enemy camp.

Left off balance, the warriors turned back to see tents blazing as flame drones scurried about, and hear the screams of their women and children as the larger corelings broke through charred and scorched inner wards.

The warriors cried out and rushed to their loved ones, all semblance of order lost. In moments the tight, invincible units had fragmented into thousands of separate creatures, little more than prey.

It seemed as if the camp would be overrun and burned to the ground, but then a figure appeared from the central pavilion. He was clad in black, like the warriors, but his outer robe, headwrap, and veil were the purest white. At his brow was a circlet of gold, and in his hands was a great spear of shining metal. The coreling princes hissed at the sight.

There were cries at the man's approach. The mind demons sneered at the primitive grunts and yelps that passed for communication among men, but the meaning was clear. The others were drones. This one was their mind.

Under the domination of the newcomer, the warriors remembered their castes and returned to their previous cohesion. A unit broke off to seal the outer breach. Another two fought fire. One more ushered the defenseless to safety.

Thus freed, the remainder scoured the camp, and the drones could not long stand against them. In minutes the camp was as littered with coreling bodies as the field outside. The mimic, still disguised as a rock demon, was soon the only coreling left, too quick to be taken by spear but unable to break through the wall of shields without revealing its true self.

There was a throb from the rise, and the mimic vanished into a shadow, dematerializing and seeping out of the camp through a tiny gap in the wards. The enemy was still searching for it when the mimic returned to its place by its master's side.

The two slender corelings stood atop the rise for several minutes, silent vibrations passing between them. Then, as one, the coreling princes turned their eyes to the north, where the other human mind was said to be.

One of the mind demons turned to its mimic, kneeling back in the form of a gigantic wind demon, and walked up its extended wing. As it vanished into the night, the remaining mind demon turned back to regard the smoldering enemy camp.

SECTION I

VICTORY WITHOUT HONOR

CHAPTER 1

FORT RIZON

:: 333 AR WINTER ::

FORT RIZON'S WALL WAS A JOKE.

Barely ten feet high and only one thick, the entire city's defenses were less than the meanest of a *Damaji's* dozen palaces. The Watchers didn't even need their steel-shod ladders; most simply leapt to catch the lip of the tiny wall and pulled themselves up and over.

"People so weak and negligent deserve to be conquered," Hasik said. Jardir grunted but said nothing.

The advance guard of Jardir's elite warriors had come under cover of darkness, thousands of sandaled feet crunching the fallow, snow-covered fields surrounding the city proper. As the greenlanders cowered behind their wards, the Krasians had braved the demon-infested night to advance. Even corelings gave berth to so many Holy Warriors on the move.

They gathered before the city, but the veiled warriors did not attack immediately. Men did not attack other men in the night. When dawn's light began to fill the sky, they lowered their veils, that their enemies might see their faces.

There were a few brief grunts as the Watchers subdued the guards in the gatehouse, and then a creak as the city gates opened wide to admit Jardir's host. With a roar, six thousand *dal'Sharum* warriors poured into the city.

Before the Rizonans even knew what was happening, the Krasians were upon them, kicking in doors and dragging the men out of their beds, hurling them naked into the snow.

With its seemingly endless arable land, Fort Rizon was more populous by far than Krasia, but Rizonan men were not warriors, and they fell before Jardir's trained ranks like grass before the scythe. Those who struggled suffered torn muscle and broken bone. Those who fought, died.

Jardir looked at all of these in sorrow. Every man crippled or killed was one who could not find glory in Sharak Ka, the Great War, but it was a necessary evil. He could not forge the men of the North into a weapon against demonkind without first tempering them as the smith's hammer did the speartip.

Women screamed as Jardir's men tempered them in another fashion. Another necessary evil. Sharak Ka was nigh, and the coming generation of warriors had to spring from the seeds of men, not cowards.

After some time, Jardir's son Jayan dropped to one knee in the snow before him, his speartip red with blood. "The inner city is ours, Father," Jayan said.

Jardir nodded. "If we control the inner city, we control the plain."

Jayan had done well on his first command. Had this been a battle against demons, Jardir would have led the charge himself, but he would not stain the Spear of Kaji with human blood. Jayan was young to wear the white veil of captain, but he was Jardir's firstborn, Blood of the Deliverer himself. He was strong, impervious to pain, and warrior and cleric alike stepped with reverence around him.

"Many have fled," Asome added, appearing at his brother's back. "They will warn the hamlets, who will flee also, escaping the cleansing of Evejan law."

Jardir looked at him. Asome was a year younger than his brother, smaller and more slender. He was clad in a *dama's* white robes without armor or weapon, but Jardir was not fooled. His second son was easily the more ambitious and dangerous of the two, and they more so than any of their dozens of younger brothers.

"They escape for now," Jardir said, "but they leave their food stores behind and flee into the soft ice that covers the green lands in winter. The weak will die, sparing us the trouble of killing them, and my yoke will find the strong in due time. You have done well, my sons. Jayan, assign men to find buildings suitable to hold the captives before they die from cold. Separate the boys for *Hannu Pash*. If we can beat the Northern weakness out of them, perhaps some can rise above their fathers. The strong men we will use as fodder in battle, and the weak will be slaves. Any women of fertile age may be bred."

Jayan struck a fist to his chest and nodded.

"Asome, signal the other *dama* to begin," Jardir said, and Asome bowed.

Jardir watched his white-clad son as he strode off to obey. The clerics would spread the word of Everam to the *chin,* and those who did not accept it into their hearts would have it thrust down their throats.

Necessary evil.

ぅ

That afternoon, Jardir paced the thick-carpeted floors of the manse he had taken as his Rizonan palace. It was a pitiful place compared with his palaces in Krasia, but after months of sleeping in tents since leaving the Desert Spear, it was a welcome touch of civilization.

In his right hand, Jardir clutched the Spear of Kaji, using it as one might a walking stick. He needed no support, of course, but the ancient weapon had brought about his rise to power, and it was never far from his grasp. The butt thumped against the carpet with each step.

"Abban is late," Jardir said. "Even traveling with the women after dawn, he should have been here by now."

"I will never understand why you tolerate that *khaffit* in your presence, Father," Asome said. "The pig-eater should be put to death for even having raised his eyes to look upon you, and yet you take his counsel as if he were an equal in your court."

"Kaji himself bent *khaffit* to the tasks that suited them," Jardir said. "Abban knows more about the green lands than anyone, and that is knowledge a wise leader must use."

"What is there to know?" Jayan asked. "The greenlanders are all cowards and weaklings, no better than *khaffit* themselves. They are not even worthy to fight as slaves and fodder."

"Do not be so quick to claim you know all there is," Jardir said. "Only Everam knows all things. The Evejah tells us to know our enemies, and we know very little of the North. If I am to bring them into the Great War, I must do more than just kill them, more than just dominate. I must *understand* them. And if all the men of the green lands are no better than *khaffit,* who better than a *khaffit* to explain their hearts to me?"

Just then, there was a knock at the door, and Abban came limping into the room. As always, the fat merchant was dressed in rich, womanly silks and fur—a garish display that he seemed to wear intentionally for the offense it gave to the austere *dama* and *dal'Sharum.*

The guards mocked and shoved him as he passed, but they knew better than to deny Abban entry. Whatever their personal feelings, hindering Abban risked Jardir's wrath, something no man wanted.

The crippled *khaffit* leaned heavily on his cane as he approached Jardir's throne, sweat pearling on his reddened, doughy face despite the cold. Jardir looked at him in disgust. It was clear he brought important news, but Abban stood panting, attempting to catch his breath, instead of sharing it.

"What is it?" Jardir snapped when his patience grew thin.

"You must do something!" Abban gasped. "They are burning the granaries!"

"What?!" Jardir demanded, leaping to his feet and grabbing Abban's arm, squeezing so hard the *khaffit* cried out in pain. "Where?"

"The north ward of the city," Abban said. "You can see the smoke from your door."

Jardir rushed out onto the front steps, immediately spotting the rising column. He turned to Jayan. "Go," he said. "I want the fires out, and those responsible brought before me."

Jayan nodded and vanished into the streets, trained warriors flowing in behind him like birds in formation. Jardir turned back to Abban.

"You need that grain if you are to feed the people through the winter," Abban said. "Every seed. Every crumb. I warned you."

Asome shot forward, snatching Abban's wrist and twisting his arm hard behind him. Abban screamed. "You will not address the Shar'Dama Ka in such a tone!" Asome growled.

"Enough," Jardir said.

Abban fell to his knees the moment Asome released him, placing both hands on the steps and pressing his forehead between them. "Ten thousand pardons, Deliverer," he said.

"I heard your coward's counsel against advancing into the Northern cold," Jardir said as Abban whimpered on the ground. "But I will not delay Everam's work because of this . . ." he kicked at the snow on the steps, "sandstorm of ice. If we need food, we will take it from the *chin* in the surrounding land, who live in plenty."

"Of course, Shar'Dama Ka," Abban said into the floor.

"You took far too long to arrive, *khaffit*," Jardir said. "I need you to find your merchant contacts among the captives."

"If they are still alive," Abban said. "Hundreds lie dead in the streets."

Jardir shrugged. "Your fault for being so slow. Go, question your fellow traders and find me the leaders of these men."

"The *dama* will have me killed the moment I issue a command, even if it be in your name, great Shar'Dama Ka," Abban said.

It was true enough. Under Evejan law, any *khaffit* daring to command his betters was put to death on the spot, and there were many who envied Abban's place on Jardir's council and would be glad to see his end.

"I will send Asome with you," Jardir said. "Not even the most fanatical cleric will challenge you then."

Abban blanched as Asome came forward, but he nodded. "As the Shar'-Dama Ka commands."

CHAPTER 2

ABBAN

:: 305–308 AR ::

JARDIR WAS NINE WHEN the *dal'Sharum* took him from his mother. It was young, even in Krasia, but the Kaji tribe had lost many warriors that year and needed to bolster their ranks lest one of the other tribes attempt to encroach on their domain.

Jardir, his three younger sisters, and their mother, Kajivah, shared a single room in the Kaji adobe slum by the dry well. His father, Hoshkamin, had died in battle two years before, slain in a well raid by the Majah tribe. It was customary for one of a fallen warrior's companions to take his widows as wives and provide for his children, but Kajivah had given birth to three daughters in a row, an ill omen that no man would bring into his household. They lived on a small stipend of food from the local *dama*, and if they had nothing else, they had each other.

"Ahmann asu Hoshkamin am'Jardir am'Kaji," Drillmaster Qeran said, "you will come with us to the Kaji'sharaj to find your *Hannu Pash*, the path Everam wills for you." He stood in the doorway with Drillmaster Kaval, the two warriors tall and forbidding in their black robes with the red drillmaster veils. They looked on impassively as Jardir's mother wept and embraced him.

"You must be man for our family now, Ahmann," Kajivah told him, "for me and your sisters. We have no one else."

"I will, Mother," Jardir promised. "I'll become a great warrior and build you a palace."

"Of that, I have no doubt," Kajivah said. "They say I was cursed, to bear three girls after you, but I say Everam blessed our family with a son so great, he needed no brothers." She hugged him tightly, her tears wet on his cheek.

"Enough weeping," Drillmaster Kaval said, taking Jardir's arm and pulling him away. Jardir's young sisters stared as they led him from the tiny apartment.

"It is always this way," Qeran said. "Mothers can never let go."

"She has no man to care for her," Jardir replied.

"You were not told to speak, boy," Kaval barked, cuffing him hard on the back of the head. Jardir bit back a cry of pain as his knee struck the sandstone street. His heart screamed at him to strike back, but he checked himself. However much the Kaji might need warriors, the *dal'Sharum* would kill him for such an affront with no more thought than a man might give to squashing a scorpion under his sandal.

"Every man in Krasia cares for her," Qeran said, jerking his head back toward the door, "spilling blood in the night to keep her safe as she weeps over her sorry excuse for a son."

They turned down the street, heading toward the Great Bazaar. Jardir knew the way well, for he went to the market often, though he had no money. The scents of spice and perfume were a heady mix, and he liked to gaze at the spears and wicked curved blades in the armorers' kiosks. Sometimes he fought with other boys, readying himself for the day he would be a warrior.

It was rare for *dal'Sharum* to enter the bazaar; such places were beneath them. Women, children, and *khaffit* scurried out of the drillmasters' path. Jardir watched the warriors carefully, doing his best to imitate their carriage.

Someday, he thought, *it will be* my *path that others scramble to clear.*

Kaval checked a chalked slate and looked up at a large tent, streaming with colored banners. "This is the place," he said, and Qeran grunted. Jardir followed as they lifted the flap and strode inside without bothering to announce themselves.

The inside of the tent smelled of incense smoke, and it was richly carpeted, filled with piles of silk pillows, racks of hanging carpets, painted pottery, and other treasures. Jardir ran a finger along a bolt of silk, shivering at its smoothness.

My mother and sisters should be clad in such cloth, he thought. He looked at his own tan pantaloons and vest, grimy and torn, and longed for the day he could don a warrior's blacks.

A woman at the counter gave a shriek as she caught sight of the drillmasters, and Jardir looked up at her just as she pulled her veil over her face.

"Omara vah'Haman vah'Kaji?" Qeran asked. The woman nodded, eyes wide with fear.

"We have come for your son, Abban," Qeran said.

"He's not here," Omara said, but her eyes and hands, the only parts of her visible beneath the thick black cloth, trembled. "I sent him out this morning, delivering goods."

"Search the back," Qeran told Kaval. The drillmaster nodded and headed for the dividing flap behind the counter.

"No, please!" Omara cried, stepping in his path. Kaval ignored her, shoving her aside and disappearing into the back. There were more shrieks, and a moment later the drillmaster reemerged clutching the arm of a young boy in a tan vest, cap, and pantaloons—though of much finer cloth than Jardir's. He was perhaps a year or two older than Jardir, stocky and well fed. A number of older girls followed him out, two in tans and three more in the black, open-faced headwraps of unmarried women.

"Abban am'Haman am'Kaji," Qeran said, "you will come with us to the Kaji'sharaj to find your *Hannu Pash,* the path Everam wills for you." The boy trembled at the words.

Omara wailed, grabbing at her son, trying to pull him back. "Please! He is too young! Another year, I beg!"

"Silence, woman," Kaval said, shoving her to the floor. "The boy is old and fat enough as it is. If he is left to you another day, he will end up *khaffit* like his father."

"Be proud, woman," Qeran told her. "Your son is being given the chance to rise above his father and serve Everam and the Kaji."

Omara clenched her fists, but she stayed where she had landed, head down, and wept quietly. No woman would dare defy a *dal'Sharum.* Abban's sisters clutched at her, sharing in her grief. Abban reached for them, but Kaval jerked him away. The boy cried and wailed as they dragged him out of the tent. Jardir could hear the women crying even after the heavy flap fell closed and the clamor of the market surrounded them.

The warriors all but ignored the boys as they led the way to the training grounds, letting them trail after. Abban continued to weep and shake as they went.

"Why are you crying?" Jardir asked him. "The road ahead is bright with glory."

"I don't want to be a warrior," Abban said. "I don't want to die."

Jardir shrugged. "Maybe you'll be called to be *dama.*"

Abban shuddered. "That would be worse. A *dama* killed my father."

"Why?" Jardir asked.

"My father accidentally spilled ink on his robe," Abban said.

"The *dama* killed him just for that?" Jardir asked.

Abban nodded, fresh tears welling in his eyes. "He broke my father's neck right then. It happened so fast . . . he reached out, there was a snap, and my father was falling." He swallowed hard. "Now I'm the only man left to look out for my mother and sisters."

Jardir took his hand. "My father's dead, too, and they say my mother's cursed for having three daughters in a row. But we are men of Kaji. We can surpass our fathers and bring honor back to our women."

"But I'm scared," Abban sniffed.

"I am, too, a little," Jardir admitted, looking down as he said it. A moment later, he brightened. "Let's make a pact."

Abban, raised in the cutthroat business of the bazaar, looked at him suspiciously. "What kind of pact?"

"We'll help each other through *Hannu Pash*," Jardir said. "If you stumble, I will catch you, and if I fall, you," he smirked and slapped Abban's round belly, "will cushion it."

Abban yelped and rubbed his belly, but he did not complain, looking at Jardir in wonder. "You mean that?" he asked, drying his eyes with the back of his hand.

Jardir nodded. They were walking in the shade of the bazaar's awnings, but he grabbed Abban's arm and pulled him into the sunlight. "I swear it by Everam's light."

Abban smiled widely. "And I swear it by the jeweled Crown of Kaji."

"Keep up!" Kaval barked, and they chased after, but Abban moved with confidence now.

The drillmasters drew wards in the air as they passed the great temple Sharik Hora, mumbling prayers to Everam, the Creator. Beyond Sharik Hora lay the training grounds, and Jardir and Abban tried to look everywhere at once, taking in the warriors at their practice. Some worked with shield and spear or net, while others marched or ran in lockstep. Watchers stood upon the top rungs of ladders braced against nothing, honing their balance. Still more *dal'Sharum* hammered spearheads and warded shields, or practiced *sharusahk*—the art of empty-handed battle.

There were twelve *sharaji*, or schools, surrounding the training grounds, one for each tribe. Jardir and Abban were Kaji tribe, and thus were taken to the Kaji'sharaj. Here they would begin the *Hannu Pash* and emerge as *dama*, *dal'Sharum*, or *khaffit*.

"The Kaji'sharaj is so much larger than the others," Abban said, looking up at the huge pavilion tent. "Only the Majah'sharaj is even close."

"Of course it is," Kaval said. "Did you think it coincidence that our tribe is named Kaji, after Shar'Dama Ka, the Deliverer? We are the get of his thousand wives, blood of his blood. The Majah," he spat, "are only the blood of the weakling who ruled after the Shar'Dama Ka left this world. The other tribes are inferior to us in every way. Never forget that."

They were taken into the pavilion and given bidos—simple white loincloths—and their tans were taken to be burned. They were *nie'Sharum* now; not warriors, but not boys, either.

"A month of gruel and hard training will burn the fat from you, boy," Kaval said as Abban removed his shirt. The drillmaster punched Abban's round belly in disgust. Abban doubled over from the blow, but Jardir caught him before he fell, steadying him until he caught his breath. When they were finished changing, the drillmasters took them to the barrack.

"New blood!" Qeran shouted as they were shoved into a large, unfurnished room filled with other *nie'Sharum*. "Ahmann asu Hoshkamin am'-Jardir am'Kaji, and Abban am'Haman am'Kaji! They are your brothers now."

Abban colored, and Jardir knew immediately why, as did every other boy present. By leaving out his father's name, Qeran had as much as announced that Abban's father was *khaffit*—the lowest and most despised caste in Krasian society. *Khaffit* were cowards and weaklings, men who could not hold to the warrior way.

"Ha! You bring us a fat pig-eater's son and a scrawny rat!" the largest of the *nie'Sharum* cried. "Throw them back!" The other boys all laughed.

Drillmaster Qeran growled and punched the boy in the face. He hit the stone floor hard, spitting up a gob of blood. All laughing ceased.

"Make mock when you have lost your bido, Hasik," Qeran said. "Until then, you are *all* scrawny, pig-eating *khaffit* rats." With that, he and Kaval turned on their heels and strode out.

"You'll pay for that, rats," Hasik said, the last word ending in a strange whistle. He tore the loose tooth from his mouth and threw it at Abban, who flinched when it struck. Jardir stepped in front of him and snarled, but Hasik and his cohorts had already turned away.

Soon after they arrived, they were given bowls, and the gruel pot was set out. Famished, Jardir went right for the pot, and Abban hurried even faster, but one of the older boys blocked their path. "You think you eat before me?" he demanded. He shoved Jardir into Abban, and they both fell to the floor.

"Get up, if you mean to eat," said the drillmaster who had brought the gruel. "The boys at the end of the line go hungry."

Abban shrieked, and they scrambled to their feet. Already most of the boys had lined up, roughly in order of size and strength, with Hasik at the very front. At the back of the line, the smallest boys fought fiercely to avoid the spots at the end.

"What are we going to do?" Abban asked.

"We're going to get on that line," Jardir said, grabbing Abban's arm and dragging him toward the center, where the boys were still outweighed by well-fed Abban. "My father said that weakness shown is worse than weakness felt."

"But I don't know how to fight!" Abban protested, shaking.

"You're about to learn," Jardir said. "When I knock someone down, fall on him with all your weight."

"I can do that," Abban agreed. Jardir guided them right up to a boy who snarled in challenge. He puffed out his chest and faced up against Abban, the larger of the two boys.

"Get to the back of the line, new rats!" he growled.

Jardir said nothing, punching the boy in the stomach and kicking at his knees. When he fell, Abban took his cue, falling on the boy like a sandstone pillar. By the time Abban got up, Jardir had already taken the boy's place in line. He glared at those behind, and they made room for Abban, as well.

A single ladle of gruel slopped into their bowls was their reward. "That's it?" Abban asked in shock. The server glared at him, and Jardir quickly ushered him away. The corners of the room had already been taken by the older boys, so they retreated to one of the walls.

"I'll starve on this," Abban said, swirling the watery gruel in his bowl.

"We're still better off than some," Jardir said, pointing to a pair of bruised boys with nothing to eat at all. "You can have some of mine," he added when Abban did not brighten. "I never got much more than this at home."

🖣

They slept on the sandstone floor of the barrack, thin blankets their only shield against the cold. Used to sharing the warmth of his mother and sisters, Jardir nestled against Abban's warm bulk. In the distance, he heard the Horn of Sharak, and knew battle was being joined. It took a long time for him to drift off, dreaming of glory.

He woke with a start when another of the thin blankets was thrown over his face. He struggled hard, but the cloth was twisted behind his head and held tight. He heard Abban's muffled scream next to him.

Blows began to rain down on him from all sides, kicks and punches blasting the breath from his body and rattling his brains. Jardir flailed his limbs wildly, but though he felt several of his blows connect, it did nothing to lessen the onslaught. Before long, he was hanging limply, supported wholly by the suffocating blanket.

When he thought he could endure no more and must surely die, never having gained paradise or glory, a familiar voice said, "Welcome to the Kaji'sharaj, rats," the *s* at the end whistling through Hasik's missing tooth. The blankets were released, dropping them to the floor.

The other boys laughed and went back to their blankets as Jardir and Abban curled tight and wept in the darkness.

5

"Stand up straight," Jardir hissed as they awaited morning inspection.

"I can't," Abban whined. "Not a bit of sleep, and I ache to my bones."

"Don't let it show," Jardir said. "My father said the weakest camel draws the wolves."

"Mine told me to hide until the wolves go away," Abban replied.

"No talking!" Kaval barked. "The *dama* is coming to inspect you pathetic wretches."

He and Qeran took no notice of their cuts and bruises as they walked past. Jardir's left eye was swollen nearly shut, but the only thing the drillmasters noticed was Abban's slump. "Stand straight!" Qeran said, and Kaval punctuated the command with a crack of his leather strap across Abban's legs. Abban screamed in pain and nearly fell, but Jardir steadied him in time.

There was a snicker, and Jardir snarled at Hasik, who only smirked in response.

In truth, Jardir felt little steadier than Abban, but he refused to show it. Though his head spun and his limbs ached, Jardir arched his back and kept his good eye attentive as Dama Khevat approached. The drillmasters stepped aside for the cleric, bowing in submission.

"It is a sad day that the warriors of Kaji, the bloodline of Shar'Dama Ka, the Deliverer himself, should be reduced to such a sorry lot," the *dama* sneered, spitting in the dust. "Your mothers must have mixed camel's piss with the seeds of men."

"That's a lie!" Jardir shouted before he could help himself. Abban looked at him incredulously, but it had been an insult past his ability to bear. As Qeran sprang at him with frightening speed, Jardir knew he'd made a grave mistake. The drillmaster's strap laid a line of fire where it struck his bare skin, knocking him to the ground.

But the *dal'Sharum* did not stop there. "If the *dama* tells you that you are the son of piss, then it is so!" he shouted, whipping Jardir repeatedly. Clad only in his bido, Jardir could do nothing to ward off the blows. Whenever he twisted or turned to protect a wounded area, Qeran found a fresh patch of skin to strip. He screamed, but it only encouraged the assault.

"Enough," Khevat said. The blows stopped instantly.

"Are you the son of piss?" Qeran asked.

Jardir's limbs felt like wet bread as he forced himself to his feet. He kept his eyes on the strap, raised and ready to strike again. He knew if he continued his insolence, the drillmaster would kill him. He would die with no glory, and his spirit would spend millennia outside the gates of paradise with the *khaffit*, looking in at those in Everam's embrace and waiting for reincarnation. The thought terrified him, but his father's name was the only thing he owned in the world, and he would not forsake it.

"I am Ahmann, son of Hoshkamin, of the line of Jardir," he said as evenly as he could manage. He heard the other boys gasp, and steeled himself for the attack to come.

Qeran's face contorted in rage, and he raised the strap, but a slight gesture from the *dama* checked him.

"I knew your father, boy," Khevat said. "He stood among men, but he won no great glory in his short life."

"Then I'll win glory for both of us," Jardir promised.

The *dama* grunted. "Perhaps you will at that. But not today. Today you are less than *khaffit*." He turned to Qeran. "Throw him in the waste pits, for true men to shit and piss upon."

The drillmaster smiled, punching Jardir in the stomach. When he doubled over, Qeran grabbed him by his hair and dragged him toward the pits. As he went, Jardir glanced at Hasik, expecting another smirk, but the older boy's face, like all the assembled *nie'Sharum*, was a mix of disbelief and ashen fear.

5

"Everam saw the cold blackness of Nie, and felt no satisfaction there. He created the sun to give light and warmth, staving off the void. He created Ala, the world, and set it spinning around the sun. He created man, and the beasts to serve him, and watched as His sun gave them life and love.

"But for half its time, Ala faced the dark of Nie, and Everam's creatures were fearful. So He made the moon and stars to reflect the sun's light, a reminder in the night that they had not been forgotten.

"Everam did this, and He was satisfied.

"But Nie, too, had a will. She looked upon creation, marring Her perfect blackness, and was vexed. She reached out to crush Ala, but Everam stood fast, and Her hand was stayed.

"But Everam had not been quick enough to stave off Nie's touch completely. The barest brush of Her dark fingers grew on His perfect world like a plague. The inky blackness of Her evil seeped across the rocks and sand, blew on the winds, and was an oily stain on Ala's pure water. It swept across the woods, and the molten fire that bubbled up from beneath the world.

"And in those places, alagai *took root and grew. Creatures of the blackness, their only purpose to uncreate; killing Everam's creatures their only joy.*

"But lo, the world turned, and the sun shone light and warmth across Nie's creatures of cold dark, and they were undone. The life-giver burned away their unlife, and the alagai *screamed.*

"Desperate to escape, they fled to the shadows, oozing deep into the world, infecting its very core.

"There, in the dark abyss at the heart of creation, grew Alagai'ting Ka, the Mother of Demons. Handmaiden of Nie Herself, she waited only for the world to turn that she might send her children forth again to ravage creation.

"Everam saw this, and reached out His hand to purge the evil from His world, but Nie stood fast, and His hand was stayed.

"But He, too, touched the world one last time, giving men the means to turn alagai *magic against itself. Giving them wards.*

"Locked then in a struggle for the sake of all He had made, Everam had no choice but to turn His back on the world and throw Himself fully upon Nie, struggling endlessly against Her cold strength.

"And as above, so below."

Every day of Jardir's first month in *sharaj* was the same. At dawn, the drill-masters brought the *nie'Sharum* out into the hot sun to stand for hours as the *dama* spoke of the glory of Everam. Their bellies were empty and their knees weak from exertion and lack of sleep, but the boys did not protest. The sight of Jardir, returned reeking and bloody from his punishment, had taught them all to obey without question.

Drillmaster Qeran struck Jardir hard with his strap. "Why do you suffer?" he demanded.

"Alagai!" Jardir shouted.

Qeran turned and whipped Abban. "Why is the *Hannu Pash* necessary?"

"Alagai!" Abban screamed.

"Without the *alagai*, all the world would be the paradise of Heaven, suffused in Everam's embrace," Dama Khevat said.

The drillmaster's strap cracked on Jardir's back again. Since his insolence the first day, he had taken two lashes for every one suffered by another boy.

"What is your purpose in this life?" Qeran cried.

"To kill *alagai*!" Jardir screamed.

His hand shot out, clutching Jardir around the throat and pulling him close. "And how will you die?" he asked quietly.

"On *alagai* talons," Jardir choked. The drillmaster released him, and he gasped in a breath, standing back to attention before Qeran could find further reason to beat him.

"On *alagai* talons!" Khevat cried. "*Dal'Sharum* do not die old in their beds! They do not fall prey to sickness or hunger! *Dal'Sharum* die in battle, and win into paradise. Basking in Everam's glory, they bathe and drink from rivers of sweet cool milk, and have virgins beyond count devoted to them."

"Death to *alagai*!" the boys all screamed at once, pumping their fists. "Glory to Everam!"

After these sessions, they were given their bowls, and the gruel pot was set out. There was never enough for all, and more than one boy each day went hungry. The older and larger boys, led by Hasik, had established their pecking order and filled their bowls first, but even they took but one ladle each. To take more, or to spill gruel in a scuffle at the pot, was to invite the wrath of the ever-present drillmasters.

As the older boys ate, the youngest and weakest of *nie'Sharum* fought hard among themselves for a place in line. After his first night's beating and the day in the pits, Jardir was in no shape to fight for days, but Abban had taken well to using his weight as a weapon, and always secured them a place, even if it was close to the back.

When the bowls were emptied, the training began.

There were obstacle courses to build endurance, and long sessions practicing the *sharukin*—groups of movements that made up the forms of *sharusahk*. They learned to march and move in step even at speed. With nothing in their bellies but the thin gruel, the boys became like speartips, thin and hard as the weapons they drilled with.

Sometimes the drillmasters sent groups of boys to ambush *nie'Sharum* in neighboring *sharaji*, beating them severely. Nowhere was safe, not even when sitting at the waste pits. Sometimes the older boys like Hasik and his friends would mount the defeated boys from other tribes from behind, thrusting into them as if they were women. It was a grave dishonor, and Jardir had been forced to kick more than one attacker between the legs to avoid such a fate for himself. A Majah boy managed to pull down Abban's bido once, but Jardir kicked him in the face so hard blood spurted from his nose.

"At any moment, the Majah could attack to take a well," Kaval told Jardir when they came to him after the assault, "or the Nanji come to carry off our women. We must be ready at every moment of every day to kill or be killed."

"I hate this place," Abban whined, close to tears, when the drillmaster left. "I cannot wait for the Waning, when I can go home to my mother and sisters, if only for the new moon."

Jardir shook his head. "He's right. Letting your guard down, even for a moment, invites death." He clenched his fist. "That may have happened to my father, but it won't happen to me."

After the drillmasters completed their lessons each day, the older boys supervised repetition, and they were no less quick to punish than the *dal'Sharum*.

"Keep your knees bent as you pivot, rat," Hasik growled as Jardir performed a complicated *sharukin*. He punctuated his advice by kicking behind Jardir's knees, driving him into the dust.

"The son of piss cannot perform a simple pivot!" Hasik cried to the other boys, laughing. His *s*'s still came out with a whistle through the gap where Qeran had knocked out one of his teeth.

Jardir growled and launched himself at the older boy. He might have to obey the *dama* and *dal'Sharum*, but Hasik was only *nie'Sharum*, and he would accept no insult to his father from the likes of him.

But Hasik was also five years his senior, and soon to lose his bido. He was larger than Jardir by far, and had years of experience at the deadly art of the empty hand. He caught Jardir's wrist, twisting and pulling the arm straight, then pivoted to bring his elbow down hard on the locked limb.

Jardir heard the snap and saw the bone jut free of his skin, but there was a long moment of dawning horror before the blast of pain hit him.

And he screamed.

Hasik's hand snapped over Jardir's mouth, cutting off his howls and pulling him close.

"The next time you come for me, son of piss, I will kill you," he promised.

ऽ

Abban ducked under Jardir's good arm and half carried him to the *dama'ting* pavilion at the far end of the training grounds. The tent opened as they approached, as if they had been expected. A tall woman clad in white from head to toe held the flap open, only her hands and eyes visible. She gestured to a table inside, and Abban hurried to place Jardir there, beside a girl who was clad all in white like a *dama'ting*. But her face, young and beautiful, was uncovered.

Dama'ting did not speak to *nie'Sharum*.

Abban bowed deeply when Jardir was in place. The *dama'ting* nodded toward the flaps, and he practically fell over himself in his haste to exit. It was said the *dama'ting* could see the future, and knew a man's death just by looking at him.

The woman glided over to Jardir, a blur of white to his pain-clouded eyes. He could not tell if she was young or old, beautiful or ugly, stern or kind. She seemed above such petty things, her devotion to Everam transcending all mortal concern.

The girl lifted a small stick wrapped many times in white cloth and placed it in Jardir's mouth, gently pushing his jaw closed. Jardir understood, and bit down.

"*Dal'Sharum* embrace their pain," the girl whispered as the *dama'ting* moved to a table to gather instruments.

There was a sharp sting as the *dama'ting* cleansed the wound, and a flare of agony as she wrenched his arm to set the bone. Jardir bit hard into the stick, and tried to do as the girl said, opening himself to the pain, though he did not fully understand. For a moment the pain seemed more than he could endure, but then, as if he were passing through a doorway, it became a distant thing, a suffering he was aware of but not part of. His jaw unclenched, and the stick fell away unneeded.

As Jardir relaxed into the pain, he turned to watch the *dama'ting*. She worked with calm efficiency, murmuring prayers to Everam as she stitched muscle and skin. She ground herbs into a paste she slathered on the wound, wrapping it in clean cloth soaked in a thick white mixture.

With surprising strength, she lifted him from the table and set him on a hard cot. She put a flask to his lips and Jardir drank, immediately feeling warm and woozy.

The *dama'ting* turned away, but the girl lingered a moment. "Bones become stronger after being broken," she whispered, giving comfort as Jardir drifted off to sleep.

ॐ

He woke to find the girl sitting beside his cot. She pressed a damp cloth to his forehead. It was the coolness that had woken him. His eyes danced over her uncovered face. He had once thought his mother beautiful, but it was nothing compared with this girl.

"The young warrior awakens," she said, smiling at him.

"You speak," Jardir said through parched lips. His arm seemed encased in white stone; the *dama'ting*'s wrappings had hardened while he slept.

"Am I a beast, that I should not?" the girl asked.

"To me, I mean," Jardir said. "I am only *nie'Sharum*." *And not yet worthy of you by half*, he added silently.

The girl nodded. "And I am *nie'dama'ting*. I will earn my veil soon, but I do not wear it yet, and thus may speak to whomever I wish."

She set the cloth aside, lifting a steaming bowl of porridge to his lips. "I expect they are starving you in the Kaji'sharaj. Eat. It will help the *dama'ting*'s spells to heal you."

Jardir swallowed the hot food quickly. "What is your name?" he asked when done.

The girl smiled as she wiped his mouth with a soft cloth. "Bold, for a boy barely old enough for his bido."

"I'm sorry," Jardir said.

She laughed. "Boldness is no cause for sorrow. Everam has no love for the timid. My name is Inevera."

"As Everam wills," Jardir translated. It was a common saying in Krasia. Inevera nodded.

"Ahmann," Jardir introduced himself, "son of Hoshkamin."

The girl nodded as if this were grave news, but there was amusement in her eyes.

ॐ

"He is strong and may return to training," the *dama'ting* told Qeran the next day, "but he must eat regularly, and if further harm comes to the arm before I remove the wrappings, I will hold you to account."

The drillmaster bowed. "It will be as the *dama'ting* commands." Jardir was given his bowl and allowed to go to the front of the line. None of the other boys, even Hasik, dared question this, but Jardir could feel their looks of resentment at his back. He would have preferred fighting for his meals, even with his arm in a cast, rather than weather those stares, but the *dama'ting* had given an order. If he did not eat willingly, the drillmasters would not hesitate to force the gruel down his throat.

"Will you be all right?" Abban asked as they ate in their customary spot.

Jardir nodded. "Bones heal stronger after being broken."

"I'd rather not test that," Abban said. Jardir shrugged. "At least the Waning begins tomorrow," Abban added. "You can have a few days at home."

Jardir looked at the cast and felt profound shame. There would be no hiding this from his mother and sisters. Barely in *sharaj* a cycle, and he was already a disgrace to them.

五

The Waning was the three-day cycle of the new moon, when Nie's power was said to be strongest. Boys in *Hannu Pash* spent this period at home with their families, so that fathers could look upon their sons and remember what they fought for in the night.

But Jardir's father was gone, and Jardir doubted he would fill the man's heart with pride in any event. His mother, Kajivah, made no mention of his injury when he returned home, but Jardir's younger sisters lacked her discretion.

Among the other *nie'Sharum,* Jardir had gotten used to living in only his bido and sandals. Among his sisters, all covered head-to-toe in tan robes revealing only their hands and faces, he felt naked, and there was no way to disguise his cast.

"What happened to your arm?" his youngest sister Hanya asked the moment he arrived.

"I broke it in my training," Jardir said.

"How?" Imisandre, the eldest of his sisters and the one Jardir was closest to, asked. She put her hand on his other arm.

Her sympathetic touch, once a balm to Jardir, now multiplied his shame tenfold. He pulled his arm away. "It was broken in *sharusahk* practice. It is nothing."

"How many boys did it take?" Hanya said, and Jardir remembered the time he had beaten two older boys in the bazaar after one of them had mocked her. "At least ten, I bet."

Jardir scowled. "One," he snapped.

Hoshvah, his middle sister, shook her head. "He must have been ten feet tall." Jardir wanted to scream.

"Enough pestering your brother!" Kajivah said. "Prepare a place for him at the table and leave him in peace."

Hanya took Jardir's sandals while Imisandre pulled out the bench at the head of the table. There were no pillows, but she laid a clean cloth on the wood for him to sit upon. After a month sitting on the floor of the *sharaj*, even that seemed a luxury. Hoshvah hurried with the chipped clay bowls Kajivah filled from the steaming pot.

Most nights, Jardir's family ate only plain couscous, but Kajivah saved her stipend, and on Waning there were always vegetables and seasoning mixed in. On this, his first Waning home from *Hannu Pash*, there were even a few hard bits of unidentifiable meat mixed into Jardir's bowl. It was more food than Jardir had seen in quite some time and it smelled of a mother's love, but Jardir found he had little appetite, especially when he noted that the bowls of his mother and sisters lacked the bits of meat. He forced the food down so as not to insult his mother, but the fact that he ate with his left hand only made his shame worse.

After the meal, they prayed as a family until the call came from the minarets of Sharik Hora, signaling dusk. Evejan law dictated that when the call sounded from the minarets of Sharik Hora, all women and children were to go below.

Even Kajivah's mean adobe hovel had a barred and warded basement with a connection to the Undercity, a vast network of caverns that connected all of the Desert Spear in the event of a breach.

"Go below," Kajivah told his sisters. "I will speak privately with your brother." The girls followed her command, and Kajivah beckoned Jardir to the corner where his father's spear and shield hung.

As always, the arms seemed to look down on him in judgment. Jardir felt the weight of his cast keenly, but there was something that had been weighing on him even more. He looked to his mother.

"Dama Khevat said father took no honor with him when he died," Jardir said.

"Then Dama Khevat did not know your father as I did," Kajivah said. "He spoke only truth, and never raised a hand to me in anger, though I bore him three daughters in succession. He kept me with child and put meat in our bellies." She looked Jardir in the eyes. "There is honor in those things, as much as there is in killing *alagai*. Repeat that under the sun and remember it."

Jardir nodded. "I will."

"You wear the bido now," Kajivah said. "That means you are no longer a boy, and cannot go below with us. You must wait at the door."

Jardir nodded. "I am not afraid."

"Perhaps you should be," Kajivah said. "The Evejah tells us that on the Waning, Alagai Ka, father of demons, stalks the surface of Ala."

"Not even he could get past the warriors of the Desert Spear," Jardir said.

Kajivah stood, lifting Hoshkamin's spear from the wall. "Perhaps not," she said, thrusting the weapon into his good left hand, "but if he does, it will fall to you to keep him from our door."

Shocked, Jardir took the weapon, and Kajivah nodded once before following his sisters below. Jardir immediately moved to the door, his back straight as he stood throughout the night, and the two that followed.

"I'll need a target," Jardir said, "for when the *dama'ting* remove my cast, and I need to get back in the food line."

"We can do it together," Abban said, "like we did before."

Jardir shook his head. "If I need your help, they'll think I'm weak. I've got to show them I've healed stronger than before, or I'll be a target for everyone."

Abban nodded, considering the problem. "You'll have to strike higher in the line than the place you left, but not so high as to provoke Hasik and his cronies."

"You think like a merchant," Jardir said.

Abban smiled. "I grew up in the bazaar."

They watched the line carefully over the next few days, their eyes settling just past the center, where Jardir had waited before his injury. The boys there were a few years his senior and larger than him by far. They marked potential targets and began to observe those boys carefully during training.

Training was much as it had been before. The hard cast kept Jardir's arm in place as he ran the obstacles, and the drillmasters made him throw left-handed during spear and net practice. He was given no special treatment, nor would he have wished it. The strap found his back no less often than before, and Jardir welcomed it, embracing the pain and knowing every blow proved to the other boys that he was not weak, despite his injury.

Weeks passed, and Jardir worked hard, practicing the *sharukin* whenever he had the chance, and repeating them in his mind as he drifted off to sleep each night. Surprisingly, he found he could throw and punch as well with his left hand as he had with the right. He even took to bludgeoning opponents with the cast, embracing the rush of pain as it swept over him like a hot desert wind. He knew that when the *dama'ting* finally cut the cast from him, he would be better for the injury.

"Jurim, I think," Abban said at last, the evening before Jardir's cast was removed. "He's tall and strong, but he forgets his lessons and simply tries to overpower his opponents."

Jardir nodded. "Perhaps. He's slow, and no one would challenge me if I took him down, but I was thinking of Shanjat." He nodded to a slender boy just ahead of Jurim in the line.

Abban shook his head. "Don't be fooled by his size. There's reason why Shanjat stands ahead of Jurim. His arms and legs crack like whips."

"But he's not precise," Jardir said. "And he overbalances when his blows miss."

"Which is rare," Abban warned. "You have a better chance of defeating Jurim. Don't haggle so much you spoil the sale."

It was midmorning the next day when Jardir returned from the *dama'-ting* pavilion, and the boys were already assembled in the gruel line. Jardir sucked in a breath, flexed his right arm, and strode in, heading right for the center of the line. Abban had already taken his place, farther back, and would not help him, as they had agreed.

It is the weakest camel that draws the wolves, he heard his father say, and the simple advice steeled him against his fear.

"To the back with you, cripple!" Shanjat barked, seeing him approach.

Jardir ignored him and forced himself to smile widely. "Everam shine upon you for holding my place," he said.

The look in Shanjat's eyes was incredulous; he was three years Jardir's senior, and considerably larger. He hesitated in that moment, and Jardir took the opportunity to shove him hard, knocking him from the line.

Shanjat stumbled, but he was quick and kept his feet, kicking up a cloud of dust as he regained his balance. Jardir could have kicked his hands or feet from under him and struck while he was off balance, but he needed more than mere victory if he was to ward off any rumors that his injury had left him weak.

There were hoots of delight, and the gruel line curved in on itself, surrounding the two boys. The shocked look vanished from Shanjat's face as it twisted in rage, and he came back in hard.

Jardir flowed like a dancer to avoid Shanjat's initial blows, which were just as fast as Abban had warned. Finally, as expected, Shanjat launched a wild swing that put him off balance when it failed to connect. Jardir stepped to the left, ducking the arm and driving his right elbow into Shanjat's kidney like a spear. Shanjat screamed in pain as he stumbled past.

Jardir whipped around and followed through with another elbow strike to Shanjat's back, driving him to the ground. His arm was thin and pale from weeks in the cast, but the bones did feel stronger now, just as the *dama'ting* had said.

But Shanjat caught Jardir's ankle, yanking him from his feet and falling on him. They wrestled in the dust, where Shanjat's weight and greater reach were to his advantage. He caught Jardir in a headlock, pulling his right fist into Jardir's windpipe with his left hand.

As the world began to blacken, Jardir began to fear he had taken on too much, but he embraced the feeling as he did pain, refusing to give up. He kicked hard behind him, a crushing blow between the legs that made Shanjat loosen his choke hold with a howl. Jardir twisted free and got in close to Shanjat's joints, where his blows held little force when they could reach Jardir at all. Slowly, laboriously, he worked his way behind Shanjat, striking hard at any vulnerable spots—eyes, throat, gut—as he went.

Finally in position, Jardir caught Shanjat's right arm and twisted it behind him, driving his full weight into the older boy's back with both knees. When he felt the elbow lock, he braced it on his own shoulder and heaved the arm upward.

"Aaahhh!" Shanjat cried, and Jardir knew it would be a simple thing now to break the boy's arm, as Hasik had done to him.

"You were saving my place, were you not?" Jardir asked loudly.

"I will kill you, rat!" Shanjat screamed, beating the dust with his free hand as he twisted and thrashed, but he could not dislodge Jardir.

"Say it!" Jardir demanded, lifting Shanjat's arm higher. He felt the strain in that limb, and knew it could not withstand much more.

"I would sooner go to Nie's abyss!" Shanjat cried.

Jardir shrugged. "Bones become stronger after being broken. Enjoy your stay with the *dama'ting*." With a heave, he felt bone snap and muscle tear. Shanjat screamed in agony.

Jardir stood slowly, scanning the gathered boys for signs that another meant to challenge him, but while there were many wide-eyed stares, none seemed ready to avenge Shanjat, who lay howling in the dust.

"Make way!" Drillmaster Kaval barked, pushing through the crowd. He looked to Shanjat, then to Jardir. "Hope for you yet, boy," he grunted. "Back in line, all of you," he shouted, "or we'll empty the gruel pot in the waste pits!" The boys quickly flowed back to their places, but Jardir beckoned to

Abban amid the confusion, gesturing for his friend to take the place behind him in line.

"Hey!" cried Jurim, the next boy in line, but Jardir glared at him and he backed off, making room for Abban.

Kaval kicked at Shanjat. "On your feet, rat!" he shouted. "Your legs aren't broken, so don't expect to be carried to the *dama'ting* after being bested by a boy half your size!" He grabbed Shanjat's good arm and hauled the boy to his feet, dragging him off toward the healing pavilion. The boys still in line hooted and catcalled at his back.

"I don't understand," Abban said. "Why didn't he just yield?"

"Because he's a warrior," Jardir said. "Will you yield when the *alagai* come for you?"

Abban shuddered at the thought. "That's different."

Jardir shook his head. "No, it isn't."

Hasik and some of the other older boys began training on the Maze walls not long after Jardir lost his cast. They lost their bidos in the Maze a year later, and those who survived, Hasik among them, could be seen strutting about the training grounds in their new blacks, visiting the great harem. Like all *dal'Sharum*, they had as little as possible to do with *nie'Sharum* after that.

Time passed quickly for Jardir, days blending together into an endless loop. In the mornings, he listened to *dama* extolling the glories of Everam and the Kaji tribe. He learned of the other Krasian tribes and why they were inferior, and why the Majah, most of all, were blind to Everam's truths. The *dama* spoke, too, of other lands, and the cowardly *chin* to the north who had forsaken the spear and lived like *khaffit*, quailing before the *alagai*.

Jardir was never satisfied with their place in the gruel line, always focused on moving up to where the bowls became fuller. He targeted the boys ahead of him and sent them to the *dama'ting* pavilion one by one, always bringing Abban in his wake. By the time Jardir was eleven, they were at the front of the line, ahead of several older boys, all of whom gave them a wide berth.

Afternoons were spent training or running as practice targets for *dal'Sharum* netters. At night, Jardir lay on the cold stone of the Kaji'sharaj floor, his ears straining to hear the sounds of *alagai'sharak* outside, and dreaming of the day he might stand among men.

As *Hannu Pash* progressed, some of the boys were selected by the *dama* for special training, putting them on the path to wear the white. They left the Kaji'sharaj and were never seen again. Jardir was not chosen for this honor, but he did not mind. He had no desire to spend his days poring over ancient scrolls or shouting praise to Everam. He was bred for the spear.

The *dama* showed more interest in Abban, who had letters and numbers, but his father was *khaffit,* something they did not take to, even though the shame did not technically carry to a man's sons.

"Better you fight," the *dama* told Abban at last, poking his broad chest. Abban had kept much of his bulk, but the constant rigor of training had hardened the fat to muscle. Indeed, he was becoming a formidable warrior, and he blew out a breath of relief when it became clear he would not be called to the white.

Other boys, too weak or slow, were cast out of the Kaji'sharaj as *khaffit*—forced to return to the tan clothes of children for the rest of their lives. This was a worse fate by far, shaming their families and denying them hope of paradise. Those with warrior's hearts often volunteered as Baiters, taunting demons and luring them into traps in the Maze. It was a brief life, but one that brought honor and entrance into Heaven for those otherwise lost.

In his twelfth year, Jardir was allowed his first look at the Maze. Drillmaster Qeran took the oldest and strongest of the *nie'Sharum* up the great wardwall—a sheer thirty feet of sandstone looking down on the demon killing ground that had once been an entire district of the city, back in ancient times when Krasia was more populous. It was filled with the remnants of ancient hovels and dozens of smaller sandstone walls. These were twenty feet high, with pitted wards cut into their surfaces. Some ran great distances and turned sharp corners, while others were just a single slab or angle. Together they formed a maze studded with hidden pitfalls, designed to trap and hold the *alagai* for the morning sun.

"The wall beneath your feet," Qeran said, stamping his foot, "shields our women and children, even the *khaffit,*" he spit over the side of the wall, "from the *alagai.* The other walls," he swept his hands out over the endlessly twisting walls of the Maze, "keep the *alagai* trapped in with *us.*" He clenched his fist at that, and the obvious pride he felt was shared by all the boys. Jardir imagined himself running through that maze, spear and shield in hand, and his heart soared. Glory awaited him on that blood-soaked sand.

They walked along the top of the thick wall until they came to a wooden bridge that could be drawn up with a great crank. This led down to one of the Maze walls, all connected by stone arches or close enough to jump. The Maze walls were thinner, less than a foot thick in some places.

"The walltops are treacherous for older warriors," Qeran said, "apart from the Watchers." The Watchers were *dal'Sharum* of the Krevakh and Nanji tribes. They were laddermen, each man carrying an iron-shod ladder twelve feet in length. The ladders could be joined to one another or used alone, and Watchers were so agile they could stand balanced at the top of an unsupported ladder as they surveyed the battlefield. The Krevakh Watchers were subordinate to the Kaji tribe, the Nanji to the Majah.

"For the next year, you boys will assist the Krevakh Watchers," Qeran said, "tracking *alagai* movements and calling them down to the *dal'Sharum* in the Maze, as well as running orders back and forth from the *kai'Sharum*."

They spent the rest of the day running the walltops. "You must know every inch of the Maze as well as you know your spears!" Qeran said as they went. Quick and agile, the *nie'Sharum* shouted in exhilaration as they leapt from wall to wall and darted over the small arched bridges. Jardir and Abban laughed at the joy of it.

But Abban's big frame did not lend itself to balance, and on one slender bridge he slipped, falling off the wall. Jardir dove for his hand, but he was not fast enough. "Nie take me!" he cursed as their fingers brushed slightly and the boy dropped away.

Abban let out a brief wail before striking the ground, and Jardir could see even from twenty feet above that his legs were broken.

A braying laugh, like a camel's honk, rang out behind him. Jardir turned to see Jurim slapping his knee.

"Abban is more camel than cat!" Jurim cried.

Jardir snarled and clenched a fist, but before he could rise, Drillmaster Qeran appeared. "You think your training is a joke?" he demanded. Before Jurim could gasp a reply, Qeran grabbed him by his bido and hurled him down after Abban. He screamed as he fell the twenty feet and struck hard, then lay unmoving.

The drillmaster turned to face the other boys. "*Alagai'sharak* is no joke," he said. "Better you all die here than shame your brothers in the night." The boys took a step back, nodding.

Qeran turned to Jardir. "Run now and inform Drillmaster Kaval. He'll send men to bring them to the *dama'ting*."

"It would be faster if we fetched them ourselves," Jardir dared, knowing Abban's fate might depend on those precious minutes.

"Only men are allowed in the Maze, *nie'Sharum*," Qeran said. "Be off before the *dal'Sharum* are forced to fetch three."

Jardir edged as close as he dared when the *dama'ting* came to speak with Drillmaster Qeran after gruel that evening, straining to hear her quiet words.

"Jurim broke several bones, and there was much bleeding within, but he will recover," she said, speaking as if she were discussing nothing more significant than the color of sand. Her veils hid all expression. "The other, Abban, had his legs broken in many places. He will walk again, but he may not run."

"Will he be able to fight?" Qeran asked.

"It is too soon to tell," the *dama'ting* said.

"If that is the case, you should kill him now," Qeran said. "Better dead than *khaffit*."

The *dama'ting* raised a finger at him, and the drillmaster recoiled. "It is not for *you* to dictate what goes on in the *dama'ting* pavilion, *dal'Sharum*," she hissed.

Immediately the drillmaster laced his hands as if in prayer and bowed so deeply that his beard nearly touched the ground.

"I beg the *dama'ting*'s forgiveness," he said. "I meant no disrespect."

The *dama'ting* nodded. "Of course you did not. "You are a *dal'Sharum* drillmaster, and will add the glory of your charges to your own in the afterlife, sitting among Everam's most honored."

"The *dama'ting* honors me," Qeran said.

"Still," the *dama'ting* said, "a reminder of your place will serve you well. Ask Dama Khevat for a penance. Twenty lashes of the alagai tail should do."

Jardir gasped. The alagai tail was the most painful of whips—three strips of leather braided with metal barbs all along their four-foot length.

"The *dama'ting* is forgiving," Qeran said, still bent low. Jardir fled before either one could catch sight of him and wonder what he might have heard.

5

"You shouldn't be here," Abban hissed as Jardir ducked under the flap of the *dama'ting* pavilion. "They will kill you if you're caught!"

"I just wanted to see that you were well," Jardir said. It was true enough, but his eyes scanned the tent carefully, hoping against hope that he might see Inevera again. There had been no sign of the girl since the day Jardir broke his arm, but he had not forgotten her beauty.

Abban looked to his shattered legs, bound tight in hardening casts. "I don't know that I will ever be well again, my friend."

"Nonsense," Jardir said. "Bones heal stronger when they are broken. You will be back on the walls in no time."

"Maybe," Abban sighed.

Jardir bit his lip. "I failed you. I promised to catch you if you should fall. I swore it by Everam's light."

Abban took Jardir's hand. "And so you would have, I do not doubt. I saw you dive to catch my hand. It is not your fault I struck the ground. I hold your oath fulfilled."

Jardir's eyes filled with tears. "I will not fail you again," he promised.

Just then a *dama'ting* entered their partition, floating in silently from deeper within the pavilion. She looked their way, and she met Jardir's eyes. His heart thudded to a stop in his chest, and his face went cold. It seemed they stared at each other forever. The *dama'ting*'s expression was unreadable beneath her opaque white veils.

At last, she tilted her head toward the exit flap. Jardir nodded, hardly believing his luck. He squeezed Abban's hand one last time and darted out of the tent.

5

"You will encounter wind demons upon the walls, but you are not to engage," Qeran said, pacing before the *nie'Sharum*. "That duty will be for the *dal'Sharum* you serve. Still, it is important you understand your foes."

Jardir listened closely, sitting in his usual spot at the front of the group, but he was keenly aware of Abban's absence at his side. Jardir had grown up with three younger sisters, and then found Abban the day he came to the Kaji'sharaj. Loneliness was a strange feeling.

"The *dama* tell us the wind demon resides on the fourth layer of Nie's abyss," Qeran told the boys, gesturing with his spear at a winged image chalked on the sandstone wall.

"Some, like the fools of the Majah tribe, underestimate the wind demon because it lacks the heavy armor of the sand demon," he said, "but do not be fooled. The wind demon is farther from Everam's sight, and a fouler creature by far. Its hide will still turn the point of a man's spear, and the speed of its flight makes it difficult to hit. Its long talons," he outlined the wicked weapons with the point of his spear, "can take a man's head off before he realizes it's there, and its beaklike jaws can tear off a man's face in a single bite."

He turned to the boys. "So. What are its weaknesses?"

Jardir's hand immediately shot up. The drillmaster nodded at him.

"The wings," Jardir said.

"Correct," Qeran said. "Though made of the same tough membrane as its skin, the wings of a wind demon are stretched thin across cartilage and bone. A strong man can puncture them with his spear, or saw them off if his blade is sharp and the creature is prone. What else?"

Again, Jardir's hand was the first to rise. The drillmaster's eyes flicked to the other boys, but none of them raised their hands. Jardir was the youngest of the group by more than two years, but the other boys deferred to him here as they did in the gruel line.

"They are clumsy and slow on the ground," Jardir said when Qeran nodded to him.

"Correct," Qeran said. "If forced to land, wind demons need a running start or something to climb and leap from to take to the air again. The close quarters of the Maze are designed to deny them this. The *dal'Sharum* atop the walls will seek to net them or tangle them with weighted bolas. It will be your duty to report their location to the warriors on the ground."

He eyed the children. "Who can tell me the signal for 'wind demon down'?"

Jardir's hand shot up.

᠊᠊᠊5᠊᠊᠊

It was three months before Abban and Jurim rejoined the *nie'Sharum*. Abban walked back to the training grounds with a pronounced limp, and Jardir frowned to see it.

"Do your legs still pain you?" he asked.

Abban nodded. "My bones may have healed stronger," he said, "but not straighter."

"It's early yet," Jardir said. "They will heal in time."

"*Inevera*," Abban said. "Who can say what Everam wills?"

"Are you ready to fight in the gruel line?" Jardir asked, nodding to the drillmaster coming out with the pot.

Abban paled. "Not yet, I beg," he said. "If my legs give way, I will be marked forever."

Jardir frowned, but he nodded. "Just don't take too long," he said, "lest your inaction mark you as plainly." As he spoke, they walked to the front of the line, and the other boys gave way to Jardir like mice before a cat, allowing them to have the first bowls. A few glared at Abban resentfully, but none dared give challenge.

Jurim had no such luxury, and Jardir watched him coldly, still remembering the older boy's honking laugh as Abban fell. Jurim walked a bit stiffly, but there was nothing of the limp that marred Abban's once straight stride. The boys in the gruel line glared at him, but Jurim strode right up to his usual spot behind Shanjat.

"This place is taken, cripple," Esam, another of the *nie'Sharum* under Jardir's command, said. "To the back of the line with you!" Esam was a fine fighter, and Jardir watched the confrontation with some interest.

Jurim smiled and spread his hands as if in supplication, but Jardir saw the way he positioned his feet and was not fooled. Jurim leapt forward, grappling Esam and bearing him to the ground. It was over in a moment, and Jurim back in his rightful place. Jardir nodded. Jurim had a warrior's heart. He glanced at Abban, who had already finished his bowl of gruel, having missed the fight entirely, and shook his head sadly.

"Gather 'round, rats," Kaval called after the bowls were stacked. Jardir immediately went to the drillmasters, and the other boys followed.

"What do you suppose this is about?" Abban asked.

Jardir shrugged. "They will tell us soon enough."

"A test of manhood is upon you all," Qeran said. "You will pass through the night, and we will learn which of you has a warrior's heart and which does not." Abban inhaled sharply in fear, but Jardir felt a burst of excitement. Every test brought him that much closer to the coveted black robe.

"There has been no word from the village of Baha kad'Everam in some months, and we fear the *alagai* may have breached their wards," Qeran went on. "The Bahavans are *khaffit*, true, but they are descended from the Kaji, and the *Damaji* has decreed that we cannot abandon them."

"Cannot abandon the valuable pottery they sell us, he means," Abban murmured. "Baha is home to Dravazi the master potter, whose work graces every palace in Krasia."

"Is money all you think of?" Jardir snapped. "If they were the lowliest dogs on Ala, they are still infinitely above the *alagai*, and should be protected."

"Ahmann!" Kaval barked. "Do you have something to add?"

Jardir snapped back to attention. "No, Drillmaster!"

"Then hold your tongue," Kaval said, "or I will cut it out."

Jardir nodded, and Qeran went on. "Fifty warriors, volunteers all, will take the weeklong trek to Baha, led by Dama Khevat. You will go to assist them, carrying their equipment, feeding the camels, cooking their meals, and sharpening their spears." He looked to Jardir. "You will be *Nie Ka* for this journey, son of Hoshkamin."

Jardir's eyes widened. *Nie Ka*, meaning "first of none," meant Jardir was first of the *nie'Sharum*—not just in the gruel line, but in the eyes of the drillmasters, as well—and could command and discipline the other boys at will. There had not been a *Nie Ka* in years, since Hasik earned his blacks. It was a tremendous honor, and one not given, or accepted, lightly. For with the power it conveyed, there was also responsibility. He would be held accountable by Qeran and Kaval for the failings of the other boys, and punished accordingly.

Jardir bowed deeply. "You honor me, Drillmaster. I pray to Everam that I do not disappoint."

"You'd better not, if you wish to keep your hide intact," Kaval said as Qeran took a strip of knotted leather and tied it around Jardir's bicep as a symbol of rank.

Jardir's heart thudded in his chest. It was only a strip of leather, but at the moment, it felt like the Crown of Kaji, itself. Jardir thought of how the *dama* would tell his mother of this when she went for her weekly stipend, and swelled with pride. Already he began to bring back honor to the women of his family.

And not only that, but a true test of manhood, as well. Weeks of travel in the open night. He would see the *alagai* up close and come to know his enemy as more than chalk on slate, or something glimpsed at a distance while running the walltop. Truly, it was a day of new beginnings.

Abban turned to Jardir after the *nie'Sharum* were dismissed to their tasks. He smiled, punching Jardir's bicep and the knotted strip of leather around it. *"Nie Ka,"* he said. "You deserve it, my friend. You'll be *kai'Sharum* soon enough, commanding true warriors in battle."

Jardir shrugged. *"Inevera,"* he said. "Let tomorrow bring what it will. For today, this honor is enough."

"You were right before, of course," Abban said. "My heart is sometimes bitter when I see how *khaffit* are treated, and I gave voice to that bitterness before. The Bahavans deserve our protection, and more."

Jardir nodded. "I knew it was so," he said. "I, too, spoke out of turn, my friend. I know there is more to your heart than a merchant's greed."

He squeezed Abban's shoulder, and the boys ran to their tasks preparing for the expedition.

5

They left at midday, fifty Kaji warriors, including Hasik, along with Dama Khevat, Drillmaster Kaval, a pair of Krevakh Watchers, and Jardir's squad of elite *nie'Sharum*. A few of the warriors, the eldest, took turns driving provision carts pulled by camels, but the rest marched on foot, leading the procession through the Maze to the great gate of the city. Jardir and the other boys rode the provision carts through the Maze so as not to sully the sacred ground.

"Only *dama* and *dal'Sharum* may put their feet down on the blood of their brothers and ancestors," Kaval had warned. "Do so at your peril."

Once they were out of the city, the drillmaster smacked his spear against the carts. "Everyone off!" Kaval barked. "We march to Baha!"

Abban looked at Jardir incredulously. "It is a week's travel through the desert, with only our bidos to protect us from the sun!"

Jardir jumped down from the cart. "It is the same sun that beats upon us in the training ground." He pointed to the *dal'Sharum* marching ahead of the supply carts. "Be thankful you have only your bido," he said. "They wear the black, absorbing the heat, and still, each man carries shield and spear, and his armor beneath. If they can march, so can we."

"Come, don't you wish to stretch your legs, after all those weeks we spent in cast?" Jurim asked, slapping Abban's shoulder with a smirk and hopping down.

The rest of the *nie'Sharum* followed, marching as Jardir called the steps to keep pace with the carts and warriors. Kaval trailed behind, keeping watch, but he left command to Jardir. He felt a surge of pride at the drillmaster's trust.

The desert road was a string of ancient signposts along a path of packed sand and hard clay. The ever-present wind whipped hot sand over them; it collected on the road, making footing poor. The sun heated the sand to the point that it burned even through their sandals. But for all that, the *nie'Sharum*, hard from years of training, marched without complaint. Jardir looked at them and was proud.

It quickly became clear, however, that Abban could not keep the pace. Lathered in sweat, his limp grew increasingly pronounced on the uneven footing, and he stumbled frequently. Once, he staggered into Esam, who shoved him violently into Shanjat. Shanjat shoved him back, and Abban hit the ground hard. The other boys laughed as Abban spat sand from his mouth.

"Keep moving, rats!" Kaval called, thumping his spear against his shield.

Jardir wanted to help his friend to his feet, but he knew it would only make matters worse. "Get up!" he barked instead. Abban looked at him with pleading eyes, but Jardir only shook his head, giving Abban a kick for his own good. "Embrace the pain and get up, fool," he said in a low, harsh voice, "or you'll end up *khaffit* like your father!"

The hurt in Abban's eyes cut at him, but Jardir spoke the truth. Abban knew it, too. He sucked in a breath and got to his feet, stumbling after the others. He kept up for some time, but again began to drift to the back of the line, frequently bumping into other boys and being shoved about. Kaval, ever watching, took note and moved up to walk next to Jardir.

"If he slows our march, boy," he said, "it is you I will take the strap to, for all to see."

Jardir nodded. "As you should, Drillmaster. I am *Nie Ka*." Kaval grunted and left it at that.

Jardir went to the others. "Jurim, Abban, get on the carts," he ordered. "You're fresh from the *dama'ting* pavilion, and not ready for a full day's march."

"Camel's piss!" Jurim snarled, pointing a finger in Jardir's face. "I'm not riding the cart like a woman just because the pig-eater's son can't keep up!"

The words were barely out of Jurim's mouth before Jardir struck. He grabbed Jurim's wrist and twisted around to push hard against Jurim's shoulder. The boy had no choice but to go limp lest Jardir break his arm, and the throw landed him heavily on his back. Jardir kept hold of the arm, pulling hard as he put his foot on Jurim's throat.

"You're riding on the cart because your *Nie Ka* commands it," he said loudly as Jurim's face reddened. "Forget that again at your peril."

Jurim's face was turning purple by the time he managed to nod, and he gasped air desperately when Jardir released the hold. "The *dama'ting* commanded that you walk farther each day until you are at full strength," Jardir lied. "Tomorrow you march an hour longer." He looked at Abban coldly. "Both of you."

Abban nodded eagerly, and the two boys headed for the carts. Jardir watched them go, praying for Abban's swift recovery. He could not save face for him forever.

He looked to the other *nie'Sharum*, staring at him, and snarled. "Did I call a halt?" he demanded, and the boys quickly resumed their march. Jardir called the steps at double time until they caught back up.

Night came, and Jardir had his *nie'Sharum* prepare the meals and lay bedrolls as the *dama* and Pit Warders prepared the warding circle. When the circle was ready, the warriors stood at its perimeter, facing outward with shields locked and spears at the ready as the sun set and the demons rose.

This near to the city, sand demons rose in force, hissing at the *dal'Sharum* and flinging themselves at the warriors. It was the first time he had seen them up close, and Jardir watched the *alagai* with a cold eye, memorizing their movements as they leapt to the attack.

The Pit Warders had done their work well, and magic flared to keep the demons at bay. As they struck the wards, the *dal'Sharum* gave a shout and thrust their spears. Most blows were turned by the sand demons' armor, but a few precise blows to eyes or down open throats scored a kill. It seemed a game to the warriors, attempting to deliver such a pinpoint blow in the momentary flash of the magic's light, and they laughed and congratulated the handful of warriors who managed it. Those who had went to their meal, while those who had not kept trying as the demons began to gather. Hasik was one of the first to fill his bowl, Jardir noted.

He looked to Drillmaster Kaval, coming out of the circle after killing a demon of his own. His red night veil was raised, the first time Jardir had ever seen it so. He caught the drillmaster's eye, and when the man nodded Jardir approached, bowing deeply.

"Drillmaster," he said, "this is not *alagai'sharak* as we were taught it."

Kaval laughed. "This is not *alagai'sharak* at all, boy, just a game to keep our spears sharp. The Evejah commands that *alagai'sharak* only be fought on prepared ground. There are no demon pits here, no maze walls or ambush pockets. We would be fools to leave our circle, but that is no reason why we cannot show a few *alagai* the sun."

Jardir bowed again. "Thank you, Drillmaster. I understand now."

The game went on for hours more, until the remaining demons decided there was no gap in the wards and began to circle the camp or sat back on their haunches out of spear's reach, watching. The warriors with full stomachs then went to take watch, hooting and catcalling at those who had failed to make a kill as they went to their meal.

After all had eaten, half the warriors went to their bedrolls, and the other half stood like statues in a ring around the camp. After a few hours' sleep, the warriors relieved their brothers.

The next day, they passed through a *khaffit* village. Jardir had never seen one before, though there were many small oases in the desert, mostly to the south and east of the city, where a trickle of water sprouted from the ground and filled a small pool. *Khaffit* who had fled the city would often cluster at these, but so long as they fed themselves and did not beg at the city wall or prey on passing merchants, the *dama* were content to ignore them.

There were larger oases, as well, where a large pool meant a hundred or more *khaffit* might gather, often with women and children in tow. These the *dama* did pay some mind to, with the warrior tribes claiming individual oases as they did the wells of the city, taxing the *khaffit* in labor and goods for the right to live there. *Dama* would occasionally travel to the villages closest to the city, taking any young boys to *Hannu Pash* and the most beautiful girls as *jiwah'Sharum* for the great harems.

The village they passed through had no wall, just a series of sandstone monoliths around its perimeter with ancient wards cut deep into the stone. "What is this place?" Jardir wondered aloud as they marched.

"They call the village Sandstone," Abban said. "Over three hundred *khaffit* live here. They are known as pit dogs."

"Pit dogs?" Jardir asked.

Abban pointed to a giant pit in the ground, one of several in the village, where men and women toiled together, harvesting sandstone with shovel, pick, and saw. The folk were broad of shoulder and packed with muscle, quite unlike the *khaffit* Jardir knew from the city. Children worked alongside them, loading carts and leading the camels that hauled the stone up out of the pits. All wore tan clothes—man and boy alike in vest and cap, and the women and girls in tan dresses that left little to the imagination, their faces, arms, and even legs mostly uncovered.

"These are strong people," Jardir said. "By what rule are these men *khaffit*? Are they all cowards? What about the girls and boys? Why are they not called to marriage or *Hannu Pash*?"

"Their ancestors were *khaffit* by their own failing, perhaps, my friend," Abban said, "but these people are *khaffit* by birth."

"I don't understand," Jardir said. "There are no *khaffit* by birth."

Abban sighed. "You say all I think of is merchanting, but perhaps it is you who does not think of it enough. The *Damaji* want the stone these people harvest, and a healthy stock to do the work. In exchange, they instruct the *dama* not to come for the *khaffit's* children."

"Condemning the children to spending their lives as *khaffit*, as well," Jardir said. "Why would their parents want that?"

"Parents can behave strangely when men come to take their children," Abban said.

Jardir remembered his mother's tears, and the shrieks of Abban's mother, and could not disagree. "Still, these men would make fine warriors, and their women fine wives who breed strong sons. It is a waste to see them squandered so."

Abban shrugged. "At least when one of them is injured, his brothers don't turn on him like a pack of wolves."

It was another six days of travel before they reached the cliff face overlooking the river that fed the village of Baha kad'Everam. They encountered no more *khaffit* villages along the way. Abban, whose family traded with many of the villages, said it was because an underground river fed many oases near the city, but it did not stretch so far east. Most of the villages were south of the city, between the Desert Spear and the distant southern mountains, along the path of that river. Jardir had never heard of a river underground, but he trusted his friend.

The river before them was not precisely underground, but it had eroded a deep valley over time, cutting through countless layers of sandstone and clay. They could see its bed far below, though the water seemed only a trickle from such a height.

They marched south along the cliff until the path leading down to the village came into sight, invisible until they were almost on top of it. The *dal'Sharum* blew horns of greeting, but there was no response as they made their way down the steep, narrow road to the village square. Even there in the center of town, there were no inhabitants to be found.

The village of Baha kad'Everam was built in tiers cut into the cliff face. A wide, uneven stair led up in zigzag, forming a terrace for the adobe buildings on each level. There were no signs of life in the village, and cloth door flaps drifted lazily in the breeze. It reminded Jardir of some of the older parts of the Desert Spear; large parts of the city were abandoned as the population dwindled. The ancient buildings were a testament to when Krasians were numberless.

"What happened here?" Jardir wondered aloud.

"Isn't it obvious?" Abban asked. Jardir looked at him curiously.

"Stop staring at the village and take a wider look," Abban said. Jardir turned and saw that the river had not appeared to be a trickle merely because of a trick of height. The waters hardly reached a third of the way up the deep bed.

"Not enough rain," Abban said, "or a diversion of the water's path upriver. The change likely robbed the Bahavans of the fish they depended on to survive."

"That wouldn't explain the death of a whole village," Jardir said.

Abban shrugged. "Perhaps the water turned sour as it shallowed, picking up silt from the riverbed. Either way, by sickness or hunger, the Bahavans must not have been able to maintain their wards." He gestured to the deep claw marks in the adobe walls of some of the buildings.

Kaval turned to Jardir. "Search the village for signs of survivors," he said. Jardir bowed and turned to his *nie'Sharum*, breaking them into groups of two and sending each to a different level. The boys darted up the uneven stairs as easily as they ran the walltops of the Maze.

It quickly became apparent that Abban had been right. There were signs of demons in almost every building, claw marks on walls and furniture and signs of struggle everywhere.

"No bodies, though," Abban noted.

"Eaten," Jardir said, pointing to what appeared to be black stone with a few bits of white sticking from it, sitting on the floor.

"What's that?" Abban asked.

"Demon dung," Jardir said. "*Alagai* eat their victims whole and shit out the bones." Abban slapped a hand to his mouth, but it was not enough. He ran to the side of the room to retch.

They reported their findings to Drillmaster Kaval, who nodded as if this were no surprise. "Walk at my back, *Nie Ka*," he said, and Jardir followed him as the drillmaster walked over to where Dama Khevat stood with the *kai'Sharum*.

"The *nie'Sharum* confirm there are no survivors, Dama," Kaval said. The *kai'Sharum* outranked him, but Kaval was a drillmaster and had likely trained every warrior on the expedition, including the *kai'Sharum*. As it was said, *The words of the red veil carry more weight than the white.*

Dama Khevat nodded. "The *alagai* cursed the ground when they broke through the wards, trapping the spirits of the dead *khaffit* in this world. I can feel their screams in the air." He looked up at Kaval. "A Waning is upon us. We will spend the first two days and nights preparing the village and praying."

"And on the third night of Waning?" Kaval asked.

"On the third night, we will dance *alagai'sharak*," Khevat said, "to hallow the ground and set their spirits free, that they might be reincarnated in hope of a better caste."

Kaval bowed. "Of course, Dama." He looked up at the stairs and buildings built into the cliff face, and the wide courtyard beneath leading down to the riverbank. "It will be mostly clay demons here," he guessed, "though likely a few wind and sand as well." He turned to the *kai'Sharum*. "With your permission, I will have the *dal'Sharum* dig warded demon pits in the courtyard, and set ambush points on the stairs to drive the *alagai* off the cliff and into the pits to await the sun."

The *kai'Sharum* nodded, and the drillmaster turned to Jardir. "Set the *nie'Sharum* to clearing the buildings of any debris we can make into barricades." Jardir nodded and turned to go, but Kaval caught his arm. "See that they loot nothing," he warned. "All must go as sacrifice to *alagai'sharak*."

〜

"You and I will clear the first level," Jardir told Abban.

"Seven is a luckier number," Abban said. "Let Jurim and Shanjat clear the first."

Jardir looked at Abban's leg skeptically. Abban had managed to keep up with the march, but his limp had not gone away, and Jardir often saw him massaging the limb when he thought no one was watching.

"I thought the first would be an easier ascent, with your leg not fully healed," Jardir said.

Abban put his hands on his hips. "My friend, you wound me!" he said. "I am fit as the finest camel in the bazaar. You were right to push me to exceed myself each day, and a climb to the seventh level will only help."

Jardir shrugged. "As you wish," he said, and they set off climbing the steps after he had given instructions to the other *nie'Sharum*.

The irregular stone steps of Baha were cut into the cliff face, shored at key points with sandstone and clay. They were sometimes as narrow as a man's foot, and other times required many paces to the next step. Worn stone showed the passage of many laden wagons pulled by beasts of burden. The steps changed direction with each tier, branching off a path to the buildings of that level.

They had not gone far before Abban's breath labored, his round face beading with sweat. His limp grew worse, and by the fifth level he was hissing in pain with every step.

"Perhaps we've gone far enough for one day," Jardir ventured.

"Nonsense, my friend," Abban said. "I am . . ." he groaned and blew out a breath, ". . . strong as a camel."

Jardir smiled and slapped him on the back. "We'll make a warrior of you yet."

They reached the seventh level at last, and Jardir turned to look out over the low wall. Far below, the *dal'Sharum* bent their backs, digging wide demon pits with short spades. The pits were set right at the edge of the first tier, so that a demon hurled from the very wall Jardir looked over would land within. Jardir felt a flash of excitement for the battle to come, even though he and the other *nie'Sharum* would not be allowed to fight.

He turned to Abban, but his friend had moved on down the terrace, ignoring the view.

"We should start clearing the buildings," Jardir said, but Abban seemed not to hear, limping purposefully away. Jardir caught up just as Abban stopped in front of a great archway, breaking into a wide smile as he looked up at the symbols carved into the arch.

"Level seven, I knew it!" Abban said. "The same as the number of pillars between Heaven and Ala."

"I've never seen wards like those," Jardir said, looking at the symbols.

"Those aren't wards, they are drawn words," Abban said.

Jardir looked at him curiously. "Like those written in the Evejah?"

Abban nodded. "They read: 'Here, seven tiers from Ala to honor He who is Everything, is the humble workshop of Master Dravazi.' "

"The potter you spoke of," Jardir growled. Abban nodded, moving to push back the bright curtain that hung in the doorway, but Jardir grabbed his arm, pulling Abban to face him.

"So you can embrace pain when it comes to profit, but not to honor?" he demanded.

Abban smiled. "I am merely practical, my friend. You cannot spend honor."

"You can in Heaven," Jardir said.

Abban snorted. "We cannot clothe our mothers and sisters from Heaven." He pulled his arm free and entered the shop. Jardir had no choice but to follow, walking right into Abban, who had stopped short just within the doorway, his mouth hanging open.

"The shipment is intact," Abban whispered, his eyes taking on a covetous gleam. Jardir followed his gaze, and his own eyes widened as well. There, stacked neatly upon great pallets, was the most exquisite pottery he had ever seen. It filled the room—pots and vases and chalices, lamps and plates and bowls. All of it painted in bright color and gold leaf, fire-glazed to a pristine shine.

Abban rubbed his hands together with excitement. "Do you have any idea what this is worth, my friend?" he asked.

"It doesn't matter," Jardir said. "It isn't ours."

Abban looked at him as if he were a fool. "It isn't stealing if the owners are dead, Ahmann."

"It is worse than stealing, to loot from the dead," Jardir said. "It is desecration."

"Desecration would be casting a master artisan's life's work into a rubbish pile," Abban said. "There is plenty of other debris to use in the barricades."

Jardir considered the pottery. "Very well," he said at last. "We will leave it here. Let it tell the story of the craft of this greatest of *khaffit*, that Everam may look down upon his works and reincarnate his spirit to a higher caste."

"What need to tell tales to Everam, if He is all-knowing?" Abban asked.

Jardir balled a fist, and Abban took a step back. "I will not hear Everam blasphemed," he growled. "Not even from you."

Abban held his hands up in supplication. "No blasphemy intended. I merely meant Everam could see the pottery as well in a *Damaji's* palace as in this forgotten workshop."

"That may be," Jardir conceded, "but Kaval said everything must be sacrificed to *alagai'sharak*, and that means this, too."

Abban's eyes flicked to Jardir's fist, still tightly closed, and he nodded. "Of course, my friend," he agreed. "But if we are truly to honor this great *khaffit* and recommend him to Heaven, let us use his fine pots to carry dirt for the *dal'Sharum* digging the demon pits. It will put the pottery to work in fighting *alagai'sharak*, and show Dravazi's worth to Everam."

Jardir relaxed, his fist falling into five loose fingers once more. He smiled at Abban and nodded. "That is a fine idea." They selected the pieces most suited to the task and carried them back to the camp. The rest they left neatly stacked, just as they had found them.

Jardir and the others fell into their work, and the two full days and nights passed quickly as the battlefield for *alagai'sharak* began to form. Each night they took shelter behind their circles, studying the demons and laying their plans. The terraced tiers of the village became a maze of debris piles hiding warded alcoves the *dal'Sharum* would use as ambush points, leaping out to drive the *alagai* over the sides into the demon pits, or to net them long enough to trap them in portable circles. Supply depots were warded on every level; there the *nie'Sharum* would wait, ready to run fresh spears or nets to the warriors.

"Stay behind the wards until you are called for," Kaval instructed the novices, "and when you must cross them, do so quickly, heading directly from one warded area to the next until you reach your destination. Keep ducked low behind the wall, using every bit of cover." He made the boys memorize the makeshift maze until they could find the warded alcoves with their eyes closed, if need be. The warriors would set bonfires to see and fight by, driving off the cold of the desert night, but there would still be great pockets of shadow where the demons, which could see in the dark, would hold every advantage.

Before long Jardir and Abban were waiting in a supply depot on the third level as the sun set. The cliff wall faced east, so they watched as its shadow reached out to envelop the river valley, creeping up the far cliff wall like an inky stain. And in the shadow of the valley, the *alagai* began to rise.

The mist seeped from the clay and sandstone, coalescing into demonic form. Jardir and Abban watched in fascination as the demons rose in the courtyard thirty feet below, illuminated by the great bonfires as the *dal'Sharum* put everything flammable in Baha to the torch.

For the first time, Jardir truly understood what the *dama* had been telling them all these years. The *alagai* were abominations, hidden from Everam's light. All of Ala would be the Creator's paradise if not for their foul taint. He was filled with loathing to the core of his being, and knew he would give his life gladly for their destruction. He gripped one of the spare spears in the alcove, imagining the day he might hunt them with his *dal'Sharum* brothers.

Abban gripped Jardir's arm, and he turned to see his friend point a shaking hand at the terrace wall just a few feet away. All along the terrace, the mists were rising, and there on the wall a wind demon was forming. It crouched, wings folded, as it solidified. Neither boy had ever been so close to a demon, and while the sight filled Abban with obvious terror, Jardir felt only rage. He gripped the spear tighter and wondered if he could charge the creature, knocking it from the wall before it was fully formed and dropping it into one of the demon pits below.

Abban squeezed Jardir's arm so tightly it became painful. Jardir looked at his friend and saw Abban looking right into his eyes.

"Don't be a fool," Abban said.

Jardir looked back to the demon, but the choice was taken from him in that moment as the *alagai* loosed its talons from their grip on the sandstone wall and dropped away into the darkness. There was a sudden snapping sound, and the wind demon soared back upward, its huge wings blocking out the stars as it swooped by.

Not far off, an orange clay demon formed, barely distinguishable from the adobe wall it clung to. The demon was small and snub, no larger than a small dog, but a compact killer of bunched muscle, talon, and thick, overlapping armor plates. It lifted its blunt head, sniffing the air. Kaval had taught that the head of a clay demon could smash through almost anything, shattering stone and denting fine steel. They witnessed its power firsthand as the demon charged them, smashing headfirst into the wards around their alcove. Silver magic spiderwebbed from the point of impact, and the clay demon was thrown back. It moved back up to the wards immediately, though, digging its talons into the cliff face as its head shot forward repeatedly, hammering at the wards and sending magic rippling through the air.

Jardir took his spear and thrust it at the demon's maw, as he had seen the *dal'Sharum* do on the trek across the desert. But the demon was too fast, and caught the point in its jaws. The metal speartip twisted like clay as the demon shook its head, tearing the weapon from Jardir's grasp and nearly pulling him out of the safety of the alcove. The demon whipped its head aside, sending the spear spinning over the wall and into the darkness.

Hasik saw the exchange from his alcove farther down the terrace. He was stationed as a Baiter, and would soon emerge to lead the demons to their doom.

"Waste another spear, rat," he cried, his *s*'s still whistling after all these years, "and I'll throw you over the wall after it!" Jardir felt a burst of shame and bowed, withdrawing farther into the alcove to wait for commands.

The Krevakh Watchers, balanced atop their ladders, could move from one level to the next in seconds. They surveyed the battlefield from above and gave signal to the *kai'Sharum,* who blew the Horn of Sharak, beginning the dance.

Hasik immediately stepped from his alcove, yelling and cavorting about to draw the attention of the demons nearby. Jardir watched in fascination. Whatever his feelings about Hasik, the man's honor knew no bounds.

Several clay demons shrieked as they caught sight of him, leaping to give chase. Their short, powerful legs pumped with terrifying speed, but Hasik stood unafraid, letting them commit to the chase before taking off himself, running for the ambush point up ahead, past the first barriers. The clay demon on the wall by Jardir's alcove leapt at him as he went by, but Hasik twisted and brought up his shield, not only deflecting the attack but also angling the shield so that the magic sent the demon hurling over the wall and shrieking all the way down into the pits—the first kill of the night.

Hasik sprinted into the maze of debris, dodging around the barriers with a speed and agility that belied his heavy frame. He moved out of Jardir and Abban's sight, but they heard him cry *"Oot!"* as he approached the ambush pocket. The call was a traditional one for Baiters, signaling to the *dal'Sharum* at an ambush point that *alagai* approached.

There were shouts and flashes of magic as the hidden warriors fell upon the unsuspecting demons. *Alagai* shrieks filled the night, and the sound sent a chill down Jardir's spine. He longed to make demons shriek their suffering, as well. One day . . .

As he mused, a Watcher, Aday, popped up over the wall right in front of them. Their twelve-foot ladders were just enough to make it up the wall from one level to the next.

Aday pulled on the stout leathern thong attached to his wrist, drawing the ladder up after him. He moved to set it to scale the next level, but a growl above halted him. He glanced up just as a clay demon leapt at him.

Jardir tensed, but he need not have worried. Quick as a snake, the Watcher had his ladder turned crosswise to catch the demon at arm's length before it struck. Aday kicked cleanly through the rungs, knocking the *alagai* down to the terrace floor.

In the time it took the clay demon to recover, Aday skittered back several feet, extending the full twelve feet of the ladder between them. The demon leapt again, but Aday caught it between the side poles and lifted the ladder with a twist, easily hurling the small demon over the wall. In seconds he was back to setting his ladder.

"Bring extra spears to the Push Guard in the courtyard," he called to them as he sprinted up to the next level, his hands never even touching the rungs.

Jardir grabbed a pair of spears, and Abban did likewise, but Jardir could see the fear in his eyes. "Stay close to me, and do as I do," he told his friend. "This is no different from the drills we did all day."

"Except that this is night," Abban said. But he followed as Jardir glanced both ways and darted for Hasik's alcove, keeping crouched low behind the wall to avoid the notice of the wind demons circling high above the village.

They made it to the alcove, and from there down the steps to the courtyard. Clay demons fell like rain from above as the *dal'Sharum* drove them over the terrace walls. The ambush points were precisely placed, and the majority of the *alagai* fell directly into the makeshift demon pits. As for the rest, and the sand demons that had formed in the courtyard, the Push Guard harried them into the pits with spear and shield. One-way wards were staked around the mouth and floor of each pit; *alagai* could enter, but not escape. The spears of the warriors could not pierce *alagai* armor, but they could sting and shove and harry, sending the demons stumbling back over the edge.

"Boy! Spear!" Kaval called, and Jardir saw that the drillmaster's own spear was snapped in half as he faced a sand demon. Seemingly unhindered, Kaval spun the broken shaft so quickly it blurred, driving it into the demon's shoulder and hip joints, preventing it from finding balance or any footing save in the direction the drillmaster wanted it to go. All along, Kaval continued to advance, pivoting smoothly to add force to thrusts and to bring his shield into play as he forced the demon ever closer to the pit's edge.

But while the drillmaster seemed to be in no danger from the demon before him, more were falling from the terraces at every moment, and the inferior weapon was slowing him at a time he needed to finish the demon quickly.

"*Acha!*" Jardir called, throwing a fresh spear. At the call, Kaval shoved the broken shaft down the demon's throat and caught the new one in a smooth turn that brought him right back in to attack with the new weapon. In moments the sand demon fell shrieking into the pit.

"Don't just stand there!" Kaval barked. "Finish and get back to your post!" Jardir nodded and scurried off, he and Abban similarly supplying other warriors.

When they were out of spears, they turned to head back up the steps. They had not gone far when a thump behind them turned their heads. Jardir looked back to see an angry clay demon roll back to its feet and shake its head. It was far from the Push Guard, and spotted easier prey in Abban and Jardir.

"The ambush pocket!" Jardir shouted, pointing to the small warded alcove where the Push Guard had hidden until the demons began to fall from above. As the clay demon charged after them, the two boys broke for it. Abban, in his fear, even managed to take the lead.

But just shy of the pocket's safety, Abban gave a cry as his leg collapsed under him. He hit the ground hard, and it was clear he would not be able to rise in time.

Jardir picked up speed, leaping to tackle Abban as he struggled to rise. He took the brunt of the impact himself, rolling them both over and turning the momentum into a perfect *sharusahk* throw that sent Abban's bulky frame tumbling the last few feet to safety.

Jardir fell flat and remained prone when the move was completed. The demon, predictably, followed the motion and leapt at Abban, only to strike the wards of the pocket.

Jardir got quickly to his feet as the clay demon shook off the shock of the wards, but the demon spotted him immediately, and worse, it stood between him and the safety of the wards.

Jardir had no weapon or net, and knew the demon could outrun him on open ground. He felt a moment of panic until he remembered the words of Drillmaster Qeran.

Alagai *have no guile,* his teacher had taught. *They may be stronger and faster than you, but their brains are those of a slow-witted dog. They reveal their intent in their bearing, and the humblest feint will confuse them. Never forget your wits, and you will always see the dawn.*

Jardir made as if to run toward the nearest demon pit, then turned sharply and ran instead for the steps. He dodged around the rubble and barricades on sheer memory, wasting no time in confirming with eyes what his head knew. The demon shrieked and gave chase, but Jardir gave it no more thought, focusing only on his path ahead.

"*Oot!*" he cried as Hasik's alcove came into sight, signaling the demon behind him. He could shelter there, and Hasik could lead the demon into ambush.

But Hasik's alcove was empty. The warrior must have just sprung another trap, and was at the ambush point fighting.

Jardir knew he could shelter in the alcove, but then what of this demon? At best, it might escape the killing field, and at worst, it could catch some warrior or *nie'Sharum* unawares and be on him before he understood what was happening.

He put his head down and ran on.

He managed to put some ground between himself and the clay demon in the makeshift maze, but it was still close behind when the ambush point came in sight.

"Oot!" Jardir called. *"Oot! Oot!"* He put on a last burst of speed, hoping the warriors within heard his call and would be ready.

He darted around the last barrier, and a pair of quick hands grabbed him and yanked him off to the side. "You think this is a game, rat?" Hasik demanded.

Jardir had no reply, and thankfully needed none as the demon came charging into the ambush point. A *dal'Sharum* threw a net over it, tripping it up.

The demon thrashed, snapping the thick strands of the woven horsehair net like thread, and seemed about to tear itself free when several warriors tackled it and pinned it to the ground. One *dal'Sharum* took a rake of claws to the face and fell away screaming, but another took his place, grabbing two of the demon's overlapping armor plates and pulling them apart with his hands, revealing the vulnerable flesh beneath.

Hasik flung Jardir aside, running in and driving his spear into the opening. The demon shrieked and writhed about in agony, but Hasik twisted the weapon savagely. The demon gave a final wrack and lay still. Jardir gave a whoop and thrust his fist into the air.

His delight was short-lived, though, as Hasik let go the spear, leaving it jutting from the dead *alagai,* and stormed over to him.

"You think yourself a Baiter, *nie'Sharum?*" he demanded. "You could have gotten men killed, taking it upon yourself to drive *alagai* into a trap that had not been reset."

"I meant no—" Jardir began, but Hasik punched him hard in the stomach, and the response was blown from his lips.

"I gave you no leave to speak, boy!" Hasik shouted. Jardir saw his rage and wisely held his tongue. "Your orders were to stay in your alcove, not lead *alagai* to the backs of unprepared warriors!"

"Better he brought it here with some warning than left it loose on the terrace, Hasik," Jesan said. Hasik glared at him, but held his tongue. Jesan was an older warrior, perhaps even forty winters, and the others in the group deferred to him in the absence of Kaval or the *kai'Sharum*. He was bleeding freely from where the demon had clawed his face, but he showed no sign of pain.

"You would not have been injured—" Hasik began, but Jesan cut him off.

"These will not be my first demon scars, Whistler," he said, "and every one is a glory to be cherished. Now get back to your post. There are demons yet to kill this night."

Hasik scowled, but he bowed. "As you say, the night is young," he agreed. His eyes shot spears at Jardir as he left for his alcove.

"You get back to your post, too, boy," Jesan said, clapping Jardir on the shoulder.

Dawn came at last, and all the company gathered at the demon pits to watch the *alagai* burn. Baha kad'Everam faced east, and the rising sun quickly flooded the valley. The demons howled in the pits as light filled the sky and their flesh began to smolder.

The insides of the *dal'Sharum* shields were polished to a mirror finish, and as Dama Khevat spoke a prayer for the souls of the Bahavans, one by one the warriors turned them to catch the light, angling rays down into the pits to strike the demons directly.

Wherever the light touched the demons, they burst into flame. Soon all the *alagai* were ablaze, and the *nie'Sharum* cheered. Seeing warriors doing likewise, some even lowered their bidos to piss on the demons as Everam's light burned them from the world. Jardir had never felt so alive as he did in that moment, and he turned to Abban to share his joy.

But Abban was nowhere to be seen.

Thinking his friend still distressed over his fall the night before, Jardir went looking for him. Abban was injured, that was all. It was not the same as being weak. They would bide their time and ignore the sniggers of the other *nie'Sharum* until Abban had regained his strength, and then they would deal with the sniggerers directly and end the mocking once and for all.

He searched through the camp and almost missed Abban, at last spotting his friend crawling out from under one of the provision carts.

"What are you doing?" Jardir asked.

"Oh!" Abban said, turning in surprise. "I was just . . ."

Jardir ignored him, pushing past Abban and looking under the cart.

Abban had strung a net there, filling it with the Dravazi pottery they had used as tools, cleverly packed with cloth to keep the pieces from clattering or breaking on the journey back.

Abban spread his hands as Jardir turned to him, smiling. "My friend—"

Jardir cut him off. "Put them back."

"Ahmann," Abban started.

"Put them back or I will break your other leg," Jardir growled.

Abban sighed, but it was more in exasperation than submission. "Again I ask you to be practical, my friend. We both know that with this leg, I have more chance of helping my family through profit than honor. And if I somehow still manage to become *dal'Sharum*, how long will I last? Even the strong veterans who came here to Baha will not all go home alive. For myself, I will be lucky to last through my first night. And what of my family then, if I leave this world with no glory? I don't want my mother to end up selling my sisters as *jiwah'Sharum* because they have no dowry save my spilled blood."

"*Jiwah'Sharum* are sold?" Jardir asked, thinking of his own sisters, poorer than Abban's by far. *Jiwah'Sharum* were group wives, kept in the great harem for all *dal'Sharum* to use.

"Did you think girls volunteered?" Abban asked. "Being *jiwah'Sharum* may appear glorious for the young and beautiful, but they seldom even know whose children grow in their bellies, and their honor fades once their wombs grow barren and their features less fair. Better by far a proper husband, even a *khaffit*, than that."

Jardir said nothing, digesting the information, and Abban moved closer, leaning in as if to speak in confidence, though they were quite alone.

"We could split the profits, my friend," he said. "Half to my mother, and half to yours. When was the last time she or your sisters had meat? Or more than rags to wear? Honor may help them years from this day, but a quick profit can help them now."

Jardir looked at him skeptically. "How will a handful of pots make any difference?"

"These are not just any pots, Ahmann," Abban said. "Think of it! These last works of master Dravazi, used by the *dal'Sharum* to help avenge his death and set free the *khaffit* souls of Baha. They will be priceless! The *Damaji* themselves would buy and display them. We need not even clean them! The dirt of Baha will be better than any glaze of gold."

"Kaval said all must be sacrificed, to hallow the ground of Baha," Jardir said.

"And so everything has," Abban said. "These are just tools, Ahmann, no

different from the spades the *dal'Sharum* used to dig the pits. It is not looting
to keep our tools."

"Then why hide them under the cart like a thief?"

Abban smiled. "Do you think Hasik and his cronies would let us keep the
profits if they knew?"

"I suppose not," Jardir conceded.

"It's settled then," Abban said, clapping Jardir on the shoulder. Quickly
they packed the rest of the pottery in the secret sling.

They were almost finished when Abban took a delicate cup and deliberately started rolling it in the dirt.

"What are you doing?" Jardir asked.

Abban shrugged. "This cup was too small to be of use in the work," he
said, holding up the cup and admiring the dust upon it. "But the dust of Baha
will increase its value tenfold."

"But it's a lie," Jardir said.

Abban winked. "The buyer will never know that, my friend."

"*I* will know!" Jardir shouted, taking the cup and hurling it to the
ground. It struck the ground and shattered.

Abban shrieked. "You idiot, do you have any idea what that was worth?"
But at Jardir's seething glare, he wisely put up his hands and took a step
back.

"Of course, my friend, you are right," he agreed. As if to drive the point
home, he lifted another similarly clean piece and smashed that on the ground
as well.

Jardir eyed the broken shards and sighed. "Send nothing to my family,"
he said. "I want no profit to come to the line of Jardir from this . . . low deed.
I would rather see my sisters chew hard grain than eat tainted meat."

Abban looked at him with incredulity, but at last he simply shrugged. "As
you wish, my friend. But if your mind ever changes . . ."

"If that day comes, and you are my true friend, you will refuse me,"
Jardir said. "And if I ever catch you at something like this again, I will bring
you before the *dama* myself."

Abban looked at him a moment longer, and nodded.

It was nighttime on the Krasian wall, and all about him Jardir could feel the
thrum of battle. It made him proud that he would one day die as a Kaji warrior in the Maze.

"*Alagai* down!" Watcher Aday called. "Northeast quad! Second layer!"

Jardir nodded, turning to the other boys. "Jurim, inform the Majah in layer three that glory is near. Shanjat, let the Anjha know the Majah will be moving away from their position."

"I can go," Abban volunteered. Jardir glanced at him doubtfully. He knew it dishonored his friend to hold him back, but Abban's limp had not subsided in the weeks since they had returned from Baha, and *alagai'sharak* was no game.

"Stay with me for now," he said. The other boys smirked and ran off.

Drillmaster Qeran noticed the exchange, and his lip curled in disgust as he looked at Abban. "Make yourself useful, boy, and untangle the nets."

Jardir pretended not to notice Abban's limp as he complied. He returned to Qeran's side.

"You can't spare him forever," the drillmaster said quietly, raising his far-seeing glass to search the skies. "Better he die a man in the Maze than return from the walls in shame."

Jardir wondered at the words. What was the true path? If he sent Abban, there was a risk he would fail in his duty, putting fighting men at risk. But if he did not, then Qeran would eventually declare the boy *khaffit*—a fate far worse than death. Abban's spirit would sit outside the gates of Heaven, never knowing Everam's embrace as he waited, perhaps millennia, for reincarnation.

Ever since Qeran had made him *Nie Ka,* responsibility had weighed upon Jardir heavily. He wondered if Hasik, who had once held the same honor, had felt the same pressure. It was doubtful. Hasik would have killed Abban or driven him out of the pack long since.

He sighed, resolving to send Abban on the next run. "Better dead than *khaffit,*" he murmured, the words bitter on his tongue.

"Ware!" Qeran cried as a wind demon dove at them. He and Jardir got down in time, but Aday was not as quick. His head thumped along the wall toward Jardir as his body fell into the Maze. Abban screamed.

"It's banking for another pass!" Qeran warned.

"Abban! Net!" Jardir called.

Abban was quick to comply, favoring his good leg as he dragged the heavily weighted net to Qeran. He had folded it properly for throwing, Jardir noted. That was something, at least.

Qeran snatched the net, never taking his eyes from the returning wind demon. Jardir saw with his warrior's eye, and knew the drillmaster was calculating its speed and trajectory. He was taut as a bowstring, and Jardir knew he would not miss.

As the *alagai* came in range, Qeran uncoiled like a cobra and threw with a smooth snap. But the net opened too soon, and Jardir immediately saw why: Abban had accidentally tangled his foot in one of the weight ropes. He was thrown from his feet by the force of Qeran's throw.

The wind demon pulled up short of the opening net, buffeting both the net and Qeran with its wings. The *alagai* dropped from sight, and the drill-master went down, hopelessly tangled in the net.

"Nie take you, boy!" Qeran cried, kicking out from the tangle to knock Abban's legs from under him. With a shriek, Abban fell from the wall a second time, this time into a maze alive with *alagai*.

Before Jardir had time to react, there was a shriek, and he realized the *alagai* was righting itself to come at them again. With Qeran tangled, there were no *dal'Sharum* to stop it.

"Flee while you can!" Qeran shouted.

Jardir ignored him, racing for the nets Abban had folded. He lifted one, grunting at its weight. He and the other boys trained with lighter versions.

The wind demon shot past in a flap of leathern wings, banking hard in the sky for another dive. For a moment it blocked the moon, vanishing in the sky, but Jardir was not fooled, and tracked its approach calmly. If he was to die, he would do so with honor, and take this *alagai* with him to pay his way into Heaven.

When the demon was close enough that Jardir could see its teeth, he threw. The horsehair net spun as the weights pulled it open, and the wind demon hit the web head-on. Yanking the cord to tighten the net, Jardir pivoted smoothly out of the way and watched the creature plummet into the Maze.

"*Alagai* down!" he cried. "Northeast quadrant! Layer seven!" A moment later there was an answering cry.

He was about to turn back and free Qeran when movement in the darkness caught his eye. Abban hung from the top of the wall, his fingernails bleeding as they scraped and strained against the stone.

"Don't let me fall!" Abban cried.

"If you fall, you will die a man, and Heaven await you!" Jardir said. He left unsaid the fact that Abban would never see Heaven any other way. Qeran would see that he ended his *Hannu Pash* as *khaffit*, and paradise would be denied him. It tore at Jardir's heart, but he began to turn away.

"No! Please!" Abban begged, tears streaming down his dirty cheeks. "You swore! You swore by Everam's light to catch me. I don't want to die!"

"Better dead than *khaffit*!" Jardir growled.

"I don't care if I'm *khaffit*!" Abban said. "Don't let me fall! Please!"

Jardir snarled, disgusted, but he bent despite himself, lying flat on the wall and pulling hard on Abban's arm. Abban kicked and strained, finally managing to crawl up Jardir's back and onto the wall. He threw himself on Jardir, sobbing.

"Everam bless you," Abban wept. "I owe my life to you."

Jardir shoved him away. "You disgust me, coward," he said. "Begone from my sight before I change my mind and throw you back."

Abban's eyes widened in shock, but he bowed and scurried away as fast as his lame leg would allow.

As Jardir watched him go, a fist connected hard with his kidney, sending him sprawling. Agony fired over him, but he opened himself to it, and the pain washed away as he turned to face his assaulter.

"You should have let him fall," Qeran said. "You did him no favors this night. A *dal'Sharum's* duty is to support his brothers in death as well as life." His spittle splattered on Jardir's shoulder. "No gruel for three days," he said. "Now fetch my far-seer. *Alagai'sharak* does not wait for cowards and fools."

CHAPTER 3

CHIN

:: 333 AR ::

ABBAN RETURNED WITH JAYAN and Asome some time later. They dragged with them a number of Northern *chin* and a single *dama*.

"This is Dama Rajin, of the Mehnding," Jayan said, ushering the cleric forward. "It is he who ordered the silos burned." He shoved the *dama* hard, and the man fell to his knees.

"How many?" Jardir asked.

"Three, before he could be stopped," Jayan said, "but he would have kept on burning."

"Losses?" Jardir looked to Abban.

"It will be some time before I know for sure, Shar'Dama Ka," Abban said, "but it could be close to two hundred tons. Grain enough to feed thousands through the winter months."

Jardir looked to the *dama*. "And what have you to say?"

"It is written in the Evejah's treatise on war to burn the enemy's stores, so they cannot make further war," Dama Rajin said. "There remains grain enough to feed our people many times over."

"Fool!" Jardir shouted, backhanding the man. There were gasps around the room. "I need to levy the Northerners, not starve and kill them! The true enemies are the *alagai*—something you have forgotten!"

He reached out and took hold of the *dama's* white robe, tearing it from his body. "You are *dama* no more. You will burn your whites and wear tan in shame for the rest of your days."

The man screamed as he was dragged out of the manse and cast into the snow. He would likely take his own life, if the other *dama* didn't kill him first.

Jardir looked to Abban once more. "I want the losses and remainder totaled."

"There may not be enough to feed everyone," Abban warned.

Jardir nodded. "If there isn't grain enough, have the *chin* too old to work or fight put to the spear until there is."

The color left Abban's face. "I will . . . find a way to make it stretch."

Jardir smiled without humor. "I thought you might. Now, what of these *chin* you bring before me? I wanted leaders, but these men look like *khaffit* merchants."

"Merchants rule the North, Deliverer," Abban said.

"Disgusting," Asome said.

"Nevertheless, it is so," Abban said. "These are men who can help ease your conquest."

"My father needs no . . . ," Jayan began, but Jardir silenced him with a wave. He gestured to the guards to bring the *chin* forward.

"Which of you leads the others?" Jardir asked, switching to the savage tongue of the North. The prisoners' eyes widened, and the men looked at one another. Finally, one stepped forward, arching his back and holding his head high as he met Jardir's eyes. He was bald, with a gray-shot beard, and was dressed in a soiled and torn silk robe. His face was blotched where he had been beaten, and his left arm was in a crude sling. He stood almost a foot shorter than Jardir, but still he had the look of a man who was accustomed to his words carrying weight.

"I am Edon the Seventh, duke of Fort Rizon and lord of its peoples," the man said.

"Fort Rizon no longer exists," Jardir said. "This land is known as Everam's Bounty now, and it belongs to me."

"The Core it does!" the duke growled.

"Do you know who I am, Duke Edon?" Jardir asked softly.

"The duke of Fort Krasia," Duke Edon said. "Abban claims you are the Deliverer."

"But you do not believe it is so," Jardir said.

"The Deliverer will not bring murder, rape, and pillage with him," Edon spat.

The warriors in the room tensed, expecting an outburst, but Jardir only nodded. "It comes as no surprise that the weak men of the North hold to a weak Deliverer," he said. "But it is no matter. I do not ask for your belief, only your allegiance."

The duke looked at him incredulously.

"If you prostrate before me and swear an oath to submit to Everam in all things, your life, and those of your councilors, will be spared," Jardir said. "Your sons will be taken and trained as *dal'Sharum*, and they will be honored above all other Northern *chin*. Your wealth and property will be returned to you, minus a tithe of fealty. All this I offer to you in exchange for helping me to dominate the green lands."

"And if I refuse?" the duke asked.

"Then all you possessed belongs to me," Jardir said. "You will watch as your sons are put to the spear and my men impregnate your wives and daughters, and you will spend the rest of your days in rags, eating shit and drinking piss until someone pities you enough to kill you."

And so Edon VII, duke of Fort Rizon and lord of its peoples, became the first Northern duke to kneel and put his head to the floor before Ahmann Jardir.

ᔓ

Jardir sat on his throne as Abban again brought a group of *chin* before him. It was a bitter irony that the fat *khaffit* should be the most indispensable member of his court, but so few of Jardir's men spoke the Northern tongue. Some of the other *khaffit* merchants spoke a smattering, but only Abban and Jardir's inner council were truly fluent. And of those, only Abban would rather talk to the *chin* than kill them.

Like all the prisoners Abban found, these were starved and beaten, clad in filthy rags against the cold. "More *khaffit* merchant lords?" Jardir asked.

Abban shook his head. "No, Deliverer. These men are Warders."

Jardir's eyes widened, and he sat up quickly in his seat. "Why have they been so ill treated?" he demanded.

"Because in the North, warding is considered a craft, like milling or carpentry," Abban said. "The *dal'Sharum* who sacked the city could not tell them from the rest of the *chin*, and many were killed, or fled with the tools of their profession."

Jardir cursed softly. In Krasia, Warders were considered the elite of the warrior caste, and it was written in the Evejah that they be accorded all honor. Even Northern ones had value, if Sharak Ka was to be won.

He turned to the men, shifting smoothly to their tongue and bowing. "You have my apologies for your treatment. You will be fed and clad in fine robes, your lands and women returned to you. Had we known you were Warders, you would have been honored as your station deserves."

"You killed my son," one of the men choked. "Raped my wife and daughter; burned my house. And now you apologize?" He spat at Jardir, striking him on the cheek.

The guards at the door gave a shout and lowered their spears, but Jardir waved them off, wiping the spittle from his cheek calmly.

"I will pay a death price for your son," he said, "and recompense you others for your losses as well." He strode up to the anguished man, towering over him. "But I warn you, do not test my mercy further." He signaled the guards, and the men were escorted out.

"It is regrettable," he said, as he sat heavily on his throne, "that our first conquest in the North should bring such waste."

"We could have treated with them, Ahmann," Abban said softly. He tensed, ready to fall to his knees if his words were not well received, but Jardir only shook his head.

"The greenlanders are too numerous," he said. "The Rizonan men outnumbered us eight to one. If they had been given time to muster, not even our superior fighting skills could have taken the city without losses we could ill afford. Now that the duke has embraced Everam, it should go easier on the hamlets until we move on to conquer the *chin* city built on the oasis."

"Lakton," Abban supplied. "But I warn you, this greenland 'lake' is, by all accounts, far bigger than any oasis. Messengers have told me it is a body of water so great that you cannot see the far side, even on a clear day, and the city itself is so far out on the water that even a scorpion could not shoot so far."

"They exaggerate, surely," Jardir said. "If these . . . fish men fight anything like the men of Rizon, they will fall easily enough when the time comes."

Just then a *dal'Sharum* entered, thumping his spear on the floor.

"Forgive the intrusion, Shar'Dama Ka," the warrior said, going down to both knees and laying his spear next to him before placing his hands flat on the floor. "You asked to be informed when your wives arrived."

Jardir scowled.

CHAPTER 4

LOSING THE BIDO

:: 308 AR ::

JARDIR WAS WHIPPED WITH the alagai tail for letting Abban live, the barbs tearing the flesh off his back, and the days without food were hard, but he embraced the penance as he did all pain. It did not matter.

He had netted an *alagai*.

Other warriors had cut the wings from the wind demon, staking it down in a warded circle to await the sun, but it was Jardir who brought it down, and everyone knew it. He could see it in the awed eyes of the other *nie'Sharum*, and the grudging respect of the *dal'Sharum*. Even the *dama* eyed him when they thought no one was looking.

On the fourth day, Jardir was weak with hunger as he made his way to the gruel line. He doubted he had the strength to fight even the weakest of the boys, but he strode to his usual place at the front of the line with a straight back. The others backed away, eyes respectfully down.

He was reaching out his bowl when Qeran caught his arm.

"No gruel for you today," the drillmaster said. "Come with me."

Jardir felt like a sand demon was trying to claw its way from his stomach, but he gave no complaint, handing his bowl to another boy and following the drillmaster across the camp.

Toward the Kaji pavilion.

Jardir's face went cold. It could not be.

"No boy your age has entered the warrior's pavilion in three hundred years," Qeran said, as if reading his thoughts. "I think you are too young, and this may prove the end of you and a terrible waste for the Kaji, but the law is the law. When a boy nets his first demon on the wall, he is called to *ala-gai'sharak*."

They entered the tent, and dozens of black-clad figures turned to eye him before returning to their food. Women served them, but not women like Jardir had seen before, covered from head to toe in thick black cloth. The veils of these women were gossamer and brightly colored, diaphanous clothes pulled tight against soft curves. Their arms and bellies were bare, save for jeweled adornments, and long slits in the sides of their pantaloons bared their smooth legs.

Jardir felt his face heat up at the sight, but no one else seemed to find it amiss. One warrior eyed the woman serving him for a moment, then dropped his kebab and grabbed her, slinging her over his shoulder. She laughed as he carried her to a curtained room filled with bright pillows.

"That will be your right, too, should you survive the coming night," Qeran advised. "The Kaji need more warriors. It is the duty of men to provide them. If you acquit yourself well, you may earn yourself a wife to keep your home, but all *dal'Sharum* are expected to keep the *jiwah'Sharum* of their tribe with child."

The sight of so many women in revealing clothes was overwhelming to Jardir, and he scanned their young faces, half expecting to see his sisters among them. He was speechless as the drillmaster led him to a pillow at the great table.

There was more food than he had ever seen in his life. Dates and raisins and rice and spiced lamb on skewers. Couscous and grape leaves wrapping steaming meats. His stomach churned, caught between hunger and lust.

"Eat well, and rest," Qeran advised. "Tonight you will stand among men." He slapped Jardir's back and left the tent.

Jardir reached tentatively for a skewer of meat, but a hand quickly snatched it away. He looked to the offender, only to find Hasik staring back at him.

"You got lucky the other night, rat," Hasik said. "Pray to Everam this day, for it will take more than luck to survive a night in the Maze."

Jardir went with the other warriors to Sharik Hora to receive the blessings of the *Damaji* before the night's battle. He had never been inside the temple of heroes' bones before, and the sight dwarfed anything he might have imagined.

Everything inside Sharik Hora was built from the bleached and lacquered bones of *dal'Sharum* who had fallen in *alagai'sharak*. The twelve chairs of the *Damaji* on the great altar stood on calf bones and rested on warriors' feet. The arms had once held spear and shield against demonkind. The seats were polished rib that had housed heroes' hearts. The backs were made from spines that had stood tall in the night. The headrests were made from the skulls of men who sat at Everam's side in Heaven. The twelve seats ringed the throne of the Andrah, built from the skulls of *kai'Sharum*, the captains of *alagai'sharak*.

Hundreds of skulls and spines made each of the dozens of huge chandeliers. Bones made up hundreds of benches where worshippers prayed. The altar. The chalices. The walls. The great domed ceiling. Warriors beyond count had protected this temple with their flesh, and built it with their bones.

The massive nave was circular, and its walls were pocked with a hundred small alcoves, housing whole skeletons on bone pedestals. These were Sharum Ka, First Warriors of the city.

Under the eyes of the *dama*, the *kai'Sharum* commanded the warriors of their respective tribes, but when the sun set, the Sharum Ka, appointed by the Andrah, commanded the *kai'Sharum*. The current Sharum Ka was Kaji like Jardir—a fact that filled him with great pride.

Jardir's hands shook as he took it all in. The entire temple thrummed with honor and glory. His father, killed in a Majah raid and not *alagai'sharak*, was not remembered here, but Jardir dreamed that one day he might add his own bones to this hallowed place, bringing honor to his father, his sacrifice remembered long after he was gone. There was no greater honor than to become one, in this world and the next, with those who had given their lives before him, and those unborn, perhaps centuries hence, whose lives were yet to be given.

The *Sharum* stood at attention as the *Damaji* begged the blessings of Everam for the coming battle, and those of Kaji, the first Deliverer.

"Kaji," they called, "Spear of Everam, Shar'Dama Ka, who unified the world and delivered us from the *alagai* in the first age, look down upon these brave warriors who go out into the night to carry on the eternal struggle, battling *gai* on Ala even as Everam battles Nie in Heaven. Bless them with courage and strength, that they might stand tall in the night, and see through to the dawn."

The warded shield and heavy spear were the smallest and lightest Qeran could find, but Jardir still felt dwarfed by them. He was twelve, and the youngest of the assembled warriors was five years his senior. He pretended nothing was amiss as he headed to stand with them, but even the smallest towered over him.

"*Nie'Sharum* are tethered to another warrior their first night in the Maze," Qeran said, "to ensure their will does not break when the *alagai* first come at them. It is a moment that tests the hearts of even the bravest warriors. The warrior assigned to you will be your *ajin'pal*, your blood brother. You will obey his every command and be bonded until death."

Jardir nodded.

"If you survive the night, the *dama'ting* will come for you at dawn," Qeran went on.

Jardir's gaze snapped to his mentor. "The *dama'ting*?" he asked. He was not afraid to face *alagai*, but *dama'ting* still filled him with fear.

Qeran nodded. "One of them will come to predict your death," he said, suppressing a shudder. "Only with her blessing will you be *dal'Sharum*."

"They tell you when you'll die?" Jardir asked, aghast. "I don't wish to know."

Qeran snorted. "They don't *tell* you, boy. The future is for the *dama'ting* alone to know. But if a coward's death is in your future, or greatness, they will know before you ever lose the bido."

"I will not die a coward's death," Jardir said.

"No," Qeran agreed, "I don't think you will. But you may still die a fool's death, if you don't listen to your *ajin'pal*, or are not careful."

"I will listen well," Jardir promised.

"Hasik has volunteered to be your *ajin'pal*," Qeran said, gesturing to the warrior.

Hasik had grown much in the two years since he had lost his bido. Seventeen years old and fleshed out with hard muscle by the rich food of the *dal'Sharum*, he was easily a foot taller than Jardir and twice his weight.

"Never fear." Hasik smiled. "The son of piss will be safe with me."

"The son of piss took down his first *alagai* a full three years sooner than you, Whistler," Qeran reminded him. Hasik kept his smile in place, but his lip twitched.

"He will honor the Kaji tribe," Hasik agreed. "If he survives."

Jardir remembered the sound of his arm breaking, and Hasik's promise afterward. He knew that Hasik would be looking for any sign of insubordination, any excuse to kill him before he lost his bido and became an equal.

So Jardir embraced the insult as he did pain, letting it pass through him harmlessly. He would not be provoked into failure right when a chance for glory was in his grasp. If he made it through this night, he would be *dal'Sharum*, the youngest in memory, and Hasik be damned.

5

Their unit waited in the second layer, hiding in an ambush pocket. A hidden pit stood at the center of a small clearing, soon to be filled with *alagai* awaiting the killing rays of the sun. Jardir tightened his grip on his spear and adjusted his shield to ease his shoulder. But for all their weight, the tether was heaviest of all. Four feet of leather connected his ankle to Hasik's waist. He shifted his foot uncomfortably.

"If you do not keep up with me, I will spear you and cut the tether," Hasik said. "I will not have my glory cut short because of you."

"I will be as your shadow," Jardir promised, and Hasik grunted. He slipped a small flask from his robes and removed the stopper, taking a long swig. He handed the flask to Jardir.

"Drink this, for courage," he said.

"What is it?" Jardir asked, taking the flask and sniffing at the neck. He smelled cinnamon, but the scent stung his nostrils.

"Couzi," Hasik said. "Fermented grain and cinnamon."

Jardir's eyes widened. "Dama Khevat says to drink of fermented grain or fruit is forbidden by the Evejah."

Hasik laughed. "Nothing is forbidden to *dal'Sharum* in the Maze! Drink! The night is almost upon us!"

Jardir looked at him doubtfully, but throughout the ambush pocket, he saw other warriors swigging from similar flasks. He shrugged, putting the bottle to his lips and drinking deeply.

The couzi burned his throat, and he coughed, spitting some back up. He could feel the strong drink burning his insides and roiling in his stomach like a snake. Hasik laughed and slapped his back. "Now you are ready to face the *alagai*, rat!"

The couzi worked quickly, and Jardir looked up through glazed eyes. The Maze was filled with shadows as the sun dipped. Jardir watched the sky turn red, and then purple, finally becoming full dark. He could sense the *alagai* rising outside the city walls, and shuddered.

Great Kaji, Spear of Everam, he prayed, *if it is true that across the centuries I come of your line, grant me courage to honor you and my ancestors.*

Before long he heard the Horn of Sharak, followed by the retort of rock slingers on the outer wall. The cries of *alagai* began to echo through the Maze. "Ware!" a call came from above, and Jardir thought he recognized Shanjat's voice. "Baiters approach! Four sand and one flame!"

Jardir swallowed hard. Glory was upon him.

With a cry of *"Oot!"* the Baiters ran full-tilt through the ambush point, veering only slightly to avoid the pits. Above, the Watchers lit oil fires in front of polished metal mirrors, and light flooded the area.

The sand demons ran in a pack, long tongues slavering over rows of razor-sharp teeth. They were the size of a man, but seemed smaller hunched down on all fours. Their long talons tore at the sand and stone of the Maze floor, and their spiked tails whipped back and forth through the air. Their gritty armor plates had few weaknesses.

The flame demon was smaller, the size of a small boy, with wicked talons and terrifying speed. Its tiny, diamond-hard iridescent scales overlapped seamlessly. Its eyes and mouth glowed with orange light, and Jardir recalled his lessons about the creature's deadly firespit. Across the ambush point was a pool in which the warriors would attempt to drown it.

Once again, the sight of the *alagai* filled Jardir with utter loathing. The creatures were a plague upon the Ala, Nie's taint come to infect the surface. And tonight, he would help send them screaming back into the abyss.

"Hold," Hasik warned, feeling him tense. Jardir nodded, forcing himself to relax. The couzi continued to work its way through him, warming him from the night's chill.

The *alagai* passed them by, intent on the Baiters. Two of them ran right out onto the tarp covering the demon pit, falling in with a shriek. The other sand demons pulled up short, but the flame dodged around, leaping onto the back of the slower Baiter. It dug its claws into the man's back and bit hard into his shoulder. The warrior was knocked down, but he did not scream.

"Now!" the *kai'Sharum* cried, and led the charge from the ambush pocket.

Jardir let the warrior's roar explode from his chest, thrumming in unison with his brothers in the night and carrying him forward with the others. They smashed into the two sand demons from behind, knocking them into the pit.

The *kai'Sharum* pivoted, launching his spear and knocking the flame demon from the Baiter's back. The other Baiter dragged him to the safety of the wards, doing his best to stem the flow of blood.

There was a cry, and Jardir turned to see that the first sand demon to fall into the pit had caught its edge, the concealing tarp protecting its talons from the wards. It swung up out of the pit easily, biting off the nearest warrior's leg at the knee. The warrior screamed as he was knocked into his fellows, opening a gap in the shield wall. The demon shrieked and dove into the opening, talons raking.

"Shield up!" Hasik called, and Jardir complied just in time to catch the full weight of the demon. He was knocked down, but not before the wards flared, throwing the *alagai* back. The demon landed in a coil and sprang at him again, but Jardir thrust his spear from his prone position, catching the demon between its breastplates. He braced the butt of the spear against the ground to create a fulcrum, and used the demon's own momentum to hurl it away.

Still in midair, bolas from half a dozen warriors struck the demon, and it hit the ground bound tight. It began tearing at the ropes with its teeth, and Jardir could hear the bindings snap under pressure from its corded muscles. It would be free in moments.

The *kai'Sharum* signaled, and a pair of warriors broke off to harry the flame demon while the rest encircled the sand demon with a wall of interlocked shields. Whenever the demon struck at a warrior, those behind it stabbed with their spears. The weapons could not pierce its armor, but they stung nonetheless. When it turned to face its attackers, their shields snapped into place and those behind struck.

The Pit Warder had cleared the tarp from the wards, preventing the other *alagai* from escaping the pit, as the warriors began to force the demon toward it by advancing the shield wall. Eventually, the creature backed up to the pit's edge, and the warriors there melted away.

Jardir was among those who thrust their spears to drive the demon past the one-way wards. "Everam's light burn you!" he screamed as he stabbed. The demon backpedaled, and then fell into the pit.

It was the greatest moment of his life.

Jardir looked around the ambush point. Two *dal'Sharum* had the flame demon pinned underwater with their spears in a shallow drowning pool. The water steamed and boiled as the demon thrashed, but the warriors held it steady until the last twitch.

The wounded Baiter seemed well enough, but Moshkama, the warrior with the severed leg, lay in a pool of blood, gasping and pale. He caught Jardir's eye and beckoned to him and Hasik, who went to him.

"Finish it," he breathed. "I have no wish to live as a cripple."

Jardir glanced at Hasik.

"Do it," Hasik ordered. "It is not right to let him suffer."

Jardir's thoughts flashed to Abban. How much suffering had he condemned his friend to by not granting him a warrior's death?

A dal'Sharum's *duty is to support his brothers in death, as well as life,* Qeran had said.

"My spirit is ready," Moshkama croaked. With weak, shaking fingers, he pulled open his robe, moving aside the fired-clay armor plates sewn into the cloth and baring his chest. Jardir looked in his eyes and saw honor and courage. Things Abban had been severely lacking.

He thrust his spear with pride.

כ

"You did well, rat," Hasik said when the horns had blown, signaling that there were no *alagai* left alive and untrapped in the Maze. "I expected you to soak your bido, but you stood like a man." He took another pull from the couzi flask and handed it to Jardir.

"Thank you," Jardir said, drinking deeply, and pretending the harsh liquid did not burn his throat. Hasik still intimidated him, but it was true what the drillmasters said: Shedding blood together in the Maze had changed things. They were brothers now.

Hasik paced back and forth. "My blood is always on fire after *alagai'sharak*," he said. "Nie damn the *Damaji* who decreed the great harem be sealed till dawn." Several warriors grunted assent.

Jardir thought of the warrior carrying a *jiwah'Sharum* through the curtains that morning, and his face flushed.

Hasik caught the look. "That excites you, rat?" he laughed. "The son of piss is eager to take his first woman?"

Jardir said nothing.

"Bido or no, I think this one will still be a boy tomorrow!" another warrior, Manik, laughed. "He's too young to know what the pillow dancers are truly for!"

Jardir opened his mouth, then snapped it shut again. They were provoking him on purpose. Whatever had happened in the Maze, he was still *nie'Sharum* until the *dama'ting* foresaw his death. Any of the warriors could still kill him for the slightest insolence.

Surprisingly, Hasik came to his defense.

"Leave the rat alone," he said. "He's my *ajin'pal*. You mock him, you mock me."

Manik puffed up at the challenge, but Hasik was young and strong. They eyed each other for a moment before Manik spat in the dust.

"Bah," he said. "It's not worth the trouble of gutting you just to mock a boy." He turned and strode off.

"Thank you," Jardir said.

"It's nothing," Hasik replied, putting a hand on his shoulder. "It is the duty of *ajin'pal* to look out for each other, and you would not be the first boy to fear the pillow dancers more than the *alagai*. The *dama'ting* teach sexcraft to the *jiwah'Sharum*, but the drillmasters give no such lessons in the *sharaji*."

Jardir felt his face flush, wondering what lay in store for him in the pillows behind the curtains when the veils were lifted.

"Do not fear," Hasik said, clapping him on the shoulder. "I will teach you how to make a woman howl."

They finished off the flask, and a wicked smile crossed Hasik's face. "Come on, rat. I know of some fun we can find in the meantime."

ॐ

"Where are we going?" Jardir asked, stumbling as Hasik led him through the Maze. The couzi made his head spin, and his limbs watery. The walls seemed to move of their own accord.

Hasik turned, his smile wide. The gap in his teeth where Qeran had hit him on Jardir's first night in the Kaji'sharaj was a black hole in the moonlight.

"Going?" Hasik asked. "We're here."

Jardir looked around in confusion, and in that moment, colored light exploded before his eyes as Hasik hit him hard in the face.

Before he could react, Hasik was upon him, pinning him facedown in the dust. "I promised to teach you to make a woman howl," he said. "For this lesson, you will be the woman."

"No!" Jardir cried, thrashing, but Hasik smashed his face into the ground, making his ears ring. Twisting one of Jardir's arms behind his back, the heavy warrior held him down with one hand as he pulled down Jardir's bido with the other.

"Looks like you get to lose the bido twice in one night, rat!" he laughed.

Jardir tasted blood and dirt in his mouth. He tried to open himself to the pain, but for once, the power was beyond him, and his cries echoed through the Maze.

ॐ

He was still weeping when the *dama'ting* found him.

She glided like a ghost, her white robes softly stirring the dust with her passage. Jardir stopped his sobbing and stared. Then reality suddenly focused, and he scrambled to pull up his bido. Shame filled him, and he hid his face.

The *dama'ting* clicked her tongue. "On your feet, boy!" she snapped. "You stand your ground against *alagai*, but weep like a woman over this? Everam needs *dal'Sharum*, not *khaffit*!"

Jardir wished the walls of the Maze would fall and crush him, but one did not refuse the orders of a *dama'ting*. He got to his feet, palming away his tears and wiping his nose.

"That's better," the *dama'ting* said, "if late. I would hate to have come all the way out here to foretell the life of a coward."

The words stung Jardir. He was no coward. "How did you find me?"

She psshed, waving a hand at him. "I knew to find you here years ago."

Jardir stared at her, unbelieving, but it was clear from her stance that his belief mattered not at all to her. "Come here, boy, that I may have a better look at you," she commanded.

Jardir did as he was told, and the *dama'ting* grabbed his face, turning it this way and that to catch the moonlight. "Young and strong," she said. "But so are all who get this far. You're younger than most, but that's seldom a good thing."

"Are you here to foretell my death?"

"Bold, too," she muttered. "There may be hope for you yet. Kneel, boy."

He did, and the *dama'ting* knelt with him, spreading a white cloth to protect her pristine robes from the dust of the Maze.

"What do I care for your death?" she asked. "I am here to foretell your life. Death is between you and Everam."

She reached into her robes, pulling forth a small pouch made from thick black felt. She loosened the drawstrings, pouring its contents into her free hand with a clatter. Jardir saw over a dozen objects, black and smooth like obsidian, carved with wards that glowed redly in the dark.

"The *alagai hora*," she said, lifting the objects toward him. Jardir gasped and recoiled at the name. She held the polished bones of demons, cut into many-sided dice. Even without touching them, Jardir could feel the dull throb of their evil magic.

"Back to cowardice?" the *dama'ting* asked mildly. "What is the purpose of wards, if not to turn *alagai* magic to our own ends?"

Jardir steeled himself, leaning back in.

"Hold out your arm," she commanded, placing the felt bag in her lap and laying the dice on it. She reached into her robes, drawing forth a sharp curved blade etched with wards.

Jardir held out his arm, willing it not to shake. The cut was quick, and the *dama'ting* squeezed the wound, smearing her hand with blood. She took up the *alagai hora* in both hands, shaking them.

"Everam, giver of light and life, I beseech you, give this lowly servant knowledge of what is to come. Tell me of Ahmann, son of Hoshkamin, last scion of the line of Jardir, the seventh son of Kaji."

As she shook the dice, their glow increased, flaring through her fingers until it seemed she held hot coals. She cast them down, scattering the bones on the ground before them.

She put her hands on her knees and hunched forward, studying the glowing markings. Her eyes widened and she hissed. Suddenly oblivious to the dirt that marred her pure white robes, the *dama'ting* crawled about intently, reading the pattern as the pulsing glow of the wards slowly faded. "These bones must have been exposed to light," she muttered, gathering them up.

Again she cut him and made the incantation, shaking vigorously, and again the dice flared. She threw them down.

"This cannot be!" she cried, snatching up the dice and throwing a third time. Even Jardir could tell that the pattern remained unchanged.

"What is it?" he dared to ask. "What do you see?"

The *dama'ting* looked up at him, and her eyes narrowed. "The future is not yours to know, boy," she said. Jardir recoiled at the anger in her tone, unsure if it was due to his impertinence or what she had seen.

Or both. What had the dice told her? His mind flashed back to the pottery he had allowed Abban to steal from Baha kad'Everam, and wondered if she could see that sin, as well.

The *dama'ting* collected the bones and returned them to the pouch before rising. She tucked the pouch away and shook the dust from her robes.

"Return to the Kaji pavilion and spend the remainder of the night in prayer," she ordered, vanishing in the shadows so quickly Jardir wondered if she had truly been there at all.

5

Qeran kicked him awake while the warriors still slept all around him. "Up, rat," the drillmaster said. "The *dama* has called for you."

"Am I to lose my bido?" Jardir asked.

"The men say you fought well in the night," Qeran said, "but that's not for me to decide. Only *dama* may give a *nie'Sharum* his blacks."

The drillmaster escorted him to the inner chambers of Sharik Hora. The cool stone floor felt hallowed under Jardir's bare feet.

"Drillmaster, may I ask a question?" Jardir said.

"This may be the last you ask of me as your instructor," Qeran said, "so make it good."

"When the *dama'ting* came for you, how many times did she throw the dice?"

The drillmaster glanced at him. "Once. They only ever throw once. The dice never lie."

Jardir wanted to say more, but they turned a corner and Dama Khevat was waiting for him. Khevat was the harshest of Jardir's instructors, the one who had called him the son of camel's piss and thrown him into the waste pits for his insolence.

The drillmaster put a hand on Jardir's shoulder. "Mind your tongue if you would keep it, boy," he muttered.

"Everam be with you," Khevat greeted them. The drillmaster bowed, and Jardir did the same. A nod from the *dama,* and Qeran turned on his heel and vanished.

Khevat ushered Jardir into a small, windowless room filled with sheaves of paper and smelling of ink and lamp oil. It seemed a place more suited to a *khaffit* or a woman, but even here the bones of men filled the room. They formed the seat Jardir was directed to, and the desk Khevat sat behind. Even the sheaves of paper were held down by skulls.

"You continue to surprise me, son of Hoshkamin," Khevat said. "I did not believe you when you said you would win glory enough for you and your father both, but you seem determined to prove me wrong."

Jardir shrugged. "I have only done as any warrior would do."

Khevat chuckled. "The warriors I have known are not so modest. A kill wholly your own and five assists, at what? Thirteen?"

"Twelve," Jardir said.

"Twelve," Khevat repeated. "And you helped Moshkama die last night. Few *nie'Sharum* would have the heart for that."

"It was his time," Jardir said.

"Indeed," Khevat said. "Moshkama had no sons. As his brother in death, it will fall to you to bleach his bones for Sharik Hora."

Jardir bowed. "I am honored."

"Your *dama'ting* came to me last night," Khevat said.

Jardir looked up eagerly. "I am to lose my bido?"

Khevat shook his head. "You are too young, she says. Returning you to *alagai'sharak* without further training and time to grow will only cost the Kaji a warrior."

"I am not afraid to die," Jardir said, "if that is *inevera.*"

"Spoken like a true *Sharum,*" Khevat said, "but it is not that simple. You are denied the Maze by her decree until you are older."

Jardir scowled. "So I must return to the Kaji'sharaj in shame after standing among men?"

The *dama* shook his head. "The law is clear on that. No boy who sees the *Sharum* pavilion is permitted to return to the *sharaj.*"

"But if I cannot go there, and I cannot stand with the men . . . ," Jardir began, and suddenly the depth of his predicament became clear.

"I . . . will become *khaffit*?" he asked, stark terror overcoming him for the first time in his life. His fear of the *dama'ting* was nothing compared to this. He felt the blood leave his face as he remembered the sight of Abban begging for his life.

I will die first, he thought. *I will attack the first* dal'Sharum *I see, and give him no choice but to kill me. Better dead than* khaffit.

"No," the *dama* said, and Jardir felt his heart begin to beat again. "Perhaps such things do not matter to the *dama'ting,* since even the lowliest *khaffit* is above a woman, but I will see no warrior fall so low when his every challenge has been met. Since the time of Shar'Dama Ka, no boy who has shed *alagai* blood in the Maze has been refused the black. The *dama'ting* dishonors us all with her decree, and handmaiden of Everam or not, she is only a woman, and cannot understand what that would do to the hearts of all *Sharum.*"

"Then what will become of me?" Jardir asked.

"You will be taken into Sharik Hora," Khevat said. "I have already spoken to Damaji Amadeveram. With his blessing, not even the *dama'ting* can deny you that."

"I am to become a cleric?" Jardir asked. He tried to mask his displeasure, but his voice cracked, and he knew he had failed.

Khevat chuckled. "No, boy, your destiny is still the Maze, but you will train here with us until you are ready. Study hard, and you may make *kai'Sharum* while others your age still wear bidos."

"This will be your cell," Khevat said, leading Jardir to a chamber deep in the bowels of Sharik Hora. The room was a ten-by-ten square cut into the sandstone with a hard cot in one corner. There was a heavy wooden door, but it had no latch or bar. The only light came from a lamp in the corridor, filtering through the barred window in the door. Compared to the communal space and stone floor of the Kaji'sharaj, even this would have seemed luxury, if not for the shame that brought him here, and the pleasures of the Kaji pavilion that he was denied.

"You will fast here and excise the demons from your mind," Khevat said. "Your training begins on the morrow." He left, his footsteps receding in the hall until all was silent.

Jardir fell upon the cot, crossing his arms in front of him to support his head. But lying on his stomach made him think of Hasik, and rage and shame flared in him until it became unbearable. He leapt to his feet and grasped the cot, shouting as he smashed it against the wall. He threw it down, kicking the wood and tearing the cloth until he stood panting and hoarse amid a pile of splinters and thread.

Suddenly realizing what he had done, Jardir straightened, but there was no response to his commotion. He swept the wreckage into a corner and began a *sharukin*. The practiced series of *sharusahk* movements centered him as no prayer ever could.

The events of the last week swirled around him. Abban was *khaffit* now. Jardir felt shame at that, but he embraced the feeling, and saw the truth beneath. Abban had been *khaffit* all along, and *Hannu Pash* had shown it. Jardir had delayed Everam's will, but he had not stopped it. No man could.

Inevera, he thought, and embraced the loss.

He thought of the glory and elation at killing demons in the Maze, and accepted that it might be many years before he could feel such joy again. The dice had spoken.

Inevera.

He thought again of Hasik, but it was not *inevera*. There, he had failed. He had been a fool to drink couzi in the Maze. A fool to trust Hasik. A fool to lower his guard.

The pain of his body and the passing of blood he had already embraced. Even the humiliation. He had seen other boys in *sharaj* mounted, and could embrace the feeling. What he could not embrace was the fact that even now Hasik strutted among the *dal'Sharum* thinking he had won, that Jardir was broken.

Jardir scowled. *Perhaps I am broken,* he conceded silently, *but broken bones heal stronger, and I will have my day in the sun.*

Night came, signaled only by the extinguishing of the lamp in the hall, leaving his cell in utter blackness. Jardir didn't mind the dark. No wards in the world could match those of Sharik Hora, and even without them, the spirits of warriors without number guarded the temple. Any *alagai* setting foot in this hallowed place would be burned away as if it had seen the sun.

Jardir could not have slept even if he had wanted to, so he continued his *sharukin,* repeating the movements over and over until they were a part of him, as natural as breathing.

When the door of his cell creaked open, Jardir was instantly aware. Recalling his first night in the Kaji'sharaj, he slipped silently to the side of the door in the darkness and assumed a fighting stance. If the *nie'dama* sought to give him a similar welcome, it would be to their regret.

"If I wished you harm, I would not have sent you here for training," said a familiar woman's voice. A red light sprang to life, illuminating the *dama'-ting* he had met the night before. She held a small flame demon skull, carved with wards that glowed fiercely in the darkness. The light found her already staring right into his eyes, as if she had known where he stood all along.

"You didn't send me here," Jardir dared to say. "You told Dama Khevat to send me back to the Kaji'sharaj in shame!"

"As I knew he would never do," the *dama'ting* said, ignoring his accusatory tone. "Nor would he have made you *khaffit*. The only path left to him was to send you here."

"Without honor," Jardir said, clenching his fists.

"In safety!" the *dama'ting* hissed, raising the *alagai* skull. The wards flared brighter, and a gout of flame coughed from its maw. Jardir felt the flash of heat on his face and recoiled.

"Do not presume to judge me, *nie'Sharum*," the *dama'ting* said. "I will act as I think best, and you will do as you are bidden."

Jardir felt his back strike the wall, and realized he could retreat no farther. He nodded.

"Learn everything you can in your time here," she commanded as she left. "Sharak Ka is coming."

The words struck Jardir like a physical blow. Sharak Ka. The final battle was coming, and he would fight in it. All his worldly concerns vanished in that instant, as she closed the door and left him in darkness once more.

5

The lamp in the hall flickered back to life after some time, and there was a light tap at the door. Jardir opened it to Khevat's youngest son, Ashan. He was a slender boy, clad in a bido that extended upward to wrap over one shoulder, marking him as *nie'dama*, a cleric in training. He wore a white veil over his mouth, and Jardir knew that meant he was in his first year of training, when *nie'dama* were not allowed to speak.

The boy nodded in greeting, then took in the wreckage of the cot in the corner. He winked and gave a slight bow, as if Jardir had somehow passed a secret test. Ashan jerked his head down the hall, then headed that way himself. Jardir took his meaning and followed.

They came to a wide chamber with a floor of polished marble. Dozens of *dama* and *nie'dama*, perhaps every one in the tribe, stood there, feet planted, practicing the *sharukin*. The boy waved a hand for Jardir to follow, and the two took their places in the *nie* lines, joining in the slow dance, bodies flowing from pose to pose, the entire room breathing in unison.

There were many forms Jardir was unfamiliar with, and the experience was quite unlike the brutal lessons to which he was accustomed, where

Qeran and Kaval shouted curses at the boys, whipping any whose form was not perfect, and demanding that they flow faster and faster still. The *dama* practiced in silence, their only instruction watching the lead *dama* and one another. Jardir thought the clerics pampered and weak.

After an hour, the session ended. Immediately a buzz of conversation started as the *dama* broke into clusters and left the room. Jardir's companion signaled him to remain, and they clustered with the other *nie'dama*.

"You have a new brother," Dama Khevat told the boys, gesturing to Jardir. "With only twelve years under his bido, Jardir, son of Hoshkamin, has *alagai* blood on his hands. He will stay and learn the ways of the *dama* until the *dama'ting* deem him old enough to don his blacks."

The other boys nodded silently, bowing to Jardir.

"Ashan," the *dama* called. "Jardir will need help with his *sharusahk*. You will teach him." Ashan nodded.

Jardir snorted. A *nie'dama*? Teach him? Ashan was no older than he was, and Jardir waited ahead of boys years his senior in the *nie'Sharum* gruel line.

"You feel you need no instruction?" Khevat asked.

"No, of course not, honored *dama*," Jardir said quickly, bowing to the cleric.

"But you feel Ashan is not worthy to instruct you?" Khevat pressed. "After all, he is only *nie'dama*, a novice not yet old enough to speak, and you have stood with men in *alagai'sharak*."

Jardir shrugged helplessly, feeling that very thing, but fearing a trap.

"Very well," Khevat said. "You will spar with Ashan. When you defeat him, I will assign you a more worthy instructor."

The other novices backed away, forming a ring on the polished marble floor. Ashan stood in its center and bowed to Jardir.

Jardir cast one last glance at Dama Khevat, then bowed in return. "Apologies, Ashan," he said as they closed, "but I must defeat you."

Ashan said nothing, assuming a *sharusahk* battle stance. Jardir did likewise, and Khevat clapped his hands.

"Begin!" the *dama* called.

Jardir shot forward, his stiffened fingers going for Ashan's throat. The move would put the boy out of the fight quickly, yet do no permanent harm.

But Ashan surprised him, pivoting smoothly from Jardir's path and delivering a kick to his side that sent him sprawling.

Jardir rolled quickly to his feet, cursing himself for underestimating the boy. He came in again, his defenses set, and feinted a punch to Ashan's jaw. When the boy moved to block, Jardir spun, feinting an elbow jab to his opposite kidney. Again Ashan shifted, positioning himself correctly, and Jardir spun back again, delivering the real blow—a leg sweep that he would complement with an elbow to the chest, putting the *nie'dama* flat on his back.

But the leg Jardir meant to sweep was not where it was supposed to be, and his kick met only air. Ashan caught his leg, using Jardir's own strength against him as he followed through with the exact move Jardir had planned. As Jardir fell, Ashan drove an elbow into his chest that blasted the breath from him. He hit the marble floor hard, banging his head, but was moving to rise before he felt the pain. He would not allow himself to be defeated!

Before he had set his hands and feet, though, they were kicked out from under him. He hit the floor again and felt a foot pin the small of his back. His flailing left leg was caught, as was his right arm, and Ashan pulled hard, threatening to twist the limbs from their sockets.

Jardir screamed, his eyes blurring in pain. He embraced the feeling, and when his vision cleared, he caught a glimpse of a *dama'ting,* watching him from the shadowed arch to the hall.

She shook her veiled head and walked away.

Deep in the bowels of Sharik Hora, Jardir could not tell night from day. He slept when the *dama* told him to sleep, ate when they gave him food, and followed their commands in between. There were a handful of *dal'Sharum* in the temple as well, training to be *kai'Sharum,* but no *nie'Sharum* save him. He was the least of the least, and when he thought of how those who had once leapt to his commands, Shanjat and Jurim and the others, might be losing their bidos even now, the shame threatened to overwhelm him.

For the first year, he was Ashan's shadow. Without uttering a sound, the *nie'dama* taught Jardir what he needed to survive among the clerics. When to pray, when to kneel, how to bow, and how to fight.

Jardir had severely underestimated the fighting skills of the *dama.* They might be denied the spear, but the least of them was a match for any two *dal'Sharum* in the art of the empty hand.

But combat was something Jardir understood. He threw himself into the training, losing his shame in the endlessly flowing forms. Even after the lamps were extinguished each night, Jardir practiced the *sharukin* for hours in the darkness of his tiny cell.

After the tanners had taken Moshkama's skin, Jardir and Ashan took the body and boiled it in oil, fishing out the bones and bleaching them in the sun atop the bone minarets that climbed into the desert sky. The *jiwah'Sharum* had filled three tear bottles over his body, and these were mixed with the lacquer they used to paint the bones before laying them out for the artisans. Moshkama's bones and the tears of his mourners would add to the glory of Sharik Hora, and Jardir dreamed of the day he, too, would become one with the holy temple.

There were other tasks, less satisfying, less honorable. He spent hours each day learning to speak on paper, using a stick to copy the words of the Evejah into a box of sand as he recited them aloud. It seemed a useless art, unfit for a warrior, but Jardir heeded the *dama'ting*'s words and worked hard, mastering the letters quickly. From there he learned mathematics, history, philosophy, and finally warding. This, he devoured hungrily. Anything that might hurt or hinder the *alagai* received his utter devotion.

Drillmaster Qeran came several times a week, spending hours honing Jardir's spearwork, while the *dama* loremasters taught him tactics and the history of war dating back to the time of the Deliverer.

"War is more than prowess on the field," Dama Khevat said. "The Evejah tells us that war is, at its crux, deception."

"Deception?" Jardir asked.

Khevat nodded. "As you might feint with your spear, so too must the wise leader misdirect his foe before battle is ever joined. When strong, he must appear weak. When weak, he must seem ready to fight. When near enough to strike, he must seem too far to threaten. When regrouping, he must make his enemies believe attack is imminent. It is thus he makes the enemy waste their strength while husbanding his own."

Jardir cocked his head. "Is it not more honorable to meet the enemy head-on?"

"We did not build the Great Maze so that we could sally forth and meet the *alagai* head-on," Khevat said. "There is no greater honor than victory, and to achieve victory, you must seize every advantage, great and small. This is the essence of war, and war is the essence of all things, from the lowest *khaffit* haggling in the bazaar to the Andrah hearing petitions in his palace."

"I understand," Jardir said.

"Deceit depends on secrecy," Khevat went on. "If spies can learn of your deceptions, they take away all your strength. A great leader must hold his deceit so close that even his inner circle and sometimes even he himself does not think on it until the time to strike."

"But why make war at all, Dama?" Jardir dared to ask.

"Eh?" Khevat replied.

"We are all Everam's children," Jardir said. "The enemy is the *alagai*.

We need every man to stand against him, yet we kill one another under the sun every day." Khevat looked at him, and Jardir was not sure if the *dama* was annoyed or pleased with the question.

"Unity," the *dama* replied at last. "In war men stand together, and it is that collective power that makes them strong. In the words of Kaji himself during his conquest of the green lands, *Unity is worth any price of blood. Against the night and Nie's untold legions, better a hundred thousand men standing together than a hundred million cowering by themselves.* Remember that always, Ahmann."

Jardir bowed. "I will, Dama."

CHAPTER 5

JIWAH KA

:: 313–316 AR ::

THREE *NIE'DAMA* APPROACHED HIM from all sides, and though he could not see her, Jardir sensed that the *dama'ting* was watching. She was always watching.

He embraced the moment as he did pain, letting all worldly concern fall away. After more than five years in Sharik Hora, the peace came effortlessly when he called it now. There was no him. There was no them. There was no her. There was only the dance.

Ashan came at him first, but Jardir feinted a block, then pivoted and leapt aside to punch Halvan in the chest, Ashan's kick meeting only air. He caught Halvan's arm and twisted him to the ground easily. He could have torn the arm from its socket, but it was a greater test of skill to leave his opponents unharmed.

Shevali waited for Ashan to recover before coming at him, the two attacking with a unity that would do any *dal'Sharum* unit proud.

It mattered little. Jardir's arms and thighs were a blur, their blocked blows a drumbeat as he followed the rhythm to its inevitable conclusion. On his fifth blow, Shevali left his throat exposed for an instant, and then, as it always was in the end, Jardir and Ashan faced off.

Knowing Jardir's speed, Ashan attempted to grapple, but the years had put meat on Jardir's bones. At seventeen, he was taller than most men, and constant training had turned his wiry sinews into lean, packed muscle. No sooner had they closed than Ashan was pinned.

Ashan laughed, his year of silence long past. "One day we will have you, *nie'Sharum!*"

Jardir gave him a hand up. "You will never find that day."

"That is true," Dama Khevat said. Jardir turned as the ring of boys and instructors broke and the cleric strode in, the *dama'ting* at his side. Jardir felt his face grow cold.

The *dama'ting* carried black robes.

5

The *dama'ting* led him to a private chamber and with her own hands unwrapped his bido, pulling it away. Jardir tried to embrace the feeling of her hands on his bare skin, but she was the only woman who had ever touched him so intimately, and for the first time in years, he could not find peace. His body responded to her touch, and he feared she might kill him for his disrespect.

But the *dama'ting* made no mention of his arousal as she wrapped a black loincloth in place of his bido, then dressed him in the loose pantaloons, heavy sandals, and robe of a *dal'Sharum.*

After eight years in a bido, Jardir expected any clothing to feel odd, but he was unprepared for the weight of a *dal'Sharum's* armored blacks. Plates and strips of fired clay were held tight in sewn pockets throughout the garb. The plates could absorb a great blow, Jardir knew, but they shattered on impact, and needed to be replaced after every hit.

So distracted was he that he did not notice at first that the veil she tied about his throat was white. When he did, he gasped aloud.

"Did you think your time among the *dama* meaningless, son of Hoshkamin?" the *dama'ting* asked. "You will rejoin your *dal'Sharum* brothers as their master, a *kai'Sharum.*"

"I am but seventeen!" Jardir said.

The *dama'ting* nodded. "The youngest *kai'Sharum* in centuries. Just as you were the youngest to bring down a wind demon, and the youngest to survive *alagai'sharak.* Who can say what else you may accomplish?"

"You can," Jardir said. "The dice told you."

The *dama'ting* shook her head. "I have seen the fate your spirit reaches for, but it is a path fraught with peril, and you may still fail to reach it." She drew the white veil about his face. Her touch seemed almost a caress. "You have many tests before you. Bring your focus to the now. When you return to the Kaji pavilion today, one of the *Sharum* will challenge you. You must—"

Jardir held up a hand, cutting her off. The *dama'ting*'s eyes flared at his audacity.

"With respect," Jardir said, recalling the gruel lines of the Kaji'sharaj, "the world of *Sharum*, I understand. I will break the challenger publicly before any dare follow his example."

The *dama'ting* regarded him a moment, then shrugged, a smile in her eyes.

ᴣ

Jardir strode with pride into the Kaji training grounds, followed by Dama Khevat and the *dama'ting*. The *dal'Sharum* paused in their training at the sight, and there were murmurs of recognition as they saw Jardir's face. One of them barked a laugh.

"Look! The rat returns!" Hasik cried, his *s*'s still whistling after all these years. The big warrior planted his spear with a thump. "It only took him five years to change out of his bido!" Several other warriors laughed at that.

Jardir smiled. It was natural for *Sharum* to test the mettle of a new *kai*, and it was *inevera* that it should be Hasik. The powerful warrior was still larger than Jardir, but he felt no fear as he strode forward.

Hasik stared him down coldly, unafraid. "You may have a white veil loose about your throat, but you are still the son of piss," he sneered, too low for the others to hear.

"Ah, Hasik, my *ajin'pal*!" Jardir called loudly. "Do they still call you Whistler? I would be happy to remove a few more teeth and cure your affliction, if you wish."

All around, *Sharum* laughed. Jardir looked among them and saw many who had served under him when he was *Nie Ka*.

Hasik growled and lunged, but Jardir sidestepped, spinning into a kick that knocked the big warrior onto his backside in the dust. He stood patiently as Hasik scowled and scrambled back to his feet unharmed.

"I will kill you for that," Hasik promised.

Jardir smiled, reading Hasik's every movement like writing in the sand. Hasik charged in, thrusting hard with his spear, but Jardir pivoted, slapping the point to one side, and Hasik stumbled past, overbalanced. He turned and swung the spear like a staff, but Jardir bent backward like a palm tree in the wind, avoiding the blow without moving his feet an inch. Before Hasik could recover, he whipped upright and grabbed the weapon with both hands, kicking up between his hands and breaking through the thick shaft of wood. He followed through on the kick, taking Hasik in the face.

There was a satisfying crack as Hasik's jaw shattered, but Jardir did not stop there. He dropped the speartip but held on to the butt, advancing as Hasik struggled back to his feet.

Hasik punched at him, and Jardir marveled that he had once found those punches too fast to follow. After years among the *dama,* the fist seemed to move at a crawl. He caught Hasik's wrist and twisted hard, feeling his shoulder pop from its socket. Hasik screamed as Jardir swung the spear butt, shattering the warrior's knee. Hasik collapsed, and Jardir kicked him over onto his stomach. He was well within his rights to kill Hasik, and those gathered likely expected him to, but Jardir had not forgotten what Hasik had done to him in the Maze.

"Now, Hasik," he said, as all the *dal'Sharum* of the Kaji tribe looked on, "I will teach *you* to be a woman." He held up the spear butt. "And this will be the man."

5

"Watch to ensure he does not fall on his spear in shame," Jardir told Shanjat as Hasik was hauled off to the *dama'ting* pavilion, howling in pain and humiliation. "I would not see any permanent harm befall my *ajin'pal.*"

"As my *kai'Sharum* wills," Shanjat said, "though they will have to remove the spear before he can fall on it." He smirked as he bowed to Jardir and hurried after the injured warrior. Jardir followed Shanjat with his eyes, marveling at how quickly they fell back into old patterns, despite Shanjat having earned the black years ago, and him just this day.

Jardir had planned his revenge on Hasik for years, while he danced *sharusahk* in his tiny cell in Sharik Hora. It wasn't enough for the man to suffer defeat; Jardir's revenge had to be an abject lesson to any who would ever seek to challenge him again. If Hasik had not challenged him, he would have sought the man out and initiated the challenge himself.

By Everam's infinite justice, every step played out exactly as he had imagined it, but now that his triumph was complete, he found no more satisfaction in it than when he fought Shanjat for his place in the *nie'Sharum* food line.

"You seem to have things well in hand," Dama Khevat said, slapping Jardir on the back. "Go to the Kaji pavilion and take a woman before tonight's battle." He laughed. "Take two! The *jiwah'Sharum* will be eager to bed the youngest *kai'Sharum* in a thousand years."

Jardir forced himself to laugh and nod, though he felt a clench in his stomach. He had never known a woman. Except for a few glimpses of the *jiwah'Sharum* that one night in the Kaji pavilion, he had never even seen one without her robes. *Kai'Sharum* or no, he had one last test of manhood in front of him, and unlike the crushing of Hasik or the killing of *alagai,* this was one none of his training had prepared him for.

Khevat left him, and Jardir took a deep breath, looking toward the Kaji pavilion.

They are only women, he told himself, taking a tentative step forward. *They are there to please you, not the other way around.* His second step came with more confidence.

"A word," the *dama'ting* whispered, grabbing his attention. Relief and fear clutched him at once. How had he forgotten her?

"In private," she said, and Jardir nodded, walking to the edge of the training grounds with her, out of earshot from the *dal'Sharum* in the yard.

He was much taller than her now, but she still intimidated him. He remembered the blast of fire from her flame demon skull, and tried to convince himself that her *alagai* magics would not work in the day, with Everam's light shining down upon them.

"I cast the *alagai hora* before bringing you the blacks," she said. "If you sleep among the *jiwah'Sharum,* one of them will kill you."

Jardir's eyes widened. Such a thing was unheard of. "Why?" he asked.

"The bones give us no 'why,' son of Hoshkamin," the *dama'ting* said. "They tell what is, and what may be. Perhaps a lover of Hasik will seek revenge, or some woman with a blood feud with your family." She shrugged. "But sleep among the *jiwah'Sharum* at your peril."

"So I am never to know a woman?" Jardir asked. "What kind of life is that for a man?"

"Don't exaggerate," the *dama'ting* said. "You may still take wives. I will cast the bones to find ones suitable for you."

"Why would you do this?" Jardir asked.

"My reasons are my own," the *dama'ting* said.

"And the price?" Jardir asked. The tales in the Evejah always spoke of a hidden price for those who would use *hora* magic for more than *sharak.*

"Ah," the *dama'ting* said. "No longer so innocent as you seem. That is good. The price is that you take me to wife."

Jardir froze. His face went cold. Take her as his wife? Unthinkable. She terrified him.

"I did not know *dama'ting* could marry," he said, fumbling for time as his mind reeled.

"We can, when we wish it," she said. "The first *dama'ting* were the Deliverer's wives."

Jardir looked at her again, the thick white robes hiding every contour and curve of her body. Her headwrap covered every hair, and the opaque veil was drawn high over her nose, muffling even her voice. Only her eyes could be seen, bright and full of zeal. There was something familiar about them, but he could not even guess at her age, much less her beauty. Was she a virgin? Of good family? There was no way to know. *Dama'ting* were taken from their mothers early and raised in secret.

"It is a man's right to see a woman's face before he agrees to marry her," he said.

"Not this time," the *dama'ting* said. "It matters not if my beauty moves you, or if my womb is fertile. Your future swirls with hidden knives. I will be your *Jiwah Ka,* or you will spend your days looking for them without my foretellings to aid you."

Jiwah Ka. She didn't just want to marry him, she wanted to be first among his wives. A *Jiwah Ka* had the right to vet and refuse any *Jiwah Sen,* subsequent wives, all of whom would be subservient to her. She would have absolute control of his household and children, second only to him, and Jardir was not fool enough to think she didn't intend to control him as well.

But could he afford to refuse? He feared no challenger face-to-face, but war was deception, as Khevat had taught him, and not all men fought their enemies with spear and fist. A poisoned drink, or blade in the back, and he could still go to Everam with little glory to buy his way into Heaven, and none to spare his mother and sisters.

And Sharak Ka was coming.

"You ask that I give everything to you," he said thickly, his mouth gone dry.

The *dama'ting* shook her head. "I leave you *sharak,*" she said. "That is all a *Sharum* need concern himself with."

Jardir stared at her for a long time. Finally, he nodded his assent.

The *dama'ting* wasted no time once the agreement was made. Before a week was through, Jardir found himself before Dama Khevat, watching as she made her vows.

Jardir looked into the *dama'ting*'s eyes. Who was she? Was she older than his mother? Young enough to give him sons? What would he find when they retired to the marriage bed?

"I offer you myself in marriage in accordance with the instructions of the Evejah," she said, "as set down by Kaji, Spear of Everam, who sits at the foot of Everam's table until he is reborn in the time of Sharak Ka. I pledge, with honesty and in sincerity, to be for you an obedient and faithful wife."

Does she mean those words, Jardir wondered, *or is this just a new way to control my life, now that I wear the black?*

Khevat turned to him. Jardir started, fumbling for his vow. "I swear before Everam," he said, forcing the words out, "Creator of all that is, and be-fore Kaji, the Shar'Dama Ka, to take you into my home, and to be a fair and tolerant husband."

"Do you accept this *dama'ting* as your *Jiwah Ka*?" Khevat asked, and something in his tone reminded Jardir of the *dama's* words when Jardir first asked him to perform the ceremony.

Are you sure you wish to do this? Khevat had asked. *A* dama'ting *is no ordinary wife you can order about, or beat when she is disobedient.*

Jardir swallowed. Was he sure?

"I do," he said thickly, and the assembled *dal'Sharum* gave a great shout, clattering their spears against their shields. His mother, Kajivah, clutched at his young sisters, all of them weeping in pride.

Jardir could feel his heart pounding, and part of him wished he was in the Maze, dancing *alagai'sharak*, rather than the dimly lit, pillowed chamber they retired to.

"Do not fear, *alagai'sharak* shall still be there tomorrow!" Shanjat had laughed. "You fight a different kind of battle tonight!"

"You seem ill at ease," the *dama'ting* said as she drew the heavy curtains behind them.

"Should I be another way?" Jardir asked bitterly. "You are my *Jiwah Ka*, and I do not even know your name."

The *dama'ting* laughed, the first time he had ever heard her do such. It was a beautiful, tinkling sound. "Do you not?" she asked, slipping off her veil and headwrap. His eyes widened, but it was not at the youth and beauty he saw.

He did indeed know her.

"Inevera," he breathed, remembering the *nie'dama'ting* who had spoken to him in the pavilion so many years ago.

She nodded, smiling at him, more beautiful than he had ever dared to dream.

"The night we met," Inevera said, "I finished carving my first *alagai hora*. It was fate; Everam's will, like my name. The demon bones are carved in utter darkness, by feel alone. It can take weeks to carve a single die; years to complete a set. And only then, when the set is complete, can they be tested. If they fail, they are exposed to light, and the carving must begin anew. If they succeed, then *nie'dama'ting* becomes *dama'ting*, and we don our veil.

"On that night, I finished my set and needed a question to ask. A test to see if the dice held the power of fate. But what question? Then I remembered the boy I had met that day, with the bold eyes and brash manner, and as I shook the demon dice, I asked, 'Will I ever see Ahmann Jardir again?'

"And from that night on," she said, "I knew I would find you in the Maze after your first *alagai'sharak*, and more, that I would marry you and bear you many children."

With that, she shrugged her shoulders, and her white robes fell away. Jardir had feared this moment, but as the flickering light caught her naked form, his body began to respond, and he knew that he would pass this last test of manhood as he had all the others before it.

5

"Jardir, you will take your men to the tenth layer," the Sharum Ka said.

It was a fool's decision. Three years after he had donned the white veil, every *kai'Sharum* assembled knew that Jardir's unit was the fiercest and best trained in all of Krasia. Jardir pressed his men hard, but the *dal'Sharum* gloried in it, their kill counts exceeding any three other units combined. They were wasted in the tenth layer. It was unheard of for the *alagai* to penetrate the Maze so deeply.

The Sharum Ka sneered at Jardir, daring dissent, but Jardir embraced the dishonor and let it pass through him. "As the Sharum Ka commands," he said, bowing low from his pillow to touch his forehead to the thick carpet of the First Warrior's audience room. As he sat back up, his face was serene despite his disgust at the man before him. The Sharum Ka was supposed to be the strongest warrior in the city. This man was anything but. His hair was streaked with gray, his face deeply wrinkled like a *Damaji's*. It had been long years since he had stood in the Maze, and it showed in a belly gone to fat. The First Warrior was supposed to lead the charge in *alagai'sharak* and inspire the men to glory, not conduct the war from behind his palace walls.

But for all that, so long as he wore the white turban, his will in the night was inviolate.

Dama Ashan, his unit's cleric, and his lieutenants, Hasik and Shanjat, were waiting outside the Sharum Ka's palace to escort Jardir back to the Kaji pavilion. He was only a *kai'Sharum*, but there had already been attempts on his life from jealous rivals, even within his own tribe. The Sharum Ka would not live forever, and with the Andrah having come from the Kaji tribe, it was all but certain one of the Kaji *kai'Sharum* would be appointed to take his place. Jardir stood in the way of many older *kai'Sharum's* hopes of ascension.

The three men were never far from his side ever since Inevera had arranged marriages between them and Jardir's sisters. Imisandre, Hoshvah, and Hanya had been in rags when Jardir left Sharik Hora three years ago, but now they were *Jiwah Ka* to his most trusted lieutenants, and had borne nephews and nieces to strengthen those loyalties.

"Our orders?" Shanjat asked.

"Tenth layer," Jardir said.

Hasik spat in the dust. "The Sharum Ka insults you!"

"Calm yourself, Hasik," Jardir said softly, and the big warrior immediately quieted. "Embrace the insult and it will pass through you, allowing you to see Everam's path."

Hasik nodded, falling in behind Jardir as he strode away from the palace. Hasik had returned from the *dama'ting* pavilion a changed man three years ago. He was still one of the Kaji's fiercest warriors, but like a wolf brought to heel, he had given his loyalty fully to Jardir—the only way to preserve his honor after the humiliating defeat.

"The Sharum Ka fears you," Ashan advised. "As he should. If you continue to gather all the glory, the Andrah may tire of having a weak old man commanding his forces and allow you to challenge him to single combat."

"And seconds after he shouts 'begin,' we will have a new First Warrior," Shanjat said.

"That isn't going to happen," Jardir said. "The Andrah and Sharum Ka are friends from of old. The Andrah will not betray his loyal servant even if the *Damaji* themselves demand it."

"So what do we do?" Hasik asked.

"You go home to my sister and thank her for the meal she has no doubt prepared you," Jardir said. "And when night falls, we go to the tenth layer and pray that Everam sends us *alagai* to show the sun."

As always, Inevera was waiting for him when he reached his quarters in the Kaji palace. Her robe was lowered to uncover the breast where his daughter Anjha suckled. Jardir's sons, Jayan and Asome, clung to her robes, young and strong.

Jardir knelt and spread his arms, and the boys fell into them, laughing as he lifted them high. He set them back down, and they ran back to their mother. The sight of his sons pricked at his serenity for a moment before he could embrace the feeling. It wasn't just his reputation the Sharum Ka sullied. It was theirs, as well.

"Something troubles you, my husband?" Inevera asked.

"It is nothing," Jardir said, but Inevera clicked her tongue at him.

"I am your *Jiwah Ka*," she said. "You need not embrace your feelings with me."

Jardir looked at her and let the tight lashes of his control ease.

"The Sharum Ka sends me to the tenth layer tonight," he spat. "How many warriors will he lose while his best unit guards an empty layer?"

"It is a good sign, husband," Inevera said. "It means the Sharum Ka fears you and your ambitions."

"What good is that," Jardir said, "if he robs me of every future glory?"

"He cannot be allowed to do that," Inevera agreed. "You must find glory in the Maze now more than ever. The bones tell me the First Warrior is not long for this world. Your glory must outshine all others when he goes to Everam, if you are to take his place."

"How am I to do that waving my spear at empty air?" Jardir growled.

Inevera shrugged. "*Sharak* is yours. You must find a way."

Jardir grunted, nodding. She was right, of course. There were some things even a *dama'ting* could not advise upon.

"The sun will not set for hours," Inevera advised. "A bout of lovemaking and a short sleep will clear your head."

Jardir smiled and went to her. "I will call my mother to take the children."

But Inevera shook her head, stepping away from his reaching arms. "Not me. The bones say Everalia is ripe. If you take her from behind with great force, she will bear you a strong son."

Jardir scowled. Everalia was his third wife. Inevera hadn't even bothered to show her to him before they were betrothed, saying the *Jiwah Sen* was selected for her breeder's hips and the fortune the *alagai hora* cast, not her beauty.

"Always the bones!" Jardir snapped. "For once I would bed the wife I choose!"

Inevera shrugged. "Take Thalaja if you prefer," she said, referring to his more beautiful second wife. "She is ripe as well. I simply thought you would prefer a son to another daughter."

Jardir gritted his teeth. She was the one he wanted, but as Khevat had warned, wife or no, Inevera was *dama'ting*, and he could not simply take her the way he would another woman. He opened his mouth, and then closed it again.

Did she really cast the bones for everything? Sometimes it seemed Inevera just used claims of their foretellings to get him to act as she wished, but she had not been wrong yet, and it was true he needed more sons if he was to restore the line of Jardir to its former glory. Did it really matter which wife he took? Everalia was comely enough from behind.

He headed for the bedchamber, pulling off his robes.

5

They waited.

As cries of battle rang through the outer layers, and wind demons shrieked in the sky, they waited.

As other men went to Everam in glory, they waited.

"No *alagai* sighted," Shanjat relayed, signaling back to the *nie'Sharum* on the wall.

"None *will* be sighted!" Hasik growled, and there was a rumble of assent from Jardir's men. Fifty of the best warriors of the Kaji crouched with them in the ambush pocket. Wasted.

"There is still time to find glory, if we join other units," Jurim said.

Jardir knew he must kill the idea before it could take root in the minds of the others. He thrust his spear butt between Jurim's eyes, knocking him to the ground.

"I will personally spear anyone who leaves their post without my orders," he said loudly. The others nodded as Jurim struggled to his feet, clutching his bloodied face.

Jardir looked upon the men, the finest *dal'Sharum* the Desert Spear had to offer, and felt profound shame. The Sharum Ka's jealousy was directed at him, but it was the men who suffered. Men bred and born to kill *alagai*, denied their destiny by an old man afraid of losing power. Not for the first time, Jardir envisioned killing the First Warrior, fair challenge or no, but such a crime would be without honor, and would likely cost his life as well as his legacy.

Just then a horn sounded, and Jardir snapped back to attention. The pattern told him it was a cry for assistance.

"Watchers!" he called, and the two Watchers from his unit, Amkaji and Coliv, sprang forward. They attached the ends of their twelve-foot, iron-shod ladders in an instant, running to the wall. No sooner had Amkaji set the ladder than Coliv was running up it, taking the rungs three at a time, his weight never seeming to fully come down on a foot before he was lifting it again. He reached the walltop in an instant, scanning the terrain. A moment later he signaled that it was safe for Jardir's ascent.

Jardir had been wary of the Watchers when he first took command of his unit, for they were of another tribe, the Krevakh. But he had come to know their hearts, and Amkaji and Coliv were as loyal to him and as devoted to *alagai'sharak* as any of his own tribesmen. The Krevakh were wholly devoted to serving the Kaji, as their nemesis tribe, the Nanji, served the Majah.

By law, the two Watchers were embedded with Jardir's unit day and night, for the Watchers had specialized training in exotic weapons and fighting styles, and had skills essential to any *kai'Sharum*. Acrobatics. Information gathering. Hit-and-run combat.

Assassination.

As Amkaji held the ladder, Jardir and Shanjat ran up the wall. Coliv held his far-seeing glass out to Jardir.

"Sharach tribe, fourth layer," he supplied, pointing.

"Learn more," Jardir ordered, taking the glass, and Coliv ran off, his balance perfect across the narrow wall. Watchers carried neither spear nor shield to weigh them, and Coliv was fast gone from sight.

"The Sharach are a small tribe," Shanjat said. "They bring barely two dozen warriors to *alagai'sharak*. Only a fool would put such a small unit in the fourth layer."

"A fool like the Sharum Ka," Jardir replied.

Coliv returned a moment later. "A cluster of *alagai* reached them, and avoided the pit. They have many warriors down, and no reinforcements close enough who are not engaged themselves. They will be overrun in minutes."

Jardir gritted his teeth. "No, they will not. Ready the men."

Shanjat laid a hand on his arm. "The Sharum Ka ordered us to guard the tenth," he reminded him, but when Jardir nodded and did not say more, he broke into a wide smile.

"We will never get to the fourth layer in time, *kai'Sharum*," Coliv said, scanning the Maze with his sharp eyes. "Many battles rage in between. The way is not clear."

"Then lower ropes," Jardir ordered. "I want every man on the wall now."

They ran the walltops like *nie'Sharum;* fifty adult warriors in full battle dress. Treacherous enough for barefoot and agile boys in nothing but their bidos, it was far more so for men in sandals and heavy armored robes, carrying spear and shield.

But these were Kaji *dal'Sharum*, Jardir's elite. They ran fearlessly, whooping with delight as they leapt from wall to wall, feeling like boys as the night wind whipped their faces, ready to die like men.

Jardir, running in the lead, felt it more than anyone. The Sharum Ka would be furious with him, but Nie take him before he let an entire tribe die out to appease the First Warrior's pride.

A trip that would have taken many times as long in the Maze was accomplished in minutes atop the walls, and the Sharach unit quickly came into view. There were more than a dozen *alagai* in the ambush pocket, cutting off all avenues of escape. At least half the Sharach were down, and those who remained stood on the defensive, back-to-back and shield-to-shield as demons came at them from all sides.

They stood as men before an overwhelming force of *alagai,* and the sight enraged Jardir's Krasian heart. He would let no more *dal'Sharum* die this night.

"Take heart, Sharach!" he cried. "The Kaji come to your aid!" He was the first to set his hook and throw a rope down into the pocket, rappelling the twenty feet in two quick hops. He didn't even wait for his men, charging in with his warded shield leading, taking a sand demon in the back. The wards flared, and the demon was thrown away from the failing Sharach circle.

Jardir paid the stunned creature no further mind, moving on to the next demon with a thrust of his spear, driving it back with a series of precise strikes to the weakest parts of its armor. Behind him, he heard the roar of his fifty as they poured down the wall, and knew his back was secure.

"Everam watched your stand with pride, brother!" Jardir cried to the Sharach *kai'Sharum,* whose white veil was red with blood. "See to your wounded now! We will finish your glorious start and see that the Sharach fight another day!"

The third demon Jardir charged turned to face him and caught his spear in its jaws, splintering the wood. The impact threw Jardir off balance, and the creature hooked the edge of his shield on its talon. It flexed its corded arm, and the shield straps snapped. Jardir hit the ground hard, dodging aside as the creature came at him. For a moment, the demon had the advantage, but the Sharach *kai'Sharum* slammed into it from the side, knocking it away from him.

"The Sharach will fight to the last, my brother!" the *kai'Sharum* cried, but the sand demon struck back, its tail whipping under the warrior's guard to knock him down. It tensed to spring for the kill.

Jardir glanced about. His warriors were all engaged, and there was no weapon in reach.

I was born to die on alagai *talons,* he reminded himself, and growled as he leapt to his feet, intercepting the sand demon in midair as it launched itself at the Sharach *kai'Sharum.*

The demon was stronger than him by far, but it fought on instinct, knowing nothing of the brutal art of *sharusahk*. Jardir caught its arm and pivoted, diverting the force of its attack and throwing it fifteen feet into the demon pit at the center of the ambush pocket. The *alagai* fell away with a howl, trapped until the sun rose to burn it from the world forever.

Another sand demon came at him, but Jardir punched it hard in the throat and kicked at the backs of its knees, grappling the creature and bearing it to the ground, twisting to avoid its teeth and claws while turning the thrashing *alagai's* own force against it.

The demon's gritty armor plates cut through his robes, slicing his skin, and his muscles screamed as they were stretched to their limits, but inch by inch, Jardir twisted farther behind the demon until he reached the desired hold and rose to his feet. He was taller than the creature, and with his arms locked under its pits and behind its head, he easily lifted it off the ground. It kicked and shrieked, but Jardir whipped it about, keeping its hind legs far from his body as he stumbled toward the demon pit.

With a shout, he threw the second demon into the pit, gratified to see that his warriors had already driven most of the other *alagai* into it as well. The pit floor was a seethe of scale and talon, the wards cut into the walls sparking angrily as they tried to climb out.

"I will watch as the sun takes you all!" Jardir shouted.

He turned back to the battle, flush with victory and ready to fight on, but only a few warriors still fought, and they had their *alagai* well in hand.

The rest of the men simply stared at him, eyes wide.

Jardir and the Sharach *kai'Sharum* stood watch over the pit for the rest of the night. Their men stood clustered about them, and there was a great cheer when the sunlight reached the pit. The demons shrieked and smoked before finally bursting into flame, and the men were proud to bear witness as Everam's light burned them back into the nothingness from which they came.

Jardir and the other *Sharum* lowered their veils, as was proper in the sun. By day, the Sharach, beholden to the Majah, were blood enemies of the Kaji. Jardir eyed the *kai'Sharum* warily. It would dishonor them both to turn on each other in the neutral ground of the Maze, but such things were not unheard of.

Instead, the Sharach captain bowed. "My people owe you a blood debt."

Jardir shook his head. "We did nothing that Everam did not command.

No *dal'Sharum* would ever abandon a brother, and all men are brothers in the night."

"I was there when the Sharum Ka sent you to the tenth, where we should have been," the Sharach said. "You came far and dared much for us."

Other warriors, their own pits burning, came across them as they left the Maze. Two blood enemies, standing together. A crowd began to form, and Jardir heard the buzz of their conversation. Again and again, he heard his men and the Sharach tell of how he had fought the *alagai* unarmed. The tale grew with each telling, and before long men were saying he had killed five demons with his bare hands. Jardir had seen warriors exaggerating deeds before. By nightfall, it would be a dozen he sent into the pit, and a month from now, fifty.

A Majah *kai'Sharum* approached them. "On behalf of the Majah," he said, "I thank you for protecting the Sharach. The Sharum Ka was . . . unwise to put them in such danger."

The man's words were near treason, but Jardir only nodded. "The Sharach stood tall," he said. "It was *inevera* that they live to fight again."

"*Inevera*," the Majah agreed, bowing lower than one *kai'Sharum* need bow to another. "Did you truly wrestle six demons into the pit yourself?"

Jardir shook his head and opened his mouth to reply, but he was cut off by a shout as the elite guard of the Sharum Ka stormed into view, clearing the way for the First Warrior.

"You disobeyed orders and left your post!" the Sharum Ka shouted, pointing at Jardir.

"The Sharach called for aid and we were unengaged," Jardir said. "The Evejah tells us to protect our brothers in the night above all things."

"Do not quote the sacred text to me," the Sharum Ka snapped. "I was teaching it to my sons when your father was in his bido, and I know its truths far better than you! There is nothing that tells you to have your men scale the Maze walls and leave your layer unguarded while you protect one half the Maze away."

"Unguarded!" Jardir goggled. "There were no demons in the eighth, much less the tenth!"

"It is not your place to disregard orders and seek glory that is not yours, *kai'Sharum*!" the Sharum Ka shouted.

Jardir's temper flared. "Perhaps my orders would have been less foolish if the one giving them did not hide in his palace until dawn," he said, knowing even as he did that he might as well have pulled his spear. Such an insult to the First Warrior could not be allowed to pass. If he were any kind of man, he would grab a spear and attack Jardir now, killing him before all the assembled men.

But the Sharum Ka was old, and men whispered of how Jardir had killed half a dozen demons with *sharusahk* alone. Jardir could not attack the First Warrior himself, but if the Sharum Ka attacked *him*, Jardir would be free to kill him and open a succession that might well put him in the Sharum Ka's palace. He wondered if this was the fate Inevera's bones had foretold so many years before.

They locked stares, and Jardir knew the Sharum Ka was thinking the same things he was, and did not have the courage to attack. He sneered.

"Arrest him!" the Sharum Ka commanded. Immediately his guards moved to comply.

Jardir's hands were bound, a grave dishonor, but though he bared his teeth at the guards, he did not resist. There was a rumble of discontent from the assembled warriors, even the Majah. They gripped spears and lifted shields, greatly outnumbering the First Warrior's guards.

"What are you doing?" the Sharum Ka demanded of the crowd. "Stand down!"

But the rumbling only grew, and men moved to block the exits from the Maze. The Sharum Ka took a tentative step back. Jardir met his eyes, and smiled.

"Do nothing," Jardir said loudly, without taking his eyes from the Sharum Ka. "The Sharum Ka has given a command, and all *Sharum* are bound to comply. Everam will decide my fate."

The grumbling quieted immediately, men clearing the path, and the Sharum Ka's rage seemed doubled at Jardir's control of the men. Jardir sneered at him again, daring him to attack.

"Take him away!" the Sharum Ka cried. Jardir kept his back straight and walked proudly as the guards gripped his arms and escorted him from the Maze.

$$\overline{3}$$

Inevera was waiting in the palace of the Andrah when Jardir arrived.

Did she know of this day years ago, as well? he wondered.

His guards tightened their grip on his arms as she approached, but it was not in fear of anything Jardir might do. It was Inevera that terrified them.

"Leave us," Inevera ordered. "Tell your master that my husband will meet him in the Andrah's audience hall one hour hence."

The guards immediately dropped Jardir's arms and bowed. "As the *dama'ting* commands," one stuttered, and they scurried away. Inevera snorted, pulling her warded blade to cut his bonds.

"You did well this night," she whispered as they walked. "Stand tall in the coming hours. When the audience with the Andrah comes, you must provoke the Sharum Ka with words while standing in submission. Enrage him, but give him no excuse to attack you."

"I will do no such thing," Jardir said.

"You did it in the Maze," Inevera snapped. "It is trebly important now."

"You see all," Jardir acknowledged, "but you understand little, if you think I will lower my eyes to this man. I was daring him to attack me then."

Inevera shrugged. "Do it that way if you wish, but keep your feet planted and your hands still. He will never dare attack you himself, but if you pose a threat, his men will cut you down."

"Do you think me a fool?" Jardir asked.

Inevera snorted. "Just enrage him. The rest is *inevera*."

"As the *dama'ting* commands," Jardir sighed.

Inevera nodded. They reached a pillowed waiting room. "Wait here," she commanded. "I go now to meet with the Andrah privately before your trial."

"Trial?" Jardir asked, but she had already slipped from the room.

Jardir had never before been close enough to the Andrah to see the man's face. It was old and lined, his beard a stark white. He was a round man, clearly given to rich foods. His corpulence was disgusting, and Jardir had to remind himself that this man was once the greatest *sharusahk* master of his day, having defeated the most skilled *Damaji* in single combat in order to achieve the Skull Throne. In his days beneath Sharik Hora, Jardir had seen the Kaji *Damaji*, Amadeveram, a man of some sixty years, leave half a dozen young and skilled *dama* on their backs in the *sharusahk* circle.

He looked closer, seeking a sign of that training in the Andrah's movements, but it seemed his ever-present bodyguards and servants had made the man lax. Even here, he picked at a plate of sugar dates during the proceedings.

Jardir's eyes flicked to the sides of the Andrah's throne. At his right hand stood the twelve *Damaji*, leaders of all the tribes of Krasia. Dressed in white robes and black turbans, they muttered among themselves about being pulled from their business and dragged to the palace when the sun had barely topped the horizon. At the Andrah's left, two steps back from the throne, stood the *Damaji'ting.* Like the *Damaji,* they wore headwraps and veils of black, falling in sharp contrast over their white robes. Unlike the *Damaji,* they were utterly silent, watching with eyes that seemed to penetrate everything.

Do they too know my fate? Jardir wondered, then glanced at his *Jiwah Ka,* standing beside him. *Or do they only know what Inevera tells them?*

"Son of Hoshkamin," Damaji Amadeveram greeted Jardir, "please tell us your version of last night's events." He was Kaji and the Andrah's First Minister, perhaps the most powerful cleric in all of Krasia save the Andrah himself. The Andrah was said to represent all tribes, but it was he who appointed the Sharum Ka and First Minister, and Jardir knew from his lessons that it had been centuries since an Andrah had filled either position with someone from another tribe. It was considered a sign of weakness.

The Sharum Ka scowled, clearly expecting to have been invited to relate his version first. He stormed over to the tea service laid for him and took a cup. Jardir could tell from the erratic way the steam rose that his old hands were shaking.

"At the *kai'Sharum* supper this evening, the Sharum Ka gave orders, as he always does," Jardir began. "My men have found much success in the night and were eager to send more *alagai* back to Nie as ashes."

The *Damaji* nodded. "Your successes have not gone without note," he said. "And your teachers in Sharik Hora speak highly of you. Go on."

"We were dismayed to learn we would be sent to the tenth layer," Jardir said. "Not so long ago, we stood in the first, showing a hundred *alagai* the sun for every man we lost. Then, recently, we were moved to the second, followed soon after by the third. We took it with pride; there is glory enough for all in the lower levels. But instead of moving us to the fourth, as expected, the Sharum Ka sent the Sharach there, giving us their traditional place in the tenth."

Jardir saw Damaji Kevera of the Sharach tense, but he was not sure if it was at the dishonor of having his tribe's "traditional place" be one so lacking glory, or at the sudden change.

He glanced at the *Damaji'ting,* but they were faceless, and he did not know which of them was Sharach. It mattered little; none of them showed the slightest reaction to his words.

"The men of Sharach are brave warriors," he said. "They accepted this assignment with pride. But the Sharach do not bring many warriors to *alagai'sharak.* Even if every man fought as two," he glanced at Kevera, "and they do, they do not have enough warriors to fully man an ambush point in the fourth."

The Sharach *Damaji* nodded, and Jardir felt a surge of relief.

"So what did you do?" Amadeveram asked.

Jardir shrugged. "The Sharum Ka gave an order, and we followed it."

"Liar!" the Sharum Ka shouted. "You left your post, you son of a camel's piss!"

The insult, one no man had dared utter since he had broken Hasik, struck Jardir hard. For a split second he considered leaping across the room and killing the man outright, even though it would likely earn him a quick death at the hands of the Andrah's guards. Instead he embraced the insult and it passed through him, leaving in its wake a cold, calm anger.

"We spent half the night in the tenth," Jardir said, not even turning his head to acknowledge that the man had spoken. "The Watchers saw no *alagai* in our layer, or the ninth, or the eighth. Still we waited."

"Liar!" the Sharum Ka shouted again.

This time Jardir did turn to him. "Were you there, First Warrior, to deny the truth of my words? Were you even in the Maze at all?" The Sharum Ka's eyes widened, then a look of rage came over him. The truth of the words struck harder than any blow could.

The Sharum Ka opened his mouth to retort, but there was a hiss from the Andrah. All eyes turned to the man.

"Peace, my friend," the Andrah told the Sharum Ka. "Let him tell his tale. You will have the last word."

It struck Jardir then just how close these men were. Both had held their respective palaces for nearly four decades. Jardir had held some hope that the Andrah might still desire a strong Sharum Ka, but seeing his bloated form gave him grave doubts. If the Andrah himself had forgotten the warrior way, could he condemn his loyal Sharum Ka for the same offense?

"There was a horn call for aid," Jardir said. "Since we were unengaged, I scaled the wall to see if we could answer it. But the call came from the fourth layer, and many battles raged in between them and our position. I was about to descend back into the Maze when the Watcher I sent returned with news that the Sharach were being overrun, and would soon pass from this world."

He paused. "All *dal'Sharum* expect to die in the Maze. A dozen warriors, two dozen, even a hundred in a night, what does it matter when we do Everam's work?

"Yet there is a difference between losing men and losing a tribe. What honor would I have if I stood idly by?"

"You said yourself the way was blocked," Amadeveram noted.

Jardir nodded. "But my Watcher made it there, and I remember running the walltops with my men as *nie'Sharum*. I asked myself, *Is there anything a boy can do that a man cannot?* So we ran the walls, praying to Everam that we would be in time."

"And what did you find when you arrived?" Amadeveram asked.

"Half the Sharach were down," Jardir said. "Perhaps a dozen remained, none without injury himself. They faced a like number of *alagai*, and with their pit revealed, the demons knew to avoid it."

Again, Jardir looked to the Sharach *Damaji*. "The remaining men stood tall in the night. The blood of Sharach, who stood with the Shar'Dama Ka himself, runs strong in their veins."

"And then?" the *Damaji* pressed.

"My men joined our Sharach brothers, and we routed the *alagai*, throwing them in the pit and showing them the sun."

"It is said you slew several yourself," Amadeveram said, pride evident in his voice, "using *sharusahk* alone."

"It was only two I sent to the pit that way," Jardir said. He knew his wife was scowling behind her veil, but he did not care. He would not lie to his *Damaji*, or claim glory that was not rightfully his.

"Still, no small feat," Amadeveram said. "Sand demons have many times a man's strength."

"My years in Sharik Hora taught me strength is relative," Jardir replied, bowing.

"This makes him no less a traitor!" the Sharum Ka snarled.

"How did I betray?" Jardir asked.

"I gave an order!" the Sharum Ka cried.

"You gave a fool's order," Jardir replied. "You gave an order that wasted your best warriors while condemning the Sharach to destruction. And *still* I complied!"

The Majah *Damaji*, Aleverak, stepped forward. He was an ancient man, older even than Amadeveram. He was like a spear, stick-thin but tall and straight despite close to seventy years.

"The only traitor I see is you," Aleverak snapped at the Sharum Ka. "You are supposed to stand for all the *Sharum* in Krasia, but you would sacrifice the Sharach just to quell a rival!"

The Sharum Ka took a step toward the *Damaji*, but Aleverak did not back off, striding forward and assuming a *sharusahk* stance. Unlike Jardir, a mere *kai'Sharum*, a *Damaji* could challenge and kill a Sharum Ka, opening a succession.

"Enough!" the Andrah cried. "Back to your places!" Both men complied, dropping their eyes in submission.

"I won't have you fighting in my throne room like . . . like . . ."

"Men?" Inevera supplied.

Jardir almost choked at her audacity, but the Andrah merely scowled and did not reprimand her.

The Andrah sighed, looking very tired, and Jardir could see the weight of years upon him. *Everam grant I die young,* he prayed silently.

"I see no crime here," the Andrah said at last. He looked pointedly at the Majah. "On *either* side. The Sharum Ka gave orders as he should, and the *kai'Sharum* made a decision in the heat of battle."

"He insulted me before my men!" the Sharum Ka cried. "For that alone, I am within my rights to have him killed."

"Your pardon, Sharum Ka, but that is not so," Amadeveram said. "His insult gives you the right to kill him yourself, not to have him killed by other men. If you had done so, the matter would be closed. May I ask why you did not?"

There was a pause as the Sharum Ka groped for a response. Inevera nudged him gently.

Jardir glanced at her. *Have we not won?* his eyes asked, but hers were hard in response.

"Because he is a coward," Jardir announced. "Not strong enough to defend the white turban, he hides in his palace and sends others to fight on his behalf, waiting for death to find him like a *khaffit* instead of seeking it in the Maze like a *Sharum*."

The Sharum Ka's eyes bulged, and veins stood sharply on his face and neck as he gnashed his teeth. Jardir tensed, expecting the man to leap upon him. In his mind's eye, he imagined all the ways he might kill the old man.

But there was no need, for the Sharum Ka gripped his chest and fell to the floor, twitching and foaming at the mouth before lying still.

"You knew that would happen," Jardir accused when they were alone. "You knew if I enraged him enough, his heart would give way."

Inevera shrugged. "What if I did?"

"Fool woman!" Jardir shouted. "There is no honor in killing a man in such a way!"

"Ware your tongue," Inevera warned, raising a finger. "You are not Sharum Ka yet, and never will be without me."

Jardir scowled, wondering at the truth of her words. Was it his fate to be Sharum Ka? And if so, could fate be changed? "I will be lucky to even remain a *kai'Sharum* after this," he said. "I killed the Andrah's friend."

"Nonsense," Inevera said, smiling wickedly. "The Andrah is . . . pliable. The post is empty now, and you have won glory that even the Majah acknowledge. I will convince him that he can only gain face by appointing you."

"How?" Jardir asked.

"Leave it to me," Inevera said. "You have other concerns. When the Andrah places the white turban on your head, your first announcement will be an offer to take a fertile wife from each tribe as a symbol of unity."

Jardir was scandalized. "Mix the blood of Kaji, the first Deliverer, with lesser tribes?"

Inevera poked him hard in the chest. "You will be Sharum Ka, if you stop acting the fool and do as you're told. If you can produce heirs with ties to each tribe . . ."

"Krasia will unite as never before," Jardir caught on. "I could invite the *Damaji* to select my brides," he mused. "That should gain me favor."

"No," Inevera said. "Leave that to me. The *Damaji* will choose for politics. The *alagai hora* will choose for Everam."

"Always the bones," Jardir muttered. "Was Kaji himself bound to them?"

"It was Kaji who first gave us the wards of prophecy," Inevera said.

The next day, Jardir found himself in the Andrah's throne room once more. The *Damaji* murmured to one another as he entered, and *Damaji'ting* watched him, inscrutable as ever.

The Andrah sat on his throne, toying with the white turban of the Sharum Ka. The steel under the cloth rang with a clear note as the Andrah flicked it with a long, painted nail.

"The Sharum Ka was a great warrior," the Andrah said as if reading his mind. He rose from his throne, and Jardir immediately sank to his knees, spreading his arms in supplication.

"Yes, Holiness," he said.

The Andrah waved a dismissive hand at him. "You do not remember him as such, of course. By the time you were in your bido, he already had more years than most *Sharum* ever see, and could no longer stand toe-to-toe with the *alagai* as a young man."

Jardir bowed his head.

"It is a failing of the young to think a man's worth lies only in the strength of his arm," the Andrah said. "Would you judge me so?"

"Your pardon, Holiness," Jardir said, "but you are not *Sharum*. The *Sharum* are your arm in the night, and that arm must be strong."

The Andrah grunted. "Bold," he said. "Though I guess any man who took a *dama'ting* to wife would have to be."

Jardir said nothing.

"You sought to provoke him into attacking you," the Andrah said. "No doubt you thought such was the way a brave man should die."

Again, Jardir said nothing.

"But if he had attacked you, it would have only shown that he was a fool," the Andrah said. "And Everam has little patience for fools."

"Yes, Holiness," Jardir said.

"And now he is dead," the Andrah said. "My friend, a man who showed countless *alagai* the sun, dead on the floor in disgrace because *you* could not show him the respect he was owed!"

Jardir swallowed hard. The Andrah looked ready to strike him. This was not going as Inevera had promised, and she was conspicuously absent from the audience. He scanned the room for support, but the eyes of the *Damaji* were downcast as the Andrah spoke, and the *Damaji'ting* simply watched him as if he were a bug.

The Andrah sighed and seemed to deflate, waddling back to his throne and sitting heavily. "It pains me to see a man who achieved such glory in life die in shame. My heart cries for vengeance, but the fact remains the Sharum Ka is dead, and I would be a fool to ignore the fact that for the first time in centuries, the *Damaji* are in agreement over who should succeed him."

Jardir glanced at the *Damaji* again. He might have imagined it, but it seemed as if Amadeveram nodded slightly to him.

"You will be Sharum Ka," the Andrah said curtly. "The night will belong to you."

Jardir spread his hands and leaned forward on his knees, pressing his forehead into the thick woven carpet before the throne. "I will be your strong arm in the night," he swore.

"I will make the announcement at Sharik Hora tonight," the Andrah said. "You may go."

Jardir touched his forehead to the floor again, remembering Inevera's instructions. Already the *Damaji* were beginning to murmur. If he was going to speak, it must be now.

"Holiness," he began, watching the Andrah's eyes return to him with irritation, "I ask your blessing, and that of the *Damaji*, to take a fertile wife from each tribe, as a show of unity among the *Sharum*."

The Andrah goggled at him, as did the *Damaji*. Even the *Damaji'ting* stirred, betraying their sudden interest.

"That is an unusual request," the Andrah said at last.

"Unusual?" Amadeveram demanded. "It is unheard of! You are Kaji! I will not bless your wedding to some—"

"You need not," Aleverak cut in, smiling openly. "I am more than willing to perform the ceremony, should the Sharum Ka wish a Majah wife."

"You would be happy to dilute the pure blood of Kaji, I have no doubt," Amadeveram growled, but Aleverak did not rise to the bait, simply grinning.

"I will bless a wedding to a daughter of Sharach, as well," Damaji Kevera of the Sharach said. Within moments the remaining *Damaji* followed suit, all of them eager to have a permanent voice in the First Warrior's court.

"Surely you cannot agree to this!" Amadeveram said, turning to the Andrah.

"I am Andrah, not you, Amadeveram," the Andrah said. "If the Sharum Ka wishes unity and the *Damaji* agree, I see no reason to refuse. Like me, the First Warrior relinquishes tribe when he dons his turban."

He turned to regard the *Damaji'ting* for the first time Jardir had seen. "This matter lies more in the realm of women than who carries the first spear," he said, addressing none of the women in particular. "What do the *Damaji'ting* say to this proposal?"

The women turned their backs on the men and clustered together in a buzz of muffled whispers, impossible to understand. In moments, they finished and turned back to the Andrah.

"The *Damaji'ting* have no objection," one of them said.

Amadeveram scowled, and Jardir knew he had angered the man, perhaps irrevocably, but there was nothing to be done for it now. He had three Kaji wives already, including his *Jiwah Ka*. That would have to be enough.

"It's settled then," Aleverak said. "My own granddaughter is just fourteen, Sharum Ka, beautiful and unknown to man. She will bear you strong sons."

Jardir bowed deeply. "My apologies, Damaji, but the duty of choosing my brides must fall to my *Jiwah Ka*. She will cast the *alagai hora* to ensure the blessings of Everam for each union."

There was another buzz among the *Damaji'ting*, and Aleverak's wide smile vanished in an instant, as did those of many other *Damaji*. But it was too late for them to take back their support. Amadeveram's scowl became a look of smug satisfaction.

"Enough talk of brides!" the Andrah barked. "You have your boon, Sharum Ka. Go now before you disturb my court further!"

Jardir bowed and left.

ऽ

"Are you a fool?" Amadeveram demanded. Jardir had not made it out of the Andrah's palace before the old *Damaji* had caught up to him, dragging him into a private room.

"Of course not, my Damaji," Jardir said.

"Only 'yours' for a few hours more, it seems," Amadeveram said.

Jardir shrugged. "I will still be ruled by the council of *Damaji*, who speak with your voice. But as Sharum Ka, I must represent warriors of all tribes."

"The Sharum Ka does not represent warriors, he rules them!" Amadeveram shouted. "That you are Kaji is proof that Everam wishes the Kaji to rule! You cannot go through with this mad plan."

"For the good of all Krasia, I can and will," Jardir said. "I will not be a weak figurehead for you, like the last Sharum Ka. The warriors need unity if they are to be strong. Becoming one with all of them is the only way to win their devotion."

"You are turning your back on your tribe!" Amadeveram shouted.

"No, I am turning to face the others," Jardir said. "I implore you, turn with me."

"Face our blood enemies?" Amadeveram said, aghast. "I would sooner die in shame!"

"There was only one tribe in the time of Kaji," Jardir reminded him. "Our blood enemies are also our blood."

"You are no blood of Kaji," Amadeveram said, spitting at Jardir's feet. "The blood of the Shar'Dama Ka has turned to camel's piss in your veins."

Jardir's face grew dark and, for a moment, he considered attacking him. Amadeveram was a *sharusahk* grand master, but Jardir was younger and stronger and faster. He could kill the old man.

But he was not Sharum Ka yet. Killing Amadeveram would only unravel Inevera's plans and cost him the Spear Throne.

Am I doomed to always have success without pride? he asked himself.

ऽ

"The Sharum Ka is dead!" the Andrah cried to the assembled warriors in Sharik Hora. The *Sharum* filling the rows of the great temple howled at the news, banging spear against shield in a great cacophony meant to announce the First Warrior's coming to Everam.

"But we will not cede the night like those to the north!" the Andrah cried when the noise died down. "We are Krasian! Blood of Shar'Dama Ka himself! And we will fight till the Deliverer returns, or the spear falls from the hands of the last *nie'Sharum* and Krasia is buried in the sand!"

The warriors hooted at that, thrusting spears in the air.

"And thus, I have chosen a new Sharum Ka to lead *alagai'sharak*," the Andrah said. "When he was *nie'Sharum*, he was made *Nie Ka* and stood on the walls at twelve, the youngest in a hundred years! He was not there six months before he netted a wind demon that had killed his Watcher and knocked his drillmaster prone. For this, he was brought to the Kaji pavilion, the youngest to come since the Return. He fought so well on his first night of *alagai'sharak* that he was sent to Sharik Hora, studying five years with the *dama* to first don his blacks as *kai'Sharum*, the youngest such since the time of the Deliverer himself!"

There was a murmur at this among the Kaji, who knew Jardir's accomplishments well. The Andrah paused a moment to let the sense of excitement travel, then continued. "Two nights ago, he led his warriors in a daring rescue of the Sharach, who stood on the brink of destruction, killing *alagai* with his bare hands while his men still readied their spears!"

The murmuring grew to a buzz. There was not a man, woman, or child in all Krasia who had not heard that tale by now.

"Ahmann asu Hoshkamin am'Jardir am'Kaji, stand before the Skull Throne!" the Andrah commanded, and the warriors cheered and banged spear and shield as Jardir appeared, dressed in his *Sharum* blacks, his head bare.

Inevera walked silently at his side as he went to the Skull Throne and prostrated himself, kneeling quickly to lay the Andrah's Evejah under his forehead as he pressed it to the rug. The holy book was inked with *dal'Sharum* blood on vellum made from *kai'Sharum* skin, bound in leather from a Sharum Ka. It would sear his skull if he should utter a lie while touching it.

"Do you serve Everam in all things?" the Andrah asked.

"I do, Holiness," Jardir swore.

"Will you be His strong arm in the night, giving all honor to the thrones of Sharik Hora?"

"I will, Holiness."

"Are you prepared to hold the reins of *alagai'sharak* until the Shar'Dama Ka comes again, or you be dead?" the Andrah asked.

"I am, Holiness."

"Then rise," the Andrah said, lifting the white turban of the Sharum **Ka** high for all to see. "The night awaits its Sharum Ka."

Jardir rose, and the Andrah turned to Inevera. He handed her the turban, and she placed it on Jardir's head.

The *Sharum* roared and stamped their feet, but Jardir barely noticed. Why did the Andrah not put the turban on his head himself, as was the custom? Why give the honor to Inevera?

"Stop basking in your glory and speak your words," Inevera whispered, breaking him from his musing. Jardir started, then turned to face the assembled *Sharum*—nearly six thousand spears. It had been ten thousand not long ago, but the previous Sharum Ka had wasted lives. Jardir promised himself he would not do the same.

"My brothers in the night," Jardir said. "This is a glorious time to be *Sharum*! Alone, the tribes of Krasia make the *alagai* quail with fear, but when we stand together, there is nothing we cannot do!"

The warriors roared, and Jardir waited until it died. "But when I look out at you, I see division!" he cried. "The Majah sit across the aisle from the Kaji! The Jama avoid the Khanjin! There is not one tribe who does not see enemies in this room! We are supposed to be brothers in the night, but who among you has volunteered to stand with the Sharach, whose numbers have been decimated?"

There was silence now, the warriors unsure how to respond. They knew the truth of his words, but tribal hatreds ran deep and were not easily let go even if one wished it—and few did.

"The Sharum Ka is said to be of no tribe," Jardir continued, "but to me, that is worse! What loyalty might a tribeless man have? The Evejah tells us that the only true loyalty is that of blood. And so," he swept a hand back toward the Andrah and the *Damaji* on their thrones, "I have beseeched our leaders to join my blood to all of you.

"With the Andrah's blessing," Jardir said, "the *Damaji* have each agreed to wed me to one fertile daughter of their tribe, to bear me a *Sharum* son to whom I will be forever loyal."

There was a shocked silence, then the room erupted in a roar of approval from every tribe save the Kaji. Clearly, they had believed Jardir would retain his loyalty to their tribe, as all previous Sharum Ka had done, no matter what the Evejah said.

Let them sulk, Jardir thought. *I will win them back in the Maze.*

"And so," he intoned, quieting the temple once more, "once my *Jiwah Ka* selects my brides, the *Damaji* will perform the wedding rites."

But then Inevera stepped forward unrehearsed, surprising Jardir no less than the *Sharum* or assembled leaders. Did she mean to speak? Any woman, *dama'ting* or no, speaking in Sharik Hora was unheard of.

But it seemed everything Inevera did was unheard of.

"There need be no delay," she said loudly. "Let the brides of the Sharum Ka step forth!"

Jardir's jaw dropped. She had chosen his brides already? Impossible!

But eleven women strode out onto the great altar of Sharik Hora, kneeling before the flabbergasted *Damaji* of their tribes. Jardir saw them, and his heart sank.

They were all *dama'ting*.

5

The palace of the Sharum Ka was smaller than the Kaji palace, but where that housed dozens of *kai'Sharum, dama,* and their families, this palace was Jardir's alone. He remembered his years spent sleeping on a filthy cloth on the crowded stone floor of the Kaji'sharaj, and gazed in wonder at the splendor of it all. Everywhere he stepped was plush carpet, velvet, and silk. He dined off porcelain plates so delicate he feared to touch them, and drank from golden goblets studded with gems. And the fountains! There was nothing in Krasia more valuable than water, yet even his mother's bedroom tinkled with fresh flowing water.

He threw Qasha down onto a pile of pillows, delighting in the sway of her soft breasts, clearly visible through her diaphanous top. Her legs were clad in the same gossamer material, leaving her sex bare, shaved and perfumed. Lust filled him as he fell on her, and he mused that being wed to twelve *dama'ting* was not the chore he had feared.

Qasha of the Sharach was by far Jardir's favorite of his new wives. Almost as beautiful as Inevera, she was far more obedient, dropping her robes at a moment's notice. Her belly was still flat, but already, six weeks wed, she carried a son—the first that would come from his new brides. He knew he should be taking another now, filling the palace with swollen bellies to tie him to the tribes, but Qasha's condition only aroused Jardir's lust for her further. Inevera didn't seem to care. Far less strict with her *dama'ting Jiwah Sen,* she let Jardir bed them as he pleased. He liked to keep Qasha close by, for she served him as a proper wife should.

Laughing, Qasha pushed him onto his back, mounting him wantonly.

"Everam's bones, woman!" Jardir cried, gasping as she lowered herself down upon him.

"Should I seem demure when I am in the pillows with the Sharum Ka?" Qasha asked, rising up and slapping down hard. "Just last night, the Andrah himself spoke of the glory you've won in the Maze since ascending. It is an honor to sheathe your spear." She leaned in close, moving rhythmically.

"A woman may bear two children in the same womb," Qasha whispered between perfumed kisses. "Perhaps you can plant yet another son within me." Jardir started to reply, but she giggled and muffled his words by giving him a full breast to suckle. For long minutes, they sweated and struggled in the only battle to rival *alagai'sharak*.

When they were finished, Qasha rolled off him, raising her legs to hold his seed.

"You were in the palace last night when I left at dusk," Jardir said after a moment.

Qasha looked at him, and for an instant fear washed over her lovely face before being replaced with the cold *dama'ting* mask he had come to expect from his wives whenever he spoke of things other than lovemaking and children.

"I was," she agreed.

"Then when did you see the Andrah?" Jardir asked. "Women with child, even *dama'ting*, are forbidden to leave the palace at night."

"I misspoke," Qasha said. "It was another night."

"Which night?" Jardir pressed. "Which night did you take my unborn son from the safety of my palace without permission?"

Qasha drew herself up. "I am *dama'ting*, and owe you no—"

"You are my *jiwah*!" Jardir roared, and she quailed in the face of it. "The Evejah grants no exceptions to *dama'ting* when it commands wives to obedience!" It was bad enough that Inevera flaunted that sacred law as she pleased, but Jardir would be damned if he gave all his wives the same power. He was Sharum Ka!

"I did not leave the wards!" Qasha cried, holding out her hands. "I swear it!"

"Did you lie about the Andrah's words?" Jardir asked, clenching a fist.

"No!" Qasha cried.

"Then the Andrah was here, in my palace?" Jardir asked.

"Please, I am forbidden to speak of it," Qasha said, casting her eyes down in submission.

Jardir grabbed her roughly, forcing her to look him in the eye. "No one may forbid you anything over me!"

Qasha thrashed and pulled from his grasp, losing her balance and falling to the floor. She burst into tears, shaking as she covered her face in her hands. She looked so frail and afraid that all the anger fell from him. He knelt and put his hands gently on her shoulders.

"Of all my wives," he said, "you are the most favored. I ask only your loyalty. You will not be punished for your answer, I swear."

She looked up at him with round, wet eyes, and he pushed back her hair, brushing away tears with his thumb. She pulled back, looking to the floor. When she spoke, it was so low he could barely make out her words.

"All is not always still in the palace of the Sharum Ka at night," she said, "when the master is at *alagai'sharak*."

Jardir choked down a blast of anger. "And when will the palace next be stirred?"

Qasha shook her head. "I do not know," she whimpered.

"Then cast the bones and find out," Jardir ordered.

She looked up at him, scandalized. "I could never!"

Jardir growled, his anger flaring again, as he silently cursed the day he had married *dama'ting*. Even if she were not carrying his child, Jardir could not strike Qasha, and she knew it. There was a layer of Nie's abyss reserved for any man who harmed a *dama'ting*.

But Jardir refused to be dominated by every one of his wives because he could not discipline as the Evejah taught. There were other ways to frighten her.

"I tire of your disobedience, *jiwah*," he said. "Cast them, or I will send the Sharach to the first layer, and your tribe will be consumed by the night. The boys will be cast from *Hannu Pash* as *khaffit*, and the women left to whore for lesser tribes." He would do no such thing, of course, but she need not know that.

"You would not dare!" Qasha said.

"Why should I allow your tribe honor, when you deny me mine?" Jardir demanded.

She was crying openly now, but Qasha nevertheless reached for the thick bag of black felt every *dama'ting* carried at all times. Hers was secured to her bare waist with a strand of colored beads.

Used to the practice by now, Jardir moved to draw the heavy velvet curtains, blocking any hint of sunlight that might break the magic and render the dice useless.

Qasha lit a candle. She looked at him, fear in her eyes. "Swear to me," she begged. "Swear that you will never tell the *Jiwah Ka* that I did this for you."

Inevera. Of course Jardir expected his First Wife to be at the center of any intrigue in his palace, but it cut him to hear it. He was Sharum Ka now, and still not fit to know her plans.

"I swear by Everam and the blood of my sons," Jardir said.

Qasha nodded and cast the bones. Jardir watched their evil light and wondered for the first time if perhaps they were not Everam's voice on Ala.

"Tonight," Qasha whispered.

Jardir nodded. "Put the bones away. We will speak no more of this."

"And the Sharach?" Qasha asked.

"I would never have vented my rage upon my son's tribe," Jardir said, laying a hand on her belly. Qasha sighed and rested her head on his shoulder, deflating as the tension left her.

丂

As the sun came to the end of its arc, Jardir left Qasha sleeping on the bed of pillows and donned his blacks and white turban. He chose his favorite spear and shield, and went down to meet his *kai'Sharum* at dinner.

They feasted on spiced meat and cool water, served by Jardir's mother, *dal'ting* wives, and sisters. His *dama'ting* wives were no doubt lurking in the shadows, listening in, but they would never deign to serve at his table, *jiwah* or no. Ashan, his spiritual advisor, sat at the foot of the table, facing him. Shanjat, who had succeeded Jardir as *kai'Sharum* of his personal unit, sat at Jardir's right hand, and Hasik, his personal bodyguard, at his left.

"What were our losses last night?" Jardir asked as they had their tea.

"We lost four last night, First Warrior," Ashan said.

Jardir looked at him in surprise. "The Kaji lost four?"

Ashan smiled. "No, my friend. *Krasia* lost four. Two Baiters and two Watchers. All *dal'Sharum* past their primes and gone to glory."

Jardir returned the smile. Since he'd become Sharum Ka, nightly losses had dwindled as demon kills had increased.

"And *alagai*?" he asked. "How many saw the sun?"

"More than five hundred," Ashan said.

Jardir laughed. He doubted the true number was half that, with every tribe habitually exaggerating their kills, but it was still a fine night's work, far more that the previous Sharum Ka had achieved.

"The tribes in the eighth layer still saw no glory," Ashan said. "We were considering leaving the Maze gates open longer tonight to ensure there are enough *alagai* for all to kill."

Jardir nodded. "An extra ten minutes. If that is not enough, add another ten tomorrow. I will be on the walls tonight, inspecting the new scorpions and rock slingers."

Ashan bowed. "As the Sharum Ka commands."

After the meal, they left for Sharik Hora, where the *Damaji* praised their successes and blessed the coming night's battle. As the warriors left for the Maze, Jardir held his two lieutenants back.

"You will wear the white turban tonight, Hasik," Jardir said.

A wild light came to Hasik's eyes. "As the Sharum Ka commands." He bowed.

"You cannot be serious!" Ashan said. "To have a *dal'Sharum* impersonate the Sharum Ka is a violation of our sacred oaths!"

"Nonsense," Jardir said. "There are tales in the Evejah of Kaji playing such games frequently, when he did not wish his movements known."

"Forgive me, First Warrior," Ashan said, "but you are not the Deliverer."

Jardir smiled. "Perhaps. But what is the Evejah, if not something the Shar'Dama Ka left for us to learn from?"

Ashan frowned. "What if Hasik is discovered?"

"He won't be," Jardir said. "With his night veil, the sling teams will not recognize him, for they have seldom seen me save at a distance. Hasik, however, will be seen on the walltops by all, and there will be no question among the *Sharum* that I was in the Maze tonight."

"If you are wrong, he will be put to death," Ashan warned.

Jardir shrugged. "Hasik has killed hundreds of *alagai*. If that is his fate, he will wake in paradise."

"I am not afraid, Sharum Ka," Hasik said.

Ashan snorted. "Fools seldom are," he muttered. "But where will you go," he asked Jardir, "while others think you on the wall?"

"Ah," Jardir said, taking Hasik's black turban and tying the veil, "that is for me to know."

🖏

The streets of Fort Krasia were quiet at night, the true men all gone to battle, and the common *khaffit*, women, and children locked in the Undercity. Like all the city's palaces, the palace of the Sharum Ka had its own walls and wards, its lower levels connected to the Undercity in several places. The palace was as safe from *alagai* as any in the world, and that was if a demon could even get past Krasia's outer walls, which, as far as Jardir knew, had never happened.

Jardir kept to the shadows, his *dal'Sharum* blacks making him invisible in the darkness. Even if someone had been there to see, none would have marked his passing.

The gates of his palace were closed, but his years as a *nie'Sharum* had taught him to scale walls with ease. In a twinkling he was dropping into the darkness on the lee side.

Nothing seemed amiss as he crossed the compound to the palace. The windows were dark, and the keep was silent. Still, Qasha's words nagged at him. *All is not always still in the palace of the Sharum Ka at night.*

Jardir moved about dark and silent in the halls of his own home like a thief, using all the skills he had learned stalking *alagai* in the Maze. He did not leave so much as a curtain stirring in his wake as, one by one, he checked the audience halls and receiving rooms—anywhere that might be fitting for a gathering of those bold enough to defy curfew—but he found no one.

As it should be, he mused. *They are all in lower levels, barred from within, as is the law. You were a fool to come. Ashan was right. You play games with your duty in order to satisfy your own curiosity. Men are dying in the night while you skulk about your own home.*

He was about to leave, heading back to the Maze, when he caught a sound coming from his bedchambers. The noise grew louder as he padded closer. He peeked around a curtain and saw two *kai'Sharum* bearing the white sash of the Andrah's personal guard standing before the door to his bedroom. The sounds became clearer, and he realized what they were.

Inevera's cries.

Rage flared in him, hotter than he had ever imagined possible. Before he even realized he was moving, his fist was shattering the spine of one of the *kai'Sharum*. The man grunted, but it was quickly silenced as he struck the floor and Jardir crushed his throat with a stomp of his heel.

The other warrior spun deftly, moving with the grace one would expect from a *Sharum* trained in Sharik Hora, but Jardir's rage knew no bounds. The warrior tried to grapple, but Jardir ducked his outstretched arms and came up behind him, gripping the man's chin with one hand and the back of his head with another. A sharp twist, and the man was falling to the carpet, dead.

Jardir spun, kicking hard against the door. It was barred from within, but he only gritted his teeth and kicked again, this time knocking out the braces and sending the door slamming inward.

He pulled up short at the scene before him, feeling as if he had taken a spear in the chest. He had expected to find the Andrah holding Inevera down, forcing himself upon her, but just the opposite, his wife, nude, rode the fat man as wantonly as Qasha had ridden him that morning. The Andrah looked up at him fearfully, but he was pinned by Inevera's soft weight. She turned to him, and in his rage he wasn't sure if he imagined it, or if a bit of a smirk touched the corners of her mouth as she took the last bit of honor from him.

If his anger was a furnace before, it was the fifth layer of Nie's abyss now. He strode to the rack on the wall, selecting a short, stabbing spear. When he turned back, the Andrah had struggled out from under Inevera. He stood naked in Jardir's bedchamber, his flaccid member all but hidden in the shadows of his massive belly. The sight filled Jardir with disgust.

"Stop! I command you!" the Andrah cried as Jardir charged, but Jardir ignored him, striking the man across the jaw with the butt of the spear.

"Not even you can deny a husband his rights in this!" Jardir cried as the Andrah hit the floor. "I do Krasia a favor this night!" He raised the spear to impale the man.

Inevera grabbed his arm. "Fool!" she cried. "You will ruin everything!"

Jardir pivoted to backhand Inevera across the face, knocking her away. "Have no fear, faithless *jiwah*," he said, turning back to the Andrah. "My spear will find you soon enough."

He raised the spear again and the Andrah screamed, but then everything turned orange and red, and Jardir was struck by an incredible force, knocking him away from his victim. The plates of fired clay sewn within his heavy warrior's garb took the brunt of the blast, but when he recovered from striking the wall, he found his robes in flames. With a shout, he tore them off.

He looked to Inevera, holding the fire demon skull she had brought to their first meeting in Sharik Hora. She stood naked before two men with no shame, knowing that even now, her beauty had no equal. Hatred and arousal swirled in him, warring for dominance.

"Stop this foolishness!" she snapped.

"I take no more orders from you," Jardir said. "Burn down this whole palace if you wish, I will still kill that fat pig and take you on his corpse!" The Andrah whimpered, but Jardir snarled, silencing him.

Inevera did not even flinch, producing a small object in her other hand. It looked like a lump of coal until the ward carved upon it flared, and Jardir realized that it, too, was *alagai hora*. The blackened piece of bone crackled, and silver magic leapt from it, like a bolt of lightning, to strike Jardir.

Jardir was lifted from his feet and thrown back into the wall, his body racked with agony beyond anything he could imagine. He tried to open himself to it, but the pain ended as quickly as it had begun, leaving only a stark terror in its wake. He turned back to Inevera, but she raised the stone again, and the lightning struck a second time, and again after that when he still managed to put his feet under him. He struggled to rise a third time, but his limbs did not respond to his commands, muscles spasming uncontrollably.

"Finally, we understand each other," Inevera said. "I am Everam's will, and you had best put aside thoughts of resisting me. If bedding a fat pig gets you the white turban, then you should be thanking me for my sacrifice, not trying to ruin things."

"Fat pig?!" the Andrah demanded, rising to his feet at last. "I am—!"

"—alive because I wish it," Inevera said, raising the demon skull. Flames licked from its jaws, and the Andrah blanched.

"I needed your support of Jardir until he won over the *Sharum* and *Damaji* of the other tribes," she said, "but now that Qasha is with child, the *Sharum* will see that he is brother to all of them in day as well as night. You can never depose him now."

"I am the Andrah!" the man shouted. "I can raze this palace with a wave of my hand!"

Inevera laughed. "Then you will have civil war. And even if you did kill Ahmann, what of his *dama'ting* wives? Will you rape and slaughter them, as is the custom? The Evejah is clear about the fate of any who would dare harm a *dama'ting*."

The Andrah scowled, having no reply.

"The gates of Heaven are closed," she said, slinging silk across her shoulders to cover her nakedness. "Perhaps they will open again the next time I need a proclamation from you, or perhaps I will send Ahmann to write it in your blood. But until then, take your withered old spear back to your palace."

Not even bothering to dress, the Andrah gathered his clothes in his arms and scurried from the room.

Inevera approached Jardir, kneeling beside him. The lump of demon bone she had used to throw lightning disintegrated, and she brushed the ash from her hand bemusedly. "You are strong," she said. "Few men could rise after one strike, much less three. I'll have to use a larger bone when I carve a new one tonight."

She reached out to him, gentling his hair and caressing his face. "Ah, my love," she said sadly. "How I wish you had not seen this."

Jardir fought with his tongue, which felt as if it had swollen to fill his entire mouth. "Why?" he finally managed to croak.

Inevera sighed. "The Andrah was going to have you executed for killing his friend with such dishonor. I did what was needed to save your life and gain you power. But fear not. The day is fast approaching when you will take his throne, and on that day, you may cut the manhood from him yourself."

"Did . . ." Jardir began, unable to manage more. He swallowed hard, trying to lubricate his tongue, but even that seemed beyond him.

Inevera rose and brought him water, running it over his lips and massaging his throat to help him swallow. She used her silk wrap to dry his mouth, revealing one of her breasts. He wondered how, even now, he could desire her, but it was undeniable.

"Did you know it would come to this," he asked, "when you had me kill the Sharum Ka?" Again he called upon his limbs to move, and again they failed to respond.

Inevera sighed again. "You have lived but twenty winters, my love, and even you can recall a time when Krasia had ten thousand *dal'Sharum*. The eldest *Damaji* can recall when it was ten times that, and the ancient scrolls show our numbers in the millions before the Return. Our people are dying, Ahmann, because they lack a leader. They need more than a strong Sharum Ka, more than a powerful Andrah. They need Shar'Dama Ka, before Nie scatters the last of us to the sands."

Inevera paused, breaking eye contact, and it seemed she considered her next words carefully. "I didn't ask the dice if I would ever see you again, that first night," she admitted. "I asked if there was a man in all Krasia who could pull us from attrition and lead us back to glory, and they pointed to a boy I would find weeping in the Maze, years hence."

"I am the Deliverer?" Jardir asked, his voice hoarse and disbelieving.

Inevera shrugged. "The dice never lie, but neither do they give absolutes. There are futures where men believe you so, and unite behind you, and others where they unite behind another, or not at all."

"Then what good are they?" Jardir asked. "If that is *inevera*, fate will decide it."

"There is no fate as you understand it," Inevera said, "save that Sharak Ka, the final battle, is coming, and soon. We dare not let the future go unguided. I have watched you since you first took the bido, my sweet. You are Krasia's best hope of salvation, and I will seize for you every advantage, even at the cost of my body's honor, or your own."

Jardir looked at her with wide eyes. Words failed him as surely as his limbs continued to do. Inevera bent and kissed his forehead, her lips soft and cool. She rose to her feet, looking down sadly as he continued to twitch helplessly on the floor.

"Everything I do, I do for you, and for Sharak Ka," she said, and left the room.

CHAPTER 6

FALSE PROPHET

:: 333 AR WINTER ::

"THE *CHIN* ARE PROVING ideal slaves," Jayan said. "Even the least of them put such high value on their own lives that they will never muster the courage to resist. Truly it is a great conquest, Father. Your glory knows no bounds."

Jardir shook his head. "To shift a few grains of sand is no more a sign of great strength than to see the sun a sign of great sight. There is no glory in dominating the weak."

"Still, it is a great boon to us," Jayan pressed. "Our victory is complete, and at no cost to ourselves."

Across the room, Abban snorted at his tiny writing desk.

"You have something to add, *khaffit?*" Jayan demanded.

"Nothing, my prince," Abban said quickly, looking up from his ledgers. He stood and braced himself on his camel-headed crutch, bowing deeply. "It was but a cough."

"No, please," Jayan said. "Tell us what amused you so."

Abban's eyes flicked to Jardir, who nodded.

"There may have been no loss of *dal'Sharum*, my prince, but there has definitely been cost," Abban said. "Food, clothing, shelter, transportation. Keeping such a vast army as ours on the move is costly beyond measure. Your father may control the riches of all twelve tribes, and Everam's Bounty besides, but even his wealth has an end."

Asome nodded. "The Evejah tells us: *When a man's purse is empty, his rivals grow bolder.*"

Jayan laughed. "Who would dare oppose Father? Besides, why should the Shar'Dama Ka pay for anything? We have conquered this land. We can take whatever we wish."

Abban nodded. "That is so, but a robbed merchant has no capital to replenish his stock. You can take all the chandler's candles, but if you do not pay at least their cost, you will find yourself sitting in the dark when the last one burns out."

Jayan snorted. "Candles are for weak *khaffit* scroll worshippers. They make no difference to warriors in the night."

"Wood and steel for spears, then," Abban said patiently, as if speaking to a child. "Cloth for uniforms and fired clay for armor. Leather and oil for saddle harness. These things do not appear from thin air, and if we steal every seed and goat now, there will be nothing to fill our bellies a year hence."

"I do not care for your tone, pig-eater," Jayan growled.

"Be silent and attend his words," Jardir snapped. "The *khaffit* is offering you wisdom, my son, and you would be wise to take it."

Jayan looked at his father in shock, but quickly bowed. "Of course, Father." His eyes shot daggers at Abban.

Jardir looked to Asome, who had stood quietly through all this. "And you, my son? What say you to the *khaffit's* words?"

"The unworthy one makes a fair point," Asome conceded. "There are still those among the *Damaji* who resent your rise, and they would use any privation of their tribesmen as excuse to sow discord."

Jardir nodded. "And what would you do to attend this problem?"

Asome shrugged. "Kill and replace the disloyal *Damaji* before they grow bold."

"That would sow discord of its own," Jardir noted. He looked to Abban.

"It's too costly to keep our army together in the city," Abban said. "And so they must be dispersed into the hamlets." Jardir's sons looked at the fat merchant incredulously.

"Disband our army? What foolishness is this?" Jayan demanded. "Father, this *khaffit* is a coward and a fool! I beg you, let me kill him!"

"Idiot boy!" Jardir snapped. "Do you think the *khaffit* speaks words unknown to me?"

Jayan looked at him in shock.

"One day, my sons," Jardir said, looking from Jayan to Asome and back, "I will die. If you have any wish to survive the days that follow, you must listen for wisdom from every side."

Jayan turned to Abban and bowed. It was a minuscule thing, barely a nod, and his eyes shot death at the fat merchant for shaming him. "Please, *khaffit*, do share your wisdom."

Abban bowed in return, though even with his crutch he could have gone lower. "With the lost granaries, the central city cannot support all of Krasia's peoples without privation, my prince. But there are hundreds of small villages, arranged around this city like the spokes of a wheel. We will have the greenland duke provide lists, and divide them among the tribes."

"That is a vast territory to hold," Asome noted.

Abban shrugged. "Hold from whom? No army threatens us, and as my prince says, the *chin* are ideal slaves. Better to let the Shar'Dama Ka's armies disperse until needed, saving him the need to provide for them. Instead, they each take a territory to forage on and tax, hunting its *alagai* at night. They can form greenland *sharaji* to train the boys in their territories, and leave the women and elderly to plant another crop in the spring. A year from now, the tribes will be richer than they have ever been, with thousands of greenland *nie'Sharum*. Give the tribes wealth instead of privations, and by the time the novices come of age, the Shar'Dama Ka will control the largest army the world has ever known, fanatically loyal, and, best of all, paying for itself."

Jardir looked at his sons. "Do you see now the use of *khaffit*?"

"Yes, Father," the boys answered, dipping identical bows.

Damaji Ashan entered the throne room, sweeping smoothly onto his hands and knees, touching his forehead to the floor. His white robes were flecked with blood, and there was a grim set to his eyes beneath his black turban.

"Rise, my friend," Jardir said. Ashan had always been his most loyal counselor, even before his rise to power. Now he spoke for the whole of the Kaji, the most powerful tribe in Krasia, and he had named as his successor his eldest son, Asukaji, Jardir's nephew by his sister Imisandre. After Jardir himself, there was no man in all the world as powerful.

"Shar'Dama Ka, there is news you must hear," Ashan said.

Jardir nodded. "Your counsel is always welcome, my friend. Speak."

Ashan shook his head. "Best you hear the words directly from their source, Deliverer."

Jardir raised an eyebrow at this, but he nodded, following Ashan out of the manse and onto the frozen city streets. Not far from Jardir's palace lay one of the *chin* houses of worship. It was mean and unadorned compared with the great Sharik Hora, but it was an impressive structure by Northland standards—three stories of thick stone, and powerfully warded.

Ashan led the way inside, and Jardir saw that the *dama* had done more than simply claim the Holy House. Already they were decorating it with the bleached and lacquered bones of the *dal'Sharum* who had died in battle since leaving the Desert Spear. With the spirits of the honored dead to guard it, no building in the North would be more secure.

Down they went, stone steps leading into a maze of cold catacombs below the structure.

"The *chin* interred their honored dead here," Ashan explained as Jardir studied the empty nooks in the walls. "We have since cleaned it of such unworthy filth and turned these tunnels to better purpose."

As if on cue, a man screamed, his cries of agony echoing through the sunken halls. Ashan paid the sound no mind, leading Jardir through the tunnels to a particular room. Within, several of the Northern clerics—Tenders, as they were called—hung by their wrists, suspended from a ceiling beam in the middle of the room. The tops of their robes were torn away, and their flesh was streaked with the deep cuts of the alagai tail—a whip that could break the will of even the strongest men.

Ashan waved away the *dal'Sharum* torturers, striding up to one of the prisoners.

"You," he said, pointing, "repeat what you told me to the Shar'Dama Ka, if you dare."

The Tender raised his head weakly. One of his eyes was puffed shut, and tears ran freely from the other, streaking the blood and filth on his face.

"Go t' th' Core," he slurred, and attempted to spit at Ashan. It was a weak effort, and the bloody spittle only ran down his lower lip.

In response, the torturer came forward, a pliers in his hands. He gripped the Tender's face firmly, forcing his mouth open and clamping the pliers on one of his front teeth. The man's screams filled the room.

"Enough," Jardir said after a moment. The torturer stopped immediately, bowing and receding to the wall. The Tender hung limply from the shackles at his wrists. Jardir went up to him, looking at him sadly. "I am the Shar'Dama Ka, sent by Everam, who is infinitely merciful. Speak and speak truly, and I will put an end to your suffering."

The Tender looked up at him, and seemed to regain something of himself. "I know you," he croaked. "You claim to be the Deliverer, but you are not him."

"And how do you know that?" Jardir asked.

"Because the Deliverer has already come," the Tender said. "The Warded Man walks in darkness, and the corelings flee from his sight. He saved Deliverer's Hollow from the brink of destruction, and he will deal with you in your turn."

Jardir looked to Ashan in surprise.

"This is not just one man's word, Shar'Dama Ka," the *Damaji* said. "Other *chin* speak of this warded infidel. You will need to destroy this false prophet, and quickly, if you are to secure your rightful place."

Jardir shook his head. "You sound like my wife, old friend."

CHAPTER 7

GREENLANDER

:: 326 AR ::

"ONE DAY, *I* WILL be Sharum Ka!" Jayan shouted, thrusting his spear at the rag-stuffed dummy Jardir had made for him. It swung lazily from a rope tied to a ceiling beam.

Jardir laughed, delighting in his son's energy. Jayan was twelve now, already in his bido, and never hungry in the food line. Jardir had begun teaching his sons the *sharukin* the day they took their first steps.

"*I* want to be Sharum Ka," Asome, eleven, lamented. "I don't want to be a stupid *dama*." He plucked at the white cloth he wore over one shoulder.

"Ah, but you will be the Sharum Ka's connection to Everam," Jardir said. "And perhaps one day, *Damaji* to all the Kaji. Even Andrah." He smiled, but inwardly, he agreed with the boy. He wanted warriors for sons, not clerics. Sharak Ka was coming.

Inevera had originally wanted Jayan to wear the white, but Jardir had categorically refused. It was one of his few victories over her, but he wondered just how much of a victory it was. It was as likely she had wanted Asome to wear the white all along.

The other boys clustered about, watching their older brothers with awe. Most of Jardir's other sons were too young for *Hannu Pash,* and had to wait to find their path. The second sons would be *dama,* the others, *Sharum.* It was the first night of Waning, when the forces of Nie were said to be their strongest and Alagai Ka stalked the night. Nothing gave a warrior strength in the night like seeing his sons.

And daughters, he thought, turning to Inevera. "It would please me if my daughters could return home for Waning each month, as well."

Inevera shook her head. "Their training must not be disturbed, husband. The *Hannu Pash* of the *nie'dama'ting* is . . . rigorous." Indeed, the girls were taken much younger than his sons. He had not seen his eldest daughters in years.

"Surely they cannot all become *dama'ting,*" Jardir said. "I must have daughters to marry to my loyal men."

"And so you shall," Inevera replied. "Daughters no man dare harm, who are loyal to you over even their husbands."

"And to Everam, over even their father," Jardir muttered.

"Of course," Inevera said, and he could sense his wife's smile behind her veil. He was about to retort when Ashan came into the room. His son Asukaji, the same age as Asome, trailed behind him in his *nie'dama* bido. Ashan bowed to Jardir.

"Sharum Ka, there is a matter the *kai'Sharum* wish you to settle."

"I am with my sons, Ashan," Jardir said. "Can it not wait?"

"Apologies, First Warrior, but I do not think it can."

"Very well," Jardir sighed. "What is it?"

Ashan bowed again. "I think it best the Sharum Ka see the problem for himself," he said.

Jardir raised an eyebrow. Ashan had never been reluctant to give his assessment of anything before, even when he knew Jardir would disagree.

"Jayan!" he called. "Fetch my spear and shield! Asome! My robes!"

The boys scurried to comply as Jardir stood. To his surprise, Inevera rose as well. "I will walk with my husband."

Ashan bowed. "Of course, *dama'ting.*"

Jardir looked at her sharply. What did she know? What had the cursed bones told her about this night?

Leaving the children behind, the three of them were soon on their way, descending the great stone stairs of the palace of the Sharum Ka, which faced the *Sharum* training grounds. At the far end was Sharik Hora, and on the long sides between were the pavilions of the tribes.

Near the base of his steps, well inside the palace walls, a group of *Sharum* and *dama* surrounded a pair of *khaffit*. Jardir grew angry at the sight. It was an insult to have the feet of *khaffit* sully the grounds of the Sharum Ka's keep. He opened his mouth to say just that when one of the *khaffit* caught his eye.

Abban.

Jardir had not thought of his old friend in years, as if the boy had indeed died the night he broke his oaths. More than fifteen years had passed since then, and if Jardir had changed from the small, skinny boy in a bido he had been, the change in Abban was even more pronounced.

The former *nie'Sharum* had grown enormously fat, almost as grotesque as the Andrah. He still wore the tan vest and cap of *khaffit*, but under the vest were a bright shirt and pantaloons of multicolored silk, and he had wrapped the tan conical cap in a turban of red silk with a gem set at the center. His belt and slippers were of snakeskin. He leaned on an ivory crutch, carved in the likeness of a camel, with his armpit resting between its humps.

"What makes you think you are worthy to stand here among men?" Jardir demanded.

"Apologies, great one," Abban said, dropping to his hands and knees in the dirt and pressing his forehead down. Shanjat, now a *kai'Sharum*, laughed and kicked his backside.

"Look at you," Jardir snarled. "You dress like a woman and flaunt your tainted wealth as if it is not an insult to everything we believe. I should have let you fall."

"Please, great master," Abban said. "I mean no insult. I am only here to translate."

"Translate?" Jardir glanced up at the other *khaffit* who had come with Abban.

But the other man was not *khaffit* at all. It was instantly apparent from his light skin and hair, his clothes, and even more so from the well-worn spear the man carried. He was a *chin*. An outsider from the green lands to the north.

"A *chin*?" Jardir asked, turning to his *dama*. "You called me here to speak to a *chin*?"

"Listen to his words," Ashan urged. "You will see."

Jardir looked at the greenlander, having never seen a *chin* up close before. He knew Northern Messengers sometimes came to the Great Bazaar, but that was not a place for men, and his memories of it from childhood were vague things, tainted by hunger and shame.

This *chin* was different than Jardir had imagined. He was young—no older than Jardir had been when he first donned his blacks—and not a particularly large man, but he had a hard air about him. He stood and moved like a warrior, meeting Jardir's eyes boldly, as a man should.

Jardir knew that the Northern men had given up *alagai'sharak*, cowering behind their wards like women, but the sands of Krasia went on for hundreds of miles with no succor. A man who passed through that must have stared *alagai* in the face night after night. He might not be *Sharum*, but he was no coward.

Jardir looked down at Abban's sniveling form and bit back his disgust. "Speak, and be quick about it. Your presence offends me."

Abban nodded and turned to the Northerner, speaking a few words in a harsh, guttural tongue. The Northerner replied sternly, stamping his spear for emphasis.

"This is Arlen asu Jeph am'Bales am'Brook," Abban said, turning back to Jardir but keeping his eyes on the ground. "Late out of Fort Rizon to the north, he brings you greetings, and begs to fight alongside the men of Krasia tonight in *alagai'sharak*."

Jardir was stunned. A Northerner who wished to fight? It was unheard of.

"He is a *chin*, First Warrior," Hasik growled. "Come from a race of cowards. He is not worthy to fight!"

"If he was a coward, he would not be here," Ashan advised. "Many Messengers have come to Krasia, but only this one has come to your palace. It would be an insult to Everam not to let the man fight, if he wishes it."

"I'll not put my back to a greenlander in battle," Hasik said, spitting at the Messenger's feet. Many of the *Sharum* nodded and grunted their agreement despite the *dama's* words. It seemed there was a limit to the clerics' powers, after all.

Jardir considered carefully. He saw now why Ashan had wanted to defer the decision to him. Either choice could have grave repercussions.

He looked at the greenlander again, curious to see his mettle in battle. Inevera had foretold he might conquer the green lands one day, and the Evejah taught men to know their enemy before battle was joined.

"Husband," Inevera said quietly, touching his arm. "If the *chin* wishes to stand in the Maze like a *Sharum*, then he must have a foretelling."

No wonder she had come. She knew there was something special about this man, and needed his blood for a true divination. Jardir narrowed his eyes, wondering what she was not telling, but she had offered him an escape from a difficult situation and he would be a fool not to take it. He turned back to Abban, still hunched in the dirt.

"Tell the *chin* that the *dama'ting* will cast the bones for him. If they are favorable, he may fight."

Abban nodded, turning back to the greenlander and speaking his harsh Northern tongue. A flash of irritation crossed the *chin's* face—a feeling Jardir knew well, having been a slave to the bones for more than half his life. They exchanged words for some time before the *chin* gritted his teeth and nodded in acceptance.

"I will take him back to the palace for the foretelling," Inevera said.

Jardir nodded. "I will accompany you through the ritual, for your own protection."

"That will not be necessary," Inevera said. "No man would dare harm a *dama'ting*."

"No Krasian man," Jardir corrected. "There is no telling what these Northern barbarians are capable of." He smirked. "I will not risk having your impeccable virtue sullied by leaving you alone with one."

Jardir knew she was snarling under her veil, but he did not care. Whatever went on between her and the greenlander, he was determined to see it. He signaled Hasik and Ashan to follow them back so she could not expel him from her presence at the palace without witnesses. Abban was dragged along with them, though his presence sullied the palace floors. They would need to be washed with blood to remove the taint.

Soon Jardir, Inevera, and the *chin* were alone in a darkened room. Jardir looked to the greenlander. "Hold out your arm, Arlen, son of Jeph."

The *chin* only looked at him curiously.

Jardir held out his own arm, miming a shallow cut, and holding it over the *alagai hora*.

The *chin* frowned, but he did not hesitate to roll up his sleeve and step forward, holding out his arm.

Braver than I was the first time, Jardir thought.

Inevera made the cut, and soon the dice were glowing fiercely in her hands. The *chin's* eyes widened at this, and he watched intently. She threw, and Jardir quickly scanned the results. He did not have a *dama'ting's* training, but his lessons in Sharik Hora had taught him many of the symbols on the dice. Each demon bone had only one ward, a ward of foretelling. The other symbols were simply words. The words and their pattern told a tale of what would be . . . or at least what might.

Jardir caught the symbols for "*Sharum,*" "*dama,*" and "one" among the clutter before Inevera snatched them back up. Shar'Dama Ka. What could that mean? Surely a *chin* could not be the Deliverer. Was he tied to Jardir in some way?

To Jardir's surprise, Inevera shook the dice and threw them again, as he had not seen her or any *dama'ting* do since that first night in the Maze. There was nothing but *dama'ting* calm about her, but the very fact of a second throw was telling.

As was the third.

Whatever she sees, Jardir thought, *she wants to be sure of it.*

He looked to the greenlander, but though he watched the proceedings closely, it was clear he saw this only as some primitive ritual required for access to the Maze.

Ah, son of Jeph, if only it were that simple.

"He can fight," Inevera said, removing a clay jar from her robes and smearing the *chin's* wound with a foul paste before wrapping it in clean cloth.

Jardir nodded, not having expected more than a yes or no. He escorted the *chin* out of the room.

"*Khaffit,*" he called to Abban. "Tell the son of Jeph he may start on the wall. When he nets an *alagai,* he may set foot in the Maze."

"Surely not!" Hasik said.

"Everam has spoken, Hasik," Jardir said sharply, and the warrior calmed.

Abban quickly translated, and the *chin* snorted, as if netting a wind demon were no great feat. Jardir smiled. He could come to like this man.

"Return to whatever hole you crawled out of," he told Abban. "The son of Jeph may be worthy to stand atop the wall, but you have lost that right. He will have to speak the language of the spear."

Abban bowed and turned to the greenlander, explaining. The *chin* looked up at Jardir and nodded his understanding. His face was grim, but Jardir recognized the eagerness in his eyes. He had the look of a *dal'Sharum* at dusk.

Jardir moved to head down to the training ground with the others, but Inevera held his arm. Ashan and Hasik turned, hesitating.

"Go on and see if you might teach the *chin* some of our hand signals," Jardir said. "I will join you shortly."

"The *chin* will be instrumental in your rise to Shar'Dama Ka," Inevera said bluntly as soon as they were alone. "Embrace him as a brother, but keep him within reach of your spear. One day you must kill him, if you are to be hailed as Deliverer."

Jardir stared hard at his inscrutable wife's eyes. *What aren't you telling me?* he wondered.

The greenlander showed no hint of fear or trepidation as the sun set that night. He stood tall atop the walls, looking out at the sands eagerly, waiting for the first signs of the enemy rising.

Truly, he was nothing like Jardir had imagined from his lessons about the weak half-men of the North. How long since a Krasian had gone to the green lands and seen its people for himself? A hundred years? Two? Had anyone left the Desert Spear since the Return?

Two warriors snickered at his back. They were Mehnding tribe, the most powerful after the Majah. The Mehnding were devoted wholly to the art of ranged weapons. They built the rock slingers and scorpions, quarried stones for hurling, and made the giant scorpion stingers—great spears that could punch through a sand demon's armor at a thousand feet. Though they were less proficient with the spear than other tribes, their honor knew no bounds, for the Mehnding killed more *alagai* than the Kaji and the Majah combined.

"I wonder how long he will last before an *alagai* kills him," one of the Mehnding said.

"More likely he will soil himself and run in fear the moment they rise," the other laughed.

The greenlander glanced at them. His expression made it clear he knew he was being mocked, but he paid the warriors no mind, returning his focus on the shifting sands.

He embraces pain when his goal is in sight, Jardir thought, remembering the mockery he had endured on his first night in the Maze.

Jardir moved to the two warriors. "The sun sets, and you have nothing better to do than mock your spear-brother?" he demanded loudly. Everyone on the wall turned to look.

"But Sharum Ka," one of the men protested, "he is only a savage."

"A savage who looks to the enemy while you snicker at his back like a *khaffit*!" Jardir growled. "Mock him again, and you will have weeks in the *dama'ting* pavilion to learn to keep a civil tongue." He spoke the words calmly, but the *dal'Sharum* recoiled as if struck.

A shout from the greenlander caught Jardir's attention. The man stomped his spear on the wall, bellowing something in his guttural tongue. He pointed to the sands, and Jardir suddenly understood.

The *alagai* were rising.

"To your places!" he ordered, and the Mehnding turned back to their scorpions.

Oil fires were lit and reflected with mirrors onto the battlefield, giving the Mehnding light for their deadly art.

The greenlander watched the scorpion teams carefully. One man wound the springs while another set the stinger in place. A third aimed and fired. The Mehnding could complete the whole process in seconds.

When the first stinger speared a sand demon, the greenlander gave a whoop, punching his fist into the air much as Jardir had done the first time he witnessed it as a *nie'Sharum*.

They have no scorpions in the North, he surmised, filing the information away.

For a time, the stingers hummed and the sling teams hauled great stones into place, cutting the ropes to free the counterweights and hurl the missiles into the growing ranks of *alagai,* killing them one by one or in groups.

But as always, it was like taking grains off a dune. There were dozens of flame and wind demons, but the sand demons were an endless storm that could wear down a mountain.

The Mehnding focused in a wide arc around the great gate to the Maze, preparing for the invitation. When the *alagai* were positioned correctly, Jardir signaled a *nie'Sharum,* who blew a long, clear note on the Horn of Sharak. Almost instantly the gates opened. The oldest warriors in the tribes stood within, beating their shields and jeering at the demons, daring them to give chase.

Their glory was endless. Even the greenlander breathed a word that rang of awe.

The *alagai* shrieked and charged into the Maze. The Baiters whooped and ran, leading the demons deeper through twists and turns to where their respective tribesmen hid in wait.

After several minutes, Jardir signaled for the gates to be closed again. The scorpions cleared the way, and the gates closed with a thunderous boom.

"Fetch the nets," Jardir told the *nie'Sharum.* "We shall head deeper into the Maze and put the greenlander to his test."

But the boy did not move. Jardir glanced at him in irritation and saw open terror on his face. He turned along the boy's line of sight, and saw many of his warriors standing similarly dumbfounded.

"What are you . . ." he began to shout, but then, in the light of the oil fires, he saw an *alagai* bounding over the dunes toward the city.

But this was no ordinary demon. Even at a distance, Jardir could tell it was enormous. Sand demons were bigger than their flame and wind cousins, not counting wingspan, but even the sand demons were no larger than a man, and they ran on all fours like dogs, standing perhaps three feet at the shoulder.

The demon that approached stood erect on hind legs jointed with sharp bone, and stood more than twice the height of a tall man. Even its spiked tail seemed longer than a man was tall. Its horns were like spears, its talons like butchering knives, and its black carapace was thick and hard. One of its arms ended at the elbow—a club that could crush a warrior's skull.

Jardir had never imagined a demon so big. His men stood frozen—in fear or surprise he could not tell. Only the greenlander seemed unsurprised, staring hard at the giant with undisguised hatred.

But why? It seemed too great a coincidence that such a creature should arrive on the same night a *chin* appeared on his palace steps, begging to fight. What was his connection to the demon?

Jardir cursed his inability to speak the greenlander's barbaric tongue.

"What are you waiting for?" he roared to the scorpion teams. "*Alagai* are *alagai*! Kill it!"

His words broke the spell, and the men leapt to obey. The greenlander clenched his fist as they took aim and let fly their stingers, massive spears with heavy heads of iron. They shot high in the sky to arc the missiles down with crushing impact.

The giant demon was struck full on by almost a dozen stingers, but all splintered against its armor, leaving the creature unfazed. It shrieked its fury and came on again.

Suddenly the city seemed vulnerable. Jardir had learned warding in Sharik Hora, and knew that each ward only found its full power against a single breed of demon. The wards carved into Krasia's walls were ancient and had never been breached, but had they ever been tested against one such as this?

He grabbed the greenlander by the shoulders, turning him about to face him. "What do you know?" he demanded. "What do we face, damn you?!"

The greenlander nodded, seeming to understand, and looked about. He moved to a rock slinger and touched the stone in the sling. Then he pointed to the demon. "*Alagai,*" he said.

Jardir nodded, moving to the Mehnding in command of the engine.

"Can you hit it?" Jardir asked.

The *dal'Sharum* snorted. "An *alagai* that big? I can take just its other arm, if you wish."

Jardir slapped his back. "Take its head, and we'll tar it as a trophy."

"Start boiling the tar," the warrior said, adjusting the tension and angle of the weapon.

The greenlander rushed over to Jardir, speaking rapidly in his ugly tongue. He waved his arms, seeming increasingly frantic that he could not make his meaning clear. Again and again he pointed to the sling, shouting what seemed the only Krasian word he knew, "*Alagai!*"

"He brays like a camel," Hasik said.

"Be silent," Jardir snapped. He narrowed his eyes, but then the slinger called, "Ready!"

"Fire!" Jardir said. The greenlander leapt for the warrior who went to cut the rope, but Hasik grabbed him, hurling him roughly away.

"I knew we could not trust a *chin*, First Warrior," he growled. "He protects the demon!"

Jardir wasn't so sure, staring hard at the man, who struggled wildly in Hasik's grip. He pointed again, this time down at the wall, shouting, *"Ala-gai!"*

Lessons long dismissed as legend returned to Jardir in a rush—tales of the great demons that had assaulted Krasia's walls in the time of the first De-liverer, and everything came into sharp focus. The greenlander hadn't been pointing to the sling; he was pointing to the stone.

Rock demon, Jardir realized in dawning horror.

"Rock demon!" he shouted, but it was too late. He heard the report as the sling arm released its cargo, and turned helplessly to watch. Behind him, the greenlander wailed.

The stone soared through the air, and it seemed as if man and *alagai* alike held their breath. The one-armed rock demon looked up at the stone—a boulder that had taken three warriors to lift into place.

And then, impossibly, the demon caught the stone in the crook of its good arm and hurled it back with terrible force.

The boulder struck the great gate, smashing a hole and sending cracks spiderwebbing from the point of impact. The rock demon charged, striking that same spot again and again. Magic sparked and flared, but the warding was too damaged to have any real effect. The gate shook with each blow, and one side tore from its hinges, smashing to the ground inside.

The rock demon leapt through, roaring as it ran into the Maze. Behind it, demons poured through the breach.

Jardir's face flared hot, then went suddenly cold. The great gates of Kra-sia had not been breached in living memory. The *dal'Sharum* trapped in the Maze would be hunted like animals, and it was his own fault for not listening to the greenlander.

I have brought my people to ruin, he thought, and for a moment, all he could do was watch dumbly as the *alagai* invaded the Maze.

Embrace the fear, you fool! he shouted to himself. *The night may yet be saved!*

"Scorpions!" he cried. "Shift positions and lay down cover fire while we close off the breach! Sling teams! I want stones falling to crush any *alagai* getting in and to block the way for the rest!"

"We can't fire so close," one slinger said. Others nodded, and Jardir could see the same terror on their faces that he had felt a moment before. They needed a more immediate terror to snap them from their stupor.

He punched the slinger in the face, laying him flat on the walltop. "I don't care if you have to drop the stones by hand! Do as I command!"

The man's night veil grew wet with blood and his response was unintelligible, but he punched a fist to his chest and staggered to his feet, moving to obey. The other Mehnding did the same, their fear lost in a flurry of activity.

He looked at the *nie'Sharum*. "Sound the breach." As the boy raised the horn to his lips, he felt a wave of failure and shame that such a command be given on his watch.

But the feeling was quickly shaken. There was too much to do. He turned to Hasik. "Gather as many men and Warders as you can and meet us at the gate. We go to seal the breach."

Hasik gave a whoop and charged off, seeming thrilled at the prospect of leaping into a sandstorm of *alagai*. Jardir ran the walltops toward the spot where his personal unit fought under Shanjat. He needed his own men behind him for this. The other Kaji might still resent Jardir for betraying their tribe, but the men who had fought with him nightly for years were still his utterly.

The greenlander kept pace with him, and Jardir wished he had the words to send him away, or the time to make him understand. Even if he wanted to help, an untrained warrior would only get in the way of Jardir's tight, cohesive unit.

There was a shriek in the sky, and the greenlander shouted, *"Alagai!"*

The man crashed into Jardir, bearing them both down to the wall. Jardir felt the wind as leathern wings passed just above them.

Jardir cursed as they rolled apart, casting about for a net, but of course there was none to be found. The greenlander was quicker to his feet, standing crouched with his spear at the ready as the wind demon banked and came back.

He is brave, if a fool, Jardir thought. *What does he hope to do without a net?*

But as the demon came in, the greenlander dropped suddenly to one knee, stabbing hard with his long spear. The barbed head broke through the thin membrane of the *alagai's* wing right at the shoulder joint, and with a twist he used the spear as a lever to turn the demon's own momentum against it and flip it over onto its back on the wall.

The demon was not seriously harmed, but the greenlander moved quickly, grabbing the straps of the shield that hung loosely on his arm and pressing its warded surface against the demon's chest.

Magic flared at the contact, jolting the creature so that it thrashed and shrieked madly. Jardir wasted no time in planting his spear deep in the stunned creature's eye. It kicked and screamed, and Jardir pulled his weapon free and drove it into its other eye, twisting until the creature lay still.

The greenlander looked up at him, his eyes alive with excitement, and said something in his Northern tongue.

Jardir laughed, clapping him on the shoulder. "You surprise me, Arlen, son of Jeph!"

Together, they ran the walltops to Jardir's men.

5

Everywhere, there were warriors fighting for their lives in the Maze, but Jardir could not pause to save them. If the breach was not sealed, the sun would rise to find every *Sharum* in the Maze torn to shreds.

"Sell your lives dearly!" he shouted as his men thundered past. "Everam is watching!"

A roar and accompanying screams echoed through the Maze, seeming to shake the very walls. Somewhere behind them, the giant rock demon was laying waste to his men.

Leap the hurdles before you, he told himself. *Nothing else matters if the breach cannot be sealed.*

They found the courtyard before the great gate in ruin. *Alagai* and *dal'Sharum* alike lay dead and dying, speared by scorpion bolts or torn from tooth and claw. The Mehnding had managed to pile some rubble before the broken door, but the nimble *alagai* scrambled over it effortlessly.

"Fall off!" Jardir cried, and the few ragged *dal'Sharum* still fighting in the courtyard broke off and quickly got out of the way.

Shields locked, Jardir's warriors ran at full speed for the breach, ten wide and ten deep. Beside him in the first rank, the greenlander ran, matching their pace as if he had been drilling with the *dal'Sharum* all his life. A *chin* he might be, but the man was no stranger to spear and shield.

The warriors on the edges picked up speed as they went, forming the ranks into a shallow V as they scooped up entering sand demons and drove them back toward the gate.

There was a sharp impact as they hit the incoming tide of *alagai*, but the wards on their shields flared, and the *alagai* were thrown back. The warriors roared at the resistance, those behind adding force to the press, keeping a bright flare of magic between them and the demons. Slowly, Jardir's hundred began to force their way to the gate.

"Back ranks!" Jardir shouted, and the ranks farthest back spun about with a snap, locking shields and advancing, opening up a wide area between the forward and backward ranks where the Pit Warders could work. The elite *dal'Sharum* dropped their spears and slung their shields over their backs, producing lacquered ceramic plates from their battle bags. Two Warders laid the plates out in order across the yard before the breach. The other two took up their spears and used them as straightsticks, lining up the plates one by one.

Jardir put his spear into a sand demon's eye—one of the only vulnerable spots on the *alagai*. Next to him, the greenlander found the other, driving his spearhead down the throat of a roaring demon. Swiping claws came at them through gaps in the shields between flares of magic, and they all had to twist this way and that to avoid being gored.

As they moved closer to the gate, Jardir's eyes widened at the host gathered outside. It seemed the dunes were covered with sand demons, all pressing to enter the stronghold of their enemies. Stingers and boulders fell upon the *alagai*, but they were like pebbles dropped in a pool of water, quickly swallowed.

Then the Warders gave the call, and Jardir and his men began to withdraw. "Another night," Jardir promised the demons that came up short at the flare of magic from the ceramic wards. "Krasia will fight again tomorrow."

He turned to find the courtyard otherwise clear of battle. The remaining demons had escaped into the Maze.

"Watcher!" Jardir called as he stepped away from his men, and in seconds Coliv dropped a ladder from the wall and ran down it to report.

"Tidings are grim, First Warrior," the Watcher said. "The Majah have gathered in the sixth to hold off the majority of sand demons, but there are scattered tribes fighting throughout the Maze, and few battles go well. The giant roams even deeper, cutting apart whole units as it claws its way toward the main gate. It was just spotted in the eighth."

"Surely it cannot navigate all the turns of the Maze," Jardir said.

"It seems to be following a trail of sorts, First Warrior," Coliv said. "It pauses to sniff the air, and has yet to miss a turn. A handful of sand and flame demons dance at its feet, but it pays them no mind."

Jardir lifted his veil to spit the dust from his mouth. "Get back on the wall and set Watchers to plot me a path to gather the scattered units as we drive toward the Majah."

Coliv punched a fist to his chest and ran to his ladder, scrambling back up the wall. Jardir turned to gather his men and noticed the greenlander attempting to communicate with one of the Pit Warders, waving his hands wildly while the warrior looked at him in confusion.

"Nie is strong this Waning," Jardir shouted, drawing everyone's attention, "but Everam is stronger! We must trust in Him to see us through to the sun, or all of Ala be consumed with Nie's black! Show the *alagai* what it means to face warriors of the Desert Spear, and know that Heaven awaits you!"

He punched his spear into the air, and the *Sharum* did the same, giving a great shout as Jardir led them off into the Maze.

Throughout the night, Jardir's men charged into demon hordes, driving them into warded pits and linking with the survivors of scattered units. He had more than a thousand warriors at his back when they joined the Majah, holding the narrow corridor that gave entrance to the sixth level.

Jardir's men drove hard into the *alagai* ranks from behind, using their warded shields to force a wedge and push through. The Majah made an opening in their shield wall, and Jardir's men flowed through as smoothly as if they were drilling in Sharaj.

"Report," Jardir told one of the Majah *kai'Sharum*.

"We're holding, First Warrior," the captain said, "but we have no way to force the *alagai* into pits."

"Then don't," Jardir said. "Have the Warders seal off this level. Leave a hundred of your best men to keep watch, and then head to the east seventh to assist the Bajin."

"Where will you go?" the *kai'Sharum* asked.

"To find the giant and send him back to Nie's abyss," Jardir said. He took as many men as the Majah could spare and headed for the city gates, praying he was not too late.

The one-armed rock demon stood before the main gate to the city, pounding against the wards. Great flares of magic lit the night, and the thundering could be heard throughout the city, but the ancient wards held strong against the assault. The demon howled in impotent fury.

At its feet, warriors charged, stabbing with spears of hard desert steel, but the demon was unaffected by the assault. As Jardir watched, it gave almost a casual swipe of its tail, crushing shields, splintering spears, and sending the brave warriors flying.

"Everam protect us," Jardir whispered.

"The gate seems to be holding, at least," Shanjat said.

Jardir grunted. "But will it last until dawn? Dare we take that chance?"

"What else can we do?" Shanjat asked. "Even the scorpions can't pierce its hide, and it's too big to trick into a demon pit. Its head would be above the rim!"

"Bah, it's just a big demon!" Hasik said. "With enough warriors we can bring it down and bind its arms."

"Arm," Shanjat corrected. "We would lose many warriors that way, and there's no guarantee it will work. I've never seen an *alagai* so strong. I fear it is Alagai Ka himself, come with the Waning."

"Nonsense," Jardir said, watching the demon as his lieutenants argued. *By Everam, I will find a way to kill you*, he swore silently.

He was about to order a charge, hoping that sheer numbers could bring the creature low, when one of his Pit Warders came running up to him.

"Your pardon, First Warrior, the *chin* has a plan," the man said. Jardir turned to see the greenlander again in animated conversation with his Warders, miming his intentions frantically.

"What is it?" Jardir asked.

"Surely you cannot still mean to trust him," Hasik said.

"Do you have a plan that doesn't involve throwing lives away charging that abyss-spawned abomination?" Jardir asked. When Hasik did not reply, he turned back to the Warder. "What is his plan?"

"The *chin* knows something of warding," the Warder said.

"He would," Hasik muttered. "Hiding behind wards is all the *chin* know how to do."

"Be silent," Jardir snapped.

The Warder ignored the exchange. "The greenlander has wardstones that should trap the creature, if we can lure him to a dead end and then uncover them. The ward for rock demons is similar to the one for sand. The walls of the Maze should serve as a pit until the dawn."

Jardir took the wardstones and examined them. Indeed, they contained wards similar to those for sand, but larger and angled differently, with a break in one of the lines. He traced them with a finger.

"There is a dead end two turns into the tenth," he said.

"I know it, First Warrior," the Warder said, bowing.

Jardir turned to Hasik and Shanjat. "Keep watch on the demon. Do nothing unless there is a sign that the wards on the gate are weakening. If that should happen, I want every man in the Maze on that monster."

The two warriors punched their chests and bowed. Jardir selected his three best Warders, and they escorted the greenlander to the alcove. When all five of them agreed the wards on the walls and at the entrance would hold, they staked the wardstones in place and covered them with a sand-colored tarp that could be quickly removed.

Again Jardir found himself impressed with the Northerner. Warding was an elite skill in Krasia, reserved only for *dama* and a few warriors they hand-selected.

"Who are you?" he asked, but the greenlander only shrugged, not understanding.

They returned to the front of the lines, where the demon continued to systematically attack every inch of the gate, searching for a weakness.

Jardir looked at the gigantic *alagai* and felt a stab of fear, but he was the First Warrior. He would ask no other to lure the beast.

Either I am the Deliverer, or I am not, he told himself, struggling to believe. But he knew Inevera lied freely about other things, so why not this?

He steeled himself, drawing a ward in the air, and took a step forward.

"No, Sharum Ka!" Hasik shouted. "I am your bodyguard! Let me lure the demon!"

Jardir shook his head. "Your courage does you great honor, but this task is for me alone."

The greenlander said something, making a chopping motion with his arm, but the time for deciphering his cryptic messages was past. Jardir embraced his fears and strode out to the demon, shouting and clattering his spear against his shield.

The demon ignored him, continuing its assault on the gate.

Jardir charged, stabbing hard at the joint in the demon's armor at the back of its knee, but the creature only flicked its massive tail at him, as a horse would a fly.

Jardir danced out of the way, ducking as the spiked appendage whooshed over his head. He looked at his spear and found that the tip had broken off.

"Camel's piss," he muttered, going back to the lines to take a fresh spear from Hasik.

"First Warrior, look!" his bodyguard cried, pointing. Jardir turned to see the greenlander striding out to the demon.

"Fool!" he cried. "What are you doing?" But the greenlander gave no indication that he had even heard, much less understood. He stopped just outside the creature's reach and gave a shout.

The demon ceased its assault at the sound, tilting its head and sniffing at the air. It turned to regard the greenlander, and there was a flare of recognition in its alien eyes.

"Nie's blood," Hasik breathed. "It knows him."

The beast gave a great roar and charged, swiping with the claws of its good arm, but the greenlander was quick to leap aside, turning to run for the trapped alcove.

"Clear the way!" Jardir shouted, and his warriors moved as one to flow out of their path. As the demon passed, Jardir darted after them, followed by all the gathered warriors.

The Maze shook with the pounding of the demon's feet, and it kicked up great clouds of dust in its wake that made it difficult to see the greenlander. But the demon kept howling and running, so Jardir could only assume the *chin* maintained his lead.

They made two sharp turns, and in the dim light of the oil lamps Jardir saw the greenlander turn into the alcove. The demon followed, and the Pit Warders sprang from concealment to reveal the wards.

The rock demon roared in triumph seeing its prey trapped, and lunged at the greenlander, who turned and darted right at the beast.

Magic flared, and the great demon's claws skittered off the greenlander's shield. He was knocked over by the blow, but he rolled back to his feet like a cat, springing past the demon before it could draw back to attack him again.

The wards were revealed, but Jardir saw immediately that the rock demon had stepped on one of the central wardstones as it stomped past. The ward was shattered beyond repair.

The greenlander saw it, too. Jardir expected him to bolt from the alcove before the demon could turn, but again the Northerner surprised him. He pointed with his spear at the broken ward, shouted something in his guttural tongue, and turned back to face the *alagai*.

"Repair that ward!" Jardir shouted, but he needn't have bothered. The Pit Warders were already at work painting a fresh symbol on slate. They would be done in less than a minute.

Again the demon struck, and again the greenlander dodged aside, catching only a glancing blow on his shield. But this time, the demon was ready, swinging the stump of its other arm like a giant club. The greenlander managed to throw himself to the ground and avoid the attack, but the demon raised a foot to crush him while he was prone, and Jardir knew he would never rise in time.

The Warders were almost done. The greenlander would die a hero's death, and Krasia would be safe. All Jardir had to do was let go the mystery of the brave Northerner, and turn his back.

Instead he gave a shout, and leapt into the alcove.

CHAPTER 8

PAR'CHIN

:: 326–328 AR ::

THE ROCK DEMON ROARED, smashing its taloned foot down. Jardir skidded on his knees underneath the blow, bracing his warded shield with his shoulder as he lifted it over them.

The blow rattled his teeth and jolted his spine. He felt his shoulder pop free of its socket, and his shield arm went limp.

But the magic flared and the great *alagai* was knocked backward, losing its balance. It struck one of the walls and the wards there flared, throwing the demon into the opposite wall, which flared as well. It shrieked in fury, knocked about like a child's ball.

The greenlander was quick to rise, grabbing Jardir's uninjured shoulder and hauling him to his feet. The Pit Warders had completed their work by then, and while the demon thrashed, they stumbled from the alcove.

A moment later the rock demon found its footing and threw itself at them, but the greenlander's wards lit the night, and it was thrown back. The Northerner shouted something at the beast and made a gesture that Jardir assumed was as obscene in the North as it was in Krasia. He laughed again.

"What news from the Watchers?" Jardir asked Shanjat.

"Half the Maze is overrun," Shanjat replied. "A few warriors succor behind the wards in ambush pockets, but most have gone to Everam's embrace. The Majah are holding at the sixth; the *alagai* have not been able to penetrate the wards there."

"How many warriors did we lose?" Jardir asked, dreading the answer.

Shanjat shrugged. "No way to know until dawn, when the men in hiding emerge and the *kai'Sharum* can make a full count."

"Guess," Jardir said.

Shanjat frowned. "No less than a third. Perhaps half."

Jardir scowled. There had not been such losses in a single night since the Return. The Andrah would have his head on a block.

"If the inner Maze is clear, begin taking the injured into the *dama'ting* pavilion," he said.

"You should be among them, First Warrior," Shanjat said. "Your shoulder . . ."

Jardir glanced down at his arm, hanging limp at his side. He had embraced the pain and forgotten it. With this reminder, it screamed at him until he suppressed it again.

He shook his head. "The arm can wait. Have the Watchers bring their reports to me here. The sun will be rising soon, and I wish to see this *alagai* burn."

Shanjat nodded and left, shouting orders. Jardir turned to regard the rock demon, clawing at the wards and roaring its fury as it tried to get to the greenlander. The greenlander stood calmly before it, and the two—human and *alagai*—had the same hatred in their eyes as they stared at each other.

"What happened between you?" Jardir asked, knowing the greenlander could not understand.

But surprisingly, the man turned to him, guessing at his tone perhaps, and made the same chopping motion with his hand that he had before. He held out his right arm, and chopped at it with the other hand, striking just below the elbow.

Jardir's eyes widened as he caught the greenlander's meaning.

"You cut its arm off?!" Others looked up at the words. When the greenlander nodded, Jardir heard the buzz of rumor that would spread like blowing sand throughout the city.

"I underestimated you, my friend," he said. "I am honored to be your *ajin'pal*."

The greenlander shrugged and smiled, not understanding his words.

Soon after, there was the deepening of color in the night sky that signaled the coming dawn. The rock demon sensed it, too, and straightened, as if concentrating. Jardir had seen this play out a thousand times, and never tired of it. In a moment the demon would discover that the cut stone beneath the sand of the Maze floor prevented it from finding a path to Nie's abyss at the center of Ala. It would shriek and thrash and claw the wards, and then the sun's rays would catch it, and Everam's light would burn it to ashes.

The *alagai* did shriek, but then it did something Jardir had never seen before. It tore at the dirt and sand of the Maze floor, finding the great stone blocks that had been laid centuries before. With its one clawed hand, the demon smashed through the stone, tearing huge pieces free.

"No!" Jardir cried. The greenlander shouted in protest as well, but it made no difference. Long before the sun rose high enough to threaten it, the creature slipped back into the abyss.

ᔧ

Inevera was waiting when they limped back to the training grounds. Seeing his arm hanging lifelessly, she turned to Hasik.

"Bring him to the palace," she said. "Drag him, if he resists."

Hasik bowed his head. "As the *dama'ting* commands."

Jardir turned to Shanjat as Hasik pulled at him. "Locate Abban and have him brought here. When he arrives, escort him and the greenlander to my audience hall."

Shanjat nodded and sent a runner. Jardir and Hasik headed for the palace, but they had not reached the steps before the training ground was swarming with *dama'ting* tending to the wounded, and women wailing for husbands and sons who could not be found.

These were followed by *dama*, who quickly broke their tribesmen away from the mass of *Sharum* returning from the Maze. In moments the force that had stood unified in the night splintered as it did each day.

Jardir had not ascended half the steps to his palace when the palanquins arrived. All twelve *Damaji* and the Andrah himself, riding the backs of *nie'-dama* and flanked by their most loyal clerics.

Jardir stopped where he was, knowing no injury could take precedence over his giving a full report of this cursed night. But what to say? He had lost at least a third of Krasia's warriors, and what did he have to show for it?

"What happened?" the Andrah demanded, storming up to him. Inevera was at Jardir's side in an instant, but in the light of day, with the *Damaji* at his back and such failure at Jardir's feet, the Andrah was uncowed even by her.

Even after years, the sight of the fat man filled Jardir with hatred and disgust. But the day Inevera had foretold, when he could feed the man his spear and cut his manhood off, seemed impossible now. Jardir would be lucky if he did not end this day as *khaffit*.

"The outer gate was breached last night," Jardir said, "letting the enemy into the Maze."

"You lost the gate?" the Andrah demanded.

Jardir nodded.

"Losses?" the Andrah asked.

"Still counting," Jardir said. "Hundreds, at the least. Possibly thousands."

The *Damaji* burst into whispered conversation. All through the training grounds, the scene was being watched closely by *Sharum* and *dama* alike.

"I will have your head on a pike above the new gate!" the Andrah promised.

Before Jardir could respond, Hasik stepped in front of him, prostrating himself before the Andrah and pressing his head to the steps.

"What are you doing, fool?" Jardir demanded, but Hasik ignored him.

"Your pardon, my Andrah," he said, "but this is not the fault of the First Warrior. Without Ahmann Jardir, we would have all been lost in the night!"

There were murmurs of accord from the gathered warriors. "He pulled me from a demon pit!" one cried. "The First Warrior led the charge that saved my unit!" another called.

"That doesn't explain how he lost the gate in the first place!" the Andrah barked.

"Alagai Ka attacked the wall last night," Hasik said. "It caught a sling stone and hurled it back, breaking the outer gate. It was only by the First Warrior's quick response that we were not completely overrun."

"It is the Waning, but Alagai Ka has not been seen in Krasia in more than three thousand years," Damaji Amadeveram said.

"It was not Alagai Ka," Jardir said. "Just a rock demon from the mountains."

"Even that is unheard of," Amadeveram said. "What could have brought one so far from its mountain home?"

Hasik looked up, scanning the crowd. Jardir hissed, but again his lieutenant ignored him.

"Him," he said, pointing to the greenlander.

All eyes turned to the greenlander, who took a step back, realizing he had become the focus of everyone's attention.

"A *chin*?" the Andrah asked. "What is a *chin* doing among the *Sharum* of Krasia? He should be in the market slums with the other *khaffit*."

A *dama* whispered in Amadeveram's ear. "I am told he came to the First Warrior last night and begged to fight," the *Damaji* said.

"And you gave him permission?" the Andrah asked Jardir, incredulous.

Inevera tensed, but Jardir stilled her with a hand. She might have power in small chambers, but if a woman, even a *dama'ting*, defended him before the assembled warriors and *dama*, she would only make matters worse.

"I did," he said.

"So this ruin brought upon us is wholly your fault!" the Andrah cried. "Your *chin*'s head shall share the gate spike with you, and let buzzards eat your eyes!"

He turned to go, but Jardir was not done. He had sacrificed too much for the greenlander to let him be executed now. Inevera had said their fates were tied, so let it be so.

His arm screamed still, and he was tired and bruised from fighting the night through. His head spun with pain and exhaustion, but he embraced it all and pushed it aside. There would be time to rest in Everam's embrace, and he was not there yet.

"So I should have turned him away?" he asked loudly, so all could hear. "He comes to us with *alagai* as his enemy, and we should show him our backs? Are we men or *khaffit*?"

The Andrah stopped short, and turned back to face Jardir. His face was a stormcloud.

"He brought a rock demon with him!" the Andrah cried.

"I don't care if his enemy really *was* Alagai Ka!" Jardir shouted back. "Woe betide Krasia when we fear the *alagai* enough to turn on a man in the night—even a *chin*!"

He beckoned to the greenlander, who ascended the steps halfway, so all could see him. He held his spear tightly, as if expecting the crowd to turn on him in an instant. His hard eyes made it clear he would not fall easily.

He is fearless, Jardir thought. *Could there be a better man to tie my fate to?*

"This is no cowardly Northerner, tilling soil like a woman," Jardir said. "This is a *par'chin*, a brave outsider who stands like a *dal'Sharum*! Let Alagai Ka come! If he wishes this greenlander's blood, then that is reason enough for any man who would stand tall before Everam to deny him!"

Shanjat gave a shout of support, echoed quickly by Jardir's hundred. In an instant every *dal'Sharum* had raised his spear to add his voice to the cacophony.

"We stood fast against Nie, this night, and denied her great servant," Jardir said. "Even now, he crawls back to the abyss in failure and defeat, quailing in fear of the *dal'Sharum* of the Desert Spear!"

The Andrah sputtered, foundering for a response, but anything he could have said was drowned away as even the *dama* in the crowd took up the cry.

The Andrah scowled, but in the face of such overwhelming support for Jardir, there was nothing he could do. He turned on his heel, sitting heavily in his palanquin. The *nie'Sharum* groaned under his bulk as they hoisted the carrying bars to their shoulders.

"You play a dangerous game," Amadeveram warned as they carried the Andrah out of earshot.

"*Sharak* is no game to me, Damaji," Jardir said.

ᔓ

"That was well done," Inevera said as she laid him on her operating table. "You sent that fat pig running with his curled tail between his legs!" She laughed as she began to cut the robes from him. His shoulder and much of his arm had gone black.

"I have rare moments of competence," Jardir said.

Inevera grunted, taking his arm and popping it back into its socket with a sharp twist. Jardir was ready for the pain, and it washed over him like a warm breeze.

"Do you need a root for the pain?" she asked.

Jardir snorted.

"So strong," she purred, running her hands over his body, searching for further injuries. Jardir was a mass of bruises and scrapes, but there was nothing that could not wait, it seemed, for Inevera's robes fell to the floor, and she climbed onto the table, straddling him.

Nothing aroused her more than victory.

"My champion," she breathed, kissing his hard chest. "My Shar'Dama Ka."

ᔓ

Jardir sat on the Spear Throne, regarding his *kai'Sharum* as they gave their reports. His left arm was in a sling, and though the pain was only a faint buzz to his focused mind, the loss of use in the limb angered him. His wives would try to keep him from *alagai'sharak* in the coming night, but he would be damned first.

Before him stood Evakh, *kai'Sharum* of the Sharach tribe.

"With but four *dal'Sharum* remaining, I regret to inform the Sharum Ka that the Sharach no longer have enough warriors to form our own unit," Evakh said, his head bowed in shame. "It will be many years before we recover." He left unsaid what they were all thinking: that the Sharach would likely never recover, dying out or being absorbed into another tribe.

Jardir shook his head. "Many units were shattered last night. I will call for *dal'Sharum* to stand up and honor their Sharach brothers with their spears. You will have warriors under your command this very night."

The *kai'Sharum's* eyes goggled. "That is too generous, First Warrior."

"Nonsense," Jardir said. "I could do no less in conscience. In addition, I will purchase wives from my own coffer to aid in your recovery." He smiled. "If your men bring as much energy for that task as they do to *alagai'sharak*, the Sharach should recover swiftly."

"The Sharach are in your eternal debt, First Warrior," the man said, prostrating himself and touching his forehead to the floor.

Jardir descended from his dais and put his good hand on the warrior's soldier.

"I am Sharach," he said, "as are my three sons and two daughters by Qasha. I will not let our tribe fade into the night." The warrior kissed his sandaled feet, and Jardir felt the tears that fell from his eyes.

"The Kaji and the Majah will not sell wives to another tribe," Ashan advised when Evakh departed, "but the Mehnding have an abundance of daughters, and are loyal to the Sharum Ka. Their losses were few last night."

Jardir nodded. "Offer to buy as many as they will allow. Money is no object. Other tribes will need fresh blood to survive this event, as well."

Ashan bowed. "It will be done. But is rebuilding the tribes not the duty of the *Damaji*?"

Jardir looked at him knowingly. "Come, my friend, you know as well as I that those old men will not lift a finger to help one another, even now. The *Sharum* must look to their own."

Ashan bowed again.

There were more reports, many just as bad. Jardir sat through them wearily, giving aid to all, and wondering at the state of the army that would assemble when dusk came that night.

Finally, the last of his commanders departed, and he sighed deeply.

"Bring in the Par'chin and the *khaffit*," he said.

Ashan signaled the guards, and they were escorted in. The *dal'Sharum* shoved Abban roughly to the floor before the dais.

"You will translate for the Sharum Ka, *khaffit*," Ashan said.

"Yes, my *dama*," Abban said, touching his head to the floor.

The greenlander said something to Abban, who mumbled a reply through gritted teeth.

"What did he say?" Jardir asked.

Abban swallowed hard, hesitating.

The guard behind Abban hit him across the back with his spear. "The Sharum Ka asked you a question, son of camel's piss!"

Abban cried out in pain, and the greenlander gave a shout, shoving the warrior back and interposing himself between them. He and the warrior glared at each other for a moment, but the warrior's eyes flicked to Jardir uncertainly.

Jardir ignored them. "I will not ask twice," he told Abban.

Abban wiped the sweat from his brow. "He said, 'It is not right that you should have to grovel so,' " he translated, ducking his head and closing his eyes, as if expecting another blow.

Jardir nodded. "Tell him that you have shamed yourself and your family in the Maze, and are no longer fit to stand among men."

Abban nodded, translating quickly. The greenlander replied, and Abban translated. "He says that should not matter. No man should crawl like a dog."

Ashan shook his head. "The ways of the savages are strange."

"Indeed," Jardir said, "but we are not here to discuss the treatment of *khaffit*. Abban, you may take your hands from the floor."

"Thank you, First Warrior," Abban said, straightening. The greenlander seemed to relax at this, and he and the guard backed away from each other.

"You fought well in the night, Par'chin," Jardir said. Abban translated quickly.

The greenlander bowed, meeting Jardir's eyes as he replied in his guttural tongue. "I was honored to stand among men of such courage," Abban translated.

"Do other men of the North fight as we do?" Jardir asked.

The greenlander shook his head. "My people fight only when they must, to save their own lives or sometimes that of another," Abban said. The greenlander scowled and added something, spitting on the floor. "Sometimes not even then," Abban said.

"They are a race of cowards, as the Evejah says," Ashan said. Abban opened his mouth, and the *dama* threw a goblet at him, soaking his fine silks in dark nectar. "Do not translate that, fool!" The greenlander clenched a fist, but kept his eyes on Jardir.

"What makes you different?" Jardir asked. Abban translated, but the greenlander only shrugged and did not reply. "You cut the arm from the rock demon?"

The greenlander nodded. "When I was a boy," Abban translated, "I ran away from my home. I made a circle of wards when the sun set, and I was surrounded by corelings . . ."

Jardir held up a hand. "Corelings?"

Abban bowed. "It is the greenland word for *alagai*, First Warrior," he said. "It means 'those who dwell in the center.' They believe Nie's abyss lies at the core of Ala, as we do."

Jardir nodded, signaling the man to continue.

"The rock demon came for me that night," Abban translated, "and in my foolishness, I made mock of it, jeering and cavorting about. But I slipped and scuffed a ward. The coreling struck, clawing my back, but I managed to repair the ward before it could cross the circle fully. When the circle reactivated, its arm was severed."

Ashan snorted. "Impossible. The *chin* is obviously lying, Sharum Ka. No one could survive a blow from such a beast."

The greenlander looked to Abban, but when the *khaffit* did not translate, he turned to Jardir. He said something, and pointed to Ashan.

"What did the Holy Man say?" Abban supplied.

Jardir glanced at Ashan, then back to the greenlander. "He said you are a liar."

The greenlander nodded, as if he had expected as much. He laid down his spear and lifted his shirt, turning his back to them.

"Nie's black heart," Abban said, turning pale at the sight of the thick scars running across the man's back. They were faded with years, but there was no doubt they were made by claws far larger than any sand demon's.

The greenlander turned back, staring hard at Ashan. "Do you still think me a liar?" Abban translated.

"Apologize," Jardir murmured.

Ashan bowed deeply. "My apologies, Par'chin." The greenlander nodded as Abban translated.

"The demon has stalked you ever since?" Jardir asked.

The greenlander nodded. "Almost seven years now," Abban translated, "but one day, I will show it the sun."

Jardir nodded. "Why did you not tell us such a great enemy pursued you? You put my city at risk."

The greenlander replied, and Abban's eyes widened. He said something in response, but the greenlander shook his head and spoke again.

"You are not here to hold your own conversations, *khaffit*!" Jardir shouted, rising from his seat. The *dal'Sharum* at the door lowered their spears and advanced.

"Apologies, First Warrior!" Abban cried, pressing his forehead back to the floor. "I sought only to clarify his meaning!"

"I will decide what needs clarifying," Jardir said. "The next time you speak out of turn, I will cut off your thumbs. Now translate everything that was spoken."

Abban nodded eagerly. "The greenlander said, 'It was only a rock demon. They are common in the North, and I did not think it worth mentioning that one bore me personal enmity,' to which I replied, 'Surely you exaggerate, my friend! There cannot be two *alagai* so great,' and he said, 'No, in the mountains of the North, there are many such.'"

Jardir nodded. "What are the weaknesses of the rock demons?"

"So far as I know," the greenlander said through Abban, "they have none. And I have looked hard."

"We will find one, Par'chin," Jardir said. "Together."

ॐ

"This level of communication is unacceptable," Jardir said when the greenlander had been escorted out.

"The Par'chin is a quick study," Abban said, "and has committed himself to learning our tongue. He will speak it soon, I promise."

"Not good enough," Jardir said. "There will be other greenlanders, and I would speak to them, as well. Since none of our learned men," he looked at Ashan with disdain, "has seen fit to study the tongue of the savages, it will fall to you to instruct us, beginning with me."

Abban paled. "Me?" he squeaked. "Instruct you?"

Jardir felt a wave of disgust. "Stop your sniveling. Yes, you! Are there any others who speak it?"

Abban shrugged. "It is a valuable skill in the marketplace. My wives and daughters speak a few words, so they might listen in secret as the Messengers talk. Many other women in the bazaar do the same."

"You expect the Sharum Ka to learn from a woman?" Ashan demanded, and Jardir swallowed the irony. If not for Inevera, he would still be an illiterate *dal'Sharum.*

"Another merchant then," Abban said. "I am not the only one who trades with the North."

"But you trade the most," Jardir said. "It is obvious from your womanish silks, and the fact that a sniveling fat *khaffit* like you has more wives than most warriors. More than that, the Par'chin knows and trusts you. Unless there is a true man who speaks the greenland tongue, it shall be you."

"But . . ." Abban said, his eyes pleading. Jardir held up a hand, and he fell silent.

"You said once you owed me your life," Jardir said. "The time has come for you to begin repaying that debt."

Abban bowed deeply, touching his forehead to the floor.

ॐ

The city gates were patched by nightfall, and though the giant rock demon continued to attack the walls, the sling teams gave it no more ammunition with which to breach the wards. The Par'chin joined in *alagai'sharak* again that night, and every night for a week to come. By day, he drilled hard with the *dal'Sharum*.

"I cannot speak for other greenland Messengers," Drillmaster Kaval said, spitting in the dust, "but the Par'chin has been trained well. His spearwork is excellent, and he has taken to *sharusahk* like he was born to it. I started him training with the *nie'Sharum*, but his form has already surpassed even those ready for the wall."

Jardir nodded. He had expected no less.

As if he had known they spoke of him, the Par'chin approached them, Abban trailing dutifully behind. He bowed and spoke.

"I will be returning to the North tomorrow, First Warrior," Abban translated.

Keep him close. Inevera's words echoed in Jardir's head.

"So soon?" he asked. "You have only just arrived, Par'chin!"

"I feel that way as well," the Par'chin said, "but I have commitments to deliver goods and messages that must be kept."

"Commitments to *chin*!" Jardir snapped, knowing he had made a mistake the moment the words left his mouth. It was a deep insult. He wondered if the greenlander would attack him.

But the Par'chin only raised an eyebrow. "Should that matter?" he asked through Abban.

"No, of course not," Jardir said, bowing deeply to everyone's surprise. "I apologize. I am simply disappointed to see you go."

"I will return soon," the Par'chin promised. He held up a sheaf of papers bound in leather. "Abban has been most helpful; I have a long list of words to memorize. When next we meet, I hope to be more adept at your tongue."

"No doubt," Jardir said. He embraced the Par'chin, kissing his hairless cheeks. "You will always be welcome in Krasia, my brother, but you will draw less attention if you grow a proper man's beard."

The Par'chin smiled. "I will," he promised.

Jardir slapped him on the back. "Come, my friend. Night is falling. We will kill *alagai* once more before you cross the hot sands."

In the months following the Par'chin's departure, Jardir began observing the other Messengers from the North more closely. Abban's contacts in the bazaar were extensive, and word came quickly when a Northerner arrived.

Jardir invited each to his palace in turn—an honor unheard of in the past.

The men came eagerly after centuries of being treated as filth beneath even *khaffit*.

"I welcome the chance to practice the Northland tongue," he told the Messengers as they sat at his table, served by his own wives. He spoke to each at length, indeed honing his speech, but seeking something more.

And when the meals were finished, he always made the same request.

"You carry a spear in the night like a man," he said. "Come stand with us in the Maze tonight as a brother."

The men looked at him, and he could see in their eyes that they had no idea of the enormity of the honor he was offering them.

And to a one, they refused him.

In the meantime, the Par'chin kept his word, visiting at least twice every year. Sometimes his visits would last mere days, and other times he would spend months in the Desert Spear and the surrounding villages. Again and again, he arrived at the training grounds, begging leave to join in *ala-gai'sharak*.

Is the Par'chin the only true man in the North? Jardir wondered.

The Pit Warder, falling in a spray of blood, had not hit the ground before the Par'chin was there. He hooked the sand demon's legs with his own and dropped to the ground, twisting for leverage in a flawless *sharusahk* move. The demon's knees buckled, and it dropped into the pit.

As if it had all been one smooth motion, the Par'chin produced a stick of charcoal, repairing the damaged ward and resealing the circle before another demon could escape. He was at the Warder's side in an instant, cutting at his robes and tossing aside the steel plates pocketed in the fabric to ward off *ala-gai* claws. The metal was a special protection granted to the Pit Warders, but it was still poor compensation for a shield and spear. Pit Warders needed their hands free.

The Par'chin's hands and arms grew slick with blood, but he paid it no mind, digging in his battle bag for herbs and implements. Jardir shook his head in amazement. This was not the first time the greenlander had treated an injured warrior on the Maze floor. Were the Northerners all Warders and *dama'ting* combined?

The Warder struggled weakly, but the Par'chin straddled him, pinning him with his knees as he continued to clean the wound.

"Help me!" the Par'chin called in Krasian, but the *dal'Sharum* only watched in confusion. Jardir felt it, too. These were no simple wounds. Could he not see the man was doomed to life as a cripple if he should survive?

Jardir walked over to the pair. The Par'chin was trying to thread a hooked needle while keeping pressure on the bandages with his elbow. The warrior continued to struggle, making the task impossible.

"Hold him still!" the Par'chin cried, seeing his approach. Jardir ignored him, looking in the warrior's eyes. The *dal'Sharum* gave a slight shake of his head.

Jardir plunged his spear into the man's heart.

The Par'chin shrieked, dropping his needle and launching himself at Jardir. He grabbed Jardir's robes and shoved him back hard, slamming him against the Maze wall.

"What are you about?" the Par'chin demanded.

All around the ambush point, warriors raised their spears and approached. No man was allowed to lay hands on the First Warrior.

Jardir raised a hand to forestall them, keeping his eyes on the greenlander, who had no idea how close he was to death.

Upon seeing the Par'chin's eyes, Jardir revised that assessment. Perhaps he did know, and simply didn't care. Killing the Warder had offended the greenlander beyond reason.

"I am about letting men die with honor, son of Jeph," Jardir said. "He did not want your help. He did not need it. He had done his duty, and now he is in Heaven."

"There is no Heaven," the Par'chin growled. "All you did was murder a man."

Jardir flexed, breaking the Par'chin's hold easily. The man had learned *sharusahk* quickly over the last two years, but he was not yet a match for most *dal'Sharum,* much less one trained in Sharik Hora. He punched the Par'chin in the jaw, easily ducking his return swing. He twisted the man's arm behind him and slammed him to the ground.

"Just this once," he whispered in the Par'chin's ear, "I will pretend I did not hear you say that. Speak your Northern blasphemies again in Krasia, and your life will be forfeit."

Keep him close, Inevera had said, but he had failed.

Jardir stood alone atop the wall, watching as the *alagai* fled the coming sun. The great rock demon, which his men had taken to calling Alagai Ka, paced before the restored gates, but the wards were strong. Soon he, too, would sink back down to Nie's abyss for another day.

Jardir kept remembering the desperation in the Par'chin's eyes, the need to save the Warder's life. Jardir knew he had been right to end it and ensure the man glory over a life as a cripple, but he knew, too, that he had deliberately antagonized the Par'chin in the process.

Among his people, such abject lessons were common, and no man would try to assault his betters for the life of a cripple. But as Jardir had learned again and again, the greenlanders were not like his people, not even the Par'chin. They did not embrace death as part of life. They fought it as hard as any *dal'Sharum* fought *alagai*.

There was honor in that, of a sort. The *dama* were wrong to call the greenlanders savages. Inevera's command notwithstanding, Jardir liked the Par'chin. The rift between them gnawed at him, and he wondered at how to repair it.

"Thought I'd find you here," a voice behind him said. Jardir chuckled. The greenlander had a way of appearing when Jardir's thoughts were turned his way.

The Par'chin stood atop the wall, looking down. He hawked loudly and spit, his phlegm striking the head of the rock demon, twenty feet below. The demon roared at him, and they laughed together as it sank beneath the dunes.

"One day he will lie dead at your feet," Jardir said, "and Everam's light will burn his body away."

"One day," the Par'chin agreed.

The two men stood quietly for a time, lost in their own thoughts. The greenlander had grown a beard as Jardir had suggested, but the yellow hair on his pale face only made him seem more of an outsider than his bare cheeks had.

"Came to apologize," the Par'chin said at last. "It's not my right to judge your ways."

Jardir nodded. "Nor I yours. You acted in loyalty, and I was wrong to spit upon that. I know you have grown quite close to the Warders since you learned our tongue. They have learned much from you."

"And I from them," the Par'chin said. "I meant no insult."

"It seems our cultures are a natural insult to each other, Par'chin," Jardir said. "We must resist the urge to take offense, if we are to continue to learn from each other."

"Thank you," the Par'chin said. "That means a great deal to me."

Jardir gave a dismissive wave. "We will speak on it no more, my friend."

The greenlander nodded and turned to go.

"Do all men in the North believe as you do?" Jardir asked. "That Heaven is not truth?"

The Par'chin shook his head. "The Tenders in the North tell of a Creator who lives in Heaven and gathers the spirits of his faithful there, much as your *dama* do. Most people believe their words."

"But you do not," Jardir said.

"The Tenders also say the corelings are a Plague," the Par'chin said. "That the sins of man were so great that the Creator sent the demons to punish us." He shook his head. "I will never believe that. And if the Tenders are wrong about that, what faith should I put in the rest of their words?"

"Then why do you fight, if not for the glory of the Creator?" Jardir asked.

"I don't need Holy Men to tell me corelings are an evil to be destroyed," the Par'chin said. "They killed my mother and broke my father. They've murdered my friends and neighbors and family. And somewhere out there," he swept a hand over the horizon, "is a way to destroy them. I will seek until I find it."

"You are right to doubt these Tenders of yours," Jardir said. "The *alagai* are no plague, they are a test."

"A test?"

"Yes. A test of our loyalty to Everam. A test of our courage and will to fight Nie's darkness. But you are mistaken, too. The way to their destruction is not out there," he waved his hand at the horizon dismissively, "it is in here." He touched a finger to the Par'chin's heart. "And on the day all men find their hearts and stand united, Nie will not be able to stand against us."

The Par'chin was silent a long time. "I dream of that day," he said at last.

"As do I, my friend," Jardir said. "As do I."

More than two years after his first visit, Par'chin returned once again. Jardir looked up from chalked slates of battle plans, seeing the man cross the training ground, and felt as if his own brother had returned from a long journey.

"Par'chin!" he called, spreading his arms to embrace him. "Welcome back to the Desert Spear!" He spoke the greenlander's language fluidly now, though the words still felt ugly on his tongue. "I did not know you had returned. The *alagai* will quail in fear tonight!"

It was then Jardir noticed the Par'chin came with Abban in tow, though neither he nor Jardir needed the fat *khaffit* to communicate any longer.

Jardir looked at Abban in disgust. He had grown even fatter since Jardir saw him last, and still draped himself in silk like a *Damaji's* favored wife. It was said he dominated trade in the bazaar, due in no small part to his extensive contacts in the North. He was a leech, putting profit above Everam, above honor, and above Krasia.

"What are you doing here among men, *khaffit*?" he demanded. "I have not summoned you."

"He's with me," the Par'chin said.

"He *was* with you," Jardir said pointedly. Abban bowed and scurried off.

"I don't know why you waste your time with that *khaffit*, Par'chin," Jardir spat.

"Where I come from, a man's worth does not end with lifting the spear," the Par'chin said.

Jardir laughed. "Where you come from, Par'chin, they do not lift the spear at all!"

"Your Thesan is much improved," the Par'chin noted.

Jardir grunted. "Your *chin* tongue is not easy, and twice as hard for needing a *khaffit* to practice it while you are away." He scowled at Abban's back. "Look at that one. He dresses like a woman."

"I've never seen a woman dressed like that," the Par'chin said.

"Only because you won't let me find you a wife whose veils you can lift," Jardir said. He had tried many times to find a bride for the Par'chin, to tie him to Krasia and keep him close, as Inevera commanded.

One day, you will have to kill him, Inevera's voice echoed in his head, but he did not wish to believe it. If Jardir could find him a wife, the greenlander would cease to be a *chin* and be reborn as *dal'Sharum*. Perhaps that "death" would fulfill the prophecy.

"I doubt the *dama* would allow one of your women to marry a tribeless *chin*," the Par'chin said.

Jardir waved his hand. "Nonsense," he said. "We have shed blood together in the Maze, my brother. If I take you into my tribe, not even the Andrah himself would dare protest!"

"I don't think I'm ready for a wife just yet," the Par'chin said.

Jardir scowled. As close as they were, the greenlander continued to baffle him. Among his people, a warrior's lusts were as great off the battlefield as on. He had seen no evidence that the Par'chin preferred the company of men, but he seemed more interested in battle than the spoils that rightly came to those who lived to see the dawn.

"Well don't wait too long, or men will think you *push'ting*," he said, using the word for "false woman." It was not a sin before Everam to lie with another man, but *push'ting* shunned women entirely, denying their tribe future generations—something his people could ill afford.

"How long have you been in the city, my friend?" Jardir asked.

"Only a few hours," the Par'chin said. "I just delivered my messages to the palace."

"And already you come to offer your spear!" Jardir cried loudly for all to hear. "By Everam, the Par'chin must have Krasian blood in him!" The men laughed.

"Walk with me," Jardir said, putting his arm around the Par'chin as he mentally reviewed the night's battle plan, seeking a place of honor for his brave friend.

"The Bajin lost a Pit Warder last night," he said. "You could fill in there."

"Push Guard, I would prefer," the Par'chin replied.

Jardir shook his head, but he was smiling. "Always the most dangerous duty for you," he chided. "If you are killed, who will carry our letters?"

"Not so dangerous, this night," the Par'chin said. He produced a rolled cloth, uncovering a spear.

But not just any spear. Its length was of a bright, silvery metal, and wards etched along the head and haft glittered in the sunlight. Jardir's trained eye ran along its length, and he felt his heart thump loudly in his chest. Many of the wards were unfamiliar, but he could sense their power.

The Par'chin stood proudly, waiting for him to react. Jardir swallowed his wonder and blinked the covetous gleam from his eyes, hoping his friend had not seen it.

"A kingly weapon," he agreed, "but it is the warrior that wins through in the night, Par'chin, not the spear." He put his hand on the Par'chin's shoulder and looked him in the eyes. "Do not put too much faith in your weapon. I have seen warriors more seasoned than you paint their spears and come to a bitter end."

"I did not make it," the Par'chin said. "I found it in the ruins of Anoch Sun."

Jardir's thumping heart came to a stop. Could it be true? He forced himself to laugh.

"The birthplace of the Deliverer?" he asked. "The Spear of Kaji is a myth, Par'chin, and the lost city has been reclaimed by the sands."

The Par'chin shook his head. "I've been there. I can take you there."

Jardir hesitated. The Par'chin was no liar, and there was no jest in his voice. He meant his words. For a moment, an image flashed in his mind: he and the Par'chin out on the sands together, uncovering the combat wards of old. It was only with great effort he recalled his responsibilities and shook the image away.

"I am Sharum Ka of the Desert Spear, Par'chin," he replied. "I cannot just pack a camel and ride off into the sand looking for a city that exists only in ancient texts."

"I think I will convince you when night falls," the Par'chin said.

Jardir bent his mouth into a smile. "Promise me that you will not try any-thing foolish. Warded spear or no, you are not the Deliverer. It would be sad to bury you."

🗲

"Tonight is the night," Inevera said. "Long have I foreseen this. Kill him and take the spear. At dawn, you will declare yourself Shar'Dama Ka, and a month from now you will rule all Krasia."

"No," Jardir said.

For a moment, Inevera did not hear him. ". . . and the Sharach will de-clare for you immediately," she was saying, "but the Kaji and Majah will take a hard line against . . . Eh?" She turned back to him, her eyebrow disappear-ing into her headwrap.

"The prophecy . . ." she began.

"The prophecy be damned," Jardir said. "I will not murder my friend, no matter what the demon bones tell you. I will not rob him. I am the Sharum Ka, not a thief in the night."

She slapped him, the retort echoing off the stone walls. "A fool is what you are!" she snapped. "Now is the moment of divergence, when what *might* be becomes what *will*. By dawn, one of you will be declared Deliverer. It is up to you to decide if it will be the Sharum Ka of the Desert Spear, or a grave-robbing *chin* from the North."

"I tire of your prophecies and divergences," Jardir said, "you and all the *dama'ting*! All just guesses meant to manipulate men to your will. But I will not betray my friend for you, no matter what you pretend to see in those warded lumps of *alagai* shit!"

Inevera shrieked and raised her hand to strike him again, but Jardir caught her wrist and lifted it high. She struggled for a moment, but she might as well have struggled with a stone wall.

"Do not force me to hurt you," Jardir warned.

Inevera's eyes narrowed, and she twisted suddenly, driving the stiffened index and middle fingers of her free hand into his shoulder. Immediately the arm holding her wrist went numb, and she twisted out of his grasp, slipping back a step and straightening her robes.

"You keep thinking the *dama'ting* defenseless, my husband," she said as he goggled at her, "though you of all people should know better."

Jardir looked down at his arm in horror. It hung limply, refusing his com-mands to move.

Inevera moved over to him, taking his numb hand in hers, and pressing her free hand to his shoulder. She twisted his arm and pressed hard, and suddenly the numbness was replaced with a sharp tingle of pins.

"You are no thief," she agreed, her voice calm once more, "if you are only reclaiming what is already yours by right."

"Mine?" Jardir asked, staring at his hand as its fingers began to flex once more.

"Who is the thief?" Inevera asked. "The *chin* who robs the grave of Kaji, or you, his blood kin, who takes back what was stolen?"

"We do not know it is the Spear of Kaji he holds," Jardir said.

Inevera crossed her arms. "You know. You knew the moment you laid eyes on it, just as you've known all along that this day would come. I never hid this fate from you."

Jardir said nothing.

Inevera touched his arm gently. "If you prefer, I can put a potion in his tea. His passing will be quick."

"No!" Jardir shouted, tearing his arm away. "Always the path of least honor with you! The Par'chin is no *khaffit*, to be put down like a dog! He deserves a warrior's death."

"Then give him one," Inevera urged. "Now, before *alagai'sharak* begins and the power of the spear is known."

Jardir shook his head. "If it is to be done, I will do it in the Maze."

But as he walked away from her, he was not sure it was to be done at all. How could he stand tall as Shar'Dama Ka if it was atop the body of a friend?

"Par'chin! Par'chin!"

The cries echoed throughout the Maze. Jardir watched from the walltop as the greenlander led the *dal'Sharum* to victory after victory. No *alagai* could resist the Spear of Kaji.

He is the brave outsider tonight, Jardir thought. *Shar'Dama Ka tomorrow.*

But perhaps this was Everam's will? When He formed the world from Nie's void, had He not created the greenlanders, as well? Must He not have a plan for them?

"But the Par'chin does not believe in Everam," he said aloud.

"How can a man who does not bow to the Creator be the Deliverer?" Hasik asked.

Jardir drew a deep breath. "He cannot. Gather Shanjat and our most loyal men. For the sake of all the world, it must be someone else."

5

Jardir found the Par'chin at the head of a host of *Sharum* chanting his name as they thundered through the Maze. He was covered in black demon ichor, but his eyes were alive with fierce joy. He thrust his spear high in salute, and Jardir's heart wrenched for what he must do to his *ajin'pal*—worse by far than Hasik had done to him.

"*Sharum Ka!*" the Par'chin cried. "No demon will escape your Maze alive tonight!"

War is deception, Jardir reminded himself, and forced himself to laugh and raise his spear to return the Par'chin's salute. He came and embraced the man for the last time.

"I underestimated you, Par'chin," he said. "I won't do so again."

The Par'chin smiled. "You say that every time." He was surrounded by warriors, glorying in their victory. Already they could not be trusted to do what must be done.

"*Dal'Sharum!*" he called to the warriors, gesturing to the slaughtered *alagai* on the streets of the Maze. "Gather up these filthy things and haul them atop the outer wall! Our sling teams need target practice! Let the *alagai* beyond the walls see the folly of attacking the Desert Spear!"

A cheer rose from the men, and they hastened to his bidding. As they did, Jardir turned to Arlen. "The Watchers report there is still battle in one of the eastern ambush points. Have you any fight left in you, Par'chin?"

The Par'chin showed Jardir his teeth. "Lead the way."

Leaving the *Sharum* behind, they sprinted through the Maze, down a route already cleared of witnesses. Like a Baiter, Jardir led the Par'chin to his doom. At last, they came to the ambush point. "*Oot!*" Jardir called, and with that, Hasik stuck out a leg, tripping the Par'chin.

The greenlander rolled with the impact as he hit the ground, coming right back to his feet, but by then Jardir's most trusted men had cut off his escape.

"What is this?" the Par'chin demanded.

Jardir's heart ached at the look of betrayal on his friend's face. He deserved no better, but now that the trap was sprung, he was committed to its course. "The Spear of Kaji belongs in the hands of the Shar'Dama Ka," he said. "You are not he."

"I don't want to fight you," the Par'chin said.

"Then don't, my friend," Jardir begged. "Give me the weapon, take your horse, and go with the dawn, never to return." Inevera would call him a fool for the offer. Even his lieutenants murmured in surprise, but he did not care.

He prayed his friend would accept, though he knew in his heart that he would not. The son of Jeph was no coward. Behind him in the demon pit, there was a growl. A warrior's death awaited him.

He fought hard as the *dal'Sharum* fell upon him, breaking bones but refusing, even now, to kill men. Jardir stayed out of the fray, consumed by his shame.

Finally, it was done, the Par'chin held tight by Hasik and Shanjat as Jardir bent to pick up the spear. Immediately he felt its power and a sense of belonging as his fingers tightened about the haft. Indeed, it was the weapon of Kaji, whose seventh son had been the first Jardir.

"I am truly sorry, my friend," he said. "I wish there could be another way."

The Par'chin spat in his face. "Everam is watching your betrayal!"

Jardir felt a flash of anger. The Par'chin did not believe in Heaven, but he was willing to use the Creator's name when it suited his purpose. He had no wives or children, no ties to family or tribe, but he thought he knew what was best for all. His arrogance knew no bounds.

"Do not speak of Everam, *chin,*" Jardir said. "I am his Sharum Ka, not you. Without me, Krasia falls."

ⵣ

They rode out of the city secretly in the predawn light. Most of the *alagai* had already returned to the abyss, but a sand demon must have heard their approach and waited, because it leapt out at them from the shadow of a dune mere minutes before dawn.

Jardir was ready, and the defensive wards on the shaft of the spear flared as he parried the attack. The *alagai* was thrown to the ground and glanced at the brightening sky, but before it could dematerialize, Jardir leapt from the back of his horse and skewered it.

There was a pulse of light as the warded spearhead punched through the gritty armor of the demon, and Jardir felt the spear come to life in his hand. A shock ran through him like Inevera's lightning stone, but where that was agony, this was ecstasy. Immediately he felt stronger, faster. Old aches from injuries long forgotten, pains he had become so accustomed to he no longer noticed them, suddenly vanished, revealing themselves by their absence. He felt immortal. Invincible. He swung his arms effortlessly, hurling the demon's corpse thirty feet to await the rising sun.

The sense of power faded quickly after the kill, but the healing remained. Jardir was over thirty, but he suddenly remembered what it had felt like when his body was twenty, and wondered how he had ever forgotten.

All this from a single sand demon, he mused. *What must the Par'chin have felt when he used it on dozens of* alagai *in the Maze?*

But he would never know the answer, for they left the unconscious Par'chin facedown on the dunes moments before sunrise, miles from the city and more than a day's walk from the nearest village.

Jardir looked down at him, and the greenlander's words flashed in his mind. *Everam is watching your betrayal!* he had shouted.

"Why could you not have left when I begged it of you, my friend?" Jardir asked—one more question the Par'chin could never answer for him.

Jardir regarded his friend sadly as Hasik and Shanjat climbed back into their saddles. He took the skin of cool water from his saddle horn, throwing it to land with a thump in the sand beside the greenlander's prone form.

"What are you doing?" Ashan asked. "We should kill him now, not help him."

"I will not stab an unconscious warrior," Jardir said. "The skin will not fly him across the sands to succor, but he will wake, and drink, and when the *alagai* come, he will die on his feet like a man, and find his way to paradise."

"What if he returns to the city?" Shanjat asked.

"Post Mehnding on the walls through the day to shoot him if he tries," Jardir said.

He looked back. *But you won't, will you, Par'chin?* he thought. *You have a* Sharum's *spirit, and will die fighting* alagai *with your bare hands.*

"He is a *chin,*" Ashan said. "An unbeliever. What makes you think Everam will welcome him in Heaven?"

Jardir raised the spear, catching the light from the rising sun. "Because I am Shar'Dama Ka, and I say it is so."

The others goggled, but no one disputed the claim.

Inevera's words from just hours ago came to him again.

At dawn, you will declare yourself Shar'Dama Ka.

He looked back to the body of the Par'chin.

Die well, he prayed, *and when we meet in Heaven, if I have not fulfilled both our dreams, we shall have a reckoning.*

He turned his horse, riding back to the city.

His city.

CHAPTER 9

SHAR'DAMA KA

:: 329 AR ::

"GO NO FARTHER, TRAITOR," Dama Everal said, moving to block the entrance to the Andrah's throne room. He was the oldest of the Andrah's sons, almost certain to become *Damaji* on the death of Amadeveram, and likely Andrah after that. At fifty, he was still robust and black-haired, a *sharusahk* master said to have no equal.

He was also the last of the Andrah's sons Jardir would have to kill before he could gut the fat old man.

It was not yet a month since, covered in demon gore, Jardir had announced himself the Deliverer in the Maze. Three-quarters of the *Sharum* had declared for him on the spot. Half the *dama* as well, with more converting daily. The remainder rallied to their *Damaji*, who attempted to defend their own palaces at first, but finally, as Jardir's power grew, fled through the Undercity and barricaded themselves behind the walls of the Andrah's palace.

His conquest might have lasted days rather than the weeks it had taken, but each nightfall, Jardir blew the Horn of Sharak, calling his warriors to the Maze. The meanest soldier had a battle-warded spear now, and the *alagai* greeted the sun in droves.

Free to regroup at night, the Andrah and *Damaji* had thought this a great advantage, but they had not reckoned with the shame this caused their remaining *Sharum*, denied *alagai'sharak* by their leaders while Jardir's men saw endless glory. Warriors deserted nightly, and were welcomed in the

Maze without question. At last, there were not enough to hold even the An-drah's walls. Jardir's men had taken the gates shortly after dawn, and breached the palace doors soon after. Now there was only one man between Jardir and his vengeance.

"Your forgiveness, Dama," Jardir said, bowing to Everal, "but I cannot offer you surrender as I have other men, for who could trust a man not will-ing to die for his own father? Better that you die with honor."

"Pretender!" Everal spat. "You are no Deliverer, just a murderer with a stolen spear. You would be nothing without it!"

Jardir stopped short, holding up a hand to halt the warriors behind him. "Think you truly so?" Jardir asked.

Everal spat at his feet. "Put the weapon down and face me without its tainted magic, if it is not so."

"*Acha!*" Jardir said, and tossed the spear to Everal. The *dama* caught the weapon reflexively, his eyes widening as he realized what he now held.

Something changed in Everal then, a subtle shift in his stance and dispo-sition. The others might not have noticed, but it was as clear to Jardir as if the *dama* had spoken. Before, he had thought himself a doomed man, deter-mined only to inflict some damage before he died. Now Dama Everal had a glimmer of hope in his eyes, a belief that he might kill Jardir and end the re-bellion that had pierced the heart of Krasia.

Jardir nodded. "Now your soul is prepared to meet Everam with honor," he said, and launched himself at the *dama*.

Everal was a *sharusahk* master, but the Evejah forbade clerics the spear, and in all Jardir's years in Sharik Hora he had never seen that law broken. He expected the *dama's* spearwork to be poor and easily defeated.

Seek every advantage, Khevat taught.

But Everal surprised him, spinning the spear about like a whip staff. It moved invisibly fast as the *dama* came at him, and for a few moments it was all Jardir could do to keep from its path. Everal's moves were fast and pre-cise, one attack flowing smoothly into the next as one would expect from a man who had spent four decades in Sharik Hora. Everal brought the point into play at last, scoring a line on Jardir's cheek, and another cut in his arm.

At last, Jardir saw the rhythm behind the *dama's* attacks and came in quick to hook his arm around the spear's shaft and pivot, throwing the *dama* across the hall where he struck a column and landed heavily.

Jardir waited for Everal to roll to his feet, then laid the spear on the floor. The *dama's* eyes widened.

"You are a fool to give up your advantage," Everal said, but Jardir only smiled, having taken the cleric's measure. He came in with his arms spread, and Everal met him, more than willing to grapple.

To the untrained eyes of the *Sharum,* what followed must have appeared a simple struggle that strength would tell, but in truth the hundreds of subtle shifts and twists were *sharukin,* designed to turn an opponent's own energy against him.

Little by little, Jardir worked his way toward a death hold. It was inevitable, and he could see in the *dama's* eyes that Everal knew it, too.

"Impossible," Everal gasped as Jardir's hand came around his throat.

"There is a difference, *dama,*" Jardir said, "between strength gained fighting air, and strength gained fighting *alagai.*" He pulled hard, and Everal's neck snapped with a sound that echoed in the hall.

The *Damaji* were clustered at the foot of the dais to the Andrah's throne. They looked up as one when Jardir's men smashed in the doors. The Andrah cowered and cringed on the Skull Throne, gripping the arms so tightly his knuckles showed white.

Jardir looked at the cluster of old men with a predatory eye. Evejan law gave each of them the right to challenge him to single combat on his way to the dais. Jardir did not fear the *Damaji,* but he had no wish to kill them.

"Kill them if you must," Inevera had said, "but your conquest will be more complete if you break their will for the fight." She had even told him what to offer.

"Damaji," he said. "All of you are loyal servants of Everam, and I wish no quarrel with you. I ask only that you step aside."

"And what will become of us, after you sit the Skull Throne?" Kevera of the Sharach asked. As *Damaji* to Krasia's smallest tribe, it was his place to offer the first challenge.

Jardir smiled. "Nothing, my friend. You *Damaji* fear for your palaces? Keep them, and minister to your tribes as you always have. I ask only a symbolic gesture of support."

Kevera's eyes narrowed. "And that is?"

"My second son by Qasha is *nie'dama,*" Jardir noted.

Kevera nodded. "A promising one."

Jardir smiled. "I would ask that you keep him ever at your side, that he may learn at your sandals."

"And one day succeed me," Kevera stated more than asked.

Jardir shrugged. "If that is *inevera.*"

Jardir eyed the other *Damaji* as they digested the offer, and again marveled at the completeness of Inevera's planning. His *dama'ting* wives had been fertile, and the dice never failed to predict the right moments to conceive. Each bride had presented Jardir with two sons and a daughter by their fourth year of marriage, and their bellies had continued to swell afterward. He had a *nie'dama* son in every tribe now, to take the black turban when the current *Damaji* died, even as his own wives would do on the passing of their tribe's *Damaji'ting*. Inevera had laid the groundwork for him to assume power more than a decade ago. It was . . . unsettling.

The *Damaji* continued to consider. Their titles were not hereditary, but to a man they had sons and grandsons among their tribes' *dama*, and it was not uncommon for the black turban to be passed along bloodlines. Still, retaining their own power would take some of the sting from his ascension, and if it grated on the *Damaji* to give up aspiration for their sons, it remained preferable to seeing them put to the spear, as Kaji had done to the sons of his defeated enemies. Jardir could easily do that as well, and they knew it. There was no need for him to offer his own sons as hostages, save in a sincere gesture of unity.

For the lesser tribes, this was enough.

"Shar'Dama Ka," Kevera of the Sharach said, bowing and stepping aside.

The others followed suit, parting before him like *ala* before the plow: The Bajin, Anjha, Jama, Khanjin, Halvas, and Shunjin all let him pass without challenge. Jardir tensed as he approached the Krevakh and Nanji *Damaji*. The Watcher tribes were intensely loyal, and practiced their own schools of *sharusahk,* said to be the deadliest in all the Desert Spear. Jardir felt Everam's will thrumming in him, and did not fear any man, but he kept on guard, respecting their skills.

He needn't have worried. The Watcher *Damaji* were much as their *Sharum,* preferring to observe and advise, not lead. They stepped aside, leaving only the three most powerful *Damaji* standing between him and the Skull Throne: Enkaji of the Mehnding, Aleverak of the Majah, and Amadeveram of the Kaji. These men ruled thousands and lived in lavish excess. Their tribes had dozens of *dama*, including their own sons and grandsons. They would not surrender so easily.

Enkaji of the Mehnding was a powerfully built man, still robust at fifty-five. He was known as a man of great cleverness as well, leader of a tribe filled with battle engineers. His tribe may have been smaller, but Enkaji was wealthier than the Majah and Kaji *Damaji* combined, and it was no secret the *Damaji* had long meant to pass that wealth to his eldest son.

Their eyes met, and Jardir thought for a moment the man might actually challenge him. He was readying for the fight when the *Damaji* laughed rue-fully and spread his hands in an exaggerated bow as he cleared the path to the dais.

Aleverak of the Majah was next. The ancient *Damaji* was nearly eighty, but nonetheless he bowed and assumed a *sharusahk* stance. Jardir nodded, and the *Sharum* and *Damaji* at his back spread wide to give the men room to fight.

Jardir bowed deeply. "You honor me, Damaji," he said, assuming a stance of his own. He was impressed the old man was still alive, much less still possessed of his warrior's spirit. He deserved an honorable death.

"Begin!" Amadeveram shouted, and Jardir shot forward, meaning to grapple and end the battle swiftly and bloodlessly. He might yet force a sub-mission from the *Damaji's* living lips.

But Aleverak surprised him, twisting sharply and much more quickly than Jardir would have believed possible. He caught hold of Jardir's arm and used his own momentum against him.

Feeling his joints scream, Jardir had no choice but to go limp and follow the *Damaji's* throw. He landed on his back, and the gathered crowd gasped in amazement. Aleverak advanced quickly, driving a bony heel down at Jardir's throat, but Jardir caught the foot in both hands, twisting in opposite directions as he got his feet under him.

Aleverak accepted the twist, leaping into it and again using Jardir's own strength against him as he kicked Jardir in the mouth with his free foot. Again Jardir found himself hitting the marble floor, with Aleverak still on his feet.

Everyone watched the battle with great interest now. A moment ago the fight had been about giving an old man an honorable death—a footnote in the tale of Jardir's ascension. But suddenly everything Jardir had built was in jeopardy. His sons were still too young to properly defend themselves if his enemies bared knives at them without Jardir's protection. The Andrah leaned forward on this throne, watching intently.

Aleverak charged again, but Jardir managed to get his feet back under him in time and met him head-on. This time, he kept his feet firmly planted, giving the old man no energy to turn back on him. Aleverak's blows were amazingly quick, but Jardir still blocked the first two. The third he let go through, accepting the punch in exchange for the opportunity to lock on to the *Damaji's* arm.

Aleverak offered Jardir no energy for a throw of his own, but whereas the ancient Damaji was little more than tough skin over sharp bone, Jardir was thick with muscle, a warrior in his prime. He did not need to steal energy to throw a man who weighed little more than his age.

Jardir flexed and pivoted sharply, hurling Aleverak away from him. The *Damaji* twisted with the move, never losing his balance even as he was thrown, and Jardir knew he would land on his feet and come right back in.

Jardir kept hold of Aleverak's arm, ducking under it to aid his twist and putting a foot into the old man's back as he hit the floor. He pulled hard, and the snap of Aleverak's shoulder echoed up to the great domed ceiling above. Bone tore through the *Damaji's* white robes, which quickly ran red.

Jardir moved to finish him quickly before pain could unman him, but Aleverak never screamed, never offered submission. Jardir met the ancient *Damaji's* eyes and saw a focus that denied all pain as Aleverak struggled back to his feet. His honor was boundless as he took a new stance, his left arm leading as his right hung twisted, limp, and bloody.

"You cannot prevent my ascending to the Skull Throne, Damaji," Jardir said as they slowly circled. "And most of your tribe has already sworn to me. See reason, I beg. Is a grave for you and your sons so preferable to being advisor to the Shar'Dama Ka?"

"My sons will no more turn our tribe over to you without a fight than I will," Aleverak said. Jardir knew it was true, but he was loath to kill Aleverak all the same. Too many honorable men had died already, and with Sharak Ka coming, Ala had none to spare. His thoughts flashed back to the Par'chin, lying facedown in the sand, and shame brought mercy to his lips.

"I will let your sons offer one challenge to mine, on your death," Jardir offered at last. "Let them decide among themselves who it will be."

There was a buzz of angry chatter among the surrendered *Damaji* at that, but Jardir glared at them. "Silence!" he roared, and they all fell still. He turned back to Aleverak.

"Will you be at my side, Damaji, as Krasia rises back to glory?" he asked. The *Damaji* was growing paler by the second from blood loss. If he did not acquiesce, Jardir would kill him quickly, that he might die on his feet.

But Aleverak bowed, glancing to his bleeding shoulder. "I accept your offer, though that challenge may come sooner than you think."

It was true. Jardir's Majah son, Maji, was only eleven, and would prove no match to one of Aleverak's sons should the *Damaji* die from his wound. "Hasik, escort Damaji Aleverak to the *dama'ting* for healing," Jardir ordered.

Hasik moved to the old man's side, but Aleverak held up a hand. "I will see this through, and Everam decide if I live or die this day." The steel in his voice held Hasik at bay, and Jardir nodded, turning to Amadeveram, the last *Damaji* between him and the cowering Andrah.

Amadeveram was younger than Aleverak, but still a man in his seventies. Jardir knew better than to underestimate him, though, especially after the fine showing of the older cleric.

"Me, you will have to kill," Amadeveram said. "I will not be bought with honeyed promises."

"I am sorry, Damaji," Jardir said, bowing, "but I will do what I must to unite the tribes."

"Murder me now, or when your son comes of age," Amadeveram said, "it is still murder."

"You will be dead by then anyway, old man!" Jardir snapped. "What does it matter?"

"The sovereignty of the Kaji tribe matters!" Amadeveram shouted. "We have held the Skull Throne for a hundred years, and will hold it a hundred more!"

"No," Jardir said, "you will not. I bring an end to tribes. Krasia will be one again, as it was in the time of Kaji himself."

"That remains to be seen," Amadeveram said, assuming a *sharusahk* pose.

"Everam will welcome you," Jardir promised, bowing. "You have a *Sharum's* heart."

🜋

Less than a minute later, Jardir looked up at the cowering Andrah atop the dais. "You are an insult to the skulls of the brave *Sharum* that support your fat backside," Jardir told him. "Come down and let us end this."

The Andrah made no effort to rise, instead seeming to shrink farther into the great chair. Jardir scowled, taking the Spear of Kaji and climbing the seven steps to the Skull Throne.

"No!" the Andrah cried, curling into a ball and hiding his face as Jardir raised his spear.

For more than a dozen years, since seeing the fat man with his wife in their marriage bed, Jardir had envisioned killing the Andrah every single day. Inevera's dice had told him he would one day have his vengeance, and he had clung to that prophecy desperately. Only *alagai'sharak* offered him distraction, and each sunrise the Andrah still lived was a blow to his honor. How many times had he practiced the speech he would recite to the man at this moment?

But now, disgust welled in Jardir's throat like bile. The pathetic ball of flesh before him had commanded all of Krasia for Jardir's lifetime and more, and yet he had not even the courage to look his death in the face. He was less than *khaffit*. Less even than the filthy pigs *khaffit* ate. He was not worthy of a speech.

The kill brought none of the satisfaction it had in Jardir's fantasies. It was more of a mercy to rid the world of such a man.

�

The Andrah's white outer robe was stained with blood when Jardir pulled it on over his *Sharum* blacks. He felt the eyes of all in the throne room lying heavily upon him, but he straightened under the weight and turned to face them.

Aleverak lay on the floor now, with Dama Shevali putting pressure on his wound. Amadeveram lay dead halfway down the steps. Jardir bent to the *Damaji* and pulled the black turban from his head.

"Dama Ashan of the Kaji, step forth," he commanded. Ashan came to the foot of the steps and knelt, placing both hands and his forehead on the floor. Jardir lifted away his friend's white turban, replacing it with the *Damaji's* black.

"Damaji Ashan shall lead the Kaji," Jardir announced, "and may pass the black turban to his sons by my sister Imisandre." He embraced Ashan like a brother.

"The Daylight War is over," Ashan said.

Jardir shook his head. "No, my friend. It has yet to begin. We shall rebuild our forces, fill the bellies of our women, and make ready for Sharak Sun."

"You mean . . . ?" Ashan asked.

"North," Jardir agreed, "to conquer the green lands and levy their men for Sharak Ka." There was a gasp from the remaining *Damaji*, but none dared question him.

A moment later the *Sharum* guarding the entrance gasped and hurriedly parted. In through the gap flowed the *Damaji'ting* and Jardir's wives. It was against Evejan law for any man to harm a *dama'ting*, and so his power over the women was limited, but they had their own intrigues in the *dama'ting* pavilion, and it seemed Inevera had proven as adept there as in manipulating the politics of men. Each of his wives wore a black headscarf with a white veil over her *dama'ting* white robe, showing that she was heir to succeed her tribe's *Damaji'ting*. Jardir had no idea how Inevera had done it.

Belina, his Majah wife, separated herself from the others to rush to

Aleverak's side. Jardir could recognize any of his wives at a glance, even in their full robes. Qasha could not hide her curves, nor Umshala her height. Belina had a walk that marked her as clearly as her face. The Majah *Damaji'ting* followed after her, seeming more the student than the mistress.

For a moment there was no sign of Inevera, but then he heard the *Sharum* gasp and saw men stiffen in fear. He looked up and saw his First Wife enter the room—but as only he should see her. Her brightly colored scarf and veil were diaphanous, as were the gossamer wisps of material that seemed to float about her like smoke, leaving nothing of her beauty to the imagination. Her night-black hair was netted in gold and oil-scented. Her arms and legs tinkled with jewelry of gem and warded gold. She wore no mark of caste or rank. Only her *hora* pouch, secure at her belt, marked her as more than a wealthy *Damaji's* most favored pillow dancer.

Inevera held all eyes as she glided into the room—both the dumbstruck gapes of the men, and the cold assessment of the *Damaji'ting*. Jardir's face heated as she went to him, and against his will, he felt stirrings best left to the bedchamber. He tried to retain his composure, but she went right up to him, pulling aside her veil to kiss him deeply. She draped her soft body about him as if she were posing for a statue, marking him before all like a bitch marked a corner.

"What in Nie's abyss are you playing at?" he whispered sharply.

"Reminding them that the Shar'Dama Ka is not bound by the laws of men," Inevera said. "Take me right on the Skull Throne with all watching, if you wish. None will dare protest." She slipped a hand between his legs and caressed him softly. Jardir gasped.

"*I* would protest," he hissed, pushing her out to arm's length. Inevera shrugged, smiling widely and caressing his face.

"All Krasia rejoices in your victory today, husband," she said loudly for the room to hear.

Jardir knew he should respond in kind, making some bold speech, but such political posturing sickened him still, and he had other concerns.

"Will he live?" Jardir asked, nodding to Aleverak. The *Damaji* had lost great pools of blood, and his arm was a twisted ruin.

Belina shook her head. "Doubtful, husband," she said, bowing her head as a proper wife—something his *dama'ting* wives had never done before.

"Save him," Jardir murmured to Inevera.

"To what end?" Inevera breathed through her veil for his ears alone. "Aleverak is stubborn and too powerful. Better to remove him."

"I promised him that when he dies, his heir may challenge Maji for the Majah palace," Jardir said.

Inevera's eyes bulged. "You did *what*?!" Everyone glanced her way, but the look was gone in an instant, and her body eased once more. She pulled away and sashayed down the dais steps, the sway of her hips, visible through her diaphanous robe, drawing the gaze of every man in the room. Jardir's honor howled for him to gouge out every eye for feasting on what should be his alone.

Belina and the Majah *Damaji'ting* both bowed deeply and moved from Inevera's path. "Damajah," they greeted her in unison.

Aleverak had passed out from the loss of blood by the time Inevera finished examining the wound. She stood and looked to the *Sharum*. "Draw every curtain and close every door," she commanded, and as several warriors rushed to comply, she had the others encircle her and the injured *Damaji* with their backs to her, holding up and interlocking their shields to bathe her and Aleverak in darkness.

In the darkened room, Jardir could see the faint glow of *alagai hora* pulsing through the living wall, accompanied by the rhythmic sound of Inevera's chanted prayers. The glow throbbed for several minutes as the men in the room stood in awe.

Inevera gave a command, and the circle of *dal'Sharum* broke. Warriors rushed to open curtains, restoring light to the room, and there, lying calm next to Inevera, was Damaji Aleverak. Stripped to the waist, his flesh had lost its gray pallor, and he breathed comfortably. Gone were any signs of his wound, the bone or bleeding or even a scar. There was only smooth flesh across his shoulder.

Smooth flesh where there should have been an arm. The limb was nowhere to be seen.

"Everam has accepted Damaji Aleverak's arm as a token of his submission," Inevera announced loudly. "Aleverak is forgiven for doubting the Deliverer, and if he walks Everam's true path from now on, he will rejoin his lost limb in Heaven."

She went back to Jardir, draping herself over him once more. "My husband must cool his blood after such a victory as today's," she said loudly, addressing the entire room. "Leave us, that I may tend him in private, as only a wife can."

There was a shocked murmuring among the men at this. It was unheard of for a woman, even a *Damaji'ting,* to give such orders to *Damaji.* They looked to Jardir, but when he did not contradict her, they had no choice but to comply.

"Are you an idiot?" Inevera snapped, when they were alone. "Putting your control of the Majah—not to mention your son—at risk, and for what?"

Jardir noted how she put Maji second. "I do not expect you to understand why it had to be done."

"Oh?" Inevera asked, her tone venomous. "Is your *Jiwah Ka* such a fool, then? Why should she be unable to understand the wisdom here?"

"Because it is a matter of honor!" Jardir snapped. "And you have shown you do not waste a moment's thought on such foolish things."

Inevera glared at him for a moment, and then turned away, her *dama'ting* serenity back in place. "It is no matter. Aleverak's heirs can be dealt with in time."

"You will not interfere in this," Jardir said. "Maji will just have to prove the stronger."

"And if he fails?" Inevera asked.

"Then Everam does not wish him to lead the Majah," Jardir said.

Inevera looked ready to respond, but only shook her head. "It isn't a total loss. Word of your crippling Aleverak but allowing him to live and serve you still will only add to your legend."

"You sound like Abban," Jardir muttered.

"Eh?" she asked, though he knew she heard full well.

"Enough," he said. "It is done and there is nothing for it. Now put on a decent robe and veil before you put impure thoughts into the minds of my men."

"Bold as ever," Inevera said, but she smiled behind her translucent veil, seeming more amused than irritated. "The Evejah commands women to wear veils so no man covet what is not his, but you are the Deliverer. Who would dare covet your woman? I have nothing to fear if I walk naked through the streets."

"Nothing to fear, perhaps, but what advantage comes with the baring of your sex like a whore for any man to see?" Jardir asked.

Inevera's eyebrows tightened, though her face remained serene. "I bare my face that none might mistake me. I bare my body that your power might be increased, for having such manly lusts that even the leader of the *Dama-ji'ting* must be prepared to service you instantly."

"Another deception," Jardir said wearily, sitting upon the throne.

"Not at all," Inevera purred, sliding into his lap. "I am fully prepared to stand responsible for the lusts of Shar'Dama Ka."

"You make it sound a task," Jardir said. "A tedious price of power."

"Not so tedious," Inevera said, tracing a finger down his chest. She undid the fastenings of his pantaloons and moved to mount him.

Jardir could not deny the lust her beauty roused in him, but he felt, too, the Skull Throne under him, and he looked up as Inevera sheathed herself upon him, much as she had ridden the Andrah. Killing the man had done nothing to excise the image from his mind. It haunted him like a spirit denied passage to the next life.

Did Inevera truly feel passion at his touch, or were her moans and gyrations just another mask, like the opaque veil she had cast aside? Jardir honestly did not know.

He stood up, lifting her off him. "I am in no mood for such games."

Inevera's eyes widened, but she held her temper. "This says differently," she purred, squeezing his stiffened member.

Jardir pushed her away. "It does not rule me," he said, redoing the fastenings at his waist.

Inevera gave him the look of a coiled snake, and for a moment he thought she would attack him, but then her *dama'ting* serenity returned. She shrugged as if his refusal was no matter, glided from the dais, hers hips swaying hypnotically as she descended.

ॼ

Hasik touched his forehead to the marble floor before the dais of the Skull Throne.

"I have brought the *khaffit*, Deliverer," he said with distaste. When Jardir nodded, the guards opened the door and Abban limped in. When he drew close to the dais, Hasik shoved Abban forward, meaning to drive him to his knees, but Abban was quick with his crutch and somehow managed to keep his feet.

"Kneel before Shar'Dama Ka!" Hasik roared, but Jardir raised a hand to stay him.

"If I am to die, at least allow me to do it on my feet," Abban said.

Jardir smiled. "What makes you think I wish to kill you?"

"Am I not another loose thread to be clipped?" Abban asked. "Like the Par'chin before me?" Hasik growled and his grip tightened on his spear as his eyes filled with murderous rage.

"Leave us," Jardir said, whisking a hand at Hasik and the other guards. As they complied, Jardir descended from the dais to stand before Abban.

"You speak things best left unspoken," he said quietly.

"He was your friend, Ahmann," Abban said, ignoring him. "But then, I suppose I was once, as well."

"The Par'chin showed you the spear," Jardir realized suddenly. "You, a simpering fat *khaffit*, laid eyes on the Spear of Kaji before me!"

"I did," Abban agreed, "and I knew it for what it was. But I did not steal it from him, though I could have. A simpering fat *khaffit* I may be, but I am no thief."

Jardir laughed. "No thief? Abban, that is *all* you are! You steal relics from the dead and cheat men in the bazaar every day!"

Abban shrugged. "I see no crime in salvaging what no man claims is his, and haggling is just another form of battle, with no dishonor to the victor. I speak of killing a man—a friend—that you might take what is his."

Jardir snarled and his arm shot out, taking Abban by the throat. The fat merchant gasped and clutched at Jardir's fingers, but he might as well have tried to bend steel. His knees buckled, putting his full weight on the arm, but still Jardir held him up. Abban's face began to turn purple.

"I will not have my honor questioned by a *khaffit*," he said. "My loyalty is to Krasia and Everam before friends, however brave they may be.

"Where are *your* loyalties, Abban?" he asked. "Do you even have any, beyond protecting your own fat skin?" He released Abban, who fell to the floor, gasping for air.

"What does it matter?" Abban choked out after a moment. "With the Par'chin dead, Krasia has no use for me."

"The Par'chin is not the only greenlander in the world," Jardir said, "and no Krasian knows of the green lands like Abban the *khaffit*. You are of use to me yet."

Abban raised an eyebrow. "Why?" he asked, the fear leaving his voice.

"I don't have to answer your questions, *khaffit*," Jardir said. "You will tell me what I wish to know either way."

"Of course," Abban said with a nod, "but it might be easier to simply answer my question than to call your torturers and sift the knowledge from my screams."

Jardir considered him a moment, then shook his head and chuckled despite himself. "I had forgotten that you find your courage when there is a scent of profit in the air," he said, reaching out a hand to pull Abban to his feet.

Abban bowed with a smile. "*Inevera*, my friend. We are all as Everam made us." For a moment, the years fell away, and they were to each other as they once had been.

"I am going to begin Sharak Sun, the Daylight War," Jardir said. "As Kaji before me, I will conquer the green lands and unite them all for Sharak Ka."

"Ambitious," Abban said, but there was doubtful condescension in his tone.

"You do not think I can do this?" Jardir asked. "I am the Deliverer!"

"No, Ahmann, you are not," Abban said quietly. "If it was anyone, we both know it was the Par'chin."

Jardir glared at him, and Abban glared right back, as if daring Jardir to strike him.

"So you won't help me willingly," Jardir said.

Abban smiled. "I never said *that*, my friend. There is great profit in war."

"But you doubt I can succeed," Jardir said.

Abban shrugged. "The Northland is far bigger than you think, Ahmann, and more populous than Krasia by far."

Jardir scoffed. "You doubt any ten, any *hundred* Northern cowards can match even one *dal'Sharum?*"

Abban shook his head. "I would never doubt you about great things like battle. But I am *khaffit*, and doubt small things." He looked at Jardir pointedly. "Like the food and water supplies you would need to cross the desert. The men you would need to leave behind to hold the Desert Spear and captured territory. The wagonloads of *khaffit* to serve the army's needs, and women to sate their lusts. And who would protect the women and children you leave behind? The *dama?* What will they turn this city into while you are gone?"

Jardir was taken aback. Indeed, in his dreams of conquest in battle, such things had seemed too inconsequential to matter. Inevera had been masterful in manipulating his rise, but somehow he doubted she considered such things, either. He looked at Abban with new respect.

"My coffers would open wide to someone who could care for such small things," he said.

Abban smiled, bowing as low as his crutch would allow. "It would be my pleasure to serve the Shar'Dama Ka."

Jardir nodded. "I want to march in three summers." He put his arm around Abban, drawing him close like a friend and putting his lips within inches of Abban's ear.

"And if you ever try to cheat me like some mark in the bazaar," he added in a low voice, "I will tan your skin and use it as a dung sack. That is a promise you should remember."

Abban paled and nodded quickly. "I will never forget it."

CHAPTER 10

KHA'SHARUM

:: 331 AR ::

JARDIR HISSED, EMBRACING THE CUT.

"Am I hurting you?" Inevera asked.

"I've taken far worse in the Maze," Jardir scoffed. "But if you should slip at a tendon . . ."

Inevera snorted. "I know the course of a man's flesh far better than you, husband. This is no different than carving *alagai hora.*"

Jardir looked at the silver tray that held the thin strips of flesh she had sliced from the palm of his hand. He let the sting pass through him as Inevera packed herbs into the wounds. "I fail to see the need for this."

"According to the Canon we took from one of the Northern Messengers in the dungeon, the greenlanders believe the Deliverer will have marked flesh that corelings cannot abide," Inevera said. She let go of his hand, allowing him to raise it before his eyes, marveling at the precision of the ward she had cut into the skin.

"Will they work?" he asked, flexing his hand experimentally.

Inevera nodded. "When I am through, your touch will bring more harm to the *alagai* than a thrust from the Spear of Kaji itself."

Jardir felt a thrill run through him. The thought of wrestling a demon on its own terms and killing it with his bare hands was intoxicating.

Inevera had just finished binding the hand when Damaji Ashan entered the throne room, followed by his son Asukaji and Jardir's second son,

Asome. Both young to be wearing the white robes of *dama*, but they were Blood of the Deliverer, and none dared question it.

"Deliverer," Ashan greeted him, bowing. "The *khaffit*," he spat the word as if it had a foul taste, "is here with the tallies." Jardir nodded, and Abban limped into the room on his ivory camel crutch while Inevera draped herself at Jardir's feet. Damaji Aleverak followed Abban in, the empty right sleeve of his robe pinned back. Jardir's son Maji, in his *nie'dama* bido, shadowed his steps. They joined Ashan, Asukaji, and Asome to the right of the Skull Throne.

Abban bowed and pulled a small vial from his belt. He threw it to Jardir. "Dama Qavan of the Mehnding asked me to give you that," he said.

Jardir caught the vial and looked at it curiously. "He asked you to give this?"

"The contents, anyway," Abban said. "Mixed in your food or drink."

Inevera snatched the vial from Jardir and pulled the stopper, sniffing the contents. She put a drop on the tip of her finger, tasting it.

"Tunnel asp venom," she said, spitting. "Enough to kill ten men."

Jardir tilted his head at Abban "What did he pay you?"

Abban smiled, lifting a jingling sack of coins. "A *Damaji's* ransom."

Jardir nodded. Damaji Enkaji of the Mehnding had proven a vocal supporter of him in public, but this was not the first assassination attempt to come from one of his minions.

"I'll have Dama Qavan arrested and put to the question," Ashan said.

"It's a waste of time," Abban said. "He won't betray his *Damaji* to your torturers. He is better left alone."

"No one asked your opinion, *khaffit*!" Damaji Aleverak growled, making Abban jump. "We can't let the man live to further plot against the Shar'-Dama Ka."

"Perhaps the *khaffit* has a point, husband," Inevera interrupted, drawing the outraged glare Aleverak always gave when the woman dared speak her mind before the Skull Throne. "Abban can tell Qavan you ate the poison without so much as a cramp, and seed the tale in the bazaar to spread it everywhere. Project such invincibility, and even the bravest assassin may reconsider his course."

"The Damajah is wise," Abban said with a bow. They were two of a kind, he and Inevera, always twisting others to their wishes. Jardir saw the *khaffit's* eyes flick to her, just for an instant, drinking of his wife's wantonly displayed beauty. He swallowed a flare of anger. Inevera said it should make him feel powerful to flaunt something other men coveted, but even after two years the opposite still held true.

But like it or not, both Abban and Inevera had skills Jardir needed, skills that the *dama* and *Sharum* sorely lacked. Abban's tallies and Inevera's dice gave only brutal truth, while every other man in Krasia fell over himself to say only what they thought Jardir wished to hear, even if the words held no truth at all.

Jardir had grown to depend on them, and both knew it, continuing to dress outlandishly, adorned with golden trinkets, as if daring Jardir to punish them.

"Damaji Enkaji is powerful, Deliverer," Abban reminded him, "and his tribe's engineering skills are essential to your preparations for war. You already slight him by denying him a place in your inner council. Perhaps now is not the time to follow a trail that may lead to him and force you to act publicly."

"Savas is not yet old enough to become *Damaji* of the Mehnding," Inevera added, speaking of Jardir's Mehnding son. "They will not follow a boy still in his bido."

They were right. If Jardir killed Enkaji before Savas earned the white robe, the black turban would simply pass on to one of Enjaki's sons, who would bear Jardir the same animosity their father did, if not more.

"Very well," he said at last, though it sickened him to play Inevera and Abban's games. "Spin your web over Qavan. Now on to the tallies."

"As of this morning, there are 217 *dama*, 322 *dama'ting*, 5,012 *Sharum*, 17,256 women, 15,623 children, including those in *Hannu Pash*, and 21,733 *khaffit* living in the Desert Spear," Abban said.

"That isn't enough warriors if we are to march in another summer," Jardir said. "Only a few hundred come out of *Hannu Pash* each year."

"Perhaps you should delay your plans," Abban suggested. "In a decade, you could double your forces."

Jardir felt Inevera's hand squeeze his leg, her long nails digging into flesh, and shook his head. "We delay too long as it is."

Abban shrugged. "Then you will have to march with the warriors you have next year. Not six thousand."

"I need more," Jardir insisted.

Abban shrugged. "What can I do? It's not as if *dal'Sharum* are stores of grain hidden in the bazaar, with merchants waiting for the price to go up before bringing them out."

Jardir looked at him so sharply that Abban flinched.

"Something I said?" he asked.

"The bazaar," Jardir said. "I haven't been there since the day Kaval and Qeran took us from our homes." He stood up, drawing a white outer robe over the *Sharum* blacks he still wore. "Show it to me now."

"Me?" Abban asked. "You wish to walk the street next to a *khaffit*?"

"Is there anyone better suited?" Jardir asked. Everyone else in the room turned to stare at Jardir in horror.

"Deliverer," Ashan protested, "the bazaar is a place for women and *khaffit* . . ."

Aleverak nodded. "That ground is not worthy of the Shar'Dama Ka's feet."

"I will decide that," Jardir said. "Perhaps there is yet some worthiness to be found there."

Ashan frowned, but he bowed. "Of course, Deliverer. I will prepare your bodyguard. A hundred loyal *Sharum*—"

"No bodyguard is necessary," Jardir cut in. "I can protect myself from women and *khaffit*."

Inevera stood, helping Jardir arrange his robes. "At least let me throw the dice first," she whispered. "You will draw assassins like a dung cart draws flies."

Jardir shook his head. "Not this time, *jiwah*. I feel Everam's hand today without that crutch."

Inevera did not seem convinced, but she stepped aside.

A weight lifted off Jardir as he strode from the palace. He could not remember the last time he had left its walls in daylight. He had loved the feel of the sun, once. His back straightened as he walked, and something in Jardir . . . hummed. He felt a rightness to his actions, as if Everam Himself guided them.

Time seemed to stop as Jardir and Abban walked through the Great Bazaar, merchants and customers alike freezing in place as they passed. Some stared in wonder at the Deliverer, and others stared in greater shock at the *khaffit* by his side. Whispers grew in their wake, and many began to drift after them.

The bazaar ran along the lee side of the city's inner wall for miles to either side of the great gate. Seemingly endless tents and carts, great pavilions and tiny kiosks were arrayed, not to mention countless roving food and trinket vendors, porters to carry purchases, and great crowds of shoppers, haggling for bargains.

"It's bigger than I remember," Jardir said in surprise. "So many twists and turns. The Maze seems less daunting."

"It is said no man may walk so far as to pass every vendor in a single day," Abban said, "and more than one fool has been left trying to find their way clear of it when the *dama* sound the curfew from the minarets of Sharik Hora."

"So many *khaffit*," Jardir said in wonder, looking out at a sea of shaved faces and tan vests. "Even though I hear them in the tallies every morning, the number never truly struck me. You outnumber everyone else in Krasia."

"There are benefits to being denied the Maze," Abban said. "Long life is one of them."

Jardir nodded. Another thing he had never considered before. "Does your heart ever miss it? Beneath the cowardice, do you ever wish you had seen the inside of the Maze?"

Abban limped quietly for a long time. "What does it matter?" he asked at last. "It was not meant to be."

They walked a bit farther, when Jardir stopped suddenly, staring. Across the street stood a giant *khaffit*, easily seven feet tall and rippling with muscle under his tan vest and cap. He had a huge barrel of water slung under each long arm, seeming no more strained than if he were holding a pair of sandals.

"You there!" Jardir called, but the giant did not reply. Jardir strode across the street to him, grabbing him by the arm. The *khaffit* turned suddenly, startled, and nearly dropped the water barrels before he caught himself. "I called to you, *khaffit*," Jardir growled.

Abban put a hand on Jardir's arm. "He did not hear you, Deliverer. The man was born without hearing." Indeed, the giant was moaning and pointing frantically toward his ears. Abban made a few quick gestures with his hands that calmed him.

"Deaf?" Jardir asked. "Did that cause him to fail at *Hannu Pash*?"

Abban laughed. "Children with such faults are never called to *Hannu Pash* in the first place, Deliverer. This man was *khaffit* the moment he was born."

Another *khaffit*, a fit-looking man of some thirty-five years, came out of a booth, stopping short in shock at the sight of them.

"Hold," Jardir commanded as the man tried to escape. Immediately the *khaffit* fell to his knees, pressing his face into the dirt.

"O great Shar'Dama Ka," the man said, groveling. "I am unworthy of your notice."

"Have no fear, my brother," Jardir said, laying a gentle hand on the terrified man's shoulder. "I have no tribe. No caste. I stand for all Krasia, *dama*, *Sharum*, and *khaffit* alike."

The tension in the man seemed to ease at Jardir's words. "Tell me, why do you wear the tan, brother?"

"I am a coward, Deliverer," the man said, his voice tightening with shame. "My will broke on my first night in the Maze. I cut my tether, and I . . . ran from my *ajin'pal*." He began to weep, and Jardir let it run its course. Then he squeezed the man's shoulder, making him look up.

"You may walk behind me on my tour of the bazaar," he said, and the man gasped in shock. "The earless one, as well," Jardir told Abban, who made more signs to the giant. The two men fell obediently in behind Abban and Jardir, followed by all who had witnessed the event, man and woman. Even the vendors left their wares unattended to walk behind the Deliverer.

Everywhere he looked, Jardir saw more and more fit men in the tan, each with his own reasons for being denied the black. None dared lie to him when pressed as to why.

"I was sickly as a child," one said.

"I cannot see colors," another said.

"My father bribed the *dama* to overlook me," a third dared admit.

"I need lenses for my eyes," many told him, and others had been thrown from the *sharaj* simply for being left-handed.

Jardir squeezed the shoulder of each one, and gave them permission to follow him. Before long, a huge crowd trailed him, sweeping everyone it passed up in its wake. Finally, Jardir looked back at them all, a throng of thousands, and nodded. He leapt atop a vendor's cart to stand above the crowd, looking over the women and *khaffit*.

"I am Ahmann asu Hoshkamin am'Jardir asu Kaji!" he cried, holding up the Spear of Kaji. "I am Shar'Dama Ka!" The crowd roared in response, startling Jardir with a strength and power he had never dreamed existed.

"Everam has charged me with destroying the *alagai*," Jardir shouted, "but to do that I need *Sharum*!" He swept his hand out over the crowd. "I see among you fit men who were denied the spear as children, forcing you to live in shame and poverty as your brothers and cousins walked in Everam's glory. Putting shame upon your parents and children, as well."

The men Jardir had asked to follow him were nodding and agreeing with his words. "We have the magic to destroy the *alagai* now," he said. "Our spears skewer them by the hundreds, but we have more spears than men to carry them. And so I offer you all this second chance! Any able-bodied *khaffit* who wishes to join in *alagai'sharak* may present himself to the training grounds tomorrow, where every tribe shall raise a *khaffit'sharaj* to train you. Those who complete the training shall be named *kha'Sharum*, and given warded weapons to buy your way back to glory and Heaven for yourselves and your families!"

There was a shocked silence as his words sank in. Men who had spent their lives under the heel of the *Sharum,* bent and toiling under the weight of their caste, began to straighten their backs. Jardir could see into their minds, it seemed, as they imagined the glory that might await them, the chance for a better life.

"Sharak Ka is coming!" Jardir shouted. "There is honor enough for all in the Great War. Who among you will swear to fight it alongside me?"

The first man Jardir had asked to follow him, the one who had run from his *ajin'pal* in the Maze, pushed to the front of the crowd, kneeling.

"Deliverer," he said, "my heart has been heavy since my failure in the Maze. I beg you for a second chance." Jardir reached down with the Spear of Kaji, touching his shoulder.

"Rise, *kha'Sharum,*" Jardir said.

The man did as he was bade, but before he had risen fully, a spear struck him in the back. Jardir caught him before he could fall, looking deep into his eyes as he coughed a gout of blood.

"You are saved," Jardir told him. "The gates of Heaven will be open to you, brother."

The man smiled as the light left his eyes, and Jardir set him down, looking at the spear jutting from his back. It was one of the short, close-quarter weapons favored by Nanji Watchers.

Jardir looked up and saw three Nanji approaching, holding short spears in one hand and weighted lines in the other. Though it was day, their night veils were drawn, hiding their faces.

"You go too far, Sharum Ka, offering spears to *khaffit,*" one of the warriors called.

"We must end your life," another agreed.

They began to advance, but several *khaffit* broke from the crowd, moving to stand protectively in front of Jardir.

The Nanji laughed. "It was foolish of you to leave your palace without a bodyguard," one said. "These *khaffit* cannot protect you."

It wasn't surprising that the warriors thought the women and *khaffit* no threat, but Jardir, having felt the crowd's power just a moment before, wasn't so sure. Even so, he would ask no one to die needlessly for his sake.

Project invincibility, Inevera said, *and even the bravest assassin may reconsider his course.*

"Clear their path!" Jardir shouted as he leapt down from the cart. The startled men stepped aside immediately.

"You think three warriors can kill me?" Jardir laughed. "If a hundred Nanji skulk in the shadows, I would need no more bodyguard than now." He rested the point of the Spear of Kaji down in the dirt and threw out his chest, inviting attack. "I am Shar'Dama Ka!" he cried, feeling the rightness of the words. "Strike at me if you dare!"

The Nanji approached, but Jardir could see hesitation in them now. His very presence unnerved them. Their spears shook in their hands, and they glanced to one another uncertainly as if to decide which should lead the attack.

"Strike or kneel!" Jardir roared. He brought up the Spear of Kaji, and the bright metal caught the sunlight and seemed to flare with power.

One of the Nanji warriors dropped his spear and fell to his knees. "Traitor!" the one next to him cried, turning to stab at him, but the third was quicker, darting in and putting his spear through the aggressor's chest.

There was a creak behind Jardir. A whisper of sandal on canvas. Knowing Nanji tactics, he turned around, looking up at the true assassin, crouched hidden atop the pavilion behind him. This Watcher should have struck while Jardir was distracted by the others, ensuring a kill.

Their eyes met, but Jardir said nothing, waiting. After a moment, the man threw down his spear and somersaulted down after it, kneeling at Jardir's feet.

Jardir went to the fallen man, pulling the spear free of his back and holding it up for all to see. "This is not *khaffit* blood!" he cried. "This is the blood of a warrior, the first *kha'Sharum*, and I will lacquer his skull and add it to my throne to remember him always." He looked out at the *khaffit*. "Will any step forth to take his place?"

There was a dissonant moan, and the seven-foot deaf giant pushed to the front of the crowd, kneeling at Jardir's feet. Others quickly followed, and there was a frantic press to kneel before Jardir. As Jardir touched each in turn, Abban seized an opportunity to speak.

"Fear not, those of you who cannot carry a spear from age or infirmity!" he cried. "Fear not, you women, you children! The Deliverer needs more than just *Sharum*! He needs weavers to make nets and smiths for spearheads. Canvas for the *kha'Sharum* pavilion, and food for its warriors. Come to my pavilion on the morrow, if you wish to put aid to Krasia's glory and bring honor to your families!"

Jardir frowned, knowing Abban acted as much to profit from cheap labor as to aid in the war, but he did not contradict him. The labor would be needed if they were to march in a year.

The crowd began to chant his name as Jardir continued to touch men with the Spear of Kaji and name them *kha'Sharum*. Soon it thundered from the bazaar, echoing throughout the city.

"Jardir! Jardir! Jardir!"

"Masterfully done," Abban said in his ear when he had touched the last *khaffit*. "You've bought ten thousand warriors and twice as many slaves for naught but a taste of self-respect."

"Is that all you see with your merchant's heart?" Jardir asked, looking at him. "A business transaction?"

Abban at least had the decency to look ashamed, though Jardir doubted it was sincere.

The next day, two thousand men presented themselves at the training grounds, as the tribes were still erecting *khaffit'sharaj*. A week later, the number had tripled. A week after that, a steady stream flowed in from the outer villages as men who had been *khaffit* for ten generations came to break their caste, bringing their families with them to share in the war effort. In less than a month, Jardir tripled the size of his army, and the city swelled with people as it hadn't in decades.

"Next summer," Jardir said again as Abban finished his morning tallies.

"The greenlanders will still outnumber us greatly," Abban said.

Jardir nodded. "Perhaps, but the best of the Northern weaklings will not be able to stand up to even a *kha'Sharum* by then."

"How many will you leave here, to secure the Desert Spear?" Ashan asked.

"None," Jardir said, drawing looks of surprise from all in the room, even Inevera.

"You will take every warrior?" Aleverak asked. "Who will defend the city?"

"Not just every warrior, Damaji," Jardir said. "Every *one*. We must leave the Sunlit Land behind. All of us. Even the old. Even the crippled and sick. Every man, woman, and child, city dwellers and villagers alike. We will empty the Desert Spear and lock its gates behind us, letting its impregnable walls stand in defiance of the *alagai* until we choose to reclaim it."

Aleverak's eyes lit up with a fanatical gleam.

"This is a dangerous plan, Deliverer," Ashan warned. "Our army will move at a crawl when it must be swift."

"At first perhaps," Jardir said. "But we will need to hold the green lands we conquer, without leaving troops behind. Everam set the *khaffit* in the Land of Sun the same as us. In the green lands, a *khaffit* who follows the Eve-jah will still rank above the *chin*. Let them settle in our wake, holding the land for Everam as the *Sharum* march on."

Jardir saw Inevera fingering her *alagai hora* pouch absently. She would excuse herself to throw the dice as soon as the audience was over, but Jardir had no doubt they would confirm his course. The rightness of it sang within him, and even Abban nodded his approval.

"When will you tell the other *Damaji*?" Ashan asked.

"Not until we're ready to leave," Jardir said, "giving Enkaji and the others no time to oppose the decision. I want the great gate at everyone's back before they have their bearings."

"And from there?" Abban asked. "Fort Rizon?"

Jardir shook his head. "First, Anoch Sun. Then the green lands."

"You have found the lost city?" Abban asked.

Jardir gestured to a table covered in maps. "It was never truly lost. There were detailed maps in Sharik Hora all along. We simply stopped going there after the Return."

"Unbelievable," Abban said.

Jardir looked at him. "What I don't understand is how the Par'chin found it. Searching the desert would take a lifetime. He must have had help. Who would he have gone to in search of that?"

Abban shrugged. "There are a hundred merchants in the bazaar claiming to sell maps to Anoch Sun."

"Forgeries," Jardir said.

"Not all, apparently," Abban said.

Jardir knew the *khaffit* could dance between truth and lie as easily as a man might breathe in and out. "*Inevera*," he said at last, holding up the Spear of Kaji. "No thing happens, but that Everam wills it."

CHAPTER 11

ANOCH SUN

:: 332 AR ::

THE OASIS OF DAWN was a place of great beauty, a series of warded sandstone monoliths protecting a wide grassy area, several clusters of fruit trees, and a broad pool of fresh, clean water, fed by the same underground river that supplied the Desert Spear. There was a stair cut into the *ala* beneath one monolith, leading to a torchlit underground chamber where a man could cast nets into the river and easily catch a feast.

It was a small oasis, meant as a way station for merchant caravans but more often used by lone Messengers. It was, of course, never meant to supply the greatest army the world had seen in centuries.

Jardir's host fell upon it like locusts, surrounding the monoliths with thousands of tents and pavilions. Before most of the Krasians had even arrived, the trees were stripped of fruit and cut for firewood, the grasses mown clean by grazing livestock and trampled flat. Thousands of men wading into the pool to wash their feet and fill their skins left only a fetid, muddy puddle in their wake. They cast nets in the underground fishing chamber, but what would have been a rich catch to a caravan was not even a morsel to the Krasian horde.

"Deliverer," Abban said, approaching Jardir as he surveyed the camp. "There is something I think you should see."

Jardir nodded, and Abban led him to a large block of sandstone covered in carvings. Some were the barest etchings, faded over many years, and others sharp and fresh. Some were crude scratches, and others great designs worked in artful script. They were all in the Northern style of writing, an ugly form with which Jardir was only passingly familiar.

"What is this?" he asked.

"Messenger markings, Deliverer," Abban said. "They are all over the oasis, naming every man who has succored here on his way to the Desert Spear."

Jardir shrugged. "What of it?"

Abban pointed to a large portion of the stone carved in flowing calligraphy. Jardir could not read the letters, but even he could appreciate their beauty.

"This," Abban said, "reads 'Arlen Bales of Tibbet's Brook.' "

"The Par'chin," Jardir said. Abban nodded.

"What else does it say?" Jardir asked.

"It says, 'Student of Messenger Cob of Miln, Messenger to dukes, known as Par'chin in Krasia, and true friend of Ahmann Jardir, Sharum Ka of the Desert Spear.' "

Abban paused, letting the words sink in, and Jardir grimaced. "Read on," he growled.

"I have been to the five living forts," Abban read, pointing to the names of the cities marked with an upward-pointing spear, "and nearly every known hamlet in Thesa." Abban pointed to another, longer list, this one showing dozens of names.

"These names, marked with the downward spear, are ruins he has visited," Abban noted, pointing to another long list. "The Par'chin was busy in the time he spent away from the Desert Spear. There are even Krasian ruins listed here."

"Oh?" Jardir asked.

"The Par'chin was always hunting the bazaar for maps and histories," Abban said.

Jardir looked back at the list. "Is Baha kad'Everam on the list?" When Abban did not immediately reply, he turned to the *khaffit*. "Do not make me ask twice. If I ask one of our *chin* prisoners to translate the wall and learn you lied . . ."

"It's there," Abban said.

Jardir nodded. "So Abban finally claimed the rest of his Dravazi pottery," he said more than asked. Abban did not reply, but he did not need to.

"What's this last one?" Jardir asked, pointing to the large carving at the end of the list, though he could well guess.

"The last place the Par'chin went before coming to the Desert Spear," Abban said.

"Anoch Sun," Jardir said. Abban nodded.

"Can any of the other merchants read this tongue?" Jardir asked.

Abban shrugged. "A few, perhaps."

Jardir grunted. "Have men with mauls smash this stone back into sand."

"So none may learn the Shar'Dama Ka is chasing a dead *chin's* footsteps?" Abban asked.

Jardir hit him, knocking Abban to the ground. The fat *khaffit* wiped blood from his mouth, but without his usual simpering and piteous cries. Their eyes met, and immediately the rage left Jardir and he was filled with shame. He turned away, looking out at the great swath his people had cut through the sand, and wondered if any of them had trodden unknowingly upon the buried bones of his friend.

🜋

"You are troubled," Inevera said when Jardir retired to his pavilion. It was not a question.

"I wonder if the true Deliverer was troubled at every turn," Jardir said, "or if he sensed Everam guiding his actions, and simply followed the path before him."

"You *are* the true Deliverer," Inevera said, "so I imagine it was much the same for Kaji as it is for you."

"Am I?" Jardir asked.

"You think it a coincidence that the Spear of Kaji was delivered into your hands right at the time you were in position to seize control of all Krasia?" Inevera asked.

"Coincidence?" Jardir asked. "No. But you have been 'positioning' me for more than twenty years. There's more of demon dice in my rise than deservedness."

"Was it demon dice that claimed the hearts of the *khaffit* and unified our people?" Inevera asked. "Was it demon dice that saw you to victory again and again in the Maze, before you ever laid eyes on Kaji's Spear? Is it for the dice that you march now?"

Jardir shook his head. "No, of course not."

"This is about the Par'chin's sandstone carving," Inevera said.

"How do you know of that?" Jardir asked.

Inevera dismissed the question with a wave. "The Par'chin was a grave robber, nothing more. A brave one," she allowed, putting a finger to Jardir's lips to forestall his protest, "cunning and bold, but a thief all the same."

"And what am I, but the one who robbed him in turn?" Jardir asked.

"You are what you choose to be," Inevera said. "You can choose to be the savior of all men, or you can sulk over past deeds and let pass the opportunity before you."

She leaned in, kissing him. It was deep and warm, a kiss that gave without asking, one that reminded Jardir that even now, he still loved her. "I have faith in you, even if you do not. The dice speak Everam's will, and neither they nor I would have aided in your rise if we did not believe that you, you and no other, could shoulder this burden. Killing the Par'chin was a necessary evil, like killing Amadeveram. You would have spared them, if you could."

She slid into his arms, and as he embraced her, he felt something of his strength return. Necessary evil. The Evejah spoke of it, as Kaji accounted his own subjugation of the northern *chin*. Every *alagai* killed helped to balance those scales, and Jardir meant to kill them all before he went to the Creator to have his life's deeds weighed and judged.

כ

The scout rode his camel up to Jardir on his white horse, stopping at a respectful distance and punching a fist to his chest.

"Shar'Dama Ka," he greeted him. "We have found the lost city. It is half buried in the sand, but much of it seems intact. There are several wells that we believe can be restored to service, but little in the way of food or grazing."

Jardir nodded. "Everam has preserved the holy city for us. Send an advance group to map the city and prepare the wells. We will slaughter the livestock and preserve the meat to save our grain stores."

"Dangerous," Abban said. "Slaughtering all the animals gives no way to replenish stock."

"We must trust in the green lands to provide," Jardir said. "For now, we need as much time as possible to explore the sacred city."

The bulk of his people moved slowly, and it was days before they caught up to the scouts, who by then had mapped the sprawling city in some detail, though it was larger by far than the Desert Spear, and there might yet be parts undiscovered. There were discrepancies between the maps of the scouts and the ancient scrolls taken from Sharik Hora.

"We will divide the city by tribe, and set each *Damaji* to oversee excavation of his section, advised by his most learned *dama* and Warders. Every relic uncovered is to be catalogued and presented to me each day."

Ashan nodded. "It shall be made so, Deliverer," he said, and he moved off to instruct the other *Damaji*.

Over the next week, the tribes ransacked the ancient city, breaking through walls, looting tombs, and removing whole sections of warded walls and pillars. There had been little sign of the Par'chin's passing when they arrived, but the Krasians took no such care to leave the city intact. Rubble piled everywhere, and whole sections of street and buildings collapsed as the tunnels beneath them were compromised.

Each afternoon, the *Damaji* came before Jardir and piled high their findings. Hundreds of new wards, many of them designed to harm demons or to create other magical effects. Warded weapons and armor, mosaics, and paintings of ancient battles, some even of Kaji himself.

Each night, they fought. Demons still came thick to the city, and as the sun set Jardir's men put aside their work and took up spear and shield. With powerful wards on even the weakest *kha'Sharum's* spear, the *alagai* died by the thousands, and soon there were none left to haunt the sacred sands. *Sharum* continued to patrol, but it seemed the city was scoured clean, like a sign from Everam of the rightness of their path.

"Deliverer," Ashan said, entering the tent with Asome and Asukaji. "We've found it."

Jardir had no need to ask what "it" was, putting down his maps of the green lands and throwing on his white robe. He had not yet made it to the tent flap when Inevera appeared at the head of his *dama'ting* wives, their very presence confirming Ashan's claim. The women fell silently in behind as he walked through the city.

"Which tribe had the honor?" Jardir asked.

"The Mehnding, Father," Asome said. He was sixteen now, a man in his own right, and moved with the grace one expected of a *sharusahk* master. His soft voice seemed all the more dangerous coming from the tall, lean frame in its white robe, like a spear wrapped in silk.

"Of course," Jardir muttered. How fitting that his least loyal *Damaji* should find the tomb of Kaji.

Enkaji was waiting with Jardir's Mehnding son Savas, still in his *nie'dama* bido, when they arrived.

"Shar'Dama Ka!" the *Damaji* cried, prostrating himself on the dusty floor of the burial chamber. "It is my honor to present Kaji's tomb to you."

Jardir nodded. "Is it intact?"

Enkaji stood, sweeping his arm out toward the great sarcophagus, the stone lid of which had been removed.

"The Par'chin did his looting well, I'm afraid," Enkaji said. "The spear is missing, of course, but you have reclaimed that." He gestured to the dusty rags worn by the skeleton within. "If ever these scraps were the sacred Cloak of Kaji, I cannot say."

"And the crown?" Jardir asked as if the item were of no import, though all knew it was.

Enkaji shrugged. "Taken. The Par'chin—"

"Didn't have it with him when he came to the Desert Spear," Jardir cut him off.

"He must have hidden it somewhere," Enkaji said.

"He's lying," Abban whispered in Jardir's ear.

"How do you know?" Jardir asked.

"Trust a liar to know," Abban said.

Jardir turned to Hasik. "Seal the tomb," he commanded. Hasik signaled the *Sharum* in the hall, and they heaved the great stone back into place.

"What is this?" Enkaji asked as the torchlight from the hall winked out. Only a few guttering torches ensconced in the tomb still gave flickering light.

"Put them out," Jardir ordered. "The Damajah will cast the bones to learn who has stolen Kaji's crown."

Enkaji paled, and Jardir knew then that Abban had spoken truth. He advanced on the *Damaji,* backing him up until his back struck the tomb wall.

"For every minute that the crown is not in my hands," he promised, "I will castrate one of your sons and grandsons, starting with the eldest."

Moments later Jardir held the Crown of Kaji, found in the burial chamber of one of Kaji's great-grandsons.

It was a thin circlet of gold and jewels, worked into a pattern of unknown wards that formed a net around the wearer's head. It seemed delicate, but all Jardir's strength couldn't make the slightest bend in the gold.

Inevera bowed and took the crown, slipping it over his turban. Though light as a feather, Jardir nevertheless felt a great weight lay upon him as it settled at his brow.

"Now, we can invade the green lands," he said.

SECTION 2

OUTSIDE FORCES

CHAPTER 12

WITCHES

:: 333 AR WINTER ::

LEESHA'S PARENTS' HOME CAME into sight. It was a modest house, considering her father's means, but it served her family well enough, built against the back wall of her father's paper shop. The path leading to the front door was warded.

Not that Rojer was paying much attention. He walked slightly behind Leesha, so he could gaze at her without her noticing. Her pale skin was a sharp contrast to her night-black hair, and her eyes were the color of sky on a clear day. His eyes drifted over her curves.

Leesha turned to him suddenly, and Rojer started, quickly raising his eyes.

"Thanks again for doing this, Rojer," Leesha said.

As if Rojer could refuse Leesha anything. "It's hardly a chore to sit through a meal, even if your mother's cooking could try a coreling's teeth," he said.

"For you, maybe," Leesha said. "If I show up alone, she'll plague me until I'm ready to spit over when I'm going to find a husband. With you there, she may at least cover her fangs. Perhaps she'll even take us for a pair and draw off entirely."

Rojer looked at her, his heart stopping. He slipped into his Jongleur's mask, face and voice betraying not a bit of what he was feeling, and asked, "You wouldn't mind your mother thinking us a pair?"

Leesha laughed. "I'd love it. Most of the town would accept it, too. Only you and Arlen and I would know how ridiculous it is."

Rojer felt like she had slapped him, but his heart resumed beating, and with his mask in place Leesha noticed nothing.

"I wish you wouldn't call him that," Rojer said, changing the subject.

"Arlen?" Leesha asked, and Rojer winced. "Arlen! Arlen! Arlen!" she said, laughing. "It's just his name, Rojer. I'm not going to pretend he doesn't have one, however mysterious he wants to seem."

"I say let him seem as he likes," Rojer said. "Arrick always said, if you rehearse an act you never mean the audience to see, sooner or later they'll see it. All you need is one slip, and his name will be on every lip in town."

"So what if it is?" Leesha asked. "The 'Warded Man' isn't comfortable in town because folk treat him differently. Admitting he has a name might go a ways toward fixing that."

"You don't know what he's left behind him," Rojer said. "Could be some folk might get hurt if his name got out, or others might come hunting him with some account to settle. I know what it's like to live like that, Leesha. The Warded Man saved my life, and if he doesn't want his name out, I mean to forget I know it, even if it means giving up the song of the century."

"You can't just forget things you've learned," Leesha said.

"Not all of us have as much space upstairs as you," Rojer said, tapping his temple. "Some of us fill right up, and forget the old things we have no use for."

"That's nonsense," Leesha said. Rojer shrugged.

"Anyway, thank you again," Leesha said. "I've no end of men volunteering to stand in front of demons for me, but not one who'll stand in front of my mother."

"Reckon Gared Cutter would do both," Rojer said.

Leesha snorted. "He's as much my mother's creature as any. Gared destroyed my life, and she wants me to forgive him and make him babies still, as if him taking so well to demon killing somehow makes him a catch worth having. She's nothing but a manipulative witch, poisoning everyone around her."

"Bah!" Rojer said. "She's not so bad. Understand her, and you can play her like a fiddle."

"You're underestimating her," Leesha said. "Men see her beauty and refuse to look past it. You may think it's you doing the charming, but in truth she'll be seducing you like she does every man, turning them against me."

"That's tampweed talk," Rojer said. "Elona isn't some corespawned genius bent on destroying your life."

"You just don't know her well enough," Leesha said.

Rojer shook his head. "Arrick taught me all about women, and he said the ones like your mum, who were really beautiful once but are starting to show their age, are all the same. Elona was always the center of attention when she was young, and that's the only way she knows how to interact with the world. You and your father have long conversations about warding that she's no part of, and it makes her starve to be noticed, any way she can. Make her think she's the center of attention, even if she's not, and she'll eat out of your hand."

Leesha looked at him a moment, then barked a laugh. "Your master didn't know a thing about women."

"He sure seemed to," Rojer replied, "considering how adept he was at bedding them."

Leesha raised an eyebrow at him. "And how many has his apprentice bedded using these brilliant techniques?"

Rojer smiled. "Kissing tales aren't the kind I spin, but a Milnese sun says they work on your mum."

"Taken," Leesha said.

"So the merchant tells Arrick, 'I paid you to teach my wife to dance!'" Rojer said, "and Arrick, calm as dawn, looks at him and says, 'I *did*. Ent my fault she preferred to do it lying down.'"

Elona burst out laughing, sloshing wine from her cup as she banged it on the table. Rojer joined her, and they clapped their cups together and drank.

Leesha scowled at them from the other end of the table where she and her father were talking. She honestly didn't know which she dreaded more: winning the bet with Rojer, or losing it. Perhaps bringing him was a bad idea. The bawdy stories were bad enough, but worse was the way Rojer's eyes kept flicking to her mother's cleavage, though she could hardly blame him, the way Elona had it on display.

The plates had long since been cleared. Erny sat leafing through the book Leesha had brought him, his eyes tiny behind the thin, wire-framed glasses that never seemed to leave the edge of his nose. Finally, he grunted and set it aside for later, gesturing at the stack of bound leather books in front of Leesha.

"Only had time to make a few more," he said. "You fill them faster than I can bind."

"Blame my apprentices," Leesha said, fetching the teakettle from the fire. "They make three copies for every book I fill."

"Still," Erny said. "I only had one grimoire of wards my entire life, and never filled it. How many is this you've made now? A dozen?"

"Seventeen," Leesha said, "but it's as much demonology as wards, and more comes from the Warded Man than me. Just copying the wards on his skin filled several books."

"Oh?" Elona asked, looking up. "And how much of his skin have you seen?"

"Mother!" Leesha cried.

"Creator knows, I'm not judging," Elona said. "You could do worse than bear the Deliverer's child, even if he's a horror to look at. But you'd best get to it, if that's your plan. Plenty younger and more fertile than you will soon be vying for the privilege."

"He's not the Deliverer, Mum," Leesha said.

"That's not how everyone else tells," Elona said. "Even Gared worships him."

"Oh, and if Gared Cutter thinks something, it *must* be right," Leesha said rolling her eyes.

Rojer whispered something in Elona's ear, and she laughed again, turning her attention back to him. Leesha blew out a sigh of relief.

"Speaking of the Warded Man," Erny said, "where has he got off to? Smitt tells me another Messenger's come from the duke, summoning him to an audience, but again he's nowhere to be found on Messenger day."

Leesha shrugged. "I doubt he much cares about an audience with the duke. He doesn't consider himself one of Rhinebeck's subjects."

"You'd best tell him to think twice," Erny said. "The Hollow isn't producing wood like it should, and Rhinebeck is getting angry. Ignoring Messengers may hold him off now, while the road is choked with snow and he can't send a sizable force, but come spring melt the duke will want answers, and assurance that Deliverer's Hollow remains loyal."

"Does it?" Rojer asked, looking up. "If the Warded Man sets himself at odds with Rhinebeck, the Hollow would likely flock to his banner in an instant."

"Yes," Erny agreed. "Other hamlets, as well, and probably a great many folk in Fort Angiers itself. The Warded Man could start a civil war with a word, which is why it's all the more important he declare his intentions before Rhinebeck does something rash."

Leesha nodded. "I'll talk to him. I have unfinished business in Angiers, myself."

"The only unfinished business you have is under your skirts," Elona muttered. Rojer choked and wine spilled from his nose. Elona smiled smugly as she sipped from her cup.

"At least I can keep mine around my ankles!" Leesha snapped.

"Don't you take that tone with me," Elona said. "I may not know anything about politics or demonology, but I know you're a winter away from becoming a spinster crone, and no matter how many corelings you leave dead behind you, you'll still go to your grave regretting not having *added* life to the world."

"I'm the town Herb Gatherer," Leesha said. "Saving those who would have otherwise died doesn't count as adding life to the world?"

"Vika saves lives," Elona said, referring to one of Leesha's fellow Gatherers. "Din't stop her raising a brood for Tender Jona. Midwife Darsy'd do the same in an instant, if she could find a man able to close his eyes and stiffen long enough to put a child in her homely womb."

"Darsy's done more for this town than you ever will, Mother," Leesha said. She and Darsy, both former apprentices of Hag Bruna, had been at odds once, but no longer. Darsy was now Leesha's most devoted student, if not her best.

"Nonsense," Elona said. "I did my duty, and gave the town *you*. You may be ungrateful for it, but I think the Hollow benefits well enough for my troubles."

Leesha scowled.

"Any fool watching you and the Warded Man together can tell there's been something between you," Elona pressed, "and that it's not to either of your satisfaction. Did he fail abed?" she asked. "Darsy gives me herbs for your father when he—"

"That's ridiculous!" Rojer cried as Erny flushed red. "Leesha would never—"

Elona cut him off with a snort. "Well she sure ent going with you. It's plain as day you got the eye for her, but you ent good enough, fiddle boy, and you know it." Rojer's face turned beet red. His mouth opened, but no sound came out.

"You've got no right to talk to him like that, Mother," Leesha said. "You don't know—"

"Always what I don't know!" Elona barked. "Like your poor mum is too dim to see the sun shining in her face!" She gulped her wine, and her face took on a cruel cast Leesha knew well, and feared.

"Like I know the boy's song about how the Warded Man found you after you was left for dead by bandits on the road," Elona said. "And I know how men treat women like us, when there ent no one to stop them."

"Mother," Leesha warned, her voice hardening.

"Not how I'd wanted you to lose your flower," Elona said, "but it was time it was done somehow, and I expect you're the better for it."

Leesha slapped her hand down on the table, glaring. "Get your cloak, Rojer," she said. "It's getting dark, and we're safer out among the demons." She shoved the blank books into her satchel and set it over her shoulder as she snatched her richly embroidered cloak from the peg by the door and threw it about her shoulders, clasping it at her throat with a silver ward pin.

Erny came over, hands spread in apology. Leesha embraced him as Rojer put on his cloak. Elona stayed at the table with the wine.

"I really wish you wouldn't walk around after dark, magic cloak or no," Erny said. "We can't exactly replace you."

"Rojer has his fiddle," Leesha said, "and I have more tricks than wards of unsight, if a coreling were to somehow find us. We're quite safe."

"You can witch all the Core to your bidding, but not a simple man," Elona sneered into her glass.

Leesha ignored her, putting up her hood and stepping out into the dusk.

"Now do you believe me?" she asked Rojer as the door closed behind them.

"Seems I owe you a sun," Rojer admitted.

The snow crunched under Leesha's booted feet as she and Rojer headed to the village proper. Their breath fogged in the crisp winter air, but their cloaks were lined with fur and kept them warm enough.

Rojer hadn't said a word since Elona's comment. His head was down, face buried under long locks of red hair. His fiddle was tucked in its case, slung beneath his motley cloak, but she could tell from the way his fingers flexed that he longed to hold it. He always played the fiddle when he was upset.

Leesha knew Rojer shined on her. Most everyone knew, really. Half the women in town thought she was mad for not snatching him up. And why not? Rojer had a boyishly pretty face and a quick wit. His music was beautiful beyond words, and he could bring a laugh from Leesha when she was at her lowest. He'd shown more than once that he was willing to die for her.

But try as she might, Leesha could not bring herself to see him as a lover. Rojer had barely seen eighteen winters, a full ten years younger than her, and he was her friend. In many ways, Rojer was her only friend. The only person she trusted. He was the little brother she'd never had. She didn't want to hurt him.

"Your apprentice Kendall saw me the other day," Leesha said. "Pretty girl."

Rojer nodded. "My best student, too."

"She asked if I knew how to brew a love potion," Leesha said.

"Ha!" Rojer barked. Then he stopped short and looked at her. "Wait, can you?"

Leesha laughed. "Of course not. But the girl doesn't need to know that. I gave her a tincture of sweet tea instead and told her to share it with her would-be love. Watch out if she offers you tea, or you might be in for a night of kissing."

Rojer shook his head. "Never stick your apprentice."

"Another of Master Arrick's brilliant maxims?" Leesha quipped.

Rojer nodded. "And one I'm happy to report he practiced as well as preached. I knew other apprentices in the guild who weren't so lucky."

"This hardly compares," Leesha said. "Kendall's nearly as old as you are, and she's the one buying love potions."

Rojer shrugged and put his hood up, pulling the edges of his motley cloak together to strengthen the wardnet. The last of the light had faded, and all around them misty forms were rising from the snow, solidifying into corelings that hissed and cast about, scenting them in the air but unable to find them.

Erny had set his house away from the village so that he would not have to endure complaints about the smell of his papermaking chemicals, but that distance also put it outside the great ward of forbidding that protected the village proper.

A wood demon wandered into Rojer's path, sniffing the air. Rojer froze, not daring to move as it searched. There was a sharp movement under the cloak, and she knew one of the warded throwing knives he kept strapped to his wrists had fallen into the palm of his good hand.

"Just walk around it, Rojer," Leesha said, continuing down the path. "It can't see or hear you." Rojer tiptoed around the demon, twirling the knife nervously in his fingers. He had grown up juggling blades and could put one into a coreling's eye at twenty paces.

"It's just unnatural," Rojer said, "walking plain as day through hordes of corelings."

"How many times must we do it before you tire of saying that?" Leesha sighed. "The cloaks are safe as houses." The Cloaks of Unsight were her own invention, based on wards of confusion the Warded Man had taught her. Leesha had modified the wards and embroidered them with gold thread into a fine cloak. Demons ignored her when she wore it, even if she walked right up to them, so long as she moved at a slow, steady pace and kept it wrapped around her.

She'd made Rojer's cloak next, embroidering the wards in bright colors to match his Jongleur's motley, and she was pleased to see that he seldom removed it, even in daylight. The Warded Man never seemed to wear the one she had made for him.

"Nothing against your wards, but I don't think I ever will," Rojer said.

"I trust your fiddle magic to keep me safe," Leesha said. "Why don't you trust mine?"

"I'm out here in the dark, aren't I?" Rojer asked, fingering his cloak. "It's just eerie. I hate to say it, but your mother wasn't far off the mark when she called you a witch."

Leesha glared at him.

"A Ward Witch, at least," Rojer clarified.

"They used to call Herb Gathering witching, too," Leesha said. "I'm just warding, same as anyone."

"You're not the same as anyone, Leesha," Rojer said. "A year ago, you couldn't ward a windowsill, and now the Warded Man himself takes lessons from you."

Leesha snorted. "Hardly."

"See the light," Rojer said. "You argue his own wards with him all the time."

"Arlen is still thrice the Warder I am," Leesha said. "It's just . . . it's hard to explain, but after looking at enough wards, the patterns started . . . speaking to me. I can look at a new ward and just by studying the lines of power, guess its purpose more often than not. Sometimes I can even change the lines to alter the effects. I've been trying to teach the knack to others, but none seems to get past rote."

"That's what fiddling's like for me," Rojer said. "The music speaks to me. I can teach my apprentices to play songs well enough, but you don't play 'The Battle of Cutter's Hollow' for the corelings to pacify them. You have to . . . massage their mood."

"I wish someone could massage my mother's mood," Leesha muttered.

"About time," Rojer said.

"Ay?" Leesha asked.

"We'll be in town soon," Rojer said. "The sooner we talk about your mum, the sooner we'll be done talking about it, and can get on with our business there."

Leesha stopped short and looked at him. "What would I do without you, Rojer? You're my best friend in the world." She put just the right emphasis on the word *friend*.

Rojer shifted awkwardly, walking on. "I just know how she gets to you."

Leesha hurried after. "I hate to think my mum could be right about anything . . ."

"But she often is," Rojer said. "She sees the world with cold clarity."

"Heartless clarity is more like it," Leesha said.

Rojer shrugged. "Rabbit in one hat, bunny in the other."

Leesha casually reached out to take snow from a low branch in her gloved hand, but Rojer noted the move and easily dodged the snowball she threw at him. It struck a wood demon, which looked about frantically for its assailant.

"You want children," Rojer said bluntly.

"Of course I do," Leesha said. "I always have. Just never seemed to find the right time."

"The right time, or the right father?" Rojer asked.

Leesha blew out a breath. "Both. I'm only twenty-eight. With the help of herbs, I can likely carry a child to term for another two decades, but never as easily as I might have ten, or even five years ago. If I'd married Gared, our first child might be fourteen now, and there would likely have been several more after that."

"Arrick used to say, *There's nothing gained in lamenting what never was,*" Rojer said. "Of course, he was living proof of how hard those words are to live by."

Leesha sighed, touching her belly and imagining the womb within. It wasn't Gared she lamented, really. Her mother had been right about the bandits on the road, as Rojer well knew. But what she had never told him, or anyone, was that it had been her fertile time when it happened, and she had feared a child might come of it.

Leesha had hoped Arlen would add his seed when she seduced him a few days later. If he had, she would have raised the child, if one came, in the hope it sprang from tenderness and not violence. But the Warded Man had refused, vowing to have no children lest the demon magic that gave him his strength infect them somehow.

So Leesha had brewed the tea she had sworn never to brew, and ensured that the bandits' seed could find no purchase. When it was done, she had wept bitterly over the empty cup.

The memory brought fresh tears, cold lines streaking her cheeks in the winter night. Rojer reached out, and she thought he meant to wipe them away, but instead he put his hand into her hood and withdrew it suddenly, producing a multicolored handkerchief as if from her ear.

Leesha laughed despite herself, and took it to dry her tears.

By the time they reached town, half a dozen corelings were trailing them, sniffing at the footprints in the snow beyond the radius of the cloaks' magic. A woman at the edge of the forbidding raised her bow, and warded arrows struck the demons like thunderbolts, killing those that failed to flee.

All the young women in Deliverer's Hollow studied the bow now, starting as soon as they could hold one. Many of the older women, not strong enough to pull a great bow, had begun learning to aim a loaded crank bow so they could throw in. The women worked in shifts to patrol the edge of town, killing any demons that ventured too close.

As they came into the light, Leesha saw Wonda waiting for them. Tall, strong, and homely, it was easy to forget the girl was only coming to her fifteenth summer. Her father, Flinn, had died in the Battle of Cutter's Hollow, and Wonda was sorely wounded. She'd recovered fully, though she was badly scarred, and had become attached to Leesha during her time in the hospit. Wonda followed Leesha like a hound, ready to kill any coreling that came near. She carried the yew great bow the Warded Man had given her, and could put it to deadly use.

"I wish you'd let me escort you, Mistress Leesha," Wonda said. "You're too important to walk alone outside the forbidding."

"That's what my father says," Leesha said.

"Your father is right, mistress," Wonda said.

Leesha smiled. "Perhaps when your Cloak of Unsight is finished."

"Really?" Wonda asked, her eyes widening. Each cloak took many, many hours to make, and was a royal gift.

"If you're determined to shadow my steps," Leesha said, "I don't see there's much alternative. I gave the pattern to my apprentices to embroider last week."

"Oh, thank you, mistress!" Wonda said, throwing her long arms around Leesha and hugging her in a girlish fashion that seemed unfit for one taller and stronger than most men.

"Air," Leesha gasped at last, and Wonda let go and drew back quickly, looking sheepish.

"Isn't she a little young to be venturing outside the forbidding?" Rojer asked quietly as they headed into town. The cobbled streets of Deliverer's Hollow looped and twisted awkwardly and often inconveniently, but in so doing they formed a huge, complex ward of protection designed by the Warded Man himself. No coreling, big or small, could rise through the soil of the town proper, nor set foot upon it, nor fly above. The streets glowed softly, warm with magic.

"She does it already," Leesha said. "Arlen caught her out hunting demons alone twice last week. The girl's determined to get herself cored. I want to keep her where I can see her."

Once, the village would have been dark and silent after sunset, but now the glowing cobbles cast light for dozens of people moving to and fro. The Hollow had lost many in the battle almost a year ago, but its numbers had swelled as folk filtered in from nearby hamlets, drawn to the growing legend of the Warded Man. These newcomers stared and whispered to one another as Rojer and Leesha, the Warded Man's only known confidants, passed.

They entered the Corelings' Graveyard, which was once the old town square where so many demons and Hollowers had perished. Despite its name, the graveyard was still the center of activity for the town: the place where the villagers trained and where the Cutters assembled each night to receive the blessings of Tender Jona before heading out to hunt demons. They stood there now, heads and broad shoulders bowed, drawing wards in the air as Jona prayed for their safety in the naked night.

Other villagers stood by, heads bowed to join in the blessing. There was no sign of the Warded Man. He spared no time for blessings, likely already out hunting. Sometimes days passed with no sign of him other than demon bodies left freezing in the snow until the morning sun rose to burn them from the world.

"There's your promised," Rojer said, nodding toward Gared Cutter, who stood at the forefront of the Cutters, stooping low so that Tender Jona, whom Gared had bullied as a child, could take a charcoal stick and draw a ward on his forehead.

A giant, Leesha's former betrothed towered over even the other Cutters, few of whom stood under six feet. His hair was long and blond, and his bronzed arms were thick with muscle. A pair of warded axe handles jutted over his shoulders, and his gauntlets, tough leather bolted to hammered steel etched with wards, hung from his belt. They would soon be black with sizzling demon ichor.

Gared was not the oldest of the Cutters, nor the wisest by any means, but he had emerged from the Battle of Cutter's Hollow a leader whom even the eldest followed without question. It was he who shouted at the men to train harder in the day, led the charge at night, and left more dead corelings in his wake than any save the Warded Man himself.

"Whatever he's done to you," Rojer said, "you have to admit, he's the sort that gets songs sung and statues made for him."

"Oh, there's no denying he's beautiful," Leesha said looking at Gared. "He always was, and drew others to worship him like iron to a magnet. I was one of them, once."

She shook her head wistfully. "His da was the same way. My mother broke her wedding vows repeatedly with him, and on an animal level, I even understand it. Both men were perfect specimens on the outside."

She turned to Rojer. "It's the inside that worries me. The Cutters follow Gared without question, but does he lead them in defense of the Hollow, or out of love of carnage?"

"We thought the same about the Warded Man, once," Rojer reminded her. "He proved us wrong. Perhaps Gared will, too."

"I wouldn't gamble on it," Leesha said, turning away from the scene and continuing on.

At the far end of the graveyard stood the Holy House, and built onto the side of the stone building was the new hospit, completed before the first snows.

"Ay, Mistress Leesha! Rojer!" Benn called, spotting them. The glass-blower was standing with his apprentices, who where carrying blown items and large sheets of glass. Nearby, a group of fiddlers stood, tuning their instruments in a clamor. Benn gave a few quick instructions to his apprentices and came over to meet them.

"Ready to charge when you are, Rojer," he said.

"How were last night's results?" Leesha asked.

Benn reached into a pocket, producing a small glass vial. Leesha took the item, running her fingers over the wards thoughtfully. It seemed like ordinary glass, but the wards were smooth, as if the bottle had been heated again after they were etched.

"Try and break it," Benn encouraged.

Leesha cast the vial down onto the cobbles as hard as she could, but the glass only bounced, ringing a clear note. She picked it up, studying it closely; there wasn't the slightest mark upon it.

"Impressive," she said. "Your warding is improving."

Benn smiled and bowed. "You can break one on an anvil, if you're determined, but it ent easy."

Leesha frowned and shook her head. "They should resist even that. Let me see one you haven't charged yet."

Benn nodded, signaling an apprentice who brought another vial, almost identical to the first. "Here's one of those we mean to charge tonight."

Leesha studied the vial closely, tracing her fingernail down into the grooves of the etching. "Might be that the depth of the groove affects the power of the charge," she mused. "I'll think on it." She slipped the vials into a pocket in her apron for later study.

"We've got production running smoothly now," Rojer said. "Benn and his apprentices blow and ward by day, and my apprentices and I lure corelings in to charge them at night. Soon every home will have windows of warded glass, and we'll be able to store liquid demonfire in quantity without fear."

Leesha nodded. "I'd like to observe the charging tonight."

"Of course," Rojer said.

Darsy and Vika were waiting by the hospit doors. "Mistress Leesha." Vika greeted her with a curtsy as they arrived at the hospit. She was a plain woman, neither beautiful nor ugly, sturdily built with breeder's hips and a round face.

"You don't have to curtsy every night, Vika," Leesha said.

"Course I do," Vika said. "You're town Gatherer." Vika was a full Herb Gatherer herself, but she and Darsy, both years Leesha's senior, accepted Leesha as their leader.

"I doubt Bruna put up with that," Leesha said. Her mentor, the town's last Gatherer, had been a woman of terrible temper who spat upon meaningless formality.

"The old crone was too blind to see it," Darsy said, coming up and giving Leesha a nod of greeting. Bowing and scraping was not Darsy's way, but there was as much deference in that nod as in all Vika's curtsies and *mistresses*.

The daughter of Cutter stock, Darsy was tall and heavyset, though more with muscle than fat. She could overmatch most men at festival feats of strength, and the heavy warded blade at her waist had cut the limbs from more than one demon seeking to finish off an injured person on the battlefield.

"Hospit's ready, if the Cutters come back with wounded," Darsy said.

"Thank you, Darsy," Leesha said. The hospit was always busiest at midnight, when Cutters came back from the hunt. Even against warded axes, wood demons could be a terrifying foe. Under the canopy of trees, their skin blended into the bark as if they wore Cloaks of Unsight, and while some walked the forest floor, looking much like trees themselves, others stalked the limbs like monkeys, dropping unexpectedly on their prey.

Even so, fatalities among the Cutters were few. When a warded weapon struck a demon and flared to life, there was always feedback. The magic jolted through the wielder, bringing with it a flash of ecstasy and a feeling of invincibility. Those who tasted the magic were stronger and healed faster, at least until the dawn. Only Arlen still had power in the day.

"What are the apprentices working on?" she asked Vika.

"Eldest are embroidering your cloak patterns," Vika said. "The rest are sterilizing instruments and practicing their letters."

"I've brought fresh books and a new grimoire I've completed," Leesha said, handing her the satchel.

Vika nodded. "I'll have it copied right away."

"You have your Gatherer's apprentices copying wards?" Rojer asked. "Isn't that better handled by Warders' apprentices? I could have a word . . ."

Leesha shook her head. "Every one of my girls gets warding lessons now. I won't have them left helpless at sunset like we were."

Leaving Leesha to make her rounds in the hospit, Rojer went over to the music shell at the edge of the square where his apprentices gathered. They were a mixed bunch, as motley as Rojer's pants. Some were Hollowers, but most had come from other towns, drawn to the tales of the Warded Man. Half of them were too old to lift a tool or weapon, and so they decided to try the fiddle, only to find that their fingers lacked the necessary dexterity. Several others were children whose skill might not tell for many years.

Only a handful of the remainder showed promise, pretty Kendall most of all. She was Rizonan, and new to the Hollow. Old enough to handle complex arrangements, but young enough to still learn quickly, she had a real aptitude for music. She was slender and quick, as adept at tumbling and acrobatics as fiddling. She would make a fine Jongleur one day.

Rojer did not immediately acknowledge his apprentices, and they knew to keep back until he did. He took out his fiddle and plucked the strings, checking their tune. Satisfied, he took up the bow in his crippled hand. He was missing his index and middle fingers, bitten off by a flame demon when he was only a child, but his two remaining fingers were limber and strong, and the bow became like an extension of his arm.

All the feelings he had hidden behind his Jongleur's mask that night found voice in his music then, as he filled the square with a haunting melody. Layer by layer, he added complexities to the music, limbering his muscles and readying himself for the night's work.

The apprentices applauded when he was finished, and Rojer bowed before taking them through a series of simpler melodies to warm them up. He winced at all the discordant notes. Only Kendall was able to keep pace with him, her face knit tight in concentration.

"Terrible!" he snapped. "Has anyone other than Kendall even lifted their fiddle since last night? Practice! All day, every day!"

Some of the apprentices grumbled at that, but Rojer played a jarring series of notes on his fiddle, startling them. "Don't want to hear your grumbles, either!" he barked. "We're looking to charm demons, not spin a wedding reel. If you ent gonna take that seriously, it's time to put your fiddle back in its case!"

Everyone looked at their feet, and Rojer knew he had been too harsh. Not half as harsh as Arrick would have been, but more than felt fair. He knew he should say something encouraging, but nothing came to mind. Arrick hadn't set much example there.

He walked away, breathing deeply. Without even thinking about it, he put his bow back to work, turning his guilt and frustration into music. He let the emotions drift off with the sounds, and he looked back to his apprentices and made the music speak to them, giving the hope and encouragement his words lacked. As he played, folk began to straighten, their eyes growing determined once more.

"That was beautiful, Rojer," a voice said when he finally took bow from string. Rojer saw Kendall standing beside him. He hadn't even noticed her approach—lost in his music.

"Are you thirsty?" Kendall asked, holding up a stone jug. "I brewed sweet tea. Still hot."

Did Leesha know all along she meant it for me? Rojer wondered.

You ent good enough, fiddle boy, Elona had said, *and you know it.*

Leesha knew it, too, it seemed. She might as well have tied Kendall with a bow.

"Never much cared for sweet tea," Rojer said. "Makes my hands shake."

"Oh," Kendall said, deflating. "Well . . . that's all right."

"I want you to solo tonight," Rojer said. "I think you're ready."

Kendall brightened. "Really?" She gave a squeal and threw her arms around him, hugging a bit longer than was precisely necessary.

Of course, that was when Leesha chose to arrive. Rojer stiffened, and Kendall pulled back in confusion until she saw Leesha. She quickly stepped away from Rojer and dipped into a curtsy. "Mistress Leesha."

"Kendall." Leesha greeted her with a smile. "Is that sweet tea I smell?"

Kendall blushed a deep red. "I, ah . . ."

Rojer scowled. "Run and fetch your fiddle, Kendall." He turned to Leesha. "Kendall is going to try a solo tonight."

"Is she ready for that?" Leesha asked.

Rojer shrugged. "Is Wonda ready to hunt corelings? I was younger than Kendall when I first charmed a demon."

"Your need was more dire," Leesha said.

"It's safe," Rojer said. "I'll be ready to take over if I'm needed, and the women will be watching with arrows nocked." He nodded to the edge of the wards, where archers, including Wonda, had gathered in force.

They began preparations by ordering the archers to keep clear a wide area of ground past the edge of the forbiddance. Rojer then led his fiddlers into a series of loud, jarring notes, filling the air with an atonal cacophony that corelings hated. The music shell focused the sound to the area just outside the forbidding, where corelings tended to gather, sometimes in force.

Thus secure, the glassblower's apprentices rushed out from the forbidding and placed warded glass throughout the clearing. There were large sheets, blown bottles, vials, even a glass axe that must have taken weeks to make and ward.

When the glassblowers were safely returned, the fiddlers changed their tune. Rojer led the music, calling out instructions to the others as he did, using them to amplify his special magic as he coaxed demons out of the woods and into the clearing. He then walked alone outside the forbiddance, calling with his music, controlling each step forward the corelings took until they were arranged as he liked.

"Kendall!" he called, and the girl stepped forward and began to play. Rojer softened his music and backed away from the corelings as she strengthened hers and approached them, until he was able to stop playing entirely, leaving the mesmerized demons to her sole control.

Rojer went to where Leesha waited by the ward's edge. "She really is quite good," he said proudly. "The demons will follow her around like puppies, charging everything they touch."

Indeed, the corelings drifted after Kendall as she stepped carefully about the field. There were flares of light as demons touched the glass in their path, the etched wards siphoning off a tiny fraction of the demons' magic and guiding it to new purpose.

The corelings hissed, clawing at the areas where they had felt the drain. Kendall tried to change her music to calm them again, but her fear was apparent in her playing as she began to miss notes. She tried to increase her tempo to compensate, and that only made things worse. The demons started to shake the confusion from their heads.

Rojer moved toward her slowly in his warded cloak, with plenty of time to reach her before the corelings turned ugly, but then Kendall misstepped. A bottle shattered under her foot, sending glass through the soft leather of her shoe. She cried out, and her bow slipped from the strings with a jarring sound.

Immediately the corelings perked up, and her spell shattered. Their nostrils flared as they caught the scent of her blood, and they shrieked, launching themselves at her.

Rojer broke into a run, but he had drifted far away to speak to Leesha, and one of the corelings buried its talons deep in Kendall's body, pulling her close and sinking rows of teeth into her shoulder before he could get in range. Blood soaked her dress, and other demons leapt in, prepared to fight one another for a share of the kill.

"Archers!" Rojer cried desperately.

"We'll hit Kendall!" Wonda cried back, and Rojer saw that all the women had bows drawn, but none dared risk the shot.

He put his fiddle to work, notes meant to frighten and drive off the demons. They shrieked and broke off their attack, Kendall collapsing to the ground, but there was blood in the air now, and they were not easily driven back. They hissed and swiped, blocking Rojer's path.

"Kendall!" Rojer screamed. "Kendall!" Weakly, she lifted her head, gasping air as she reached a bloodied hand his way.

Suddenly a huge shape swept by Rojer, nearly bowling him over. He looked up to see Gared tackle one of the wood demons into another. Both corelings were brought down under the burly Cutter's weight, and the wards on his gauntlets flared brightly as he laid heavy blows on the one he had landed upon. By the time the other recovered, he was up again, but the coreling was quick and bit hard into his arm.

Gared screamed and grabbed the demon's crotch with his free hand. He flexed his mighty arms, lifting the huge wood demon and using it as a ram to drive into its fellows. He and the demons all went down in a tumble just as other Cutters rushed in, hacking at the prone creatures with warded axes.

His fiddle useless amid the commotion, Rojer hurried to Kendall's side, staining his cloak with blood as he threw it over her. Kendall croaked weakly at him as Rojer struggled to lift her. The commotion had drawn more demons from the woods, though, faster than the archers could pick them off.

Gared, an axe in each hand and blood streaming down his arm, hacked his way to them. He dropped the weapons and lifted Kendall like a feather. With the archers and Cutters providing cover, he ran her to the hospit.

"I need a blood donor!" Leesha cried as Gared kicked in the hospit door. They laid Kendall on a bed, and apprentices ran for Leesha's instruments.

"I'll do it," Rojer said, rolling up his sleeve.

"Check if he's a match," Leesha told Vika as she moved to scrub her hands and arms. Vika quickly lanced a sample from Rojer as Darsy tried to have a look at Gared's arm.

"Worry about those that are hurt worse," Gared said, pulling away. He pointed to the door, where other injured Cutters were being carried in.

There was a whirlwind of bloodied activity as the Herb Gatherers worked. Leesha cut and clamped and sewed Kendall for two hours as Rojer looked on, dizzy from the blood transfusion.

At last, Leesha paused to drag the back of a bloodied hand over her sweating brow. "Will she be all right?" Rojer asked.

Leesha sighed. "She'll live. Gared, I'll have a look at that arm now."

"It's just a scratch," Gared said.

Leesha bit back a scowl, reminding herself how brave Gared had just been, but try as she might, she could not forget how his lies had almost ruined her life, and how he had brutally beaten any man caught speaking to her after she broke off their betrothal.

"You were bit by a demon, Gar," she said. "You let the wound fester, and I'll be cutting that arm off before you know it. Get over here."

Gared grunted and complied. "It's not so bad," Leesha said, after she had washed the wound out with hogroot tincture. Charged by the magic he had absorbed, the clean cuts from the demon's sharp teeth were already closing. She wrapped the arm in a clean bandage, and then took Rojer aside.

"I told you Kendall wasn't ready for a solo," she whispered angrily.

"I thought . . ." Rojer began.

"You didn't think," Leesha said. "You were showing off, and it almost cost that girl her life! This isn't a game, Rojer!"

"I know it isn't a game!" Rojer snapped.

"Then act like it," Leesha said.

Rojer scowled. "We're not all as perfect as you, Leesha." His eyes were seething, but Leesha saw right through to the pain they hid.

"Come to my office," she said, taking him by the arm. Rojer yanked his arm away, but followed Leesha to her office, where she poured him a glass of hard alcohol more suited to antiseptics than consumption.

"I'm sorry," she said. "I was out of the light."

Rojer seemed to deflate, falling into a chair and downing the glass in one gulp. "No, you weren't," he said. "I'm a fraud."

"Nonsense," Leesha replied. "We all make mistakes."

"I didn't make a mistake," Rojer said. "I lied. I lied and said I could teach people how to charm corelings when in truth, I don't even understand how I do it myself. Just like I lied last year and told you I could see you safely here from Angiers. It's how I made my way in the hamlets after Arrick died, and how I got into the Jongleurs' Guild. Seems lying is all I ever do."

"But why?" Leesha asked.

Rojer shrugged. "Keep telling myself pretending to be something's the same as being it. Like if I just pretend to be great like you and the Warded Man, it will be so."

Leesha looked at him in surprise. "There's nothing so great about me, Rojer. You know that better than anyone."

But Rojer laughed out loud. "You don't even see it!" he cried. "An endless line of weapons and wards comes from your hut, the sick and injured cured with a wave of your hand. All I can do is play my fiddle, and I can't even save a life when I do. You and the Warded Man have become giants while I spend months teaching my apprentices, and all they're good for is getting folk to dance."

"Don't belittle the joy you and your apprentices have brought to a town fraught with hardship," Leesha said.

Rojer shrugged. "I do nothing a keg of ale can't do on its own."

Leesha took his hands in hers. "That's ridiculous. Your magic is as strong as Arlen's or mine. The fact that you have such trouble teaching it is just proof of how special you are."

She laughed mirthlessly. "Besides, however big I grow, I'll always have my mum to cut me back down."

It was a moonless night, and where Leesha and Rojer walked, far from the glow of the greatward, the darkness was near complete. Leesha walked with a tall staff, the end of which held a flask of chemics that glowed fiercely, casting light for them to make their way by. The flask and staff were etched with wards of unsight; corelings could see the light, but they could no more find the source than they could find the two of them in their warded cloaks.

"Don't see why he couldn't meet us in town," Rojer muttered. "*He* might not feel the cold, but *I* do."

"Some things are best said in private," Leesha said, "and he tends to draw a crowd."

The Warded Man was waiting for them on the warded path leading to Leesha's cottage. Twilight Dancer, his enormous black stallion, was in full barding and horns, nearly invisible in the darkness. The Warded Man himself wore only a loincloth, his tattooed skin bare to the cold.

"You're late," the Warded Man said.

"Had some problems at the hospit," Leesha said. "An accident while we were charging glass. Why aren't you wearing your cloak?" She tried to make the question seem casual, but it hurt her that for all the hours she spent on it, Leesha had never seen him wear the garment apart from the one time she threw it across his shoulders to check the fit.

"It's in my saddlebag," the Warded Man said. "Not looking to hide from corelings. They want to come at me, let them. World could do with a few less."

They tied Twilight Dancer to a hitching post in the yard and went inside. Leesha took a match from her apron and lit the fire, filling a kettle and hanging it over the blaze.

"How are the fiddle wizards coming along?" the Warded Man asked Rojer.

"More fiddle than wizard, I'm afraid," Rojer said. "They're not ready."

The Warded Man frowned. "Cutter patrols would be stronger with a fiddler who can manipulate the demons' emotions."

"I can patrol with them," Rojer said. "I have my cloak to keep me safe."

The Warded Man shook his head. "Need you teaching."

Rojer, blew out a breath, glancing at Leesha. "I'll do what I can."

"And the Hollow?" the Warded Man asked when Leesha joined them at the table.

"Expanding quickly," Leesha said. "Already we have twice as many people as we had before the flux last year, and more come in daily. We planned the new town to accommodate growth, but not at this rate."

The Warded Man nodded. "We can have the Cutters clear more land and plot another greatward."

"We need the lumber, anyway," Leesha agreed. "We haven't sent a shipment to Duke Rhinebeck in over a year."

"Had to rebuild the entire village," the Warded Man said.

Leesha shrugged. "Perhaps you'd like to explain that to the duke. He sent another Messenger, requesting an audience. They fear you, and your plans for the Hollow."

The Warded Man shook his head. "Ent got any plans, beyond making the Hollow secure from corelings. When that's done, I'll be on my way."

"But what about the Great War on demonkind?" Rojer asked. "You have to lead the people to it."

"Corespawn it, boy, I'm not the ripping Deliverer!" the Warded Man growled. "This isn't some fantasy from a Tender's Canon, and I wasn't sent from Heaven to unite mankind. I'm just Arlen Bales of Tibbet's Brook, a stupid boy with more luck than he deserved, most of it bad."

"But there's no one else!" Rojer said. "If you don't lead the war, who will?"

The Warded Man shrugged. "Not my problem. I won't force war on anyone. All I aim to do is make sure that anyone who wants to fight, can. Once that boulder shifts, I mean to get out of the way."

"But why?" Rojer asked.

"Because he doesn't think he's human," Leesha said, reproach clear in her tone. "He thinks he's so tainted by coreling magic that he's as much a danger to us as they are, even though there's not a shred of proof."

The Warded Man glared, but Leesha glared right back. "There's proof," he said finally.

"What?" Leesha asked, her voice softening but still skeptical.

The Warded Man looked at Rojer, who shrank back under the glare. "What I say stays in this cottage," he warned. "If I hear even a *hint* of it in a song or tale . . ."

Rojer held his hands up. "Swear by the sun as it shines. Not a whisper."

The Warded Man eyed him, finally nodding. His eyes dropped as he spoke. "It's . . . uncomfortable for me, in the forbidding."

Rojer's eyes went wide, and Leesha inhaled a sharp breath, holding it as her mind raced. Finally, she forced herself to exhale. She had sworn to find a cure for the Warded Man, or at least the details of his condition, and she meant to keep that vow. He'd saved her life, and that of everyone in the Hollow. She owed him that much and more.

"What are the symptoms?" she asked. "What happens when you step onto the ward?"

"There's . . . resistance," the Warded Man said. "Like I'm walking against a strong gust of wind. I feel the ward warming beneath my feet, and myself getting cold. When I walk through the town, it's like wading through hip-deep water. I pretend otherwise, and no one seems to notice, but I know."

He turned to Leesha, his eyes sad. "The forbiddance wants to expel me, Leesha, as it would any demon. It knows I don't belong among men any longer."

Leesha shook her head. "Nonsense. The ward's siphon is just drawing away some of the magic you've absorbed."

"It's not just that," the Warded Man said. "The Cloaks of Unsight make me dizzy, and I can feel warded blades warm and sharpen at my touch. I fear I become more demon every day."

Leesha took one of the warded glass vials from her apron pocket and handed it to him. "Crush it."

The Warded Man shrugged, squeezing as hard as he could. Stronger than ten men, he could easily shatter glass, but the vial resisted even his grip.

"Warded glass," the Warded Man said, examining the vial. "So what? I taught you that trick myself."

"That wasn't charged till you touched it," Leesha said. The Warded Man's eyes widened.

"Proof of what I'm saying," he said.

"The only thing it proves is that we need more tests," Leesha said. "I've finished copying your tattoos and studying them. I think the next step is to start experimenting on volunteers."

"What?!" Rojer and the Warded Man asked in unison.

"I can make a stain from blackstem leaves that will stay in the skin no more than two weeks," Leesha said. "I can perform controlled tests and mark the results. I'm certain we can—"

"Absolutely not," Arlen said. "I forbid it."

"You *forbid*?" Leesha asked. "Are you the Deliverer, to order folk about? You can forbid me nothing, Arlen Bales of Tibbet's Brook."

He glared at her, and Leesha wondered if perhaps she had pushed him too far. His back arched like a hissing cat, and for a moment she was afraid he would leap at her, but she stood fast. Finally, he deflated.

"Please," he said, his tone softening. "Don't risk it."

"People are going to imitate you," Leesha said. "Already Jona is drawing wards on people with charcoal sticks."

"He'll stop if I tell him to," the Warded Man said.

"Only because he thinks you're the Deliverer," Rojer noted, and flinched at the look the Warded Man gave him in return.

"It won't make any difference," Leesha said. "It's only a matter of time before your legend draws a tattooist to the Hollow, and then there will be no stopping it. Better we experiment now, in control."

"Please," the Warded Man said again. "Don't curse anyone else with my condition."

Leesha looked at him wryly. "You're not cursed."

"Oh?" he asked. He looked at Rojer. "Do you have one of your throwing knives?"

Rojer flicked his wrist, and a knife appeared in his hand. He spun it deftly and moved to give it to the Warded Man, handle-first, but the Warded Man shook his head. He rose and took a few steps back from the table. "Throw it at me."

"What?" Rojer asked.

"The knife," the Warded Man said. "Throw it. Right at my heart."

Rojer shook his head. "No."

"You throw knives at people all the time," the Warded Man said.

"As a trick," Rojer said. "I'm not going to throw one at your heart, are you insane? Even if you can use your demon speed to dodge . . ."

The Warded Man sighed and turned to Leesha. "You, then. Throw something—"

He hadn't even finished the sentence before Leesha snatched a frying pan off a hook by the fire and hurled it at him.

But the pan never struck home. The Warded Man turned into mist as the iron passed through, dissipating his body as if waved through smoke. It clattered against the far wall and fell to the floor. Leesha gasped, and Rojer's mouth fell open.

It took several seconds for the mists to coalesce again, re-forming into the body of the Warded Man. He breathed deeply as he became solid.

"Been practicing," he said. "Dissipation is easy. Like relaxing your molecules and spreading them the way boiling spreads water into steam. Can't do it in sunlight, but at night I can do it at will. Pulling back together is harder. Sometimes I worry I'll spread too thin, and just . . . drift away on the wind."

"That sounds horrible," Rojer said.

The Warded Man nodded. "But that's not the worst of it. When I dissipate, I can feel the Core pulling at me. When the dawn is near, the pull can become . . . insistent."

"Like that day on the road, in the predawn light," Leesha said.

"What day?" Rojer asked, but Leesha barely heard him, reliving that terrible morning.

Three days after the attack on the road, Leesha's body had healed, but the pain had not lessened. All she could think of was her womb and what might be growing there. There was a tea Bruna had taught her of, one that would flush a man's seed from a woman before it could take root.

"Why would I ever want to brew such a vile thing?" Leesha had asked. "There are few enough children in the world as it is."

Bruna had looked at her sadly. "I hope, child, that you never find out."

But Leesha understood when the bandits had left her. If she'd had her herb pouch, she would have brewed the tea as soon as she'd washed her body, but the men had taken that, too. The decision was out of her hands. By the time they reached the Hollow, it would be too late.

But when the pouch was returned to her, so too was the choice. The only missing ingredient of the tea was tampweed root, and she had seen some just off the road as they ran to a cave for shelter from the rain.

Unable to sleep, Leesha had risen before full dawn while Rojer and the Warded Man were still sleeping and snuck out to cut a few stalks of the weed. Even then, she was unsure if she could bring herself to drink the tea, but she meant to brew it all the same.

The Warded Man had come upon her, startling her, but she forced herself to smile and speak with him, rambling on about plants and demons to distract from her true purpose. All the while, her thoughts roiled in chaos.

But then she unintentionally insulted him, and the hurt in his eyes brought her out of it. Suddenly she saw something of the man he had once been. A good man, who had been hurt as she was, but embraced his pain like a lover rather than give it up.

She felt that pain, so resonant with her own, and all her swirling thoughts suddenly clicked together like the gears of a clock, and she knew what she must do.

Moments later she and Arlen lay together in the mud, a frantic coupling born of mutual desperation, cut short when a wood demon attacked. The man who had been caressing her vanished, becoming the Warded Man again as he wrestled the coreling away from her. As the sun rose, both of them began to dissipate. She stared in terror as they began to sink into the ground.

But then the mist drifted back to the surface and they solidified, the demon burning away in the sun. Leesha reached for Arlen then, but the Warded Man turned away, and she cursed him for it. So caught in her own feelings, she had barely given thought to what he must have been going through.

Leesha shook her head, coming back to herself.

"I'm so sorry," she told the Warded Man.

He waved a hand dismissively. "You didn't make my choices for me."

Rojer looked at her, then at him, then back to her. "Creator, your mum was right," he realized. Leesha knew the news was a blow to him, but there was nothing to be done for it. In a way, she was glad to have the secret out.

"This can't just be the tattoos," she said, returning to the topic at hand. "It makes no sense." She looked at the Warded Man. "I want your grimoires. All of them. Everything I learn from you is filtered by your understanding. I need the source material to understand what's causing this."

"I don't have them here," the Warded Man said.

"Then we'll go to them," Leesha said. "Where are they?"

"The nearest cache is in Angiers," the Warded Man said, "though I have others in Lakton, and out on the Krasian Desert."

"Angiers will do nicely," Leesha said. "I have unfinished business with Mistress Jizell, and perhaps you can convince the duke you're not after his crown while we're there."

"I might be able to help there," Rojer said. "I grew up in Rhinebeck's court while Arrick was his herald. I'll visit the Jongleurs' Guild while we're there, maybe hire some proper teachers for my apprentices."

"All right," the Warded Man said. "We'll go at first melt."

The broad wings of the mimic ate the miles, but the coreling prince hated the brightness of the surface, and twice took shelter in the Core for all but the darkest hours of the night. It was now the night after new moon, and even the effects of that minute sliver were bright to the demon's corespawned eyes. When it returned to the Core, it would not rise again until the cursed orb waxed and waned a full turn.

The greatward of Deliverer's Hollow came into sight below, its stolen magic shining like a beacon. The mind demon hissed at the sight, and its forehead pulsed as it sent the image hundreds of miles to the south in an instant, resonating in the mind of its brother.

A reply came instantly, the demon's cranium reverberating with its brother's frustration.

The mimic landed silently, and the mind demon dismounted. Immediately the mimic shed its wings and became a nimble flame demon, darting ahead to ensure that the path of the coreling prince was clear as it made its way toward the village.

The greatward was too large to mar, and too powerful for even a coreling prince to overcome. The demon could see the accumulated magic shimmering around the village—a barrier more solid than stone. It reached out with its thoughts, the soft nodules on its cranium pulsing as it tried to touch the minds of those within, but the sheer concentration of magic blocked even mental intrusion.

The demon circled the town, noting the terrain around the twists and turns of the ward. A strong defense with few weaknesses, and those not easily exploited. Drones drifted out of the trees, drawn to the coreling prince's presence, but a thought drove them off.

It found a place where two human females stood at the edge of the ward, armed with primitive weapons. The demon listened carefully to their grunts and yelps, waiting for a particular intonation that signaled address. It came soon, and the females clutched each other before dividing to walk the edge in different directions, their weapons at the ready.

The mind demon ran ahead of the elder of the two, waiting in an isolated spot until the woman reappeared. It signaled the mimic, and its servant swelled, scales melting away to be replaced by pink skin and the outer wrappings of the surface stock.

The mimic fell to the ground in the shadows just outside the forbidding as the elder female approached. It cried the elder female's name, its voice as perfect a copy of the younger female as its form. "Mala!"

"Wonda?" its chosen victim cried. She looked about frantically, but seeing no demons, she ran to what she assumed was her friend. "I just left you! How did you get out here?"

The mind demon stepped from behind a tree, and the female gasped, raising her bow. The nodules on the coreling prince's cranium throbbed softly, and the female stiffened, hands lowering her weapon against her will. The mind demon approached, and the female held out the projectile she had meant to launch for its inspection.

The wards on the projectile were powerfully shaped; the mind demon could feel them tugging at its own potent magic. It waved a taloned hand at them, marveling at how they began to glow even with its flesh still inches away.

The demon prince probed the mind of its victim deeply, sifting through images and memories as one might rummage in an old trunk. It learned much; too much to act upon without further consideration.

It was hours before dawn, but already the sky was brightening. Far to the south, it sensed its brother's agreement. There was time to reflect upon the problem.

The mind demon regarded the female. It could steal the memory of this event from her—send her back into the forbidding never knowing what had happened—but the touch of the human's mind, fat and largely unused, aroused its hunger.

Sensing its master's desire, the mimic sent a sharp tentacle to sever the female's head. It caught the prize and slithered over, peeling the skull open with a talon to present the meal.

The coreling prince tore at the sweet gray matter within, gorging itself. The meat was not as tender as the ignorant brains of its personal stock, but there was a satisfaction to hunting on the surface that added pleasure to the repast.

The demon looked to its mimic, standing vigilant as the coreling prince feasted. A throb of permission, and the mimic swelled, opening an enormous, many-toothed maw and slithering over to the female, swallowing the remainder of her body whole.

When master and servant alike were sated, they dissolved into mist, slipping back down to the Core as the sky continued to brighten.

CHAPTER 13

RENNA

:: 333 AR SPRING ::

RENNA'S STRONG ARMS BURNED, coated in a thin sheen of sweat as she worked the butter churn. It was early spring, but she was clad only in her shift. Her father would have a fit if he saw her, but he was around back cutting wardposts, and Lucik and the boys were out in the fields.

The farm had grown in the fourteen years since Lucik came to live with them, marrying Beni and putting children in her. There had been a hard season after Ilain ran off with Jeph Bales. Harl had raged and taken it out on them—mostly on Beni, since she was elder. But that had all stopped when Lucik, with his thick arms and broad shoulders, came to live with them. Harl hadn't touched either of them since, and the fields, once little more than a large garden, had gotten bigger every year.

Thinking of that time made her think again of Arlen Bales, and what might have been. When they were promised, it was agreed that she was to be the one to go and live on Jeph's farm, not Ilain. But Arlen had run off into the woods after his mother passed, and was never heard from again. Folk said he must be dead, especially after Jeph went to Sunny Pasture to search and hadn't found him. The Free Cities were weeks away on foot, and no one could survive that many nights without succor.

But Renna had never given up hope. Her eyes were always searching the road east, praying that one day he would come and take her away.

She looked up just then and saw a horseman coming down the road. Her heart stopped for a moment, but the rider came from the west, and after a moment, she recognized him.

Cobie Fisher sat tall on Pinecone, one of Old Hog's dappled mares, his patchwork armor and hammered cookpot helmet polished carefully. His spear and shield were strapped to the saddle in easy reach, though she had never heard tell of him using them.

Cobie fancied himself a Messenger, but he didn't brave the night like real Messengers; he simply ferried goods and word from one end of the Brook to another for Rusco Hog, who ran the general store. Once or twice, Cobie had slept in their barn on his way north to Sunny Pasture.

"Ay, Renna!" Cobie called, lifting a hand in greeting. She wiped the sweat from her brow with the back of her hand and straightened as he approached.

Cobie's eyes bulged suddenly, and he blushed. Renna remembered then that she was only half dressed. Her shift ended above her knees, and swooped low in front, showing a fair bit of cleavage. She smirked, amused at his embarrassment.

"Off to Sunny Pasture again?" she asked, making no effort to cover herself.

Cobie shook his head. "I've a message for Lucik."

"So late in the day?" Renna asked. "What could be so . . ." She caught a look in Cobie's eye, and began to worry. The last time someone had come with a message for Lucik, barely two years past, it was that his brother Kenner had gotten drunk testing ale from the vats and stumbled out beyond the wards. By the time the sun banished the demons, there was barely anything left of him to burn.

"Everyone's alright, ent they?" she asked, dreading the answer.

Cobie shook his head. He bent in close, lowering his voice though no one was around. "Lucik's da passed this morning," he confided.

Renna gasped, putting her hands to her mouth. Fernan Boggin had always been kind to her when he came to see his grandchildren. She would miss him. And poor Lucik . . .

"Renna!" came her father's bark. "Get inside and cover yourself, girl! This ent no Angierian house of sin!" He pointed to the door with his prized hunting knife. The blade was Milnese steel, with a bone handle, and was never far from his hands.

Renna knew that tone, and left Cobie with his mouth open as she turned and hurried inside. She stopped at the door to watch Harl stride out to meet Cobie, who was tying Pinecone to the hitching post.

Her father was wrinkled and gray, but he seemed to only toughen with age, his wiry muscles hard from working the fields and his skin leathern and rough. Harl had wanted to find Renna a husband before Ilain left, but since, he had scared off any boy who even looked her way.

Cobie was taller than Harl, though, and wider, one of the biggest men in Tibbet's Brook. Hog had chosen him as his messenger because he had more than a little bully in him still and didn't scare easily, especially with his armor on. Renna couldn't hear what they said, but her father's rumbling tone was respectful as they clasped wrists.

"What's the commotion?" Beni asked from the fire where she was chopping vegetables into the stew.

"Cobie Fisher's come in from Town Square," Renna said.

"Did he say why?" Beni asked, her face clouding with worry. "Messengers don't just come to say hello."

Renna swallowed hard. "Da called me in before he could say," she lied, and hurried to the curtain in her corner of the common room, pulling off her dirty shift and putting on a dress. She was still lacing the stays when she exited the curtain and caught Cobie looking at her again.

"Corespawn it, Renna!" Harl roared, and she vanished behind the curtain until she was properly done up.

Harl scowled when she reemerged. "Run and fetch Lucik from the fields, girl, and keep the boys out in the barn. Messenger's come with dark news."

Renna nodded, darting out the door. She found Lucik tending the wardposts at the far end of the fields, just before the ground turned black, scorched clean by flame demons.

Cal and Jace were with him, digging weeds while their father worked. They were seven and ten.

"Suppertime?" Cal asked hopefully.

"No, poppet," Renna said, tousling his dirty blond hair. "But we're going to put the animals back in the barn. Your da has a visitor."

"Eh?" Lucik said.

"Cobie Fisher," Renna said, "with news from your mam."

Fear flashed on Lucik's face, and he set off at once. Renna led the boys back and set them to work leading the hogs and cows from the day pens into the big barn. Renna untethered Pinecone herself, leading the mare into the small barn off the back of the house where they kept their mollies and the chickens. Their last horse had given out two summers past, so there was an empty stall. Renna undid the girth, slipping off the saddle and bridle. She turned to get the brushes and caught Jace reaching for Cobie's spear.

"Hands off, 'less you want a whipping," she said, slapping his hand away. "Get the brushes and rub the horse down, then go slop the pigs."

She fed the chickens while the boys went about their chores, but her eyes kept glancing to the door to the house. She had seen twenty-four summers, but Harl still treated her like a child, sheltering her as much as he did the boys.

After a time, the door opened and Beni stuck her head in. "Supper's ready. Everyone wash up."

The boys whooped and ran inside, but Renna lingered, meeting her sister's eyes. Since they were children, the two had been able to speak volumes to each other with but a look, and this time was no different. Renna put her arms around Beni and hugged her as she cried.

After a brief bout of sobbing, Beni straightened and wiped her eyes with her apron before going back inside. Renna drew a deep breath and followed.

The dinner table only sat six, so the boys were sent to eat by the fire in the common room. Having no idea anything was amiss, they scampered off happily, and the elders could hear them laughing and wrestling the dogs through the thin curtain that served as a divider between the dining area and the common.

"We'll head out first thing in the morning," Lucik said when Renna had cleared the bowls. "With Da and Kenner gone, Mam is going to need a man around afore Hog starts buying Marsh Ale again."

"Can't someone else take it on?" Harl said, his face sour as he whittled the end of a wardpost. "Fernan young's near a man." Fernan young was Kenner's son, named after his grandfather.

"Fernie's only twelve, Harl," Lucik said. "He can't be trusted to run the brewery."

"Then what about yer sister?" Harl pressed. "She married that Fisher boy couple summers ago."

"Jash," Cobie supplied.

"He's a Fisher," Lucik said. "He might be able to scale and gut, but he won't know night about brewing." He glanced at Cobie. "No offense."

"None taken," Cobie said. "Jash is apt to drink more than he brews, anyway."

"You're one to talk," Harl snapped. "Way's I hear, Hog made you his message boy when you couldn't pay all the ale credits you owed. Maybe it's you, ort be up at the brewery, working off your drink."

"You got some stones, old man," Cobie said, scowling and half rising from his seat. Harl rose with him, pointing at him with his long hunting knife.

"Know what's good for you, boy, you'll sit'cher ass back down," he growled.

"Corespawn it!" Lucik barked, slamming his hands down on the table. Both men looked at him in shock, and Lucik glared in return. He was of a size with Cobie, and flushed red with anger. They returned to their seats, and Harl picked up his post end, whittling furiously.

"So just like that, you up and desert us," he said. "What about the farm?"

"Spring planting's done," Lucik said. "You and Renna should be able to weed and keep the wardposts till harvest time, and me and the boys'll come back for that. Fernie, too."

"And next year?" Harl asked.

Lucik shrugged. "I don't know. We can all come to plant, and might be I can spare one of the boys for the summer."

"Thought we was family, boy," Harl said, spitting on the floor, "but it looks like you've always been a Boggin at heart." He pushed back from the table. "Do as you want. Take my daughter and grandsons away from me. But don't expect a slap on the back for it."

"Harl," Lucik began, but the old man waved him off, stomping over to his room and slamming the door.

Beni laid a hand over Lucik's clenched fist. "He din't mean it like that."

"Oh, Ben," he said sadly, laying his free hand over hers, "course he did."

"Come on," Renna said, grabbing Cobie's arm and pulling him from his seat. "Let's leave them in peace and find you some blankets and a clean spot in the barn." Cobie nodded, following her out of the curtain.

"Your da always like this?" he asked as they left the house proper.

"He took it better than I expected," Renna said, taking a broom and sweeping out one of the empty stalls. Outside, the sun had set, and there were shrieks and flashes of light as the corelings tested the wards. The animals were used to the sound, but still they shifted nervously, knowing instinctively what would happen if the wards failed.

"Lucik just lost his da," Cobie said. "You'd think Harl would show a little heart."

Renna shook her head. "Not my da. He don't care about any needs but his own." She bit her lip, remembering what things were like before Lucik came.

After Cobie was safely settled in the barn, Renna came back in to the house to find Lucik in the common room, explaining things to the boys. She slipped quietly by and went into Beni's room, finding her sister folding clothes and packing her few belongings.

"Take me with you," Renna said bluntly.

"What?" Beni asked, surprised.

"I don't want to be alone with him," Renna said. "I can't."

"Renna, what are you . . ." Beni began, but Renna grabbed her shoulders.

"Don't pretend you don't know what I'm talking about!" she snapped. "You know what he was like before Lucik came."

Beni hissed and pulled away, going to the door and pushing it shut. "What do you know of it?" she asked, her voice a harsh whisper. "You were always the baby. You never had to endure—" She broke off, her face twisting with anger and shame.

Renna glanced pointedly at her bosom. "I'm not a baby anymore, Beni."

"Then bind your breasts," Beni said. "Stop running about in just your shift. Don't give him a reason to notice you."

"That won't stop him, and you know it," Renna said.

"Been almost fifteen years, Ren," Beni said. "You don't know what he'll do."

But Renna did know. In her heart, she had no doubt. She had seen her father looking at her, his eyes running over her like greedy hands. Why else did he react so jealously whenever a man glanced her way? More than one had come courting when she was younger. They knew better now.

"Please," she begged, gripping Beni's hands as tears filled her eyes. "Take me with you."

"And what will I tell Lucik?" Beni snapped. "He feels bad enough, leaving the farm untended. Without you, Da ent never gonna be able to handle the load."

"You could tell him the truth," Renna said.

Beni slapped her. Renna fell back, clutching her cheek in shock. Her sister had never struck her in her life.

But Beni showed no sign of remorse. "You get that out of your head," she growled. "I ent gonna make my family bear that shame. Lucik would turn me out if he knew, and before long the whole town would hear tell. And what of Ilain? Should Jeph and her children have to carry that stain, too, all 'cause of you being a baby?"

"I'm not being a baby!" Renna shouted.

"Keep your voice down!" Beni hissed.

Renna took a deep breath, trying to calm herself. "I'm not being a baby," she said again, "just because I don't want to be left alone with that monster."

"He ent a demon, Renna, he's our da," Beni said. "He's given us succor and put food on the table all our lives, even though his heart broke when Mam died. Ilain and I took it, and if it comes to that, you can, too."

"Ilain took it by running to hide behind Jeph," Renna said, "just like you hide behind Lucik. But who do I have to hide behind, Ben?"

"You can't come with us, Renna," Beni said again.

Just then, Lucik walked into the room. "Everything all right? I heard raised voices."

"Everything's fine," Beni said, glaring at Renna, who sobbed and pushed past Lucik, running to her little curtained corner of the common.

Renna lay awake that night, listening to the shrieks of the corelings in the yard and the grunting from Beni's room, her and Lucik at it like most every night. The same sound used to come from Harl's room when her mother was alive. And after that, when Harl had made their eldest sister Ilain take her place. And when Ilain left, those sounds had come again on the nights when Harl pulled Beni in there. She hadn't been so accepting of it then.

Renna sat up, bathed in sweat, her heart pounding. She peeked around the curtain and saw the boys fast asleep on their blankets. Clad only in her shift, she crept through the common and eased open the barn door, slipping quietly within.

Inside, she took the striker and lit a lantern, casting the barn in a flickering light.

"Eh?" Cobie asked, squinting and raising a hand over his eyes. "Whozzat?"

"It's Renna," she said, coming over and sitting beside him in the hay. The lantern light danced around the stall, flickering over Cobie's broad chest as his blanket slipped down.

"Don't get visitors often," she said. "Thought we could sit and talk a spell."

"Sounds nice," Cobie said, rubbing the sleep from his face.

"Have to be quiet, though," Renna said. "If Da catches us, there'll be the Core to pay."

Cobie nodded, flicking a nervous eye in the direction of the house door.

"What's it like, being a Messenger?" Renna asked.

"Well, I ent a real Messenger," Cobie admitted. "Ent licensed by the guild in the Free Cities, and don't think I'd be fool enough to sleep outside with the demons even if I were. But workin' for Mr. Hog beats fishin'. Always hated that."

"Way I hear tell, you never did much of it," Renna said.

Cobie laughed. "True enough. Used to just run and fool about with Gart and Willum, but they got promised and stopped having time for it. Can't laugh out on the boats. Scares the fish."

"How come you never got promised yourself?" Renna asked.

Cobie shrugged. "Da said it's because girls' fathers didn't think I could settle and provide for a wife and young'uns. He was right, I guess. I was always more interested in hanging around the general store than working. Fished when I had to, but never had enough credits to pay for all the ale I drank. Your da was right that Mr. Hog started sending me to fetch this or deliver that just to balance the log. But when the Speaker started asking Mr. Hog to have me ferry messages around, too, he said I could stay in the little room behind the store to be on hand.

"People treat me with respect now," Cobie said, "because I'm on town business. They give me meals, and succor when it's too far to go back to Town Square before dark."

"Bet it's nice," Renna said, "traveling all over the Brook and seeing everyone all the time. I never see anyone."

Cobie nodded. "I earn more than I drink, now, and when I have enough credits, I'm going to buy a horse of my own, and change my name to Cobie Messenger. Maybe build a house in Town Square, and have sons to take on the job when I'm old."

"So you think you could settle and provide now?" Renna asked. Cobie wasn't handsome, but he was a good strong man with prospects. She was coming to realize Arlen might never come back for her, and life had to go on.

Cobie nodded, looking in her eyes. "I might," he said, "if a girl took her chances on me."

Renna leaned in and kissed him on the mouth. Cobie's eyes widened a moment, but then he kissed her back, enveloping her in his strong arms.

"I know a wife's tricks," Renna whispered, pulling down her shift to expose her breasts. "I seen Beni and Lucik at it plenty of times. I could be a good wife." Cobie groaned, nuzzling her bosom as his hands ran up her legs.

There was a crash from behind, startling them both.

"What in the Core is going on here?!" Harl demanded, grabbing Renna by the hair and pulling her off Cobie. In his free hand, he held his long hunting knife, sharp as a razor. He threw Renna aside and put the point up to Cobie's throat.

"We . . . we were just . . ." Cobie stuttered, drawing back as far as he could, but his back was against the wall of the stall, and there was nowhere to go.

"I ent no fool, boy," Harl said. "I know what you were 'just'! You think because I give you succor behind my wards, you can go and treat my daughter like some Angierian whore? I orta gut you right here."

"Please!" Cobie begged. "It ent like that! I really like Renna! I want her hand!"

"'Spect you wanted more than that," Harl growled, pressing the point in and drawing a drop of blood from Cobie's throat. "You think that's how it works? Come stick a girl, then ask for her hand?"

Cobie pulled his head back as far as he could, tears and sweat mixing on his face.

"That's enough!" Lucik cried, grabbing Harl's arm and pulling the knife away. Harl whirled to his feet, and the two men stood glaring at each other.

"You wouldn't say that if it were your daughter," Harl said.

"That may be," Lucik said, "but I ent gonna let you kill a man in fronta my boys, either!"

Harl glanced back, seeing Cal and Jace watching wide-eyed from the house door while Renna cried in Beni's arms. Some of the anger went out of him, and his shoulders slumped.

"Fine," he said. "Renna, you're sleeping in my room tonight, so's I can keep an eye on you. And you," he pointed his knife at Cobie again, who went rigid with fright, "you so much as look at my girl again, and I'll cut yer stones off and feed 'em to the corelings."

He grabbed Renna by the arm and dragged her along as he stormed into the house.

Renna was still shaking when Harl threw her down on the bed. She had pulled her shift back in place, but it seemed woefully inadequate, and she could feel her father's eyes on her.

"This is what you do when we have a visitor in the barn?" Harl snapped at her. "I bet half the town is laughing behind my back!"

"I never!" Renna said.

"Oh, I'm supposed to believe that, now?" Harl sneered. "I saw the way you paraded around half dressed for him today. Reckon the hogs aren't all that's grunting in the barn when the messenger boy's about."

Renna had no reply, sniffling as she pulled the blanket around her bare shoulders.

"Now yer shy and trying to cover?" Harl asked. "Mite late, you ask me." He undid his overalls and slung them over the bedpost, snatching the edge of the blanket and sliding in beside her. Renna shuddered.

"Quit yer whining and get some sleep, girl," Harl said. "Another of yer sisters up and deserted us, and there'll be extra chores for both of us from now on."

Renna woke early, finding her father snuggled close with an arm over her. She shivered with revulsion, easing out of his grasp and leaving him snoring as she fled the room.

Remembering Beni's advice, she tore a long strip from the sheet on her pallet, wrapping the cloth around her chest several times, binding her breasts tight. When she was done, she looked down and sighed. Even flattened, no one would ever mistake her for a boy.

She dressed quickly, lacing her dress loosely to hide her curves and tying her long brown hair in an unkempt knot.

The boys stirred as she put the porridge on and laid bowls on the table. By the time the sun rose, the whole house was bustling, and Lucik sent the boys out to their morning chores one last time.

Cobie was gone before breakfast was ready, but Renna supposed it was just as well. Harl might not deny a man succor, but that didn't mean he would share his table. She wished she'd had a chance to apologize for his actions, and for hers. She'd ruined things for both of them.

After morning chores, Harl hitched the cart and drove them all up through Town Square to Boggin's Hill for the cremation. It was afternoon by the time they arrived, and by then there was a big gathering on the hill. Most everyone in Tibbet's Brook drank Boggin's Ale, and many came to pay their respects as Fernan Boggin was burned.

The Holy House crowned the hill, and Tender Harral welcomed everyone warmly. He was a big man, not yet fifty, with powerful arms reaching out from the rolled sleeves of his brown robe. "Your da was a good friend, and a good man," he told Lucik, wrapping him in a tight hug. "We'll all miss him."

Harral gestured to the great doors. "Go on inside and sit in the front pew with your mam." The Tender smiled at Renna, winking at her for some reason as she passed.

"Looks like the ingrate's come down from hiding," Harl muttered as they slid into the pew behind Lucik, Beni, and the boys. Renna followed his gaze to see her eldest sister Ilain a few rows back. She stood with Jeph, Norine Cutter, and her children. They had all gotten so big!

"Don't even think about it," Harl muttered, grabbing her arm and squeezing hard as she moved to go and greet them. Harl had never forgiven Ilain for running off, though it was near fifteen years gone, and meant that he never knew his grandchildren by her.

"That sumbitch got a lot of nerve, coming here," Harl muttered, glaring at Jeph. "Another corespawned thief, thinking just because I give them succor, they can run off with one of my girls. Just as well you didn't end up married to that good-for-nothing son of his."

"Arlen wasn't good for nothing," Renna said sadly, remembering how he had kissed her when they were children. She'd admired him from afar for years, and being promised to him had seemed a dream come true. She had always refused to believe he'd been cored, but if he hadn't, why didn't he come back for her?

"What's that, girl?" Harl asked, distracted.

"Nothing," Renna said.

The ceremony went on, with Harral singing the praises of Fernan Boggin as he painted wards on the tarp wrapping the body to protect Fernan's spirit as it made its way to the Creator.

When it was done, they carried the body out to the pyre Harral had built, and laid him to rest as the fire burned. Renna drew wards in the air along with everyone else, praying that Fernan's soul would escape this demon-infested world as the flames consumed his body.

On the other side of the fire, Ilain stared sadly at her. She raised a hand to wave, and Renna started to cry.

People began to drift off as the fire burned down, some to Meada Boggin's house, where she had refreshments ready for her husband's mourners, and others beginning the trek back to their homes. Some had come from a ways off, and the corelings rose no later on funeral days.

"C'mon, girl, we'd best be getting back," Harl said, taking her arm.

"Harl Tanner!" Tender Harral called. "A moment of your time!"

Harl and Renna turned to see the Tender approaching with Cobie Fisher in tow. Cobie's eyes were firmly on his feet.

"Oh, what now?" Harl muttered.

"Cobie told me what happened last night," Tender Harral said.

"Oh, did he?" Harl said. "Did he tell you I caught him and my daughter in sinful embrace under my own wards?"

Harral nodded. "He did, and he has something to say now. Don't you, Cobie?"

Cobie nodded, coming forward while still studying his boots. "I'm sorry for what I done. Din't mean to shame no one, and I intend to make an honest woman of Renna, if you'll allow it."

"The Core I will!" Harl barked, and Cobie paled and took a step back.

"Now, Harl, wait just a minute," Tender Harral said.

"No, you wait, Tender!" Harl said. "This boy disrespected me, my daughter, and the sanctity of my wards, and you want me to take him as a son, just like that? I'd sooner let Renna marry a wood demon."

"Renna's past the age where she ought to be married and raising young'uns of her own," Harral said.

"That don't mean I got to hand her to some drunken wastrel just cuz he bent her over a hay bale," Harl said. He grabbed Renna and dragged her toward the cart. Renna looked longingly at Cobie as they rode off.

CHAPTER 14

A TRIP TO THE OUTHOUSE

:: 333 AR SPRING ::

RENNA CAST A WISTFUL eye back up the road as the farm came into sight. "I know what yer thinkin', girl," Harl said. "Yer thinkin' of bein' like yer ingrate sister and runnin' off t'be with that boy."

Renna said nothing, but she felt her cheeks burn, and that was damning enough.

"Well, you think twice about it," Harl said. "I won't let you shame our family like Lainie did, runnin' off with a man whose wife just died the night before. Whole town still talks of it, and they all cast a dark eye on old Harl for raising such a corespawned whore.

"Yer on your way to getting the same reputation," Harl said. "Not this time, girlie. I'd rather scar the wards than go through that again. You even think about runnin', and you'll have yerself a trip to the outhouse, even if I have to go all the way to Southwatch to collect you."

Renna glanced at the tiny, ramshackle structure in the yard, and her blood went cold. Her father had never put her in there, but he had done it to Ilain a few times, and to Beni once. She remembered their screams vividly.

Renna reclaimed Beni and Lucik's small room, which she had once shared with her sister, moving in her few possessions and barring the door with a trembling hand.

As she lay back in the bed, she stroked Miss Scratch, her favorite cat, who was pregnant and soon to litter. As she did she thought of Cobie, of a house in Town Square and children of her own. The images warmed and comforted her, but she kept one eye on the door for a long time before drifting off to sleep.

For the next few days, Renna avoided her father whenever she could. It wasn't difficult. Spring planting might have been done, but even so, they were two splitting chores once shared by six. Just feeding the animals and cleaning their stalls was half a morning's work for Renna, and she still had to milk and shear and slaughter, ready meals thrice a day, mend clothing, make butter and cheese, tan skins, and an endless array of other tasks. She fell into the work almost gratefully for the protection it offered.

Each morning she bound her breasts, leaving her hair a tangle and her face smudged, and there was enough work to keep lewd thoughts from Harl's mind. Just checking the wardposts around the fields took hours. Each had to be examined carefully to make sure the wards were clear and sharp and aligned properly to overlap their neighbors without gap. A simple bird dropping or a warp in the wood could weaken a ward sufficiently for a demon to pass through if it found the gap.

After that, the fields still needed weeding, and the ripest produce had to be harvested for the day's meals, or for pickling and preserves. After all that, there was still always something around the farm that needed fixing, or sharpening.

The only time they really spent together was at meals, and they said little. Renna was careful not to bend close as she served and cleared. Harl never gave any sign he was looking at her differently, but he grew increasingly irritable as the days wore on.

"Creator, my back hurts," he said one night at supper as he bent to fill another mug from the keg of Boggin's Ale that Meada had sent back with them after the burning. Renna had lost count of how many he had filled that night.

Harl gasped in pain as he tried to straighten, and stumbled, sloshing his ale. Renna was there in an instant, steadying him and catching the mug before it spilled. Harl leaned heavily on her as she dragged him back to his chair.

Renna and Beni had often been called upon to knead the pain from Harl's bad back, and she did it now without thinking, working her father's tensed muscles with strong, skilled fingers.

"Atta girl," her father groaned, closing his eyes and pressing against her hands. "You were always the good one, Ren. Not like yer sisters, with no loyalty to kith and kin. Dunno how you turned out all right, with those two deserters as an example."

Renna finished her ministrations, but Harl grabbed her about the waist and pulled her close before she could pull out of reach. He looked up at her with tears in his eyes.

"You'll never leave me, girl, will you?" he asked.

"No, Da," Renna said. "Course not." She squeezed him briefly, and then pulled quickly back, taking his mug to the keg and refilling it.

Renna awoke that night to a crash as something struck her door. She leapt from bed, pulling on her dress, but there was no other sound. She crept to the door and pressed her ear to the wood, hearing a low wheeze.

Carefully, she lifted the bar and opened the door a crack, seeing her father passed out on the floor, regurgitated ale staining the front of his nightshirt.

"Creator make me strong," Renna begged as she soaked a rag to clean the vomit from him and the floor, then half carried, half dragged her father back to his room.

Harl wept as she heaved him into his bed, clinging to her desperately. "Can't lose you, too," he sobbed over and over. Renna sat awkwardly on the edge of the bed, holding him as he cried, and then disengaged as he drifted off to sleep. She went quickly back to her room and barred the door again.

The next morning, Renna came back into the house after collecting eggs in the barn and found Harl popping the pins out of the hinges of her door.

"The door broke?" she asked, her heart clutching.

"Nope," Harl grunted. "Need the wood to patch a hole in the barn wall. Don't matter none, you don't need it. Ent no marital relations going on in this room no more." He hefted the door and carried it off to the barn, leaving Renna stunned.

She felt like a frightened animal for the rest of the day, and didn't sleep at all that night, all her senses attuned toward the thick curtain hung over the doorway.

But nothing stirred the curtain that night, or the night that followed, or for a week after.

Renna wasn't sure what woke her. Corelings had tested the wards earlier in the night, but the sounds had faded to silence as they gave over to search out easier prey.

The only light was a soft glow around the edges of the curtain in the doorway from the fire in the common room, burned low in the night. It threw a dim light over her bed, though the rest of the tiny room was bathed in darkness.

But Renna knew immediately that she wasn't alone. Her father was in the room.

Careful to keep still, she reached out into the darkness with her senses, trying to convince herself it was only a dream, but she could smell the stink of ale and sweat, and hear his tense breathing. Floorboards creaked as he shifted from foot to foot. She kept waiting for him to do something, but he just stood there, watching her.

Had he done this before? Snuck into her room and watched her sleep? The thought sickened her. Afraid to stir, her eyes flicked to the curtain, but escape that way seemed unlikely. It would take her four steps to reach the doorway. Harl could intercept her in one.

The window was closer, but even if she could unlatch the shutters and throw them open before he got to her, it was deep in the night, and demons prowled the darkness outside.

Time seemed to slow as Renna desperately tried to think of a way to escape. If she ran through the yard, she might make it to the barn before a coreling caught her. The big barn was warded, and not connected to the house. If she made it there, Harl couldn't follow till morning, and perhaps by then he would have slept off his drink.

Running into the night went against her every instinct. It was suicide. But where else was there to go? She was trapped in the house with him until sunrise.

Just then Harl shifted, and she caught her breath. He came slowly over to the bed, and Renna froze, like a rabbit paralyzed with fear. As he came into the light, she saw he was clad only in his nightshirt, his arousal jutting through the cloth. He came close to her, reaching out to touch her hair. He ran his fingers through it, and then sniffed at them, his hand dropping again to gently caress her face.

"Jus' like yer mam," he mumbled, and ran his hand lower, past her throat and collar, tracing the smooth skin to her breast.

He squeezed, and Renna shrieked. Miss Scratch woke with a start and hissed, sinking claws deep into Harl's arm. He cried out, and terror gave Renna strength. She shoved at him, throwing him backward. Drunk, Harl stumbled and fell to the floor. Renna was through the curtain in an instant.

"Girl, you get back here!" Harl cried, but she ignored him, running hard for the back door to the small barn. He stumbled after her, tangling in the curtain and ripping it from the rod.

She was through the barn door before he freed himself, but there was no lock from the inside. She grabbed a heavy old saddle, throwing it against the door, and ran through the stalls.

"Corespawn it, Renna! What's gotten into you?" Harl cried as he burst through the door. There was a cry as he fell over the saddle, cursing loudly.

"Girl, I will tan the skin off your arse, you don't come out of hiding!" he called, and there was a crack like a whip. He had pulled a set of leather reins off the barn wall.

Renna made no reply, crouching in the darkness of an empty stall behind an old rain barrel as Harl fumbled with the striker to light a lantern. He finally managed to catch the wick, and a flickering light sprang to life, sending shadows dancing around the barn.

"Where you gone to, girl?" Harl called, as he began to search the stalls. "Gonna be worse, I have to drag you out." He cracked the reins again to accentuate his point, and Renna's heart jumped. Outside, the demons, drawn to the commotion, flung themselves against the wards with renewed fervor. Wardlight flashed through cracks in the wood, accompanied by coreling shrieks and the crackle of magic.

She wound like a spring as he drew closer, every muscle coiling tighter and tighter until she was certain she would burst. His muttered curses grew fouler and fouler as he went, and he began flailing around with the reins in frustration.

He was only inches from her hiding place when Renna burst free, running deeper into the barn. She came to the back wall, cornered, and turned to face him.

"Dunno what's taken you, girl," Harl said. "'Spect I need to beat some sense into you."

There was no way to get past this time, so Renna turned and scampered up the ladder to the hayloft. She tried to pull it up after her, but Harl gave a shout and caught the bottom rung, yanking it back down and almost pulling Renna down with it. She only barely managed to catch herself on the trap, and lost her grip on the ladder completely. Harl hooked the lantern and began to climb up after her, the reins in his teeth.

Renna kicked out in desperation, catching her father full in the face. He was knocked back off the ladder, but the floor was covered with hay and broke the worst of his fall. He grabbed the ladder again before she could pull it away, and came up fast. She kicked again, but he caught her foot and shoved hard, sending her sprawling.

And then he was up in the loft with her, and there was nowhere to run.

She was only half on her feet when his fist connected with her face, and light exploded behind her eyes.

"You brung this on yourself, girl," Harl said, punching her again in the stomach. The air exploded from her lungs, and she gasped in pain. He gripped her nightshirt in one sinewy fist and yanked, tearing half of it away.

"Please, Da!" she cried. "Don't!"

"Don't?" he echoed with a harsh laugh. "Since when do you say *don't* to boys in the hayloft, girl? Ent this where you do your sinning? Ent this where you bring shame to our family? You'll stick any drunk that falls asleep in a stall, but yer too good for your own da?"

"No!" Renna cried.

"Corespawned right, yer not," Harl said, grabbing the back of her neck and pushing her face down into the hay as he lifted his nightshirt with his free hand.

When it was over, Renna lay crying in the hay. Harl's weight was still on her, but the strength seemed to have gone out of him. She shoved hard, and he rolled off her without resistance.

She wanted to shove him right off the side of the loft and break his neck, but she couldn't stop sobbing enough to rise. Her cheek and lip throbbed where he had struck her, and her stomach was on fire, but it was nothing compared with the burning between her legs. If Harl had even noticed the evidence that she had never been with a man before, he gave no sign.

"That's it, girl," Harl said, patting her shoulder weakly. "You go ahead and have yerself a good cry. It used to help Ilain, before she got to liking it."

Renna scowled. Ilain had never liked it, no matter what he said.

"You ever do that again," she said, "I'll tell everyone in Town Square what you done."

Harl barked a laugh. "No one will believe you. The goodwives'll just think the town tramp is looking for an excuse to move close enough to get her claws into their husbands, and none of them will care for that.

"And besides," he added, wrapping a gnarled hand around her throat, "you tell anyone, girl, and I'll kill you."

Renna watched the sun set from the warded porch, hugging herself as the sky washed with color. Not long ago, she had stood every night looking to the east, dreaming of the day Arlen Bales would return from the Free Cities to fulfill his promise and take her away.

She still watched the road each evening, but now she looked to the west, praying to see Cobie Fisher come for her. Did he still think of her? Had he meant what he said? Wouldn't he have come by now if he had?

Her hope faded further each night, till it was little more than a flicker, and then nothing but a coal buried in sand, a warmth buried away for a use that might never come.

But anything that kept her outside a moment longer was worth it, even a dream that cut as much as it soothed. Soon she would have to go inside and serve her father dinner, and work her evening chores with his eyes on her until he said it was time for bed.

And then she would go obediently to his bed, and lie still as he had his way. She thought of Ilain, and all the years she had undergone this torment, back when Renna was too young to understand. How she had survived with her mind intact was beyond Renna, but Ilain and Beni had always been stronger than her.

"Gettin' dark, girl," Harl called. "Come and shut the door 'fore the corelings get you."

For a moment, the image danced across her mind. The corelings would rise in a moment. It would be a simple matter to step across the wards and end her torment.

But Renna found she didn't have the strength for that, either. She turned and went inside.

"Oh, don't you grumble at me, Wooly," Renna told the sheep as she sheared. "You'll thank me to be rid of your coat in this heat."

Beni and the boys used to make mock of her when she spoke to the animals like people, but with them gone, Renna found herself doing it more and more. The cats and dogs and the animals in the stalls were the only friends she had in the world, and when Harl was in the fields, they lent sympathetic ears as Renna poured her heart out to them.

"Renna," came a whisper behind her. She jumped and Wooly bleated as she accidentally cut him, but Renna barely noticed, spinning to find Cobie Fisher just a few feet away.

She dropped the shears, looking around frantically, but Harl was nowhere to be seen. Out weeding the fields, he would likely be gone hours more, but she took no chances, grabbing Cobie's arm and pulling him behind the big barn.

"What are you doing here?" she whispered.

"Bringing a few casks of rice out to Mack Pasture's farm up the road," Cobie said. "I'll succor there, and head back to the Square in the morning."

"My father will kill you if he sees you," Renna said.

Cobie nodded. "I know. I don't care." He fumbled with his message pouch, pulling out a long necklace of smooth brook stones threaded on a stout leather cord with a fishbone clasp.

"It ent much, but it's what I could afford," he said, handing the necklace to Renna.

"It's beautiful," she said, taking the gift. It wrapped around her neck twice and still hung past her breasts.

"Keep thinking about you, Renna," Cobie said. "Tender Harral and my da told me to forget you, but I can't do it. I see you every time I close my eyes. I want you to come back with me tomorrow. The Tender will marry us if we go to him and beg; I know he will. He did it for your sister, when she ran off with Jeph Bales, and once we're joined before the Creator, nothing your da says can pull us apart."

"Honest word?" Renna asked, her eyes brimming with tears.

Cobie nodded and pulled her to him, kissing her deeply.

But Cobie only kept control for a moment, as Renna pushed him back against the barn wall and sank to her knees. He gasped and his nails dug grooves in the wood of the barn wall while she worked. His knees bucked, and as he slipped down to the ground, Renna straddled him and lifted her skirts.

"I . . . I've never . . ." Cobie stuttered, but she put a finger to his lips to silence him and sank herself onto him.

Cobie threw his head back in pleasure, and Renna smiled. This wasn't like it was with Harl, rough and unfeeling. This was how it should be. She covered Cobie's face in kisses as she rose and fell, finding her own pleasure as his hands roamed her body.

"I love you," he whispered, and spent himself inside her. She cried and kissed him. They held each other in that warm glowing embrace for a time, and then stood, readjusting their clothes. Renna cast a wary eye around the corner of the barn, but there was no sign of her father.

"My father goes out into the fields early," Renna said. "Right after breakfast. If you come then, he'll be gone till lunchtime."

"We'll be at the Holy House before he even realizes you're gone," Cobie said, squeezing her tightly. "Pack your things tonight and have them ready. I'll come as early as I can."

"There's nothing to pack," Renna said. "I've no dowry but myself, but I promise I can be a good wife. I can cook and ward and keep your home . . ."

Cobie laughed, kissing her. "I want no dowry. Only you."

Renna hid the necklace in her apron pocket, and was obedient the rest of the day and night, giving her father no reason to doubt her. It was true that she had nothing to pack, but she went to each of her friends, the animals, to whisper her goodbyes. She cried over Miss Scratch, lamenting the kittens she would never see.

"You'll be Mrs. Scratch when the kits come," Renna said, "even if that good-for-nothing tabby don't help you care for 'em."

She scanned the animals in the room, spotting the likely sire. "You take care of your kits," she admonished, keeping her voice low so her father wouldn't hear, "or I'll come back and throw you in the water trough."

She lay awake all night as Harl snored beside her, and before the first crack of light came through the shutters, she had porridge on the fire and was out collecting eggs from the coop in the barn. She went about the rest of her chores that morning aware that she was performing each for the last time, and as she worked, she kept casting eyes up the road.

She didn't have to wait long. There was a galloping in the distance, but it faded before it came too close. Soon after, Cobie came around the bend in the road, sweaty and breathless.

"Galloped all the way," he said, kissing her. "Couldn't wait to see you."

Pinecone needed a rest, so Cobie tethered her behind the barn while Renna drew water from the well. The mare drank greedily and began grazing while they fell into each other's arms. Before long, she was bent over against the barn with her skirts around her waist.

And it was there Harl found them.

"I knew it!" he cried, swinging his pitchfork hard at Cobie's head. The shaft caught him on the temple and sent him reeling.

"Cobie!" Renna shouted, running to him and cradling him in her arms as he tried to rise.

"I knew sumpthin' was up when I saw you weepin' over them cats, girl," Harl said. "You think yer da's an idiot?"

"I don't care!" Renna shouted. "Cobie and I are in love, and I'm leaving with him!"

"The Core you are," Harl said, grabbing her arm. "You'll get your ass in the house this instant, you want to keep the skin on it."

But Cobie's meaty hand locked over Harl's wrist, twisting and pulling it off Renna.

"I'm sorry, sir," he said, "but I ent gonna let you do that."

Harl turned to face him and snorted. "Well, boy, don't say you didn't ask for this," he said, and kicked Cobie hard in the crotch.

His pants still around his ankles, Cobie had no protection whatsoever from Harl's heavy boot, and he crumpled in a heap, clutching between his legs. Harl shoved Renna to the ground and raised his pitchfork, striking merciless blows as Cobie lay helpless.

"Typical bully boy," Harl spat. "Bet you never been in a real fight in your life." Cobie let go his crotch and tried to get out of the way, but his pants were still a tangle, tripping him up, and he screamed as each blow struck home.

Finally, as he lay gasping and bloody on the ground, Harl stuck the fork in the dirt and pulled his long knife from the sheath on his belt.

"Told you what I'd do if I caught you with my daughter again," he said, advancing. "Say goodbye to yer stones, boy." Cobie's eyes widened in terror.

"No!" Renna screamed, leaping on Harl's back and tangling him with her arms and legs. "Run, Cobie! *Run!*"

Harl shouted, and the two of them struggled. A lifetime of hard work had made Renna strong, but Harl turned and kicked back, slamming her into the wall of the barn. The wind was knocked from her, and before she could take another breath Harl slammed her again. And again. Her grip loosened, and he caught her arm, flipping her over onto the ground.

Pain flared through Renna on impact, but even through the haze she saw Cobie pulling up his pants and leaping onto his horse. Before Harl could snatch up his pitchfork, he had kicked Pinecone's flanks and was galloping down the road.

"This is yer last warning, boy! Stay away from my daughter or I ent gonna leave you an inch to piss with!"

"As for you, girlie," Harl said, "I told you what we do to tramps around here!" He grabbed Renna's hair in a fist and dragged her toward the house. She cried out in pain but, still dazed, she could do little more than stumble along.

Halfway across the yard, she realized they weren't going to the house at all. Harl was taking her to the outhouse.

"No!" she screamed, accepting the pain from her pulled hair as she planted her feet and began to pull away. "Creator, please! *No!*"

"Think the Creator's gonna help you with you out sinnin' in broad daylight, girl?" Harl asked. "I'm doing His corespawned work!" He yanked hard, keeping her moving.

"Da! Please!" she cried. "I promise I'll be good!"

"You made that promise before, girl, and see where it's got us," Harl replied. "Shoulda done this right away; made sure you took me serious."

He shoved hard, and Renna fell into the outhouse, landing hard against the bench and wrenching her back. She ignored the pain and surged forward to escape, but Harl punched her right in the face as she charged, and everything went black.

ᛞ

Renna came to a few hours later. At first, she forgot where she was, but the fire in her back where she had struck the bench, and the blinding pain in her cheek when she flexed her face, brought it all back. She opened her eyes in terror.

Harl heard her screaming and pounding on the door, and came over, rapping sharply on the wall with the bone handle of his knife. "You quiet down in there! This is for your own good."

Renna ignored him, continuing to scream and kick at the door.

"Wouldn't do that, if I were you," Harl said, loudly enough to be heard over her tantrum. "Them boards're old enough as is, and you'll want 'em good and strong for when the sun sets. Keep kicking and you'll knock the wards out of place."

Renna quieted immediately.

"Please," she sobbed through the door. "Don't leave me out at night! I'll be good!"

"Corespawned right you will," Harl said. "After tonight, you'll chase that boy off yourself, he comes callin'!"

ᛞ

It was hot in the tiny outhouse, and the air was thick with the stench of excrement. There was a vent, but Renna didn't dare open it for fear of creating a hole in the wardnet. Flies buzzed noisily in the midden barrel in the pit below the crude waste bench.

Through the cracks in the wood, Renna watched the light dim as the sun began to set. She kept hoping, praying, that Harl would come back, that it was just a scare, but as the last glimmer of light died, so too did her hopes. Outside, the corelings were rising. She felt in her apron pocket, clutching the polished stones of Cobie's necklace tightly for strength.

The demons came silently; the day's heat drifting up from the ground gave them a path from the Core, it was said, and their misty forms even now would be coalescing into claws and scales and razor teeth. Renna could feel her heart pounding in her chest.

There was a snuffling at the outhouse door. Renna stiffened, biting her lip in fear, and in the silence of her stillness she could hear claws digging at the dirt of the yard, quick sniffs as the coreling inhaled the sharp tang of her fear.

Suddenly the demon shrieked and struck hard at the wards. There was a flare of magic, so bright it came through the cracks in the wood and illuminated the interior of the outhouse, and Renna screamed so hard it felt as if her throat would tear.

The wards held, but the demon was undeterred. There was a flap of leathery wings, and another flare of magic from the roof. The entire outhouse shook with the impact, and Renna screamed again as dust and dirt clattered down on her, shaken loose by the blow.

The wind demon tried again and again, shrieking its rage at the prey so near and yet so far. The wards threw the coreling back each time, but the rebounds shook the outhouse, and the old wood groaned in protest. How many blows could it withstand?

At last, the coreling gave up. Renna heard the flap of wings and its receding cries as it soared off in search of easier prey.

But the ordeal did not end there. Every coreling in the yard caught her scent before long. She endured the sparks of magic as flame demons raked at the wood with their tiny claws, shivering at the blasts of cold air as the wards converted their firespit. Worse were the wood demons, which drove off the others before long and pounded the wards so hard that the entire structure rocked with the force of each rebound. Renna felt every flare of the wards like a physical blow, and sank down to the floor, curling into a ball and sobbing uncontrollably.

It seemed to go on for an eternity. After Creator only knew how many hours, Renna found herself praying for the wards to fail—as they surely must before the night was through—just to put an end to it. If she'd been able to muster the strength to stand, she would have opened the door herself to let them in.

More interminable time passed, and she found she lacked even the strength to cry. The flare of magic, the shrieks in the night, the stench of the midden pit, all faded as she sank deeper and deeper into a primal fear so powerful that the details ceased to exist.

She lay curled tight, every muscle tensed at once, and tears flowed silently from her wide eyes as they stared into the darkness. Her breath came in short, sharp intakes, and her heart was a hummingbird's wing. Her nails dug grooves into the wood of the floor, oblivious to the resulting blood and splinters.

She didn't even notice when the sounds and flashes ceased, and the demons returned to the Core.

There was a thump as the outside bar was lifted, but Renna didn't react until the door opened wide to the blinding light of the rising sun. After hours of staring into darkness, the light seared her eyes, snapping her mind from its retreat. She gasped deeply and bolted upright, throwing an arm up against the light, screaming as she kicked back until she was scrunched against the rear wall of the outhouse.

Harl put his arms around her, soothing her hair. "There, there, girl," he whispered, gentling her hair. "That hurt me as much as it did you." He hugged her, firmly but gently, and rocked her from side to side as she sobbed.

"That's it, girl," he said. "You have yerself a good cry. Get it all out."

And she did, clutching at him as she convulsed in sorrow, before she finally calmed.

"Think you can mind me now?" Harl asked when her composure began to return. "Don't want to have to do this again."

Renna nodded eagerly. "I promise, Da." Her voice was hoarse from screaming.

"That a girl," Harl said, and lifted her in his arms, carrying her into the house. He put her in her own bed, and made her a hot broth, bringing lunch and dinner to her on a board she could lay across her lap. It was the first time Renna had ever seen him prepare food, but it was warm and good and filling.

"You sleep in tomorrow," he said that night. "Rest up, and you'll be right as rain by afternoon."

Indeed, Renna did feel better the next day, and better still the day after that. Harl did not come to her at night, and he let her work at her own pace by day. Time passed, and it became clear that Cobie wasn't coming back. It was just as well, Renna thought.

Sometimes, between chores, she remembered flashes of the night in the outhouse, but she blocked them quickly from her mind. It was over, and she would be a good daughter from now on, so she need not fear going back there again.

CHAPTER 15

MARICK'S TALE

:: 333 AR WINTER ::

THE CROWD HAD GATHERED at Leesha's hut early in the evening, while the sky was still awash in lavender and orange. At first it was just Darsy, Vika, and their apprentices, but then Gared and the other Cutters began to filter in, carrying their warded axes on their shoulders, and Erny and the rest of the Warders in the Hollow, along with their apprentices. Rojer arrived soon after, and Benn the glassblower. More and more came, until the yard was filled with onlookers, more than she could hope to house for the night. Some had brought tents to sleep in after the lesson.

Many of the visitors shifted nervously as the sun set, but they trusted in Leesha and the strength of her wards. Lanterns were lit to illuminate the stone table at the center of the gathering.

A few misty forms seeped from the ground as full dark came, but the corelings fled as soon as they solidified. They had learned that attempting to breach Leesha's wards could bring more than simple forbiddance.

Soon after, the Warded Man arrived, walking beside his giant stallion. Slung over the horse's back were the carcasses of several demons.

The Warders moved quickly, deactivating a portion of the wardnet long enough for the Warded Man to bring the coreling bodies through. The Cutters took over then, hauling the carcasses over to the stone table as the Warders reestablished the net.

"That didn't take you very long," Leesha told the Warded Man as he drew close.

The man shrugged. "You wanted one of each breed. It wasn't exactly a challenge."

Leesha grinned and took up her warded scalpels. "Rapt attention, all," she called loudly as she went to the wood demon and prepared to make the first incision. "Class is in session."

There was a communal breakfast in the morning for those who had remained at the hut. The Cutters had left soon after Leesha's lesson with the Warded Man at their lead, looking to reinforce their learning with practical application, but most others had stayed safe behind her wards until dawn.

Leesha had her apprentices cook a great vat of porridge, and brewed tea by the cauldron. They passed out the bowls and mugs as guests emerged from their tents, rubbing sleep from their eyes after the late night.

Rojer sat away from the others, tuning his fiddle on the porch of Leesha's hut.

"It's not like you to sit off by yourself," Leesha said, handing him a bowl and sitting beside him.

"Not really hungry," Rojer said, swirling his spoon in the porridge halfheartedly.

"Kendall is going to be all right," Leesha said. "She's recovering quickly, and she doesn't blame anyone for what happened."

"Maybe she should," Rojer said.

"You have a unique gift," Leesha said. "It's not your fault it's hard to teach."

"Is it?" Rojer asked. Leesha looked at him curiously, but he did not elucidate, instead turning away from her and looking out into the yard. "You could have told me."

"Told you what?" Leesha asked, knowing full well.

"About you and 'Arlen,' " Rojer said.

"I don't see that it's any of your business," Leesha said.

"But Kendall's love potions are yours?" Rojer snapped. "Maybe my teaching's not so bad after all. Maybe the girl just had her mind on sweet tea when it should have been on the demons."

"That's not fair," Leesha said. "I thought I was doing you a favor."

Rojer snarled at her, a look she'd never seen on his face outside of mummery. "No, you thought you were shoving me off on some other girl to make yourself feel better about not being interested yourself. You're more like your mother than you know."

Leesha opened her mouth to respond, but no words came to her. Rojer set down his bowl and walked off, putting his fiddle under his chin and playing an angry melody that drowned out anything Leesha might have said to call him back.

The Corelings' Graveyard was in chaos when Leesha and the others returned to town. Hundreds of folk, many of them injured and none of them familiar, filled the square. All were filthy, ragged, and half starved. Exhausted, they rested in grim misery on the frozen cobbles.

Tender Jona was running to and fro, shouting orders to his acolytes as they tried to give comfort to those in need. The Cutters were dragging logs out to the square so people would at least have a place to sit, but it seemed an impossible task.

"Thank the Creator!" the Tender called when he caught sight of them. Vika, his wife, ran to embrace him as he hurried over.

"What happened?" Leesha asked.

"Refugees from Fort Rizon," Jona said. "They just started pouring in this morning, a couple hours past dawn. More arrive at every moment."

"Where is the Deliverer?" a woman in the crowd cried. "They said he was here!"

"The wards in the entire city failed?" Leesha asked.

"Impossible," Erny said. "Rizon has over a hundred hamlets, all individually warded. Why flee all this way?"

"Wasn't the corelings we fled," a familiar voice said. Leesha turned, her eyes widening.

"Marick!" she cried. "What are you doing here?" The Messenger was as handsome as ever, but there were yellowed bruises on his face only partially obscured by his long hair and beard, and he favored one leg slightly as he approached.

"Made the mistake of wintering in Rizon," Marick said. "Usually a good idea; the cold doesn't bite so hard in the South." He chuckled mirthlessly. "Not this year."

"If it wasn't demons, what happened?" Leesha asked.

"Krasians," Marick said, spitting in the snow. "Seems the desert rats got sick of eating sand and decided to start preying on civilized folk."

Leesha turned to Rojer. "Find Arlen," she murmured. "Have him come in secret and meet us in the back room of Smitt's Tavern. Go now." Rojer nodded and vanished.

"Darsy. Vika," Leesha said. "Have the apprentices triage the wounded and bring them to the hospit in order of severity."

The two Herb Gatherers nodded and hurried off.

"Jona," Leesha said. "Have your acolytes fetch stretchers from the hospit and help the apprentices." Jona bowed and left.

Seeing Leesha giving direction, others drifted over. Even Smitt, the Town Speaker and innkeep, waited on her word.

"We can hold on food a moment," Leesha told him, "but these people need water and warm shelter immediately. Put up the wedding pavilions and any tents you can find, and have every spare hand you can find hauling water. If the wells and stream don't provide fast enough, put cauldrons on a fire and fill them with snow."

"I'll see to it," Smitt said.

"Since when does the whole Hollow hop to your commands?" Marick asked with a grin.

Leesha looked at him. "I need to see to the wounded now, Master Marick, but I'll have many questions for you when I'm through."

"I'll be at your disposal," Marick said, bowing.

"Thank you," Leesha said. "It would help if you could gather the other leaders of your group who might have something to add to your story."

"Of course," Marick said.

"I'll settle them in the inn," Stefny, Smitt's wife, said. "Surely you could use a cold ale and a bite," she told the Messenger.

"More than you could imagine," Marick said.

There were broken bones to set and infections to treat, many from blistered feet that had burst and been left untreated as folk spent more than a week on the road, knowing that to fall behind the main group meant almost certain death. More than a few of the travelers had coreling wounds, as well, from crowding into hastily put-together circles. It was a wonder any had made it to Deliverer's Hollow at all. She knew from their tales that many had not.

There were several Herb Gatherers of varying skill among the refugees, and after a quick check of their own state, Leesha put them to work. None of the women complained; it was ever the lot of the Herb Gatherer to put aside her own needs for those of her charges.

"We would never have made it without Messenger Marick," one woman said as Leesha treated her frostbitten toes. "He rode ahead each day and warded campsites for our group to succor when the corelings came. Wouldn't have lasted a night without him. He even felled deer with his bow and left them on the road for us to find."

By the time Rojer reappeared, the worst of the wounds had been treated.

She left control of the hospit to Darsy and Vika and went with him to her office.

When the door closed behind them, Leesha slumped against Rojer, finally allowing her exhaustion to show. It was late in the afternoon, and she had been working for hours without a break, treating patients and fielding questions from apprentices and town elders alike. It would be dark in a few short hours.

"You need to rest," Rojer said, but Leesha shook her head, filling a basin with water and splashing it on her face.

"No time for it now," she said. "Have we found shelter for everyone?"

"Barely," Rojer said. "All told, there's more refugees than the entire population of Deliverer's Hollow twice over, and I've no doubt there will be more tomorrow. Folk have opened their homes, but Tender Jona still has people sleeping sitting up in his pews, just to keep a roof over them. If this keeps up, every inch of the greatward will be covered in makeshift tents by week's end."

Leesha nodded. "We'll worry over that come morning. Arlen is waiting at Smitt's?"

"The *Warded Man* is there," Rojer said. "Don't call him Arlen in front of those people."

"It's his name, Rojer," Leesha said.

"I don't care," Rojer snapped, surprising her with his vehemence. "These people need something bigger than themselves to believe in, and right now it's him. No one is asking you to call him Deliverer."

Leesha blinked, taken aback. "I've gotten used to everyone leaping when I say *hop*."

"Well you can trust me never to do that," Rojer said.

Leesha smiled. "I want it no other way. Come. Let's go see the Warded Man."

The taproom of Smitt's Tavern was filled to capacity when Rojer and Leesha arrived, even though the new inn was twice the size it had been when it burned down the year previous.

Smitt nodded to them as they entered, and jerked his head toward the back room. They hurried through the crowd and ducked through the heavy door.

The Warded Man was in the room, pacing like an animal.

"I should be out hunting for more survivors before nightfall, not waiting on council meetings," he said.

"We'll be as swift as we can," Leesha said, "but it's best we do this together."

The Warded Man nodded, though she could see his impatience in his clenching hands. Smitt entered a moment later, ushering in Marick, along with Stefny, Tender Jona, Erny, and Elona.

Marick stared at the Warded Man, though his hood was drawn and his tattooed hands were hidden in the voluminous sleeves of his robe.

"Are you . . . him?" Marick asked.

The Warded Man pulled back his hood, revealing his painted flesh, and Marick gasped.

"You the Deliverer, as they say?" Marick asked.

The Warded Man shook his head. "Just a man who learned to kill demons."

Jona snorted.

"Something caught in your throat, Tender?" the Warded Man asked.

"The other Deliverers never named themselves as such," Jona said. "They were all given the title by others." The Warded Man scowled at him, but Jona only bowed his head.

"I guess it doesn't matter," Marick said, though he sounded a little disappointed. "I didn't really expect you to have a halo."

"What happened?" the Warded Man asked.

"Twelve days ago, the Krasians sacked Fort Rizon," Marick said. "They came in the night, bypassed the hamlets, and took out the wall guards, opening the gates of the central city wide at the crack of dawn. We were all still in our beds when the killing started."

"They came in the night?" Leesha asked. "How is that possible?"

"They've got warded weapons that kill demons," Marick said, "same as you Hollow folk. They talk like there ent nothing in the world more important than demon killing, and taking Rizon was just something to keep them busy till the sun set."

"Go on," the Warded Man pressed.

"Well," Marick said, "it's clear their eyes were on the central grain silos, because they took those first. Their warriors killed any man that resisted, and bent any woman that looked old enough to bleed." He glanced at the women present, and his face flushed.

"It's no shock what men will do when they think they can get away with it," Elona said bitterly. "Get on with your tale, Messenger."

Marick nodded. "They must have killed thousands, that first morning, and took the city walls to keep the rest of us in. We were beaten, tied together, and dragged into warehouses like cattle."

"How did you escape?" the Warded Man asked.

"At first I didn't think any of the desert rats spoke a civilized tongue," Marick said. "I know a couple of sand words I picked up from other Messengers, but it's mostly curses, not much to start a conversation with. I figured I was done for, but after a day, a fat one came who spoke Thesan like a native. He started rounding up the royals, landowners, and skilled laborers, bringing them to the Krasian duke. I was among those."

"You saw their leader?" the Warded Man asked.

"Oh, I saw that big bastard all right," Marick said. "They brought me before him, bound and battered, and when he heard I was a Warder, he set me free like nothing had happened. Even gave me a purse of gold for my troubles! I think he meant for me to teach them our wards, but I was over the wall and out of the city at dawn the next morning."

"Their leader," the Warded Man pressed. "What was he wearing?"

Marick blinked. "Open white robe and head rag," he said, "with black underneath, like their warriors wear. And he wore a crown; that's how I knew he was their duke."

"A crown?" the Warded Man asked. "Are you sure? He didn't just have a jewel set in his turban?"

Marick nodded. "I'm sure. It was gold, and covered in jewels and wards. Ripping thing must have been worth more than every other duke's crown combined."

"And this duke, did he speak our tongue?" the Warded Man asked.

"Better than some Angierians I know," Marick said.

"What was his name?" the Warded Man asked.

Marick shrugged. "Don't think anyone said it. They all called him some sand word. Shamaka, or somesuch. I figured it meant 'duke.' "

"Shar'Dama Ka?" the Warded Man asked.

"Ay." Marick nodded. "That was it."

The Warded Man swore under his breath.

"What is it?" Leesha asked, but he ignored her, leaning in to the Messenger.

"Was he about this tall?" he asked, holding up a hand above his own head. "With a forked, oiled beard and a sharp, hooked nose?"

Marick nodded.

"Did he carry a warded spear?" the Warded Man asked.

"They all carried warded spears," Marick said.

"You would remember this one," the Warded Man said.

Marick nodded again. "Metal, it was, point-to-butt. And covered in etched wards."

The growl that issued from the Warded Man's throat was so feral that even Marick, usually fearless, took a step back.

"What is it?" Leesha asked again.

"Ahmann Jardir," the Warded Man said. "I know him."

"What does this mean?" she asked, but the Warded Man waved the question away.

"It makes no difference now," he said. "Go on," he told Marick. "What happened next?"

"As I said, I scaled the wall and fled the city the moment they set me free," Marick said. "The hamlets I passed through were half deserted by the time I arrived. When word of the attack reached them, the smart folk grabbed what they could and were on the road before the blood on the cobbles of the central city was dry. Those too weak to travel or too scared of the night stayed behind. I think more stayed than left, but there were still tens of thousands on the road.

"I bought a horse from an old fellow got left behind, and galloped off. I caught up to the folk on the road soon after. The groups were too large to stick together; no city could absorb so many. Most went to Lakton and its hamlets, where any with a hook and line can fill their belly, but the Jongleurs have had a lot to say about you," he pointed to the Warded Man, "and them that believed you were really the Deliverer come again flocked here. I needed to get back to Angiers and report to the duke, but I couldn't just leave folk on the road with so few to ward for them, so I offered up my services."

"It was a good thing you did, Marick," Leesha said, laying a hand on his arm. "These people never would have made it without you. Go and take your ease out into the taproom while we discuss your news."

"I have a room reserved for you upstairs," Smitt added. "Stefny will see you there."

The Warded Man put his hood up as soon as the Messenger left. "Daylight is fading. If there are more on the road, I need to make sure they see the dawn."

Leesha nodded. "Take Gared and as many Cutters as can sit a horse."

"Get your cloak," the Warded Man told Rojer. "You're coming with us." Rojer nodded, and they headed for the rear exit.

"You'll need Warders," Erny said, pushing back his wire-framed glasses and rising from his seat. "I'll go."

Elona was on her feet instantly grabbing his arm. "You'll do no such thing, Ernal."

Erny blinked. "You're always complaining I'm not brave enough. Now you want me to hide when people need my help?"

"You'll prove nothing to me by getting yourself killed," Elona said. "You haven't sat a horse in years."

"She has a point, Da," Leesha said.

"Stay out of this," Erny said. "The town may hop at your word, but I'm still your father."

"There's no time for this," the Warded Man said. "Are you coming or not?"

"Not," Elona said firmly.

"Coming," Erny said, pulling his arm from her grasp and following the other men out.

"That idiot!" Elona shrieked as the door slammed shut. Everyone else glanced at one another.

"Take as long back here as you like," Smitt said, "I need to get out front." He, Stefny, and Jona quickly filed out of the room, leaving Leesha alone with her fuming mother.

"He'll be all right, Mum," Leesha said. "There's nowhere in all the world safer than traveling with Rojer and the Warded Man."

"He's a frail man!" Elona said. "He can't ride with young men, and he'll catch his death of cold! He's never been the same after the flux took him last year."

"Why, Mother," Leesha said, surprised, "it sounds like you truly care."

"Don't take that tone with me," Elona snapped. "Of course I care. He's my husband. If you knew what it was like to be married almost thirty years, you wouldn't say such things."

Leesha wanted to snap back, to shout out all the horrible things her mother had done to her father over the years, not the least of which being her repeated infidelity with Gared's father, Steave, but the sincerity in her mother's voice checked her.

"You're right, Mum, I'm sorry," she said.

Elona blinked. "I'm right? Did you just say I was right?"

"I did." Leesha smiled.

Elona opened her arms. "Hug me now, child, while it lasts." Leesha laughed and embraced her tightly.

"He'll be fine," Leesha said, as much for herself as her mother.

Elona nodded. "You're right, of course. He may look a terror, but no demon can stand up to your tattooed friend."

"Both of us right in one night, and Da not here to witness," Leesha said.

"He'll never believe it," Elona agreed. She dabbed at her eyes with a kerchief, and Leesha pretended not to notice.

"So was that the same Marick you used to shine on?" Elona asked. "The one you ran off to Angiers with?"

"I never shined on him, Mother," Leesha said.

Elona scoffed. "Sell that tampweed tale to someone who doesn't know you. The whole town knew you wanted him, even if you were too prudish to act on it. And why not? He's handsome as a wolf, and a Messenger on top. That's man enough for any woman. Why do you think he used to make Gared so jealous?"

"Everything made Gared jealous, Mum," Leesha said.

Elona nodded. "He's just like his father: simple men, ruled by their passions." She smiled wistfully, and Leesha knew she was thinking of Steave, her first love, who had died the year previous when flux took Cutter's Hollow and the wards failed.

"The Marick I saw when we were alone on the road wasn't much different," Leesha said.

"And you used Gatherer's tricks to keep him off you," Elona guessed, "instead of taking it as the perfect opportunity to have a romp with no one the wiser." It was true enough; Leesha had secretly drugged Marick into impotence to prevent his taking advantage of her on the road.

"Like you would have?" Leesha asked, unable to keep the bite from her tone.

"Yes," Elona said, "and why not? Skirts lift up for a reason. Women have needs down below, just as men. Don't lie to yourself and pretend otherwise."

"I know that, Mum," Leesha said.

"You know it," Elona agreed, "and yet still you sew your petticoats shut, and think denying yourself somehow makes you heroic. How can you treat every body in the Hollow when you don't understand the needs of your own?"

Leesha said nothing. Her mother had a most unsettling way of reading her thoughts.

"You should go up and talk to Marick while your other suitors are out of town," Elona said. "He's had years and tragedy to season him, and come out a hero. The folk outside can't stop singing his praises. Perhaps he'll be more to your liking now."

"I don't know . . ." Leesha said.

"Oh, go on!" Elona said. "Take a plate of food up to his room and talk to him. It's not like you have to let him stick you this very night." She smiled and winked. "Though if you did, it'd be a better use of your night than fretting over problems that will remain come morning."

Leesha laughed despite herself, and hugged her mother again.

Several times they passed scenes of slaughter; bodies, alone and in groups, torn apart by corelings when night fell upon them without succor.

The Warded Man cursed the sights, spurring Twilight Dancer on harder, not bothering to stop after the first. The others who followed him, even Gared and the Cutters, were inexperienced riders falling well behind his powerful stallion, but he didn't care. There were refugees on the road, driven out of their homes by Ahmann Jardir, the man he had been fool enough to call friend, and he needed to find and protect as many of them as he could before night fell.

But he would hold Jardir to account for every life lost. Corespawn him if he did not.

More than an hour of hard riding brought him to a large group of refugees. The sky was awash with color as the sun set, but the folk were still working on their wards. They had painted the magical symbols on wooden boards, but the area they needed to secure was irregularly shaped, and the net was out of alignment.

He galloped right to the edge of the wardnet, pulling Twilight Dancer up short and leaping down with his warding kit. People cried out at the sight of him, but he ignored them, inspecting their wards.

"It's him," one Warder whispered to another. "The Deliverer." The Warded Man paid him no mind, focusing on the task at hand. Some of their wards he turned or twisted to align properly with others, but many he altered with charcoal, or turned the boards over and replaced entirely.

A crowd began to gather around him, folk clutching one another and whispering as they stared at his tattooed hands and tried to get a peek under his hood. None dared approach him, though, and his work went uninterrupted. When his companions finally caught up, Erny fumbled his way down off his horse to assist. Rojer and the others placed themselves protectively between him and the crowd.

"Deliverer!" a woman screamed at him. He glanced over to see her struggling vainly toward him against the pull of Gared's trunklike arms, her eyes alight with fanatical fire. He turned back to his work.

"Please!" the woman cried. "My sister is still on the road!"

The Warded Man looked up sharply at that. "Take over the warding," he told Erny. "Draft as many of their Warders as you need. I'll leave a couple of archers to buy you time to finish." Erny gulped, but he nodded and called to the Rizonan Warders, who had been standing back with the rest of the refugees.

"Let her go," the Warded Man told Gared when he reached the pair. Gared complied immediately, and the woman fell to her knees before him, clutching at his feet.

"Please, Deliverer," she said. "My sister is with child; too far along to sit a horse. She and our gray parents couldn't keep up with the group, so our husbands bade me take the children on ahead while they set a slower pace."

"And they haven't caught up," the Warded Man finished for her.

"It is nearly dark," the woman said, weeping upon his feet and clutching at the hem of his robes. "Please, Deliverer, save them."

The Warded Man reached down to her, placing a hand on her chin and gently pulling her to her feet. "I'm not the Deliverer," he said. "But I swear I'll save your family if I can."

He turned to Gared. "Pick two archers to stay with Erny while the wards here are completed," he said. "The rest of you are with me." Gared nodded, and moments later they thundered out of the camp, riding even more frantically than before.

It was dark when they found them: five people, as the desperate woman had said. They stood in a tiny makeshift ward circle, surrounded by dozens of corelings. Flame demons spat fire and wind demons swooped down from the sky. There was even a rock demon, towering over the rest.

Each time the demons struck and the wardnet flared to life, Rojer could see the holes in the web; holes more than large enough for a demon to squeeze through.

The two young men stood by those holes, stabbing out with pitchforks to drive the demons back as an elderly couple tended to the obvious reason why they had fallen behind.

The young woman at the circle's center was giving birth.

The Warded Man growled and kicked his stallion forward, leaping ahead of the others. He cast his robe aside, and it floated to the ground in his wake. Gared and the Cutters gave a cry and followed suit, freeing their warded axes as they galloped toward the fray.

The Warded Man rode Twilight Dancer right into the rock demon, the warded metal horns welded to the horse's barding crackling with power as they punched through the black carapace of the demon's abdomen. The

Warded Man leapt from his horse as the demon was driven back, grabbing one of its horns to hold on to as he rode the coreling to the ground, punching it repeatedly in the throat with warded fists as it went down.

He was up in an instant, tackling a flame demon and tearing its lower jaw clean off. The Cutters caught up to him then, catching flame bursts on their warded shields and hacking at the demons as if they were sectioning lumber.

Wonda and the archers took a different tack, halting their horses several dozen yards back and sighting the wind demons that filled the sky. They came crashing down one after another, feathered shafts jutting from their leathery bodies.

Rojer slipped from his horse, leaving it with the archers, and took up his fiddle, playing even as he ran for the small circle. Much like Leesha's Cloaks of Unsight, his music made him effectively invisible to the corelings as he waded through their lines, but without the need for a slow pace. In moments he was inside the circle, and changed his tune to the jarring notes that would drive the demons away from the small family.

The young woman screamed as battle raged about them, black demon ichor flying free in the night air. Her parents were doing what they could to make her comfortable, but it was clear from their fumbling that they had no idea how to assist in the delivery.

"She needs help!" Rojer cried. "We need to get her to an Herb Gatherer!"

The Warded Man broke away from the demons he was engaging and was at Rojer's side in an instant. He was clad only in a loincloth, covered in tattoos and demon ichor. The Rizonans backed away from him in fear, but the girl was too far gone to even notice.

"Get my herb pouch," the Warded Man said, kneeling by the girl and examining her with a surprisingly gentle touch. "Her water's broken and her contractions are close. There's no time to get her to a Gatherer."

Rojer ran out to Twilight Dancer, but the stallion was in a wild rage, trampling a pair of flame demons into the snow and mud. Drawing his warded cloak about him, Rojer took up his fiddle again. As with the corelings, Rojer's special magic found resonance with the beast, and in short order the horse stood calmly while Rojer retrieved the precious herb pouch.

He brought the pouch to the Warded Man, who quickly began grinding herbs into powder and mixing them with water. The girl's family kept back, watching the scene in horror as the Cutters laid waste to demons all around them.

"Do you know what you're doing?" Rojer asked nervously, as the Warded Man brought his potion to the moaning woman's lips.

"I was apprenticed to an Herb Gatherer for six months as part of my Messenger training," the Warded Man said. "I've seen it done."

"Seen?!" Rojer asked.

"Do you want to do it?" the Warded Man asked, looking at him. Rojer blanched and shook his head. "Then just play your ripping fiddle and keep the demons back while I work." Rojer nodded and put bow back to string.

Hours later, with the sounds of battle long faded, a shrill cry broke the night. Rojer looked at the screaming babe and smiled.

"There will be no denying it when people call you Deliverer now," he said.

The Warded Man scowled at him, and Rojer laughed.

Leesha carried the steaming tray up the steps of Smitt's inn, her heart beating nervously. Twice before, she had considered giving herself to Marick, whom she could not deny was handsome and quick-witted. Both times, Marick's character had failed at the key moment, making Leesha feel that in his mind, her needs were second to his own, if he was considering them at all.

But her mother was right again. She often was, even as she used the insight to cut at people. Leesha was tired of being alone, and she knew in her heart that Arlen would never fill that place for her. Not for the first time, she wished she could see Rojer in that light, but it was impossible. She loved Rojer, but had no desire for him to share her bed. Marick had shown the people of Fort Rizon that he was a man who could be counted upon in times of need. Perhaps it was time to look beyond his past failings.

She tugged the wrinkles from her dress, then felt foolish for it, and knocked on his door.

"Ay?" Marick asked as he opened the door. He was shirtless and damp, having just come from the warm basin of water in his room. His eyes widened as he caught sight of Leesha.

"I didn't mean to disturb you," Leesha said. "Just thought you might do with a hot meal before you sleep."

"I . . . yes, thank you," Marick said, grabbing his tunic and pulling it on. Leesha looked away as he did so, though the image of his muscled body lingered in her mind.

Marick took the tray, inhaling its aroma deeply as he brought it over to the small table and chair by the bed. He lifted the lid to reveal a hot joint of meat, moist with its own juices, nestled amid spiced potatoes and fresh steamed greens.

"Food in Deliverer's Hollow is soon to grow short," Leesha said, "but Smitt's stores have held out for a night, at least."

"A bed is glorious enough, after lying down in snow for near two weeks," Marick said. "This is a gift from the Creator Himself." He tore into the meat, and Leesha took a strange satisfaction in watching him eat the food she had prepared. She remembered the feeling, distantly, from the time she and Gared had been promised, and she first cooked for him. It seemed a century ago, in another life.

"That was delicious," Marick said when he was done, wiping his mouth on his sleeve.

"It's small thanks for what you did," Leesha said, "bringing those people to safety in their time of need."

"Even after I failed you in yours?" Marick asked. Leesha looked at him in surprise.

"Last year," Marick said, "when flux caught the Hollow and you needed to get home. I made . . . unfair demands for my assistance."

"Marick . . ." Leesha began softly.

"No, let me speak," Marick said. "When we were on the road to Angiers that first time, I was so taken with you, I thought we would be raising children together within a year. But then, in the tent, when I couldn't . . . be a man with you, I . . ."

"Marick . . ." Leesha said again.

"It made me crazy," Marick said. "I felt like I needed to get far away from you, but when I did, I couldn't stop thinking of you, even when I . . . lay with other women." He looked away.

"But when I saw you again," he went on, "I felt so . . . hard, and I wanted to make up for my past failing quickly, before something else prevented it. It was unfair to you, and I'm sorry."

Leesha laid a hand on his arm. "I'm not a child," she said. "I was as responsible for what happened as you." It was more true than he would ever know, and at that moment she felt horrified at her own actions. It felt so righteous at the time, but the truth was she had drugged and used him for her own convenience, leaving him scarred for years over the ordeal. Perhaps Rojer was right, and she was more like her mother than she knew.

"That's kind of you to say," Marick said, squeezing her arm, "but you and I both know it isn't so. I'm glad you managed to make it home," he added, "and without having to surrender your virtue."

Leesha had been leaning in toward him, but she flinched back from him at the words, for indeed, her virtue had been torn from her on the trip, taken by bandits on the road because she went without proper escort. All because of Marick's impatience and inability to think of others before himself.

Marick seemed not to notice her change in demeanor. He chuckled and shook his head. "Can't get over how you run the Hollow now. What happened to the soft girl who turned the head of every man that saw her? Overnight you've become Hag Bruna. I'll wager even the corelings are scared of you now."

Hag Bruna? Was that how folk saw her? The lonesome crone who bullied and intimidated everyone in town? Was that what she'd become when her virtue was stripped from her?

Her mother sensed the change, too. *Time it was done somehow,* Elona had said, *and I expect you're the better for it.*

Leesha shook her head to clear it, sensing the moment they had been about to share slipping away. "What are your plans now?" she asked. "Will you help us hunt for more survivors on the road, or do you mean to take your group of refugees directly on to Angiers?"

Marick looked at her in surprise. "Neither."

"What do you mean?" Leesha asked.

"Now that the Rizonans are safe, it's time I moved on," Marick said. "The duke needs word of the Krasian attack, and I've let them slow me long enough."

"Slow you?" Leesha asked. "Their lives depended on you!"

Marick nodded. "I couldn't leave people out on the road without succor, but they have succor now. I'm not Rizonan. I have no further responsibility to them."

"But Deliverer's Hollow can't possibly absorb so many!" Leesha cried.

Marick shrugged. "I'll tell the duke. Let it be his problem."

"They're not a problem, Marick, they're people!" Leesha said.

"What do you expect me to do?" Marick asked. "Devote the rest of my life to looking out for them? That's not a Messenger's way."

"Well, I'm glad we never ended up raising children together, then," Leesha snapped. "Enjoy your bed, Messenger." She took the tray and left, slamming the door behind her.

"What are we going to do?" Smitt asked. Leesha had called a late meeting of the town council to discuss Marick's revelation that he was leaving the refugees in Deliverer's Hollow and pressing on alone in the morning.

"Take them in, of course," Leesha said. "Open our homes while helping them build their own. We can't just leave these folk without food or shelter."

"The greatward can't accommodate so many new houses," Smitt said.

"So we'll build another," Leesha said. "We have near two thousand hands to do the work, and miles of forest for material."

"Not to scuff the wards," Darsy said, "but just how're we supposed to feed so many in the dead of winter? If more keep coming, we'll all be eating snow before long."

Leesha had been considering the same problem. "Every young woman in the Hollow can shoot a bow now. We'll put them to hunting, and the boys to trapping."

"That will only go so far," Vika said.

Leesha nodded. "Corkweed may be tough and bitter, but it's nutritious enough, grows on just about everything, and survives year-round. Put the younger children to work gathering it, and I'll think of a way to cook and season it in bulk. If that's not enough, there are edible barks and even insects that can fill a starving belly."

"Weeds and insects?" Elona asked. "You're going to ask folk to eat bugs?"

"I'm seeing to it they don't starve, Mother," Leesha said. "If I have to sit and eat bugs in front of them to set an example, that's what I'll do."

"Well enough for you," Elona said, "but don't expect me to do the same."

"You'll have your own part to play," Leesha said.

Elona looked at her. "I'm not making my house into an inn for every vagabond that comes down the road."

Leesha sighed. "It's getting dark, Mother. You'd best head home. We'll talk in the morning."

The others took this as the meeting's end and filed out of the room after Elona, leaving Leesha alone with Stefny.

"Don't fret," Stefny said. "I'm sure your mother will be more than willing to do her part, opening her home to the Rizonan men with the biggest dangles."

Leesha glared at her. "My mum isn't the only woman in this village who broke her wedding vows," she reminded her. Stefny's youngest son Keet, now nearly twenty, was fathered not by Smitt but by the village's previous Tender, Michel. It was still unknown to Smitt and the rest of town, but Bruna, who had midwifed the child, knew from the outset.

"Don't ever make the mistake of thinking Bruna's secrets died with her," Leesha warned. "Keep your hypocrisy to yourself."

Stefny blanched white and nodded meekly. Leesha gave an amused snort at how she scurried out of the room, and then started suddenly, realizing she sounded just like Bruna.

It was well over a week after Marick rode off—to the cheers and adulation of those he was deserting—before the Warded Man and Rojer returned. Erny and the Cutters had drifted back into the city over the first few days, each bringing groups of refugees with them, but the Warded Man and Rojer kept ranging ever farther, and all who came to the Hollow told stories of encountering them.

Leesha was proud of Arlen and Rojer for the lives they were saving, but by the time they returned, so many folk had come that she despaired of feeding them all, weeds and bugs or no.

"We went as close to Rizon as we dared," Rojer said over hot tea at her cottage the day they returned. "I think we found everyone who took the road, though there are likely some who tried to cut overland. The Krasians have dug in firmly, and send out regular patrols on the road."

"They've only dug in temporarily," the Warded Man said. "It won't be long before they're on the move again."

"Back to the ripping desert, I hope," Rojer said.

The Warded Man shook his head. "No. They'll conquer Lakton, and then they'll turn north and head right for the Hollow."

Leesha felt her face grow cold, and Rojer looked like he might be sick.

"How can you know that?" she asked.

"The Krasians believe that Kaji, the first Deliverer, unified the tribes of Krasia and then rode out of the desert, spending two decades conquering the lands to the north," the Warded Man said. "He called it Sharak Sun, the Daylight War, and levied the men into Sharak Ka, the great holy war against demonkind. If Ahmann Jardir thinks he is the Deliverer come again, he will attempt to follow the same path."

"What are we to do?" Leesha asked.

"Build defenses," the Warded Man said. "Fight them, every inch of the way."

Leesha shook her head. "No. I won't support that. These aren't demons you're talking about killing, Arlen. They're human beings."

"You think I don't know that?" the Warded Man said. "I have Krasian friends, Leesha! Can you say the same?" Leesha looked at him in shock, but she recovered and shook her head.

"Make no mistake," the Warded Man said, his voice quieter, but no less vehement, "the Krasians believe every single person in the North is inferior to the least of them. They may make a show of being merciful to leaders they can use to further their goals, but there will be no such concessions to regular folk. They will kill or enslave everyone who does not swear utter submission to Jardir and the Evejah. We *have* to fight."

"We could retreat to Angiers," Leesha said. "Hide within the city walls."

The Warded Man shook his head. "We can't give them any ground. I know these people. If we show fear and retreat, they will think us weak, and only press the attack harder."

"I still don't like it," Leesha said.

The Warded Man shrugged. "Your liking it is irrelevant. The good news is that I doubt they have more than six thousand warriors of fighting age. The bad news is that the least of those can outfight any three Cutters, and when they're ready to move, they'll have levied thousands of slave troops from Rizon."

"How are we supposed to fight against that?" Rojer said.

"Unity," the Warded Man said. "We need to open dialogue with Lakton now, while the lines of communication are still clear, and petition the dukes of Angiers and Miln to put aside their differences and commit to a common defense."

"I don't know the duke of Miln," Rojer said, "but I grew up in Rhinebeck's court when my master Arrick was his herald. Rhinebeck is more likely to put aside his differences with the corelings than with Duke Euchor."

"Then we'll have to convince him personally," Leesha said. She looked at the Warded Man. "All of us."

The Warded Man sighed. "Just as well I not go to Lakton. I'm . . . not very welcome there."

"So the tale's true then?" Rojer asked. "The dockmasters tried to kill you?"

"After a fashion," the Warded Man said.

Rojer sat in the music shell that night, playing to soothe the hundreds of refugees still living in tents in the Corelings' Graveyard. Many of them drifted over to sit by the shell, basking in the warm glow of the greatward as they fell under Rojer's spell. His music swept them up and carried them far away to forget, at least for a short time, that their lives had been shattered.

It seemed a terribly inadequate gift, but it was all he had to give. He kept his Jongleur's mask in place, letting them see nothing of the bleakness he felt inside.

Tender Jona was waiting for him when he finished playing. The Holy Man was young, not yet thirty, but he was well loved by the Hollowers, and no one had worked harder to bring comfort and necessities to the refugees. In addition to organizing most of the food and shelter rationing, the Tender walked among the refugees, learning their names and letting them know they were not alone. He led prayers for the dead, found caregivers for orphans, and married lovers brought together by tragedy.

"Thank you for doing this," Jona said. "I could feel their spirits lifting as they watched you play. My own, as well."

"I'll perform every evening I'm not needed elsewhere," Rojer said.

"Bless you," Jona said. "Your music gives such strength to them."

"I wish it could give some to me," Rojer said. "Sometimes I think in my case the opposite is true."

"Nonsense," Jona said. "Strength of spirit is not some finite thing, where one man must lose for another to gain. The Creator grants strength and weakness to us all. What has you feeling weak, child?"

"Child?" Rojer laughed. "I'm not part of your audience, Tender. I have my fiddle," he held up the instrument, "and you have yours." He pointed with his bow at the heavy leather-bound Canon that Jona held in his hands.

Rojer knew his words hurt the Tender, and that the man deserved better, but his mood was black and Jona had picked the wrong time to condescend. He waited for the Holy Man to shout at him, ready and willing to shout right back.

But Jona never grew vexed. He slipped the book into a satchel he wore for just that purpose, and spread his hands to show they were empty. "As your friend, then. And someone who understands your pain."

"How could *you* possibly understand my pain?" Rojer snapped.

Jona smiled. "I love her, too, Rojer. I don't think I've ever met a man who didn't. She used to come almost every day to read at the Holy House, and we would talk for hours. I've seen her shine on men who didn't deserve her, never even noticing that I was a man as well."

Rojer tried to keep his Jongleur's mask in place, but there was an honesty in Jona's tone that cut through his defenses. "How did you deal with it? How do you stop loving someone?"

"The Creator didn't make love conditional," Jona said. "Love is what makes us human. What separates us from the corelings. There is value in it, even when it is not requited."

"You love her still?" Rojer asked.

Jona nodded. "But I love my Vika and our children even more. Love is as infinite as spirit." He put his hand on Rojer's shoulder. "Do not waste years lamenting what you do not have with her. Instead, cherish what you do. And if ever you need to speak with someone who understands your trial, come to me. I promise to leave the Canon in its satchel."

He slapped Rojer on the shoulder and walked off, leaving Rojer feeling as if a weight had been lifted from him.

The lamps were lit in Leesha's cottage when Rojer arrived, and the front door was open. Neglecting his warded cloak, Rojer had held the corelings off with his fiddle, which meant Leesha had heard him coming long before he arrived.

It was a ritual they shared. Leesha was always awake and working, but she would leave the door open when she heard his fiddle in the distance. Rojer would find her with her nose in a book or embroidering, grinding herbs or tending her gardens.

Rojer stopped playing when he reached Leesha's warded path, and the cold night grew quiet save for the distant shrieks of demons. But in the silence between the sounds of corelings, Rojer heard weeping.

He found Leesha curled in an ancient rocking chair, wrapped in a tattered old shawl. They had belonged to her teacher, Bruna, and Leesha always went to them when she had doubt.

Her eyes were red and puffy, the crumpled kerchief in her hand soaked through. He looked at her and understood what Jona meant about cherishing what they had. Even when she was at her lowest, she left her door open for him. Could the other men in her life say the same?

"You're not still mad at me?" Leesha asked.

"Course not," Rojer said. "We both did a little spitting, is all."

Leesha gave a strained smile. "I'm glad."

"Your kerchief is soaked," Rojer said. He flicked his wrist, pulling out one of the many colored kerchiefs in his sleeve. He held it out to her, but when she reached for it, he tossed it into the air, quickly adding several more as if from empty air. Rojer began to juggle them, creating a circle of colored cloth floating in the air. Leesha laughed and clapped.

Arrick, Rojer's master, could have juggled anything in the room, but with Rojer's crippled hand, kerchiefs were the only thing he could keep going indefinitely. "Pick a color."

"Green," Leesha said, and faster than her eye could see his hand snatched that cloth and tossed it her way, making it seem to have leapt from the circle of its own accord. Rojer caught the rest and tucked them back away as Leesha dried her face.

"What is it?" he asked.

"Bad enough that demons hunt us at night," Leesha said, "but now men are killing one another in the daylight. Arlen wants us to make war with both, but how can I support that?"

"I don't know that you have much choice," Rojer said. "If he's right, the Daylight War will find us whether we support it or not."

Leesha sighed, hugging the shawl tightly even though the heat wards around her yard kept things comfortably warm. "Do you remember the night in the cave?"

Rojer nodded. It had been the previous summer, a few days after the Warded Man had rescued them on the road. The three of them had taken shelter from the rain, and while there, Leesha had learned that Rojer and the Warded Man had killed the bandits who had robbed them and ravished Leesha. She had been furious with them, and called them murderers.

"Do you know why I was so angry with you and Arlen?" Leesha asked. Rojer shook his head. "Because I could have killed those men if I'd wanted." She reached into her dress pocket, producing a slim needle coated in some greenish mixture.

"I carry these needles for putting down mad animals," Leesha said. "I keep them in my dress pocket because they are too dangerous to leave lying in the herb cloth, or even my apron, which I take off sometimes. No man would long survive a puncture from one of these, and even a scratch might kill him in time."

"I'll ware my tongue around you in the future," Rojer said, but Leesha didn't laugh.

"I had one in my free hand when I threw the blinding powder at the bandit leader," Leesha said. "If I had struck the mute with it when he grabbed me, he would have been dead before the leader recovered, and I could have struck him, too."

"And I could have handled the third," Rojer said. He lifted an empty hand, and suddenly a knife appeared in it. He thrust quick and twisted the knife in the air. "So why didn't you?"

"Because it's one thing to kill a coreling," Leesha said, "and another to kill a person. Even a bad person. I wanted to. Sometimes I even look back and wish I had. But when the time to do it came, I couldn't."

Rojer looked at the knife in his hand a moment, then sighed and slipped it back into the special harness on his forearm, rebuttoning his cuff.

"Don't think I could, either," he admitted sadly. "I started learning knife tricks when I was five, but it's all mummery. I've never so much as cut someone."

"Once I knew I couldn't do it, I just stopped fighting when they pushed me down," Leesha said. "Night, I even spit on my hand to wet myself when the first one fumbled with his breeches. But even when they left me sobbing in the dirt, I didn't wish I'd killed them."

"You wished they'd killed you, instead," Rojer said.

Leesha nodded.

"I felt the same way, after Master Jaycob was killed," Rojer said. "I didn't want revenge, I just wanted the pain to end."

"I remember," Leesha said. "You begged me to let you die."

Rojer nodded. "That's why I went with the Warded Man to the bandit camp."

"For me?" Leesha asked.

Rojer shook his head. "Those men needed to be put down like any mad horse, Leesha. We weren't the first folk they robbed, and we wouldn't have been the last, especially once they had my portable circle. But we didn't kill them. The Warded Man walked in and stole your horse, I grabbed the circle, and we ran. They were all breathing and relatively unbroken when we left."

"Food for the demons," Leesha said.

Rojer shrugged. "The Warded Man had killed most of the demons in the area. We didn't see a one when we walked to their camp, and dawn was only a few hours away. It was a better chance than they gave us by far."

Leesha sighed, but she said nothing. He looked at her. "Why do folk call an Herb Gatherer to put down an animal? Any axe or mallet will do the job."

Leesha shrugged. "Can't bring themselves to kill a loyal animal, or they hold out hope I can heal it. But sometimes I can't and the animal is suffering. The needles are quick and kind."

"Maybe the Warded Man is, too," Rojer said.

"Are you saying you think we should fight the Krasians?" Leesha asked.

Rojer shrugged. "I don't know. But I think we need to keep a needle in our hand, even if we don't use it."

CHAPTER 16

ONE CUP AND ONE PLATE

:: 333 AR SPRING ::

LEESHA WATCHED AS WONDA and Gared faced off in the Corelings' Graveyard, circling slowly. Wonda was taller than any other woman in the Hollow, including the refugees, but giant Gared dwarfed her regardless. She was fifteen, and Gared near to thirty. Still, Gared wore a look of intense concentration, while Wonda's face was calm.

Suddenly he lunged, grabbing for her, but Wonda caught his wrist in one hand and pivoted, pressing his elbow hard with her other hand as she sidestepped and used the force of his own attack to throw him onto his back on the cobbles.

"Corespawn it!" Gared roared.

"Well done," the Warded Man congratulated Wonda as she gave Gared a hand to help him up. Since he had begun giving *sharusahk* lessons to the Hollowers, she had shown herself to be his best student by far.

"*Sharusahk* teaches diverting force," the Warded Man reminded Gared. "You can't keep using the wild swings you would against a coreling."

"Or a tree," Wonda added, bringing titters from many of the female students. The Cutters glared. More than a few of them had found themselves defeated by female students, something no man was used to.

"Try again," the Warded Man said. "Keep your limbs in close and your balance centered. Don't give her an opening.

"And you," he added, turning to Wonda, "don't grow overconfident. The weakest *dal'Sharum* still has a lifetime of training against your few months. They'll be your true test." Wonda nodded, her smile disappearing, and she and Gared bowed and began to circle again.

"They're learning quickly," Leesha said as the Warded Man came to join her and Rojer. She never trained with the other Hollowers, but she watched carefully each day as they practiced the *sharukin*, her quick mind cataloguing every move.

Again, Wonda threw Gared onto his back. Leesha shook her head wistfully. "It really is a beautiful art. It's a shame its only purpose is to maim and kill."

"The people that invented it are no different," the Warded Man said. "Brilliant, beautiful, and deadly beyond reckoning."

"And you're sure they're coming?" Leesha asked.

"There isn't a doubt in my mind," the Warded Man said, "much as I wish otherwise."

"What do you think Duke Rhinebeck will do?" she asked.

The Warded Man shrugged. "I met him a handful of times in my Messenger days, but I know little of his heart."

"There's not much to know," Rojer said. "Rhinebeck spends his hours doing three things: counting money, drinking wine, and bedding younger and younger brides, hoping one of them will bear him an heir."

"He's seedless?" Leesha asked in surprise.

"I wouldn't call him that anyplace where it might be overheard," Rojer warned. "He's hung Herb Gatherers for less insult. He blames his wives."

"They always do," Leesha said. "As if being seedless somehow makes them less a man."

"Doesn't it?" Rojer asked.

"Don't be absurd," Leesha said, but even the Warded Man looked at her doubtfully.

"Regardless," Leesha said, "fertility was one of Bruna's specialties, and she taught me well. Perhaps I can win favor by curing him."

"Favor?" Rojer asked. "He'd make you his duchess for it, and get the child on you."

"It doesn't matter," the Warded Man said. "Even if your herbs can awaken his seed, it could be months before there was any proof of it. We'll need more leverage than that."

"More leverage than an army of desert warriors on his doorstep?" Rojer asked.

"Rhinebeck will need to mobilize well before it comes to that, if he's to have any hope of stopping Jardir," the Warded Man said, "and dukes are not men apt to take such risks without great convincing."

"You'll have Rhinebeck's brothers to contend with, as well," Rojer said. "Prince Mickael will take the throne if Rhinebeck dies without an heir, and Prince Pether is Shepherd of the Tenders of the Creator. Thamos, the youngest, leads Rhinebeck's guards, the Wooden Soldiers."

"Are any of them likely to see reason?" Leesha asked.

"Not likely," Rojer said. "The one to convince is Lord Janson, the first minister. None of the princes could find their boots without Janson. Not a thing goes on in Angiers that Janson doesn't track in his neat ledgers, and the royal family delegates almost everything to him."

"So if Janson doesn't support us, it's unlikely the duke will, either," the Warded Man said.

Rojer nodded. "Janson is a coward," he warned. "Getting him to agree to war . . ." He shrugged. "It won't be easy. You may have to resort to other methods." The Warded Man and Leesha looked at him curiously.

"You're the ripping Warded Man," Rojer said. "Half the people south of Miln think you're the Deliverer already. A few meetings with the Tenders and the right tales spun at the Jongleurs' Guildhouse, and the other half will believe it, too."

"No," the Warded Man said. "I won't pretend to be something I'm not, even for this."

"Who is to say you're not?" Leesha asked.

The Warded Man turned to her in surprise. "Not you, too. It's bad enough from the Jongleur eager for tales and the Tender blind with faith, but you're an Herb Gatherer. Knowledge cures your patients, not prayer."

"I'm also a ward witch," Leesha said, "and you made me so. It's honest word I put more store in books of science than the Tenders' Canon, but science falls short of explaining why a few squiggles in the dirt can bar a coreling or do it harm. There's more to the universe than science. Perhaps there's room for a Deliverer, too."

"I'm not Heaven-sent," the Warded Man said. "The things I've done . . . no Heaven would have me."

"Many believe the Deliverers of old were just men, like you," Leesha said. "Generals who arose when the time was right and the people needed them. Will you turn your back on humanity over semantics?"

"It ent semantics," the Warded Man said. "Folk start looking to me to solve all their problems, they'll never learn to solve their own."

He turned to Rojer. "Everything set?"

Rojer nodded. "Horses laden and saddled. We can leave when you're ready."

It had been over a month since spring melt, and the trees lining the Messenger road to Angiers were green with fresh leaves. Rojer held tightly to Leesha as they rode. He had never been much of a rider and generally mistrusted horses, especially those not hitched to a cart. Fortunately, he was small enough to ride behind Leesha without straining a beast too far. As with everything she turned her mind to, Leesha had mastered riding in short order, and commanded the horse with confidence.

It didn't help his churning stomach that they were returning to Angiers. When he had left the city with Leesha a year ago, it had been as much to save his own life as to help her get home. He wasn't eager to return, even alongside his powerful friends, especially when it meant letting the Jongleurs' Guild know he was still alive.

"Is he overweight?" Leesha asked.

"Hm?" Rojer said.

"Duke Rhinebeck," Leesha said. "Is he overweight? Does he drink?"

"Yes and yes," Rojer said. "He looks like he swallowed the whole beer barrel, and it's not far from the truth."

Leesha had been asking him questions about the duke all morning, her ever-active mind already working on a diagnosis and potential cure, though she had yet to meet the man. Rojer knew her work was important, but it had been close to ten years since he had lived in the palace. Many of her questions taxed his memory, and he had no idea if his answers were still accurate.

"Does he sometimes have trouble performing abed?" Leesha asked.

"How in the Core would I know?" Rojer snapped. "He wasn't the boy-buggering type."

Leesha frowned at him, and Rojer immediately felt ashamed.

"What's bothering you, Rojer?" she asked. "You've been distracted all morning."

"Nothing," Rojer said.

"Don't lie to me," Leesha said. "You've never been good at it."

"Being on this road again has me thinking about last year, I guess," Rojer said.

"Bad memories all around," Leesha agreed, casting her gaze off to the sides of the road. "I keep expecting bandits to leap from the trees."

"Not with this lot around," Rojer said, nodding ahead of them to Wonda, who rode a light courser and had her great bow strung and ready in a sheath by her saddle. She sat up straight and alert, eyes sharp within her scarred face.

Behind them, Gared rode a heavy garron, though the giant man made the huge beast look a more normal size by comparison. His huge axe handles jutted up from either shoulder, ready at a moment's notice. Trained demon hunters both, there was little to fear from mortal foes with them on guard.

But most comforting of all, even in daylight, was the Warded Man. He rode his giant black stallion at the lead of the small column, shunning idle talk, but his presence was a silent reminder that no harm could come to any of them while he was near.

"So is it the road that bothers you, or what lies at its end?" Leesha asked.

Rojer looked at her, wondering how she could just pick thoughts right out of his head.

"What do you mean?" he asked, though he knew full well.

"You never told me how you came to be at my hospit last year, beaten near to death," Leesha said. "And you never went to the guard over it, or told the Jongleurs' Guild you were still alive, even after they buried Master Jaycob."

Rojer thought of Jaycob, Arrick's former master who had been like a grandfather to him after Arrick died. Jaycob took him in when he had nowhere else to go, and put his own reputation in the hat to start Rojer's career. The old man paid a heavy price for his kindness, beaten to death for Rojer's crime.

Rojer tried to speak, but his voice caught, and tears filled his eyes.

"Shhh, shhh," Leesha whispered, taking his hands and drawing them tighter around her. "We'll talk about it when you're ready." He leaned into her, inhaling the sweet scent of her hair, and he felt himself grow calm again.

They were two days from the city, not far from where the Warded Man had first found Rojer and Leesha on the road, when he turned his horse and rode into the trees.

Leesha kicked her horse ahead, picking her way through the trees until she came alongside the Warded Man. With no natural path to follow, much less one wide enough for two, they had to continually shift and duck to avoid low-hanging limbs. Gared was forced to get down from his horse entirely and walk.

"Where are we going?" Leesha asked.

"To get your grimoires," the Warded Man replied.

"I thought you said they were in Angiers," she said.

"The duchy, not the city," the Warded Man said with a grin.

The path soon widened, but still in a way that seemed natural to the untrained eye. Leesha was an Herb Gatherer, though, and knew plants better than anything.

"You cultivated this," she said. "You felled trees and widened the path, then hid your work so it doesn't seem a path at all."

"I value my privacy," the Warded Man said.

"It must have taken years!" Leesha said.

The Warded Man shook his head. "My strength has some uses. I can fell a tree almost as fast as Gared, and drag it off easier than a team of horses."

They followed the secret path deep into the woods until it veered off to the left. Ignoring the clear path, the Warded Man turned right, and again plunged into the trees. The others followed, and when they pushed through the branches they gasped as one.

There, hidden in a hollow, was a stone wall, so covered in ivy and moss that it had been invisible until they were upon it.

"I can't believe this is just sitting here, so close to the road," Rojer said.

"There are hundreds of ruins like this in the forest," the Warded Man said. "The trees reclaimed land quickly after the Return. A few are common Messenger stops, but others, like this one, have gone unnoticed for centuries."

They followed the wall to a gate, ancient and rusted shut. The Warded Man took a key from his robes and inserted it in the lock, which turned with a smooth oiled click. The gates opened silently.

Inside was a stable that seemed collapsed from the front, but the rear half of the structure was intact and clear, with a large covered cart and more than enough space for the four horses.

"Miraculous that half the stable should survive the years so well, and the other half not," Leesha noted with a grin, lifting some ivy out of the way to reveal fresh wards on the stable's walls. The Warded Man said nothing as they brushed down the horses.

Like the rest of the compound, the main house was in ruins, the roof caved and looking decidedly unsafe. The Warded Man led them around the back to a servant's house, still quite large by the standards of anyone raised in the hamlets. The place was half collapsed, like the stable, but the door the Warded Man led them through was heavy, thick, and locked.

The door opened into one great room, restored to function as a workshop. Warding equipment lay on every surface, along with sealed jars of ink and paint, various half-finished projects, and piles of materials.

There was a small cupboard by the fireplace. Leesha opened it to find one cup and one plate, one bowl and one spoon. A knife was stuck in a small cutting board by the cold pot hanging in the hearth.

"So cold," Leesha whispered. "So lonely."

"He doesn't even have a bed," Rojer murmured. "He must sleep on the floor."

"I used to think I was alone, living in Bruna's hut," Leesha said, "but this . . ."

"Over here," the Warded Man said, moving to a corner of the room with a large bookshelf. That got Leesha's attention immediately, and she headed over.

"Are those the grimoires?" she asked, unable to keep the eagerness from her voice.

The Warded Man glanced at the shelf and shook his head. "Those are nothing," he said. "Common wards and books, histories and basic maps. Nothing you can't find in the library of any Warder or Messenger worth the name."

"Then where . . . ?" Leesha began, but the Warded Man moved over to a nondescript section of the floor and stamped his heel down hard in a precise spot. The board was on a fulcrum, and as one end dipped into a hollow in the floor, the other rose, revealing a small metal ring. The Warded Man grasped the ring and pulled, opening a trapdoor in the flooring, its edges uneven and filled with sawdust, making them indistinguishable from the surrounding floorboards.

He lit a lantern and led the way down the steps into a large basement. The walls were stone, and the room was cool and dry. There was a hall leading in the direction of the collapsed main house, but a giant stone block had fallen to bar the path.

Warded weapons lay stacked and hung everywhere. Axes, spears of varying length, polearms, and knives, all delicately etched with battle wards. Dozens of crank bow bolts. Literally thousands of arrows, stacked in gross bundles.

There were trophies of a sort, as well, demon skulls, horns, and talons, dented shields and broken spears. Gared and Wonda drew wards in the air.

"Here," the Warded Man said to Wonda, handing her a bundle of arrows, delicate wards entwined along their wooden shafts and metal heads. "These will bite coreling flesh deeper than the ones in your quiver."

Wonda's hands shook as she accepted the gift. Speechless, she bowed her head, and the Warded Man bowed in return.

"Gared . . ." the Warded Man said, looking around as Gared stepped forward. He selected a heavy machete, its blade etched with hundreds of tiny wards. "You can hack through wood demon limbs like errant vines with this," he said, handing the weapon to Gared hilt-first. Gared dropped to his knees.

"Get up," the Warded Man snapped. "I ent the ripping Deliverer!"

"Ent callin' you any names," Gared said, keeping his eyes down. "All I know is I spent my whole life acting the selfish fool, but since you come to the Hollow, I seen the sun. I seen how I let my pride and my . . . lusts," his eyes flicked to Leesha, just for an instant, "blind me. The Creator blessed me with strong arms to kill demons, not to take whatever I wanted."

The Warded Man held out his hand, and when Gared took it, he pulled the man roughly to his feet. Gared weighed more than three hundred pounds, but he might as well have been a child.

"Maybe you seen the sun, Gared," he said, "but that doesn't mean I showed it to you. You'd lost your da just a day before. That'll grow any man. Show him what's important in life."

He held out the machete again, and Gared took it. It was a huge blade, but it seemed little more than a dagger in Gared's giant hand. He looked at the delicate warding in wonder.

The Warded Man looked at Leesha. "Those," he pointed to a series of shelves at the far end of the room, "are the grimoires." Leesha immediately moved toward the shelves, but he caught her arm. "I let you go there and we'll lose you for the next ten hours."

Leesha frowned, wanting nothing more than to pull her arm away and bury herself in the heavy, leather-bound tomes, but she suppressed the urge. This was not her home. She nodded.

"We'll bring the books with us when we leave," the Warded Man said. "I have other copies. Those will be yours to keep."

Rojer looked to the Warded Man. "Everyone gets a gift but me?"

The Warded Man smiled. "We'll find you something." He moved over to the blocked corridor. The keystone that had collapsed from the archway looked to weigh hundreds of pounds, but he lifted it away easily, leading them to a heavy, locked door that had been hidden in the darkness.

He produced another key from his robes and turned it in the lock, opening the door and stepping inside. He touched a taper to a huge stand lamp by the door, and it flared to life, reflecting off large mirrors carefully placed around the room. Instantly the huge chamber was filled with bright light, and the visitors gasped collectively.

Carpets, rich and thick, woven in faded design from ages past, covered the stone floor. The walls were hung with dozens of paintings of forgotten people and events, masterworks in gilded frames, along with metal-framed mirrors and polished furniture. Treasures lay piled in rain barrels around the room, filled to bursting with ancient gold coins, gems, and jewelry. Machines of unknown purpose lay partially disassembled alongside great marble statues and busts, musical instruments, and countless other riches. There were bookshelves everywhere.

"How is this possible?" Leesha asked.

"Corelings care little for riches," the Warded Man said. "Messengers picked the easily accessible ruins clean, but there are countless places they've never been, whole cities lost to demons and swallowed up by the land. I've tried to preserve whatever survived the elements."

"You're richer than all the dukes combined," Rojer said in awe.

The Warded Man shrugged. "I have little use for it. Take whatever you like."

Rojer gave a whoop and ran through the room, running his fingers through piles of coins and jewelry, picking up statuettes and ancient weapons. He played a tune on a brass horn, then gave a cry and ducked behind a broken statue, reappearing with a fiddle in his hands. The strings had rotted away, but the wood was still strong and polished. He laughed aloud, holding the prize up in delight.

Gared looked around the room. "Liked the other room better," he told Wonda, and she nodded her agreement.

The gates of Fort Angiers were closed.

"During the day?" Rojer asked in surprise. "They're usually open wide for the loggers and their carts." He sat now in the driver's seat of the cart from the Warded Man's keep, pulled by Leesha's horse. She sat beside him, in front of several bags of books and other items used to disguise the cart's false bottom. The hidden hold was filled with warded weapons and more than a little gold.

"Maybe Rhinebeck's taking the Krasian threat more seriously than we thought," Leesha said. Indeed, as they drew closer to the city, they saw guards armed with loaded crank bows patrolling the walltop, and woodworkers carving arrow slits at the lower levels of the wall. Where the gate had once had a single pair of guards, now there were several, standing alert with their spears at the ready.

"Marick's tale likely set things in a frenzy," the Warded Man agreed, "but I'll wager those guards are there more to prevent thousands of refugees from pouring into the city than they are to ward off any Krasian attack."

"The duke couldn't possibly refuse all those people succor," Leesha said.

"Why not?" the Warded Man said. "Duke Euchor lets the Beggars of Miln sleep on the unwarded streets every night."

"Ay, state your business!" a guard called as they approached. The Warded Man pulled his hood lower and drifted toward the back of the group.

"We come by way of Deliverer's Hollow," Rojer said. "I'm Rojer Halfgrip, licensed to the Jongleurs' Guild, and these are my companions."

"Halfgrip?" one guard asked. "The fiddler?"

"The same," Rojer said, lifting the newly strung fiddle the Warded Man had given him.

"Saw you play once," the guard grunted. "Who are the others?"

"This is Leesha, Herb Gatherer of Deliverer's Hollow, formerly of the hospit of Mistress Jizell in Angiers," Rojer said, gesturing to Leesha. "The others are Cutters come to guard us on the road; Gared, Wonda, and, er . . . Flinn."

Wonda gasped. Flinn Cutter was her father's name, a man killed in the Battle of Cutter's Hollow less than a year earlier. Rojer immediately regretted the improvisation.

"Why's he all covered?" the guard asked, pointing his chin at the Warded Man.

Rojer leaned in close, dropping his voice to a whisper. "He's badly demon-scarred, I'm afraid. Doesn't like people looking on his deformity."

"It true what they say?" the guard asked. "Do they kill corelings in the Hollow? They say the Deliverer has come there, bringing with him the battle wards of old."

Rojer nodded. "Gared here has killed dozens himself."

"What I wouldn't give to have my spear warded to kill demons," one guard said.

"We've come to trade," Rojer said. "You'll have your wish soon enough."

"That what you got in the cart?" the guard asked. "Weapons?" As he spoke, a few other guards walked back to inspect the contents.

"No weapons," Rojer said, his throat tightening at the thought of them discovering the hidden compartment.

"Just looks like warding books," one of the guards said, opening one of the sacks.

"They're mine," Leesha said. "I'm a Warder."

"Thought he said you was an Herb Gatherer," the guard said.

"I'm both," Leesha said.

The guard looked at her, then at Wonda, then shook his head. "Women warriors, women Warders," he snorted. "They'll let 'em do anything out in the hamlets." Leesha bristled at that, but Rojer laid a hand on her arm and she calmed.

One of the guards had moved back to where the Warded Man sat atop Twilight Dancer. Much of the stallion's magnificent warded barding was hidden away, but the giant animal himself stood out, as did his cloaked rider. The guard moved in, trying to peek under the Warded Man's hood. The Warded Man obliged him, lifting his head slightly so a sliver of light could reach under the shadows of his cowl.

The guard gasped and backed away, hurrying over to his superior, who was still speaking to Rojer. He whispered in the lieutenant's ear, and his eyes widened.

"Clear the way!" the lieutenant shouted to the other guards. "Let them pass!" He waved them through, and the gate opened, allowing them passage into the city.

"I'm not sure if that went well or not," Rojer said.

"What's done is done," the Warded Man said. "Let's move quickly before word spreads."

They headed into the bustling city streets, boardwalked to prevent corelings from finding a path to rise within the city's wardnet. They had to dismount and lead the horses, which slowed things considerably, but it also allowed the Warded Man to virtually disappear between the horses and behind the cart.

Still, their passage did not go unobserved. "We're being followed," the Warded Man said at one point when the boardwalk street was wide enough for him to come up alongside the cart. "One of the guards has been drifting along in our wake since we left the gate."

Rojer looked back and caught a glimpse of a city guard's uniform just before the man ducked behind a vendor's stall.

"What should we do?" he asked.

"Not much we *can* do," the Warded Man said. "Just thought you should know."

Rojer knew the mazelike streets of Angiers well, and took them on a circuitous route through the most crowded areas to their destination, hoping to shake the pursuit. He kept glancing over his shoulder, pretending to look appreciatively at passing women or vendors' wares, but always the guard was there, just on the edge of sight.

"We can't keep circling forever, Rojer," Leesha said at last. "Let's just get to Jizell's before it starts to get dark."

Rojer nodded and turned the cart directly for Mistress Jizell's hospit, which quickly came in sight. It was a wide, two-story building, made almost entirely of wood, as were all the buildings in Angiers. There was a small visitors' stable around the side.

"Mistress Leesha?" the girl minding the stable asked in surprise, seeing them pull up.

"Yes, it's me, Roni." Leesha smiled. "Look how you've grown! Have you been keeping to your studies while I was gone?"

"Oh, yes, ma'am!" Roni said, but her eyes had already flicked to Rojer, and then drifted on to Gared, where they lingered. Roni was a promising apprentice, but she was easily distracted, especially by men. Fifteen and full-flowered, she would already be married and raising children of her own if she had grown up in the hamlets, but women married later in the Free Cities, and Leesha was thankful for that.

"Run and tell Mistress Jizell we've arrived," Leesha said. "I didn't have time to write, and she may not have room for all of us."

Roni nodded and ran off, and before they were done brushing down the horses, a woman shouted "Leesha!" Leesha turned, only to find herself smothered against Mistress Jizell's prodigious bosom as the older woman swept her into a tight hug.

Just shy of sixty, Mistress Jizell was still strong and robust despite the heavy frame under her pocketed apron. A former apprentice of Bruna much as Leesha was, Jizell had been running her hospit in Angiers for more than twenty years.

"It's good to have you back," Jizell said, pulling back only after all the air had been squeezed from Leesha's slender frame.

"It's good to be back," Leesha said, returning Jizell's smile.

"And young Master Rojer!" Jizell boomed, sweeping poor Rojer into a similarly crushing embrace. "It seems I owe you thrice! Once for escorting Leesha home, and twice more for bringing her back!"

"It was nothing," Rojer said. "I owe you both more than I can repay."

"You can help work that off by playing your fiddle for the patients tonight," Jizell said.

"We don't want to put you out if there's no room," Leesha said. "We can stay at an inn."

"The Core you can," Jizell said. "You'll all stay with us, and that's final. We have a great deal of catching up to do, and all the girls will want to see you."

"Thank you," Leesha said.

"Now, who are your companions?" Jizell asked, turning to the others. "No, let me guess," she said when Leesha opened her mouth. "Let's see if the descriptions in your letters do them justice." She looked Gared up and down, craning her head back to meet his eyes. "You must be Gared Cutter," she guessed.

Gared bowed. "Yes'm," he said.

"Built like a bear, but with good manners," Jizell said, slapping one of Gared's burly biceps. "We'll get along fine."

She turned to Wonda, not flinching in the least at the angry red scars on the young woman's face. "Wonda, I take it?" she asked.

"Yes, mistress," Wonda said, bowing.

"It seems the Hollow is full of polite giants," Jizell said. She was by no means short by Angierian standards, but Wonda still towered over her. "Welcome."

"Thank you, mistress," Wonda said.

Jizell turned last to the Warded Man, still hidden in his hooded robe. "Well, I guess you need no introduction," she said. "Let's see, then."

The Warded Man's loose sleeves fell to his elbows as he reached up to draw back his hood. Jizell's eyes widened slightly at the sight of his tattoos, but she took his hands and squeezed them warmly as she looked into his eyes.

"Thank you for saving Leesha's life," she said. Before he could react, she hugged him tightly. The Warded Man looked at Leesha in surprise, awkwardly returning the embrace.

"Now, if the rest of you can tend the horses, I'd like a few minutes to speak to Leesha alone," she said. The others nodded, and Jizell escorted Leesha into the hospit.

Jizell's hospit had been home to Leesha for several years, and still held a warm familiarity, but somehow it seemed smaller than it had just a year earlier.

"Your room is the same as you remember it," Jizell said, as if reading her thoughts. "Kadie and some of the older girls grumble about it, but as far as I'm concerned, that's your room until you say otherwise. You can bed there, and we can put the others in spare cots in the patient wards." She broke into a smile. "Unless you'd like one of the men to share your room." She gave Leesha a wink.

Leesha laughed. Jizell hadn't changed at all, still trying to find Leesha a match. "That's quite all right."

"Seems a waste," Jizell said. "You told me Gared was handsome, but you shorted him even so, and half the Jongleurs and Tenders in the city whisper that your Warded Man may be the Deliverer himself. Not to mention Rojer, a fine catch by any girl's standards, and we all know he shines on you."

"Rojer and I are just friends, Jizell," Leesha said, "and the same goes for the others."

Jizell shrugged and let the matter drop. "Just good to have you home."

Leesha put a hand on her arm. "It's only for a short time. Deliverer's Hollow is my home now. The village has swollen into a small city, and they need all the Herb Gatherers they can get. I can't stay away long; not ever again."

Jizell sighed. "Bad enough I lost Vika to the Hollow, but now you, too. If the place is going to keep stealing my apprentices, I might as well sell the hospit and set up shop there."

"We could use the extra Gatherers," Leesha said, "but the town's got threefold more refugees than we can feed. It's no place for you and the girls right now."

"Or the place we're needed most," Jizell said.

Leesha shook her head. "I expect you'll have refugees aplenty in Angiers, before long."

CHAPTER 17

KEEPING UP WITH THE DANCE

:: 333 AR SPRING ::

"OPEN UP, IN THE name of the duke!" a voice barked shortly after dawn. The shouted command was accompanied by a loud pounding on the hospit door, still barred for the night.

Everyone at the breakfast table froze, looking at the door. The apprentices had long since eaten and were bustling about serving breakfast to the patients, leaving Jizell and the others alone in the kitchen.

It seemed to Rojer that long minutes passed in stillness, but in truth it could not have been more than seconds before Mistress Jizell looked up at them all.

"Well," she said, wiping her mouth and rising to her feet, "I'd best see to that. The rest of you keep your seats and clean your plates. Whatever the duke wants, it's best you not handle it on an empty stomach." She straightened her dress and strode out to the door.

She had not been gone more than a second before Rojer sprang from his seat, putting his back to the wall next to the doorway to listen in.

"Where is he?!" a man's deep voice barked when Jizell opened the door. Rojer crouched low and tilted his head to peek around the door frame, revealing little more than his eye and a strand of red hair. A tall, powerfully built man in bright lacquered armor loomed over Mistress Jizell. He had a fine gilded spear strapped across his back, and his breastplate was emblazoned with a wooden soldier. Rojer recognized his strong-jawed face immediately.

Rojer turned quickly to the others. "Duke Rhinebeck's brother, Prince Thamos!" he hissed, putting his eye back around the frame.

"We have many patients, Your Highness," Jizell said, sounding more bemused than threatened, "you'll have to be more specific."

"Don't toy with me, woman!" the prince barked, putting a finger in Jizell's face. "You know well—"

"Highness, please!" a high male voice cut the prince off. "There's no need for this!"

A man appeared, spreading his arms between them to passively ease the prince's arm and pointing finger away from Jizell's face. He was in many ways the exact opposite of the prince, small and uncomely, with a bald crown and a pinched face. His lank black hair was long, falling into his high collar, and his thin beard drew to a point at his chin. His wire-framed glasses sat halfway down his long nose, making his eyes seem like two tiny black dots.

"Lord Janson, the duke's first minister," Rojer advised the others.

Thamos glanced at the minister, who flinched back as if afraid the prince might strike him. The prince glanced at Jizell, then back to the small man, but his stance eased, and after a moment, he nodded. "All right, Janson, it's your stage."

"My apologies for the . . . urgency, Mistress Jizell," the first minister said, bowing, "but we wanted to arrive before your . . . ah, guest had a chance to move on." He hugged a leather paper case to his chest with one hand and pushed his glasses back up his nose with the other.

"Guest?" Jizell asked. Prince Thamos growled.

"Flinn Cutter," Janson said. Jizell looked at him blankly.

"The . . . ah, Warded Man," Janson said. Jizell's look became more guarded.

"He is in no trouble, I assure you," Janson added quickly. "His Grace the duke simply wishes me to ask a few questions before he decides whether to grant an audience."

There was a thump, and Rojer turned from the door to see the Warded Man rise from the table. He nodded to Rojer.

"It's all right, mistress," Rojer said, stepping through the doorway.

Janson looked over at him, and his nose twitched. "Rojer Inn," he said more than asked.

"I'm honored you remember me, Minister," Rojer said, bowing as the others followed him out of the kitchen.

"Of course I remember you, Rojer," Janson said. "How could I forget the boy Arrick brought back with him, sole survivor of the destruction of Riverbridge?" The others looked at Rojer in surprise.

"Still," Janson went on, his nose twitching again, "I would swear I read a report last year from Guildmaster Cholls that said you were missing and presumed dead."

He looked down his glasses at Rojer. "Leaving a considerable unpaid debt to the Jongleurs' Guild, as I recall."

"Rojer!" Leesha cried.

Rojer put his Jongleur's mask in place. The money had been restitution for breaking the nose of Janson's nephew, Jasin Goldentone. Of course, Jasin had already taken payment in blood.

"Did you come all this way to discuss the Jongleur?" the Warded Man asked, moving in front of Rojer. His hood cast his face in shadow, giving him a dark countenance frightening even to those who knew him. Prince Thamos put a hand to the short spear strapped to his back.

Janson twitched nervously, his tiny eyes darting from one man to the other, but he recovered quickly. "Indeed not," he agreed, turning his attention from Rojer as if he had been doing nothing more significant than examining a ledger. He shifted his feet as if he were ready to run and hide behind the prince if anyone made a sudden move.

"You'd be . . . him, then?" he asked.

The Warded Man pulled back his hood, showing his tattooed face to the prince and minister. Both of their eyes widened at the sight, but they gave no other sign that they had seen anything out of the ordinary.

Janson bowed deeply. "It is an honor to meet you, Mr. Flinn. Allow me to present Prince Thamos, captain of the Wooden Soldiers, youngest brother to Duke Euchor, and third in line for the ivy throne. His Highness is here as my escort." He gestured to the prince, who nodded politely, though his eyes lost none of their challenge.

"Your Highness," the Warded Man said, bowing smoothly in accordance with Angierian custom. Leesha dropped into a curtsy, and Rojer made his best leg. Rojer knew the Warded Man had met both men before, in his Messenger days, but it was clear that even Janson, whose memory was legendary, did not recognize him.

Janson turned to his left, where a boy who had been lingering in the doorway appeared. "My son and assistant, Pawl," he noted. The boy was no more than ten summers old, small like his father, with the same lank black hair and ferretlike face.

The Warded Man nodded to the boy. "An honor to meet you and your son as well, Lord Janson."

"Please, please, just Janson," the first minister said. "I'm as common-born as any; just a clerk with a visible post. Forgive me if I seem a bit awkward at this. The duke's herald, my nephew, usually handles this sort of thing, but as luck would have it, he's out in the hamlets."

"Jasin Goldentone is the duke's new herald?!" Rojer exclaimed.

All eyes turned back to him, but Rojer hardly noticed. Jasin Goldentone and his apprentices beat Rojer and his guild sponsor Jaycob a year ago, leaving them for dead as night fell. Rojer had survived only because Leesha and a few brave city guardsmen had risked their lives for him. Master Jaycob had not. Rojer never made charges, however, pretending not to recall his assailants for fear Jasin might use his uncle's connections to escape punishment and come after him again.

Janson, however, seemed to know none of this. He looked at Rojer curiously, his eyes flitting to the side, as if checking some forgotten ledger.

"Ah, yes," he said after a moment. "Master Arrick and Jasin had something of a rivalry once, didn't they? I'm sure he won't be pleased to hear about this."

"He won't hear," Rojer said. "He was cored on the road to Woodsend three years ago."

"Eh?" Janson said, his eyes widening. "I'm sorry to hear it. For all his faults, Arrick was a very good herald and served the duke well, not only for his heroism at Riverbridge. It's a shame about the brothel incident."

"Brothel incident?" Leesha asked, half amused as she turned to Rojer.

Janson turned bright red, and he turned to Leesha, bowing deeply.

"Ah . . . Ah . . . Forgive me, good woman, for bringing up such indelicate matters in the presence of a lady. I meant no disrespect."

"None taken, Minister," Leesha said. "I'm an Herb Gatherer, and used to indelicate matters. Leesha Paper," she extended a hand for him to take, "Herb Gatherer to Deliverer's Hollow."

The prince's nostrils flared and the clerk's nose twitched again at the new name the people of Cutter's Hollow had chosen, but Janson only nodded, saying, "I've watched your career with some interest since you apprenticed to Mistress Bruna."

"Oh?" Leesha said, surprised.

Janson gave her that same curious look. "It should come as no surprise. I review the duke's censuses every year, and take special note of prominent citizens in the duchy, especially ones like Bruna, a woman who registered every year since the first census, taken by Rhinebeck the First more than a century ago. I've kept watch over all her apprentices, wondering which would inherit her mantle. It was a great loss when she passed last year."

Leesha nodded sadly.

Minister Janson gave a respectful pause for the deceased, then cleared his throat. "While we're on the subject, Mistress Leesha," he looked down his glasses and affixed her with the same reproachful stare he had given Rojer, "your annual census report is months late."

Leesha blushed as Rojer snickered behind her.

"I . . . Ah . . . We've been a bit . . ."

"Preoccupied with the flux," Janson nodded, "and," he glanced at the Warded Man, "other concerns, of course, I understand. But as I'm sure your father can tell you, mistress, paper makes the engine of state run."

"Yes, minister," Leesha nodded.

"Please, Janson," Prince Thamos interposed himself, pushing the first minister to the side. His sharp eyes took in Leesha's body with a predatory seeming, and Rojer bristled. "The Hollow has been through enough of late. Spare them a moment of your endless paperwork!"

Janson frowned, but he bowed. "Of course, Highness."

"Prince Thamos, at your command," the prince told Leesha, bowing low and kissing her hand. Rojer scowled as Leesha's cheeks colored.

Janson cleared his throat and turned to the Warded Man. "Enough shuffling the papers. Shall we address the duke's business?"

When the Warded Man nodded, Janson turned to Jizell. "Mistress, if there were a place we could speak quietly . . ."

Jizell nodded, escorting them to her study. "I'll bring in a fresh pot of tea," she said, and returned to the kitchen.

Prince Thamos offered Leesha his arm on the way, and she took it with a bemused look on her face. Gared hovered near them protectively, but if Leesha or the prince took any notice of him, they gave no sign.

Pawl took his father's paper case and scurried to Mistress Jizell's desk, laying out a sheaf of notes and some blank pages. He set a quill and inkwell at the ready with a blotter, then pulled out the chair for his father, who sat and dipped the pen.

He looked up suddenly. "No one minds, of course, my penning our discussion for the duke?" Janson asked. "I will, of course, strike anything you consider inaccurate or indiscreet."

"It's fine," the Warded Man said. Janson nodded, looking back to his paper.

"Well then," he said. "As I told Mistress Jizell, the duke is eager for an audience with the representatives of . . . ahem, Deliverer's Hollow, but he is concerned about the authenticity of that representation. May I ask why Mr. Smitt, the Town Speaker, has not come in person? Is it not the first and only legal duty of the Speaker to represent the town in instances such as these?" As he spoke, his hand was almost a blur, taking down even his own words in an indecipherable shorthand, his quill flicking back to the inkwell every few seconds, with never a drop spilled.

Leesha snorted. "Anyone who thinks that has never spent any time in the hamlets, minister. The people look to their Speaker in a crisis, and with refugees from Rizon still trickling in, and those already arrived lacking even basic necessities, he couldn't pull away. He sent me in his stead."

"You?" Thamos asked, incredulous. "A woman?"

Leesha scowled, but Janson cleared his throat loudly before she could retort. "I believe what His Highness means is that proper succession should have had your Tender, Jona, come in Mr. Smitt's stead."

"The Holy House is overflowing with refugees seeking succor," Leesha said. "Jona could no more come than Smitt."

"But the Hollow can spare its Herb Gatherer in this time of need?" Thamos asked.

"This presents a problem for His Grace," Janson said, looking up at Leesha even as his hand continued to take down their words. "How would it look at court if he received a delegation from one of his vassalages who did not think enough of the ivy throne to even send their proper Speaker? It would be seen as an insult."

"I assure you, no insult was meant," Leesha said.

"How not?" Thamos demanded. "Regardless of crisis, your Speaker could have come. *Cutter's* Hollow is only six nights hence," he looked to the Warded Man, "but it appears that this *Deliverer's* Hollow has moved farther off."

"What would you have me do, Highness?" Leesha asked. "Spend a fortnight fetching Smitt when there's an army at our doorstep?"

Prince Thamos snorted.

"Please don't exaggerate, Miss Paper," Janson said, still writing. "The royal family knows all about the Krasian raids on Rizon, but the threat to Angierian lands is minimal."

"For now," the Warded Man said. "But those were no simple raids; Fort Rizon and its hamlets, the grain belt of all Thesa, are now under Krasian control. They will dig in for a year at least, levying troops from the Rizonans and training them. Then they will move on to swallow Lakton and its hamlets. It may be years before they turn north and head for your city, but I assure you, they will, and you will need allies if you hope to stand against them."

"Fort Angiers isn't afraid of a handful of desert rats, even if your tampweed tales were true!" Thamos barked.

"Highness, please!" Janson squeaked. When the prince fell silent again,

Janson looked back to the Warded Man. "May I ask how is it you know so much of the Krasians' plans, Mr. Flinn?"

"Do you have a copy of the Krasian holy book in your archives, minister?" the Warded Man asked.

Janson's eyes flicked away for a moment, as if checking an invisible list. "The Evejah, yes."

"I suggest you read it," the Warded Man said. "The Krasians believe their leader is the reincarnation of Kaji, the Deliverer. They are fighting the Daylight War."

"The Daylight War?" Janson asked.

The Warded Man nodded. "The Evejah details how Kaji conquered the known world before turning its collective spears on the corelings. Jardir will seek to do the same. His advancements may be followed by consolidation periods, where the conquered people are broken to Evejan law," he fixed Janson and the prince with a hard look, "but don't let that fool you for a moment into thinking that they've ceased their advance."

The prince glared defiantly, but the color slowly drained from Janson's face. Beads of sweat had broken out on his forehead, even in the cool spring morning. "You know much about the Krasian people for a Cutter, Mr. Flinn," he noted.

"I spent some time in Fort Krasia," the Warded Man said simply. Janson made another mark in his strange shorthand.

"You see why we must speak with His Grace, minister," Leesha said. "The Krasians can afford to take their time. With their grain silos, Rizon has resources to support an army indefinitely, even as they cut off the flow of food to the north."

Janson did not seem to notice she had spoken. "There are some who say you are the Deliverer, yourself," he said to the Warded Man.

Thamos snorted. "And I'm a friendly coreling," he muttered.

The Warded Man didn't look at him, keeping eye contact with the minister. "I make no such claim, Lord Janson."

Janson nodded, writing. "His Grace will be relieved to hear that. But on the matter of the fighting wards . . ."

"They—" Leesha began.

"They will be shared with all who want them, free of cost," the Warded Man cut her off, drawing looks of shock from everyone.

"The corelings are the enemies of all humanity, minister," the Warded Man said. "In this, the Krasians and I agree. I will deny no man the wards to combat them."

"If they even work," Thamos muttered.

The Warded Man turned to face Thamos fully, and even a prince could not long weather his glare. Thamos dropped his eyes, and the Warded Man nodded.

"Wonda," he said without turning to the young woman, who started at the sound of her name, "give me an arrow from your quiver." Wonda took an arrow and placed it in the waiting hand he threw over his shoulder. The Warded Man laid the missile flat across his hands and presented it to the prince, but he did not bow, standing as an equal.

"Test them, Your Highness," he said. "Stand atop the wall tonight and have a marksman fire this at the largest demon you can find. Decide for yourself if they work."

Thamos drew back slightly, and then straightened quickly, as if trying not to appear intimidated. He nodded and took the arrow. "I will."

The first minister pushed back from his seat, and Pawl darted forward to blot the wet pages and shuffle them back into the leather paper case. He collected the writing implements and wiped down the table as Janson got to his feet and went over to Prince Thamos.

"I believe that should be all for now," Janson said. "His Grace will receive you in his keep tomorrow, an hour past dawn. I will send a coach here for you in the morning, to avoid any . . . unpleasantness, should you," his eyes flicked to the Warded Man, "be seen on the street."

The Warded Man bowed. "That will do well, minister, thank you," he said. Leesha curtsied, and Rojer bowed.

"Minister," Leesha said, moving close to the man and dropping her voice. "I have heard that His Grace . . . has yet to produce an heir."

Prince Thamos bristled visibly, but Janson held up a hand to forestall him. "It is no secret that the ivy throne is heirless, Miss Paper," he told Leesha calmly.

"Fertility was a specialty of Mistress Bruna's," Leesha said, "and it is one of mine, as well. I would be honored to offer my expertise, if it were desired."

"My brother is quite capable of producing an heir without your help," Thamos growled.

"Of course, Highness," Leesha said, dipping a curtsy, "but I thought perhaps the duchess might bear examination, in case the difficulty is hers."

Janson frowned. "Thank you for your generous offer, but Her Highness has Herb Gatherers of her own, and I would strongly advise you not to broach this topic before His Grace. I will mention it along the proper channels."

It was a vague response, but Leesha nodded and said no more, curtsying again. Janson nodded, and he and Thamos headed for the door. Just before he left, the minister turned to Rojer.

"I trust that you will be visiting the Jongleurs' Guild to clarify your status and settle your outstanding debts before leaving town again?" he asked.

"Yes, sir," Rojer said glumly.

"I am certain tales of your recent adventures will be of great value to the guild, and likely pay your debt in full, but I hope you will show discretion regarding certain," he glanced at the Warded Man, "*subjective* interpretations of events, however tempting it may be to use the more . . . sensational interpretations."

"Of course, minister," Rojer said, bowing deeply.

Janson nodded. "Good day, then," he said, and he and the prince left the hospit.

Leesha turned to Rojer. "Brothel incident?"

"A copse of wood demons couldn't get me to tell you about it," Rojer said, "so you might as well quit asking."

Leesha watched from Jizell's kitchen window as a coach pulled up the next morning, its wide doors emblazoned with Rhinebeck's seal—a wooden crown hovering over a throne overgrown with ivy. The coach was accompanied by Prince Thamos in full armor astride a great charger, and a squad of his elite guardsmen, the Wooden Soldiers, following on foot.

"They brought an army," Rojer said, coming up beside her and peeking out. "I can't tell if we're being protected or imprisoned."

"Why should the day feel any different from the night?" the Warded Man asked.

"Maybe it's normal for those the duke has invited to audience," Leesha said.

Rojer shook his head. "I rode in that coach plenty of times when Arrick was herald. Never needed a squad of Wooden Soldiers at our backs for a ride across town."

"They must've tested the arrow last night," Leesha said, "which means they know that what we're offering them is real."

The Warded Man shrugged. "What will be, will be. Either they're here as escorts, or Rhinebeck will have a squad of crippled soldiers." Leesha's mouth fell open, but the Warded Man walked out into Jizell's courtyard before she could respond. The others followed him.

The coach's footman placed a stair beside the coach and held the door. Thamos watched them from astride his charger, nodding to the Warded Man slightly as they climbed into the coach. They were quickly clattering along the boardwalk toward Rhinebeck's palace.

The duke's keep was the only structure in the city made entirely of stone, a tremendous show of wealth. As with Duke Euchor of Miln, Rhinebeck's keep was a self-sufficient mini-fortress within the larger fort of the city proper. There was open ground on all sides of the thirty-foot-high outer walls, which were carved with great wards, the grooves filled with bright lacquer. They were impressively permanent, though they had likely never been tested by anything more than a lone wind demon. If the walls of Fort Angiers were breached and demons entered the city in numbers, Rhinebeck could shut the gates and await the dawn in safety, even if the entire city were in flames around his keep.

Inside the walls, they passed the duke's private gardens and herds, along with dozens of buildings for his personal servants and craftsmen, before reaching the palace. Its sheer walls climbed several stories, with lookout spires reaching even higher, past the keep's wardnet.

The palace wards were works of art as well as function, and Leesha could sense the strength of the symbols, her eyes dancing along the invisible lines of power they created.

"Please follow me," Prince Thamos said to the Warded Man when the carriage pulled to a stop at the palace entrance. Leesha frowned as they followed the prince into the palace, wondering if she was to be ignored in favor of the Warded Man throughout the interview. He had said repeatedly that he took no responsibility for the Hollow, any more than Marick did the Rizonan refugees. Could she trust him to speak the town's needs before his own?

The vaulted ceiling of the entrance hall soared overhead, but the great room was empty of petitioners. The prince led them away from the main throne room, down halls thick with carpet and covered in tapestries and oil paintings. They came to a waiting room with velvet couches and a warm fire, set in a marble mantel. "Please wait here on the duke's pleasure," Thamos told the Warded Man. "The attendants will see to your refreshment."

"Thank you," the Warded Man said as a valet arrived with a tray of drinks and small sandwiches. Two Wooden Soldiers stood rigid outside the door, spears at the ready.

Time went by, and Rojer, bored, began to juggle their empty teacups. "How long do you think Rhinebeck will have us wait?" he asked, his feet beating a pattern on the floor as he moved to keep his crippled hand in position to throw and catch.

"Long enough to establish that he's holding the reins," the Warded Man said. "Dukes make everyone wait. The more important the guests, the longer they're left to count rug threads. It's a tiresome game, but if it makes Rhinebeck feel secure, there's no harm letting him play it."

"I should have brought my needlepoint," Leesha said.

"I have a great number of unfinished hoops, dear," a voice behind her said. "I've always been good at starting patterns, but somehow I never get to the end." Leesha turned to find Minister Janson standing in the doorway, holding the arm of a venerable woman who looked to be in her late seventies.

Rojer gave a start, and Leesha winced as one of the cups he was juggling hit the floor. Thankfully, it bounced on the thick carpet and did not break.

The woman fixed Rojer with a look that would have done Elona proud. "Arrick never got around to teaching you manners, I take it." Rojer's face turned redder than his hair.

The woman was small, even for an Angierian, barely five feet tall from the white Krasian lace at the hem of her wide, green velvet gown to the top of the lacquered wooden circlet resting upon the severely pinned gray hair atop her head. The circlet's points were banded in gold and set with precious stones. She was thin like a reed, and stooped slightly, leaning on the first minister's arm. The hands that clutched him were covered in wrinkled, translucent skin. A velvet choker around her neck was set with an emerald the size of a baby's fist.

"Please allow me to present Her Grace the Lady Araine, Duchess Mum, mother to His Grace, Duke Rhinebeck the Third, Guardian of the Forest Fortress—"

"Yes, yes," Araine cut him off. "Everyone in the world knows my son's titles, and I'm not getting younger as you recite them for the thousandth time this week, Janson."

"Apologies, my lady," Janson said, bowing slightly.

Leesha dipped into a curtsy at the introduction, and the men bowed. In her men's breeches, Wonda had no skirts to spread, and assumed an awkward posture that was neither.

"If you're going to dress like a man, girl, then bow like one," Araine said, looking down her nose. Wonda blushed and bowed deeply.

The duchess mum grunted in satisfaction and turned to Leesha. "I've come to rescue you from all this tiresome men's business, dear." She glanced at Wonda. "The young lady, as well."

"Apologies, Your Grace," Leesha said, curtsying again, "but I am serving as Speaker for Deliverer's Hollow, and must remain for the audience."

"Nonsense," Araine tsked. "A woman Speaker? They may practice such frivolity in Miln, but Angiers has the right of things. Women were not meant to handle affairs of state." The duchess mum let go Janson's arm and latched on to Leesha's, pulling her toward the door even as she pretended to lean on it for support.

"Leave the men to their ledgers and proclamations," Araine said. "We will speak of more feminine matters."

Leesha was mildly surprised at the woman's strength. She wasn't quite as frail as she appeared. Still, the idea of sitting around with a bunch of pampered women vapidly discussing weather and fashion while the men charted the course of Deliverer's Hollow was unacceptable.

Janson leaned in to Leesha as she resisted the old woman's pull. "It isn't wise to upset the duchess mum," he whispered. "Best humor her for now. The duke will not receive the others for quite some time, and I will come for you before you're needed."

Leesha looked at him, his face unreadable, and frowned. Not wanting to antagonize the royal family, she reluctantly allowed herself to be led away.

"The women's wing is this way, dear," Araine said, leading Leesha down a long, richly appointed hall. Outside of the Warded Man's treasure room, Leesha had never seen such largesse as in the duke's palace. Her father had been the richest man in Cutter's Hollow while she was growing up, but the duke made Erny's wealth seem like the scraps that one might throw to a dog after a great feast. Lush carpets caressed and cushioned her every step, woven with vibrant patterns, and tapestries and statues on marble pedestals lined the walls. The ceiling was painted gold, and glittered in the light of the chandeliers.

Throughout the duchy Rizonan refugees were starving, but could the royal family ever truly understand what that meant, surrounded by such opulence? It reminded Leesha of her mother, always seeing to her own comfort first and others' only when someone was watching.

Araine's shuffling steps became firmer as they went, the frail-looking old woman guiding Leesha through the vast palace as a man might lead a woman through a dance. Wonda trailed along silently behind until they passed through a final door and Araine looked back at her.

"Be a dear and close the door, there's a good child," she said. Wonda complied, pulling the sturdy oak portal shut with a click.

"All right then, let's have a look at you," Araine said, releasing Leesha's arm with a push that sent her into a spin for the duchess mum's inspection.

Araine looked her up and down, her lip curling slightly. "So *you're* the young prodigy Bruna was so proud of." She sounded less than impressed. "How many summers have you seen, girl? Twenty-five?"

"Twenty-eight," Leesha said.

Araine snorted. "Bruna used to say a Gatherer wasn't worth two klats before fifty."

"You knew Mistress Bruna, Your Grace?" Leesha asked, surprised.

Araine cackled. "Knew her? The old witch pulled two princes from between my legs, so yes, I'd say I knew her. Pether was nigh fifty years ago, and Bruna was almost as old then as I am now. Thamos was a decade later, a giant babe like his brothers, but I wasn't as young then as I was for the others, and needed more than some glorified midwife. Bruna was in her eighties by then, and reluctant to leave the Hollow even when I sent my herald to get on his knees and beg. She grumbled the whole time, but came just the same, and stayed in the palace for months. She even took on a pair of apprentices, Jizell and Jessa, while she was here."

"Jessa?" Leesha asked. "Bruna never mentioned a Jessa."

"Hah!" Araine barked. "That's no surprise." Leesha waited for the woman to elucidate further, but she did not.

"I'd have made Bruna Royal Gatherer if she'd wanted it," Araine went on, "but the wretched old woman turned and headed back to the Hollow the moment Thamos' cord was cut. Said titles meant nothing to her. All that mattered were her children in the Hollow."

The duchess mum looked at Leesha. "That how you feel as well, girl? Putting the Hollow above all, even your duty to the ivy throne?"

Leesha met her eyes and nodded. "It is."

Araine locked stares with her for a moment, as if daring Leesha to blink, but she finally grunted in satisfaction. "I wouldn't have trusted another word from you if you'd said otherwise. Now, Janson tells me you claim some of Bruna's skill with fertility."

Leesha nodded again. "Bruna gave intensive lessons on the topic, and I have years of practical experience."

Araine looked down her nose at Leesha again. "Not too many years, I expect, but we'll forgive you that for now. Can't hurt, you checking her. Everyone else has."

"Her?" Leesha asked.

"The duchess," Araine said. "My latest daughter-in-law. I want to know if the girl is barren, or if it's my son that's seedless."

"I won't be able to determine the latter by examining the duchess," Leesha said.

Araine snorted. "You'd be out on your pert bottom if you claimed you could. But first things first. Have a look at the girl."

"Of course," Leesha said. "Is there anything you can tell me about Her Highness, before I examine her?"

"She's fit as a courser, with a sturdy frame and wide breeder's hips," Araine said. "Not the sharpest spear on the rack, but that's how an Angierian lady of quality is expected to be. Her brothers are canny enough, so we'll call it nurture and not nature. After Rhinebeck's last divorce, I picked her out of all the well-bred young hopefuls myself, with an eye on the nursery. Lady Melny was the youngest of twelve children, two-thirds of them male. She has three sisters, and all have children of their own; two boys for every girl. If anyone should be able to give the ivy throne an heir, it's her. Of course, all my son cared about was the size of her paps, but Melny has meat enough there to suckle even a big baby like Rhiney."

"How long have they been wed?" Leesha asked, ignoring the comment.

"Over a year now," Araine said. "The Royal Gatherer brews fertility tea and I have Janson close the brothels when she's cycling, but still she reddens her wadding each moon."

Araine brought Leesha through the maze of private halls and stairs used by the women of the royal family. She saw many servants, but not a single man. Finally, they came to a plush bedchamber filled with velvet pillows and Krasian silks. The duchess was standing before one of the great stained-glass windows in the chamber, looking out over the city. She wore a wide dress of green and yellow silk, cut low in the front and laced tight at the waist. Her hair was put up behind a gold and gem-studded tiara, and her face painted exquisitely, ready at any moment in case the duke should summon her to his chambers. She was no more than sixteen summers old.

"Melny, this is Mistress Leesha of Cutter's Hollow," Araine introduced.

"Deliverer's Hollow," Leesha corrected. Araine gave her a look of bemused tolerance.

"Mistress Leesha is an expert in fertility," Araine went on, "and will be examining you today. Take off your dress."

The girl nodded, not hesitating in the least as she reached behind herself for the laces of her corset. It was clear who was in charge among the duke's women. Her handmaids quickly moved to help with the fastenings, and soon the duchess' dress was folded beside the bed.

"Examine as you see fit," Araine muttered while the handmaids worked, too low for anyone else to hear. "The girl's been poked and prodded more times than a two-klat inn tart."

Leesha shook her head, feeling sorry for the poor girl, but she bent and opened her herb pouch on the duchess' vanity, laying out a series of bottles and swabs. She had hoped for this opportunity, and came prepared with the proper chemics.

The young duchess stood meek and silent as Leesha went about her examination, but her heart was thudding in her chest when Leesha listened to it. The girl was likely terrified, afraid of what would happen to her if she failed to produce an heir like the duchesses before her. Leesha wondered if she had even been given a choice in the union, or, as was common throughout Thesa, it was arranged by her parents without a thought to her desires.

She took a sample of the duchess' urine and swabs of her vaginal fluids, mixing the samples with chemics and leaving them to interact. She felt at the girl's womb, even going so far as to slip in a finger to examine her cervix. Finally, she smiled at the duchess. "Everything seems in order, Your Highness. Thank you for your cooperation. You can get dressed now."

"Thank you, mistress," the duchess said. "I hope you can find what's wrong with me."

"I don't think anything's 'wrong' with you, dear," Leesha said, "but if something needs correcting, rest assured, we will." The duchess smiled weakly and nodded. Likely she had heard the same thing from a dozen other Gatherers. She had no reason to think Leesha any different.

The duchess went back to the window as Leesha went over to the vanity to check on her test results. The duchess mum drifted over to her.

"There's nothing wrong with that girl," Leesha said. "She's fit to breed an army."

Araine handed her a bit of netting full of dried herbs. "The tincture the Royal Gatherer makes to brew her fertility tea."

Leesha sniffed the packet. "Standard. It certainly doesn't hurt, but I could brew stronger . . . not that it matters."

"You think the problem is with my son," Araine said.

Leesha shrugged. "The next logical step would be to examine him, Your Grace."

Araine snorted. "The stubborn ass will barely let a Gatherer look down his throat when he's caught a chill and coughing up his innards. Little chance he'll let you anywhere near his manhood . . ." she looked Leesha up and down and smiled wryly, ". . . unless you want to examine him and collect your samples the old-fashioned way."

Leesha scowled, and Araine laughed.

"I thought not!" she cackled. "We'll make the girl do it! What else is a young duchess for?"

Minister Janson remained behind after the duchess mum left with Leesha and Wonda. He produced a slim oak box, lacquered smooth, and handed it to Rojer.

"We found this in Arrick's chambers after his dismissal," Janson said. "I messaged the Jongleurs' Guild informing him I had it held in trust, but your master never bothered to retrieve it. I confess, it baffled me; Arrick took everything but the feathers from his mattress when he left, including a few things that weren't precisely his, but this he left on a table, plain as day."

Rojer took the case and opened it. Inside, on a bed of green velvet, lay a gold medallion on a heavy braided chain. Molded into relief upon the medallion were crossed spears behind a shield with Duke Rhinebeck's crest: a leafed crown floating above an ivy-covered throne.

Rojer remembered enough of Arrick's heraldry lessons to recognize the medallion immediately: the Royal Angierian Medal of Valor. The duke's highest honor. Rojer stared at it, amazed. What had Arrick done to earn such a prize, and why would he leave it behind? Beyond even the symbolic value, the medal itself was worth a fortune. In metal-poor Angiers, the braided chain alone was worth a mountain of klats, and the gold . . .

"His Grace bestowed the medal upon Arrick for his bravery at the fall of Riverbridge," Janson said, as if reading his thoughts. "It would have been enough if he had saved himself and returned to report the fall to the duke, but to face the corelings and rescue you as well, a boy of only three summers who could not run or hide on his own . . ." He shook his head.

Rojer felt as if the minister had slapped him. "I can't imagine why he would have left it behind," he said hollowly, swallowing the lump in his throat. "Thank you for keeping it safe." He closed the case and slipped it into the multicolored bag he carried across his shoulders.

"Well," Janson said, when it became clear Rojer had no more to say. He looked to the Warded Man. "If you're ready, Mr. Flinn, His Grace is ready to receive your delegation."

"But Leesha . . ." Rojer began.

The minister pursed his lips. "His Grace does not care to receive women in his throne room," he said. "I assure you, Mistress Leesha is in good hands with the duchess mum and her ladies-in-waiting. You can relate the audience to her after His Grace has dismissed you."

The Warded Man frowned, and he locked stares with the minister. The little man seemed petrified under those hard eyes, but he did not recant. His eyes flicked to the guards by the door.

"Very well," the Warded Man said at last. "Please lead the way."

Janson masked a sigh of relief and bowed. "This way, please."

Duke Rhinebeck was tall for an Angierian, but still shorter than most of the folk of Deliverer's Hollow. He was thickly set, a man in his mid-fifties, the muscles of youth now run to flab. His gravy-stained doublet was emerald green, and his leggings brown, both of rare, Krasian silk. He wore the lacquered wooden crown of Angiers atop his oiled brown hair, shot through with gray, but his fingers and throat were bedecked with rings and necklaces of Milnese gold.

To the duke's right and on a lower dais sat his brother, Crown Prince Mickael. Almost as old as the duke if a bit more robust, Prince Mickael was clad in equal finery, his hair held in place with a gold circlet. To the duke's left sat Shepherd Pether, Rhinebeck's middle brother. The Shepherd was even fatter than Rhinebeck, despite the austerity implied by his plain brown robe and shaved head. Unlike the rough material most Tenders wore, the Shepherd's robe was made of fine wool, tied with a belt of yellow silk.

Prince Thamos kept his feet, standing at the bottom of the dais in his ward-lacquered breastplate and greaves. He held his spear at the ready, as did the Wooden Soldiers at the door, though Rojer and the others had been searched and stripped of their weapons before entering the throne room. Even so, beside Gared and the Warded Man, Rojer felt as safe as if he were standing in Deliverer's Hollow under the bright sun.

"His Grace, Duke Rhinebeck the Third," Janson announced, "Guardian of the Forest Fortress, Wearer of the Wooden Crown, and Lord of all Angiers." Rojer dropped to one knee, Gared following suit. The Warded Man, however, only bowed.

"Bend knee to your duke," Thamos growled, pointing to the Warded Man with his spear.

The Warded Man shook his head. "I mean no disrespect, Your Highness, but I am not Angierian."

"What nonsense is this?" Prince Mickael demanded. "You are Flinn Cutter of Cutter's Hollow, Angierian born and raised. Do you mean to say the Hollow no longer considers itself part of the duchy?" Thamos tightened his grip on his spear, leveling it at them, and Rojer swallowed hard, hoping the Warded Man knew what he was doing.

The Warded Man seemed not to notice the threat. He shook his head again. "I mean nothing of the sort, Your Highness. Flinn Cutter was only a name given at the gate for expedience's sake. I apologize for the deception." He bowed again.

Janson, who had retreated to a small desk beside the dais, began scribbling furiously.

"Your accent is Milnese," Shepherd Pether said. "Are you beholden to Euchor, perhaps?"

"I have spent time in Fort Miln, but I am not Milnese, either," the Warded Man said.

"Then state your name and city," Thamos said.

"My name is my own," the Warded Man said, "and I call no city my home."

"How dare you?!" Thamos sputtered, advancing with his spear. The Warded Man gave him the bemused look a man might give a young boy who put up his fists. Rojer held his breath.

"Enough!" Rhinebeck barked. "Thamos, stand down!" Prince Thamos scowled, but he did as he was told, retreating to the foot of the dais and glowering at the Warded Man.

"Keep your mysteries for now," Rhinebeck said, raising a hand to forestall any further questions. Prince Mickael glared at his older brother, but kept his tongue.

"You, I remember," Rhinebeck said to Rojer, apparently hoping to cut some of the tension in the room. "Rojer Inn, Arrick Sweetsong's brat, who thought my brothel was a nursery." He chuckled. "They called your master Sweetsong because his voice made women sweet between the legs. Has the apprentice become the master?"

"I only charm corelings with my music, Your Grace," Rojer replied with a bow, painting a smile on his face and hiding his anger behind a Jongleur's mask.

Rhinebeck laughed, slapping his knee. "As if a coreling could be taken in like some wood-brained tart! You have Arrick's humor, I'll give you that!"

Lord Janson cleared his throat. "Eh?" Rhinebeck asked, turning to look at his secretary.

"The word from Messengers passing through the Hollow is that young Mr. Inn can indeed charm demons with his music, Your Grace," he said.

The duke's eyes widened. "Honest word?" Janson nodded.

Rhinebeck coughed to hide his surprise, then turned back to them, looking at Gared. "You are Captain Gared of the Cutters?" he asked.

"Er, just Gared, Y'Worship," Gared stuttered. "I lead the Cutters, yeh, but I ent no captain. Just handy with an axe, I guess."

"Don't sell yourself short, boy," Rhinebeck said. "No one praises a man who won't praise himself. If half of what I hear about you is true, I may give you a commission myself."

Gared opened his mouth to reply, but it was clear he had no idea what the proper response was, so he simply bowed, dipping so low Rojer thought his chin might strike the floor.

☙

Leesha sipped her tea, her eyes flicking over the rim to regard the duchess mum, who watched her in return with similar quiet candor. Araine's servants had set a polished silver tea service on the table between them, along with a pile of pastries and thin sandwiches, before vanishing. A silver bell sat beside the platter to summon them back when needed.

Wonda sat rigidly, as if trying to make herself as invisible to the duchess mum as she was to corelings in her Cloak of Unsight. She stared at the plate of sandwiches longingly, but seemed terrified to take one, lest she draw attention to herself.

The duchess mum turned to her. "Girl, if you're going to dress like a man and carry a spear, stop acting like some timid young debutante whose first suitor has come to court. Eat. Those sandwiches aren't piled there for show."

"Sorry, Y'Grace," Wonda said, bowing awkwardly. She grabbed a fistful of the finger sandwiches and shoved them into her mouth, neglecting napkin and plate alike. Araine rolled her eyes, but she seemed more amused than put off.

The duchess mum then turned to Leesha. "As for you, I can see the questions on your face, so you might as well ask them. I'm not getting any younger while we wait."

"I'm just . . . surprised, Your Grace," Leesha said. "You're not what I expected."

Araine laughed. "From what, my frail crone act in front of the men? Creator, girl, Bruna said you were quick, but I've my doubts if you couldn't see through that."

"I won't be fooled again, I assure you," Leesha said, "but I confess, I don't understand why the act was needed at all. Bruna never pretended to be . . ."

"Doddering?" Araine asked with a smile as she selected a delicate sandwich from the tray and dipped it smoothly in her tea, eating it in two quick bites. Wonda attempted to mimic her but left the sandwich in her tea too long, and half of it broke off in the cup. Araine snorted as the girl quickly swallowed tea and sandwich alike in one quick gulp.

"As you say, Your Grace," Leesha said.

The duchess mum looked down her nose at Leesha in that reproachful way she had. It reminded her of Lord Janson's look, and she wondered if the first minister had learned it from her. "It's necessary," Araine said, "because men turn to hardwood around a sharp woman, but around a dullard they are soft as pulp. Live a few more decades, and you'll find my meaning."

"I'll remember that in the audience before His Grace," Leesha said.

Araine snorted. "Keep up with the dance, girl. This *is* the audience. What goes on in the throne room is all just for show. Whatever they may think, my sons no more run this city than your Smitt does the Hollow."

Leesha choked on a pastry and almost spilled her tea. She looked at Araine in shock.

"It was ill planned to come without Mr. Smitt, though," Araine tsked. "Bruna hated politics, but she could have taught you the bare rudiments. She knew them well enough. My boys take after their father, and have little use for women at court unless they're putting food on a table or kneeling under it. They've naturally assumed your Mr. Flinn—if that's even his name— leads the dance now, and will give even that ape Gared and Arrick's brat more respect than you."

"The Warded Man doesn't speak for the Hollow," Leesha said. "Nor do the others."

"You think me dim, girl?" Araine asked. "One look at them told me that. It makes no difference, though. All the decisions are already made."

"Excuse me?" Leesha asked, confused.

"I gave Janson his instructions last night after I read his report, and he's seeing to them now," Araine said. "So long as none of those peacocks starts a real fight while they strut and posture in the throne room, the result of the 'audience' will be this:

"You will return to the Hollow to await a team of my best Warders to study your combat wards. Before winter, I want every two-klat Warder in Angiers etching weapons until every wood-brained huntsman who can pull a bow has a quiver of warded arrows and warded spears are cheap at the boardwalk kiosks.

"Thamos and the Wooden Soldiers will accompany the Warders," Araine went on, "both for their protection and so your Cutters can train them in demon hunting."

Leesha nodded. "Of course, Your Grace." Araine smiled patiently at the interruption, and Leesha realized as far as the duchess mum was concerned, these were royal commands and not topics for debate.

"The Tenders of the Creator are in turmoil over your painted friend," Araine went on. "Half of them think he's the Deliverer himself, and the other half think he's worse than the mother of all demons. Neither side seems to trust your young Tender Jona, though he seems to be leaning toward the former category. They wish to inquisit him. I've exchanged missives with my advisors on the Council of Tenders, and have agreed that a replacement, Tender Hayes, will be sent to tend the faithful in the Hollow while Jona is called here to give testimony before the council. Hayes is a good man, not crazed with zealotry and no fool. He will gauge the Hollowers' beliefs about the Warded Man even as the council gauges Jona's."

Leesha cleared her throat. "Your pardon, Your Grace, but the Hollow isn't a city with dozens of Tenders. The people trust Jona to guide them because he has earned that trust over many years. They won't just follow any man in a brown robe, and they won't take well to the idea of your dragging Jona off to an inquisition."

"If Jona is loyal to his order, he'll go willingly and quell any doubts," Araine said. "If not . . . well, I wish to know where his loyalties lie as much as the council."

"And if the council's inquisition ends unfavorably?" Leesha asked.

"It's been a while since the Tenders burned a heretic," Araine said, "but I expect they still know the recipe."

"Then Tender Jona will not be going," Leesha said, putting down her cup and meeting the duchess mum's eyes, "unless you intend to test your Wooden Soldiers against men who cut trees by day and wood demons by night."

Araine's eyebrows raised, and her nostrils flared. The serene veil returned in an instant, so quickly that Leesha thought she might have imagined the flash of vexation. Araine turned to regard Wonda.

"Is that true, girl?" she asked. "Will you take arms against your duke, if the Wooden Soldiers come for your Tender?"

"I'll fight whoever Leesha tells me to fight," Wonda said, sitting up to her full height for the first time since meeting the tiny duchess mum.

Even at fifteen summers, Wonda Cutter was taller than most men in Deliverer's Hollow, men known to be the tallest in the duchy. She towered over the diminutive old woman, but Araine seemed more amused by her than cowed. The duchess mum nodded as if to dismiss Wonda back to her previous state and looked at Leesha, tapping a nail on her delicate teacup.

"Very well," she said at last. "I will personally vouch for Tender Jona's safety and return to the Hollow, though he may return stripped of his robes."

"Thank you, Your Grace," Leesha said, bowing her head in acceptance of the terms.

Araine smiled and raised her teacup. "You may be Bruna's heir after all." Leesha smiled, and they drank together.

"The Warded Man," Araine said, after a moment, "will go alone to Miln, to carry his story about the Krasians to Euchor and make our plea for aid."

"Why the Warded Man and not your herald?" Leesha asked.

Araine snorted. "Janson's fop nephew? Euchor would eat the boy alive. If you haven't heard, Euchor and my son despise each other."

Leesha looked at her, but the duchess waved the look away. "Don't try to meddle with those wards, girl. The ivy throne and the metal one have been at odds long before the current occupants sat their overweight bottoms down on them, and will be long after they're gone. It's the way of men to glower at their rivals."

"That doesn't explain why it should be the Warded Man and not a Royal Messenger," Leesha said. "I assure you, if he even agrees to go—and you may find him harder to steer than you think—he will go with his own agenda, and not yours."

"Of course he will," Araine said, "which is precisely why I want that man as far from my city as possible. Whether he means it or not, his very presence will incite people to mad zealotry, and that's no way for a state to run. Let him go and cause a stir in Miln; Euchor may agree to whatever we want, just to be rid of him."

"And what, exactly, do 'we' want?" Leesha asked.

Araine eyed, her, and Leesha could not tell if she was more amused or annoyed at her audacity. "An alliance against the Krasians, of course," the duchess mum said at last. "It's one thing to bicker over some carts of wood and minerals, but quite another for the sheepdogs to keep nipping at one another when there are wolves at the pen."

Leesha looked at the woman, wanting to argue, but she found herself agreeing. Part of her felt so safe when Arlen was around, she never wanted him to leave the Hollow. But there was another part of her, a growing part, that found his presence . . . stifling. Just as he had feared, the Hollowers and refugees were looking to him to save them rather than saving themselves, and hadn't Leesha done the same? Perhaps it was best for all that he go for a short while.

When the moment for Leesha to reply had passed with no word spoken, Araine nodded and turned back to her tea. "I have yet to decide what to do with Arrick's boy. His so-called fiddle magic bears closer examination, but I have no designs on it as yet."

"It's not magic," Leesha said. "Not as we know it, anyway. He just . . . charms the corelings, like a Jongleur works a crowd's mood. It's a useful skill, but it works only so long as he continues to play, and he hasn't been able to teach the trick to others."

"He might make a good herald," Araine mused. "Better than Janson's fop nephew, at any rate, though that says little."

"I would prefer that Rojer stay with me, Your Grace," Leesha said.

"Oho! Would you?" Araine asked, amused. She reached over the table and pinched Leesha's cheek. "I like you, girl. Not afraid to speak your mind." She sat back, looking at Leesha a moment, and then shrugged. "I'm feeling generous," she said, refilling their teacups. "Keep him. Now, for this 'Deliverer' business."

"The Warded Man does not claim to be the Deliverer, Your Grace," Leesha said. She snorted. "Night, he'll bite the head from any that suggest it."

"Whatever he claims, folk believe it," Araine said, "as evidenced by the sudden change of your hamlet's name . . . without royal permission, I might add."

Leesha shrugged. "That was the town council's decision and none of mine."

"But you did not oppose it," Araine noted.

Leesha shrugged again.

"Do *you* believe it?" Araine asked, meeting her eyes. "Is he the Deliverer come again?"

Leesha looked at the duchess mum for a long time. "No," she said at last. Wonda gasped out loud, and Leesha scowled.

"It appears your bodyguard does not agree," Araine said.

"It's not my place to tell people what or what not to believe," Leesha said.

Araine nodded. "Just so. Nor is it your town council's. Janson has already penned a royal condemnation of the name change. If your council is wise, they will repaint their signs in a hurry."

"I'll inform them, Your Grace," Leesha said. Araine narrowed her eyes at the vague response, but said nothing.

"And the refugees?" Leesha asked.

"What about them?" Araine asked.

"Will you take them in?" Leesha asked.

The duchess mum snorted. "And put them where? Feed them what? Use your head, girl. *Angiers* accepts them, but the *fort* cannot hold so many. Let them swell the hamlets like yours. The Warders and soldiers I send the Hollow will show the duke's full support for our neighbors in this time of need, and we'll forgive the lumber shipments the Hollow has failed to make."

Leesha pursed her lips. "We need more than that, Your Grace. We have groups of three sharing blankets, and children running about in rags. If you have no food to spare, then send clothing. Or wool from Shepherd's Dale, that we might make our own. It's their shearing season, is it not?"

Araine thought a moment. "I'll have a few carts of raw wool sent, and drive a hundred head of sheep, as well."

"Two hundred," Leesha said, "at least half of breeding age, and a hundred milking cows."

Araine scowled, but she nodded. "Done."

"And seed from Farmer's Stump and Woodsend," Leesha added. "It's planting season, and we have the labor to clear land and grow a full crop, if they have sufficient seed to plant."

"That's in everyone's interest," Araine agreed. "You'll get as much as we can spare."

"How can you know the men will come to these terms?" Leesha asked.

Araine cackled. "My sons couldn't tie their shoes without Janson, and Janson answers to me. Not only will they decide as he advises, they'll go to their graves thinking it was all their own ideas."

Leesha still felt doubtful, but the duchess mum only shrugged at her. "Hear it for yourself, when your men come out and tell you what they 'negotiated.' Until then, let's finish our tea."

"Why have you come before the ivy throne?" Rhinebeck asked.

"The Krasian advance threatens us all," the Warded Man said. "Refugees flood the countryside, more than the hamlets can easily absorb, and when they move on Lakton—"

"This is ridiculous," Prince Mickael cut him off. "At the very least, show your face when addressing the duke."

"Apologies, Highness," the Warded Man said with a slight bow. He drew back his hood, and in the sunlight streaming in through the windows, the wards seemed to crawl across his skin like living things. Thamos and Janson, having seen this before, kept composure, but the other princes could not entirely hide their shock.

"Creator," Pether whispered, drawing a ward in the air before him.

"Since you have no name, I suppose you'll want us to call you Lord Ward?" Mickael asked, twisting the surprised look on his face into a sneer.

The Warded Man shook his head, smiling wanly. "I'm as peasant as they come, Highness. No lord in any land."

Mickael snorted. "Circumstances of birth notwithstanding, I find it hard to believe a man who styles himself the Deliverer doesn't think himself as much a lord as any of royal blood. Or do you think yourself above such things?"

"I'm not the Deliverer, Highness," the Warded Man said. "I've never claimed otherwise."

"That's not what your Tender in Cutter's Hollow believes, by his own reports," Shepherd Pether noted, waving a sheaf of papers in the air.

"He's not my Tender," the Warded Man said, scowling. "He can believe as he wishes."

"Actually, he can't," Janson interrupted, "if he is representing the Tenders of the Creator in Angiers, he owes his loyalty to His Grace the Shepherd and the Council of Tenders. If he is preaching heresy . . ."

"That's a fair point, Janson," Pether said. "We'll have to look into that."

"You could perhaps have the Council of Tenders summon and inquisit Tender Jona, Your Grace," Janson suggested.

"Hear, hear," Mickael said. He looked to his brother. "You should do that with all haste, brother." Pether nodded.

"Your former mentor, Tender Hayes, would be fit to replace him in the Hollow and minister the refugees, Your Grace," Janson suggested. "He has experience working with the poor, and is loyal to the ivy throne. Perhaps you can convince the council to send him?"

"Convince them?!" Pether demanded. "Janson, I am their Shepherd! You *tell* them I said to send Tender Hayes!"

Janson bowed. "As you say, Your Grace."

"As for you," Pether said, turning back to the Warded Man, "why did the Hollowers rename their hamlet Deliverer's Hollow if you have no sway there?"

"I never wanted the change," the Warded Man said. "They did it against my wishes."

Mickael snorted. "Save that ale story for a taproom of drunks. Of course you wanted the change."

"To what end, Highness?" the Warded Man asked. "It does nothing but further a notion I would rather quash."

"If that is so, you will have no argument if His Grace sends the town council a royal decree commanding that they change it back, of course," Janson said.

The Warded Man shrugged.

Rhinebeck nodded. "Do it."

"As you wish, Your Grace," Janson said.

"All this is neither East nor West," Prince Thamos snapped, stamping his spear butt on the floor. He looked at the Warded Man. "We tested your wards. I killed a wood demon myself with that arrow. I want more. And the other combat wards you've developed, along with training for my men. What do you want in exchange?"

"It matters not what he wants," Rhinebeck said. "The Hollowers are my subjects, and I won't pay for what they owe the ivy throne regardless."

"As I told Prince Thamos and the Lord Janson, Your Grace," the Warded Man said, "the corelings are the real enemy. I won't withhold warded weapons from any who want them."

Rhinebeck grunted, and Thamos' eyes took on an eager light.

"I can consult with the Warders' Guild to select Warders to send to the Hollow, if Your Grace wishes," Janson said. "Perhaps with a contingent of Wooden Soldiers to guard them?"

"I'll lead them personally, brother," Prince Thamos said, turning to look at the duke.

Rhinebeck nodded. "Very well," he said.

"What of the refugees from Rizon?" the Warded Man asked. "Will you take them in?"

"My city has no room for thousands of refugees," Rhinebeck said. "Let them succor in the hamlets. We can offer them . . . what was it again, Janson?" Rhinebeck asked.

"Royal asylum," Janson said, "and the protection of the crown to any who swear an oath of loyalty to Angiers." Rhinebeck nodded.

The Warded Man bowed. "That is very generous, Your Grace, but these people are starved and penniless, lacking basic necessities of survival. Surely, in your mercy, you can offer more than that."

"Very well," Rhinebeck said. "I'm not heartless. Janson, what can we spare?"

"Well, Your Grace," Janson said, flipping open a ledger and scanning its contents, "we can forgive the Hollow its delinquent lumber shipments, of course . . ."

"Of course," Rhinebeck echoed.

"And while in the Hollow, your Royal Warders can offer their expertise in protecting the refugees in the night," Janson went on, "as can the Wooden Soldiers."

"Of course, of course," Rhinebeck said.

Janson pursed his lips. "Please allow me to review further, Your Grace, and I will present you with detailed lists of what resources we have available."

"See to it," Rhinebeck said.

Janson bowed again. "As you command."

"And what of the Krasian advance?" the Warded Man asked.

"I've seen no evidence that the Krasians *will* advance, apart from your own claims," Rhinebeck said.

"They will," the Warded Man assured. "The Evejah demands it."

"You know a lot about the desert rats and their heathen religion," Pether said. "Lord Janson says you even lived among them for a time."

The Warded Man nodded. "That's correct, Your Grace."

"Then how can we be sure of where your loyalties lie?" Pether said. "For all we know, you're a corespawned Evejan convert yourself. Night, if you won't tell us who you are and where you're from, how do we even know you're not a Krasian yourself under all those wards?"

Gared growled, but the Warded Man held up a finger, and the giant Cutter fell silent. "I assure you, that isn't the case," the Warded Man said. "My loyalty is to Thesa."

Rhinebeck smiled. "Prove it."

The Warded Man tilted his head curiously. "How shall I prove it, Your Grace?"

"My herald is out in the hamlets," Rhinebeck said, "and cannot travel as swiftly as you, in any event. Go to Fort Miln for me and speak to Duke Euchor. Invoke the Pact."

"The Pact, Your Grace?" the Warded Man asked. Rhinebeck looked to Janson, who cleared his throat.

"The Pact of the Free Cities," the minister said. "In the year zero, after the first wardwalls were finally built and a semblance of order restored to the ravaged countryside, the surviving dukes of Thesa signed a mutual nonaggression pact called the Pact of the Free Cities. In it, they recognized the death of the king of Thesa and the end of his line, and accepted one another's sovereignty over their territories. The pact bans the taking of territory by force, and promises the unity of all cities in putting down its violators."

"Did the Krasians sign this Pact?" the Warded Man asked.

Janson shook his head. "Krasia was not part of Thesa, and thus was never subject to the Pact. However," he held up a hand to forestall further response as he set his spectacles at the end of his nose and lifted an old parchment, "the exact wording of the Pact is as follows:

"*Should the territory or sovereignty of any duchy be threatened by* human *design, it shall be the obligation of all signees and their posterity to intercede in unity on behalf of the threatened party.*" Janson set the parchment down. "The Pact was so worded to outlaw all warfare among men, because there were so few of us left after the depredations of the Return. Thus, it remains binding, regardless of whether the Krasian leader signed it."

"Do you think Duke Euchor will see it so?" the Warded Man asked Janson.

"Are you in audience with my secretary, or me?" Rhinebeck demanded loudly, drawing all eyes back to him. Rojer saw that the duke had gone red in the face, as angry as he had been the night he had caught seven-year-old Rojer sleeping in the bed of one of his favorite whores.

The Warded Man bowed. "Apologies, Your Grace," he said. "No disrespect was meant."

Rhinebeck seemed somewhat mollified by the response, but his reply remained gruff. "Euchor will try to find a way out of the Pact like a coreling longs for a gap in the wards, but without support from him, Angiers cannot afford to commit to attacking the Krasian host."

"You would violate the Pact yourself?" the Warded Man asked.

"*Intercede in unity,* the Pact says," Rhinebeck growled. "Should I clash with the desert rats alone, only to have Euchor sweep in and destroy both our weakened armies and declare himself king?"

The Warded Man was silent a long time. "Why me, Your Grace?"

Rhinebeck snorted. "Don't be modest. Every Jongleur in Thesa sings of you. If your arrival causes half the stir in Miln that it has in Angiers, Euchor will have no choice but to adhere to the Pact, especially if you sweeten the call with your battle wards."

"I won't withhold them for political gain," the Warded Man said.

"Of course not," Rhinebeck said, grinning, "but Euchor need not know that, ay?"

Rojer edged closer to the Warded Man. A skilled puppeteer, he could shout or whisper without moving his lips, even making the sounds appear to come from another place.

"He's just trying to be rid of you," he warned, so the others did not hear or notice.

But if the Warded Man heard him, he gave no sign. "Very well, I'll do it. I'll need your seal, Your Grace, so Duke Euchor knows the message is authentic."

"You'll have whatever you need," Euchor promised.

"Your Grace," the lady-in-waiting said, "the Lord Janson bade me to inform you that the duke's audience with the delegation from Cutter's Hollow is at an end."

"Thank you, Ema," Araine said, not bothering to ask how things went. "Please inform Lord Janson that we will meet them in the antechamber when we have finished our tea." Ema curtsied smoothly and vanished. Wonda threw back the rest of her cup and got to her feet.

"There is no need for haste, young lady," Araine told her. "It does men good to have to wait for a woman now and again. It teaches them patience."

"Yes'm," Wonda said, bowing.

The duchess mum got to her feet. "Come here, girl, and let me have a proper look at you," she said. Wonda came closer, and Araine walked around her, examining her worn and patched clothes, the jagged scars on her homely face, and reaching out to squeeze her shoulders and arms like a butcher examining livestock.

"I can see why you chose to lead a man's life," the duchess mum said, "you being built like one. Do you regret missing out on a life of dresses and blushing at suitors?" Leesha got to her feet, but the duchess mum raised a finger at her without even turning, and Leesha kept her tongue behind her teeth.

Wonda shifted her feet uncomfortably. "Ent never given it much thought."

Araine nodded. "What's it like, girl, to stand among men when they go to war?"

Wonda shrugged. "Feels good to kill demons. They killed my da and a lot of my friends. Some of the Cutters treated us women different at first, trying to keep us behind them when the demons came, but we kill as many as they do, and after a few of them got pounced on for looking out for some woman instead of themselves, they wised up quick."

"The men here would be worse, by far," Araine said. "I had to abdicate power when my husband died, even though my eldest son was an idiot, and his brothers little better. Creator forbid a woman sit the ivy throne. I've always been a little jealous of the way old Bruna dominated men openly, but that sort of thing just isn't done here."

She eyed Wonda again. "Not yet, anyway," she allowed. "Stand tall in the night for me, girl. Stand tall for every woman in Angiers, and never let anyone, man or woman, make you stoop."

"I will, Y'Grace," Wonda said, making a proper bow at last. "I swear it by the sun."

Araine grunted and tapped her chin for a moment, then snapped her fingers. She snatched up the little silver bell on the table and rang it. In an instant one of her ladies-in-waiting appeared. "Summon my seamstress immediately," Araine said. The woman curtsied and scurried off, and moments later another woman arrived, assisted by a young girl with a leather-bound book and a feathered quill.

"The girl," Araine said, pointing to Wonda. "Take her measurements. Everything." The royal seamstress nodded and produced a series of knotted strings, calling the measurements out to the girl, who noted them in her book. Wonda stood awkwardly while the woman worked, moving Wonda's limbs about like a doll's, and running her hands over places that made the girl blush furiously. The white scars on her face became even more prominent as her cheeks colored.

The seamstress came over to Araine and Leesha when she was finished. "It's a challenge, Your Grace," she admitted. "The girl is flat where a woman should be curved, and broad where a woman should be narrow. Perhaps a few ruffles on the dress to distract the eye, and a fan to help her hide the scars . . ."

"Am I an idiot?" Araine snapped. "I'd as soon put Thamos in a gown as that girl!"

The woman paled, and dipped into a curtsy. "Apologies, Your Grace," she said. "What did you have in mind?"

"I don't know yet," Araine said. "It will come to me, I'm sure. Run along now." The woman nodded, quickly gliding out of the room with her assistant in tow.

Araine turned to Leesha as she and Wonda prepared to go. "Bruna and I were great friends, dear, something that was of great benefit to both of us. I hope we can be friends, as well."

Leesha nodded. "I hope so, too."

CHAPTER 18

GUILDMASTER CHOLLS

:: 333 AR SPRING ::

"WHY DID YOU AGREE to go?" Rojer asked in a low voice after Janson had escorted the men back to the parlor and left them alone to wait for Leesha and Wonda. "Rhinebeck is just trying to be rid of you because he's afraid his own subjects will flock to you."

"I don't want that any more than he does," the Warded Man said. "I don't want people to start thinking of me as some kind of savior. Besides, I have my own reasons for wanting to visit Miln, and going under Rhinebeck's seal is too good an opportunity to let slip past."

"You're going to give them your battle wards," Rojer said.

The Warded Man nodded. "Among other things."

"All right," Rojer said. "When do we leave?"

The Warded Man looked at him. "There is no 'we' here, Rojer. I'm going to Miln alone. I'll be traveling at speed through the nights, and I don't need you slowing me down. Besides, you have apprentices to train."

"What's the point?" Rojer asked. "Whatever it is I do to the corelings, it's not something I can teach."

"Demonshit," the Warded Man snapped. "That's quitting talk. You've only been training apprentices for a few months. We need those fiddle wizards, Rojer. You need to find a way to get them ready." He took Rojer's shoulders, looking into his eyes, and Rojer saw the endless determination that burned in the man and, more, his confidence in Rojer. "You can do this," the Warded Man said, squeezing his shoulders. He turned away, but that stare remained with Rojer, and he felt as if some of the man's determination had passed on to him. If he couldn't train the apprentices, he knew who could. All he needed to do was swallow his fear and go to them.

Gared came to the Warded Man, dropping to one knee. "Let me go with ya," he begged. "I ent afraid to gallop at night. I won't slow ya."

"Get up," the Warded Man snapped, kicking at Gared's bent knee. The giant Cutter rose to his feet quickly, but kept his eyes down. The Warded Man put a hand on his shoulder.

"I know you wouldn't slow me, Gared," he said, "but you're not going, either. I'm going to Miln alone."

"But you need someone to protect you," Gared said. "The world needs you."

"The world needs men like you more than it needs me," the Warded Man told Gared, "and I don't need a bodyguard. I have another task in mind for you."

"Anything," Gared promised.

"I don't need a guard, but Rojer does," the Warded Man said. Rojer looked at him sharply, but the Warded Man ignored him. "As Wonda guards Leesha, I want you to watch over Rojer. His fiddle magic is unique and irreplaceable, and may turn the tide if we can harness it."

Gared bowed deeply and stepped into a sunbeam streaming in from a window. "I swear it by the sun." He looked at Rojer. "I won't let him leave my sight."

Rojer looked at the giant, unpredictable Cutter with not a little apprehension, unsure if he should be comforted or terrified. "Let me use the privy in peace, at least."

Gared laughed and slapped him on the back, knocking all the air from Rojer's body and nearly throwing him to the floor.

"I'm leaving for Fort Miln before the north gate is barred tonight," the Warded Man told Leesha on the carriage ride back to Jizell's hospit, after filling her in on the rest of his audience with the duke, which had gone precisely as the duchess mum had predicted. "In fact, I mean to go as soon as I can pack Twilight Dancer for the journey."

Leesha had instructed Wonda to keep a straight face if the men confirmed Araine's words. The girl performed admirably, but Leesha herself had to force down the smile that threatened to turn up the corners of her mouth. "Oh?"

"Rhinebeck wants me to go as his agent to Duke Euchor, petitioning him for aid in driving the Krasians out of Thesan lands," the Warded Man said.

Leesha pretended to nod grimly, awed at the duchess mum's power. What she wouldn't give to bend men to her will so, without their ever knowing!

The Warded Man looked expectantly at her. "What?"

"No protests at my leaving?" He seemed almost disappointed. "No insistent offers to accompany me?"

Leesha snorted. "I have business back in the Hollow," she said, not meeting his eyes, "and you've made no secret that you want to spread the battle wards to every city and hamlet. It's for the best."

The Warded Man nodded. "I think so, too."

They passed the rest of the ride in silence, and arrived back at the hospit as the apprentices were taking the linens off the lines.

"Gared, please help the girls haul the laundry baskets," Leesha said as the empty carriage pulled away. Gared nodded and went off.

"Wonda," Leesha said. "The Warded Man will need ammunition for his ride north. Please fetch a few bundles of warded arrows."

"Ay, mistress," Wonda said, bowing, and headed inside.

"Five minutes at court, and everyone's bowing to everyone else," Rojer muttered.

"Rojer, would you ask Mistress Jizell to have the girls pack food for his saddlebags?" Leesha asked.

Rojer looked at them and scowled. "Might be best I stay and chaperone."

Leesha gave him such a withering glare that he shrank back. He bowed with a sarcastic flourish and headed off. Leesha and the Warded Man went to the stables, and he fetched his warded saddle and the stallion's barding.

"You *will* be careful, won't you?" Leesha asked him.

"I wouldn't have survived so long if I wasn't," he said.

"Fair point," Leesha said, "but I didn't just mean with the corelings. Duke Euchor has a . . . harder reputation than Rhinebeck."

"You mean he's not led around by the nose by his councilors?" the Warded Man asked. "I know. I've met Euchor before."

Leesha shook her head. "Is there anywhere you haven't been?"

The Warded Man shrugged. "Over the eastern mountain range. Through the western wood. Past the Krasian Desert to the seashore." He looked at her. "But I'll see all those places one day, if I can."

"I'd like to see them as well, Creator willing," Leesha said.

"Nothing stopping you or anyone from going anywhere, now," the Warded Man said, holding up a tattooed hand.

I meant with you, she wanted to say, but swallowed it. His words said it all. She was his Rojer. There was no point in pretending otherwise any longer.

The Warded Man reached out his hand. "You be careful, too, Leesha."

Leesha slapped his hand away and embraced him. "Goodbye."

An hour later, he was galloping north from the city, and though her eyes were wet, Leesha felt as if a great weight had lifted from her.

Leesha fell into her old patterns at the hospit, giving the apprentices a lesson and doing rounds while Jizell caught up on her correspondence. Part of her thought hungrily of the books of warding in the satchel in her room upstairs, but she resisted the temptation to immerse herself in Arlen's lore, for she knew once she did, she would be able to think of nothing else. Learning was as addictive to Leesha as the jolt of magic that came with killing a coreling with his warded axe was to Gared. But for a few hours, at least, she decided to take comfort in the simple pleasure of grinding herbs and treating patients with nothing worse than a broken bone or a bad chill.

When last rounds were completed and the apprentices shooed off to bed, Leesha brewed a pot of tea and took a cup to Jizell's sitting room. The room would be empty at this time of night, and there was a warm hearth and a small writing desk there. Leesha had her own correspondence to catch up on, Herb Gatherers throughout the duchy that she kept in touch with, many of whom had yet to be informed of Bruna's passing last year. Like grinding herbs, keeping in touch with old friends was another thing Leesha had not had time for since she and Rojer met the Warded Man.

But as she drew near the sitting room, she heard the sound of breaking glass. She entered the room to see Rojer behind Jizell's desk, a carafe of brandy open in front of him. The fire hissed and popped angrily, and there were wet shards of glass on the stone of the fireplace.

"Are you trying to burn the whole building down?" Leesha shouted, pulling a rag from her apron and running to wipe up the alcohol before it caught flame.

Rojer ignored her, taking another glass and filling it.

"Mistress Jizell won't be pleased at you shattering her glass, Rojer," Leesha said.

Rojer reached into the motley bag he carried everywhere. It was old, stained, and weather-worn, but Rojer still referred to it as his "bag of marvels." Indeed, he could reach into it at will and pull forth something to widen the eyes of even the most skeptical audience.

He threw a handful of the Warded Man's ancient gold coins on the desk. They bounced with a clatter, and half of them fell to the floor. "She can buy a hundred more now."

"Rojer, what is the matter with you?" Leesha demanded. "If this is about sending you away before . . ."

Rojer waved his hand dismissively, taking a pull from his glass. Leesha could tell he was already very drunk. "Don't care how you and Arlen said goodbye in the stable."

Leesha glared. "I didn't stick him, if that's what you're implying."

Rojer shrugged. "Your business if you did."

"Then what is it?" Leesha asked softly, coming over to him. Rojer looked at her a moment, then reached into his bag of marvels again, producing a slim wooden box he opened to reveal a heavy gold medallion.

"Minister Janson gave this to me," Rojer said. "It's a Royal Medal of Valor. The duke gave it to Arrick for saving me the night Riverbridge fell. I never knew."

"You miss him," Leesha said. "It's only natural. He saved your life."

"The Core he did!" Rojer cried, grabbing the chain and hurling the medal across the room. It struck the wall with a heavy thunk and dropped to the floor with a clatter.

Leesha put her hands on Rojer's shoulders, but his lips curled and for a moment, she thought he might strike her. "Rojer, what happened?" she asked softly.

Rojer pulled away from her hands and turned away. For a moment she thought he would remain silent, but then he began to speak.

"I used to think it was just a nightmare." His voice was strained and tight, as if it might break at any moment. "We were dancing, my mother and I, while Arrick played the fiddle. My father and a Messenger, Geral, were clapping along. It was off-season, and there was no one else in the inn that night."

He drew a deep breath, swallowing hard. "There was a crash, as something hit the door. I remember my father had been arguing that morning with Master Piter, the Warder, but he and Geral said not to worry." He chuckled mirthlessly, sniffling. "I guess we should have, because as we all turned to the sound, a rock demon burst through the door."

"Oh, Rojer!" Leesha said, covering her mouth, but Rojer did not turn.

"The rock was followed by a blaze of flame demons, pouring in around its legs as it smashed the lintel and jambs of the doorway to fit through. My mother snatched me up in her arms, and everyone started shouting at once, but I don't remember what was said, except . . ." He sobbed, and Leesha had to fight the urge to go to him.

Rojer composed himself quickly. "Geral threw his warded shield to Arrick and told him to get my mother and me to safety. Geral took his spear and my father an iron poker from the fireplace, and they turned to hold off the corelings."

Rojer was silent a long time. When he spoke again, it was a cold monotone, lacking any emotion at all. "My mother ran to him, but Arrick shoved her aside, snatched up his bag of marvels, and ran from the room."

Leesha gasped, and Rojer nodded. "Honest word. Arrick only helped me because my mother shoved me into the bolt-hole with him, just before the demons took her. Even then, he tried to leave me."

He reached out to Arrick's bag of marvels, running his fingers across the worn velvet and cracked leather patches. "It wasn't threadbare and faded then. Arrick was the duke's man, and this bag was bright and new, as befit a royal herald.

"That's the truth of Arrick's *valor*," he said through clenched teeth. "Saving a bag of toys!" He snatched up the bag in his good hand, clenching it so tightly his knuckles showed white. "A bag I carry around with me everywhere, like it's just as important to me!" He shook the bag in Leesha's face, then his eyes flicked to the fire roaring in the hearth, and he moved around the desk toward the fireplace.

"Rojer, no!" Leesha shouted, moving to intercept him and grabbing the bag. Rojer held on tightly so she could not pull it away, but he did not try to push past her. They locked stares, Rojer's eyes wide like a cornered animal. Leesha put her arms around him, and he buried his face in her bosom, weeping for some time.

When his convulsions finally eased, Leesha let go, but Rojer held her tight. His eyes were closed, but his mouth moved toward hers. She pulled back quickly, catching Rojer as he stumbled drunkenly.

"I'm sorry," he said.

"It's all right," she said, guiding him back to the desk chair where he sat heavily and held a breath, as if to suppress a roiling stomach. His face was pale and sweaty.

"Drink my tea," Leesha said. She took the bag of marvels from him, and Rojer let it go without resistance. She set the bag in a dark corner, well away from the fire, and retrieved Arrick's gold medallion from where it lay on the floor.

"Why did he leave it behind?" Rojer asked, looking at the medallion. "When the duke threw us out, he took everything in our chambers that wasn't staked to the floor. He could have sold that medal along with all the other things he peddled over the years we drifted. It could have fed and boarded us for months. Night, it could have paid every bar tab Arrick had in the city, and that's saying something."

"Maybe he knew he didn't deserve it," Leesha said. "Maybe he was ashamed of what he'd done."

Rojer nodded. "I think so. And for some reason, it's worse. I want to hate him . . ."

"But he was like a father to you, and you can't bring yourself to do it," Leesha finished. She shook her head. "I know that feeling well."

Leesha turned the medallion over in her hands, feeling the smooth back. "Rojer, what were your parents' names?"

"Kally and Jessum," Rojer said. "Why?"

Leesha laid the medallion on the desk and reached into one of the many pockets of her apron, pulling forth the small leather bundle that held her ward-etching tools. "If this medal is meant to honor your being saved from the massacre at Riverbridge, then it should honor everyone."

With a smooth, flowing script, she etched KALLY, JESSUM, and GERAL into the soft metal. When she was finished, the names glittered in the firelight. Rojer looked at them with wide eyes as Leesha took the heavy chain and put it over his head. "When you look at this, don't think of Arrick's failure. Remember those whose sacrifice went unsung."

Rojer touched the medallion, tears falling onto the gold. "I'll never let it out of reach."

Leesha put a hand on his shoulder. "I think you will, if it comes down to saving the medal, or someone's life. You're not Arrick, Rojer. You're made of sterner stuff."

Rojer nodded. "Time I proved it." He got to his feet, but wobbled so unsteadily he had to slap a hand onto the desk for balance.

"In the morning," he amended.

"Hold on to your wits and let me do the talking," Rojer told Gared as they entered the Jongleurs' Guildhouse. "Don't be fooled by the bright smiles and motley. Half the men in here can slip the purse right from your pocket without you ever knowing."

Gared reflexively slapped his hand to his pocket.

"Don't clutch it, either," Rojer added. "You're just advertising where you keep it."

"So what should I do?" Gared asked.

"Just keep your hands at your sides and don't let anyone bump into you,"

Rojer said. Gared nodded and followed close behind as Rojer navigated the halls. The giant Cutter, his warded axes crossed on his back, drew a few stares in the guildhouse, but not too many. The Jongleurs' Guild was all about spectacle, and those who stared were likely only wondering what part the big man was playing, and in what production.

Finally, they came to the offices of the guildmaster. "Rojer Halfgrip to see Guildmaster Cholls," Rojer told the receiving clerk.

The man looked up sharply. It was Daved, Cholls' secretary, whom Rojer had met before.

"Are you mad, coming here after all this time?" Daved asked in a harsh whisper, glancing down the hall to see if anyone was watching. "The guild-master will have your stones!"

"Not if he wants to keep his own, he won't," Gared growled. Daved turned to him, seeing only a pair of burly crossed arms, and had to crane his head up to look Gared in the eye.

"As you say, sir," the clerk said, swallowing hard. He got up from his tiny hallway desk. "I will inform the guildmaster you're waiting." He went to the heavy oak doors of the guildmaster's office, knocked, and vanished inside at the muffled reply.

"Here?! Now?!" a man cried from inside, and a moment later the doors burst open to reveal Guildmaster Cholls. Rather than the motley almost all Jongleurs wore, the guildmaster was dressed in a fine linen shirt and wool waistcoat, his beard trim and his hair combed neatly back with oil. He looked more like a royal than a Jongleur. As he thought about it, Rojer realized he had never once seen the guildmaster perform. He wondered if Cholls was a Jongleur at all.

The guildmaster's face was a thunderhead, pulling Rojer from his mus-ing. "You've got some stones, coming back here, Halfgrip! We had a ripping funeral for you, and you still owe me . . ." He glanced at Daved.

"Five thousand klats," Daved supplied, "give or take a few dozen."

"We can sort that first," Rojer said, pulling a purse of the Warded Man's ancient coins from his pocket and tossing it to the guildmaster. The coins were worth twice his debt, at least.

Cholls' eyes lit up at the glitter of gold as he opened the purse. He snatched a coin at random and bit it, his scowl vanishing at the imprint his teeth made in the soft metal. He looked back to Rojer.

"I suppose I can make some time to hear your excuses," he said, stepping aside to allow Rojer and Gared into his office. "Daved, bring some tea for our guests."

Daved brought in the tea, and Rojer slipped him another gold coin, likely more money than the clerk saw in a year. "That's for the paperwork to make me alive again."

Daved nodded, his smile wide. "You'll be off the pyre and back among the living by sunset." He left the office, closing the door behind him.

"All right, Rojer," Cholls said. "What in the night happened last year and where in the Core have you been? One day you and Jaycob are raking in the klats to pay your debt, and the next I get a note from some clerk, asking me to pay for the pyre for Master Jaycob's body in the city coldhouse, with you just vanished!"

"Master Jaycob and I were attacked," Rojer said. "Spent months in hospit recovering, and when I was well, I thought it best to leave town for a bit." He smiled. "But since then, I've been witnessing the greatest ripping tampweed tale anyone's ever seen, and the best part is, it's true!"

"Not good enough, Halfgrip," Cholls said. "Attacked by who?"

Rojer gave the guildmaster a knowing look. "Who do you think?"

Cholls' eyes widened, and he coughed to cover it. "Ay . . . well, what's important is that you're all right."

"Someone put ya in the hospit?" Gared asked, balling a fist. "Jus' tell me where to find 'em, and I'll—"

"We're not here for that," Rojer said, laying a hand on Gared's arm, but looking at Cholls as he did. The guildmaster blew out a breath, seeming to deflate.

"To the Core with tea," Cholls muttered, "I could do with a real drink." His hands shook a little as he reached into his desk, producing a glazed clay jug and three cups. He poured a generous portion in each and handed them out.

"To choosing our battles wisely," the guildmaster said, raising his cup and exchanging a look with Rojer as they drank.

Gared looked at them both suspiciously, and Rojer wondered if the burly Cutter was really quite as dim as everyone thought. After a moment, though, Gared shrugged and tossed back the cup, swallowing it all in one gulp.

Immediately his eyes bulged, and his face turned bright red. He bent over, coughing violently.

"Creator, boy, you don't gulp it!" Cholls scolded. "That's Angierian brandy, and likely older than you are. It's meant to be sipped."

"Sorry, sir," Gared gasped, his voice gone hoarse.

"They're used to watered ale in the Hollow," Rojer said. "Great foaming mugs that giants like Gared throw back by the dozen. What little spirit they have goes right from the fermenting tub to the glass."

"No appreciation for the subtle," Cholls agreed, nodding. "And you, Halfgrip?"

Rojer smiled. "I was Arrick's apprentice, wasn't I?" He took another pull from his cup and swished the liquid in his mouth, savoring the taste as he exhaled the alcohol burn through his nostrils. "I was drinking brandy before I had hair on my seedpods."

Cholls laughed, reaching into his desk again and producing a leather weed pouch. "They do smoke in the Hollow, ay?" he asked Gared, who was still coughing a little. Gared nodded.

The guildmaster gave a start, whipping around to look at Rojer. "The Hollow, you say?"

"Ay," Rojer said, taking a pinch from Cholls' pouch and packing it into a pipe that appeared in his crippled hand. "I did."

Cholls gaped. "*You're* the Warded Man's fiddle wizard?!"

Rojer nodded, lighting a taper from the lamp on the guildmaster's desk and puffing the pipe to a glow.

Cholls sat back, regarding Rojer. After a moment, he nodded. "Guess it's not too much of a surprise, at that. I always thought you had a bit of magic in your fiddling."

Rojer passed him the taper, and Cholls puffed his own pipe to life, passing it to Gared.

They smoked in silence for a time, but eventually Cholls sat up and knocked the dottle from his pipe, setting it on its small wooden stand on his desk. "All right, Rojer, you can sit there smugly all day, but I have a guild to run. You're telling me you were in Cutter's Hollow for the coming of the Warded Man?"

"I wasn't just in the Hollow for the *coming* of the Warded Man," Rojer said. "He *arrived* with me and Leesha Paper."

"The one they call the ward witch?" Cholls asked.

Rojer nodded.

Cholls' eyebrows narrowed. "If you're spinning some ale story at me, Rojer, I swear by the sun I'll . . ."

"It's no ale story, this," Rojer said. "Every word is true."

"You and I both know that we're talking about a story every Jongleur alive would kill for," Cholls said, "so let's skip to the end. How much do you want for it?"

"I'm not motivated by money anymore, Guildmaster," Rojer said.

"Don't tell me you've had some kind of religious awakening," Cholls said. "Arrick would roll over in his grave. This Warded Man may fill seats at a Jongleur show, but you don't actually think he's the Deliverer, do you?"

There was a loud crack, and both men looked to see one of Gared's chair arms had broken off in the big man's grip. "He *is* the Deliverer," Gared growled, "and I'll have at any man that says otherwise."

"You'll do no such thing!" Rojer snapped. "He's said himself he isn't, and unless you want me to tell him what an ass you're making of yourself, you'll keep your peace."

Gared glared at him a moment, and Rojer felt his blood run cold, but he met the stare with one of his own and didn't back down an inch. After a moment, Gared calmed and looked sheepishly at the guildmaster.

"Sorry about the chair," he said, trying lamely to put the arm back on.

"Ah . . . think nothing of it," Cholls said, though Rojer knew the chair cost more than most Jongleurs ever had in their purse at once.

"I'm not qualified to say he's the Deliverer or not," Rojer said. "Until last year, I thought the Warded Man's very existence was an ale story. I spun more than a few of them, myself, making them up as I went along." He leaned in to the guildmaster. "But he's real. He kills demons with his bare hands, and he has powers I can't explain."

"Jongleur's tricks," Cholls said skeptically.

Rojer shook his head. "I've dazzled my share of yokels with magic tricks, Guildmaster. I'm not some bumpkin taken in by sleight of hand and flash powders. I'm not calling him Creator-sent, but he has *real* magic, sure as the sun shines."

Cholls sat back, steepling his fingers. "Let's say you're telling the truth. That still doesn't explain why you're here, if you aren't looking to sell me the story."

"Oh, I'll sell it," Rojer said. "I composed a song, 'The Battle of Cutter's Hollow,' that will be called for in every ale house and square in the city, and there are enough stories from the last year to keep your Jongleurs working just to empty their collection hats so the people can fill them again."

"Then what do you want, if not money?" Cholls asked.

"I need to train others to use fiddle magic," Rojer said. "But I'm no teacher. I've had apprentices for months now, and they can fiddle well enough to spin dancers in a reel, but none of them can shift a coreling's mood from more than 'blood-crazed' to 'savage.' "

"There are two aspects of music, Rojer," Cholls said, "skill and talent. One is learned, the other is not. In all my years, I've never seen someone with talent like yours. You have a natural gift that no fiddle instructor can teach."

"So you won't help?" Rojer asked.

"I didn't say that," Cholls said. "I just want you forewarned. Perhaps there's something we can do, even so. Did Arrick teach you sound signs?"

Rojer looked at the guildmaster curiously and shook his head.

"It's using your hands to give instructions to a group of players," Cholls said.

"Like a conductor," Rojer said.

Cholls shook his head. "A conductor's players already know the piece. A sound signaler can compose on the spot, and if his players know the signs, they can immediately follow."

Rojer sat up straight in his chair. "Honest word?"

Cholls smiled. "Honest word. We have a number of masters who can teach the art. I'll send the lot of them to Deliverer's Hollow, and assign them to follow your word."

Rojer blinked.

"It's not entirely unselfish of me," Cholls said. "Whatever stories you give us now will do for a short while, but Deliverer or no, this is the defining event of our time, and the tale is still unfolding. The Hollow is clearly at the crux of it, and I've wanted to send Jongleurs there for some time, but with the flux at first and then the refugees, no one has had the stones to go. If you can promise safety and board, I'll . . . persuade them."

"I can guarantee it," Rojer said, smiling.

SECTION 3

JUDGMENTS

CHAPTER 19

THE KNIFE

:: 333 AR SUMMER ::

A FEW WEEKS AFTER Renna's night in the outhouse, there was a visitor to the farm. Her heart jumped at the sight of a traveler on the road, but it wasn't Cobie Fisher, it was his father, Garric.

Garric Fisher was a big, burly man, much like his son in appearance. In his fifties, he had only a few streaks of white in his thick curly black hair and beard. He nodded curtly to Renna as he pulled up in his cart.

"Your da around, girl?" he asked.

Renna nodded.

Garric spat over the side of his cart. "Run and fetch him, then."

Renna nodded again and ran into the fields, her heart pounding. What could he want? Had he come to speak for Cobie? Did he still think of her? She was so preoccupied that she nearly crashed into her father as he emerged from a row of cornstalks.

"Night, girl! What in the Core's gotten into you now?" Harl asked, catching her shoulders and shaking her.

"Garric Fisher just rode in," Renna said. "He's waitin' for you in the yard."

Harl scowled. "He is, is he?" He wiped his hands on a rag and touched the bone handle of his knife as if to reassure himself of its presence, then headed out of the fields.

"Tanner!" Garric called, still sitting in the cart when they came into the yard. He hopped down and held out his hand. "It's good to see you lookin' well."

Harl nodded, shaking hands. "You, too, Fisher. What brings you out these ways?"

"I brought you some fish," Garric said, gesturing to the barrels on the cart. "Good trout and catfish, still alive and swimmin'. Toss some bread in the barrels, and they'll keep a good while. Reckon it's been a while since you had fresh fish out here."

"That's real thoughtful," Harl said, helping Garric unload the cargo.

"Least I could do," Garric said. He wiped his sweaty brow when the work was done. "Sun's hot today. Long trip out and I'm mighty thirsty. Think we might set a spell under the shade of your porch afore I head back?"

Harl nodded, and the two men went and sat on the old rockers on the porch. Renna fetched a pitcher of cool water and brought it out with a pair of cups.

Garric reached into his pocket, producing a clay pipe. "Mind if I smoke?"

Harl shook his head. "Girl, fetch my pipe and leaf pouch," he said, and shared the pouch with Garric. Renna brought a taper from the fire to light them.

"Mmm," Garric said, exhaling slow and thoughtfully. "That's good leaf."

"Grow it myself," Harl said. "Hog buys most of his smokeleaf from Southwatch, and they always keep the best and sell him the stale dregs." He turned to Renna. "Girl, fill a pouch for Mr. Fisher to take back with him."

Renna nodded and went inside, but she hung by the door, listening. With the formalities done with, the real talk would begin soon, and she didn't want to miss a word.

"Sorry it took me so long to come," Garric began. "Meant no disrespect."

"None taken," Harl said, drawing on his pipe.

"Whole town's buzzing about this business between the kids," Garric said. "Got it from Hog's daughter, or summat. Goodwives ent got nothin' better to do with their time than gossip and rumormonger."

Harl spat.

"Want to apologize for my boy's behavior," Garric said. "Cobie's fond o' tellin' me he's a grown man and can handle his own affairs, but grown is as grown does, I say. Wern't right, what he done."

"That's undersaid," Harl grunted, and spat again.

"Well, you ought to know that after you sent him runnin' home with his tail between his legs, I caught wind and stepped in. I promise you, it won't happen again."

"Glad to hear it," Harl said. "I were you, I'd beat some sense into that boy."

Garric scowled. "I were you, I'd tell my daughter to keep her skirts around her ankles, steada puttin' sin in the mind of every man passes by."

"Oh, I had my words with her," Harl assured. "She won't be sinnin' no more. I put the fear o' the Creator in her, honest word."

"Been more'n words, it was one of my girls," Garric said. "I'da caned her backside raw."

"You discipline your way, Fisher," Harl said, "and I'll do mine."

Garric nodded. "Fair and true." He drew on his pipe. "That sophearted Tender woulda married them, they made it to Boggin's Hill afore you caught 'em," he warned.

Renna gasped, and her heart skipped a beat. She covered her mouth in fright, holding her breath for a long moment until she was sure they hadn't heard her.

"Harral's always been too soft," Harl said. "A Tender needs to punish wickedness, not condone it."

Garric grunted his assent. "Girl ent been sick none?" He made it sound casual, but Renna could tell it was anything but.

Harl shook his head. "Still got her moon blood."

Garric blew out a breath, clearly relieved, and suddenly Renna realized why he'd waited so long to come. Her hand strayed to her stomach, and she wished her womb had quickened, but she'd only had Cobie's seed once, and Harl was always careful not to spend in her.

"No disrespect," Garric said, "but my lazeabout son's got prospects for the first time in his life, and Nomi and I aim to find him a proper bride, not some scandal."

"Yer son ent got no prospects at all, he puts his hands on my daughter again," Harl said.

Garric scowled, but he nodded. "Can't say I'd think any different, it was one o' my girls," He tapped out his pipe. "Reckon we understand each other."

"Reckon we do," Harl said. "Girl! Where's that leaf?"

Renna jumped, having forgotten all about the pouch. She ran to the smokeleaf barrel and filled a sheepskin pouch. "Coming!"

Harl scowled at her when she returned, and gave her a slap on the rump for being slow. He gave the pouch to Garric, and they watched him climb into his cart and trundle off.

"Do you think it's true, Mrs. Scratch?" Renna asked the mother cat as she nursed her kits that night. They scrambled over one another in a great pile, fighting for the teats as Mrs. Scratch lay out behind the broken wheelbarrow in the barn where she'd hidden her litter. Renna called her Mrs. Scratch now, like a proper mam, though as expected the tabby that got the kits on her had made scarce since the birth.

"Do you think the Tender would really marry us if we went to him?" she asked. "Cobie said it was so, and Garric, too. Oh, could you imagine?" Renna picked up one of the kits, kissing its head as it mewed softly at her.

"Renna Messenger," she said, trying on the name and smiling. It sounded good. It sounded right.

"I could make it to Town Square," she said. "It's a long way, but I could run it in four hours or so. If I went late in the day, Da could never make it out in time, not with his aching joints." She glanced over at the cart.

"'Specially not if he can't ride," she added slyly.

"But what if Cobie's away when I come?" she asked. "Or if he doesn't want me anymore?" As she pondered that awful thought, the prodigal tabby returned, a fat mouse in its teeth. It laid the catch by Mrs. Scratch, and Renna thought it was a sign from the Creator himself.

She waited for days, in case her father suspected she'd overheard Garric. She went through the plan over and over in her mind, knowing this would be her last chance to escape. If he caught her and threw her back in the outhouse, she doubted she'd survive, much less dare to run again.

Her father came for lunch past noon each day, and took his time at eating before going back out into the fields. If she ran then, she could make it to Town Square with two hours of daylight left. Harl wouldn't notice she was gone in time to follow before the corelings rose, and would have to wait till morning, or at least stop for succor along the way.

If Cobie was in the Square, that left them the rest of the day to go up Boggin's Hill and see the Tender. If not, she would run on up the road to Jeph's farm. She'd never been there herself, but Lucik had, and said it was two hours' walk up the north road from the Square. She should be able to run it in plenty of time, and Ilain would hide her if Harl came looking. She knew she would.

When the day finally came, she was careful not to do anything out of the ordinary. She made her rounds and did her chores exactly as she had every day in the last week, careful to keep the pattern.

Harl came out of the fields for lunch, and she had stew ready. "Stay for seconds?" she asked her father, trying to appear unhurried. "Want to finish out the pot, so's I can scrub it and start fresh for supper."

"Ent gonna turn down another bowl o' yer stew, Ren," Harl said with a grin. "Shoulda had you at the pot all these years steada Beni." He pinched her behind as she bent to fill his bowl. Renna wanted to dump the boiling stew in his lap, but she swallowed the urge and forced a giggle, giving him the stew with a smile.

"Nice to see a smile on you, girl," Harl said. "You've had a sour puss since yer sister and the young'uns left."

"Guess I've gotten used to things," Renna managed, returning to her seat and having a second helping herself, though eating was the last thing she wanted to do.

She waited a count of a hundred after Harl left the table, then got up swiftly and went to the cutting board where she had piled vegetables for a stew she never meant to make. She took the knife and went out to the barn.

The only draft animals they had were the two mollies. Renna looked at them sadly, having cared for them ever since Harl brought the two foals home from Mack Pasture's farm.

Could she really do this? Harl's farm was the only world she knew. The few times she had been to Town Square or Boggin's Hill, she had felt suffocated by all the people, unable to understand how anyone could keep their head in such a crowd. Would they accept her? Did she really have a reputation as a whore? Would men try and force themselves on her, thinking her witless and willing?

Her heart pounded so loud it was deafening, but she drew a deep breath and steadied herself until the knife in her hand stopped shaking, and she raised it determinedly.

She cut all the saddle girths, and the harnesses to the cart, and the bridles and reins. She hammered the pin out of one of the wheels on the wagon and kicked it free, splitting the wheel with a stone axe.

Letting the axe fall to the ground, she reached into her apron pocket, pulling out the long brook stone necklace Cobie had given her. She had known better to wear it when her father might see, but she had treasured it in her secret moments. She put it on now, and it felt right about her shoulders. A proper promise gift.

Then she took up the skin of water she had hidden, slipped out the barn door, lifted her skirts, and ran down the road as fast as she could.

The run was harder than Renna thought, if not longer. She was strong, but unused to running distances. Her lungs burned before long, and her thighs cried out in protest. She stopped when she had no choice, gulping water from the skin and panting hard, but she never rested more than a few minutes before setting off again.

By the time she made it to the bridge over the brook, her eyes were blurry, and she felt drunk on Boggin's Ale. She collapsed on the bank, dunking her face in the cold running water and drinking deeply.

Her head clear for the first time in almost an hour, she looked up at the sky. The sun was dipping low, but there was time enough, if she kept on. Her legs and feet and chest all screamed as she rose, but Renna ignored the lances of pain and ran on.

She saw a few people as she ran through the Square, mostly folk checking their wards for the night. They looked at her curiously, and one called to her, but she ignored them, heading for the one place everyone in Tibbet's Brook knew, Hog's general store.

"Shopsh closhed," Stam Tailor slurred at her, heading down Hog's porch steps as Renna started her way up. He stumbled, and Renna had to stop to catch him.

"What do you mean, the shop's closed?" she asked, trying to keep the desperation out of her voice. "Hog's supposed to be open till sunset." If Cobie wasn't at the store, she had no idea where to look for him, and would have to run on to Ilain.

"Thatsh what I shaid!" Stam shouted, nodding wildly. "Ay, sho I hadda bit too much ale, and sloshed up a bit. Like thatsh reason to kick poor Stam out and lock up early?"

Renna caught a whiff of him and recoiled. The vomit on his shirt was still wet. It seemed some gossip, like that about Stam being a drunk, was all too true.

Setting him on the rail, she ran up the steps and pounded on the door. "Mister Rusco!" she cried. "It's Renna Tanner! I need to see Cobie Fisher!" She bashed her fist on the door until it hurt, but there was no response.

"He'sh alreddy gone," Stam said, holding the banister as if for dear life. He was a sickly pale, and swayed. "Jusht been setting here on 'is porch a shpell, tryin'a . . . get my feet under me."

Renna looked at him in horror, and Stam misunderstood the look. "Oh, don' you worry yourshelf on account'a ol' Shtam Tailor, girl," he said, patting the air at her. "I been worsh off than thish plenny timesh. I'll be find . . . fine!"

Renna nodded, waiting for him to stumble away before she ran around the back of the store. She doubted Hog would trust anyone, even Cobie, inside his store when he wasn't there. If Cobie lived in the back, there had to be another entrance.

She was right, and found a little room next to the stables, probably meant to store tack, but big enough for a chest and a cot. She drew a breath and knocked. A moment later Cobie opened the door, and she laughed out loud in joy.

"Renna, what are you doing here?!" Cobie's eyes nearly popped out of his head. He stuck his head out the door and looked around, then grabbed her arm and pulled her inside. She moved in to embrace him, but he had not let go her arm, and kept her away.

"Did anyone see you come?" he asked.

"Just Stam Tailor out front," Renna said, smiling, "but he's so drunk he probably won't even remember." She tried to move toward him again, but still he held her back.

"You shouldn't have come, Ren," Cobie said.

It felt as if he had hit her in the chest with a hammer.

"What?" she asked.

"You have to get out of here before someone finds you," Cobie said. "If your da doesn't kill me, mine will."

"You've seen thirty summers, and you're the size of a horse!" Renna cried. "Are you more scared of our das than I am?"

"Your da won't kill you, Ren," Cobie said. "He will me."

"No, he'll just make me pray I was dead!" Renna said.

"All the more reason you should go before he finds us together," Cobie said. "Even if the Tender marries us, they won't let it go. You don't know my da. He has it in his head that I'm to marry Eber Marsh's daughter, even if I do it with a pitchfork at my back. Paid Eber a lotta fish for the promise."

"Then let's run off," Renna said, clutching at his arm. "Go to Sunny Pasture, or even the Free Cities. You could join the real Messengers' Guild."

"And sleep out in the naked night?" Cobie asked, aghast. "Are you mad?"

"But you said you loved me," Renna said, clutching the brook stone necklace. "You said nothing could keep us apart."

"That was before your da almost cut my stones off, and mine did worse," Cobie said, looking around the room frantically. "I shouldn't stay here tonight, either," he muttered, "in case Harl comes looking before dark. You go to Boggin's Hill and stay with your sister. I'll run to my da, so he knows I din't do nothing. Come on." He put a hand behind Renna's back, propelling her toward the door. She went along, shocked and bewildered.

Cobie opened the door, only to find Harl standing there, knife in hand. Behind him, one of the mollies lay collapsed and panting in the dirt. He had ridden her bareback.

"Caught you!" Harl cried, punching Cobie hard in the face. His fist, wrapped around the heavy bone hilt of his knife, turned Cobie's head sharply to the side and knocked him to the ground. He grabbed Renna with his free hand, hard bony fingers digging painfully into her arm.

"Run on an' beg yer sister's succor," he said, his face a mask of rage. "I'll be along presently to deal with you." His eyes flicked to Cobie as he shoved her toward the door.

"It's not what it looks like!" Cobie cried, struggling to one knee and holding his hand out to ward off Harl. "I never asked her to come!"

"Core you didn't," Harl sneered, raising his knife. "Made you a promise, boy, and I aim t'keep it."

He looked back at Renna, frozen in fear. "Get going!" he barked. "You'll be a week in the outhouse as is. Don't make it two!"

Renna recoiled in horror, and Harl turned from her. The night in the outhouse flashed through her mind again, seemingly endless hours of torment relived in barely a second. She thought about the aftermath, the smell of her father's bed, and the weight of his wrinkled bones atop her as he grunted and thrust.

She thought of going back to the farm, and something inside her snapped.

"No!" she screamed, and leapt at her father, nails digging at his face like claws. He fell back in shock, knocking his head on the floor. She tried to wrest the knife from his hands, but Harl was stronger, and kept his grip.

Cobie was standing by then, but he made no move toward them. "Cobie!" she pleaded. "Help me!"

Harl punched Renna in the face, knocking her over, and leapt to pin her, but she bit his arm, and he howled in pain. His fist smashed into her face again, and then three times into her stomach until her teeth let go.

"Little bitch!" he cried, looking at the blood spurting from his arm. He growled and dropped the knife as his hands found her throat.

Renna thrashed as hard as she could, but Harl had locked on and wouldn't budge. Blood ran down his arm and dripped onto her face as she gasped for air that could not come. She saw madness in her father's eyes, and realized he meant to kill her.

Her eyes flicked to Cobie again, but he was still standing there, motionless. She managed to catch his eye, and pleaded with him silently.

With a start, Cobie seemed to find himself again, and moved toward them. "That's enough!" he shouted. "You'll kill her!"

"That's enough of you, boy," Harl said, letting go of Renna's throat with one hand and grabbing his knife when Cobie came close. As Cobie reached for him, Harl pivoted and thrust the blade between his legs.

Cobie's face went bright red, and he looked down in horror, blood pouring down the knife. He drew in a breath to scream, but Harl never gave him the chance, pulling the knife free and burying it in his heart.

Cobie gripped the blade protruding from his chest, mouthing a silent protest as he fell back, dead.

Harl got off Renna, leaving her gasping weakly on the floor, and went to Cobie, pulling the knife free. "I warned you more than once, boy," he said, wiping the blade on Cobie's shirt, "you shoulda listened."

He slipped the knife back in its sheath, where it rested barely a moment before Renna pulled it free and buried it in his back. Again and again she stabbed, screaming and crying as blood spattered her face and soaked her dress.

CHAPTER 20

RADDOCK LAWRY

:: 333 AR SUMMER ::

JEPH BALES FINISHED CHECKING the porch wards not a moment too soon. His family was already inside; children washing for supper, Iain and Norine in the kitchen. He looked out as the last rays of sun vanished and heat leached out of the ground, giving the demons a path up from the Core.

As those stinking gray mists began to rise, he moved inside, even though it would be a few moments more before the corelings solidified. Jeph didn't believe in taking chances where demons were concerned.

But as he reached to close the door, he heard a wail and looked up. Down the road, someone was running hard for the farm, screaming all the way.

Jeph took his axe, always by the door, and moved out as far as the porch wards would allow, his eyes flicking nervously to the corelings coalescing in the yard. He thought of his eldest son, and how he would not have hesitated to run out and help the stranger, but Arlen was dead fourteen years now, and Jeph had never been so brave.

"Be strong and run on!" he called. "Succor is at hand!" Corelings, still more smoke than flesh, looked up at his call, and Jeph tightened his grip on the axe. He wouldn't leave the safety of the wards, but he would strike a demon to clear the path if one came too close.

"What's happening?" Ilain called from inside.

"Keep everyone inside!" Jeph shouted back. "No matter what you hear, stay inside!"

He pulled the door shut, then looked back. The screaming stranger was closer now. It was a woman, her dress soaked in blood, running as if her life depended upon it, as well it did. She had something in her hand, but Jeph couldn't see what it was.

Corelings swiped at her as she passed, but their claws lacked substance, and merely scratched when they should have torn. The woman seemed not to notice—but then she was already screaming.

"Run on!" Jeph called again, hoping the feeble words gave some encouragement.

And then she was in the yard, and almost to the porch. Jeph recognized her just as a flame demon, fully formed, shrieked and leapt into her path.

"Renna," he breathed, but when he looked again, it was not Renna Tanner he saw, but his wife, Silvy, murdered by a flame demon fourteen years ago in that very place.

Something hardened in him then, and he was off the porch before he knew it, swinging the steel axe with all his might. A flame demon's armor could turn the edge of any weapon a man could take to hand, but the creature was small, and his blow sent it tumbling through the dust of the yard.

Other corelings shrieked and leapt for them, but the way back was clear. Jeph grabbed Renna's arm and pulled her along behind him as he charged to safety. He tripped on the porch steps, and they went down in a heap, but when a wood demon came at them it struck the outer net, sending a spiderweb of silver magic through the air before it was thrown back.

Jeph cradled Renna in his arms, calling to her, but she kept on screaming, heedless of her safety. She was drenched in blood, her dress soaked and her arms and face covered, but he could see no injury on her. Clutched tightly in her right hand was a large, bone-handled knife. It, too, was coated in blood.

"Renna, are you all right?" he asked. "Whose blood is this?" The door opened, and Ilain came out, gasping at the sight of her sister.

"Whose blood is this?" Jeph asked again, but if Renna heard him at all, she gave no sign, continuing to scream and sob, the blood and dirt on her face streaked with tears.

"That's Da's knife," Ilain said, indicating the bloody blade she clutched so tightly. "I'd recognize it anywhere. He never lets it out of his sight."

"Creator," Jeph said, blanching.

"Ren, what happened?" Ilain asked, leaning in and taking her sister's shoulders. "Are you hurt? Where's Da? Is he all right?"

But Ilain got no more response from her sister than Jeph had, and she soon fell silent, listening to Renna's cries and the answering shrieks of the corelings at the wards.

"Best bring her inside," Jeph said. "Put the young'uns in their rooms and

I'll take her to ours." Ilain nodded and went in first as Jeph lifted Renna's quivering form in his strong arms.

He laid Renna down on his straw mattress, and turned his back as Ilain came in with a bowl of warm water and a clean cloth. Renna had stopped screaming by this point, but she still gave no response as Ilain pried the bloody knife from her hand and laid it on the night table before undressing her and cleaning the blood from her with firm, even strokes of the cloth.

"What d'you suppose happened?" Jeph asked when she was bundled in the covers, still staring silently off into space.

Ilain shook her head. "Don't know. Long run from here to Da's farm, even if you leave the road and cut straight across. She must have been runnin' for hours."

"Looked like she came up from town," Jeph said.

Ilain shrugged.

"Whatever happened, it wasn't corelings that done it," Jeph said. "Not in the middle of the day."

"Jeph," Ilain said, "I need you to go out to the farm tomorrow. Maybe they were attacked by nightwolves or bandits. I don't know. I'll keep Renna hidden till you get back."

"Bandits and nightwolves, in Tibbet's Brook?" Jeph asked doubtfully.

"Just go and see," Ilain said.

"What if I see Harl lying dead of a knife wound?" Jeph asked, knowing it was what they were both thinking.

Ilain sighed deeply. "Then you mop the blood and build a pyre, and for all anyone ever need know, he slipped off the hay ladder and broke his neck."

"We can't just lie," Jeph said. "If she killed someone . . ."

Ilain whirled angrily on him. "What in the Core do you think we've been doing all these years?" she snapped. Jeph put up his hands to placate her, but she pressed on.

"Have I been a good wife?" Ilain demanded. "Kept your house? Given you sons? Do you love me?"

"Course I do," Jeph said.

"Then you'll do this for me, Jeph Bales," she said. "You'll do it for all of us, an' for Beni an' her boys, too. There ent no need for anything what's ever happened on that farm to reach the town's ears. What they make up is bad enough, and to spare."

Jeph was quiet for a long time as they matched stares and wills. Finally, he nodded. "All right. I'll leave after breakfast."

Jeph was up with the dawn, hurrying through his morning chores despite the tired ache in his bones. They had tried all night to get a response out of Renna, but she simply stared at the ceiling, neither sleeping nor eating. After breakfast, he saddled their best mare.

"Reckon I'll avoid the road myself," he told Ilain. "Take a shortcut through the fields southeast." Ilain nodded, throwing her arms around him and hugging him tightly. He returned the embrace, the pit of his stomach heavy with dread at what he might find. Finally, he let go. "Best to get going while there's still time enough for a return trip."

He had just mounted his horse when the sound of hoofbeats reached his ears. He looked up to see a cart approaching, carrying the Herb Gatherer, Coline Trigg, wringing her hands with worry, and the Town Speaker, Selia the Barren, looking grim. Selia was nearing seventy now, tall and thin, but still tough as boiled leather and sharp as a Cutter's axe.

Beside the cart on one side rode Rusco Hog, and on the other Garric Fisher and Raddock Lawry, Garric's great-uncle and the Speaker for Fishing Hole. On foot behind them were Tender Harral and what looked like half the men of Fishing Hole, armed with thin fishing spears.

Garric kicked his horse ahead when the farm came in sight, galloping right up to the porch where Ilain stood and pulling up so short the beast reared before settling.

"Where is she?" Garric demanded.

"Where is who?" Ilain asked, meeting his wild glare.

"Don't play games with me, woman!" Garric snarled. "I've come for your whorin', witchin', murderin' sister, and you well know it!" He got off his horse and strode up to her, shaking his fist.

"You stop right there, Garric Fisher," said Norine Cutter, coming out of the house holding Jeph's axe. She had lived on Jeph's farm since before his wife died, and was as much a part of the family as any. "This ent your property. You keep back an' state your business, 'less you're looking to take a coreling by the horns."

"My business is that Renna Tanner murdered her own da and my son, and I'll see her cored for it!" Garric shouted. "Ent no point in hiding her!"

Tender Harral caught up and interposed himself between Garric and the women. He was young and strong, a match for the older if just as bulky Garric. "There's no proof of anything yet, Garric! We just need to ask her a few questions, is all," he told Ilain. "And you, if she's said anything since Jeph left."

"We need to do more than that, Tender," Raddock said, getting off his horse. He was born Raddock Fisher, but everyone in the Brook called him

Raddock Lawry, because he was Speaker for the Hole on the town council, and legal arbitrator of disputes in his borough. A mass of grizzled hair from ears to chin, the crown of his head was bald as an egg. He was older than Selia but shorter-tempered, full of righteous passion with a knack for stirring it in others. "Girl needs to answer for her crimes."

Hog was the next to dismount. He was imposing as always, the man who owned half of Tibbet's Brook outright and held debts from the rest. "Garric speaks honest word when he says your father and Cobie Fisher are dead," Hog told Ilain. "My girls and I went to investigate some shouting we heard at the store last evening, and found them in the back room I rented Cobie, dead. Not just stabbed, they was . . . mutilated. Both of them. Stam Tailor says he saw your sister there just before it happened."

Ilain gasped, covering her mouth.

"Horrible," Harral agreed, "and that's why it's best we see Renna right away."

"So clear the door!" Raddock ordered, pushing forward.

"I am Speaker in Tibbet's Brook, Raddock Lawry, not you!" Selia barked, silencing everyone. Jeph reached out to help her down from the cart. As soon as her feet touched the ground, she gripped her skirts to keep them from the dirt and strode over. The younger men, outweighing her several times over, shrank back at the force of her presence.

One did not get to be Selia's age easily in Tibbet's Brook. Life in the Brook was hard; only the sharpest, most cunning and capable folk survived to see full gray, and the rest treated them accordingly. When she was younger, Selia had been forceful. Now she was a Power unto herself.

Only Raddock stood his ground. He had ousted Selia as Town Speaker more than once over the years, and if age was power in Tibbet's Brook, he was stronger, if not by much.

"Coline, Harral, Rusco, Raddock, and I will need to go in and see her," Selia told Jeph. It wasn't a request. The five of them were half the town council, and he could only nod and stand aside, allowing them entrance.

"I'm going, too!" Garric growled. The crowd of Fishers, his kith and kin, gathered angrily around him, nodding.

"No, you're not," Selia said, fixing them all with a steely glare. "Your blood is up and none can blame you, but we're here to learn what happened, not stake the girl without a trial."

Raddock put a hand on Garric's shoulder. "She ent getting away, Gar, I promise you that," he said. Garric gritted his teeth, but he nodded and stepped back as they went inside.

Renna was still lying in the same position they had placed her in the night before, staring at the ceiling. She blinked occasionally. Coline went right to her.

"Oh, dear," Selia said, spotting the bloody knife on the night table. Jeph cursed silently. Why had he left it there? He should have thrown it down the well the moment he saw it.

"Creator," Harral breathed, and drew a ward in the air.

"And here," Raddock grunted, kicking a basin by the door. Renna's dress was soaking within, the water pink with blood. "Still think we're just here to ask a few questions, Tender?"

Coline looked over the bruises on Renna's face with a concerned eye and a firm hand, then turned to the others and cleared her throat loudly. The men stared dully for a moment, then gave a start and turned their backs as she drew back the covers.

"Nothing's broken," Coline said, coming over to Selia when her inspection was complete, "but she's taken quite a beating, and there are bruises around her throat like she was choked."

Selia went and sat down on the bed beside Renna. She reached out gently, brushing the hair from Renna's sweating face. "Renna, dear, can you hear me?" The girl didn't react at all.

"Been like this all night?" Selia asked, frowning.

"Ay," Jeph said.

Selia sighed and put her hands on her knees, pushing to her feet. She took the knife, and then turned and ushered everyone out of the room, closing the door.

"Seen this before, after demon attacks, mostly," she said, with Coline nodding along. "Survivors get more of a fright than they can handle, and are left staring off into the air."

"Will she get better?" Ilain asked.

"Sometimes they snap out of it in a few days," Selia said. "Sometimes . . ." She shrugged. "Won't lie to you, Ilain Bales. This is the worst thing ever happened in Tibbet's Brook as far back as I can recall. I've been Speaker on and off for thirty years, and seen a great many folk die before their time, but there ent never been one killed in anger. That kind of thing may happen in the Free Cities, but not here."

"Renna couldn't have . . . !" Ilain choked, and Selia took her shoulders, gentling her.

"That's why I was hoping to talk to her first, dear, and get the story from her lips." She glanced at Raddock. "The Fishers have come looking for blood, and they won't be satisfied without it, or a good explanation."

"We got reason," Raddock growled. "It's our kin dead."

"Case you ent noticed, my kin's dead, too," Ilain said, glaring at him.

"All the more reason to want justice," Raddock said.

Selia hissed, and everyone fell silent. She held the bloody knife out to Tender Harral.

"Tender, if you'd be so kind as to wrap this and hide it in your robes till we get to town, I'd be grateful." Harral nodded, reaching for it.

"What in the Core you think you're doing?" Raddock shouted, snatching the knife before the Tender could take it. "The whole town's got a right to see this!" he said, waving it around.

Selia grabbed his wrist, and Raddock, outweighing her twice over, laughed until she drove her heel down on his instep. He howled in pain, letting go of the knife to clutch his foot. Selia caught it before it could hit the floor.

"Use your head, Lawry!" she snapped. "That knife's evidence and all have a right to see it, but not with two dozen men outside with spears and a defenseless girl numb with fright. The Tender ent gonna steal it."

Ilain fetched a cloth, and Selia wrapped the knife, giving it to the Tender, who stowed it safely in his robes. She gathered her skirts and strode outside, back arched and head up high as she faced the gathered men in the yard, who grumbled angrily and fingered their spears.

"She's in no condition to talk," Selia said.

"We're not looking to talk!" Garric shouted, and the Fishers all nodded their assent.

"I don't care what you're looking to do," Selia said. "No one's doing anything until the town council meets on this."

"The council?" Garric asked. "This ent some coreling attack! She murdered my son!"

"You don't know that, Garric," Harral said. "Could be he and Harl killed each other."

"Even if she didn't hold the knife, she done it," Garric said, "witchin' my son into sin and shamin' her da!"

"The law is the law, Garric," Selia said. "She gets a council meeting, where you can make your accusations and she can say her piece, before we name her guilty. Bad enough we've had two killings, I won't have your mob doing a third because you can't wait on justice."

Garric looked to Raddock for support, but the Speaker for Fishing Hole was silent, edging toward Harral. Suddenly he shoved the Tender against the wall, reaching into his robes.

"She ent tellin' you all!" Raddock shouted. "The girl had a red dress soaking!" He held Harl's knife up for all to see. "And a bloody knife!"

The Fishers gripped their spears and shouted in outrage, ready to push right into the house. "The Core with your law," Garric told Selia, "if it means I can't avenge my son."

"You'll murder that poor girl over my dead body," Selia said, moving to stand directly in front of the door with the rest of the council and Jeph's family. "That what you want?" she called. "To be named murderers yourselves? Every Fisher?"

"Bah, you can't hang us all," Raddock scoffed. "We're taking the girl, and that's that. Stand aside, or we'll go clean through you."

Hands in the air, Rusco stepped aside. Selia glared at him. "Traitor!"

But Rusco just smiled. "I'm no traitor, ma'am. Just a visiting businessman, and it isn't my place to take sides in this kind of dispute."

"You're as much a part of this town as anyone!" Selia shouted. "You've been in Town Square twenty years, and on the council near all of 'em! If you've a place that's more home than this, maybe it's time you went back to it!"

Rusco just smiled again. "I'm sorry, ma'am, but I got to be fair to all. Standing against a whole borough is just bad business."

"Once a year at least, half the town comes to me, ready to run you out for a cheat, like they did to you in Miln and Angiers and Creator knows where else," Selia said, "and every year, I talk them out of it. Remind them what a benefit your store is, and how things were before you came. But you stand aside now, and I'll see to it no decent person sets foot in your shop again."

"You can't do that!" Hog cried.

"Oh, yes I can, Rusco," Selia said. "Just you try me if you think it ent so." Raddock scowled, and it turned venomous when Hog went back to stand with Selia in the doorway.

Hog met his eyes. "I don't want to hear it, Raddock. We can wait a day or two. Any man puts hands on Renna Tanner before the council meets is banned from the store."

Selia turned to Raddock, her eyes blazing. "How long, Lawry? How long can Fishing Hole go without Bales' grain and livestock? Marsh rice? Boggin's Ale? Cutters' wood? I'm betting not nearly so long as we can go without ripping fish!"

"Fine, you call the council," Raddock said. "But we'll lock the girl up in Fishing Hole until she has her trial."

Selia barked a laugh. "You think I'd entrust her to you?"

"Then where?" he asked. "I'll be corespawned before I let her stay here with her kin, where she could run off."

Selia sighed, glancing back at the house. "We'll put her in my spinning room. It's got a stout door, and you can nail the shutters and set a guard, if you wish."

"You sure that's wise?" Rusco asked her, raising an eyebrow.

"Oh, feh," Selia said, waving dismissively. "She's just a little girl."

"A little girl that killed two grown men," Rusco reminded her.

"Nonsense," Selia said. "I doubt she could have killed one of those strong men herself, much less two."

"Fine," Raddock growled, "but I'm keeping this," he held up the knife, "and that bloody dress, until the council comes." Selia scowled, and their eyes met as they matched wills. She knew Raddock Lawry could whip the town into a frenzy with the items, but she didn't have much choice in the matter.

"I'll send runners today," Selia said, nodding. "We'll meet in three days."

Jeph carried Renna out to his cart and they took her down to Selia's house in Town Square, locking her in the spinning room. Garric nailed the shutters closed from the outside himself, testing the wood carefully before grunting and agreeing to leave.

CHAPTER 21

TOWN COUNCIL

:: 333 AR SUMMER ::

DAWN CAME THE NEXT day, and Selia's bones ached as she swung her feet out of bed. The pain had come to her joints a few years past. It was worst when it was rainy or cold, but lately she felt a twinge of it even on the warmest, driest days. She supposed it would worsen ere she died.

But Selia never complained, not even to Coline Trigg. The pain was her burden to bear. She was Speaker in Tibbet's Brook, and that meant folk expected her to be strong and stand up for what was right. No matter how her limbs screamed, no one ever saw any sign that Selia was anything other than what she had always been, a rock of support they could lean upon.

She felt that added weight heavily as she rose and made her ablutions, dressing in one of her heavy, high-necked gowns. She didn't know Renna or her sisters well, but she knew their mother, and how Harl had treated her before the corelings took her. Some said she went to the demons willingly, to escape him. If he was at all the same with his daughters, Selia could well imagine Renna needing to kill in her own defense.

When she was done, she saw to Renna, dressing her in one of her own gowns and sitting her up to take some porridge. She wiped the girl's mouth clean when she was done and left the spinning room, dropping the bar.

She had her own meal, then went outside. Rik Fisher was standing on her walk, holding his thin fishing spear. He was seventeen and not yet married, though Selia had seen him walking with Ferd Miller's daughter Jan. If Ferd approved the match, they would likely be promised soon.

"Need you to run an errand for me," Selia said.

"Sorry, ma'am," Rik said. "Raddock Lawry said to stay right here and make sure the girl dunt leave, no matter what anyone said to me."

"Oh, did he?" Selia asked. "And am I right to guess I would find your brother Borry around back, by my nice shutters that Garric nailed shut?"

"Yes'm," Rik said.

Selia went back into the house, coming out with a broom and a rake. "Won't have idle hands milling around my house, Rik Fisher. You want to stay here, you'll sweep my front walk spotless and have your brother clear the leaves and dead grass out back."

"I'm not sure I . . . ," Rik began.

"You'd leave an old woman to do work you're too lazy to?" Selia asked. "Perhaps I'll mention that to Ferd Miller, the next time I see him."

Rik had taken the broom and rake before she finished the sentence. "That's a dear boy," she said. "When you're done, you can check my wards. Anyone comes calling, have them set on my porch. I'll be back soon."

"Yes'm," Rik said.

She took a crock of butter cookies and went to where the children played in the Square, sending the swiftest to deliver messages in exchange for a cookie. By the time she made it back to her house, Rik was done with the walk and was sweeping her porch. Stam Tailor, the first person she had summoned, sat slumped on her porch steps, clutching his head in pain.

"Regretting yesterday's ale?" Selia asked, knowing the answer already. Stam was always regretting yesterday's ale, even as he reached for today's.

Stam only groaned in reply.

"Come inside then, and have a cup of tea to soothe your head," Selia said. "Want to talk about what you saw, night before last."

She interviewed Stam at length, and then the others who claimed to have seen Renna pass through on her way to the store. There were too many of these to believe, though, as if the whole town had seen her charge down the street, eyes ablaze and knife in hand. Raddock and Garric had been from one end of the Brook to the other with the bloody knife and dress, and everyone wanted to feel a part of the drama.

"Cobie may have been weak in the flesh," Tender Harral told her, recalling the scene after Fernan Boggin's funeral, "but he was honest in wanting to marry Renna, I saw it plain on his face. Hers, too. It was Harl that had murder in his eyes at the thought."

"My Lucik got in a fight with two Fishers last night," Meada Boggin told her later. "They said Renna planned to kill her da all along, and tried to trick

Cobie into doing it for her. Lucik punched one on the nose, and they broke his arm."

"Lucik punched one?" Selia asked.

"My boy lived with Renna Tanner nigh fourteen years," Meada said, "and if he says she ent a killer, that's enough for me."

"You'll speak for Boggin's Hill, now that Fernan's gone?" Selia asked.

Meada nodded. "Hill voted yesterday."

Coline Trigg came next. "Keep asking myself," the Herb Gatherer said, "why was poor Cobie stabbed twixt the legs? Must've been her done it; no man'd do that to another man. Expect she wasn't as willing as folk say when Cobie visited. Reckon he forced himself on her, and she went to kill him for it. When her father tried to stop her, she must've killed him, too."

In the afternoon, Jeph arrived with Ilain and Beni. He kept close to the women, interposing himself between Beni and Rik Fisher as they glared at each other.

"How's Lucik?" Selia asked Beni as they came inside.

Beni sighed. "Coline says the splint comes off in a couple months, but it puts us in a bad place, we want to fill Hog's ale orders. Worried for my boys, too, this feud goes on much longer."

Selia nodded. "Best keep your boys close to hand. Raddock's stirred the Fishers into a fine frenzy, and they reckon they're owed blood. Might be they're not picky about where they get it. Meantime, I'll see if I can find any idle hands around town to throw in at the brewery."

"Thank you, Speaker," Beni said.

Selia gave all three a hard look. "We all have to do our part, when times try us." She turned and led them to the spinning room. Renna sat in a chair, staring at the wall.

"She been eating?" Ilain asked, worry in her voice.

Selia nodded. "She'll swallow what you put in her mouth, and use the privy if you lead her to it. Even worked the pedal on my spinning wheel last night. Just her will that's gone."

"She was like that for me, too," Ilain agreed. Beni looked at Renna and started to cry.

"Would you mind leaving us a spell, Speaker?" Jeph asked.

"Course not," Selia said, leaving the room and closing the door behind her.

Jeph hung back, giving Ilain and Beni distance as they went to their sister. They spoke in hushed tones, but Jeph could hear a mole digging his fields at thirty yards, and he caught every word.

"She done it," Beni said. "Never believe she hurt Cobie Fisher, but she was scared to death of what Da might do if they was alone. Begged me to take her away with us . . ." She sobbed again, and Ilain joined her. They held each other until it passed.

"Oh, Ren," Ilain said, "why'd you have to go and kill him? I always just took it quiet."

"You never took nothin' quiet," Beni snapped. "You took it like I did, hiding behind the first man I saw. And we both got away with it, because we left Da another plum."

Ilain turned to her, horror in her eyes. "Din't reckon he'd turn to you," she said, reaching out. "Thought you were too young."

Beni slapped her hand away. "You knew," she spat. "I already had paps bigger than most goodwives, and was old enough to promise. You knew, and you left anyway, 'cause you were thinkin' more of yourself than your kin."

"You din't do the same?" Ilain accused. "If that ent the night callin' things dark, dunno what is!"

They went at each other, but Jeph crossed the floor in an instant, pulling them apart by the necks of their dresses. "There'll be none of that!" he said, holding them out at arm's length and glaring at them until they dropped their eyes. When he let go, the fight was out of them.

"Maybe it's time to air this all before the council," he said, making both women look up at him sharply. "Tell 'em the kinda man Harl was," he thrust his chin at Renna, "and maybe they won't blame her for what she done."

Ilain slumped into the seat next to Renna, digesting the thought, but Beni glared at him. "You expect me to stand before the likes of Raddock Lawry and Lucik's mam and say my da liked to treat his daughters like wives?" she demanded. "You expect I'll trust that tale to the tavern keeper and that old gossip Coline Trigg? Night, how'll I look my own husband in the eye after that, much less hold my head up in town? How could any of us? Worse'n what happened, everyone knowin' what happened!"

"Worse than seein' your sister staked?" Jeph asked.

"Even if it wern't," Beni said, "ent no proof it would change one mind on the council, and might be it gets three sisters staked, steada just one."

Jeph looked to Ilain, sitting very quiet as the image Beni painted danced before her eyes. "I think everyone knowing might be worse," she said softly, her voice cracking into a sob with the last word. Jeph rushed to her, going to one knee to hold her as she cried.

"You best keep your mouth shut on this, too, Jeph Bales," Beni said.

Jeph looked at his weeping wife, and nodded. "Not my place to make that decision for you two. I'll hold my peace."

Ilain looked at Renna and moaned, her face screwing up further. "I'm sorry!" she sobbed, and hurried out of the room.

"Are you all right, dear?" Selia asked Ilain as she stumbled out of the spinning room.

"Hate seein' her like that," Ilain mumbled.

Selia nodded, but she wasn't satisfied. "Sit." She pointed to a chair in her common room. "I'll make tea."

"Thank you, Speaker," Ilain said, "but we have business—"

"Sit," Selia said again, this time it was less an offer than a command, and Ilain complied instantly at the change in tone. "All of you," Selia added, as Beni and Jeph caught up.

"Town council meets tomorrow," Selia said when the tea was served. "Early, most like. If Renna ent talking by then, and I don't 'spect she will be, Raddock's going to demand a ruling without her words, and with so much evidence against her and nothing for, reckon he'll have his way. I'll try and delay till she's better, but that will be up to the council."

"What'll they rule, you reckon?" Jeph asked.

Selia blew out a breath. "Can't say for sure. This ent ever happened before. But the Fishers are in arms, and it's one more reason for Marshes and Watches to preach keeping their young'uns away from Town Square and its temptations. The Tender and Meada won't turn on the girl, but there's no telling what the rest will do. Expect she'll be strung from the nearest tree, with Garric hauling the rope."

Ilain gave a little cry.

"This ent no small crime, girl," Selia said. "We got two men dead, and one with angry kin. I'll argue in moot until I'm blue-faced, but the law is the law. Once the council votes, there ent no choice but to hold peace and abide."

She looked at Beni and Ilain. "So if there's anything—*any*thing—you can tell me that'll help me when I am fighting for that girl, I need to hear it now."

The sisters both glanced at Jeph, but neither said a word.

Selia huffed. "Jeph, Mack Pasture speaks for the farms in council. Go visit him; see if you can get an idea how he'll vote. Make sure he's got the story straight, and not whatever tampweed tale Raddock is spinning."

"Mack's farm is a long way," Jeph said. "It'll take the rest of the day just to get there."

"Then succor there, and use the time wisely," Selia said, the tone of command returning to her voice. She nodded to the door. "Now, dear. I'll see Ilain and Beni get home safe."

Jeph glanced nervously at Ilain, then nodded. "Yes'm," he said, and headed out the door.

Selia turned back to the sisters but kept her eyes down. "Always wondered about your da," she said, selecting a butter cookie from the crock on the table. "Learned to watch a man after corelings take his wife. Sometimes they . . . crack a bit. Start acting irrational. I asked folk to watch Harl, but your da liked to keep to himself, and all seemed well those first years." She dipped the cookie in her tea, eyes still on her hands.

"But then, Ilain, when you ran off with Jeph, though his lost wife wasn't even burned yet, I wondered again. What were you running from? And the Harl I knew would have fetched some men and come and dragged you home, kicking and screaming. I had half a mind to do it myself." She ate the moist cookie with quick, neat bites, and wiped her mouth delicately with a napkin. Ilain just stared at her, mouth open.

"But he didn't," Selia said, setting down the napkin and meeting Ilain's eyes. "Why?" Ilain recoiled from the force of Selia's gaze, but she dropped her eyes and shook her head.

"Dunno," she said.

Selia frowned, selecting another cookie. "And there was all the suitors that went to court Renna." She dropped her eyes again. "She's a pretty enough girl, fit as a horse, with two elder sisters shown to give strong sons. Harl could've made a good match for her after Arlen Bales ran off. Could've had another man to help about the farm; even taken a widow to wed himself. But again, he didn't. He drove them boys off time and again, sometimes at the end of a pitchfork, till your sister's best breeding years were all but gone. By then, Cobie Fisher was as good a match as she could hope for, and the farm in desperate need of a strong back, but still he refused."

Selia looked up at both of them. "I wonder what would make a man behave like that, and have my guesses, but what do I know? Saw your da maybe once or twice a year. You two lived with him every day. Reckon you know better than me. Anything to add to the slate?"

Ilain and Beni looked at her, and then at each other, and then at their hands. "No," they mumbled together.

"Ent no one seen either of you shed a tear over your da," Selia pressed.

"That ent natural, when a girl's father takes a knife in the back." Ilain and Beni didn't even lift their eyes.

Selia looked at them a moment, and then sighed deeply.

"Off with you, then!" she snapped at last. "Out of my house, before I take a cane to both your backsides! And Creator forbid you selfish little brats ever need someone to stand for you!"

The two sisters scurried out of the house, and Selia put her head in her hands, feeling her age as never before.

Selia had barely dressed the next morning before she found Raddock Lawry in her yard with Cobie's parents, Garric and Nomi, and close to a hundred folk from Fishing Hole, which was just about everyone.

"Are your words so feeble, Raddock Lawry, that you need all your kith and kin to back them?" she asked, coming out on her porch.

There was a murmur of shock through the crowd, and they turned as one to Raddock for their cue. Raddock opened his mouth to reply, but Selia cut him off.

"I will not call the town council to order in front of a mob!" she shouted, her voice making grown men cringe. "You voted yourselves a Speaker for a reason, and apart from those making accusations, you will disperse, or I'll put the meeting off until you do, even if you have to wait out the winter right on my doorstep!"

A sudden buzz of confusion started in the crowd, drowning out Raddock's reply. After a moment, they began to trickle away, some heading back up toward the Hole but most heading down the road to the Square and the general store to await the verdict. Selia didn't like that, but there was little she could do once they left her property.

Raddock scowled at her, but Selia only smiled primly, putting Nomi to work helping serve tea on the porch.

Coline Trigg was the next to arrive, having heard the commotion from her house down the road. Her apprentices, who were also her daughters, took over the tea at once while the three council members awaited the others.

There were ten seats on the council. Each borough of Tibbet's Brook held a vote each year, electing one of its own to the council, to sit with the Tender and Herb Gatherer. In addition, they cast a general vote for the Town Speaker. Selia held the head seat most years, and spoke for Town Square when she didn't.

The council seats usually went to the oldest and wisest person in each borough and were rare to change from year to year, unless someone died. Fernan Boggin had held the seat for Boggin's Hill almost ten years, and it was only natural for it to fall to his widow.

Meada Boggin was next to arrive, escorted by at least fifty from Boggin's Hill who dispersed into the Square. She came up the walk with Lucik, his arm in a sling, and Beni, her shoulders covered in a black shawl to mark the death of her father. With them came Tender Harral and two of his acolytes.

"Parading your injured young'uns around ent gonna get you sympathy," Raddock warned Meada as she took tea and sat.

"Parading," Meada said, amused. "This from the man who's ridden from one end of town to the other, waving a bloody dress like a flag."

Raddock scowled, but his response was cut off as Brine Cutter, also known as Brine Broadshoulders, stomped up the walk. "Ay, my friends!" Brine boomed as he ducked to avoid hitting his head on the porch roof. He embraced the women warmly, and squeezed the hands of the men until they ached.

A survivor of the Cluster Massacre, Brine had spent weeks in a fugue state similar to Renna's, yet now he stood tall as Speaker for the Cluster by the Woods. A widower almost fifteen years, Brine had never remarried, no matter how often pressed, saying it wouldn't be right to his lost wife and children. Folk said loyalty was rooted in him as the trees he cut were rooted in the ground.

An hour later, Coran Marsh came slowly up the walk, leaning heavily on his cane. At eighty summers, he was one of the oldest people in the Brook, and he was given every courtesy as his son Keven and grandson Fil helped him up the stairs. All of them came barefoot, as Marshes were wont to do. Toothless and shaky as he was, Coran's dark eyes were still sharp as he nodded to the other speakers.

Next to arrive was Mack Pasture, at the head of quite a few other farmers, including Jeph Bales. Jeph leaned in to Selia as they came onto the porch.

"Mack's come with no prejudice against Renna," he whispered, "and promised me to judge fair, no matter what the Fishers shout." Selia nodded, and Jeph went to stand with Ilain, Beni, and Lucik on the opposite side of the porch from Garric and Nomi Fisher.

As the morning wore on, a general buzz grew in the air, and it became clear that more than just Fishing Hole was out in force. Hundreds of folk walked the streets, trying to seem nonchalant as they glanced toward Selia's porch on their way to the tailor, or the cobbler, or any of the other shops about the Square.

Last to arrive were the Watches. Southwatch was the farthest borough, practically a town unto itself, with near three hundred inhabitants and their own Herb Gatherer and Holy House.

They came in neat procession, marked by their stark clothing. Watch men were all thickly bearded and wore black pants with black suspenders over a white shirt. A heavy black jacket, hat, and boots finished the outfit, even in the harsh heat of summer. The women all wore black dresses reaching from ankle to chin to wrist, as well as white aprons and bonnets, with white gloves and parasol when not working. Their heads were bowed, and they all drew wards in the air, over and over, to protect them from sin.

At their head was Jeorje Watch. Speaker and Tender both, Jeorje was the oldest man in Tibbet's Brook by two decades. There were children running around the Brook who hadn't been born when he celebrated his hundredth birthday. Still, his back was straight as he led the procession, his stride firm and his eyes hard. He stood in stark contrast with Coran Marsh, a quarter century his junior and ravaged by time.

With his years and his solid bloc of votes from the largest borough, Jeorje should have been Town Speaker, but he never got a single vote outside Southwatch, and he never would, not even from Tender Harral. Jeorje Watch was too strict.

Selia rose as tall as she was able, and that was very tall, as she went to greet him.

"Speaker," Jeorje said, biting back his displeasure at having to give that title to a woman, and an unmarried one at that.

"Tender," Selia said, refusing to be intimidated. They bowed respectfully to each other.

Jeorje's wives, some old and proud like him, others younger, including one great with child, flowed around them wordlessly and went into the house. They were heading for the kitchen, Selia knew. Watches always took over the kitchen, to ensure that their special eating needs were attended to. They kept to a strict diet of plain foods with no seasoning or sugar.

Selia signaled Jeph. "Go and pull Rusco from the store," she told him, and Jeph ran off.

Selia was always elected Speaker for Town Square, but on years when she was also elected Town Speaker, she appointed Rusco Hog to speak for the Square, so that it would keep an independent voice, as prescribed in town law. Few people were pleased by this, but Selia knew the general store was the heart of the Square, and when one prospered, the other most often would, as well.

"Well come in, and let's have supper," Selia said when they'd had their ease a bit. "We'll handle standing council business over coffee, and then on to this last affair when the cups are cleared."

"If it's all the same, Speaker," Raddock Lawry said, "I'd just as soon dispense supper and the rest till the next council meeting and get on to the business of my dead kin."

"It is *not* all the same, Raddock Fisher," Jeorje Watch said, thumping his polished black walking stick. "We can't just take leave of our customs and civility because someone died. This is the time of Plague, when death comes often. Creator punishes those what sin in his own time. The Tanner girl will have her judgment when the Brook's standing business is done."

He spoke with the authority of one who is never questioned, though Selia was Speaker. She accepted the slight—a common one from Jeorje—because he argued to her favor. The later the hour grew, the less likely Renna's sentence, if death, would take place that very night.

"We could all use some supper," Tender Harral said, though he and Jeorje were often at odds themselves. "As the Canon says, *There's no justice from a man with an empty stomach.*"

Raddock looked around to the other Speakers for support, but apart from Hog, who was always the last to arrive and the first to leave, all were resolute to keep the council meeting in its traditional fashion. He scowled but gave no further protest. Garric started to open his mouth, but Raddock silenced him with a shake of his head.

They had supper, and discussed the business of each borough in turn over the coffee and cakes that followed.

"Reckon it's time to see the girl," Jeorje said when the business of his borough, always handled last, was complete. The closing of old business was the Speaker's to call, but again he spoke over Selia, thumping his stick like the Speaker's gavel. She sent the witnesses out onto the porch, then led the nine council members in to see Renna.

"Girl ent faking?" Jeorje asked.

"You can have your own Gatherer examine her, if you like," Selia said, and Jeorje nodded, calling for his wife Trena, the Herb Gatherer for Southwatch, who was near ninety herself. She left the kitchen and went to the girl's side.

"Men out," Jeorje ordered, and they all trooped back out to their seats at the table. Selia sat at the head, and Jeorje, as always, the foot.

Trena emerged some time later and looked to Jeorje, who nodded permission for her to speak. "Whatever she done, girl's shock is true," she said, and he nodded again, dismissing her.

"So you've seen the state of her," Selia said, taking up the gavel before Jeorje could try to take over protocol. "I move that any decision should be postponed until she comes back to herself and can speak her own defense."

"The Core it should!" Raddock shouted. He started to rise, but Jeorje cracked his walking stick on the table, checking him.

"Din't come all this way to glance at a sleeping girl and leave, Selia," he said. "Best we hear from the witnesses and accusers now, in proper fashion." Selia scowled, but no one dared to disagree. Speaker or no, if she went against Jeorje, she would be doing it alone. She called in Garric to make his accusation, and the witnesses, one by one, for the council to question.

"I don't pretend to know what happened that evening," Selia said in her closing. "There ent no witness but the girl herself, and she ought to get to speak in her own defense before we pass judgment on her."

"No witness?!" Raddock cried. "We just heard from Stam Tailor, who seen her heading toward the murder not a moment before!"

"Stam Tailor was rot drunk that night, Raddock," Selia said, looking to Rusco, who nodded in agreement.

"He sloshed up on my floor, and I threw him out and closed early after that," Rusco said.

"Blame the one who put the drink in his hand, I say," Jeorje said. Rusco's brow furrowed, but he was wise enough to bite his tongue.

"Either he saw the girl or he didn't, Selia," Coran Marsh said. Others nodded.

"He saw her in the vicinity, yes," Selia said, "but not where she went or what she did."

"You're suggesting she's not involved?" Jeorje asked, incredulous.

"Course she's involved," Selia snapped. "Any fool can see that. But ent none of us can swear by the sun at how. Maybe the men took to fighting and killed each other. Maybe she killed in her own defense. Coline and Trena both attest she was beat bad."

"How don't matter none, Selia," Raddock said. "Two men can't kill each other with the same knife. Does knowing which man she killed, if not both, make a difference?"

Jeorje nodded. "And let us not forget it was most likely by feminine wile that the men were taken to wrath. The girl's promiscuity led them to this path, and she should be held to account."

"Two men fight over who owns a girl, and we blame the girl?" Meada broke in. "Nonsense!"

"It ent nonsense, Meada Boggin, you're just too shaded to see it, seeing how the accused's your kin," Raddock said.

"There's the night calling it dark," Meada said. "I can say the same of you."

Selia banged her gavel. "If everyone related to a problem in the Brook had to be disqualified in moot, Raddock Fisher, there would be none to argue at all. Everyone has a right to speak. That's our law."

"Law," Raddock mused. "Been reading the law," he produced a book bound in worn leather, " 'specially the law for killers." He turned to a marked page, and began to read:

"And should the foul deed of murder be committed in the confines of Tibbet's Brook or its purview, you shall erect a stake in Town Square, and shackle those responsible for all to see for a day of repentance, and a night, without ward or succor, that all may witness the Creator's wrath upon those who violate this covenant."

"You can't be serious!" Selia cried.

"That's barbaric!" Meada agreed.

"That's the law," Raddock sneered.

"See here, Raddock," Tender Harral said. "That law must be three hundred years old."

"The Canon is older still, Tender," Jeorje said. "Will you discount that next? Justice is not meant to be kind."

"We ent here to rewrite the law," Raddock said. "The law is the law, ent that what you said, Selia?"

Selia's nostrils flared, but she nodded.

"All we're here to debate is whether she's responsible," Raddock said, placing Harl's bloody knife on the table, "and I say it's clear as day she is."

"She could've picked that up after, Raddock, and you know it," Tender Harral said. "Cobie wanted Renna's hand, and Harl threatened twice to cut the stones from him if he tried."

Raddock barked a laugh. "You might convince some folk that two men could kill each other with the same knife, but they wasn't just killed. They was mutilated. My great-nephew didn't hack Harl near to pieces with his manhood gone and a knife in his heart."

"Man has a point," Hog said.

Raddock grunted. "So let's vote and have done."

"Second," Hog said. "Town Square has never seen such crowds, and I need to get back to the store."

"A girl's life is at stake, and all you care is how many credits you can make off the folk come to gape?" Selia asked.

"Don't preach to me, Selia," Hog said. "I was the one had to mop up the blood out of my back room."

"All in favor of moving to vote?" Jeorje said.

"I am Speaker, Jeorje Watch!" Selia snapped, pointing the gavel at him. But already there was a show of hands in favor of a vote, checking her. Jeorje accepted the rebuke with a mild nod.

"Fine," Selia said. "I say the girl is innocent until we can prove otherwise, and there is no proof of anything." She looked to her right for Tender Harral to continue the vote.

"You're wrong, Selia," Harral said. "There is proof of one thing: young love. I spoke to Cobie and looked in Renna's eyes. They were both grown and wanted to decide the match for themselves, as is their right. Harl had no call to refuse, and I'll stand in the sun's light and state my belief that any bloodshed started with him, and ended with him, too. Innocent."

Brine Cutter was next, the giant man's voice uncharacteristically soft. "Seems to me that anything the girl done, she done in self-defense. I know what it's like to see things so horrible that it makes your mind run for succor. I was much the same, after the corelings took my family. Selia saw me through that, and the girl deserves the same. Innocent."

"Ent no innocent," Coran Marsh said. "Whole town knows Renna Tanner's a sinner, offerin' herself to Cobie Fisher in fornication. Apt to make any man mad with lust! If she's gonna behave like a coreling, we should put 'er out among them with easy hearts. Swamp demons have cored better'n her, and the sun still comes in the morning. Guilty."

Jeorje Watch was next. "Harl's daughters were ever a trial to him. It's but by the grace of the Creator that this scene didn't occur nigh fifteen years ago with her sister. Guilty."

Raddock Lawry nodded. "We all know she's guilty." He turned to Rusco.

"Tying a girl out for the corelings, no matter what she's done, is savage," Hog said. "But if that's how you do things here . . ." He shrugged. "Can't just let people go around killing folk. I say put her out and have done. Guilty."

"See if I let you speak for the Square next year," Selia muttered.

"Sorry, ma'am, but I *am* speaking for the Square," Hog said. "Folk need to feel safe when they come to shop in town. Ent no one going to feel safe with a killer about."

"Harl was a sour old crow who never cared a whit for anyone but himself," Meada Boggin said. "I tried to broker a match for Renna myself once, but Harl wouldn't hear of it. Ent no doubt in my mind he killed young Cobie, and Renna did what she needed to keep him from killing her, too. Innocent."

"Then why was Cobie stabbed in the stones?" Coline asked. "I think he raped her, and she came to town to get him back. Stabbed him between the legs, and then they fought until she could finish the job. Harl must've gone after her, and she caught him from behind. The girl's got blood on her hands, Selia. She could have gone to one of us, or called for help, but she chose to solve her problems with a knife. I say she's guilty."

All eyes turned to Mack Pasture. With four votes of innocent and five of guilty, it was in his power to deadlock the council, or pronounce her guilty. He sat quietly for a long time, his brow furrowed as he rested his face on his steepled fingers.

"All keep saying 'innocent' or 'guilty,' " Mack said finally, "but the law don't say that. We all just heard it. It said 'responsible.' Now, I knew Harl Tanner. Knew him long years, and never liked the coreling's son one bit." He spit on the floor. "But that don't mean he deserved a knife in his back. Way I see it, that girl didn't mind her da, and now two men are dead. Whether she swung a knife or not, she's sure as the sun rises 'responsible' for what happened."

Shock stayed Selia's hand, and the gavel lay on the table untouched, though the vote was done. Jeorje thumped his walking stick on the floor. "Guilty, six to four."

"Then I'll see her cored tonight," Raddock growled.

"You'll do no such thing," Selia said, finding her voice at last. "The law says she's to have a full day to make her peace, and today's nearly over."

Jeorje thumped his stick. "Selia is correct. Renna Tanner must be staked in Town Square tomorrow dawn, for all to see and bear witness until the Creator's justice is done."

"You expect people to watch?!" Hog was aghast.

"Folk can't learn their lessons if they skip school," Jeorje said.

"I'm not going to just stand there and watch the corelings tear someone apart!" Coline shouted. Others, even Coran Marsh, voiced protest as well.

"Oh, yes you are," Selia snapped. She looked around the room, her eyes hard stones. "If we're going to . . . to *murder* this girl, then we're *all* gonna watch and remember what we did; man, woman, and child," she growled. "Law's the law."

CHAPTER 22 ·

THE ROADS NOT TAKEN

:: 333 AR SPRING ::

IT WAS A FULL day's ride from Fort Angiers to the bridge over the Dividing River, which separated the lands of Duke Rhinebeck from those of Duke Euchor. The Warded Man had left too late in the day to make it before sunset.

It was just as well. His farewell with Leesha had left him in a dark mood, and he welcomed the chance to show a few corelings the sun. Jardir had taught him the Krasian technique of embracing pain and it worked well enough, but there were few balms so sweet as choking the life from a demon with one's bare hands.

The Hollow was in good hands with Leesha, at least until the Krasians advanced. She was brilliant and a natural leader, respected by all and governed by a pure heart and good common sense. If she was not yet a better Warder than he was, she soon would be.

And she's beautiful, he thought. *No denying that.* The Warded Man had traveled far and wide, and never seen her equal. Perhaps he could have loved her once, before Jardir had left him for dead in the sand. Before he had been forced to tattoo his flesh to survive.

Now he was something less than human, and love had no place in his life.

Night fell, but his warded eyes saw clearly in the dark. He touched Twilight Dancer's barding and the wards there glowed softly granting night vision to the giant stallion as well. He kicked into a gallop as the corelings rose, but there were thick trees to either side of the road, and wood demons kept pace with him, leaping from branch to branch or running just inside the tree line. Their barklike armor made them almost invisible, but the Warded Man could see the aura of their magic glowing softly, and did not mistake them. Above, wind demons shrieked, following his course and attempting to match speed for a dive.

The Warded Man let go the reins, steering the giant stallion with knees alone as he took up his great bow. A shriek from above provided ample warning, and he spun, putting a warded arrow through the head of a diving wind demon with an explosion of magic.

The flash of light seemed to bring the wood demons all at once. They exploded from the trees all around him, shrieking their hatred and leading with teeth and talons.

The Warded Man fired repeatedly, his warded arrows punching great, blackened holes in the corelings to either side. Twilight Dancer scattered those ahead, warded hooves sparking like festival crackers as they trampled through.

The demons gave chase, loping alongside the galloping horse. The Warded Man shoved his bow back in the harness and took up a spear, spinning it in a blur as he stabbed at corelings coming from every direction. One got in close, but he kicked it in the face, the impact ward on his heel throwing it back with a flash.

All along, Twilight Dancer continued to run.

Charged from the night's killing, they remained fresh and alert when the Riverbridges came into sight at dawn, though neither man nor steed had rested all night.

It had been fifteen years since Riverbridge was destroyed. It had been a Milnese village then, but Rhinebeck had wanted a share of the bridge tolls, and had attempted to rebuild the village on the south side of the Dividing River.

The Warded Man remembered the audience where Ragen had told Duke Euchor of Rhinebeck's plan. The duke had raged and seemed ready to burn Fort Angiers to the ground rather than let Rhinebeck toll his bridge.

And so arose two merchant towns, one on either side of the river and both calling themselves Riverbridge, with little love lost between them. There were garrisons for royal guardsmen, and mounted travelers were taxed on both sides of the river. Those who refused to pay could either hire a raft to ferry them and their goods—often for more than the tax—or swim.

The Riverbridges were the only walled villages in all of Thesa. On the

Milnese side, the walls were piled stone and mortar; on the Angierian side, great tarred logs, lashed tight. Both went right to the river's edge, and the guards who patrolled the walltops often called curses to their counterparts across the water.

The guards on the Angierian side had just opened the gate to greet the morning when the Warded Man rode through. His hands were gloved, and his hood pulled low to hide his face. It may have seemed odd to the guards, but he made no effort to explain himself, holding up Rhinebeck's seal without slowing his steady pace. Royal Messengers were given free passage on both sides of the river. The guards grumbled at his rudeness but did not hinder him.

There was fog in the morning air, and most of the Bridgefolk were still warming their porridge as the Warded Man passed through the towns, all but unnoticed. It was easier this way. His painted skin tended to lead half of them to shun him like a coreling, and the other half to fall to their knees and call him Deliverer. He honestly didn't know which was worse.

From Riverbridge, the road to Miln was a straight run north. The average time for a Messenger to make the ride was two weeks. His mentor Ragen's average was better: eleven days. Astride Twilight Dancer and fearing no darkness, the Warded Man made the trip in six, a trail of demon ashes in his wake. He passed Harden's Grove, the village a day south of Miln, at a full gallop in the dead of night, and it was still hours before dawn when Fort Miln came into sight.

As much his home as Tibbet's Brook in some ways, the Warded Man was overwhelmed by the emotion he felt at again seeing the mountain city he had sworn so many times never to return to. Too distracted to fight, he set up a portable circle and made camp while he waited for dawn, trying to remember what he could about Duke Euchor.

The Warded Man had only met Euchor once, as a boy, but he had worked in Euchor's Library, and knew the duke's heart. Euchor hoarded knowledge as another man might hoard food or gold. If he gave Euchor the battle wards, the duke would not share them openly with his people. He would attempt to increase his own power by keeping them secret.

The Warded Man could not allow that. He needed to distribute the wards quickly to every Warder in the city. There was a network of Warders in Miln, a network he had helped build. If he got the wards to Cob, his former master, they could be everywhere before Euchor had time to suppress the knowledge.

Thinking of Cob opened a floodgate of memories he had long suppressed. He had not spoken to his master or anyone else in Miln for eight years. He had written letters but never found the strength to send them. Were Ragen and Elissa well? Their daughter Marya would be eight now. What of Cob, and his friend Jaik? What of Mery?

Mery. It was she who had kept him from coming back those early years. He could have faced Jaik again, or Ragen and Cob. Elissa would have railed at him for leaving without so much as a goodbye, but he knew that she would have forgiven him when she was done. It was Mery he did not want to see. Mery, the only girl he had ever allowed himself to love.

Does she still think of me? he wondered. *Did she wait, thinking I might return?* He had asked himself those questions a thousand times over the years, but after she had rejected him once, he had never dared seek the answers.

And now . . . he looked down at the tattoos covering his skin. Now he could not face any of them, could not bear for them to see the freak he had become. He would trust Cob, because he had no other choice, but better for all if the rest thought him gone forever, or even dead. He thought of the letters in his pouch. They said enough. He would see them delivered, and let all know the sender had died a good death.

A great weariness overcame him, and he lay down. As sleep took him, he saw Mery's face in his mind's eye. Saw the night they had broken.

But his dreams changed that past. This time, he did not let her go. He gave up his aspiration to become a Messenger, staying on to run Cob's warding business, and instead of feeling confined, he felt freer than he did walking the naked night.

He saw Mery's beauty in her wedding dress, saw the graceful swell as her belly grew, saw her laughing, surrounded by happy, healthy children. He saw the smiling customers whose homes he made safe, and he saw the pride in Elissa's eyes. A mother's pride.

His limbs twitched in the dirt, trying vainly to call his mind back from the vision, but the dream had hold of him, and there was no escape.

He saw the night they had broken again, this time as it truly was, with him riding off without another word after their argument. But as he left, his mind's eye followed Mery instead, watching her over long years spent walking the walls of Miln, looking out for his return. All the joy and color was washed from her face, and at first the sadness only made her more beautiful. But as the seasons passed, that sad, beautiful face grew gaunt and hollow, with lines of sorrow about her mouth and dark circles beneath lifeless eyes. The best years of her life she spent waiting atop the wall, praying, weeping.

He saw the night they broke a third time, and with this last vision the dream turned into full nightmare. For in it he left, but there was no sorrow, no great pain. Mery had spit in the dirt at the city gate and turned away, finding another instantly and forgetting he had ever existed. Ragen and Elissa, so wrapped up in their infant daughter, had not even noticed he was gone. Cob's new journeyman was more grateful, wanting nothing more than to be like a son and take over his shop. The Warded Man started awake, but the image remained, and he was ashamed of his horror, for he knew it was selfish of him.

That last vision would be best for all, he thought.

After a dozen years of beating elements, the place where One Arm had breached the wardnet of Miln was still a different color from the rest of the wall, the Warded Man noted as he broke camp in the morning, packing away Twilight Dancer's warded barding.

The three dreams still haunted his thoughts. Which would he find inside? Should he try to find out, for his own peace, if none other?

Don't, the voice in his head advised. *You came to see Cob, so see him. You're not here for the others. Spare them the pain. Spare yourself.* The voice was with him always, urging caution. He thought of it as his father's voice, though he had not seen Jeph Bales in close to fifteen years.

He was used to ignoring it.

Just a look, he thought. *She won't even see me. Wouldn't recognize me even if she did. Just one look, to take back into the night.*

He rode as slowly as he could bear, but even so the day gate was only just opening as he arrived. City guards came out first, escorting groups of Warders and apprentices to clearly demarcated sections of ground, where they bent and began to collect pieces of warded glass, checking quickly to ensure they had been charged by a coreling's touch. The Warded Man himself had brought the glass wards to Miln, but even he was shocked at this efficiency of production, as good as they had in the Hollow, if less practical. The Milnese Warders seemed to make mostly objects of luxury: walking sticks, statues, windows, and jewelry. When the blood of the bait was washed from them, all would be as clear as polished diamond, and infinitely harder.

The guards looked up as he approached. In the cool damp of morning, it did not seem so strange that he should have his hood up, but seeing the weapons in Twilight Dancer's harnesses, they raised their spears until the Warded Man showed them the pouch with Rhinebeck's seal.

"You're out early, Messenger," one guard said as they relaxed.

"Raced and tried to make it without stopping at Harden's Grove," the Warded Man said, the lie coming easily. "Thought I had it, but then I heard the last bell from afar, and knew I'd never make the gate before sunset. Set up my circles just a mile back and spent the night."

"Ripped luck," the guard said. "Cold night to be stuck outside, a mile from warm walls and sweet succor."

The Warded Man, who had not felt heat nor cold in years, nodded and forced himself to shiver, pulling his hood lower as if to ward off a lingering chill. "I could use a warm room and a hot coffee. I'd even settle for it the other way around."

The guard nodded and seemed about to wave him on when he looked up suddenly. The Warded Man tensed, wondering if he would ask him to lower his hood.

"Things in the South as bad as they say?" the guard asked instead. "Rizon lost, Beggar refugees everywhere, and this new Deliverer doing nothing for it?"

Even this far north, rumors had flown. "That's news for the duke, before I can share it with anyone else," the Warded Man said, "but ay, it's bad in the South."

The guard grunted and waved for him to head on into the city.

The Warded Man found an inn and led Twilight Dancer to the stable. There was a boy already there, mucking the stalls. He couldn't have been more than twelve years old, and he was filthy.

Servant class, the Warded Man thought, which explained why he was working so early. The boy likely slept in the stables, and counted himself lucky at that. He reached into his purse and took out a heavy gold coin, putting it in the boy's hand.

The boy's eyes bulged as he looked at the coin. It was likely more money than he had ever held in his hand, enough to purchase new clothes, food, and succor for a month.

"See my horse is well cared for, and there'll be another when I claim him," the Warded Man said. It was extravagant and might draw attention, but money meant nothing to him anymore, and he knew how easily the Servants of Miln could become Beggars. He left the boy and headed into the inn.

"I need a room for the next few nights," he told the innkeeper, pretending as if his saddlebags and gear were a troublesome weight when they felt like feathers.

"Five moons a night," the innkeeper said. He was young, seeming too young to run a business, and he bowed conspicuously, trying to peek under the Warded Man's hood.

"Flame demon spat in my face," the Warded Man said, the real irritation in his voice driving the man back. "It ent a pretty sight."

"Of course, Messenger," the innkeeper said, bowing again. "I apologize. Wern't right of me to stare."

"It's fine," the Warded Man grunted, carrying his gear up the steps and locking it in his room before heading out into the city.

The streets of Miln were bright and familiar, the stench of dung fires and coal from the ironworks almost welcoming. It was just as he remembered, and yet alien.

He was different.

The way to Cob's shop was second nature even now, but the Warded Man was shocked by what he found. Large extensions had been built to either side. The small house behind the shop that he and Cob had lived in had been torn down and replaced with a warehouse many times its size. Cob had been prosperous when Arlen left, but it was nothing compared with this. Steeling himself, he went to the main entrance.

Chimes rang as the door opened, and the sound, like a part of his soul that had been missing, sent a shudder through him. The shop was larger now, but still filled with familiar sights and scents. There was the workbench he had hunched over for countless hours. The small handcart he had pulled all over the city. He walked over to a windowsill and reverently ran his gloved fingers over wards he had etched in the stone. He felt he could almost pick up a warding tool and return to work as if the last eight years had never happened.

"Can I help you?" asked a voice, and the Warded Man froze, his blood turning to ice. He had been lost in another time and hadn't heard anyone approach, but without turning, he knew who it was. Knew, and was terrified. What was she doing here? What did it mean? Slowly, he turned to face her, keeping his face shadowed by his hood.

The years had been kind to Mother Elissa. With forty-six winters behind her, her long hair was still dark and rich, and her cheeks smooth, with only the faintest lines about her eyes and mouth. Smile lines, he'd heard them called, and it gave some relief.

Let her have spent the last eight years smiling, he thought.

Elissa opened her mouth to speak, but a young girl with long brown hair and large brown eyes came running over to them, stealing her attention. The girl wore a dress of maroon velvet, with a matching ribbon in her hair. The ribbon was askew, thick locks of hair falling in front of her face, and her cheeks and hands were white with chalk that streaked her dress as well. The Warded Man knew in an instant that she was Marya, Ragen and Elissa's daughter, whom he had held mere moments after her birth. She was innocent and beautiful, and he ached, seeing in her all the joy of the years he had missed.

"Mother, see what I drew!" the girl cried. She held out a slate, upon which a warding circle had been drawn. The Warded Man scanned the wards in a blink and knew they were strong. More, he saw that many of them were his, brought with him from Tibbet's Brook. He took comfort knowing that in some small way he had touched her life.

"These are beautiful, sweet one," Elissa congratulated, bending to secure her daughter's hair in the ribbon once more. She kissed Marya's forehead when she was done. "Soon your father will be taking you on his Warding calls." The girl gave a little squeal of delight.

"We have a customer to attend, sweet," Elissa said, turning back to the Warded Man, her arm around the girl. "I am Mother Elissa." The pride in that title was still evident in her voice after all these years. "And this is my daughter—"

"Are you a Tender?" the girl asked him, cutting her mother off.

"No," the Warded Man said, using the deep rasp of a voice he had adopted since warding his flesh. The last thing he needed was for Elissa to recognize his voice.

"Then why do you dress like one?" the girl demanded.

"I am demon-scarred," he told her, "and I don't want to frighten you."

"I'm not scared," the girl said, trying to peek under his hood. He took a step back, pulling the hood lower.

"You're being rude!" Elissa scolded her. "Run along and play with your brother."

The girl took on a rebellious look, but Elissa stared her down and she darted back across the room to a worktable where a boy of perhaps five winters was stacking blocks with wards painted on their sides. The Warded Man saw Ragen in his young face, and felt a profound gladness for his mentor, mixed with a terrible regret that he would never know the boy, or the man he would become.

Elissa looked abashed. "I am sorry for that. My husband, too, has scars he does not care for the world to see. You're a Messenger, then?"

The Warded Man nodded.

"What can I help you with, today?" she asked. "A new shield? Or perhaps repairing a portable circle?"

"Looking for a Warder named Cob," he said. "I was told he owned this shop."

Elissa looked sad as she shook her head. "Cob has been dead almost four years," she said, her words hitting harder than a demon's blow. "Taken by a cancer. He left the shop to my husband and me. Who told you to seek him here?"

"A . . . Messenger I knew," the Warded Man said, reeling.

"What Messenger?" Elissa pressed. "What was his name?"

The Warded Man hesitated, his mind racing. No name came to him, and he knew the longer he waited, the greater the risk he would be discovered. "Arlen of Tibbet's Brook," he blurted, cursing himself as he did.

Elissa's eyes lit up. "Tell me of Arlen," she begged, placing a hand on his arm. "We were very close, once. Where did you last see him? Is he well? Can you get a message to him? My husband and I would pay any price."

Seeing the sudden desperation in her eyes, the Warded Man realized how deeply he had hurt her when he left. And now, stupidly, he had given her false hope that she might somehow see Arlen again. But the boy she knew was dead, body and soul. Even if he took off his hood and told her the truth, she would not have him returned. Better to give her the closure she needed.

"Arlen spoke of you that night," he said, his decision made. "You're every bit as beautiful as he said."

Elissa smiled at the compliment, her eyes moist, but then she stopped, as what he had said fully registered. "What night?"

"The night I was scarred," he said. "Crossing the Krasian Desert. Arlen died, so that I might live." It was true enough, after a fashion.

Elissa gasped, covering her nose and mouth with her hands. Her eyes, moist a moment before with joy, now brimmed with water as her face screwed up in pain.

"His last thoughts were of you," he said, "of his friends in Miln, his . . . family. He wanted me to come here and tell you that."

Elissa barely heard him. "Oh, Arlen!" she cried, and stumbled. The Warded Man darted forward to catch her, guiding her to one of the workbenches and easing her down as she sobbed.

"Mother!" Marya cried, rushing over. "Mother, what's wrong? Why are you crying?" She looked at the Warded Man, accusation in her eyes.

He knelt before the girl, not sure if it was simply to appear less threatening to the child, or to allow her to strike him if she wished. He almost hoped she would. "I'm afraid I brought her some ill tidings, Marya," he said gently. "Sometimes it's a Messenger's duty to tell people of things they might not be happy to hear."

As if on cue, Elissa looked up at him, her sobbing cut short. She pulled herself together with a deep breath, drying her tears with a lace cuff and embracing her daughter. "He's right, sweetest. I'll be all right. Take your brother into the back a spell, if you please."

Marya shot the Warded Man one last dark glance, then nodded, gathering up her little brother and leaving the room. He watched them go, feeling wretched. He should never have come, should have sent an intermediary or found some other Warder to go to, though there were none he trusted like Cob.

"I'm sorry," the Warded Man said. "I never wished to bring you pain."

"I know," Elissa said. "I'm glad you told me. It makes things easier in some ways, if you understand."

"Easier," the Warded Man agreed. He fumbled in his pouch, pulling forth a handful of letters, and a grimoire of battle wards, wrapped in oilcloth and tied with stout cord. "These are for you. Arlen meant for you to have them."

Elissa took the bundle and nodded. "Thank you. Do you plan to stay in Miln long? My husband is out, but he will surely have questions for you. Arlen was like a son to him."

"I am only in town for the day, my lady," he said, wanting no part of a conversation with Ragen. The man would press for details where there were none. "I have a message for the duke, and a few others to pay respects to, and then I am off."

He knew he should leave it lie there, but the damage was done, and his next words came unbidden. "Tell me . . . does Mery still live at the house of Tender Ronnell?"

Elissa shook her head. "Not for many years. She—"

"No matter," the Warded Man cut her off, not wanting to hear more. Mery had found someone else. It was no great surprise, and he had no right to feel stung by the news.

"What about the boy, Jaik?" he asked. "I've a letter for him, as well."

"No more a boy," Elissa said, looking at him with piercing eyes. "He's a man now. He lives on Mill Way, in the third workers' cottage."

The Warded Man nodded. "Then, with your permission, I'll take my leave."

"You may not like what you find there," Elissa warned.

The Warded Man looked up at her, trying to read her meaning, but it was lost in her wet puffy eyes. She looked tired and guileless. He turned to go.

"How did you know my daughter's name?" Elissa asked.

The question surprised him. He hesitated. "You introduced her when she came over." The moment he said it, he cursed silently, for of course, Elissa had been cut off before she could introduce the girl, and he could have claimed the knowledge came from Arlen in any case.

"I suppose I did," Elissa agreed, surprising him. He took it as a stroke of luck and made for the door. His fingers were closing on the latch when she spoke again.

"I've missed you," she said quietly.

He paused, fighting the urge to turn and run back, crushing her in his arms and begging her forgiveness.

He left the warding shop without another word.

The Warded Man cursed himself as he strode down the street. She had recognized him. He didn't know how, but she had, and in walking out he had likely hurt her more deeply than news of his death ever could have. Elissa had been as a mother to him, and his leaving must have seemed the ultimate rejection of her love. But what could he have done? Shown her what he had done to himself? Shown her the monster her adopted son had become?

No. Better she think he had turned his back on her. Better any lie than that truth.

Even though she deserves to know? the nagging voice in his head asked.

The question pained him, so he put it from his mind, focusing on the real reason he had come to Miln. Rhinebeck's message. He presented himself at Duke Euchor's keep, but the gate guards were not welcoming.

"His Grace ent got time to see every ragamuffin Tender in town," one of them growled as they saw him approach in his hood and robes.

"He'll see me," the Warded Man said, holding up the Messenger pouch bearing Rhinebeck's seal. The guards' eyes widened, but then they turned back to him suspiciously.

"You ent any Royal Messenger I met before," the first guard said, "and I met 'em all."

"What kind of Messenger goes around in Tender's robes, anyway?" the other asked.

The Warded Man, his mind still reeling from the encounter with Elissa, had no patience for the petty posturing of minor functionaries. "The kind who will crack your skull if you don't open that gate and announce me," he said, pulling off his hood.

The guards both took a step back as they saw his tattooed face. He gestured to the gate, and they stumbled over each other in their haste to open it. One scrambled ahead to the palace.

The Warded Man pulled his hood back up, hiding a smile. There were some benefits to being a freak, at least.

He walked toward the palace at a steady pace, drawing eyes from all in the courtyard as their whispers reached his sharp ears. Before long the duke's chamberlain, Mother Jone, appeared to greet him, led by the gate guard. Gaunt the last time the Warded Man had seen her more than a decade ago, Jone had become almost desiccated in the years since, her skin translucent and pale, thinly stretched over blue veins and liver spots. But her back was still straight, and her stride quick. Ragen had likened the chamberlain to her own breed of coreling, and none of his encounters with her had given him cause to doubt that assessment. Several steps behind her, a pair of guards followed discreetly.

"That's him, Mother," one guard said.

Jone nodded and dismissed the guard with a wave. He moved back to the gatehouse, but the Warded Man could see many from the courtyard drifting in his wake, eager for gossip.

"You are the one they call the Warded Man, are you not?" Jone asked.

The Warded Man nodded. "I come with urgent tidings from Duke Rhinebeck, and an offer of my own."

Jone raised an eyebrow at that. "There are many who believe you are the Deliverer come again. How come you to be in the service of Duke Rhinebeck?"

"I serve no man," the Warded Man said. "I carry Rhinebeck's message because his interests and mine intersect. The Krasian attack on Rizon affects us all."

Jone nodded. "His Grace agrees, and so he will grant you audience . . ."

The Warded Man nodded and began to move toward the palace, but Jone held up a finger. " . . . tomorrow," she finished.

The Warded Man scowled. It was customary for dukes to make Messengers wait for short periods of time as a show of strength, but a Royal Messenger with grave tidings delayed a full day when the sun had yet to reach its zenith? Unheard of.

"Perhaps you mistake the importance of my news," the Warded Man said carefully.

"And perhaps you mistake your own," Jone replied. "You have quite a reputation south of the Dividing, but you're in the lands of Duke Euchor, Light of the Mountains and Guardian of the Northland, now. He will see you when his schedule allows, and that is tomorrow."

Posturing. Euchor wanted to show his power by turning the Warded Man away.

He could insist, of course. Claim insult and threaten to return to Angiers, or even force his way past the guards. None of them could hinder him if he did not wish it.

But he needed Euchor's goodwill. Ragen would find the grimoire of battle wards he had given Elissa and know what must be done with them, but only Euchor could provide the needed men and supplies to Angiers before it was too late. It was worth a day's wait.

"Very well. I'll be waiting at the gates at dawn tomorrow." He turned to go.

"We have curfew in Miln," Jone said. "No one is allowed on the streets before dawn."

The Warded Man turned back to face her, lifting his head to give her a view into his hood. His teeth showed bright against his tattooed lips as he smiled.

"Have the gate guards arrest me then," he suggested.

They could both posture and flex their power.

Jone's mouth was a hard line. If the sight of his tattooed flesh unnerved her, she did not show it. "Dawn," she agreed, and turned swiftly, striding back to the palace.

Several guards followed him as he left the duke's keep. They were discreet and kept distance, but there was no doubt they meant to track him back to where he was staying and make note of anyone he spoke to.

But the Warded Man had lived in Miln for years and knew the city well. He turned a corner into a dead-end alley and, once out of sight, leapt ten feet straight up to catch the sill of a second-floor window. From his perch there, it was an easy leap to the third-floor sill across the way, and from there to the opposite roof. He looked down over the roof's edge, watching the guards as they waited patiently for him to realize the dead end and emerge. Soon they would tire of waiting and one would go into the alley to investigate, but he would be long gone by then.

As he approached the third house on Mill Way, the Warded Man thought back to Elissa's last, cryptic message about Jaik. Was he well? Had something happened to him?

Jaik and Mery had been his only friends while growing up. Jaik had dreamed of being a Jongleur, and the boys had made a pact to travel together when Arlen got his Messenger license, as Messengers and Jongleurs frequently did.

But while Arlen had pursued his goals with a single-minded tenacity, Jaik had never been willing to put in the long hard hours to master a Jongleur's art. When the time came for Arlen to leave, Jaik could no more juggle than flap his arms and fly.

He seemed to have done well for himself, even so. Though it was no great manse like that of Ragen and Elissa, Jaik's cottage was sturdy and well kept, spacious by crowded Miln's standards. Jaik was likely at the mill at this time of day, which was best. He would have family at home who could receive a packet of letters, people unlikely to recognize Arlen Bales, much less the Warded Man.

Nothing could have prepared him, though, for Mery answering the door.

She gasped at the sight of him, all hooded and covered, and took a step back. Just as frightened and surprised, he did much the same.

"Yes?" Mery asked, recovering. "May I help you?" She kept her hand on the door, ready to slam it shut in an instant.

She was older than he remembered, but that did nothing to diminish her. On the contrary, the Mery he remembered was a spring bud compared with the flower before him. The thin limbs of her youth had filled out into lush curves, and her rich brown hair fell in waves over a round face and the same soft lips he had kissed a thousand times. He could feel his hands shake at the sight of her, but however unprepared he had been for her beauty, the knowledge that came with her opening this door was far more shocking.

She had married Jaik. Jaik, who taught him Tackleball and stole sweets from the baker's back window for them to share. Jaik who had followed him around with a kind of awe when Arlen told him he was going to become a Messenger. Jaik, who had always been invisible to Mery, her eyes for Arlen alone.

"Excuse me," he said, too off balance to even disguise his voice. "I must have the wrong . . ." He turned and started away, long strides taking him back down Mill Way.

He heard her gasp behind him, and moved faster.

"Arlen?" she called, and he started to run.

But even as he took off, he heard her following. "Arlen, stop! Please!" she cried, but he paid no heed, seeking only to escape, his strong legs easily outpacing her.

There was a broken cart in the road, tipped over with two men arguing amid the mess. He lost precious seconds dodging around, and Mery shortened the gap between them. He darted between a pair of cottages, hoping to cut through, but the egress he remembered was gone, the alley ending now in a stone wall too high to jump.

He closed his eyes, willing himself to dematerialize as he had in Leesha's cottage, but the sun was upon him and the magic would not come. He doubled back, but it was too late. He ran face-first into Mery as she turned into the alley, and the both of them went sprawling to the ground. The Warded Man kept his wits as he fell, managing to hold his hood in place as he struck the cobbled street. He tensed, ready to spring back to his feet, but Mery threw herself upon him, wrapping him tightly in her arms.

"Arlen," she wept, "I let you go once. I swore to the Creator I would never do it again." She clutched him tighter, crying into his robes, and he held her in his arms, rocking her back and forth, sitting on the ground in the alley's mouth. Though he had faced demons great and small, that embrace terrified him in ways he could not explain.

After a time, Mery regained herself, sniffing and wiping her nose and eyes with a sleeve. "I must look a mess," she croaked.

"You're beautiful," he said, the words less a compliment than a simple truth.

She laughed self-consciously, dropping her eyes and sniffing again. "I tried to wait," she murmured.

"It's all right," he said.

But Mery shook her head. "If I thought you were coming back, I would have waited forever." She looked up at him, peering into the shadows of his hood. "I would never have . . ."

"Married Jaik?" he asked, perhaps less kindly than he had meant.

She looked away again, even as they both rose awkwardly to their feet. "You were gone," she said, "and he was here. He's been good to me all these years, Arlen, but . . ." She looked up at him, hesitating. "If you ask me . . ."

His gut wrenched. If he asked her what? Would she leave with him? Or stay in Miln but leave Jaik to be with him? The visions from his dream flashed before his mind's eye.

"Mery, don't," he begged. "Don't say it." There was no going back for him now.

She turned away as if he had slapped her. "You didn't come back for me, did you?" she asked, breathing deeply as if to hold back tears. "This was just a stop to see your old friend Jaik, to offer a slap on the back and a tale before taking to the road again."

"It's not like that, Mery," he said, coming up behind her and taking her shoulders in his hands. The sensation was strange; familiar, yet alien. He could not remember the last time he had touched someone like that. "I hoped you had found someone while I was gone. I heard that you had, and didn't want to spoil it." He paused. "I just didn't expect it to be Jaik."

Mery turned and embraced him again, not meeting his eyes. "He's been good to me. Father spoke to the baron who owns the mill, and they made him a supervisor. I went to the Mothers' School to do the slates so we could afford the house."

"Jaik's a good man," the Warded Man agreed.

She looked up at him. "Arlen, why are you still hiding your face?"

This time it was he who turned away. For a moment, he'd dared to forget. "I gave it to the night. It's not something you want to see."

"Nonsense," Mery said, reaching for his hood. "You're alive, after all this time. Do you think I care if you've been scarred?"

He drew back sharply, blocking her hand. "It's more complicated than that."

"Arlen," she said, putting hands to hips in the same manner she had long ago, when the time for nonsense was past, "it's been eight years since you left Miln without a word to me. The least you can do is have the courage to show your face."

"As I recall, it was you who did the leaving," he said.

"Don't you think I know that?" Mery shouted at him. "I've spent all these years blaming myself, not knowing if you were dead on the road or in the arms of another woman, all because I was selfish and upset one night! How long must I be punished for reacting badly when you told me you wanted to risk your life just to get away from the prison of living here with me?"

He looked at her, knowing she was right. He had never lied to her or anyone, but he had deceived nonetheless, letting her believe his dreams of becoming a Messenger had faded.

Slowly, he lifted his hands, and drew back his hood.

Mery's eyes widened, and she covered her mouth to stifle her gasp as the tattoos were revealed. There were dozens on his face alone, running along his jaw and lips, over his nose and around his eyes, even on his ears.

She recoiled instinctively. "Your face, your beautiful face. Arlen, what have you done?"

He had imagined this reaction countless times, seen it before from people all across Thesa, but despite all, he was not prepared for how it cut him. The look in her eyes passed judgment on everything he was, making him feel small and helpless in a way he had not in years.

The feeling angered him, and Arlen of Miln, who had been gaining strength for the first time in years, fled back into darkness. The Warded Man took control, and his eyes grew hard.

"I did what I had to, to survive," he said, his voice deepening into a rasp.

"No you didn't," Mery said, shaking her head. "You could have survived here in Miln, safe in succor. You could have lived in any of the Free Cities, for that matter. You didn't . . . mutilate yourself to survive. Truer is you did it because you hate yourself so much you think you deserve no better than to be out in the naked night. You did it because you're terrified of opening your heart and loving anything the corelings might take from you."

"I'm not scared of anything the corelings can do," he said. "I walk free in the night and fear no demon, great or small. They run from *me*, Mery! Me!" He struck his chest for emphasis.

"Of course they do," Mery whispered, tears running down her smooth, round cheeks. "You've become a monster, yourself."

"Monster?!" the Warded Man shouted, making her flinch back in fright. "I've done what no man has done in centuries! What I've always dreamed! I've brought back powers lost to mankind since the First Demon War!"

Mery spat on the ground, unimpressed. The sight was unnerving; he had seen it the night before, in his third vision.

"At what cost?" she demanded. "Jaik's given me two sons, Arlen. Will you ask them to march and die in another demon war? They could have been yours, your gift to the world, but instead all you've given it is a way to destroy itself."

The Warded Man opened his mouth to let fly an angry retort, but none came. Had anyone else said such things to him, he would have lashed out, but Mery stabbed through his defenses with ease. What *had* he given the world? Would thousands of young men march with his weapons, only to be slaughtered in the night?

"It's honest word you've done what you always dreamed, Arlen," Mery said. "You've made sure no one will ever get close to you again." She shook her head, and her face twisted. A sob broke from her soft lips, and she covered her mouth, turning and running from him.

The Warded Man stood a long time, staring at the cobbles as people walked by. They saw his tattooed face and the sight sparked animated conversation, but he hardly noticed. For the second time, Mery had left him in tears, and he wished the ground would swallow him.

He wandered the streets aimlessly, trying to come to grips with what Mery had said, but there was nothing for it. Was she right? Since the night his

mother was cored, had he truly opened his heart to anyone? He knew the answer, and it lent weight to her accusations. People gave him a wide berth as
he walked, his painted flesh as much a barrier to them as to corelings. Only
Leesha had tried to break through, and he had pushed even her away.

After a time, he glanced up and realized he'd wandered instinctively back
to Cob's shop. The familiar place called to him, and he had no strength to resist. He felt empty inside. Void. Let Elissa rail and beat at him with her fists.
She could do no worse than had already been done.

Elissa was sweeping the floor of the shop when he entered. She was
alone. She looked up as the chimes rang, and their eyes met. For a long time,
neither of them said a word.

"Why didn't you tell me they were married?" he asked finally. It was
petulant and lame, but he could think of nothing else to say.

"You didn't see fit to tell me everything, either," she returned. There was
no anger in her voice, no accusation. She spoke matter-of-factly, as if discussing what she'd eaten for breakfast.

He nodded. "I didn't want you to see me like this."

"Like what?" Elissa asked gently, laying aside her broom and gliding
over to him. She put a hand on his arm. "Scarred? I've seen them before."

He turned from her, and she let her hand fall away. "My scars are self-
inflicted."

"We all have those," she said.

"Mery took one look at me and fled as if I were a coreling," he said.

"I'm so sorry," Elissa said, coming behind and wrapping her arms
around him.

The Warded Man wanted to pull away, but that part of him melted away
in her embrace. He turned and held her in return, inhaling the familiar scent
of her and closing his eyes, opening himself up to the pain and letting it flow
out of him.

After too short a time, Elissa pulled back. "I want to see what you showed
her."

He shook his head. "I . . ."

"Hush," Elissa said softly, reaching into his hood to put a finger on his
lips. He tensed as her hands came up, slowly, and gathered the hood, easing
it down. Fear ran through him, chilling his blood, but he stood like a statue,
resigned to it.

Like Mery, Elissa's eyes widened and she gasped, but she did not recoil.
She simply looked at him, taking it in.

"I never used to appreciate wards," she said after a time. "Before, they
were just another tool, like a hammer, or fire." She reached out, touching his

face. Her soft fingers traced the wards on his eyebrows, his jaw, his skull. "It's only now, working in this shop, that I see how very beautiful they can be. Anything that protects our loved ones is beautiful."

He choked, lurching clumsily as he started to sob, but Elissa caught him in a firm embrace, supporting him.

"Come home, Arlen," she said. "Even if only for a night."

CHAPTER 23

EUCHOR'S COURT

:: 333 AR SPRING ::

THE WARDED MAN LEFT the warding shop and walked some distance before again taking to the rooftops, ensuring he was not followed as he returned to Ragen and Elissa's manse.

It was smaller than he remembered. When he had first come to Fort Miln at eleven years old, Ragen and Elissa's home had seemed like a village unto itself with its great wall surrounding the gardens, Servants' cottages, and house proper. Now even the courtyard, a seemingly endless space when he was young and learning to ride and fight, seemed claustrophobic. So used to walking free in the night, any walls felt stifling to him now.

The Servants at the gate let him in without a word. Elissa had sent a runner back to the manse, and had another go to fetch Twilight Dancer and his bags from the inn. He passed through the courtyard and entered the manse, ascending the marble steps to his old room.

It was exactly as he'd left it. Arlen had acquired many things in his time in Miln—books, clothes, tools, bits of warding—too much to take Messaging, when a man was limited to what his horse could carry. He had left most of it behind, never looking back, and the room seemed untouched by time. There were fresh linens on the bed and not a speck of dust to be found, but nothing had been moved. There was even still clutter on his desk. He sat there a long time, basking in the safe familiarity of it and feeling seventeen again.

There was a sharp rap on the door, snapping him from the reverie. He opened it to find Mother Margrit, her meaty arms crossed in front of her as she glared at him. Margrit had cared for him since he first came to Miln, treating his wounds and helping him understand the ways of the city. The Warded Man was amazed to find she could still intimidate him after so long.

"Let's see, then," Margrit said.

He didn't need to ask what she meant. He steeled himself and pulled down his hood.

Margrit looked at him for some time, showing none of the horror or surprise he expected. She grunted and nodded to herself.

Then she slapped him full in the face.

"That's for breaking my lady's heart!" she cried. It was a surprisingly powerful blow, and he hadn't fully recovered before she slapped him again.

"And that's for breaking mine!" she sobbed, and clutched at him, pulling him close and crushing the air from him as she cried. "Thank the Creator you're all right," she choked.

Ragen returned soon after, and clapped the Warded Man on the shoulder, meeting his eyes and making no comment about his tattoos at all. "Good to have you back," he said.

In truth, the Warded Man was more shocked by Ragen, who wore the keyward symbol of the Warders' Guild as a heavy gold pin on his breast.

"You're the Warders' Guildmaster now?" he asked.

Ragen nodded. "Cob and I became partners after you left, and the ward brokering you started made us the dominant company in Miln. Cob served three years as guildmaster before the cancer took his strength. As his heir, I was the natural choice to succeed him."

"A decision no one in Miln regrets," Elissa put in, pride and love in her voice as she looked at her husband.

Ragen shrugged. "I've thrown in where I could. Of course," he looked at the Warded Man, "it should have been you. It still can. Cob's will made it clear his controlling share of the business was to be turned over to you, if you ever returned."

"The shop?" the Warded Man asked, shocked that his old master would have included him in his last wishes at all after all this time.

"The shop, the ward exchange, the warehouses and glasseries," Ragen said, "everything down to the apprentice contracts."

"Enough to make you one of the richest and most powerful men in Miln," Elissa said.

An image flashed in the Warded Man's mind, him walking the halls of the

Duke Euchor's keep, advising His Grace on policy and commanding dozens if not hundreds of Warders. Brokering power . . . building alliances . . .

Reading reports.

Delegating responsibility.

Surrounded by Servants to care for his every need.

Stifling in the city's walls.

He shook his head. "I don't want it. Any of it. Arlen Bales is dead."

"Arlen!" Elissa cried. "How can you say that, standing right here?"

"I can't just pick up my life where I left off, Elissa," he said, pulling off his hood and the gloves as well. "I've chosen my path. I can never live inside walls again. Even now, the air seems thicker, harder to breathe . . ."

Ragen put a hand on his shoulder. "I've Messaged, too," he reminded him. "I know what the open air tastes like, and how you thirst for it behind city walls. But the thirst dies out in time."

The Warded Man looked at him, and his eyes darkened. "Why would I want it to?" he snapped. "Why would you? Why lock yourself back in prison when you had the keys?"

"Because of Marya," Ragen said. "And because of Arlen."

"Arlen?" the Warded Man asked, confused.

"Not you," Ragen growled, his own temper rising. "My five-year-old son. Arlen. Who needs a father more than his father needs fresh air!"

It was a blow as hard as Margrit's slap, and the Warded Man knew he deserved it. For a moment, he had spoken to Ragen as if he were his true father. As if he were Jeph Bales of Tibbet's Brook, the coward who had stood by while his own wife was cored.

But Ragen was no coward. He had proven that a thousand times over. The Warded Man himself had seen him face demons with nothing but his spear and shield. Ragen didn't give up the night out of fear. He did it to conquer fear.

"I'm sorry," he said. "You're right. I had no right to . . ."

Ragen exhaled. "It's all right, boy."

The Warded Man walked to the rows of portraits on the walls of Ragen and Elissa's receiving room. They had one commissioned every year, to mark its passing. The first was only Ragen and Elissa, looking very young. The next was some years later, and the Warded Man looked at his own face staring back at him without wards, something he hadn't seen in years. Arlen Bales, a boy of twelve, sitting on a chair in front of where Ragen and Elissa stood.

He grew progressively older in the portraits until one year, he stood between Ragen and Elissa, holding infant Marya.

The next year's portrait, he was gone, but soon after, a new Arlen appeared. He touched the canvas gently. "I wish I'd been there to see him born. I wish I could be there for him now."

"You can," Elissa said firmly. "We're family, Arlen. You don't have to live life like a Beggar. You'll always have a home here."

The Warded Man nodded. "I see that now. See it in a way I never did before, and for that, I'm sorry. You deserve better than I gave, better than I can give. I'm leaving Miln once I've had my audience with the duke."

"What?!" Elissa cried. "You've only just arrived!"

The Warded Man shook his head. "I've chosen my path, and I've got to walk to its end."

"Where will you go then?" Elissa asked.

"Tibbet's Brook, to start," he said, "long enough to return battle warding to them. And then, if you can broker the wards throughout Miln and its hamlets, I'll do the same for the Angierians and Laktonians."

"You expect every tiny hamlet to rise up and fight?" Elissa asked.

The Warded Man shook his head. "I'm not asking anyone to fight. But if my da had owned a bow with warded arrows, my mam might be alive. I owe everyone the chance she didn't have. Once the wards are everywhere, spread so far and wide that they can never be lost again, people can make their own decision about what to do with them."

"And then?" Elissa pressed, her tone still hopeful that one day he might return for good.

"Then I fight," the Warded Man said. "Any that stand beside me will be welcome, and we'll kill demons until we fall, or until Marya and Arlen can watch the sun set without fear."

It was late, and the Servants had long since retired. Ragen, Elissa, and the Warded Man sat in the study, the air thick with the men's sweet pipe smoke as they shared brandy.

"I've been summoned to the duke's audience with 'the Warded Man' tomorrow," Ragen said, "though I must say I never in a century would have thought they were talking about you."

He smirked. "I'm to have Warders disguised as Servants try to copy your tattoos while you're distracted talking to His Grace."

The Warded Man nodded. "I'll keep my hood up."

"Why?" Ragen asked. "If you mean for everyone to have them, why keep them secret?"

"Because Euchor will covet them," the Warded Man said. "And I can use that to gain advantage. I want him distracted, thinking he is buying them from me, while you distribute them quietly to every Warder in the duchy. Spread them so far that Euchor can never suppress them."

Ragen grunted. "Clever," he admitted, "though Euchor will be livid when he learns you've double-dealed."

The Warded Man shrugged. "I'll be long gone, and it's no less than he deserves for locking up all the knowledge of the old world in his library for only a handful to see."

Ragen nodded. "Best for me to act as if I don't know you in the audience, then. If your identity gets out, I'll act as shocked as the rest."

"I think that's wise," the Warded Man agreed. "Who else will be there, do you think?"

"As few people as possible," Ragen said. "Euchor's actually pleased you're coming at dawn, so he can have you in and out before the Tenders and Royals even catch wind of the meeting. Apart from the duke and Jone, there will be myself, Messengers' Guildmaster Malcum, Euchor's daughters, and my Warders, dressed as Servants."

"Tell me of Euchor's daughters," the Warded Man said.

"Hypatia, Aelia, and Lorain," Ragen said, "all as thick-skulled as their father, and none of them prettier. Mothers all, with born sons. If Euchor doesn't produce a son of his own, the Mothers' Council will choose the next duke from among that group of unholy brats."

"So if Euchor dies, a boy becomes duke?" the Warded Man asked.

"Technically," Ragen said, "though truer is the boy's mother becomes duchess in everything but name and rules in his stead until he reaches manhood . . . and perhaps longer. Don't underestimate any of them."

"I won't," the Warded Man said.

"You should know, too, that the duke has a new herald," Ragen said.

The Warded Man shrugged. "What does that matter? I never knew the old one."

"It matters," Ragen said, "because the new one is Keerin."

The Warded Man looked up sharply. Keerin was Ragen's Jongleur partner when they found young Arlen on the road, unconscious and dying of demon fever after crippling One Arm. The Jongleur had been a coward, curling under his bedroll and whimpering as demons tested the wards, but years later the Warded Man had caught him giving a performance where he claimed to have crippled the demon himself, a demon that nightly tried to break into the city to revenge itself upon Arlen, and one time even succeeded in breaching the wall. Arlen had called Keerin a liar publicly, and he and Jaik were badly beaten by Keerin's apprentices as a result.

"How can a man who refuses to travel herald the duke?" the Warded Man asked.

"Euchor holds tight to power by hoarding people as well as knowledge," Ragen said. "Keerin's stupid little song about One Arm made him sought after by Royals, and that got Euchor's attention. Keerin had a ducal commission soon after, and now performs solely at the duke's pleasure."

"So he doesn't truly herald," the Warded Man said.

"Oh, he does," Ragen said. "Most of the hamlets can be reached without ever leaving proper succor, and Euchor even built some way stations on the way to others to accommodate the stoneless little weasel."

The gates to the Duke's Keep opened at dawn, and the person who strode out to greet the Warded Man was none other than Keerin.

Keerin was much as the Warded Man remembered, tall even for a Milnese, with carrot-colored hair and bright green eyes. He had fattened a bit, no doubt due to the benefits of his new patron. His thin wisp of a mustache still refused to join with the curl of hair at his chin, though powder crinkled in the lines of his face, attempting to preserve a fading youth.

But where he had last seen Keerin in a Jongleur's patchwork motley, he was now a royal herald, and dressed accordingly. His tabard was patched in Euchor's gray, white, and green, cutting a much more somber figure, though his pantaloons were still loose, should he be called upon to tumble, and the inside of his black cloak was sewn with patchwork colored silk that could be revealed with a twirl.

"An honor to meet you, sir!" Keerin said, bowing formally. "His Grace is preparing for the arrival of a few of his key councilors before your audience. If you'll come with me, I will escort you to a waiting salon."

The Warded Man followed him through the palace. The last time he had walked here, it was a bustle of activity as Servants and Mothers scurried to and fro on the duke's business. But this early in the morning, the halls were still empty save for the occasional Servant, trained to be all but invisible.

Buzzing lamps lit the way with a pulsing glow. These needed no oil or wick, no Herb Gatherer's chemics. Lectrics, it was called, another bit of old science Euchor kept only for himself. It seemed like magic, but the Warded Man knew from his time in the Duke's Library that it was just harnessed magnetics, no different from wind or running water turning a mill.

Keerin ushered him into a room plush with velvet and a warm hearth. The walls were lined with bookshelves, and there was a mahogany writing desk. If he were alone, it might be a pleasant place to wait.

But Keerin made no move to leave. He went to a silver service, pouring goblets of spiced wine, and returned to hand one to the Warded Man. "I, too, am a demon fighter of some renown. Perhaps you have heard the song I composed about it, titled 'One Arm'?"

Young Arlen would have seethed at this, Keerin still laying claim to his deeds, but the Warded Man was beyond such things. "I have indeed," he said, clapping the tall Jongleur on the shoulder. "An honor to meet one so brave. Come out with me tonight, and we will find a quake of rock demons to show the sun!"

Keerin paled at the offer, his skin taking on a sickly pallor. The Warded Man smiled in the shadow of his hood. Perhaps he was not so far above such things after all.

"I . . . er, thank you for the offer," Keerin stammered. "And I would be honored, of course, but my duties to the duke would never allow for it."

"I understand," the Warded Man said. "A good thing you were not so bound when you saved the life of that young boy in the song. What was his name again?"

"Arlen Banes," Keerin said, regaining his composure with a practiced smile. He moved in close, putting a hand around the Warded Man's shoulder and speaking in a low voice.

"One demon fighter to another," he said, "I would be honored to immortalize your deeds in song, if you would grant a short interview when your business with His Grace is concluded."

The Warded Man turned to face him, lifting his head to allow the lectric lamplight to show into his hood. Keerin gasped and removed his arm, drawing away sharply.

"I don't kill demons for glory, Jongleur," he growled, advancing on the poor herald who backed away until his back hit the bookshelf, causing it to rock unsteadily. "I kill demons," he leaned in close, "because they *deserve* killing."

Keerin's hand shook, spilling his wine. The Warded Man took a step back and smiled. "Write a song about that, perhaps," he suggested.

Keerin still did not leave, but the herald did not speak again, and for that the Warded Man was thankful.

Euchor's great hall was smaller than the Warded Man remembered, but still impressive, with soaring pillars holding up a ceiling that seemed impossibly high. It was painted to look like blue sky, with a yellow-white sunburst in the center. Mosaics covered the floor, and tapestries the walls. There was room for a crowd, as the duke held a great many balls and parties there, watching the proceedings from his high throne at the hall's end.

Duke Euchor was waiting on his throne as the Warded Man approached. Behind him on the royal dais stood three women whose uncomely faces, so like the duke's, and expensive gowns covered in jewels made it clear they were his daughters. Mother Jone stood at the foot of the dais stairs holding a writing board and pen. Opposite her were Guildmasters Ragen and Malcum. The men, retired Messengers both, stood easily with each other. Ragen whispered something to Malcum, who snickered, drawing a glare from Jone.

Next to Jone stood Tender Ronnell, the Royal Librarian. And Mery's father.

The Warded Man cursed himself. He should have expected to see Ronnell. If Mery had told him . . .

But while Ronnell looked at him with interest, there was no recognition in his eyes. His secret was safe, at least for now.

Two guards closed the door behind them and crossed their spears over it from the inside. "Servants," all with writing boards, drifted on the far side of the pillars, unobtrusive as they watched him closely.

Up close, Euchor had grown fatter and older by far than the Warded Man remembered. He still wore jewels on every stubby finger and a fortune in gold chains, but there were fewer hairs underneath his golden crown. Once an imposing figure, he now looked as if he could barely rise from his throne without help.

"Duke Euchor, Light of the Mountains and Lord of Miln," Keerin called, "may I present to you the Warded Man, Messenger on behalf of Duke Rhinebeck, Guardian of the Forest Fortress and Lord of Angiers."

Ragen's voice came to him, as it always did when meeting a duke. *Merchants and Royals will walk all over you if you let them. You need to act like a king in their presence, and never forget who it is risking their life.*

With that in mind, he squared his shoulders and strode forward. "Greetings, Your Grace," he called without waiting to be addressed. His robes whipped out as he sketched a graceful bow. There was a murmur from some at his audacity, but Euchor acted as if he did not notice.

"Welcome to Miln," the duke said. "We have heard much about you. I confess I was one of many who thought you a myth. Pray, indulge me." He mimed removing a hood.

The Warded Man nodded and removed his hood, drawing gasps from around the room. Even Ragen managed to look suitably awed.

He waited, letting them all have a good look. "Impressive," Euchor said. "The tales do not do justice." As he spoke, Ragen's Warders went to work, dipping their pens to copy every symbol they saw while trying to seem inconspicuous.

This time it was Cob's voice in his mind. *Fort Miln isn't like Tibbet's Brook, boy. Here, things cost money.* He didn't think they would get much—the multitude of symbols were too small and close together—but he pulled his hood up casually, his eyes never leaving the duke's. The message was clear. His secrets would not come free.

Euchor glanced at the Warders and scowled at their lack of subtlety.

"I bring message from Duke Rhinebeck of Angiers," the Warded Man said, producing his sealed parcel.

The duke ignored him. "Who are you?" he asked bluntly. "Where are you from?"

"I am the Warded Man," he said. "I come from Thesa."

"That name is not spoken in Miln," the duke warned.

"Nevertheless, it is so," the Warded Man replied.

Euchor's eyes widened at his audacity, and he leaned back, considering. Euchor was different from the other dukes the Warded Man had met in his travels. In Lakton and Rizon, the duke was little more than a figurehead to speak the will of the city council. In Angiers, Rhinebeck ruled, but it seemed his brothers and Janson made as many decisions as he. In Miln, Euchor made all the decisions. His advisors were clearly his, and not the other way around. The fact that he had ruled so long was a testament to his canniness.

"Can you really kill corelings with your bare hands?" the duke asked.

The Warded Man smiled again. "As I was telling your Jongleur, Your Grace, come out beyond the wall with me after dark, and I'll show you personally."

Euchor laughed, but it was forced, the color draining from his red, doughy face. "Perhaps another time."

The Warded Man nodded.

Euchor looked at him a long time, as if trying to decide something. "So?" he asked at last. "Are you, or aren't you?"

"Your Grace?" the Warded Man asked.

"The Deliverer," the duke clarified.

"Surely not," Tender Ronnell scoffed, but the duke made a sharp gesture, and he quieted immediately.

"Are you?" he asked again.

"No," the Warded Man replied. "The Deliverer is a legend, nothing more." Ronnell looked ready to speak up at that, but the librarian glanced at the duke and remained silent. "I am just a man who has found wards once lost."

"Battle wards," Malcum said, his eyes alight. The only one in the room besides Ragen to have faced corelings alone in the night, his interest was no surprise. The Messengers' Guild would likely pay anything to arm their men with warded spears and arrows.

"And how did you come by these wards?" Euchor pressed.

"There is much to be found in the ruins between cities," the Warded Man replied.

"Where?" Malcum asked. The Warded Man only smiled, letting them settle on the hook.

"Enough," Euchor said. "How much gold for the wards?"

The Warded Man shook his head. "I will not sell them for gold."

Euchor scowled. "I could have my guards persuade you otherwise," he warned, nodding toward the two at the door.

The Warded Man smiled. "Then you would find yourself with two less guards."

"Perhaps," the duke mused, "but I have men to spare. Enough, perhaps, to pin even you down while my Warders copy your flesh."

"None of my markings will help you ward a spear, or any weapon," the Warded Man lied. "Those wards are here," he tapped his hooded temple, "and there are not enough guards in all Miln to force them from me."

"I wouldn't be so sure," Euchor warned, "but I can see you have a price in mind, so name it and be done."

"First things first," the Warded Man said, handing Rhinebeck's satchel to Jone. "Duke Rhinebeck requests an alliance in driving out the Krasian invasion that has taken Rizon."

"Of course Rhinebeck wants to ally," Euchor snorted. "He sits behind wooden walls, in green lands the desert rats will covet. But what reason have I to march?"

"He invokes the Pact," the Warded Man said.

Euchor waited as Jone took the letter to him, snatching it and reading it quickly. He scowled and crumpled it in his hand.

"Rhinebeck has already broken the Pact," he growled, "when he tried to rebuild Riverbridge on his side of the river. Let them pay back the tolls from the last fifteen years, and then perhaps I will give thought to his city."

"Your Grace," the Warded Man said, swallowing the urge to leap onto the dais and throttle the man, "the matter of Riverbridge can be settled another day. This is a threat to both your peoples far beyond that petty dispute."

"Petty?!" the duke demanded. Ragen shook his head, and the Warded Man immediately regretted his choice of words. He had never been as good at handling royals as his mentor.

"The Krasians don't come for taxes, Your Grace," he pressed. "Make no mistake, they come to kill and rape until the entire Northland is levied into their army."

"I fear no desert rats," Euchor said. "Let them come and break themselves against my mountains! Let them lay siege in these frozen lands, and see if their sand wards can battle snow demons while they starve outside my walls."

"And what of your hamlets?" the Warded Man said. "Will you sacrifice them as well?"

"I can defend my duchy without aid," Euchor said. "There are books of war sciences in my library, plans for weapons and engines that can break the savages with little loss to us."

"If I may have a word, Your Grace," Tender Ronnell said, drawing all eyes to him. He bowed deeply, and when Euchor nodded, he darted up the dais steps and bent to whisper.

The Warded Man's sharp ears caught every murmured word.

"Your Grace, are you sure it's wise to return such secrets to the world?" the Tender asked. "It was the wars of men that brought the Plague."

"Would you prefer a plague of Krasians?" Euchor hissed back. "What will become of the Tenders of the Creator if the Evejans come?"

Ronnell paused. "Your point is well taken, Your Grace." He bowed away.

"So you hold the Dividing," the Warded Man said. "But how long can Miln survive without grain, fish, and lumber from the South? The Royal Gardens may supply your keep, but when the rest of the city begins to starve, they will dig you out of your own walls."

Euchor snarled, but he did not immediately reply. "No," he said at last, "I won't send Milnese soldiers to die in the South for Rhinebeck's sake without something in return from him."

The Warded Man seethed inwardly at the man's shortsightedness, but this was not unexpected. Now it was just a matter of negotiation.

"Duke Rhinebeck has empowered me to make some concessions," the Warded Man said. "He will not remove his people from their half of Riverbridge, but he will turn fifty percent of the tolls over to you for a period of ten years, in exchange for your aid."

"Only half, for a decade?" Euchor scoffed. "That will barely buy rations for the soldiers."

"There is some room to negotiate, Your Grace," the Warded Man said.

Euchor shook his head. "Not good enough. Not good enough by far. If Rhinebeck wants my help, I want that and something more."

The Warded Man inclined his head. "And that is, Your Grace?"

"Rhinebeck has still failed to produce a male heir, has he not?" Euchor said bluntly. Mother Jone gasped, and the other men in the room shifted uncomfortably at the unseemly topic.

"Much as Your Grace," the Warded Man said, fighting words that Euchor waved away.

"I have grandsons," Euchor said. "My line is secure."

"Your pardon, but what has this to do with an alliance?" the Warded Man asked.

"Because if Rhinebeck wishes one, he will have to marry one of my daughters," Euchor said, looking back at the women standing unprettily behind his throne. "With the bridge tolls as her promise gift."

"Aren't your daughters all Mothers?" the Warded Man asked in confusion.

"Indeed," Euchor said, "proven breeders, all of whom have given sons, but still in the flower of their youth."

The Warded Man glanced at the women again. They didn't seem in the flower of anything, but he made no comment. "I mean, Your Grace, aren't they all wed?"

Euchor shrugged, "To minor Royals, all. I can dissolve their vows with a wave, and any of them would be proud to sit the throne beside Rhinebeck and give him a son. I'll even let him choose which one."

Rhinebeck will die first, the Warded Man thought. *There will be no alliance.*

"I have not been empowered to negotiate such matters," he said.

"Of course not," Euchor agreed. "I'll put the offer in writing this very day, and send my herald to Rhinebeck's court to deliver it personally."

"Your Grace," Keerin squeaked, again a sickly pallor, "surely you need me here for—"

"You will go to Angiers, or I will throw you from my tower," Euchor growled.

Keerin bowed, attempting a Jongleur's mask though his distress still shone through. "Of course it is my great honor to go, if I am absolved of my local duties."

Euchor grunted, then turned his eyes back to the Warded Man. "You still haven't given me a price for your battle wards."

The Warded Man smiled and reached into his satchel, producing a grimoire of hand-sewn pages bound in leather. "These?"

"I thought you said they weren't with you," Euchor said.

The Warded Man shrugged. "I lied."

"What do you want for them?" the duke asked again.

"Warders and supplies sent to Riverbridge with your herald on the way to Angiers," the Warded Man said, "along with a royal decree accepting all refugees from across the Dividing without toll, and a guarantee of food, shelter, and succor through the winter."

"All that, for a book of wards?" Euchor demanded. "Ridiculous!"

The Warded Man shrugged. "If you wish to buy those I sold Rhinebeck, you'd best treat with him soon, before the Krasians burn his city down."

"The Warders' Guild will defray the costs to Your Grace, of course," Ragen said on cue.

"The Messengers' Guild, as well," Malcum added quickly.

Euchor's eyes narrowed at the men, and the Warded Man knew he had won. Euchor knew that if he refused, the guildmasters would buy the wards themselves, and he would lose control of the greatest advancement in magic since the First Demon War.

"I would never ask such of my guilds," the duke said. "The crown will cover the expense. After all," he nodded to the Warded Man, "the least Miln can do is take in any survivors who come so far north. Provided, of course, that they take an oath of allegiance."

The Warded Man frowned, but he nodded, and at a signal from Euchor, Tender Ronnell hurried forward to take the book from him. Malcum stared at it hungrily.

"Will you accept the shelter of the caravan back to Angiers?" the duke asked, trying to hide his eagerness for the Warded Man to be gone.

The Warded Man shook his head. "I thank you, Your Grace, but I am my own succor." He bowed and, without being dismissed, turned and strode from the room.

It was simple to lose the men Euchor sent to follow him. The city had begun its morning bustle, and the streets were crowded as the Warded Man headed for the Duke's Library. He seemed just another Tender as he ascended the marble steps of the greatest building in Thesa.

As always, the Duke's Library filled the Warded Man with both elation and sorrow. In it, Euchor and his ancestors had collected copies of nearly every remaining book from the old world that survived the flame demons burning the libraries during the Return. Science. Medicine. Magic. History. Everything. The dukes of Miln had collected all that knowledge and locked it away, denying its benefits to all mankind.

As a journeyman Warder, the Warded Man had warded the stacks and furniture of the Library, earning permanent placement in the book of access to the archives. Of course, he had no desire to reveal his identity, even to some acolyte clerk, but his objective wasn't in the stacks this time. Once inside the building, he slipped out of sight and headed down a side passage.

He was waiting in Tender Ronnell's office when the librarian returned, clutching the grimoire of battle wards. Ronnell didn't notice him at first, moving quickly to lock the door behind him. He exhaled then, turning and holding the book out before him.

"Odd that Euchor would give the book to you and not the head of his Warders' Guild, who would be better able to decipher it," the Warded Man said.

Ronnell yelped at the sound and stumbled back. His eyes widened farther when he saw who stood before him. His hand sketched a quick ward in the air before him.

When it became clear that the Warded Man intended no attack, the Tender straightened and regained his composure. "I am well qualified to decipher this book. Warding is part of an acolyte's studies. The world may not be ready for what is contained within. His Grace commanded that I assess it first."

"Is that your function, Tender? To decide what mankind is ready for? As if you or Euchor might have a right to deny men the ability to fight back against the corelings?"

Ronnell snorted. "You speak, sir, as someone who did not sell the wards at a high price rather than giving them freely."

The Warded Man walked to Ronnell's desk. The surface was impeccably neat and clear, save for a lamp, a polished mahogany writing kit, and a brass stand holding the Tender's personal copy of the Canon. He lifted the book casually, and his sharp ears caught a possessive inhalation from the Tender, but the man said nothing.

The leather-bound book was worn, its ink faded. It was no showpiece, but rather a guide often referred to, its mysteries pondered regularly. Ronnell had commanded Arlen to read from this very copy during his time at the Library, but he had none of Ronnell's faith in the book, for it was built upon two premises he could not accept: that there was an all-powerful Creator, and that the corelings were a part of His plan, a punishment upon mankind's sins.

In his mind, the book, as much as anything in the world, was responsible for the wretched state of humanity—cowering and weak when they should stand strong; always afraid, never hopeful. But for all that, many of the

Canon's sentiments about brotherhood and the fellowship of men were ones the Warded Man believed in deeply.

He flipped through the book until he found a certain passage, and began to read:

> *"There is no man in creation who is not your brother*
> *No woman not your sister, no child not your own*
> *For all suffer the Plague, righteous and sinful alike*
> *And all must band together to withstand the night."*

The Warded Man closed the book with a snap that made the librarian jump. "What price did I ask for the wards, Tender? That Euchor help the helpless who come to his door? How do I profit from that?"

"You could be in league with Rhinebeck," Ronnell suggested. "Paid to get rid of Beggars who have become a problem south of the Dividing."

"Listen to yourself, Tender!" the Warded Man said. "Making excuses not to follow your own Canon!"

"Why have you come?" Ronnell asked. "You could give the wards to everyone in Miln if you wished."

"Already have," the Warded Man said. "Neither you nor Euchor can suppress them."

Ronnell's eyes widened. "Why are you telling me this? Keerin doesn't leave until tomorrow. I could still advise the duke to rescind his promise to grant succor to the refugees."

"But you won't," the Warded Man said, placing the Canon back on its stand pointedly.

Ronnell scowled. "What is it you want of me?"

"To know more of the war engines Euchor mentioned," the Warded Man said.

Ronnell drew a deep breath. "And if I refuse to tell you?"

The Warded Man shrugged. "Then I go to the stacks and find out for myself."

"The archives are off limits save to those with the duke's seal," Ronnell said.

The Warded Man pulled his hood down. "Even to me?"

Ronnell stared in wonder at his painted skin. He was silent a long time, and when he spoke, it was another verse from the Canon. *"For he shall be marked upon his bare flesh . . ."*

"And the demons will not abide the sight, and they shall flee terrified before

him," the Warded Man finished. "You made me memorize that passage the year I warded your stacks."

Ronnell stared at him for a long moment, trying to peel back the wards and years. Suddenly his eyes flared with recognition. "Arlen?" he gasped.

The Warded Man nodded. "You gave your word that I would have access to the stacks for life," he reminded the librarian.

"Of course, of course . . ." Ronnell began, but trailed off. He shook his head as if to clear it. "How could I not have seen it?" he muttered.

"Seen what?" the Warded Man asked.

"You." Ronnell dropped to his knees. "You are the Deliverer, sent to end the Plague!"

The Warded Man scowled. "I've said no such thing. You knew me as a boy! I was willful and impulsive. Never set foot in a Holy House. I courted your daughter and then left and broke our promise." He leaned in close to the Tender. "And I'll eat demonshit before I believe humanity deserves the 'Plague.'"

"Of course not," Ronnell agreed. "The Deliverer must believe the opposite."

"I'm not the ripping Deliverer!" the Warded Man snapped, but this time the librarian did not flinch, his eyes wide with wonder.

"You are," Ronnell said. "It's the only way to explain your miracles."

"Miracles?" the Warded Man asked, incredulous. "Have you been smoking tampweed, Tender? What miracles?"

"Keerin can sing as he pleases about how you were found on the road, but I had my version from Master Cob first," Ronnell said. "You cut the arm from that rock demon, and when it breached the wall, it was you that tricked it into the Warders' trap."

The Warded Man shrugged. "So what? Anyone with basic warding skill could have done those things."

"I can't think of anyone who ever did," Ronnell said. "And you were only eleven summers old when you crippled the demon, alone in the naked night."

"I would have died from my wounds had Ragen not found me," the Warded Man said.

"You survived for several nights before the Messenger came," Ronnell said. "The Creator must have sent him when your trial was at an end."

"What trial?" the Warded Man asked, but Ronnell ignored him.

"A Beggar boy found on the road," the librarian went on, "yet you brought new wardings to Miln, and revitalized the craft before you even finished your apprenticeship!" He spoke as if he were seeing each deed in a new light as he mentioned it, filling in pieces of some great puzzle.

"You warded the Holy Library," he said in awe, pointing. "A boy, a mere apprentice, and I let you ward the most important building in the world."

"Just the furniture," the Warded Man said.

Ronnell nodded, as if fitting another piece. "The Creator wanted you here, in the Library. Its secrets were collected for you!"

"That's nonsense," the Warded Man said.

Ronnell got to his feet. "Pray, put your hood up," he said, going to the door.

The Warded Man stared at him a moment, then complied. Ronnell led him from his office to the main archive, striding through the maze of stacks as a man might swiftly cross his own home when the kettle began to whistle.

The Warded Man followed no less swiftly. After warding every shelf, table, and bench in the building, its layout was seared into his mind. They soon came to an archway with the path roped off. A burly acolyte stood there to grant entry, and above him, the letters BR were etched into the keystone.

Contained within were the most valuable books in the archive—original copies of books dating back before the Return. These were housed in glass and seldom touched, for copies had long since been penned. Also in the BR section were countless rows of manuals, philosophies, and stories the librarian, always a devout Tender of the Creator, deemed unfit for even the scholars of Miln to see.

The Warded Man had delighted in perusing these as a boy, when the acolytes who patrolled the censored stacks were not about. He had stolen more than one censored romance or unedited history for a night's reading, replacing the text before any noticed its absence.

The acolyte bowed low at the Tender's approach, and Ronnell led them to one of the censored stacks. There were literally thousands of books, but the Duke's Librarian knew every volume by heart, and did not slow to check shelf or spine as he selected a volume. He turned and handed it to the Warded Man. The hand-painted cover read: *Weapones of the Olde Wyrld*.

"The Age of Science had terrible weapons," Ronnell said. "Weapons that could kill hundreds, even thousands of men. It is no wonder the Creator grew wroth with us."

The Warded Man ignored the comment. "Euchor will seek to rebuild them?"

"The most terrible are beyond our ability to re-create, requiring vast refineries and lectric power," Ronnell said. "But there is much that can still be built by any man with access to simple chemics and a steel forge. That book," he pointed to the volume in the Warded Man's hands, "is a detailed account of those weapons and how they are built. Take it."

The Warded Man raised an eyebrow. "What will Euchor do when he learns it's gone?"

"He will grow wroth, and demand I re-create it from the original texts," Ronnell said, gesturing to the rows of glass bookcases. Glass the Warded Man had etched with wards himself.

Tender Ronnell followed his gaze. "When the Warders' Guild began charging glass, I had them put out in the night. Your wards made those cases indestructible. Another miracle."

"You mustn't tell anyone who I was," the Warded Man said. "You would endanger everyone I ever knew."

Ronnell nodded. "It is enough for now that I know."

If he hadn't told Ronnell who he was, Mery likely would have, but he had never expected the strict man to honestly believe that he, Arlen Bales, was the Deliverer. The Warded Man scowled as he put the book in his satchel.

It was the last night of the new moon when the mind demon tracked the Warded Man to Fort Miln. The coreling prince could only rise on the three darkest nights of the cycle, but it picked up its quarry's trail quickly, following a lingering scent in the air, even days after his passing. It was an intriguing scent—not quite human and warm with stolen Core magic.

Atop its winged mimic, the mind demon stared down at the net atop the human breeding ground. The walls were powerfully warded, but there were large gaps in the lines of magic crisscrossing the rooftops. A winged drone, unable to see the net unless it activated, might never find the gap save by accident, but to the coreling prince the pattern was clear, and it guided its mimic to slip neatly through into the city proper.

Windows were shuttered closed, streets dark and empty. The mind demon felt the pull as the house wards tried to leech its magic, but the mimic glided by so quickly that they could find no draw. Clumsy wardnets were cast throughout the city, but the coreling prince avoided them as easily as a man might step around a puddle.

They passed through the city following the invisible path in the air. They paused at a great inner keep, but a sniff at the gate made it clear it was not their final destination. Next they came to a giant building whose wards were so powerful, the coreling prince hissed as it felt their pull even from a distance. There was usually at least one such place at the center of every breeding ground, and they were places best avoided, especially since his quarry had not remained there. A fresher scent headed away from the building.

The trail led at last to another wardwall, this one tightly crafted and without flaw. The wards were not keyed to their castes, but the coreling prince knew they would still activate and cause great pain should it or its mimic cross the net. The demon was forced to disable some of the wards so they could pass the barrier safely.

They drifted silently up to the dwelling, and in the window, the mind demon caught sight of its quarry at last. Those with him were dull and colorless creatures, but the one had warded his flesh, and glowed fiercely with stolen magic.

Too fiercely. The coreling prince was thousands of years old, a creature of caution, consideration, and decisive action. This deep in the breeding ground, it could not summon drones to attack, and the mind demon was loath to risk its mimic. Having seen the human, there was no question he must be killed, but there would be better chances in the coming cycles when he was less protected, and there were unanswered questions about his power to answer first.

It moved to the window, absorbing the crude grunts and gestures of the human stock.

" 'You would find yourself with two less guards?' " Ragen said with a deep, rich laugh. "I thought Euchor was going to burst a vein right there! I told you to act like a king, not a suicidal Krasian!"

"I didn't expect him to demand a marriage," the Warded Man said.

"Euchor knows full well he is not going to produce a direct heir," Ragen said, "so it's wise to get at least one of his daughters out of the city before they tear Miln apart for his throne. Whichever girl Rhinebeck chooses, she'll likely welcome the escape, and the chance to put her own issue on the throne of Angiers."

"Rhinebeck will never accept it," the Warded Man said.

Ragen shook his head. "Depends on how much of a threat the Krasians prove," he said. "If it's half as bad as you say, Rhinebeck may have no choice. Will you share Euchor's book of weapons with him?"

The Warded Man shook his head. "I have no interest in ducal politics, or helping the men of Thesa kill one another with the Krasians in our lands and the corelings clawing at the wards. I've more interest in turning these weapons against the corelings, if it can be done."

"No wonder Ronnell thinks you the Deliverer," Ragen said.

The Warded Man looked at him sharply.

"Don't look at me like that," Ragen said. "I believe it no more than you do. At least, not that you're divine. But perhaps it's natural that when the time is right, a man of sufficient will and drive appears to guide the rest of us."

The Warded Man shook his head. "I don't want to guide anyone. I just want to see the fighting wards spread wide so they can never be lost again. Let men guide themselves."

He moved to the window and glanced out the curtains at the sky. "I'll leave before first light, so none will mark my . . ."

He almost missed it, his eyes on the sky and not the ground. It was just a glimpsed thing, vanished before he got a good look, but there was no mistaking the glow to his warded eyes.

There was a demon in the yard.

He turned and ran for the door, pulling off his robe and throwing it on the marble floor as he went. Elissa gasped at the sight of him.

"Arlen, what is it?" she cried.

He ignored her, lifting the bar off the heavy oak door and flinging it open as if it were weightless. He leapt out into the yard, looking about frantically.

Nothing.

Ragen was at the door an instant later, spear in hand and warded shield on his arm. "What did you see?" he demanded.

The Warded Man turned a slow circuit, scanning the courtyard for signs of magic, and straining his other senses to catch some hint confirming what he had seen.

"There's a demon in the yard," he said. "A powerful one. Stay behind the wards."

"Good advice for you as well," Elissa called. "Come inside before my heart stops."

The Warded Man ignored her, moving about the yard, scanning. There were Servants' houses inside Ragen's wall, as well as his garden and stables. Many places to hide. He drifted through the darkness, seeing all with absolute clarity, even better than he did in the light.

There was a presence in the air, like a lingering stench, but it was insubstantial and impossible to pinpoint. His muscles grew tight, ready to flex at an instant's notice.

But there was nothing. He searched the compound from one end to another, and found nothing. Had he imagined it?

"Anything?" Ragen asked, when he returned. The guildmaster was still in the doorway, safe behind the wards, but ready to spring out at a moment's notice.

"Empty my pockets," the Warded Man said with a shrug. "Maybe I imagined it."

Ragen grunted. "No one gets cored for being too careful."

The Warded Man took Ragen's spear as he came back inside. A Messenger's spear was his trusted companion on the road, and Ragen's, though he had not Messaged in nearly a decade, was still well oiled and sharp.

"Let me ward this before I leave," he said. He glanced outside. "And you check your wardnet come morning." Ragen nodded.

"Must you go so soon?" Elissa asked.

"I draw too much attention in town, and I don't want it to lead back here," the Warded Man said. "Better I be gone before sunrise, and out the dawn gate the moment it opens."

Elissa did not look pleased, but she embraced him tightly and kissed him. "We expect to see you again before another decade passes," she warned.

"You will," the Warded Man promised. "Honest word."

The Warded Man felt better than he had in years when he left Ragen and Elissa just before dawn. They had refused sleep and stayed up with him through the night, filling him in on the goings-on in Miln since his departure, and asking after the details of his life. He told them stories of his early adventures, but never spoke of his time in the desert, when Arlen Bales had died and the Warded Man been born. Or the years after.

Still, there were enough tales to fill the remainder of the night and to spare. He barely made it away before the dawn bell, and had to trot to be far enough from the manse not to draw suspicion as people began to open warded doors and unshutter warded windows.

He smiled. Likely, his missing the bell and being forced to stay another day had been Elissa's plan all along, but she had never been able to cage him.

The guards at the day gate were still stretching out morning kinks when he arrived, but the gate was open. "Seems everyone's up early this morn," one said as he passed.

The Warded Man wondered what he meant, but then he rode past the hill where he had first met Jaik and found his friend waiting there, sitting on a large rock.

"Looks like I made it out just in time," Jaik said. "Had to break curfew to do it."

The Warded Man dropped from the horse's back and came over to him. Jaik made no effort to rise or extend a hand, so he simply sat on the rock beside him. "The Jaik I met on this hill would never break curfew."

Jaik shrugged. "Didn't have much choice. Knew you'd try and skulk off with the dawn."

"Didn't Ragen's man bring you my letters?" the Warded Man asked.

Jaik pulled out the bundle and threw it to the ground. "Can't read, and you know it."

The Warded Man sighed. In truth, he had forgotten. "Came to see you in person," he offered. "Wasn't expecting to find Mery there, and she wasn't eager that I stay."

"I know," Jaik said. "She came to me at the mill in tears. Told me everything."

The Warded Man hung his head. "I'm sorry."

"You should be," Jaik said. He sat quietly for a time, looking out over the land spread out before them.

"Always knew she was just settling for me," he said at last. "You were gone a year before she saw me as anything more than a shoulder to cry on. Two more before she agreed to be my wife, and another after that before we made our vows. Even on the day she was holding her breath, hoping you'd storm in and break up the ceremony. Night, I half expected it myself."

He shrugged. "Can't blame her. She was marrying down a class, and I ent educated or much to look at. There was a reason I followed you around when we were kids. You were always better than me at everything. I wasn't even fit to be your Jongleur."

"Jaik, I'm no better than you are," the Warded Man said.

"Yeah, I see that now." Jaik spat. "I'm a better husband than you ever could have been. Know why? Because unlike you, I was there for her."

The Warded Man scowled, and any feelings of contrition fled from his thoughts. Anger and hurt he would accept from Jaik, but the condescension in his tone burned.

"That's the Jaik I remember," he said. "Shows up and does the least he can. Heard Mery's da had to call favors at the mill so you could afford to move off your parents' carpet."

But Jaik stood fast. "I was there for her here," he snapped, pointing to his temple, "and here!" He pointed to his heart. "Your head and heart were always out there." He swept a hand out over the horizon. "So why don't you just go back there? No one needs your delivering here."

The Warded Man nodded, leaping back up onto Twilight Dancer's back. "You take care of yourself, Jaik." He rode off.

CHAPTER 24

BROTHERS IN THE NIGHT

:: 333 AR SPRING ::

"HEY! WATCH THE BUMPS, I'm tuning!" Rojer cried as the cart trundled along the road. He had carefully cleaned and waxed the ancient fiddle the Warded Man had given him, and purchased expensive new strings at the Jongleurs' Guildhouse. His old fiddle had belonged to Master Jaycob, and the cheap workmanship had him forever tuning it. Before that, he had used Arrick's fiddle, which was finer, though it had seen many years of use and was worn down even before Jasin Goldentone and his apprentices smashed it.

This one, rescued from some forgotten ruin, was another class entirely. The neck and body curved differently than Rojer was used to, but the workmanship was exquisite, and the wood had passed the centuries like days. A fiddle fit for a duke to play.

"I'm sorry, Rojer," Leesha said, "but the road just doesn't seem to care that you're tuning. I don't know what's gotten into it."

Rojer stuck his tongue out at her, gently turning the last peg between the thumb and forefinger of his crippled hand while the thumb of his other hand plucked at the string.

"Got it!" he shouted at last. "Stop the cart!"

"Rojer, we have miles to go before dark," Leesha said. Rojer knew that every moment away from the Hollow ate at her, worried over its citizens as a mother worried over her children.

"Just for a minute," Rojer begged. Leesha tsked, but she complied. Gared and Wonda pulled up as well, looking at the cart curiously.

Rojer stood on the driver's seat, brandishing the fiddle and bow. He put the instrument under his chin and caressed the strings with the bow, bringing them to a resonant hum.

"Listen to that," he marveled. "Smooth like honey. Jaycob's fiddle was a toy by comparison."

"If you say so, Rojer," Leesha said.

Rojer frowned for a moment, then dismissed her with a wave of his bow. His two remaining fingers spread wide for balance, it fit his crippled hand like a part of it as it danced across the strings. Rojer let the music soar from the fiddle, sweeping him up in its whirlwind.

He could feel Arrick's medallion resting comfortably against his bare chest, hidden under his motley tunic. No longer a trigger to painful memories, it was a reassuring weight, a way to honor those who had died for him. He stood straighter knowing it was there.

This wasn't the first talisman Rojer had carried. For years, he had kept a puppet of wood and string topped with a lock of his master's golden hair in a secret pocket in the waistband of his motley pants. Before that, it was a puppet of his mother, capped with a lock of her red.

But with the medallion, Rojer could feel both Arrick and his parents looking over him, and he spoke to them through the fiddle. He played his love and played his loneliness and regret. He told them all the things he had never been able to in life.

When he finally finished, Leesha and the others were staring at him, their eyes glazed like charmed corelings. It was only after a few moments of silence that they shook their heads and came back to themselves.

"Ent never heard anything beautiful as that," Wonda said. Gared grunted, and Leesha produced a kerchief, dabbing at her eyes.

The rest of the journey to Deliverer's Hollow was filled with music, with Rojer playing every minute his hands weren't otherwise occupied. He knew they were returning to all the same problems they had left, but with the promise of aid to come from the duke and the Jongleurs' Guild, as well as the comfort of the medallion around his neck, he held new hope that all their problems could be solved.

They were still a day from the Hollow when the way became choked with refugees, many of them with tents and warding circles pitched right in the road. Leesha knew them immediately as Laktonians, for as a whole they were stocky folk, short and round-faced, and they stood as those more used to walking on a boat's deck than dry land.

"What's happened?" Leesha demanded of the first person they came to, a young mother pacing to calm a crying infant. The woman looked at her with hollow, uncomprehending eyes as Leesha got down from the cart. Then she took note of Leesha's pocketed apron and a light came back to her.

"Please," she said, holding out the screaming child. "I think he's sick."

Leesha took the babe in her arms, running sensitive fingers over it to check pulse and temperature. After a moment, she simply sat it up in the crook of one arm and stuck a knuckle in its mouth. The child quieted immediately, sucking vigorously.

"There's nothing wrong with him," she said, "apart from sensing the stress of his mum." The woman relaxed visibly, breathing a sigh of relief.

"What's happened?" Leesha asked again.

"The Krasians," the woman said.

"Creator, have they marched on Lakton so soon?" Leesha asked.

The woman shook her head. "They've spread out through Rizon's hamlets, forcing the women to cover up, and dragging the men off to fight demons. They pick and choose Rizonan girls to take as wives like a rancher picking a chicken to slaughter, and march the boys to training camps where they're taught to hate their own families."

Leesha scowled.

"Hamlets ent safe anymore," the woman said. "Those that could moved on to Lakton proper, and a few stayed to fight for their homes, but the rest of us went to the Hollow looking for the Deliverer. He wan't there, but folk said he had gone on to Angiers, so that's where we're headed. He'll put things right, you see if he doesn't."

"So we all hope," Leesha sighed, though she had her doubts. She handed back the baby and climbed back into the cart.

"We need to get to the Hollow immediately," she told the others. She looked at Gared.

"Clear the road!" the giant Cutter bellowed, a lion's roar, and folk fell over themselves to move out of his path as he stomped his garron toward them. Tents, blankets, and wards were snatched quickly away. Leesha regretted the need, but the cart could not go off-road, and her children needed her.

They galloped the horses when they finally cleared the press of refugees, thousands in number, but they were still well short of the Hollow by nightfall. It only took a mild look from Leesha to make Rojer take up his fiddle, and they rode on through the darkness with only Leesha's light staff to guide them and his music to keep the corelings at bay.

Leesha could see the demons at the edge of the light, swaying in time to the music as they ambled slowly after Rojer, mesmerized.

"I'd rather they were attacking," Wonda said. She had her great bow strung and a warded arrow nocked and ready.

"Ent natural," Gared agreed.

They made it to Leesha's cottage on the outskirts of the Hollow by midnight, and paused only long enough for Leesha to store the most precious of their cargo before they pressed on through the darkness to the village proper.

If things had seemed cramped before, they were many times worse now. The refugees from Lakton came better equipped, with tents and warding circles and covered wagons laden with supply, but they spilled over the edges of the forbidding on almost every side, weakening the greatward.

Leesha turned to Gared and Wonda. "Find the other Cutters and make a sweep of the forbidding. Any tent or carriage within ten feet of the greatward needs to be moved, or we could have corelings in the streets." The two nodded and moved off.

She turned to Rojer. "Find Smitt and Jona. I want a council meeting tonight; I don't care who's in bed."

Rojer nodded. "I don't have to ask where you'll be, I suppose." He hopped from the cart and pulled up the hood of his warded cloak as she turned the cart for the hospit.

Jardir looked up as Abban limped into the throne room. "You seem almost spry today, *khaffit*."

Abban bowed. "The spring air gives me strength, Shar'Dama Ka."

Ashan snorted at Jardir's side. Jayan and Asome kept their distance, having learned not to antagonize Abban in their father's presence.

"What do you know of the place called Deliverer's Hollow?" Jardir asked, ignoring them.

"You seek the Warded Man?" Abban asked.

Ashan lunged at Abban, taking him by the throat. "Where did you hear that name, *khaffit*?!" he demanded. "If you've been bribing the *nie'dama* for information again, I'll—"

"Ashan, enough!" Jardir shouted as Abban gasped and struggled weakly. When the *Damaji* did not comply fast enough, Jardir did not ask again, kicking him hard in the side. Ashan was knocked away and hit the polished stone floor hard.

"You would strike me, your loyal *Damaji*, over a pig-eating *khaffit*?" Ashan asked, incredulous, when he had found his breath again.

"I struck you for not attending my command," Jardir corrected, and swept his gaze over the rest of those in the room. Aleverak and Maji, Jayan and Asome, Ashan, Hasik, even the door guards. Only Inevera, stretched out in her diaphanous robes on a bed of bright silk pillows beside his throne, escaped his gaze. "I tire of this game, so I say now for all to hear, I will kill the next person to strike someone in my presence when I have not given them leave to do so."

Abban began to smirk, but Jardir whirled on him, glaring. "And you, *khaffit*," he growled. "The next time you answer a question with a question, I will tear out your right eye and make you eat it."

Abban paled as Jardir strode angrily to his throne, sitting down hard. "How did you learn of the one they call the Warded Man? The *dama* required intensive interrogation to pull his name from the *chin* Holy Men's lips."

Abban shook his head. "It's all the *chin* talk about, Deliverer. I doubt the interrogations discovered anything a few crumbs of bread or words of kindness couldn't have gathered freely on the street."

Jardir scowled. "And the stories agree he is in the village called Deliverer's Hollow?" Abban nodded. "What do you know of it?"

"Until a year ago, it was called Cutter's Hollow," Abban said, "a small village of men beholden to the duke of Angiers who felled trees for lumber and fuel. Wood is impractical to ship through the desert, so I had little business with them, though I do have one contact who might remain. A seller of fine paper."

"What good is that?" Ashan demanded.

Abban shrugged. "I do not know that it is, Damaji."

"And what have you heard of the place since its name changed?" Jardir demanded.

"That the Warded Man came to them last year when the village was rife with flux and the wards failing," Abban said. "That he killed hundreds of *alagai* with his bare hands alone, and taught the villagers to fight *alagai'sharak*."

"Impossible," Jayan said. "The *chin* are too weak and cowardly to stand up in the night."

"Perhaps not all," Abban said. "Remember the Par'chin."

Jardir glared at him. "No one remembers the Par'chin, *khaffit*," he growled. "You would do well not to remember him, either."

Abban nodded, bowing as low as his crutch would allow.

"I will see for myself," Jardir decided, "and you will come with me." Everyone looked at him in surprise. "Hasik, find Shanjat. Tell him to assemble the Spears of the Deliverer." Jardir's Maze unit had taken the name when they became his personal bodyguard. The Spears of the Deliverer were fifty of the finest *dal'Sharum* in Krasia, serving under *kai'Sharum* Shanjat.

Hasik bowed, leaving immediately.

"Are you certain this is wise, Deliverer?" Ashan asked. "It is not safe to separate yourself from your armies in enemy lands."

"Nothing in life is safe for those who fight Sharak Ka," Jardir said. He put a hand on Ashan's shoulder. "But if you are concerned, you may come with me, my friend."

Ashan bowed deeply.

"This is foolishness," Aleverak growled. "A thousand weakling *chin* can overwhelm even the Spears of the Deliverer."

Jayan snorted. "I doubt that very much, old man."

Aleverak turned to Jardir, who nodded his permission. The ancient *Damaji* reached out to Jayan, and suddenly the boy was on his back.

"I'll kill you for that, old man," Jayan growled, rolling quickly to his feet.

"Try it, boy," Aleverak dared, setting his feet in a *sharusahk* stance and beckoning with his one arm. Jayan snarled, but at the last moment, he glanced at his father.

Jardir smiled. "By all means, try and kill him."

A vicious smile broke out on Jayan's face, but a moment later he was back on the floor, Aleverak pulling on his arm to increase the slow pressure of his heel on Jayan's windpipe.

"Enough," Jardir said, and Aleverak immediately released the hold and stepped back. Jayan coughed and rubbed his throat as he rose.

"Even my own sons must respect the *Damaji*, Jayan," Jardir warned. "You would be wise to hold your tongue in the future."

He turned to Aleverak. "The *Damaji* will rule Everam's Bounty in my absence, with you leading the council."

Aleverak narrowed his eyes, as if deciding whether or not to continue his protest. Finally, he bowed deeply. "As the Shar'Dama Ka commands. Who will speak for the Kaji until Damaji Ashan returns?"

"My son, Dama Asukaji," Ashan said, nodding to the young man. Asukaji was not yet eighteen, but he was old enough for the white robe, which meant he was old enough for the black turban, if he was strong enough to hold it.

Jardir nodded. "And if Jayan will be humble, he will serve as Sharum Ka."

All eyes turned to Jayan, whose face betrayed his shock. After a moment, he put one hand and one knee on the ground, perhaps for the first time in his life. "I will serve the council of *Damaji*, of course."

Jardir nodded. "See to it the lesser tribes continue to subjugate the *chin* while I am gone," he said to Asukaji and Aleverak. "I need fresh warriors for Sharak Ka, not bickering tribes stealing one another's wells." The two men bowed.

Inevera rose from her bed of pillows, her face serene behind the diaphanous veil.

"I would speak to my husband in private," she said.

Ashan bowed. "Of course, Damajah." He ushered the others quickly out of the room, all save Asome, who stood fast behind.

"Something troubles you, my son?" Jardir asked when the others were gone.

Asome bowed. "If Jayan is to be Sharum Ka while you are gone, then by rights I should be Andrah."

Inevera laughed. Asome's eyes narrowed, but he knew better than to cross her.

"That would put you above your elder brother, my son," Jardir said. "Something no father does lightly. And Sharum Ka are appointed. Andrah is a title that must be earned."

Asome shrugged. "Summon the *Damaji*. I will kill them all, if that is what is required."

Jardir looked into his son's eyes, seeing ambition, but also a fierce pride that might indeed carry the boy, barely past his eighteenth born day, through eleven death challenges, even if it meant killing one of his own brothers or Asukaji, who was his closest friend and rumored to be his lover. Asome's white robe might forbid him to touch a weapon, but he was deadlier than Jayan by far, and even Aleverak would do well to step carefully around him.

Jardir felt a swell of pride in the boy. Already he thought his second son might well prove a better successor than Jayan, but not until he was seasoned, and firstborn Jayan would never allow his brother to surpass him while he still drew breath.

"Krasia needs no Andrah while I live," Jardir said instead. "And Jayan will only wear the white turban while I am gone. You will assist Asukaji in maintaining control of the Kaji."

Asome opened his mouth again, but Inevera cut him off.

"Enough," she said. "The matter is closed. Leave us."

Asome scowled, but he bowed and left.

"He will be a great leader one day, if he lives long enough," Jardir said when the door closed behind his son.

"I often think the same of you, husband," Inevera said, turning to face him. The words stung, but Jardir said nothing, knowing it was pointless until his wife had said her piece.

"Aleverak and Ashan were right," Inevera said. "There is no need for you to lead the expedition personally."

"Is it not the duty of the Shar'Dama Ka to gather armies to Sharak Ka?" Jardir asked. "By all accounts, these *chin* fight the Holy War. I must investigate."

"You could at least have waited until I had a chance to throw the dice," Inevera said.

Jardir scowled. "There's no need to throw the dice every time I leave the palace."

"Perhaps there is," Inevera said. "Sharak Ka is no game. We must command every advantage, if we are to succeed."

"If Everam wills me to succeed, that is all the advantage I need," Jardir said. "And if He does not . . ."

Inevera lifted her felt pouch of *alagai hora*. "Pray, indulge me."

Jardir sighed, but he nodded and they retreated to a chamber off the throne room that Inevera had claimed as her own. As always, the room was filled with bright pillows and cloying incense. Jardir felt his pulse quicken, his body conditioned to associate the smell with Inevera's sex. The *Jiwah Ka* was more than happy to share him when she was sated, but she was almost a man in her hunger, and the side chamber was used frequently for that purpose, often while the *Damaji* and Jardir's councilors waited in the throne room without.

Inevera moved to pull the curtains, and he watched her body through the translucent veils that were all she ever wore anymore. Even at more than forty years of age—she never said for certain—she was the most beautiful of his wives by far, her curves still round and firm, her skin smooth. He was tempted to take her right there, but Inevera was single-minded when the dice were concerned, and he knew she would only rebuff him until they were thrown.

They knelt on the silk pillows, allowing a broad space for the dice to fall. As always, Inevera needed his blood for the spell, releasing it with a quick slash of her warded knife. She licked the blade clean and returned it to her belt sheath, pressing her palm to the wound, and then emptying the dice into it. They glowed fiercely in the dark as she shook her hands and threw.

The demon bones scattered on the floor, and Inevera scanned them quickly. Jardir had learned that the pattern of the fall was as important as the symbols that showed, but his understanding of the dice ended there. He had seen his wives argue many times over the meaning of a throw, though none ever dared question Inevera's interpretations.

The Damajah hissed angrily at the pattern before her, looking up sharply at Jardir.

"You cannot go," she said.

Jardir scowled, moving to the window and grabbing the curtain angrily. "Cannot?" he demanded, pulling the heavy drapes aside and flooding the room with bright sunlight. Inevera barely got her dice back in the pouch in time.

"I am Shar'Dama Ka," he said. "There is nothing I cannot do."

There was a flash of rage on Inevera's face, but it was gone in an instant. "The dice promise disaster if you go," she warned.

"I tire of following your dice," Jardir said. "Especially since they always seem to tell you more than you deem me worthy to know. I will go."

"Then I am going with you," Inevera said.

Jardir shook his head. "You will do no such thing. You will stay here and keep your sons from killing one another until I return."

He strode up to her and took her shoulder in a firm grip. "I would have one last taste of my wife, though, before the trek north."

Inevera twisted, seeming only to tap his arm, but his grip lost strength for an instant, and she stepped away. "If you go alone, you can wait," she said, a cruel smile on her face. "More reason to come back alive."

Jardir scowled, but he knew better than to try to force the issue, Shar'-Dama Ka and husband or no.

Wonda opened the door to Leesha's cottage, letting Rojer and Gared in. Once the girl heard the Warded Man had commanded Gared to guard Rojer, she had insisted on doing the same for Leesha, sleeping at the cottage every night. Leesha had begun assigning her chores to try to dissuade the girl's smothering, but Wonda did the work gladly, and Leesha had to admit she had grown accustomed to her looming presence.

"The Cutters finished felling trees to clear space for the next greatward," Rojer said as they sat at her table and took tea. "It's a mile square, just like you asked."

"That's good," Leesha said. "We can start laying stones to mark the edges of the ward immediately."

"Land's thick with woodies," Gared said. "Hundreds of 'em. The cuttin' drew 'em like flies to a dungpile. Oughta gather the town and wipe 'em out 'fore we build."

Leesha looked at Gared closely. The giant Cutter was always recommending battle, as the notched and dented gauntlets at his belt showed. But Leesha was never certain if it was for love of carnage and the jolt of magic that he acted, or for the good of the town.

"He's right" Rojer added when Leesha remained silent. "The demons will be pushed to its edges when the ward activates, making them thicker still, ready to kill anyone who stumbles off the forbidding. We should just annihilate them in the open rather than try to hunt them through the trees later."

"S'what the Warded Man'd do," Gared said.

"The Warded Man would do half the killing himself," Leesha said, "but he's not here."

Gared nodded. "That's why we need yur help. Gonna need thunder-sticks and liquid demonfire. Lots of it."

"I see," Leesha said.

"Know yur busy," Gared said. "Got folk to do the mixing, if yu'll give 'em the recipe."

"You want me to give you the secrets of fire?" Leesha barked a laugh. "I would sooner let the knowledge pass from the world!"

"What's the difference 'tween that and my warded axe?" Gared asked. "Yu'll trust folk with one and not the other?"

"The difference is that your axe doesn't explode and destroy everything within fifty feet if you drop it or leave it out in the sun," Leesha said. "My own apprentices will be lucky if I teach *them* the secrets of fire one day."

"So we should build the refugee town on demon-infested land?" Gared asked.

"It's going to be an extension of the Hollow, not a refugee town," Leesha corrected, "and of course not. Draw up a plan, and if it's sound, I'll make what's needed. But," she added, "I'll be on hand to make sure no wood-brained idiot sets himself or the ripping woods on fire."

Gared shook his head. "Ent safe. Need you at the hospit, case anyone's hurt."

Leesha folded her arms. "Then you'll be fighting without the flame-work."

Wonda crossed her arms as well. "Ent no demon going to lay a claw on Mistress Leesha while I'm around, Gared Cutter, and I don't mean to wait at the hospit, either."

"We'll scour in a week," Leesha said. "Plenty of time to prepare the land and mix the chemics. Let Benn know, as well. Might as well let the demons charge some glass before we show them the sun."

Neither Gared nor Rojer seemed pleased, but Leesha knew they had no choice but to nod and agree. Perhaps not as subtle as Duchess Araine, who would have had the men convinced it was their own idea to have her at the scene, but not bad. She wondered if Bruna had secretly been the same, ruling the Hollow from her tiny hut without anyone even realizing.

They galloped across the land on black desert chargers, fifty warriors following Jardir and Ashan on their white stallions. Trailing behind but keeping them in sight, if barely, came Abban on his long-legged camel. They were forced to stop several times to allow him to catch up, usually by a stream where they could water the horses. Such things were almost commonplace in the green lands, something that never ceased to amaze the desert warriors.

"Everam's beard, these roads are stony," Abban whined when he finally reached one stream. He practically fell from his seat and groaned as he rubbed at his prodigious backside.

"I do not see why we needed to bring the *khaffit*, Deliverer," Ashan said.

"Because I want someone other than you and I who can count past his toes," Jardir said. "Abban sees things that other men do not, and I need to see all in the green lands if I am to make best use of them in Sharak Ka."

Abban continued to complain at every bump in the road or chill breeze, but Jardir found it easy to ignore the endless tirade as they rode on. He felt freer than he had in a decade, like an incredible weight had been taken from his shoulders. For however long this expedition took, weeks perhaps, he was responsible for nothing except Abban, Ashan, and the fifty hardened *dal'Sharum* at his back. Part of him wanted to keep on riding forever, away from the politics of *chin*, *Damaji*, and *dama'ting*.

They encountered some greenland refugees on the road, but these fled their path, and Jardir saw no gain in pursuing them. On foot and afraid to travel at night, there was little danger of them getting ahead and warning the Hollow, and none of them would dare attack the Spears of the Deliverer. Even the corelings at night shied from their path, for Jardir did not call halt when the sun set. Abban somehow managed to keep up in the night, though. He put his camel right in the center of the warriors, tolerating their jeers and spittle for the succor they offered.

It was on such a night that they came upon the Hollow. Shouts echoed down the road, along with sounds like thunder and great flashes of light.

They slowed their pace, and Jardir turned into the trees to follow the cacophony, his warriors following. Eventually, they came to the edge of a great swath of cleared land filled with the stumps of trees, where the *chin* fought their Northern *alagai'sharak*.

Great fires blazed in trenches, and coupled with the constant flare of wards throughout the battlefield, the clearing was lit as if it were daylight and littered with dead *alagai*. The fires and wards funneled demons into places where the Northerners stood ready to cut them to pieces.

"They've prepared their battlefield," Jardir mused.

Abban looked around, finding a suitable space, and staked his camel, removing a portable warding circle from its saddlebags, which he began to set up around them both.

"Even among so many warriors, you must hide behind wards like a coward?" Jardir asked him.

Abban shrugged. "I am *khaffit*," he said simply. Jardir snorted and turned back to watch the Northerners fight.

Unlike the *chin* from Everam's Bounty, these Northerners were tall and heavily muscled. The largest of them fought not with spear and shield but with great warded axes and mattocks. The men were of a size with the wood demons, and chopped at them like trees.

The Northerners fought well, but there were hundreds of wood demons coming at them. It seemed the *chin* would be overwhelmed when they broke apart, clearing ground for a line of archers to scour the field.

Jardir gaped to see the archers were clad in the long dresses the Northern women favored, displaying their faces and half their breasts like harlots.

"Their women join in *alagai'sharak*?" Ashan asked in shock. Jardir looked closer at the battlefield and saw that even some of those fighting in close quarters were female.

And there was a great giant, even among these tall people, who led every charge with a bellow that resonated for miles. He swung a great two-headed axe in one hand like a hatchet, and in the other he swung a machete as if it were a pocketknife.

One of the Northerners went down on one knee at the blow of an eight-foot-tall wood demon, and the giant tackled it away before it could land a killing blow. He lost his weapons in the tumble, but it made no difference as the *alagai* leapt at him. With one hand, the giant stopped the demon short, grabbing it, and with the other he landed a blow that flared with magic and sent the *alagai* reeling. Jardir saw he wore heavy gloves banded with warded metal.

The giant gave the wood demon no time to recover, falling on it and pummeling it about the head until he was covered in ichor and the demon lay still. He roared into the night, and with his thick mane of yellow hair and beard, he looked like nothing if not a lion atop its kill.

Another demon approached, but a slender boy with bright red hair and pale skin, dressed like a *khaffit* in a patchwork of bright color, stood before it and put up an instrument of some sort. He made a jarring sound, and the *alagai* grasped its head and shrieked in agony. The noise continued, and the demon fled as if in terror, right into another *chin's* waiting axe.

"Everam's beard," Abban breathed.

"What magic does that one carry?" Ashan asked.

"We must find out," Jardir agreed.

"Allow me to kill the giant and bring the boy to you, Deliverer," Hasik begged, his eyes taking on the mad light they always did before battle.

"Do nothing," Jardir said. "We are here to learn, not fight." He could tell his warriors did not like that answer, but he did not care, because two other figures had caught his eye. One was clearly a woman, carrying no weapon, only a small basket. The other was much larger, and dressed like a man, but carried a bow like the northern women. Her face was demon-scarred.

Both were clad in fine cloaks embroidered with hundreds of wards, and they wandered through the carnage unmolested by *alagai* and given a respectful berth by the other Northerners.

"They are unseen to the *alagai* as if they wear the Cloak of Kaji," Ashan said.

A demon clawed through the chest of a man, and he cried out and went down, dropping his axe. The cloaked women hurried to the man, the taller one putting an arrow in the demon as the slender one knelt by the man's side. She pulled back her hood, and Jardir saw her face.

She was even more beautiful than Inevera, her skin white like cream, a sharp contrast with her hair, black like the armor of a rock demon.

The woman tore the man's shirt, tending his wound while her female bodyguard stood watch over her, shooting any *alagai* that dared draw close.

"Some sort of Northern *dama'ting*?" Jardir mused aloud.

"A heathen parody of one, perhaps," Ashan said.

After a moment, the beautiful woman gave a command to her bodyguard, who slung her bow across her shoulders and lifted the wounded man in her arms. The way back out was blocked by a group of *alagai*, but the Northern *dama'ting* reached into her pouch and removed an object. Fire appeared in her hand, setting spark to it, and she drew back her arm and threw. An explosion blasted the *alagai* from her path, leaving them littering the ground, unmoving.

"Heathen, perhaps," Jardir said, "but these Northerners are not without power."

"The men must be cowards worse than *khaffit,* to depend on women for their rescue," Shanjat said. "I would rather die on the field."

"No," Jardir said, "the cowards are us, hiding here in the shadows while *chin* fight *alagai'sharak.*"

"They are our enemies," Ashan said.

Jardir looked at him and shook his head. "Perhaps by day, but all men are brothers in the night." He put up his night veil and lifted his spear, giving a war cry as he charged into the fight.

There was a surprised hesitation in his men, and then they, too, roared and followed.

"Krasians!" Merrem the butcher's wife screamed, and Rojer looked up in surprise, seeing that she was right. Dozens of black-clad Krasian warriors were charging into the clearing, brandishing spears and whooping. His blood went cold, and the bow slipped from his fiddle.

A demon almost killed him in that moment, but Gared cut the arm that swiped at him clean off with his machete.

"Eyes on the demons!" Gared bellowed for all the Cutters to hear. "Krasians ent gonna get a fight if we let the corelings do their work for 'em!"

But it quickly became apparent that the Krasians had no intention of attacking the Hollowers. Led by a man with a white turban and a warded spear that looked as if it was made entirely of polished silver, they fell upon the wood demons like a pack of wolves breaking into a chicken coop, killing with practiced efficiency.

The leader waded out alone into clusters of wood demons, but his fearlessness seemed justified, for he laid waste to them as easily as the Warded Man could have, his spear a blur and his limbs moving inhumanly fast.

The other warriors linked shields in fighting wedges, mowing demons like summer barley. One group was led by a man in a pristine white robe, a stark contrast with the black-clad warriors. The man in white held no weapons, but he strode through the battlefield confidently. A wood demon leapt at him and he stepped to the side, tripping it and shoving as it passed him by, driving it onto the spear of one of his warriors.

Another demon attacked him, but the man in white swung his torso left, then right, his feet never moving as he smoothly dodged the demon's clawed swipes. On its third swing, he caught its wrist and twisted, turning its own attack against it and flipping it over onto its back where a warrior casually skewered it.

Rojer and the others had assumed the scouring would take all night, and planned for reserves of fighters to be brought in as needed and much of Leesha's flamework used.

With the Krasians fighting, the battle was over in minutes.

Krasian and greenlander alike stood frozen when the last demon fell, staring at one another in shock. All continued to clutch their weapons, as if unsure the time for battle was past, but none dared make the first move, waiting for word from their leaders.

"The *chin* watch us with one eye," Jardir said to Ashan.

Ashan nodded. "The other eye looks to the giant and the red-haired *khaffit* boy who made the *alagai* run in terror."

"They stand as frozen as the others," Jardir noted.

"Not the true leaders, then," Ashan guessed. "*Kai'Sharum,* or the heathen equivalent. The giant might even be their Sharum Ka."

"Men still worthy of respect, then," Jardir said. "Come."

He strode over to the two, slipping his spear into his shoulder harness and showing his hands to indicate he meant no harm. When he stood before the men, he dipped a polite bow.

"I am Ahmann, son of Hoshkamin, of the line of Jardir, son of Kaji," he said in perfect Thesan, seeing the men's eyes flare in recognition. "This is Damaji Ashan." He gestured to Ashan, who imitated his shallow bow.

"Honored," Ashan said.

The two greenlanders looked at each other curiously. Finally, the red-haired boy shrugged, and the giant relaxed. Jardir realized with surprise that the boy was dominant.

"Rojer, son of Jessum, of the Inns of Riverbridge," the red-haired boy said, sweeping back his multicolored cloak. He set one leg forward and the other back, lowering himself in some sort of greenland bow.

"Gared Cutter," the giant said. "Er . . . son of Steave." He was even less civilized, stepping forward and sticking out his hand so quickly Jardir almost caught his wrist and broke his arm. It was only at the last moment that he realized the giant merely wanted to clasp hands in greeting. He squeezed hard, perhaps in some primitive test of manhood, and Jardir returned the pressure until both men felt their bones grinding together. The giant gave him an extra nod of respect when they finally broke apart.

"Shar'Dama Ka, more *chin* approach," Ashan said in Krasian. "One of their heretic clerics and the heathen healer."

"I've no wish to antagonize these people, Ashan," Jardir said. "Heathens or no, we will respect them as if they were *dama* and *dama'ting*."

"Shall I wash the feet of their *khaffit,* as well?" Ashan asked, disgusted.

"If I command it," Jardir replied, bowing deeply to the new arrivals. The red-haired boy stepped in smoothly to facilitate introductions. Jardir met the Holy Man, bowed, and forgot his name instantly, turning to the woman.

"Mistress Leesha Paper," Rojer introduced, "Herb Gatherer of Deliverer's Hollow." Leesha spread her skirts and dipped low, and Jardir found himself unable to take his eyes from her displayed cleavage until she rose. She looked him boldly in the eyes, and he was shocked to find hers were blue like the sky.

On impulse, Jardir took her hand and kissed it. He knew it was bold, especially among strangers, but Everam favored the bold, it was said. Leesha gasped at the move, and her pale cheeks reddened slightly. If it was possible, she became even more beautiful in that moment.

"Thank you for your assistance," Leesha said, nodding her head at the hundreds of *alagai* corpses in the clearing.

"All men are as brothers in the night," Jardir said, bowing. "We stand united."

Leesha nodded. "And during the day?"

"It seems the Northern women do more than just fight," Ashan murmured in Krasian.

Jardir smiled. "I believe all people should stand united in the day, as well."

Leesha's eyes narrowed. "United under you?"

Jardir felt Ashan and the greenland men tense. It was as if no one else on the scene mattered. Only they two would determine if the black demon ichor on the field of battle would soon be covered with red human blood.

But Jardir had no fear of that, feeling as if this meeting was destined long ago. He spread his hands helplessly. "If it is Everam's will, perhaps someday." He bowed again.

The corner of Leesha's mouth quirked in a smile. "You're honest, at least. Perhaps it's best, then, that the night is young. Will you and your councilors share tea with us?"

"We would be honored," Jardir said. "May my warriors pitch horses and tents in this clearing while they wait?"

"At the far end," Leesha said. "We have work yet to do on this side."

Jardir looked at her curiously, and then noted the greenlanders who had come out after the battle was complete. These were smaller, weaker men than the axe-wielding warriors, and they began gathering glittering objects off the battlefield.

"What are they about?" he asked, more to hear her voice again than because he actually cared what the Northern *khaffit* were doing.

Leesha looked to the side, then bent to retrieve a stoppered glass bottle, which she handed to Jardir. It was an elegant blow of glass, beautiful in its simplicity.

"Smash it with the butt of your spear," she said.

Jardir's brow furrowed at that, not understanding the significance of destroying something so beautiful. Perhaps it was some sort of friendship ritual. He pulled free the Spear of Kaji and complied with her request, but the butt of the spear ricocheted off the bottle with a clang, leaving the glass intact.

"Everam's beard," Jardir murmured. He tried repeatedly to smash the bottle, but failed every time. "Incredible."

"Warded glass," Leesha said, picking the bottle back up and giving it to him.

"A princely gift," Ashan noted in Krasian. "They are respectful, at least." Jardir nodded.

"Our peoples could learn much from each other, if we kept peace by day as well as night," Leesha said.

"I agree," Jardir said, staring into her eyes. "Let us discuss that, among other things, at our tea."

"Did you see his crown?" Leesha asked.

Rojer nodded. "And his metal spear. He's the one Marick and the Warded Man were talking about."

"Obviously," Leesha said. "I meant the crown itself. The Warded Man has the same wards on his own forehead."

"Really?" Rojer asked in surprise.

Leesha nodded, dropping her voice for only him to hear. "I don't think Arlen told us everything he knows about that man."

"Can't believe you invited him to tea," Wonda said.

"Should I have spat in his eye instead?" Leesha asked.

Wonda nodded. "Or had me shoot him. He's killed half the men in Rizon, and had his men force themselves on every flowered woman in the duchy!"

Wonda stopped short, then turned to Leesha suddenly, leaning in close. "You're going to drug him, aren't you?" she asked, her eyes glittering. "Take him and his men prisoner?"

"I'm going to do no such thing," Leesha said. "Everything we know about that man is hearsay. All we know for sure is that he and his men helped us fight off two hundred wood demons. He's our guest until his actions show he should be treated otherwise."

"Not to mention that kidnapping their Deliverer is the surest way under the sun to bring the Krasian army straight down on the Hollow," Rojer added.

"There's that, as well," Leesha agreed. "Ask Smitt to clear his taproom, and summon the town council. Let everyone see and judge this supposed demon of the desert for themselves."

"He's not what I expected, at all," Tender Jona said.

"Polite, like," Gared agreed. "All falsefaced, like the servants in the duke's palace."

"It's called manners, Gared," Leesha said. "You and the other men could use a few lessons in them yourselves."

"He has a point," Rojer said. "I expected a monster, not some royal smiling through his oiled beard."

"I know what you mean," Leesha said. "I certainly didn't expect him to be so handsome."

Jona, Rojer, and Gared all stopped short. Leesha walked several more steps before she noticed they were not keeping pace. She looked back to find the men staring at her. Even Wonda had a surprised look on her face.

"What?" she asked.

"We're just going to pretend you didn't say that," Rojer said after a moment. He resumed walking, the others following his lead. Leesha shook her head and followed.

"These greenlanders are worse than we thought," Ashan said as they walked back to join the other men. "I cannot believe they take orders from a woman!"

"But what a woman!" Jardir exclaimed. "Powerful and exotic and beautiful as the dawn."

"She dresses like a harlot," Ashan said. "You should have killed her simply for daring to meet your eyes."

Jardir hissed and waved the thought away. "It is death to kill a *dama'-ting*."

"Your pardon, Shar'Dama Ka, but she is *not* a *dama'ting*," Ashan said. "She is a heathen. All these greenlanders are infidel, praying to a false god."

Jardir shook his head. "They follow Everam whether they know it or not. There are only two Divine Laws in the Evejah: Worship one god, and dance *alagai'sharak*. Beyond that, every tribe is entitled to their own customs. Perhaps these greenlanders are not so different from us. Perhaps their customs are simply foreign to us."

Ashan opened his mouth to protest, but a look from Jardir made it clear the discussion was over. Ashan's mouth snapped shut, and he bowed. "Of course, if the Shar'Dama Ka says it, it must be so."

"Go and tell the *dal'Sharum* to make camp," Jardir ordered. "You, Hasik, Shanjat, and Abban will join me for their tea."

"We're bringing the *khaffit*?" Ashan scowled. "He is not worthy to take tea with men."

"He is more fluent in their tongue than you are, my friend," Jardir said, "and Hasik and Shanjat barely have a handful of greenland words between them. This is the very reason I chose to bring him. He will prove invaluable at this meeting."

It seemed the whole town had gathered around Smitt's Tavern by the time the Krasians arrived. Leesha let only the town council and their spouses attend, but coupled with Smitt's small army of children and grandchildren who were setting and serving, they outnumbered the Krasians greatly.

The crowd rumbled ominously as Jardir walked to the tavern. "Go back to the sand!" someone shouted, and many voices grunted in agreement.

If the Krasians were bothered at all, they gave no sign. They strutted through the crowd with their heads held high, unafraid. Only one, a rotund man clad in bright colors and limping on a cane, looked at the Hollowers warily as he passed. Leesha stood by the door, ready to rush out if the crowd turned ugly.

"You're right, he *is* handsome," Elona said at her ear.

Leesha turned to her in surprise. "Who told you I said that?" Elona only smiled.

"Welcome," Leesha said, when Jardir made it to the door. She and her mother gave identical curtsies. Jardir looked at Elona, then glanced over to Leesha. They were similar enough that no one could mistake their relation.

"Your . . . sister?" Jardir asked.

"My mother, Elona," Leesha rolled her eyes while Elona tittered and allowed Jardir to kiss her hand. "And my father, Ernal," she nodded to her father. Jardir bowed to him.

"Allow me to introduce my councilors," Jardir said, gesturing to the men behind him. "You have met Damaji Ashan. These are *kai'Sharum* Shanjat and my *dal'Sharum* bodyguard, Hasik." The men bowed with the introduction. Jardir made no effort to introduce the fifth member of his entourage, moving on down the receiving line with his men, bowing and making introductions.

The fifth was unlike any of the others. Where they were lean, he was fat. Where they dressed in somber, solid colors, he was clad as brightly as any Jongleur. And where they were fit and strong, he leaned on his crutch so heavily that it seemed he would fall over without it.

Leesha opened her mouth to greet the man as he entered, but his eyes passed over her, and he bowed to her father. "A pleasure to meet you at last, Ernal Paper."

Erny looked at him curiously. "Do I know you?"

"Abban am' Haman am'Kaji," the man introduced himself.

"I . . . used to sell you paper," Erny stumbled after a moment. "I, ah . . . actually still have your last order sitting in my shop. I was waiting on payment when the Messengers stopped coming from Rizon."

"Six hundred sheets of your daughter's flower press, I believe," Abban said.

"Night, that was you?!" Leesha exclaimed. "Do you know how many hours I slaved over those sheets, only to have them sitting in the dryhouse like . . . like compost!"

Jardir was there in an instant, breaking away from an introduction to Smitt as if it were meaningless.

"What have you said to offend our host, *khaffit?*" he demanded.

Abban bowed as low as his crutch would allow. "It seems I owe her father some money, Deliverer, for paper she and her father made for me years ago that I was not able to claim after our borders closed."

Jardir snarled, backhanding him viciously to the ground. "You will pay him triple what you owe, immediately!" Abban cried out as he struck the floor, spitting blood.

Leesha shoved Jardir aside, running to Abban's side and kneeling beside him. He tried to pull away, but she took his head firmly in her hands, examining him. His lip was split, but she didn't think it would require stitching.

She rose quickly and glared at Jardir. "Just what in the Core is the matter with you?!"

A shocked look came over Jardir's face, as if Leesha had suddenly grown horns. "He is only *khaffit*," he explained. "A weakling without honor."

"I don't care what he is!" Leesha snapped, storming up to Jardir so their noses practically touched, her eyes ablaze like blue flame. "He is a guest under our roof, as are you, and if you wish to remain so, you'll mind your ripping manners and keep your hands to yourself!"

Jardir stood there, stunned, and his councilors looked equally shocked. All turned to their leader for a cue on how to react. The warriors flexed their hands, as if readying them to reach for the short spears slung over their shoulders, and Leesha's fingers itched to reach into one of the many pockets of her apron for a handful of blinding powder in case they did.

But Jardir broke the stare and stepped back, bowing deeply. "You are right, of course. I apologize for bringing violence to your table." He turned to Abban. "I will purchase the pages from you at triple what you must pay her father," he said loudly, turning to eye Leesha. "Anything so precious to Mistress Leesha must be a treasure indeed."

Abban touched his forehead to the floor, and then braced himself on his cane to rise. Erny rushed over to help him, though the small man could do little to shift the other's great bulk.

Jardir turned and smiled at Leesha, beaming with pride as if he honestly thought he could impress her any more with a display of wealth than he had with one of violence.

"Handsome or no, he's a pompous ass," Leesha muttered quietly to Rojer.

"Perhaps," Rojer agreed, "but an ass who can crush the Hollow like a bug if he wishes."

Leesha scowled. "Don't go betting on that."

"The Northern women have steel in them," Hasik observed in Krasian as they were ushered to one of the tall greenland tables with its hard benches.

"Ours do as well," Jardir replied, "they simply hide it beneath their robes." All of them, even Abban, laughed at that and did not disagree.

Tea was served by children, along with plates of hard biscuit. The Northern Holy Man cleared his throat, and all eyes turned to him. Ashan stared at the Tender like a raptor watching a rodent. The greenland cleric paled under the *dama*'s gaze, but he pressed on.

"It is our custom to pray before meals," he said.

Elona snorted, and Jona glared at her. Jardir ignored the woman, though he was shocked at her rudeness. "That is our custom as well, Tender," he said, bowing. "It is right to give thanks to Everam for all things."

Jona's lip twitched slightly at the name Jardir attached to the Creator, but he nodded, mollified for the most part.

"Creator," Jona intoned, holding up his teacup in both hands like an offering, "we thank you for the food and drink before us, a symbol of the life and fruitful bounty you have given. We pray for the strength to better serve you, and ask your blessings for ourselves, and all those who have no table to gather at this night."

"Not so fruitful a bounty this year," Elona muttered, picking up one of the hard biscuits, her nose crinkling with distaste. The woman gave a sudden start, and Jardir guessed from the way she glared at Leesha that her daughter had kicked her under the table.

"I am sorry we cannot offer you better fare," Leesha said when Jardir caught her eye, "but depredations of war have been hard on our village, with thousands of refugees having senselessly lost everything they own, and many loved ones, as well."

"Senselessly?" Ashan whispered in Krasian. "They insult you and your holy path, Deliverer!"

"No!" Abban hissed. "It is a challenge. Answer carefully." Ashan glared at him.

"Be silent, both of you!" Jardir hissed. He took his eyes from both Leesha and her mother, turning to nod to the Tender.

"Your prayer over bread is much the same as ours," he said. "In Krasia, we pray over even an empty bowl, for with Everam's will, it can strengthen in ways a full one cannot."

He looked back to Leesha. "I am told your village was small and little different from any other a year ago," he said. "And yet now you are large and powerful. I see no hungry on your streets. No beggars or wailers or cripples. Instead, you stand tall in the night, fighting demons by the hundred. Like steel, my coming has tempered your village and made it stronger."

"Wern't you that tempered it," Gared snapped. "Warded Man done that, back when you were still eating sand out in the desert."

Hasik tensed. Jardir doubted he understood fully what the greenlander had said, but the giant's tone was clear. He whisked his fingers at Hasik, calming him.

"I would know more of this Warded Man," Jardir said. "I have heard much of him in Everam's Bounty, but nothing from one who had actually seen the man."

"He's the Deliverer, that's all ya need t'know," Gared growled. "Gave us back the magic we lost all them years ago."

"Combat wards to fight the *alagai*," Jardir said. Gared nodded.

"May I see a weapon he has warded?" Jardir asked.

Gared hesitated, his eyes flicking over to Leesha. Jardir's naturally followed, and again her blue eyes, like cool water, threatened to drown him in their hidden depths. She smiled, and a thrill went through him.

"We will show you," Leesha said, smiling coyly, "if you will show us something of yours. Your spear, perhaps."

Even Abban gasped at her audacity, but Jardir only smiled. He reached for his spear, but Ashan grabbed his hand.

"Deliverer, no!" Ashan hissed. "The Spear of Kaji is unfit for the hands of *chin*."

"It is no longer the Spear of Kaji, Ashan," Jardir said in Krasian. "It is the Spear of Ahmann, and I will do with it as I please. It will not be the first time it has been touched by *chin* hands, and its blessings remain."

"What if they try to steal it?" Hasik asked.

Jardir looked at him, his eyes calm. "If they try, we will kill every man, woman, and child in this village and raze it to the ground."

The matter closed, he lifted the spear horizontally before him. In response, Gared reached to his belt, pulling free a long blade. Hasik and Shanjat tensed, ready to strike, but the giant flipped the weapon over, holding the blade to offer Jardir the hilt. As one, they switched.

There was no pretense of decorum, then, as those skilled in warding on both sides rushed to examine the weapons.

Jardir turned the long blade over to catch the light as it ran in glittering rivers along the intricate wards etched in its surface. He saw immediately that most of the wards were the same his people used to ward their own weapons, symbols taken from the Spear of Kaji, which held almost every combat ward in existence.

But the warding went beyond cold functionality, like the harshly etched spears of the *dal'Sharum*. There was an artistry to it that rivaled anything Jardir had ever seen outside the Spear itself, hundreds of wards flowing in harmony to weave a net of incredible power that was both beautiful to look upon and terrible for an *alagai* to behold.

"Exquisite," Jardir murmured.

"Priceless," Abban said.

"Could this Warded Man have stolen the symbols from Anoch Sun?" Ashan wondered.

"Ridiculous," Jardir said. "No one has been there in a thousand years, except . . ."

He looked at his men, and all eyes had lit with the same thought.

"No," Jardir said at last. "No, he is dead."

"Of course, it must be so," Ashan echoed after a slight pause, and the others all nodded.

They looked up to see Leesha and her father, now wearing spectacles, examining the Spear of Kaji a little too closely. They had held it long enough to appreciate the grandeur, but he saw no reason to give away all its secrets yet.

"These wards are strong," he said, holding the blade back out to Gared, handle-first. He looked pointedly at the spear, and the greenlanders grudgingly returned it. The look of longing in Leesha's eyes as the spear was returned was gratifying. She was hungry for its secrets.

"Where is this Warded Man?" Jardir asked Gared when the spear was again tucked safely over his shoulder. "I would very much like to meet him."

"He comes and goes," Leesha cut in before the giant could answer.

Jardir nodded at her. "Was it he that gave you your wondrous cloak? Truly, it is like the Robe of Kaji, himself, to let you walk past *alagai* unseen."

Leesha's cheeks colored, and Jardir realized he had just complimented her in some way.

"The Cloaks of Unsight are my own creation," she said. "I altered wards of confusion and sight, along with a mild forbiddance, so that no coreling big or small can see one wearing it."

"Incredible," Jardir said. "Everam must speak in your ear, if you are altering wards, especially to make something of such divine beauty and power."

Leesha looked down at her cloak, fingering it absently. Finally, she clucked and got to her feet, unfastening the silver ward clasp at her throat. "Take it," she said, holding the cloak out to Jardir.

"Are you crazed?!" Elona shouted, moving to block her way, much as Ashan had done to him before.

"The cloak's only good against demons," she said, as much to her mother as Jardir. "Take it to remind you who the real enemy is, when the sun rises tomorrow." She pulled her arm away from her mother and held the cloak out to Jardir.

Jardir put his hands flat on the tabletop and bowed. "That is too great a gift, and I have nothing to give in return. By Everam, I cannot accept."

"The reminder is all I want in return," Leesha said. Jardir bowed again, taking the wondrous cloak with widening eyes. If the wards on this so-called Warded Man's weapon were a harmony, Leesha's Cloak of Unsight was a symphony. He folded the cloak carefully and tucked it in his robe before he or any of his councilors began to study the gift to distraction.

"Thank you, Mistress Leesha, daughter of Erny, Herb Gatherer of Deliverer's Hollow," he said, bowing again. "You honor me greatly with your gift."

Leesha smiled and returned to her seat. For a moment, the greenlanders made a great pretense of sipping their tea, murmuring to one another as they did. Jardir allowed them this conference time, looking to Abban.

"Tell me of the red-haired boy who dresses like a *khaffit,*" he commanded.

Abban bowed. "He is what the greenlanders call a Jongler, Deliverer. They are traveling storytellers and music makers who dress in bright colors to announce their craft. It is considered an honored profession, and its practitioners are often highly regarded figures of inspiration."

Jardir nodded, digesting the knowledge. "He had power over the *alagai* with his music. Commanded them with it. What of that?"

Abban shrugged. "The tales of the Warded Man speak of such a one, who charms *alagai* with his magic, but I know nothing of this power. It is not common, I imagine."

Rojer watched uneasily as the Krasians cast furtive glances his way. It was obvious they were talking about him, but while Rojer's trained ear had already begun to isolate the sounds and patterns of their surprisingly musical tongue, understanding was still far off.

The Krasians both terrified and fascinated him, much as the Warded Man did. Rojer was a teller of stories as much as a fiddler, and he had woven many a tale of Krasia yet he had never met someone from that land. A thousand questions shouted in his head, but caught in a jumble before they could reach his tongue, because these weren't the exotic princes of his stories. Rojer had ridden the road to Rizon and seen their handiwork. Cultured or no, these were murderers, rapists, and bandits.

Jardir glanced his way again, and before Rojer could avert his gaze, their eyes met. Rojer started, feeling like a cornered hare.

"Forgive me, we have been impolite," Jardir said, bowing.

Rojer pretended to scratch his chest, but it was just an excuse to touch his talisman. He drew strength both from the medallion and the reassuring presence of Gared at his side. Not for the first time, Rojer was glad for the mighty woodcutter's oath to keep him protected.

"No offense taken," he said, nodding.

"There are no Jonglers among my people," Jardir said. "Your profession interests us."

"You don't have musicians?" Rojer asked, shocked.

"We do," Jardir said, "but in Krasia, music is used only to praise Everam, not to charm demons on the battlefield. Tell me, is this power common in the North?"

Rojer barked a laugh. "Not in the least." He threw back his tea, wishing the cup held something stronger. "I can't even teach it. Don't know quite how I do it myself."

"Perhaps Everam speaks to you," Jardir suggested. "Perhaps He has blessed your line with this power. Have any of your sons shown promise?"

Rojer laughed again. "Sons? I'm not even married."

The Krasians seemed shocked at this. "A man of your power should have many brides to bear him sons," Jardir said.

Rojer chuckled, lifting his cup to them. "Agreed. I *should* have many brides."

Leesha snorted. "I'd like to see you handle one." Everyone on both sides of the table had a laugh at Rojer's expense. He weathered it silently; jokes at his expense were nothing new in the Hollow, but he felt his cheeks coloring all the same. He looked at Jardir, only to find that the Krasian leader was not among those laughing.

"May I ask you a personal question, son of Jessum?" Jardir asked.

Rojer touched the medallion at his father's name, but he nodded.

"How did you get that scar?" Jardir asked, pointing at the crippled hand Rojer had raised, missing two fingers and part of the palm besides. "It looks old, too old for you to have gotten it fighting *alagai* as a man, and it hinders you little, as if you've had it for many years."

Rojer felt his blood run cold. His eyes flicked to the fat merchant prince in his bright silks; treated with such derision by his fellows because he was crippled. He wondered if the Krasians thought him less a man for having only half a hand.

Everyone else had stopped talking, waiting on Rojer's answer. They had all been half listening anyway, but now everyone stared at them openly.

Rojer scowled. *Are the Hollowers so different?* he wondered. None of them, not even Leesha, had ever so much as mentioned his crippled hand, trying to pretend it didn't exist, and then staring when they thought he wasn't watching.

At least he's honest about his curiosity, Rojer thought, looking back to Jardir. *And I don't give a coreling's shit what he thinks of me.*

"Demons broke through our wards when I was a child of three," he said. "My father stood with an iron fireplace poker to hold them off while my mother fled with me. A flame demon leapt upon her back, biting though my hand and into her shoulder."

"How did you survive this?" Jardir asked. "Did your father save you?"

Rojer shook his head. "My father was dead by then. My mother killed the flame demon, and pushed me into a bolt-hole."

There were gasps around the table, and even Jardir's eyes widened sharply.

"Your *mother* killed a flame demon?" he asked.

Rojer nodded. "Pulled it off me and drowned it in a water trough. The water boiled and left her arms blistered and red by the time its thrashing stopped."

"Oh, Rojer, how terrible!" Leesha moaned. "You never told me any of that!"

Rojer shrugged. "You never asked. No one's ever asked me about my hand before. Everyone, even you, avoids it with their eyes."

"I always thought you wanted privacy," Leesha said. "I didn't want to make you uncomfortable by calling attention to your . . ."

"Deformity?" Rojer supplied, irritated by the pity in her voice.

Jardir stood sharply, his face enraged. Everyone on both sides of the table tensed, ready in an instant to fight or flee.

"That is an *alagai* scar!" he shouted, reaching across the table and grabbing Rojer's hand, holding it up for all to see. "Nie take any who look upon you in pity; this is a badge of honor!

"Scars show our defiance of the *alagai*!" he shouted. "And of Nie Herself! They tell Her we have looked at the maw of Her abyss, and spit in it."

"Hasik!" Jardir pointed to the largest of his warriors. At his command, the warrior stood and opened his armored robe, showing a semicircle of tooth marks that covered half his torso.

"Clay demon," he said, his accent thick. "Big," he added, spreading his arms.

Jardir turned to Gared and narrowed his eyes in challenge.

"Not bad," Gared grunted. "Reckon I got it beat, though." He pulled the shirt from his muscled chest, turning to reveal a thick line of claw marks running from his right shoulder to his left hip. "Woodie got me good," he said. "Smaller man mighta been cut in half."

Rojer watched in wonder as it went around the room like a little ripple, people on both sides of the table standing up to show scars and shouting their stories, arguing over whose were bigger. After the last year in the Hollow, there was hardly a person in town who didn't have at least one.

But there was no air of regret in the room. People were roaring with laughter as near misses were recalled and sometimes pantomimed, even the

Krasians slapping their knees in delight. Rojer looked to Wonda, the girl's face horribly scarred, and saw her smiling for the first time he could recall.

When the cacophony was at it highest, Jardir stood upon his bench like a master Jongleur. "Let the *alagai* see our scars, and despair!" he cried, removing his own robe.

Muscles rippled along his olive skin, but it was not that which drew amazed gasps from every mouth in the room. It was his scars. They were wards. Hundreds of them, perhaps thousands, cut into his skin like the tattoos of the Warded Man.

"Night, maybe he *is* the Deliverer," Rojer muttered.

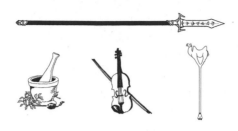

CHAPTER 25

ANY PRICE

:: 333 AR SPRING ::

"YOU'D BEST LIMP QUICKER," Hasik told Abban with a laugh, "or you will be left behind in the darkness."

Abban grimaced in pain, sweat running in rivulets down his thick-jowled face. Ahmann set a brutal pace back to the Krasian camp, and he strode ahead with Ashan, leaving poor Abban stuck between Hasik and Shanjat, two men who had tortured him since childhood and did worse now.

Just a week earlier, Hasik had raped one of Abban's daughters when he came to their pavilion to deliver a message. The time before, it was one of his wives. Jurim and Shanjat had made a point of taking Abban's *nie'Sharum* sons under their wing in the Kaji'sharaj, instilling in them such a disgust of their *khaffit* father that Abban's heart felt torn. All the Spears of the Deliverer jeered and spat at him, striking him at their pleasure when the Shar'-Dama Ka was not about. They all knew Ahmann from of old, and resented that Abban had the Deliverer's ear as they did not. Abban knew that if he ever fell from Ahmann's favor, his life would be short indeed.

But the moment they left the forbidding generated by the giant ward of Deliverer's Hollow, Abban felt his skin crawling, and he was forced to accept that there was nothing the *Sharum* could do to him that would make him too prideful to beg their protection in the night.

Such was the fate of *khaffit*.

"I do not understand why you treat these *chin* weaklings as though they were true men," Ashan said to Ahmann as they walked.

"These people are strong," Ahmann replied. "Even their women have *alagai* scars."

"Their women are brazen like harlots," Ashan said, "and should see more of the back of their husbands' hands. The one who leads them is worst of all! I cannot believe you let her scold you like a . . . a . . ."

"Dama'ting?" Ahmann asked.

"More like the Damajah," Ashan said. "And this woman is neither."

Ahmann's face twitched slightly, a barely noticeable sign of irritation that nevertheless would have sent Abban running for cover if there had been any to run to.

But Ahmann kept his temper. "Think, Ashan," he said. "Should I waste warriors conquering these people for Sharak Ka when they fight the *alagai* already?"

"They do not fight under you, Shar'Dama Ka," Ashan pointed out. "The Evejah commands that all warriors obey the Deliverer for Sharak Ka to be won."

Ahmann nodded. "And so it shall be. But I did not unite the tribes of Krasia by killing men. Unity came from mixing my blood with theirs by marrying their *dama'ting*. I see no reason not to do the same in the North."

"You would marry that . . . that . . ." Ashan was incredulous.

"That what?" Ahmann asked. "That beautiful woman who kills *alagai* with a wave of her hand, and wards like a sorceress of old?" He lifted the warded cloak she had given him and held it up to his face, closing his eyes and inhaling deeply. "Even the scent of her intoxicates me. I must have her."

"She isn't even Evejan!" Ashan spat. "She is an infidel!"

"Even infidels are part of Everam's plan, my friend," Ahmann said. "Can you not see it? The only tribe in the North that fights *alagai'sharak* is led by a woman, a Northern healer blessed with powers never before seen. By marrying her, I can add their strength to our own without a drop of red blood spilled. It is as if Everam Himself has arranged the match. I can feel His will thrumming in me, and it will not be denied."

Ashan looked ready to argue further, but it was clear Ahmann considered the matter closed. He scowled, but he bowed. "As the Deliverer wills," he said through gritted teeth.

They reached the camp at last, and Abban breathed a sigh of relief when he saw that Ahmann's pavilion was raised and waiting. The *dal'Sharum* surrounded it, sleeping in shifts and ever alert for any threat, demon or otherwise.

"Abban, meet with me," Ahmann said. "Shanjat and Ashan, see to the men."

Damaji and *kai'Sharum* exchanged a bitter look, but they gave no argument and left to comply. Hasik moved to follow Ahmann, but Ahmann stopped him with a look.

"I do not require a bodyguard to meet with a *khaffit*," Ahmann said.

Hasik bowed. "When you did not give me another assignment, Deliverer, I assumed my place was with you."

"My pavilion could use raising," Abban suggested.

Ahmann nodded. "Hasik, see to it."

Hasik looked up at Abban, murder in his eyes, but Abban, safe behind Ahmann, gave not the obsequious bow of a *khaffit* but a full mocking grin.

Abban turned and stepped into the pavilion, holding the tent flap for Ahmann to enter. The impotent rage on Hasik's face as he closed the flap was poor recompense for his daughter's virginity, but Abban took his revenge where he could find it.

Jardir turned to Abban once they were alone.

"I apologize for striking you," he said. "It was—"

"Meant to impress the woman, I know," Abban cut him off. "And it would have been a fair bargain had it worked, but these *chin* see the world differently than we do."

Jardir nodded, thinking of how the Par'chin used to defend Abban. "Our cultures are a natural insult to each other. I should have known better."

"One must take especial care when dealing with *chin*," Abban agreed.

Jardir lifted the Spear of Kaji. "I am a warrior, Abban. My strategies are for conquering men and killing *alagai*. I am not good at the sort of . . . manipulation," he spat the word, "that you and Inevera excel at."

"Lies have always been bile on your lips, Ahmann," Abban agreed, with a bow that seemed equal parts deferential and mocking.

"So how do I claim this woman?" Jardir asked. "I saw her eyes upon me. Do you think she has the liberty of *dama'ting* to choose her husband, or should I approach her father?"

"*Dama'ting* have their liberty because their fathers are not known," Abban said. "Mistress Leesha made a point of introducing us to her father, and then gave you the cloak, a clear sign she is open to courting. An ordinary maiden might give a fine robe to a suitor, but her gift is one worthy of the Deliverer."

"So it should only be a matter of arranging a dower with her father," Jardir said.

Abban shook his head. "Erny is a hard negotiator, but he will be the simple part. I would be more concerned that the Damajah might oppose the match, and the *Damaji* support her."

"I will kill any *Damaji* who defies me in this," Jardir said, "even Ashan."

"What message will that send to your army, Ahmann," Abban asked, "when their leader kills his own *Damaji* for the sake of a *chin* woman?"

Jardir scowled. "What does it matter? Inevera has no reason to oppose it."

Abban shrugged. "I only suggest it because the Damajah may find she has difficulty dominating this Northern woman as she does your other *Jiwah Sen*."

Jardir knew Abban was right. He had always thought Inevera the most powerful woman in the world, but this Leesha of Deliverer's Hollow seemed to rival her in every way. She would not play the role of a lesser wife, and Inevera would tolerate nothing less.

"But it is that very indomitability that I must have beside me, if I am to lead the *chin* to Sharak Ka," Jardir said. "Perhaps I can marry her in secret."

Abban shook his head. "Word of the union would reach the Damajah eventually, and she could cancel it with a word, which Leesha's tribe might take as an unbearable insult."

Jardir shook his head. "There is a way. This is Everam's will. I can feel it."

"Perhaps . . ." Abban began, twisting his fingers through the curl of his oiled beard.

"Yes?" Jardir asked.

Abban was silent a moment, but then shook his head and waved his hand dismissively. "Only a thought that did not hold water when filled."

"What thought?" Jardir asked, and his tone made it clear he would not ask again.

"Ah," Abban said, "I had only wondered, what if the Damajah were only your *Krasian Jiwah Ka*? If that were so, there might be wisdom to appointing a Northern *Jiwah Ka* as well, to arrange marriages to *chin* in the green lands."

Abban shook his head. "But not even Kaji ever had two *Jiwah Ka*."

Jardir rubbed his fingers together, feeling the smooth scars of the wards cut into his skin as he pondered.

"Kaji lived three thousand years ago," he said at last, "and the sacred texts are incomplete. Who is to say for certain how many *Jiwah Ka* he had?"

When clever Abban did not immediately reply, Jardir smiled. "You will go tomorrow to the house of Leesha's father to settle your debt," he commanded, "and to learn what dower he asks for her."

Abban bowed and turned to go.

Abban smiled to the greenlanders as he limped through the village on his camel-headed crutch. They stared at him, many mistrustful, but while his crutch was an invitation for violence against him in Krasia, it seemed to have the opposite effect among the *chin*. They would be ashamed of themselves to hit a man who could not properly defend himself, just as they were ashamed to hit a woman. It explained why their women took such liberties.

Abban found he liked the green lands more and more as time went by. The weather was neither unbearably hot nor unbearably cold, whereas the desert held both extremes, and there was abundance in the North like nothing Abban had ever dreamed. The possibilities for profit were endless. Already his wives and children were making a fortune in Everam's Bounty, and most of the green lands were as yet untapped. In Krasia, he was wealthy, but still only considered half a man. In the North, he could live like a *Damaji*.

Not for the first time, Abban wondered at Ahmann's true thoughts. Did he truly believe himself the Deliverer, and that such things as marrying this woman were Everam's will, or was that just a pretense for power?

If it were any other man, Abban would have thought the latter, but Ahmann had always been naïvely true about such things, and might well harbor such delusions of grandeur.

It was ridiculous, of course, but the belief in his divinity shared by almost every man, woman, and child in Krasia gave Ahmann such tremendous power that it almost didn't matter if it was true or not. Either way, Abban served the most powerful man in the world, and if they had not returned to their old friendship, they had at least fallen into its patterns.

But there was a new thread to the pattern now, the Damajah, and Abban was far too skilled a manipulator not to know another one on sight. Inevera twisted Ahmann to her own ends, and those ends were opaque even to Abban, who had made fortunes on his ability to see the desires in others' hearts.

The Damajah had some unknown power over Ahmann, but it was tenuous. He was Shar'Dama Ka. *Dama'ting* or no, if he commanded it, the people would not hesitate to tear her apart to please him.

Abban knew better than to come between them, of course. He had survived too long to make so foolish a mistake. The moment Inevera sensed his disloyalty to her, she would crush him like a scorpion beneath her sandal, and not even Ahmann could stop it. Abban was as far beneath the Damajah as she was below Ahmann. Farther.

The only man who can truly handle a woman is a woman, Abban's father had said to him many times before he died. It was good advice.

Leesha Paper would shake the very foundations of Inevera's power, perhaps freeing Ahmann of her entirely. And the best part was, the Damajah would never see Abban's hand in it.

Abban's smile widened.

Abban was pleased to learn Erny was as formidable a haggler in person as he had been through his Messengers. Abban had contempt for anyone who could not haggle. He excluded only Ahmann from that rule, because it was less that Ahmann *could* not haggle than that he *would* not.

The result was a fair price, but after Abban tripled it as Ahmann had commanded, it was a sizable sum. Erny and his wife seemed quite pleased as Abban counted out the gold.

"Stock's all here," Erny said, putting the box of Leesha's flower-pressed paper on the counter and lifting off the lid.

Abban ran his fingers lightly over the top sheet of the colorful paper, feeling the imprint of the artfully arranged flowers embedded in the weave. He closed his eyes and inhaled. "Still smells sweet after all this time," he said, smiling.

"Keep it dry, and it will last forever," Erny said, "or close enough for mortal men."

"Your daughter seems touched by Everam," Abban said. "Perfect in every way, like a Heavenly Seraph."

Elona snorted, but Erny glared at her and she fell silent.

"She is," Erny agreed.

"My master would like to purchase her as a bride," Abban said. "He has empowered me to negotiate her dower, and will be most generous."

"How generous?" Elona asked.

"It doesn't matter!" Erny snapped. "Leesha isn't for sale like some horse!"

"Of course, of course," Abban said, bowing to buy himself some time to consider the situation. Erny's reaction was unexpected, and it was difficult to tell if Abban had given honest offense, or if this was just a haggling tactic to drive up the price.

"Please forgive my poor sense of words," Abban said. "Your language eludes me at critical times, it seems. I meant no offense."

Erny seemed mollified at that, and Abban drew his face into the smile that had beguiled thousands of customers into thinking he was their friend. "My master understands that your daughter leads your tribe, and is not some common piece of merchandise," he said. "He intends her and your tribe great honor, mingling your blood with his own. At his side, your daughter would be first of all the women in the North, and wield influence in both the Deliverer's court and bed to prevent unnecessary bloodshed as my master comes north."

"Is that a threat?" Erny demanded. "Are you saying your master will come kill us to take her, if I don't sell her to you?"

Abban's face heated. He *had* given offense, and deeply. The Par'chin had always told him the Krasians were quick to temper, but it seemed the Northerners were no less so if one spoke to them too truly.

Abban bowed deeply, spreading his hands. "Please, my friend, let us begin again. My master makes no threats and wishes to give no offense. Among our people, it is the father's duty to arrange the marriages of his daughters. Part of the arrangement is that the groom's family provide the father and bride with dower symbolic of her value. I was given to understand that Northerners shared this custom."

"We do," Elona cut in before Erny could reply.

"Some folk might do that sort of thing," Erny corrected, "but that's not how I raised my Leesha. Your master wants to marry my girl, he'll have to court her just like anybody else, and if *she* decides she wants him, then he can come and ask my blessing on it."

It seemed backward to Abban, but it made little difference. He bowed once more. "I will make your terms clear to my master. I expect he will begin to court your daughter immediately."

Erny's eyes widened. "I didn't . . . ow!" he cried as Elona dug her nails into his arm most unsubtly. Abban noted the move with interest. His wives were by no means docile, but they would never dare unman him so in front of a customer.

"Ent hurtin' anyone, he comes bringin' flowers," Elona said. "You said yourself it's Leesha's choice."

Erny looked at her a long moment, then he sighed and nodded. He took the box cover and slipped it back over Leesha's paper.

"It's a heavy box," he said. "You want me to get a boy to carry it for you?"

Abban bowed. "Please."

"I think the boys are all busy," Elona said, "and I could use a stroll. I'll carry the paper."

Again Abban was confused. In Krasia, it was expected that women do such labor, but from the way Erny goggled at his wife, Abban could tell he was shocked.

He watched Elona as she came around the counter, taking in her beauty, even with her youth fading. Perhaps she was a pillow-wife, given light work to be kept close at hand should her husband's lust be aroused. Many Krasian men kept such, but Abban had never tolerated that sort of laziness, expecting his youngest and most beautiful wives to work as hard as the rest.

As they walked down the isolated path from Erny's shop, Abban turned to her. "I pray to Everam my misunderstanding of your ways gave you and your husband no lasting offense."

Elona shook her head. "We ent much different from you, only here, fathers *approve* marriages, but mothers *arrange* them. Erny ent blessing anything until the dower's set."

Abban stopped short, finally understanding. "Of course. I regret that my master's mother, Kajivah, is still in Everam's Bounty with his wives. May I negotiate in her stead?"

Elona nodded, but she raised an eyebrow. "He has other wives?"

"Of course," Abban said. "Ahmann Jardir is the Shar'Dama Ka."

Elona frowned. "Tell him if he's wise, he'll never so much as mention his other wives to my daughter. Girl gets jealous like a thundercloud."

Abban nodded. "I will be sure to advise him, thank you. I assume your daughter is a virgin?"

"Course she is," Elona snapped.

Abban bowed. "Please, take no offense. In Krasia, a man's First Wife will inspect prospective brides personally, but if that is not your custom, your word will suffice."

"It sure as the Core ent our custom to let anyone but husbands and Herb Gatherers look between our legs," Elona said, "so don't you or your master go getting any ideas about sampling the milk."

"Of course," Abban said, nodding and smiling now that the haggling had begun.

Jardir paced his pavilion like an animal, waiting for Abban to return.

"What did he say?" he demanded the moment the *khaffit* entered the tent. "Is it done?"

Abban shook his head, and Jardir took a deep breath to embrace the disappointment and let it pass through him without harm.

"Mistress Leesha is more like *dama'ting* than I thought," Abban said. "She has liberty to choose her own husband, though you must still pay a dower for her father's blessing."

"I will pay any price," Jardir said.

Abban bowed. "So you have said," he agreed, "but I, your humble servant, have nevertheless begun negotiations to minimize the impact on your treasury."

Jardir waved his hand dismissively. "So I may approach her directly?"

"Her father has given you permission to court her," Abban said, and Jardir smiled, snatching up his spear and pausing to check himself in a silvered mirror.

"What will you say to her?" Abban asked.

Jardir looked back at him. "I have no idea," he said honestly. "But this is Everam's will, so I trust that whatever I say will be the right thing."

Abban frowned. "I do not think it works that way, Ahmann."

Jardir looked at Abban, knowing all the words unspoken. Abban was much like the Par'chin in that regard. Polite. Tolerant. And utterly disbelieving.

Jardir looked at his old friend and felt great pity in his heart, understanding at last what it meant to be *khaffit*. Everam did not speak to them. Abban might use the Creator's name in every other sentence, but had never truly heard His voice or felt the rapture of submitting to His divine will. Only profit spoke to Abban, and he would ever be its slave.

But that, too, was part of Everam's plan, for the *khaffit* saw things no other man did, things essential to Jardir, if he was to win Sharak Ka.

Jardir put a hand on Abban's shoulder, smiling sadly. "I know you do not, my friend, but if you do not trust in the Creator, hold faith in me."

Abban bowed. "Of course. But at the very least, avoid mention of your other wives. Her mother tells me that Mistress Leesha's jealousy is like a storm."

Jardir nodded, not surprised in the least that such a woman would know her own worth and expect other women to make way for her. It only made him want her more.

Rojer led his apprentices through their exercises halfheartedly. They had improved a little, but whenever Kendall bent to her fiddle case, he could see the tops of the scars that ran across her chest. A mark of honor demon scars might be, but they were also a reminder to Rojer of just how far his apprentices had yet to come before they could be of any real use in the night. He hoped the instructors from the Jongleurs' Guild arrived soon.

Across the way, the Cutters trained in the Corelings' Graveyard. There was plenty of work to be done to build the new greatward, but so long as the Krasians were camped in the clearing, none of the Cutters had any interest in doing it. Gared had groups of them patrolling the town, and the rest had gathered at the graveyard to train and stand ready if needed. Leesha would be furious when she saw the work wasn't getting done, but even after all she had been through, Leesha was too trusting of people.

There was a shout, and Rojer looked up to see the Krasian leader approaching, followed by his two bodyguards, Hasik and Shanjat. They wore their spears and shields on their backs, but while Jardir looked relaxed and serene, the warriors had the look of men surrounded by enemies. Their hands flexed unconsciously for want of a spear.

Jardir headed toward Rojer, and Gared gave a shout as he and a few Cutters hurried to intercept. Jardir's bodyguards whirled to face them, spear and shield appearing in their hands instantly. The Cutters lifted their own weapons at the sight, and it seemed a clash was inevitable.

But Jardir turned, taking in Cutter and *Sharum* alike. "We are guests of Mistress Leesha!" he cried. "No blood will be shed between our peoples until she decrees otherwise."

"Then tell your men to put their spears down," Gared said, holding an axe in one hand and his warded blade in the other. Dozens of Cutters hurried across the graveyard and gathered at his back, but Hasik and Shanjat seemed unfazed—more than willing to fight the lot of them. Having seen the Krasian warriors fight, Rojer expected they would give far better than they got.

But then Jardir shouted something in Krasian, and his bodyguards sheathed their spears, though they kept their shields out.

"Din't say put 'em away, I said put 'em *down*," Gared growled.

Jardir smiled. "*Guests* are not asked to leave their knives at the door, Gared, son of Steave."

Gared opened his mouth to reply, but Rojer cut him off.

"Of course, you are correct," he said loudly, looking at Gared. "Put up your axe," he told the giant Cutter.

Gared's eyes widened. It was the first time Rojer had ever publicly given Gared an order, and it was one the Cutter might well refuse to accept, for if he put up his weapon, every other Cutter would as well.

Their eyes met, and Gared challenged him in that look, but Rojer was a mummer, and his face easily imitated the harsh look of the Warded Man, his voice deepening to the rasp Arlen used to frighten people and distance himself from them.

"Ent gonna tell you again, Gared," he said, and he felt it as the giant's will broke. Gared nodded and stepped back, returning his axe to its harness and his blade to its sheath. The other Cutters looked at him in surprise, but they did the same, taking comfort in their numbers.

Rojer turned to face Jardir. "Is there something I can help you with?"

"Indeed," said Jardir, bowing. "I wish to speak with Mistress Leesha."

"She's not in town," Rojer said.

"I see," Jardir said. "Can you tell me where I might find her?"

"The Core we will!" Gared growled, but Rojer and Jardir both ignored him.

"Why?" Rojer asked.

"She has given me a gift of incredible value in the cloak," Jardir said. "I wish to bestow a gift of equal value upon her."

"What gift?" Rojer asked.

Jardir smiled. "That is a matter between Mistress Leesha and myself."

Rojer considered him. Part of him screamed not to trust this smiling desert demon who had slaughtered and raped so many, but Jardir seemed to have his own code of honor, and he did not think the man would try to harm Leesha while the truce held. And if the gift he offered was truly magic of equal value, they might be fools to refuse it.

"I'll take you to her if you leave your warriors behind," Rojer said.

Jardir bowed. "Of course." The guards gave a cry of protest, as did Gared and a few of the Cutters, but again Rojer and Jardir ignored them. "My intentions toward Mistress Leesha are honorable, and I will of course accept a chaperone while in her presence."

It seemed an odd choice of words, but Rojer could not find further cause to argue. Soon they were walking the path to Leesha's cottage. Gared insisted on coming along, and glared at Jardir the whole way, though the Krasian leader seemed thankfully oblivious.

"Why does the mistress not live on your village's wondrous greatward?" Jardir asked. "I would think her too valuable to risk to the *alagai*."

Rojer laughed. "If all the Core rose up tonight, you'd be safer in Leesha's cottage than anywhere else in the world."

Jardir found that hard to believe, but as they came close to the cottage, he found the path laid with a walkway of stone wards, each large enough to stand upon without marring it.

Jardir stopped short, looking at the stones in amazement. He squatted, pressing against the stone with his hand. "Everam's beard. It must have taken a thousand slaves to carve these."

"We ent a bunch of filthy desert slavers like you," Gared muttered. Jardir's first impulse was to kill the man, but that was no way to impress the mistress. He embraced the insult instead and gave it no further thought, returning his focus to the path.

"The wards were poured, not carved," Rojer said, "made from a mixture of stone and water called crete, which hardens as it dries. Leesha cut them into the ground herself, and *free men* poured the stone."

Jardir scanned the path ahead in amazement. "These are combat wards. And linked."

Rojer nodded. "Any demon that sets foot on this path might as well step into a sunbeam."

Jardir realized he had been arrogant and naïve to scoff before. For all their savage ways, not even Sharik Hora held the power of some of the Northern woman's wardings.

The yard was no less stunning, filled with more crete walkways that wove a complex wardnet around the cottage and its environs. A large garden bloomed brightly, the herbs and flowers arranged in neat groupings, their lines forming yet more wards. Jardir couldn't recognize many of them, but he saw enough to know that these did far more than banish or kill corelings.

Stronger than ever, he felt Everam's will thrumming within him. This woman was destined to be his bride. With her and Inevera behind him, what in the world could he not accomplish?

Leesha listened to the comforting rhythm of Wonda chopping firewood as she prepared lunch. The simple task helped give her mind clarity as she went over the night's events and compared the men she had met with the tales of the refugees and Arlen's words of warning.

It was not that she did not trust the accounts, but Leesha preferred to form her own opinions. Many of the refugees spoke hearsay and exaggeration, and Arlen's heart could be hard and unforgiving at times. Something had happened to him in Krasia, some hurt done he could not forgive, but since he would not speak of it, Leesha could only guess as to what it was.

Whatever else might be true of the Krasians, they were warriors without equal. Leesha had seen that instantly as she watched them fight. The Cutters were generally larger and more heavily muscled, but they moved with none of the precision that marked the *dal'Sharum*. The fifty camped in the clearing could cut a swath of destruction across the Hollow before they were pulled down, and if the rest of Jardir's army had half their skill, the Hollowers would stand little chance against them, even with all the secrets of fire she could muster.

And so she had determined that they must not fight, if it could be avoided. It was one thing to kill demons, but every human life was precious. The books of the old world said mankind had once numbered in the billions, but how many remained after the Return? A quarter million? The thought of the last men in the world fighting one another sickened her.

Yet neither could she surrender. She would not spit on her hand and wet the Hollow for the Krasians. She had worked too hard to hold the Hollowers together after the flux to assimilate the refugees from Rizon and Lakton to just turn them over. If there was a way to negotiate a peace, she had to find it.

The first meeting with the Krasian leader had seemed to indicate that was a possibility. He was cultured and intelligent, nothing like the rabid animal the accounts had portrayed, and clearly held true to his beliefs, even if Leesha thought them brutal and cruel at times. She had looked deeply into his eyes, and there was no cruelty there. Like a stern father administering a needed spanking, Ahmann Jardir was doing what he thought best for humanity.

Leesha paused in her work, realizing that the chopping outside had stopped. She looked up as the door opened and Wonda stood in the threshold.

"Wash up and set the table," Leesha said. "Lunch will be another few minutes."

"Beggin' your pardon, mistress, but Rojer and Gared are here to see you," Wonda said.

"Tell them to come in and set another pair of places at the table," Leesha said.

But Wonda just stood there. "They're not alone."

Leesha set her knife on the cutting board and toweled her hands clean as she went to the door. Ahmann Jardir stood on her front porch, standing calmly and ignoring the way Gared glared at him. He wore a fine white robe over his warrior blacks, matching the white turban his crown nestled within. Leesha's eyes danced across its wards, but she forced herself not to stare. She dropped her gaze to his eyes, but that was worse, for they bored into her with such intensity that she felt as if he could see her very soul.

Jardir bowed deeply. "Forgive my appearing unannounced, mistress."

"Just say the word and I'll haul him back where he came from, Leesha," Gared said.

"Nonsense," Leesha said. "Welcome," she told Jardir. "Wonda and I were about to sit down to lunch. Would you care to join us?"

"I would be honored and delighted," Jardir said, bowing again. He followed Leesha into the cottage, pausing to remove his sandals and leave them by the door. Leesha noted that even his feet were covered in ward scars. A kick from him would likely do as much to a coreling as one by the Warded Man.

The meal Mistress Leesha had prepared was a meatless stew served with fresh bread and cheese. Jardir bowed his head as she invoked a blessing over the food, and then everyone began eating at once. He began to lift his bowl to drink when he noticed the greenlanders were leaving theirs on the table, using some sort of tool to bring the food to their lips.

He glanced at his own setting, and saw a similar utensil there—a wooden strip with a depression at the end. He looked at Leesha and mirrored her actions as he tasted the stew. It was delicious, with heavy vegetables he had never tasted. He began to eat more vigorously, using the thick greenland bread to soak the last drops from his bowl as he saw Gared and Wonda do.

"Exquisite," he told the mistress, and felt a thrill run through him as he saw her pleasure at the compliment. "We do not have such food in Krasia."

Leesha smiled. "There is much we could learn from each other, if we can find a way to live in peace."

"Peace, mistress?" Jardir asked. "There is no such thing on Ala. Not while the *alagai* hold the night and men cower before them."

"So the tales are true?" Leesha asked. "You mean to conquer us and levy our people for Sharak Ka?"

"Why should I wish to conquer you?" Jardir asked. "Your people are humble before the Creator, stand tall in the night, and shed blood in *alagai'sharak* alongside my warriors. That makes you Evejan, though you know it not."

"It don't!" the giant growled. "We ent got nothin' to do with your filthy—"

"Gared Cutter!" Leesha's voice snapped like a *dama's* whip, silencing him. "You'll keep a polite tongue at my table or I'll give it such a dose of pepper you can't talk for a month!"

Gared recoiled, and again Jardir was amazed at the power of the woman. She made the *dama'ting* seem timid.

Leesha turned to him. "I apologize, Ahmann." She seemed taken aback when he smiled brightly at her. "What did I say?"

"My name," Jardir said simply.

"I'm sorry," Leesha said. "Was that improper of me?"

"On the contrary," Jardir said. "It sounds beautiful, coming from your lips."

With no veil to cover her cheeks, Jardir saw how her pale skin reddened at his words. He had never courted a woman before, but it seemed as if Everam himself guided his words.

"More than three thousand years ago," Jardir said, "my ancestor Kaji ruled this land from the Southern Sea to the frozen waste."

"So the histories say," Leesha agreed, "though three thousand years is a long time, and accounts can become . . . blurred."

"Perhaps here in the North," Jardir said, "but the temple of Sharik Hora in the Desert Spear has stood that long and more, and our records are sharp. Kaji did rule this land, sometimes by the spear, and sometimes by building alliance with its tribes and sealing it with blood."

He looked around the table. "Kaji's blood is still strong here. Even your name, Deliverer's Hollow, honors him. You are not *chin* to be conquered, but lost brethren to be welcomed into our fold. I name you Hollow tribe, and accord you all the rights therein."

"What rights?" Leesha asked.

Jardir reached into his robe, producing his personal Evejah. Its cover was of supple leather embossed with wards, and its pages were gilded in gold. A red ribbon hung ready to mark a page. The pages were soft and thin from daily use.

"These rights," he said, giving her the volume.

Leesha took the book as one who knew its value, and he recalled she was a bookbinder's daughter as she turned it to examine the spine. She pushed her bowl aside and spread the cloth from her lap over the table before laying the book upon it and paging through.

"It's beautiful," she said after a time. "But much as I would love to learn the language, I'm afraid I can't understand a word." She closed the book and held it out to him.

Jardir held up a hand to forestall her. "Keep it. What better book to help you learn? You may find its truths more in line with your own beliefs than you imagine."

"Oh, I couldn't!" Leesha said. "This is too precious!"

Jardir laughed. "You give me a cloak that rivals Kaji's own, and you balk at a book of his truths? I can pen another."

Leesha looked back down at the book, and then up at him. "You penned this yourself?"

"In my own blood," Jardir said, "during the years I studied in Sharik Hora."

Leesha's eyes widened.

"It is not gold or jewels, I understand," Jardir said. "I would shower them upon you if I could, but I brought no such trinkets north. This is the most valuable thing I own, apart from my crown, spear, and new cloak. I hope you will accept it while Abban negotiates a proper dower with your mother."

"Dower?" Leesha asked in surprise.

"Of course," Jardir said. "Your father gave me permission to court you, and your mother will see your price is met. Did they not tell you?"

"No they corespawned didn't!" Leesha cried, rising to her feet so fast her chair skidded out behind her. In an instant everyone was on their feet. Jardir felt a sudden flash of fear. He had given offense to her, but without understanding how, he could not even apologize.

"Son of the Core!" the giant cried, and swung his meaty fist across the table at Jardir.

Jardir could not remember the last time a man had dared to strike at him. Had they been anywhere but at Mistress Leesha's table, Jardir would have killed him for the affront, but remembering Leesha's abhorrence of violence, he acted only in his own defense. He caught Gared's wrist and pivoted, pulling him clear across the table and flipping him onto his back. He put a single toe into Gared's throat and held his log of a wrist with only two fingers, but though the giant thrashed, he was held firmly prone and helpless, his face reddening more with every second.

"Your betters are speaking, *Sharum*," he said. "I have tolerated your constant rudeness out of respect to Mistress Leesha, but if you try to lay hands on me again, I will tear your arm off." He gave a slight tug, and Gared roared in pain. Everyone looked to Leesha for how to react.

Leesha crossed her arms. "Serves you right, Gared Cutter. No one asked you to attack anyone in my home." She nodded to the door. "Out with you. Rojer and Wonda, too. You can all wait in the yard."

"The Core we will!" Rojer cried, Wonda nodding along with him. "If you think we're leaving you alone with this—"

There was a bang and a flash at their feet, and they jumped in shock. Leesha said nothing, but her face was a storm cloud as she pointed at the door. Both were gone in an instant. Jardir released Gared, and he, too, scurried out.

Jardir turned to Leesha and bowed long and deep. "I apologize, mistress, though I do not understand why I have given distress. I have come to you and your family honorably, yet you act as if I tried to carry you off after stealing a well."

Leesha did not respond for a long time, and her anger was terrible to behold, such that Jardir had an urge to shield his eyes as if in a sandstorm. Slowly, she embraced the feeling, and her features grew calm once more.

"I apologize as well," she said. "My distress is not directed at you, but at being the last to find out you had come courting."

"Abban told your parents I would come immediately," Jardir said. "I assumed they sent you word."

Leesha nodded. "I believe you. My mother has a history of trying to make such arrangements without my knowledge."

Jardir bowed. "If you need time to consider, you need not answer now."

"Yes . . . ," Leesha began, "I mean, no. That is, I'm flattered, but I can't marry you."

You will, Jardir thought. *You are destined to love me as I already do you.*

"Why not?" he asked her instead. "Your mother says you are unspoken for, and I will meet any dower your family desires. Soon I will control all the Northland, and you with me. What husband could offer you more?"

Leesha paused for a moment, then shook her head as if to clear it. "It doesn't matter. I barely know you, dowers mean nothing to me, and frankly, I don't know that I want you 'controlling' anything."

"Come with me to Everam's Bounty," Jardir said. "Come see my people and what we are building. I will teach you our language as you asked, and you can come to know me and decide what I am . . . worthy to control."

Leesha looked at him a long time, but Jardir waited patiently, knowing her answer was *inevera*. "All right," she said at last, "but with proper chaperone, and no decision until I am safely returned to the Hollow."

Jardir bowed. "Of course. I swear it by Everam."

Rojer paced the yard, staring at Leesha's cottage. Gared's clenched fists were like two hams, and even Wonda had fetched and strung her bow. Finally, the door opened, and Leesha followed Jardir out onto the porch. "Wonda, escort Mr. Jardir back to town," she said. "Gared, you can finish cording the woodpile."

Gared grunted and picked up Wonda's axe as she and Jardir headed down the path. Rojer looked at Leesha, who nodded her head back to the door. She went inside, and he followed as she went right to Bruna's rocker and put on her shawl. Never a good sign.

"How did he take your refusal?" Rojer asked, not bothering to sit.

Leesha sighed. "He didn't. Told me to take my time and think it through. He's invited me back to Rizon with him."

"You can't go," Rojer said.

Leesha raised an eyebrow at that. "You have no more say over who I marry than my mother, Rojer."

"Are you saying you want to marry him?" Rojer asked. "After a single tea and an awkward lunch?"

"Of course not," Leesha said. "I have no intention of accepting his proposal."

"Then why in the Core would you deliver yourself into his hands?" Rojer asked.

"There's an army at our doorstep, Rojer," Leesha said. "You don't see value in looking at them with our own eyes? Counting tents and learning how their leader thinks?"

"Not at the cost of our own leader," Rojer said. "Duke Rhinebeck doesn't personally go to Miln to see what Euchor's up to. He sends spies."

"I don't have any spies," Leesha said.

Rojer snorted. "You have over a thousand Rizonans who owe you their lives, many who left family behind. Surely a few could be persuaded to return home and keep their ears open."

"I won't order people to put themselves at risk," Leesha said.

"But you'll put yourself?" Rojer asked.

"I don't think Ahmann would harm me," Leesha said.

"Two days ago, he was the demon of the desert," Rojer said. "Now he's Ahmann? What, do you just shine on any man who thinks he's the Deliverer?"

Leesha scowled. "I don't want to hear any more of this, Rojer."

"I don't care what you want," Rojer snapped. "You've heard how the Krasians treat women. No matter what that oily snake tells you, the moment you're out of range of the Hollowers' bows you'll be his property, and anyone with you will get a spear in the eye."

"So you won't be coming with me?" Leesha asked.

"Night, haven't you heard anything I've been saying?" Rojer demanded.

"Every word," Leesha said, "but I'm still going. If that's the kind of man Ahmann is, then war is inevitable and it doesn't matter what we do. But if there's even a chance he meant what he said at the table, then there's a chance we can find a way to coexist without killing each other, and that's worth more to the world than the fate of Leesha Paper."

Rojer sighed, plopping down in a chair. "When do we leave?"

SECTION 4

THE CALL
OF THE CORE

CHAPTER 26

RETURN TO
TIBBET'S BROOK

:: 333 AR SUMMER ::

THE WARDED MAN'S MOOD was black as Fort Miln receded in the distance. Any happiness he had felt upon leaving Ragen and Elissa's manse was swept away by the meeting with Jaik. The conversation played out over and over in his mind, all the words he should have said presented themselves too late, and did little to dispel a nagging doubt that his friend was right.

To take his mind away, he read through the book Ronnell had given him, but that brought no comfort. Laid bare were Leesha's coveted secrets of fire, with metalwork diagrams to turn their force into tools of precision killing. Tools designed for killing not demons, but men.

Did the corelings drive us to the brink of extinction, he wondered, *or did we do it to ourselves?*

He caught sight of a ruined keep off the side of the road as the sun began to set. One of Euchor's predecessors had kept a garrison there, but the keep had fallen to demons and never been rebuilt. Most Messengers, convinced it was haunted, gave it a wide berth. A rusted gate hung bent and torn from twisted moorings, and great holes had been broken in the outer wall.

He rode into the keep, staking Twilight Dancer in a warded circle. He stripped to his loincloth, selecting a spear and bow. As darkness fell, the stinking mists began to seep up between the shattered stones of the courtyard. Corelings rose thickly in unwarded ruins, instinct telling them the odds were good prey might one day return. Fifty men had died when the wards of this keep fell, likely killed by the very demons rising now. They deserved vengeance.

The Warded Man waited until the demons spotted him and charged before lifting his bow. In the lead was a flame demon, but his first arrow blasted the life from it. Next was a rock that took several shots to put down.

When the rock fell, the other demons paused, some even backpedaling to flee, but wardstones the Warded Man had placed around the gaps in the wall and gate kept them trapped in the keep with him. When he was out of arrows, he charged with spear and shield, eventually abandoning that as well and fighting with bare hands and feet.

He only grew stronger as the night wore on and he absorbed more and more magic. Lost in the killing frenzy, he thought of nothing else until at last, covered in demon ichor that sizzled on his wards, he found no more demons to kill. The sky began to lighten soon after, the few remaining corelings in the area fading into mist to flee the sun as it burned their taint away from the surface world.

But then the light reached him, and it was like fire on his skin. The glare stung his eyes, leaving him dizzy and nauseous, and his throat burned. Standing before it was agony.

This had happened before. Leesha said it was the sunlight burning the excess magic away from him, but there was another part of him, a primal part, that knew the truth.

The sun was rejecting him. He was becoming a demon, and no longer belonged on the surface of the world.

The Core called to him, beckoning with offers of succor. The paths, like vents of magic coming up from the ground, were unmistakable to his warded eyes, and they all sang the same song. No sun would burn him in the Core's embrace.

The Warded Man started to dematerialize, slipping a bit of his essence down along a path, tasting it.

Just once, he told himself. *To probe for weakness. To see if the fight can be taken there.* It was a noble thought, if not entirely true. More likely, he would be destroyed.

World's better off without me, anyway.

But before he could melt away, there was a pop and a flash of light as one of the smoldering bodies in the yard was caught in a sunbeam and burst into flame. He looked over at it, watching the bodies ignite one after another like festival flamework.

Even as the corelings burned, his own pain lessened. The sun left him weakened as it always did, but it did not destroy him.

Yet, he thought. *But soon. Best give the Brook its wards while you still can.*

&

Landmarks began to appear as the Warded Man drew closer to Tibbet's Brook, bringing his mind, lingering on thoughts of the Core, back to the present. Here was the Messenger cave where he had succored with Ragen and Keerin. There were the ruins where they had found him. Those, at least, were free of demons. A pack of nightwolves had taken up residence there, and the Warded Man wisely gave them a wide berth. Even corelings thought twice before disturbing a pack of nightwolves. Centuries of demons culling the smallest and weakest had left the few remaining predators in the wild formidable indeed. Named after their jet-black fur, adult nightwolves could weigh three hundred pounds, and a pack of them could take down even a wood demon if cornered.

Next along the road came the small clearing where he had crippled One Arm. The Warded Man had expected the place to be just as he had left it: a scorched and blackened ruin surrounding the clear spot where he had built his circle.

But it had been better than fourteen years, and that bleak place now bloomed with rich life, brighter, even, than its surroundings. It might be a good omen, if he believed in such things.

In a far-flung hamlet such as Tibbet's Brook, a Messenger, or any stranger—even someone from Sunny Pasture, the next town over—was a rare thing and apt to draw attention. When the Warded Man drew close to the town too early in the day, he pulled up and waited. Better to pass through the outskirts and town proper late in the day when folk were busy checking their wards rather than watching the road. He would arrive in Town Square close to dusk, with just enough time to rent a room at Hog's tavern. Come morning, all he would have to do was find the Town Speaker and give him or her a grimoire of battle wards, handing out a few weapons to those who wanted them in the process, and then leave before half the folk even knew he was there. He wondered if Selia still spoke for the town, as she had when he was young.

The first farm he passed was Mack Pasture's, but though he heard animals in the barn, he didn't see anyone. He reached Harl's not long after. The Tanner farm was deserted entirely. Recently, it seemed, since its wards were still intact and the fields unburned. But the livestock was gone, and the fields in disarray, as if they had not been properly tended in some time. There was no sign of a demon attack. He wondered what could have happened.

Harl's farm had special meaning for him. For eleven years, Harl's farm was the farthest he had ever gotten from home, but more than that, it was where he had kissed Beni and Renna the night before his mother died. It was ironic. He could no longer remember his mother's face, but he remembered everything about those kisses. The way his teeth had clicked clumsily with Beni's and they had both recoiled in shock, the softness and warmth of Renna's mouth, the taste of her breath.

It had been a long time since he had thought of Renna Tanner. Their fathers had promised them to each other, and if Arlen had not run away they would likely be married now, raising children and tending Jeph's farm. He wondered what had become of her.

Things only grew stranger as he went on. There was no reason for him to have taken any caution with his approach, because he didn't see a single soul on his way through the Brook; every home was locked up tight. He mentally checked the date, but it was too early for the summer solstice festival. They must have been summoned by the Great Horn.

The Great Horn was in Town Square and was blown when there was an attack, giving directions so that those closest could come and help search for survivors and rebuild if possible. Folk would lock up their livestock and leave for that, sometimes even overnight.

The Warded Man knew he had judged his people harshly when he left home. They were no different from the folk of Cutter's Hollow or any other of dozens of hamlets he had seen. Brook folk might not stand up to the corelings like Krasians, but they resisted in their own way, coming together time and again to reaffirm their bonds to one another. When they bickered, it was over petty things. No one in the Brook would allow a neighbor to go hungry or be left without succor, as happened so often in the cities.

The Warded Man sniffed the air and searched the sky, but there was no sign of smoke, the surest indicator of an attack. He strained his ears, but there was nothing to guide him, and after some casting about he headed on down the road to Town Square. There would be folk there who could tell him about the attack.

It was nearly dark as he approached Town Square, and the buzz of hundreds of voices came to his ears. He relaxed, realizing his fears were unfounded, and wondered what occasion could have drawn everyone in the Brook to spend a night in town. Had one of Hog's daughters finally married?

The streets were clear, but it seemed all the Brook had gathered. Every porch and doorway and window facing the square was packed full of people. Some, like the Watches, had even drawn their own circles, standing apart from the others and clutching their Canons, deep in prayer. It was a sharp contrast with the folk from Boggin's Hill, clutching only one another as they wept. He caught sight of Renna's sister Beni among them, holding tight to Lucik Boggin.

He followed their gaze to the square's center, where a beautiful young woman was bound to a stake in the ground.

And the sun was setting.

It was only an instant before the Warded Man recognized Renna Tanner. Perhaps it was because she had been on his mind, or that he had just seen her sister, but Renna's round face, even after so long, was unmistakable, as was the long brown hair that fell nearly to her waist.

She hung limply, held up more by the ropes wrapped around her arms and chest than her own strength. Her eyes were open, but they stared blankly, focused on nothing.

"What in the Core is going on?" he roared, digging his heels into Twilight Dancer's flanks. The giant stallion leapt forward into the square, digging great divots in the grass as he pranced before the shocked crowd. The square was lit with a dim, flickering glow from torches and lanterns, but above the sky was a deep purple. The corelings would rise in seconds.

He leapt from the horse's back, rushing to the stake to undo Renna's bonds. An old man strode out to him, waving a large hunting knife with a stained blade. The Warded Man's sharp nostrils caught the scent of dried blood as he recognized Raddock Lawry, the Speaker from Fishing Hole.

"This ent your affair, Messenger!" Lawry said, pointing the knife at him. "That girl killed my kin, as well as her own da, and we aim to see her cored for it!"

The Warded Man glanced at Renna in shock, and like a slap in the face it all came back to him. The marriage games she and Beni had wanted to play with him in the hayloft, games they said they learned from watching Ilain with their father. Ilain's secret, pleading words to Jeph, begging him to take her away. The grunting from Harl's room deep in the night.

The memories flooded back, but this time he saw them as a grown man, and not a naïve boy. Horror struck him, followed quickly by anger. He reached out faster than Raddock could react, catching the man's wrist in a *sharusahk* twist that flipped him to the ground even as the knife came free from his hands.

The Warded Man held the blade up for all to see. "If Renna Tanner killed her da," he shouted, "then I tell you, he had it comin'!"

He moved to cut Renna's bonds, but several Fishers, led by Garric, charged him with their thin spears. He stuck the bloody knife in the stake and turned to meet them.

To call it a fight would have been overly kind to the Fishers. They were strong men, but no warriors. The Warded Man was a trained fighter, and stronger than all of them together. It was only by his mercy that none of them were permanently injured when they hit the ground.

"Ent nobody getting cored while I'm around," he barked. "I'm taking her, and there ent a corespawned thing you can do about it!"

There was a thump, and he looked up, his eyes widening in disbelief. Jeorje Watch stood there, looking much as he had the last time the Warded Man had seen him, though that had been over sixteen years gone, and Jeorje in his nineties then.

"Nothing we can do, may be," he said, nodding and pointing with his stick, "but reckon we're not the ones you need to contend with, boy. The Plague take you both!"

The Warded Man followed the stick and saw he was right. Mist was rising throughout the square, and already some corelings were solidifying. The Fishers on the ground shrieked and scrambled back behind the wards.

Jeorje Watch had a grim smile on his face, one of righteous satisfaction, but the Warded Man didn't flinch. Instead he pulled off his hood and met the Southwatch Tender's eyes.

"I've contended with worse, old man," he growled, stripping off his robe, as well. The crowd gasped at the sight of his tattooed flesh.

As always, the first to come were the flame demons. One leapt at Renna, but the Warded Man caught its tail, hurling it across the square. Another pounced at him, but the wards on his skin flared to life and its claws could find no purchase. He caught the coreling's jaws before it could bite, so it spat fire in his eyes.

The wards on his face glowed briefly, absorbing the attack and turning it into nothing more than a cool breeze. All the while the wards on his palms glowed more and more fiercely until he crushed the demon's snout, hurling it aside.

A wood demon formed next, charging Twilight Dancer, but the stallion reared and trampled it, sparks flying from his warded hooves.

There was a shriek from above, and the Warded Man pivoted in time to grab the diving wind demon and turn its momentum against it, throwing it hard to the ground and crushing its throat with a stomp of his foot and a thunderclap of magic.

Two more wood demons came at him, and he kicked the first in the stomach, knocking it back with a blast of magic before grappling with the other. He caught one of its arms in a *sharusahk* hold and pulled with all his strength, tearing the demon's arm clear off. This he threw at Jeorje Watch, though the limb bounced off the wards of the Southwatch Tender's circle.

Three flame demons set upon the crippled wood demon, and soon the wounded coreling was shrieking as it was consumed in flame. The other wood demon recovered and made to come at the Warded Man, but he snarled at it, and the demon kept its distance.

"It's the Deliverer!" someone in the crowd cried. Many others echoed his words, some even falling to their knees, but the Warded Man only scowled.

"Ent here to deliver anyone that would put a girl out in the night!" he roared. He turned to Renna, pulling the knife free from the stake and slashing through her bonds. She collapsed into his arms, and their eyes met for just a moment. Focus returned to Renna's gaze, and she shook her head as if to clear it. He lifted her up onto Twilight Dancer's back.

"That witch killed my son!" Garric Fisher cried.

The Warded Man turned, remembering all too clearly the many beatings he'd suffered at Cobie Fisher's hands as a child. "Your son was a bully, and never worth a coreling's piss," he said, climbing into the saddle behind Renna. She snuggled into him like a child, shivering though the night was warm.

He looked out over the crowd, scanning the terrified faces. He saw his father there, clutching Ilain Tanner, and felt another surge of anger. Nothing had changed, if Jeph could stand there and watch Renna staked, knowing what they both did of Harl.

"I came to teach you all to fight the corelings!" he called to the crowd. "But I see Tibbet's Brook still raises only cowards and fools!"

He turned to ride off, but something gnawed at him, and he looked back, giving the crowd one last glance, one last chance.

"Any man, woman, or child who would rather kill corelings than feed them their neighbor, meet me here at dusk tomorrow," he shouted. "If not, corespawn the lot of you!"

Jeph met his eyes then, though there was no recognition in his gaze. "Renna Tanner is my kin!" he called, drawing stares from all around. "Succor at my farm up the north road! Renna knows the way!" The Warded Man needed no directions to Jeph's farm, but he nodded, turning Twilight Dancer north.

"Here now, you can't go shelterin' that murderin' witch, Jeph Bales!" Raddock Lawry called. "The council voted!"

"Then it's best I ent on the council," Jeph shouted back, " 'cause the night as my witness, you or anyone else comes to my farm looking for her, there'll be more bloodshed, and to spare!"

Raddock opened his mouth to reply, but there was an angry murmur from the crowd, and he looked around uneasily, unsure whose side they were on.

The Warded Man grunted and kicked Twilight Dancer into a gallop out of the Square and headed up the road to his father's farm.

Renna was silent the whole ride, resting against him and clinging to his robes. A few demons came at them, but Twilight Dancer dodged and put on speed, quickly leaving them behind. Twice, the stallion simply trampled demons into the road without slowing.

His father's farm was much as he remembered it, though an addition had been built onto the back of the house. Some of the wardposts in the barley field were still those he had carved himself, coated in fresh lacquer many times over the years. Jeph maintained his wards religiously, a habit he had instilled in his son that had saved Arlen's life many times since and defined much of the course of his life.

Drawn to the house, a great many corelings were in the yard, testing the wards. The Warded Man shot two to clear the way to the barn, and once safe behind its wards, he stabled Twilight Dancer and stood in the doorway, picking off the others one by one with his bow. Soon the way was clear, and he escorted Renna to the house proper.

The Warded Man was shaking as he deposited Renna in the common room and lit the lanterns, kindling a fire in the hearth. Everything about the place was so familiar, it made his heart ache. It even smelled the same. He half expected his mother to come out of the cold room and tell him to wash for supper. An old cat came and sniffed him, purring and rubbing against his leg. He picked it up and scratched its ears, remembering how its mother had birthed the litter behind the broken cart in the barn.

He went over to Renna who was sitting right where he left her, playing with her skirts. "You all right?"

Renna shook her head, eyes on the floor. "Ent sure I'll ever be all right again."

"Know the feeling," the Warded Man said. "You hungry?"

When she nodded, he set the cat down and went to the cold room, unsurprised to find it laid out just as he recalled. There was smoked ham and fresh vegetables, and bread in the bread box. He took everything to the chopping block and filled a pot from the water barrel. He soon had a stew simmering over the fire, filling the house with its aroma. He opened the cupboard and set bowls and spoons at the table. He went to fetch Renna and found the cat curled in her lap. She stroked it absently as she wept, her teardrops matting its fur.

Renna said little as they ate, and he found himself staring at her, wishing he knew what words could put life back in her eyes.

"Good stew?" he asked as she tore bread to soak the last of it from her bowl. "There's more if you like." She nodded, and he fetched the pot from the fire, ladling her another helping.

"Thanks," she said. "Feel like I haven't et in days. Haven't, really. Ent been hungry."

"You had a rough week, I imagine," he said.

She met his eyes finally. "You killed those demons. Killed 'em with your bare hands."

The Warded Man nodded.

"Why?" she asked.

The Warded Man raised a brow at her. "Need a reason to kill demons?"

"But they told you what I done," Renna said. "And they's right. None a this would've happened, I'd just minded my da. Maybe I deserve to be cored." She looked away again, but the Warded Man grabbed her shoulders roughly and forced her to turn and face him. His eyes were blazing, and hers went wide with fright.

"You listen to me, Renna Tanner," he said. "Your da din't deserve mindin'. I know what he done to you and your sisters, out on that farm. That kind of man ent worth no mind at all. It's him that brought these troubles about, not you. Ent never been you."

When she just stared at him, he shook her. "You hear me?!"

For a moment more Renna just stared, and then slowly she nodded. And then again, more decisively. "Wasn't right, what he done to us."

"That's undersaid," the Warded Man grunted.

"And poor Cobie never done nothing wrong," Renna went on, the words coming faster. She looked up at him. "He wan't no bully, least not that I ever saw. All he ever wanted was to marry me proper, and Da . . ."

"Killed him for it," the Warded Man finished, when she hesitated.

She nodded. "Man like that ent much more than a demon himself."

He nodded. "And you got to fight demons, Renna Tanner. It's the only way to live with your head held high. Can't trust no one else to do what you won't do for yourself."

Renna was curled up by the fire, fast asleep, when Jeph's cart pulled into the yard early the next morning. The Warded Man watched through the window, swallowing a lump in his throat as four children hopped down from the back of the cart, brothers and sisters he had never known.

They were followed off the cart by tough old Norine and Ilain. The Warded Man had shined on Ilain when he was young, and she was still beautiful now, but seeing his father help her down from the front seat the way he used to do for his mother gnawed at him. He didn't blame Ilain for wanting to escape Harl—not anymore, at least—but that made it no easier to see how quickly she had taken his mother's place.

He looked up the road, but there was no sign of anyone else following. He opened the door and went out to meet them. The children pulled up short, staring, as he walked over to Jeph.

"She's asleep by the fire," he said.

Jeph nodded. "Thank you, Messenger."

"I'll hold you to your promise to protect her from any looking to do her harm," the Warded Man said, pointing a tattooed finger at his father.

Jeph swallowed, but he nodded. "I will."

The Warded Man's eyes narrowed. Jeph was full of sincere-sounding promises, ones he meant full well, yet when the time came for action he was apt to fail.

But with no other option, the Warded Man nodded. "I'll fetch my horse and go."

"Wait, please," Jeph said, catching his arm. The Warded Man looked at the offending hand, and Jeph snatched it quickly away.

"I just . . ." He hesitated. "We'd like it if you stayed for breakfast. Least we can do. Whole town might be at the square come evening, like you said. You can take your ease here, till then."

The Warded Man looked at him, wanting to be gone from the place, but a part of him longed to meet his siblings, and his stomach rumbled at the thought of a proper Brook breakfast. Such things had meant little to him when he was a child, but now they were cherished memories.

"Reckon I can set a spell," he said, and allowed himself to be escorted back inside as the children ran to their chores and Norine and Ilain headed to the cold room.

"This here's Jeph Young," Jeph said, introducing his oldest son when they were gathered around the breakfast table. The boy nodded at him, but mostly stared at his tattooed hands and tried to peek into the shadows of his hood.

"Next to him is Jeni Tailor," Jeph went on. "They been promised near two seasons. At the end are our youngest, Silvy and Cholie."

Seated opposite the children, next to Renna and Norine, the Warded Man coughed at the names, those of his lost mother and uncle. He took a sip from his water cup to cover his surprise. "You have beautiful children."

"Tender Harral says you're the Deliverer, come again," little Silvy blurted.

"Well I ent," the Warded Man told her. "Just a Messenger, come to spread good word."

"Messengers all like you now, then?" Jeph asked. "All painted up?"

The Warded Man smiled. "I'm one of a kind like that," he admitted. "But I'm just a man, all the same. Din't come to deliver anyone."

"You sure did for our Renna," Ilain said. "Can't thank you enough for that."

"Shouldn't have had to," the Warded Man said.

Jeph sat quiet a moment at the rebuke. "You're right at that," he said at last, "but sometimes when a body's in a crowd, and the crowd has its say . . ."

"Stop making excuses, Jeph Bales," Norine snapped. "Man's right. What do we got in this world, 'cept kith and kin? Ent nothing should keep us from standing by them."

The Warded Man looked at her. This wasn't the Norine he remembered, the one who had stood on the porch the night his mother was cored. Stood and done nothing, except try to keep Arlen from going to her aid. He nodded, his eyes flicking back to meet Jeph's.

"She's right," he said. "You've got to stand up to those that would harm you and yours."

"You sound like my son," Jeph said, his eyes growing distant.

"Say again?" the Warded Man said, his throat tightening.

"Me?" Jeph Young asked.

Jeph shook his head. "Your elder," he told his son, and everyone at the table except Renna and the Warded Man drew a quick ward in the air.

"Had another son, name of Arlen, years back," Jeph explained, and Ilain took his hand in hers, squeezing to lend him strength. "Promised to Renna there, in fact." He nodded to Renna. "Arlen's mam was cored, and he ran off." He looked down at the table, and his voice grew tight. "Always asking about the Free Cities, Arlen was. Like to think he mighta made it there . . ." He broke off, shaking his head as if to clear it.

"But you have this beautiful family now," the Warded Man said, hoping to move the conversation toward something positive.

Jeph nodded, covering Ilain's hand in both of his and squeezing. "I thank the Creator for them every day, but that don't mean I ent carrying a weight for those gone before."

After breakfast, the Warded Man went out to the stables to check on Twilight Dancer, more to escape for a moment than for any need. He had just started to brush the horse down when the barn door opened and Renna came in. She cut an apple and held the halves out for Twilight Dancer to eat, stroking the stallion's flanks when she was done. He nickered softly.

"It was night when I came runnin' here, few days ago," she said. "Demons would've got me, Jeph hadn't crossed the wards and hit one with his axe."

"Honest word?" the Warded Man asked, and felt a lump in his throat when she nodded.

"You're not going to tell him, are you?" she asked.

"Tell him what?" the Warded Man asked.

"That you're his son," Renna said. "That you're alive and well and you forgive him. He's waited so long. Why are you still punishing him when I can see forgiveness in your eyes?"

"You know who I am?" he asked, surprised.

"Course I know!" Renna snapped. "Ent stupid, no matter what everyone thinks. How would you've known about my da and what he done, you weren't Arlen Bales? How would you know Cobie was a bully, or which farm was Jeph's? Night, you strolled around the cupboards like it was still your house!"

"Din't mean for anyone to know," the Warded Man said, suddenly realizing that his Brook accent, which he'd dropped while living in Miln, had returned. It was an old Messenger's trick to put folk in the hamlets at ease, shifting accent to match theirs. He had done it a hundred times, but this time was different, like he'd been doing the trick since he left and was finally speaking in his own voice again.

Renna kicked him hard in the shin. He yelped in pain.

"That's for thinkin' I din't know, and not sayin' anythin'!" she shouted, shoving him so hard he fell into the pile of hay at the back of the stall. "Fourteen summers I waited for you! Always thought you'd come back for me. We was promised. But you din't come back for me at all, did you? Not even now! You was gonna just stop in and leave thinkin' no one knew!" She kicked at him again, and he scrambled quickly to his feet, moving to put Twilight Dancer between them.

She was right, of course. The same as his visit to Miln, he had thought he could look in on his old life without touching it, like removing a bandage to see if the wound underneath had healed. But truer was he had left those wounds to fester, and it was time they were bled.

"Five minutes' talk between our das don't make us promised, Ren," he said.

"I *asked* my da to talk to Jeph," Renna said. "I told you we was promised then, and I said the words on the porch at sunset the day you left. That makes it so."

But the Warded Man shook his head. "Sayin' something at sunset doesn't make it so. I never promised to you, Renna. Everyone got a say that night but me."

Renna looked at him, and there were tears in her eyes. "Maybe you din't," she conceded, "but I did. It was the only thing I ever done that was really mine, and I ent gonna take it back. I knew it when we kissed, that we was meant to be."

"But you'd have married Cobie Fisher," he said, failing to keep some bitterness from his voice, "who used to beat on me with his friends."

"You fixed 'em for that," Renna said. "Cobie was always nice to me . . ." She sniffed, touching the necklace she wore. "Din't even know you were alive, and I needed to get away . . ."

He put his hand on her shoulder. "I know, Ren. Din't mean it like that. Don't blame you for doing what you did. Just meant that nothing's 'meant to be.' We all just go through life doing what we think's best."

She looked at him. "I want to go with you when you leave. That's what I think's best."

"You know what that means, Ren?" the Warded Man asked. "I don't just hide behind a circle when the sun sets. Ent a safe life."

"Like I'm safe here?" Renna asked. "Even if they don't stake me again soon as you leave, who I got to turn to now? Who, that wern't willing to stand by and watch me get cored?"

He looked at her a long time, trying to find the words to refuse her. The Fishers were no different from any bullies—he would cow them come nightfall, if he hadn't already. Renna would be safe in the Brook. She deserved to be safe.

But was simple safety enough? It wasn't for him, so who was he to say it was for her? He'd always looked with derision on those who spent their lives in fear of the night.

Being around Renna was like salt in the wound, a reminder of everything he had given up when he began warding his flesh. It was hard enough around those who never knew him before. Renna made him feel like he was still eleven years old.

But she needed him, and that kept the call of the Core away. Today was the first dawn he had looked forward to since Miln. In his heart, the Warded Man knew he would never survive if he tried to enter the demon world, but seeing his own people put Renna out at night made him want to leave humanity behind forever. If he left Tibbet's Brook alone, he might.

"All right," he said at last, "so long as you keep the pace. You slow me down, and I'll leave you at the first town we come to."

Renna looked around the barn, spotting a beam of sunlight streaming in through the hayloft doors above. She stepped carefully into the sunlight and met his eyes. "I ent gonna slow you," she promised, drawing Harl's knife, "sun as my witness."

"You clutch that knife like it could help you against a coreling," the Warded Man said. "Let me ward it for you." Renna blinked, looking at the knife, then held it out. He reached for it, but she drew it back suddenly, clutching it protectively.

"Knife's one of the only things in the world that's mine," she said. "Like to ward it myself, if you'll teach me."

The Warded Man looked at her doubtfully, remembering her poor warding when they were children. Renna noted the look and scowled.

"I ent nine years old anymore, Arlen Bales," she snapped. "Been warding my property nigh ten years now and ent no demon ever got past, so you quit looking down. Reckon I can draw a ripping circle or a heat ward good as you."

Shocked, the Warded Man shook his head to clear it. "Sorry. The Warders in the Free Cities treated me the same way when I left the Brook. Forgot how insulting it was."

Renna went over to where his gear was stored, pulling a warded knife from a sheath on his saddle. "Here," she said, coming over to him. "What's this'un do?" She pointed to the single ward at the tip. "And why's the rest of the edge just a repeat of this other ward, only rotated? How's it form a net without connectors?" She turned the weapon over in her hands, running her finger over the dozens of wards on the flat.

The Warded Man pointed to the tip. "This is a piercing ward, to break the armor. Those on the side are cutting wards, to let the blade slide in once the armor is broken. Cutting wards are self-linking, if you rotate them proper."

Renna nodded, her eyes dancing along the lines. "And these?" She pointed to the symbols inside the cutting edge.

After supper, Jeph hitched his cart, and the whole family climbed in to head to Town Square. Renna rode with the Warded Man, seated behind him on Twilight Dancer.

They arrived scant minutes before sunset. If the square had been packed the day before, it was near bursting now. Every borough of Tibbet's Brook was represented in full, man, woman, and child. They filled the street and most of the square, more than a thousand souls in all, succored only by hastily hauled and painted wardstones.

Everyone looked up when they rode in, ignoring Jeph's family entirely as they stared at the hooded stranger on his enormous warded stallion, and the girl who rode behind him. The crowd parted as the Warded Man rode through to the center of the square, turning Twilight Dancer back and forth a few times so all could see them. He reached up and pulled his hood down, drawing a collective gasp from the crowd.

"I came from the Free Cities to teach the good people of Tibbet's Brook to kill demons!" he shouted. "But so far, I've seen no 'good people.' Good people do not feed helpless girls to the corelings! Good people do not stand by while someone is cored!" As he spoke, he continued to turn his horse back and forth, meeting as many eyes as possible.

"She wern't no helpless girl, Messenger!" Raddock Lawry shouted, coming to the fore of those from Fishing Hole. "She's a cold killer, and the council voted to have her staked for it."

"Ay, they did," the Warded Man agreed loudly. "And none stood up against them for it."

"Folk trust in their Speakers," Raddock said.

"That true?" the Warded Man asked the crowd at large. "You folk trust your Speakers?"

There was a chorus of passionate *Ays* from every section. The folk of Tibbet's Brook were proud of their boroughs and the surnames they shared.

The Warded Man nodded. "Then I reckon it's your Speakers I'll test." He leapt down from the horse and, from the harnesses on Twilight Dancer's saddle, selected ten light spears he stuck point-down to stand quivering in the dirt.

"Every man or woman of the town council who stands with me and fights tonight, or their heir if they're killed, will get a battle-warded spear," he said, raising one of the weapons, "and the secrets of combat warding, so they can make their own."

There was a shocked silence as everyone looked to their Speaker.

"Kin we have some time to think on it?" Mack Pasture asked. "Don't care to be hasty."

"Of course," the Warded Man said, looking at the sky. "I'd say you have . . . ten minutes. By this time tomorrow, I intend to be back on the road to the Free Cities."

Selia Barren came out of the crowd. "You expect us, the Brook's elders, to stand in the naked night with naught but them spears?"

The Warded Man looked at her, still tall and intimidating after all these years. She'd switched his backside more than once, and always for his own good. The idea of standing up to Selia Barren was more alien to him than staring down a rock demon, but this time it was her that needed a switching.

"It's a sight more'n you gave Renna Tanner," he said.

"Not all of us voted her out, Messenger," Selia said.

The Warded Man shrugged. "You let it happen, all the same."

"Ent no one above the law," Selia said. "When the council voted, we had to put the town first, no matter how we felt."

The Warded Man spat at her feet. "The Core with your law, if it says to throw your neighbor to the night! You want to put town first, come out here and show you can get as you give. Elsewise, I'll take my spears and go."

Selia's eyes narrowed, and then she picked up her skirts, striding firmly into the square. There were gasps of shock from all sides, but Selia ignored them, taking up one of the spears. She was followed immediately by Tender Harral and Brine Broadshoulders. The giant Cutter took up his spear with a hungry look in his eyes. The Squares and Cutters gave a cheer.

"Anyone else have a question?" the Warded Man asked, looking around. As a boy in Tibbet's Brook, he'd had no voice, but now he finally meant to speak his mind. The crowd had suddenly become animated, but he picked the Speakers out easily, islands in the brook.

"Reckon I do," Jeorje Watch said.

The Warded Man faced him. "Ask, and I'll answer with honest word."

"How are we to know you're really the Deliverer?" Jeorje asked.

"Like I said, Tender," the Warded Man said, "I ent. Just a Messenger."

"The Messenger of whom?" Jeorje asked.

The Warded Man hesitated, seeing the trap. If he said no one, many would assume it was because he was a Messenger of the Creator. His best choice would be to name Euchor as his patron. Tibbet's Brook was technically part of Miln, and the people would assume the combat wards were a gift of his. But he had promised to speak honest word.

"No patron for this message," he admitted. "Found the wards in a ruin of the old world, and took it upon myself to spread them to all good folk, so we can start fighting back."

"The Plague cannot end without the coming of the Deliverer," Jeorje said, as if the Warded Man were caught in a logic trap.

But the Warded Man simply shrugged, handing Jeorje a warded spear. "Could be it's you. Kill a demon and find out."

Jeorje dropped his walking stick and took the weapon, a hard glint in his eyes.

"Seen a hundred years and more of the Plague," he said. "Seen everyone I know pass on, even my own grandkin. Always wondered why it was, Creator kept me alive so long when he called so many others to his side. Reckon it was on account of me having something left to do."

"They say in Fort Krasia that a man can't get to Heaven, 'less he takes a coreling with him," the Warded Man said.

Jeorje nodded. "Wise folk." He went to stand beside Selia, and the Watches all drew wards in the air as he passed.

Rusco Hog stomped into the square next, rolling his sleeves up thick and meaty arms. He grabbed a spear of his own.

"Da, what are you doing?" his daughter Catrin cried, running out to grasp his arm.

"Use your head, girl!" Hog snapped. "Anyone selling warded weapons is gonna make a fortune!" He yanked his arm away and went to stand by the other Speakers.

There was movement from the Marsh contingent, where Coran Marsh sat in a hard-back chair. "My da can't even stand without his cane," Keven Marsh called. "Let me fight for him."

The Warded Man shook his head. "Spear's as good a cane as any for a man thinks he can sit in council and play Creator." The Marshes began to shake their fists and shout angrily at him, but the Warded Man ignored them, keeping his eyes on Coran, daring him to step forward. The aged Marsh Speaker scowled, but he stood up from his chair and hobbled slowly over to take a spear. He left his cane on the ground beside Jeorje's walking stick.

The Warded Man's eyes came to Meada Boggin as she broke an embrace with her son and strode out of the cluster from Boggin's Hill. She looked to Coline as she passed, but the Herb Gatherer shook her head. "I got sick to tend," she said, "not to mention any of you lucky enough to make it back out of there."

Mack Pasture shook his head as well. "Ent fool enough to step over them wards," he said. "Got folk and livestock dependin' on me. Din't come here to be cored." He stepped back, and there was a roar of discontent from Baleses and Pastures alike.

"Let us call a new Speaker, if this one ent got the sack!" someone cried.

"Why should I?" the Warded Man shot back at them. "None of you had the sack to stand up for Renna Tanner!"

"That ent true!" Renna called, and the Warded Man turned to her in surprise. She met his eyes with a hard look. "Jeph Bales stood in front of a flame demon for me not five nights hence."

All eyes turned to Jeph, who shrank under the glare. The Warded Man felt like Renna had kicked him in the teeth, but his father was under the test now, and he wanted to know the result more than any.

"That honest word, Bales?" he asked. "You fight a demon in your yard?"

Jeph looked at the ground a long time, then glanced to his children. He seemed to draw strength from the sight, and his back straightened. "Ay."

The Warded Man looked to the Baleses and Pastures, farmers and shepherds from every end of the Brook. "You make Jeph Bales Speaker before sundown, and I'll let him stand."

The roar of approval was immediate, and Norine gave Jeph a shove to get him walking. The Warded Man turned at last to Raddock Lawry.

"Ent no proof them spears even work!" Lawry shouted.

The Warded Man shrugged. "You come out on trust, or you don't come out."

"Don't know you, Messenger," Lawry said. "Don't know where yer from or what you believe. Don't know nothin' but what you say, and what you say is Fishers get no justice!" Many of the Fishers nodded and grunted their agreement.

"So you'll forgive me," Raddock went on, striding into the square and looking out at not just the Fishers, but other Brook folk as well, "if I don't entirely trust your word."

The Warded Man nodded. "I forgive you." He pointed to the mist beginning to rise at the Speaker's feet. "Now I'd advise you either pick up a spear or head back to your wards."

Raddock Lawry made a most undignified sound and scampered back to the Fishers' wards as fast as his old legs would carry him.

The Warded Man turned to regard the Speakers who had stepped forward. They gripped their spears awkwardly, used to holding tools and not weapons, but there was a surprising lack of fear. Except for Jeph who looked white as a snow demon's scales, they seemed at peace. Speakers didn't question decisions once they were made.

"The demons are most vulnerable now, when they are half formed," the Warded Man said. "If you are quick . . ."

Before he even finished speaking, Hog grunted, striding over to a solidifying wood demon. The Warded Man remembered the summer solstice festivals each year from when he was a boy. Hog would have whole pigs on great spits he paid the children to turn over the fire. He lifted his spear and stuck it in the coreling's chest with the same calm efficiency he used to skewer those pigs.

The wards on the spearhead flared and the coreling screamed. The crowd roared, seeing in the semi-translucent demon's body how the magic rocked through it like forked lightning. Hog held tight as the demon thrashed, magic dancing up his arms as the spear came alive with glowing wards. Finally, the coreling's jerking stopped and Hog yanked the spear back out, letting the now solid demon drop to the ground.

"Could get used to that feeling," Hog grunted, spitting on the corpse.

Selia moved next, choosing a flame demon that was beginning to take form. She stabbed down repeatedly as if she were churning butter, and the magic flared, arcing death through it.

Coran did the same, stabbing at another forming flame demon the way he might try to spear a frog in the Marsh, but his leg buckled and he threw himself off balance, missing the demon completely. It made a gurgling noise as it solidified, hawking firespit.

"Da!" Keven Marsh cried, running out into the square. He grabbed one of the two spears still sticking in the dirt and swung it like an axe, knocking the spit right out of the demon's mouth as it rolled with the blow. The spit left a line of fire in the dirt that Keven followed, sticking the demon the same way his father had tried to.

He looked up at the Warded Man, his eyes hard. "Weren't gonna just let my da get cored," he said, baring his teeth and daring protest. His son Fil fetched Coran and helped him back behind the wards.

The Warded Man bowed to him, instead. "Good man."

Jeph hurried to stab at a nearly solid flame demon, but he was not quick enough and it spat flame at him. Jeph screamed, his spear held out diagonally as if to block the fire.

The crowd cried out in fear, but the wards along the shaft of Jeph's spear flared, and the flame was turned into nothing more than a cool breeze. Jeph recovered quickly, spearing the coreling as if he were driving a hoe through a troublesome root. He stepped on its smoking back as he pulled out the spear same as he might step on a batch of hay stuck to the teeth of his rake.

A wind demon solidified, and the Warded Man dropped his robe, grappling and driving the demon into the Boggin wardstones, where it convulsed against the wardnet before falling stunned to the ground. "Meada Boggin," he called, pointing to the prone and helpless demon.

A wood demon swept a branchlike arm at him, but the Warded Man caught its wrist and turned its force against it, flipping it onto its back in front of Jeorje Marsh, who struck his spear as if he were thumping his cane. Magic rocked through him, and his eyes took on a fanatical light.

Tender Harral and Brine Broadshoulders escorted Meada to her kill, standing ready with their spears in case it should recover itself before she could strike her blow. They needn't have worried. She leaned into the blow like she was putting a prybar into an ale barrel.

Another wood demon formed, and Brine and Harral struck it together.

The demons were all solid now. A fair number had formed in the square, but more than half were dead, and the wardstones of the crowd prevented reinforcements from coming.

A flame demon came at Renna and she cried out, but she was still astride Twilight Dancer, and the stallion reared up, trampling it.

"Group, close!" the Warded Man ordered the Speakers. "Spears out ahead of you!" They did as they were told, and cornered two wind demons, sharing the kills. The Warded Man calmly guided them around the square, directing kills, ready to step in if needed.

But he was not called upon to act again, and the remaining demons were quickly dispatched. The Speakers looked around, gripping their spears quite differently now.

"Ent felt so strong in twenty years, when I used to split my own firewood," Selia said. The others grunted in agreement.

The Warded Man looked out at the gathered crowd. "Your elders done it!" he cried. "You remember that, the next time there's a demon in your yard!"

"Ent no demons left in the square," Hog noted. "We done our part of the bargain, so the second part of your payment's due."

The Warded Man bowed. "Now?"

Hog nodded. "I've a stack of blank vellum we can fill in my back room."

"All right," the Warded Man said, and Hog bowed and gestured toward his store. The other Speakers and the Warded Man began to head that way, but Hog turned to face the crowd.

"Come morning," he called, "I'll be taking orders for warded spears at the general store, and hiring folk with a steady warding hand to make them! First come, first served!" A buzz went through the crowd at the news.

The Warded Man shook his head. He knew Hog's business would be brisk. Hog always found a way to profit off things folk could just do for themselves.

CHAPTER 27

RUNNIN' TO

:: 333 AR SUMMER ::

RENNA SAT IN A corner as Arlen taught the council combat warding in Hog's back room. Dasy and Catrin were in and out serving fresh pots of coffee. They watched Renna suspiciously, as if expecting her to suddenly leap up and attack them with Harl's knife, which lay on the table beside her. She'd painted wards on the blade in a neat hand and now worked with one of Arlen's fine etching tools, slowly imprinting them onto the metal. Arlen came by once, trying to see her work, but she turned away from him. She was done asking for help.

Dawn's light was creeping through the cracks in the shutters by the time the Speakers finished, each standing up with a roll of vellum in their hands.

Arlen spoke with Hog a few moments longer, then came over to her. "You all right?"

Renna nodded, swallowing a yawn. "Just tired."

Arlen nodded and put his hood back up. "Might be you can catch a couple hours' sleep back at the farm while Hog readies the supplies we need to head back." He snorted. "The old crook had the stones to charge for them, even after I handed him means to make a fortune."

"Dunno why you expected different," Renna said.

"Leaving town then?" Selia asked as they went for the door. "You turn the Brook on its head, and then ride off before you see what comes of it?"

"Town was already on its head when I arrived," Arlen said. "Reckon I set it aright."

Selia nodded. "Maybe you did at that. What news from the Free Cities? Are they all warding weapons and killing corelings?"

"The Free Cities ent your concern right now," Arlen said. "When the Brook is free of demons, you can look to the wider world."

Jeorje Watch thumped his new spear on the floor. *"Tend your own field, before you look to you neighbor's,"* he quoted, a popular verse from the Canon.

Arlen turned to Rusco Hog. "I want copies made and sent to the Speakers of Sunny Pasture."

"Well, that won't be cheap," Hog began. "The vellum alone will cost near twenty credits, plus having them penned—"

Arlen cut him off, holding up a heavy gold coin. Hog's eyes bulged at the size and thickness of it. "If they don't get their wards, I'll hear of it," he said when Hog took the coin, "and make vellum out of your hide."

Renna saw Hog's ruddy complexion pale, and even though he was larger by far, he shrank back from Arlen's stare and swallowed hard. "Two weeks," he said. "Honest word."

"Learned to bully a bit, yourself," she noted quietly when he came back to her. He didn't look at her, and his hood was still up. For a moment, she thought he might not have heard.

"Got whole lessons on it, during my Messenger training," he said, dropping the gravelly pitch he used when speaking to everyone else. She could picture the grin on his warded lips.

Hog opened the doors to the store, and there was a huge crowd waiting on the steps. "Back!" he bellowed. "Clear a path for the Speakers! Ent taking a single order until you do!" Folk grumbled at the risk of losing their places in line, but they made way, letting them pass.

Raddock Lawry was waiting at the front of the crowd as Renna descended the steps of Hog's porch. "This ent over, Renna Tanner! Can't hide up at Jeph's farm forever."

"Ent hidin' from no one no more," Renna said, looking him in the eye. "I'm leavin' this corespawned town, and ent ever comin' back." Raddock opened his mouth to reply, but Arlen raised a warded finger at him and he fell silent, glaring at them as Arlen laced his hands into a step to help her onto Twilight Dancer's back.

He pulled a small book from his saddlebag, turning and scanning the crowd. Spotting Coline Trigg, he strode over to her. The Herb Gatherer stumbled back from him, tripping over those behind her and going down in a shrieking heap.

Arlen waited for her to right herself, face flushed red with embarrassment, and then pressed the book into her hands. "Everything I know about treating demon wounds is in there," he told her. "You're smart, you'll learn it quick and pass it on."

Coline's eyes were wide, but she nodded. Arlen grunted and leapt into the saddle.

Arlen left Jeph's farm around noon to fetch the promised supplies from Hog. "Pack your things," he said as he left. "We'll leave as soon as I get back."

Renna nodded and watched him go. She had nothing to pack, not even back at Harl's farm. Only Selia's dress on her back, her father's knife at her waist, and the brook stone necklace Cobie had given her, still looped twice around her neck. She wished she had something to offer Arlen in exchange for taking her, but she had nothing but herself. Cobie had thought it enough, but she doubted Arlen would be so easily paid.

Ilain came out onto the porch to stand next to her as she sat etching her father's blade.

"Brought somethin' to eat on your trip," she said, holding out a basket. "Hog cooks so food'll keep more'n he does for taste. His bacon's more smoke than meat."

"Thanks," Renna said, taking the basket. She looked at her sister, whom she'd missed desperately for so many years, and wondered why she had nothing else to say to her.

"You don't have to go, Ren," Ilain said.

"Yes I do," Renna said.

"That Messenger's a hard man, Renna, and we don't know nothin' about him other than he kills demons," Ilain said. "Could be worse'n Da a long sight. You're safer here with us. After last night, folk'll hold their peace with you."

"Hold their peace," Renna said. "Reckon that makes it sunny they tried to stake me."

"So you gonna just run off with some stranger crazy enough to scar himself with wards?" Ilain asked.

Renna stood up and snorted. "If that ent the night calling it dark! You din't love Jeph Bales when you ran away with him, Lainie. Din't know anything other than he was the sort would take a new wife when the old one wasn't even cold."

Ilain slapped Renna, but she didn't flinch, her eyes hard, and it was Ilain who recoiled.

"Difference 'tween us, Lainie," she said, "is I ent running away. I'm runnin' to."

"Runnin' to?" Ilain asked.

Renna nodded. "Tibbet's Brook ent a place I want to live, where folk let a man like Da do as he will, and put me out in the night. I dunno what the Free Cities are like, but they *got* to be better than here."

She leaned in, lowering her voice so none might overhear.

"I killed Da, Lainie," she said, holding up the half-warded knife. "I did. Killed that son of the Core good. He needed killing, not just for what he done, but what he woulda done, I hadn't. Da never paid for anything an ounce of cruelty could take."

"Renna!" Ilain cried, recoiling as if her sister had become a coreling.

Renna shook her head and spat over the porch rail. "You had any stones, you'd've done it yourself long since, when Beni and I were still young'uns."

Ilain's eyes widened, but she said nothing, and Renna couldn't tell if it was guilt or shock. Renna turned away, looking out at the yard.

"Don't blame you," she said after a bit. "I'd had stones, I'd've done it myself the night he stuck me. But I din't, 'cause I was scared."

She turned back and met Ilain's eyes. "But I ent scared no more, Lainie. Not of Raddock Lawry or Garric Fisher, and not of this Messenger. I expect he's a good man, but he turns out like Da, I'll do the world a favor and kill him, too. Sure as the sun rises."

The Warded Man came riding fast into the yard a couple of hours later. Renna was waiting on the porch, and came out to him as Twilight Dancer pranced and kicked up dust in the yard.

"Light's wasting," he said, not even bothering to dismount. He held a hand out to her.

"You're not even going to say goodbye?" Renna asked.

"Life's about to get real interesting in the Brook," he said. "Best no one have cause to think I got anything more to do with Jeph and Lainie Bales than stealing you."

But Renna shook her head. "Your da deserves better than you've given him."

He glared at her. "Ent gonna tell him who I am," he growled.

Renna was uncowed. "Least tell him his son ent dead, or you got no call judgin' which folk are good enough for your wards and which ent." The Warded Man scowled, but he dismounted. Renna was right and he knew it, much as he hated to admit it.

"We're off!" she cried, and everyone came running from all over the yard. The Warded Man looked at his father and nodded away from the press. Jeph followed.

"Rode caravan with an Arlen Bales in the Messengers' Guild," he said when they were alone. "Mighta been your son. Bales name is common everywhere, but Arlen not so much."

Jeph's eyes lit up. "Honest word?"

The Warded Man nodded. "It was years ago, but I recall he worked for Cob's Warding Company in Fort Miln. Might be you can still get word of him there."

Jeph reached out, grabbing one of the Warded Man's hands in both of his own. "Sun shine on you, Messenger."

The Warded Man nodded and pulled away, going over to Renna. "Light's wasting," he said again. She nodded this time and let him lift her into Twilight Dancer's saddle. He climbed in ahead of her, and she held his waist as he trotted to the road and turned north.

"Ent the road to the Free Cities south?" Renna asked.

"Know a shortcut," he said. "Faster, and we avoid the town altogether." Twilight Dancer opened up his stride, and they flew up the road. The wind whipped through Renna's hair, and he joined her as she gave a laugh of exhilaration.

True to his word, Arlen remembered every path and pasture of the local farms in the north of Tibbet's Brook. Before Renna knew it, they were on the main road out of town, past even Mack Pasture's farm.

They rode hard for the rest of the day and were well on the way to the Free Cities when he finally pulled up, with barely a quarter hour before sunset.

"Ent we cutting it close?" she asked.

Arlen shrugged. "Got time enough to set the circles. I was alone, might not stop at all."

"Then don't," Renna said, swallowing her fear at the thought of the naked night. "Promised I wan't gonna slow you."

He ignored her, dismounting and pulling two portable circles from the saddlebags. He threw one over Twilight Dancer and the other in a small clearing, quickly aligning the wards.

Renna swallowed, but she did not protest. Stiffening, she clutched her knife and looked around, waiting for the demon mist to rise. Arlen glanced up and noticed her discomfort. He straightened from his work, going over and rummaging through his saddlebags.

"Ay, there it is," he said at last, opening a cloak with a snap and throwing it over Renna's shoulders. He tied it in place and put up the hood.

The cloth against her cheek was impossibly soft, like a kitten's fur. Used to rough homespun, the fabric was finer than she imagined possible. She looked down and gasped again. There were wards sewn into the fabric with stitches impossibly small. Hundreds of them.

"That's a Cloak of Unsight," Arlen said. "So long as you keep wrapped in it, no demon will even know you're there."

"Honest word?" she asked, amazed.

"Swear by the sun," Arlen said, and suddenly she realized that she was still clutching her knife. Her knuckles ached from the grip when she finally relaxed and let go. She took her first full breath in what seemed like an hour.

Arlen bent back to the circles and quickly had them ready, while she laid a firepit and took out Ilain's basket. They sat together a time, sharing cold meat pies and ham, fresh vegetables, bread, and cheese. Corelings threw themselves at the wards occasionally, but Renna trusted in Arlen's warding and paid them no mind.

"You sit the saddle awkward in that big dress," Arlen said.

"Eh?" Renna said.

"Can't give Dancer his full head with you not seated right," he explained.

"He goes even *faster?*" Renna asked in disbelief.

Arlen laughed. "Much."

She leaned over to him, putting her arms around his shoulders. "If you're looking to get me out of my dress, Arlen Bales, just say so." She smiled, but Arlen recoiled, putting his hands on her waist and lifting her off him like he might lift Mrs. Scratch from her lap. He was on his feet immediately.

"Din't bring you for that, Ren," he said, backing away.

"You ent takin' advantage," she said, confused.

"Ent about that," Arlen said, taking a sewing kit out of a saddlebag. He threw it to her, turning away. "Divide your skirts, and do it quick. We have business yet tonight."

"Business?" Renna asked.

"You're killing a demon by dawn," Arlen said, "or I'm dropping you in the next town."

❦

"Done," Renna called. She'd removed her petticoat and shortened the skirt, slitting it high on each side. Arlen looked up from where he sat warding an arrow at the edge of the circle, and his eyes danced across her bared thighs.

"Like what you see?" she asked, and smirked at his discomfort as he started and quickly met her eyes. "Come into the firelight, you want a better look."

Arlen looked at his hand for a moment, slowly rubbing his warded fingers together, his eyes in distant thought. Finally he shook his head and got to his feet, coming over to her.

"You trust me, Ren?" he asked.

She nodded, and he took out a brush and some thick, viscous ink. "This is blackstem," he said. "It will stain your skin for a few days; perhaps a week."

Carefully, almost lovingly, he brushed her long hair from her face and painted wards around her eyes. When he was finished, he blew gently on them to dry the ink. His lips were inches from hers, and she wanted to put her mouth against them, but she still felt the sting of his rejection and dared not.

When his warding was done, he looked at her. "What do you see beyond the firelight?"

Renna looked around. The night was near pitch dark. "Nothing."

Arlen nodded and laid his hands on her eyes. They were rough hands, scarred and callused, but gentle, as well. There was a soothing tingle in her skin where he touched, and she shivered in pleasure. He took his hands away, and the sensation faded, but the wards around her eyes felt warm now.

"What do you see now?" he asked.

Renna looked around, amazed. Trees and plants now glowed of their own accord, and there was a glowing mist seeping about her feet like a low and lazy fog. "Everything," she said in wonder. "More'n I see in the sun. It's all glowing."

"You're seeing magic," Arlen said. "It seeps up from the Core and gives all living things a spark of it that makes them glow."

"Their soul?" Renna asked.

Arlen shrugged. "I ent a Tender. Corelings are infused with it, and will flare brightly to your eyes now."

Renna turned toward a rustle in the brush, and a wood demon there, invisible a moment before, now shone in the magic-lit world. She looked at her own hands, glowing only faintly. Twilight Dancer was brighter, wards on his hooves and harness glowing like stars in the sky.

But it was Arlen who shone brightest, the wards on his skin positively brimming over with power. It looked as if they were written in light, permanently activated.

"Too many wards," Arlen said, noticing her stare and putting his hood up. "Soaked up too much demon magic to ever be just a man again."

"Why would you want to give up such power?" Renna asked.

Arlen paused, seeming confused. He opened his mouth and closed it.

"Don't know I would," he admitted at last. "But it ent a choice you can take back, and I wan't in my right head when I made it." He pointed at Renna. "You ent in your right head, either."

"Who are you, Arlen Bales, to tell me when my head is right?" Renna demanded.

He ignored her in that infuriating way he had, taking up a spear and handing it to her. She looked at it doubtfully, and made no effort to take it.

"Speakers all done it," Arlen reminded her.

"Know that," Renna said, "but if I'm gonna fight, it'll be with my own knife." She had finished etching the piercing and cutting wards, if nothing else. She held it out for him to inspect.

"It's a fine blade," Arlen noted when he took it. He touched the edge to his thumb, drawing blood with almost no pressure. "Sharp enough to shave."

"Da cared for it better than he did his own kin," Renna said.

Arlen looked at her but said nothing. He held the knife this way and that, inspecting the etched wards. "Good warding," he admitted with a touch of contrition. "Good as any I've seen. Could do with more, but this is enough to start." He handed it back, pommel-first, and Renna grunted as she took it.

"All that's left is to test it," Arlen said. "Time to leave the circle."

Renna had known all along it would be necessary, but she could not suppress the wave of fear that overcame her at that moment, like welling vomit. She'd told her sister that she wasn't scared of anything anymore, but it wasn't entirely true. She might not be scared of *men,* but corelings . . . Memories of her night in the outhouse still haunted her, startling her sometimes even when she was awake.

Arlen put a hand on her shoulder. "We're miles from nowhere, Ren. Corelings cluster where there's people to hunt, or big game. Won't be but a few out here. You got your cloak, and I'm right here."

"To save me," Renna said. He nodded, and she felt a flash of anger. She was tired of waiting for others to save her, but she looked at a wood demon stalking the edge of the road and shivered. "Ent ready for this," she admitted, hating to show her weakness.

But Arlen didn't berate her as he did the Speakers. "Know you're scared spitless," he said. "I was, too, my first time. But I learned in Krasia to *embrace* my fear."

"How's that?" Renna asked.

"Open yourself to the feeling," he said, "and then step your mind back to a place beyond."

Renna snorted. "That don't make any sense."

"Does," Arlen said. "Seen boys half my age charge demons with nothing more than a wardless spear between 'em. Seen 'em ignore pain and keep fighting like everything's sunny till they win or drop dead. Fear and pain can only touch you if you let them."

"Honest word?" Renna asked.

He nodded, and Renna closed her eyes, opening herself up to the sick feeling of her fear. The tension in her limbs and rolling of her stomach. The clenching of her fists and the coldness of her face. When she felt she was aware of it all, she ignored the lot.

Arlen lifted a finger, pointing to a small wood demon clinging to a nearby tree. It would otherwise have blended with the trunk perfectly, but now it glowed fiercely to her warded eyes, a stark contrast with the dimmer glow of the tree.

Trusting in her cloak, Renna left the circle and walked calmly to the demon. It sniffed the air with a look of vague curiosity, but gave no sign it sensed her proximity. Before she realized what she was doing, she stabbed it in the back. The wards flared, and the demon's barklike armor parted easily. There was a shock up her right arm as if she had just put the whole arm in a roaring fire, a pain that pulsed with ecstasy.

The demon threw back and shrieked, but Renna pulled the blade free and stabbed again. And again. A moment later, the demon hit the ground, sending the magic mist flowing away in tiny eddies and whorls.

Renna straightened, inhaling a breath sweet with summer air. She felt stronger, more alive, than she ever had in her life.

Across the road, she caught a glimpse of a flame demon's glowing eyes, and this time, she didn't hesitate, her eyes hard as she charged and dropped to one knee, putting the blade right through its head. This time, she relished the pain of the magic as the demon thrashed and collapsed. Black ichor struck the ground, smoking and starting small fires where it landed.

The original wood demon she had seen on the road was six feet tall, and noticed the commotion. She could have hidden behind her cloak, but the thought never occurred to her as Renna snarled and launched herself at it. The demon roared and took a swipe at her, but Renna was fast and strong like she had never dreamed, and she laughed as she dodged the clumsy attack and put her knife in its chest. This time, it was just like gutting a pig.

She looked around, breathing hard, but not in exhaustion. It felt more like . . . lust. She *wanted* there to be more demons. Wanted there to be a horde of them.

But there were none.

"Told you," Arlen said, smiling. He gathered the circles back up and took Twilight Dancer's reins. "Let's go for a ride in the naked night. Free."

Renna nodded, vaulting easily into the giant stallion's saddle without touching the stirrup. She took the front position, leaving room for Arlen to climb in behind her. He laughed and leapt into place as easily as she had. He put his arms about her and she kicked Twilight Dancer, giving a whoop of glee as the stallion leapt forward and they galloped down the glowing night road.

It had been a full turn since the coreling prince glimpsed its prey in the walled breeding ground. It was forced to spend two nights tracking the one, coming at last to soar above an abandoned ruin thick with his scent. Fresh wards protected the structure, strong ones, but easily breached nonetheless.

There was no need, however, as the mind demon spotted the human mind moving through the woods far from the walls.

With a flap of it gargantuan wings, the mimic banked and soared toward the human, silent as death. The mind demon reached out with its thoughts, seeking access to the one's thoughts, but it was turned away by powerful warding. It hissed, but as it spread its probe wider, it discovered he was not alone. The human mind traveled with a female whose mind was as open as the sky. It slipped quietly into her thoughts and rested unnoticed, seeing through her eyes.

Renna stabbed hard into the wood demon, twisting the blade up into its heart. Next to her, Arlen had wrestled the other one to the ground, holding it prone while the killing wards all over his body did their work.

There was a growl, and Renna looked up to see a third demon appear in the branches above her. She twisted as it dropped, but caught the hilt of her knife on the ridged armor of the first demon. The coreling fell dead, and the weapon was twisted from her grasp.

"Demonshit," she said, dropping to her back and coiling her legs as Arlen had taught her. She caught the wood demon's branchlike arms and pulled them aside as she kicked out, using its own momentum against it. The demon landed right in front of Arlen, who crushed its skull.

"You'd let me paint my knuckles, I could do that myself," Renna said.

"Ent no need to ward your skin," he told her. "Knife's good enough for now."

Renna went over to the wood demon, pulling her knife free. She held it up for Arlen to see. "Din't have the knife."

"You handled it well enough without."

"Only because you wern't still wrestlin' that other one," Renna said. "Ent looking to use a needle, only a brush and some blackstem."

Arlen frowned at her. "Feedback's different when the wards are on your skin, Ren. Strong enough to lose yourself in. I was lost a long time after I started doing it, and I ent myself even now. Don't want to see that happen to you. You mean too much to me."

"I do?" Renna asked.

"Good to have someone to talk to other than Dancer," Arlen said, oblivious to her sudden interest. "I . . . get lonely."

"Lonely," Renna echoed. "Know what that's like. Apt to lose yourself there, too. World's full of things to lose yourself in. Don't mean we should spend our whole lives behind the wards."

Arlen looked at her a long time. Finally, he shrugged. "Can't tell you what to do, Ren. You want to ignore me and paint your hands, it's on you."

The coreling prince observed the courting for several more minutes, amused by human mating rituals. It was clear the one barely understood his magic, oblivious to the mind demon's presence or the extent of his own powers. He had the potential to be a unifier, but here in the wilderness he was no threat and could be safely observed.

The demon let go the female's surface thoughts, probing more deeply into her mind for information on the one, but there was little of value. It planted a question on her lips.

"How'd you bring back the lost wards?" Renna asked, surprising herself. She knew Arlen hated to talk about what had happened to him after he left the Brook.

"Told you. Found them in a ruin," Arlen said.

"What ruin? Where?" she pressed.

"What does it matter?" Arlen snapped. "It ent some Jongleur's saga."

Renna shook her head to clear it. "I'm sorry. Dunno why I got so interested. Dun't matter. Ent lookin' to pry."

Arlen grunted and headed off toward the keep they had spent the last few weeks warding while he trained her to hunt demons.

The coreling prince hissed as the one refused the question. Logic said to kill them both, but there was no urgency. The number of wards around their shelter suggested they would not leave soon. It could observe another few cycles.

As the humans crossed the wards, the mind demon was cut off from the female's mind. A moment later the mimic landed in a clearing and turned to mist, guarding the path as the coreling prince slipped back down to the Core to consider.

CHAPTER 28

THE PALACE OF MIRRORS

:: 333 AR SUMMER ::

IT WAS WELL AFTER dark by the time the council meeting ended. As Leesha expected, they had voted unanimously against her going back to Rizon with Jardir, and had all been appropriately shocked when she reminded them their votes meant exactly nothing.

Leesha was without the benefit of her warded cloak for the walk back to her cottage, but Rojer layered a protective field of music around the group as potent as any wardnet. His powers seemed to have increased tenfold with his new fiddle, but Wonda and Gared kept their weapons ready as they escorted Darsy and Vika.

"Still say you're out of your skull," Darsy growled. She was as intimidating as Wonda—wider if not as tall and every bit as homely, though without the scars to account for it.

Leesha shrugged. "You're welcome to your opinion, but it isn't open for debate."

"What're we s'posed to do if they take you?" Darsy asked. "Ent like we can mount a rescue, and you're what holds this town together, especially with the Deliverer gone off to Creator knows where."

"Prince Thamos and the Wooden Soldiers will be here soon," Leesha said.

"They ent gonna come for you, either," Darsy said.

"I don't expect them to," Leesha said. "You'll just have to trust me to take care of myself."

"I'm more worried about the rest of us," Vika said. "If you marry this man, we lose you forever, and if you don't . . . We'll likely lose you that way, as well. What are we to do?"

"That's why I brought you here tonight," Leesha said. Her cottage came into sight, and they were barely inside before she signaled Wonda to lift the trapdoor to her basement workshop.

"Everyone but Vika and Darsy stays up here," Leesha ordered. "This is Gatherers' business." The others nodded, and Leesha escorted the women down the stairs, lighting her cool chemic lamps on the way.

"Creator," Darsy breathed. She had not seen the cellar in many years, since Bruna had dismissed her as an apprentice. Leesha had expanded it greatly since then, and it now covered the whole underside of the cottage and most of the yard as well, an enormous space. Warded support pillars ran along the walls of the main chamber and the many offshoot tunnels.

Where once Bruna had stored a handful of thundersticks for removing unruly stumps from the ground and a couple of jugs of liquid demonfire, Leesha had what seemed like an endless stockpile.

"There's enough flamework here to turn the Hollow into the face of the sun," Vika said.

"Why do you think I've kept my cottage so far from town?" Leesha asked. "I've been brewing demonfire and rolling thundersticks every night for a year."

"Why didn't you tell anyone?" Vika asked.

"Because no one else need know," Leesha said. "I won't have the Cutters or the town council determining how this should be used. It's Gatherers' business, and you'll dole it out sparingly while I'm gone, and only when it will preserve lives. And I'll have your words that you'll keep the same silence or I'll dose your tea so you don't remember being here at all."

The two women looked at her as if trying to determine whether she was serious, but Leesha was, and knew they could see it in her eyes.

"I swear," Vika said. Darsy hesitated a moment longer, but finally nodded.

"Swear by the sun," she said. "But even this won't last, you don't come back."

Leesha nodded, turning to a table piled high with books. "These are the secrets of fire."

Jardir smiled broadly as Leesha and her escort arrived. It was a smaller group than he had anticipated for such a powerful woman: just her parents, Rojer, giant Gared, and the female *Sharum*, Wonda.

"That one will set the *dama* in a frenzy," Abban said, indicating Wonda.

"They will demand she give up her weapons and cover herself. You should ask that she stay behind."

Jardir shook his head. "I promised Leesha that she could choose her chaperone, and I will not go back on my word. Our people must begin to accept the ways of the Hollow tribe. Perhaps showing them a woman who fights *alagai'sharak* is a good way to begin."

"If she acquits herself well before them," Abban said.

"I've seen the woman fight," Jardir said. "With proper training, she could become as formidable as any *Sharum*."

"Tread carefully, Ahmann," Abban said. "Force change on our people too quickly, and many of them will reject it."

Jardir nodded, knowing well the truth of Abban's words.

"I want you to keep close to Leesha on the trip back to Everam's Bounty," he said. "Use the pretext of teaching her our language, as she has requested. It would be unseemly for me to attend her too closely, but her greenland chaperones should accept you."

"Better than the *dal'Sharum*, I'm sure," Abban muttered.

Jardir nodded. "I want to know everything about her. The food she likes to eat, the scents that give her pleasure, everything."

"Of course," Abban said. "I will see to it."

While the *dal'Sharum* broke camp, Abban limped over to the covered wagon Leesha and her parents rode in. The woman drove the horses herself, Abban noted in surprise. No servants to attend her, nor keep her hands from work. His respect for her grew.

"May I ride with you, mistress?" he asked, bowing. "My master has asked that I instruct you in our language, as you requested."

Leesha smiled. "Of course, Abban. Rojer can take a horse." Rojer, seated next to her in the driver's seat of the cart, groaned and made a face.

Abban bowed deeply, holding tight to his crutch. As the *dama'ting* had feared, his leg had never truly healed, and even now it could buckle at inopportune times.

"If you prefer, son of Jessum, you may ride my camel," he said, gesturing to where the beast was tethered. Rojer looked at the animal dubiously until he saw the canopied and pillowed seat, spacious and richly appointed. A glitter came to his eyes.

"She is a gentle beast who will follow the other animals without direction," Abban noted.

"Well, if it will be a favor to you . . ." Rojer said.

"Of course," Abban agreed. Rojer grabbed his fiddle and somersaulted off the cart, running over to the camel. Abban had lied, of course, the beast was ill tempered at best, but no sooner had it spit at him than Rojer lifted his instrument, calming it as easily as he might an *alagai*. Leesha might have greater value to Ahmann, but Rojer, too, was an asset to cultivate.

"May I ask you a question, Abban?" Leesha asked, breaking him from his reverie.

Abban nodded. "Of course, mistress."

"Have you used that crutch since birth?" she asked.

Abban was more than a little surprised at her boldness. Among his people, his infirmity was either mocked or ignored. No one cared enough about a *khaffit* to ask such things.

"I wasn't born this way, no," Abban said. "I was injured during *Hannu Pash*."

"*Hannu Pash?*" Leesha asked.

Abban smiled. "As good a place as any to begin your lessons," he said, climbing into the cart and taking a seat next to her. "In your tongue, it means 'life's path.' All Krasian boys are taken from their mothers at a young age and brought to their tribe's *sharaj*, a . . . training barrack, to learn if Everam has meant them to be *Sharum, dama*, or *khaffit*."

He tapped his lame leg with his crutch. "This was inevitable. I was never a warrior, and knew it, right from the first day. I was born a *khaffit,* and the . . . rigors of *Hannu Pash* proved it."

"Nonsense," Leesha said.

Abban shrugged. "Ahmann thought much as you do."

"Did he?" Leesha asked, surprised. "I wouldn't guess it from the way he treats you."

Abban nodded. "I beg that you forgive him for that, mistress. My master was called to *Hannu Pash* the same day I was, and he fought against Everam's hand time and again, carrying me through the Kaji'sharaj on his back. He gave me chance after chance, and I let him down every time I was tested."

"Were they fair tests?" Leesha asked.

Abban laughed. "Nothing on Ala is fair, mistress, a warrior's life least of all. Either you are weak, or you are strong. Bloodthirsty or pious. Brave or cowardly. *Hannu Pash* reveals a boy's inner man, and in my case, at least, it was successful. I am not *Sharum* in my heart."

"That's nothing to be ashamed of," Leesha said.

Abban smiled. "Indeed not, and I am not. Ahmann knows my value, but it would be . . . unseemly for him to show me kindness in front of the other men."

"Kindness is never unseemly," Leesha said.

"Life in the desert is harsh, mistress," Abban said, "and it has made my people equally so. I beg you, do not judge us until you know us well."

Leesha nodded. "That is why I am coming. In the meantime, let me examine you. I might be able to do something for your leg."

An image flashed before Abban's eyes, of Ahmann catching sight as Abban lowered his silken pants for Leesha's examination. His life wouldn't be worth a bag of sand after that.

Abban waved her away. "I am *khaffit*, mistress. Not worthy of your attentions."

"You are a man like any other," Leesha said, "and if you're going to spend any time with me, I'll not suffer to hear you say otherwise."

Abban bowed. "I knew another greenlander once who thought as you do," he said, making it seem an offhand comment.

"Oh?" Leesha asked. "What was his name?"

"Arlen son of Jeph, from the Bales clan of Tibbet's Brook," Abban said, and saw her eyes flare with recognition, even though her face showed no other sign.

"Tibbet's Brook is far from here, in the duchy of Miln," she said. "I have never had the pleasure to meet anyone from there. What was he like?"

"He was known to my people as the Par'chin, or 'brave outsider,' " Abban said, "equally at home in the bazaar and the *Sharum's* Maze. Alas, he left our city years ago, never to return."

"Perhaps one day you will meet him again," Leesha said.

Abban shrugged. "*Inevera.* If Everam wills it, I would be pleased to see my friend again and know that he is well." They rode together for the rest of the day, speaking of many things, but the subject of the Par'chin never rose again. Leesha's silence on the matter told Abban much.

Slowed as they were by the trundling cart, the *dal'Sharum* could not give their chargers their head when the sun set, leaving them vulnerable to demons. Ahmann gave the order that they stop and make camp. Abban was erecting his tent when Ahmann summoned him.

"How went your first day?" he asked.

"She has a fast mind," Abban said. "I started by teaching her simple phrases, but she was dissecting the sentence structure in minutes. She'll be able to introduce herself to anyone and discuss the weather by the time we reach Everam's Bounty, and proficient by winter."

Ahmann nodded. "It is Everam's will that she learn our tongue."

Abban shrugged.

"What else did you learn?" Ahmann asked.

Abban smiled. "She likes apples."

"Apples?" Ahmann asked, confused.

"A Northern tree fruit," Abban said.

Ahmann frowned. "You spoke to the woman all day, and all you learned was that she likes apples?"

"Red and hard, fresh picked from the tree. She laments that with so many mouths to feed, apples have become scarce." Abban smiled as Ahmann's face deepened into a scowl. He reached into his pocket, holding up a piece of fruit. "Apples like this one."

Ahmann's smile nearly reached his ears.

Abban left Ahmann's tent, feeling a slight twinge of guilt at withholding Leesha's reaction to his mention of the Par'chin. He had not lied, but even in his own heart Abban could not explain the omission. The Par'chin was his friend, it was true, but Abban had never let friendship stand in the way of prosperity, and his prosperity was inextricably tied to Ahmann's success in conquering the North. The surest road to that success would be for Ahmann to find and kill the Par'chin quickly. The son of Jeph was not an enemy any man should take lightly.

But Abban had survived as *khaffit* by keeping secrets and waiting for the proper opportunity to exploit them, and there was no secret in all the world greater than this one.

Leesha was stirring a cookpot when Jardir came to her circle. Like the Warded Man, he walked casually through the unwarded areas of the Krasians' haphazard camp. He wore Leesha's warded cloak about his shoulders, but it was thrown back, offering him no protection from coreling eyes.

Not that he was likely to need protection, unless a wind demon spotted him from above. The *dal'Sharum* made sport of hunting the field demons that infested the camp when the sun set, piling the bodies of those stunted offshoots of wood demons into what would be an enormous bonfire when dawn came to set them alight.

"May I join you at your fire?" Jardir asked in Thesan.

"Of course, son of Hoshkamin," Leesha replied in Krasian. As Abban had taught her, she broke a piece from a fresh loaf of bread and held it out to him. "Share bread with us."

Jardir smiled widely, bowing low as he accepted the bread.

Rojer and the others came to the pot for their meal as well, but all drifted away at a meaningful look from Leesha. Only Elona stayed in earshot, which Jardir seemed to think was perfectly proper, even if Leesha resented the spying.

"Your food continues to delight my tongue," Jardir said when he finished scraping the stew from his second bowl.

"It's a simple stew," Leesha said, but she couldn't help but smile at the compliment.

"I hope your belly is not too full," Jardir said, pulling out a large red apple. "I have grown fond of this Northern fruit, and would share it with you, as you shared your bread."

Leesha felt her mouth water at the sight. How long since she had eaten a ripe apple? With starving refugees scouring the land around Deliverer's Hollow like locusts, apples were gone from the trees the moment they became edible, and often before.

"I would like that," she said, trying to keep the eagerness from her voice. Jardir produced a small knife, cutting neat round slices for them to enjoy. Leesha savored the sweet crunch of every bite, and it took them some time to finish the fruit. Leesha noticed that however fond he might be of apples, he left almost all of it to her, nibbling only on the irregular cuts and watching her chew with delight in his eyes.

"Thank you, that was wonderful," Leesha said when they were done.

Jardir bowed from where he sat across from her. "It was my pleasure. And now, if you wish, it would be my pleasure to read to you passages from the Evejah, as I have promised."

Leesha smiled and nodded, producing the slender leather-bound book from one of the deep pockets of her dress. "I would like that very much, but if you are to read me your book, you must start from the beginning, and swear to read it through, omitting nothing."

Jardir tilted his head at her, and for a moment Leesha worried that she might have offended him. But then, slowly, a smile crept across his face.

"That will take many nights," he said.

Leesha looked around at the camp and the empty plains. "My nights seem to be rather free at the moment."

Surprisingly, it was not Wonda who garnered the most attention when they reached Everam's Bounty, but Gared. Jardir watched the eyes of the *Sharum* take in the Cutter's enormous frame and powerful muscles, searching for weaknesses, sizing him up for the kill as they did everyone. It was the *Sharum* way to be ready to fight anyone—enemy, brother, father, or friend. Every one of his warriors would be eager to test his strength against the giant Northern warrior. The *Sharum* who brought him down would carry great honor.

It was only after the warriors had assessed Gared, the most obvious threat, that their eyes slipped to Wonda, and a few did a double take, realizing she was a woman.

They sent no word ahead, but when they rode into the courtyard of Jardir's palace, Inevera and the *Damaji'ting* were there waiting for them. Inevera lay on a pillowed palanquin held up by muscular *chin* slaves clad only in bidos and vests. She was dressed as scandalously as ever, and even the greenlanders gasped and colored at the sight of her as her slaves set the palanquin down and she rose to her feet. Her hips swayed hypnotically as she came to Jardir with her hands outstretched.

"Who is that?" Leesha asked.

"My First Wife, Damajah Inevera," Jardir said. "The others are my lesser wives."

Leesha looked at him sharply, and as Abban had warned, her face became a storm cloud.

"You're already married?!" she demanded.

Jardir looked at her curiously. Surely she had understood that much, even if she was prone to jealousy. "Of course. I am Shar'Dama Ka."

Leesha opened her mouth to retort, but Inevera reached them, and she swallowed whatever she had been about to say.

"Husband," Inevera said, embracing him and kissing him deeply. "How I have missed your warmth in our bed."

Jardir was taken aback for a moment, but he saw how Inevera's eyes kept flicking to Leesha, and felt as filthy as if he had been marked by a dog.

"Allow me to present my honored guest," he said. "Mistress Leesha, daughter of Erny, First Herb Gatherer of the Hollow tribe." Inevera's eyes narrowed at the title, and she glared at Jardir, then Leesha.

For her part, Leesha acquitted herself well, not backing down an inch as she met Inevera's gaze with a calm serenity and dipped into the skirt-spreading bow the women of the green lands favored. "An honor to meet you, Damajah."

Inevera's smile and return bow were equally unreadable, and Jardir knew then that Abban was right. Inevera would not accept this woman as a *Jiwah Sen,* and would certainly not take it well when Jardir married her anyway and gave her dominion over the women of the North.

"I would speak with you in private, husband," Inevera said, and Jardir nodded. Now that the moment to face her had come, he had no desire to delay. He thanked Everam that the sun was still high and she could not use her *hora* magic in its light.

"Abban, see to it that the Palace of Mirrors is made ready for Mistress

Leesha and her entourage during their stay," he said in Krasian. The palace was unfit for one such as Leesha, but it was the best Everam's Bounty had to offer, three stories, richly appointed with carpets, tapestries, and silvered mirrors.

"I believe Damaji Ichach is using the Palace of Mirrors at the moment," Abban said.

"Then Damaji Ichach will need to make new arrangements," Jardir said.

Abban bowed. "I understand."

"Please excuse me," Jardir said, bowing to Leesha. "I must consult with my wife. Abban will see to your accommodations. When you are settled, I will come to call on you."

Leesha nodded, a cool gesture that warned of fire beneath. Jardir felt his pulse quicken at the sight, and it gave him strength as he and Inevera strode into his palace.

✤

"What is the purpose of bringing that woman here?" Inevera demanded when they were alone in her pillow chamber beside the throne room.

"The bones have not told you?" Jardir smirked.

"Of course they have," Inevera snapped, "but I hold out hope that this once, they are wrong, and you are not such a fool."

"Marriages cemented my power in Krasia," Jardir said. "Is it so foolish to think that they would serve the same in the Northland?"

"These are *chin*, husband," Inevera said. "Fine for the *dal'Sharum* to breed, but there is not a woman among them worthy to carry your seed."

"I disagree," Jardir said. "This Leesha is as worthy as any woman I have ever met."

Inevera scowled. "Well it does not matter. The bones have spoken against her, and I will not approve the match."

"You are correct, it matters not," Jardir said. "I will still marry her."

"You cannot," Inevera said. "I am *Jiwah Ka*, and I decide who else you may marry."

But Jardir shook his head. "You are my *Krasian Jiwah Ka*. Leesha shall be my greenland *Jiwah Ka*, and have dominion over all my wives in the North."

Inevera's eyes bulged, and he thought for a moment they would pop right out of her face. She shrieked and came at him, long painted nails leading the way. Jardir's back, often clawed by those nails under much different circumstances, could attest to their sharpness.

He was quick to pivot out of the way. Remembering the last time she had struck him, he blocked and dodged with minimal contact as Inevera pressed her attack. Her long legs, clad only in thin, diaphanous silk, kicked high and fast as her fingers stabbed at him, seeking the weak points where a man's muscles and nerves joined. If she managed to connect, his limbs would cease to obey him.

It was the first real display of *dama'ting sharusahk* Jardir had ever seen, and he studied the precise, deadly moves with fascination, knowing Inevera could likely kill a *Damaji* before he knew she had even struck.

But Jardir was Shar'Dama Ka. He was the greatest living *sharusahk* master, and his body was stronger and faster than it had ever been thanks to the magic of the Spear of Kaji. Now that he respected her ability as a warrior and kept his guard, even Inevera was no match for him. Eventually he caught her wrist and flipped her onto the pile of pillows.

"Attack me again," he said, "and *dama'ting* or no, I will kill you."

"The heathen harlot has bewitched your mind," Inevera spat.

Jardir laughed. "Perhaps. Or perhaps she has begun to set it free."

Damaji Ichach sneered at them as he left the Palace of Mirrors with his wives and children.

"If eyes could core you, his would," Rojer said.

"You'd think he hadn't stolen that manse from some Rizonan royal," Leesha replied.

"Who knows with these people?" Rojer asked. "He might have taken it as an honor if we had done him the courtesy of killing him and his family first."

"That isn't funny, Rojer," Leesha said.

"I don't know that I was joking," Rojer said.

Abban came out of the manse soon after, bowing deeply. "Your palace awaits, mistress. My wives will be preparing the lower floors for your entourage, but your private chambers, the entire top floor, are ready to receive you."

Leesha looked up at the giant manse. There were dozens of windows on the top floor alone. That whole floor was for her personal use? It was easily ten times the size of the entire cottage she shared with Wonda.

"She gets the whole floor?" Rojer asked, gawking along with her.

"Of course your chambers shall be richly appointed as well, son of Jessum," Abban said, bowing, "but tradition dictates a virgin bride be kept alone on the top floor with her chaperones below, to ensure that she don her wedding veil with her honor intact."

"I have not agreed to Ahmann's proposal," Leesha pointed out.

Abban bowed. "That is so, but neither have you refused, and so you remain my master's intended until you make your decision. The rules of tradition are unbending here, I am afraid."

He leaned in close, shielding his lips by pretending to stroke his beard. "And I strongly advise, mistress, that unless your answer is yes, you make no final decision while in Everam's Bounty." Leesha nodded, having already come to the same conclusion.

They entered the manse, seeing black-clad women everywhere as they polished and straightened. The main entry hall was lined on either side with mirrors, reflecting the walls into infinity. The carpet running along the center of the polished stone floor was rich and thick, with bright dyes in the weave, and the banister of the wide stairwell leading up was painted in gold and ivory. Portraits, presumably of the previous owners, lined the wall, watching them ruefully as they ascended the steps. Leesha wondered what had become of them when the Krasians came.

"If you would be so kind as to wait up here with your entourage, mistress," Abban said, "I will return shortly to escort them each to their own chambers."

Leesha nodded, and Abban bowed and left them in a massive sitting room whose windows overlooked all of Rizon proper.

"Step outside and guard the door, Gared," Leesha said as Abban left. When the portal was closed, Leesha whirled on her mother.

"You told them I was a virgin?" she demanded.

Elona shrugged. "They assumed it. I just let them keep the assumption."

"And if I do marry him and he learns I am not?" Leesha asked.

Elona snorted. "You wouldn't be the first bride to go to her marriage bed a woman. Ent no man going to turn away a woman he covets over that." She glanced at Erny, who was studying his own shoes as if they were covered in writing.

Leesha scowled, but she shook her head. "It doesn't matter. I'm not going to be just another bride in a harem. The nerve of him, bringing me here without telling me!"

"Oh, for night's sake!" Rojer snapped. "You've got no excuse for not knowing. Every Krasian tale ever told starts with a lord with dozens of bored wives locked in a harem. What difference does it make, anyway? You already said you had no intention of marrying him."

"No one asked you," Elona snapped. Leesha looked at her in surprise.

"You already knew he was married, didn't you?" Leesha accused. "You knew and you still tried to trade me off like a piece of livestock!"

"I knew, yes," Elona said. "I also know that he could burn the Hollow to ashes, or make my daughter a queen. Was my choice so bad?"

"Who I marry isn't your choice to make," Leesha said.

"Well, someone has to make it," Elona snapped. "You sure as night weren't going to."

Leesha glared at her. "Just what have you promised them, Mother? And what did they offer in return?"

"Promised?" Elona laughed. "It's a marriage. All the groom wants is a bed toy and baby maker. I promised you were fertile and would provide sons. That was all."

"You're disgusting," Leesha said. "Just how could you know that, anyway?"

"I might have mentioned your six older brothers," Elona admitted, "all tragically killed fighting demons." She tsked wistfully.

"Mother!" Leesha shouted.

"Do you think six was too many?" Elona asked. "I was worried I overplayed, but Abban accepted it right away, and even seemed disappointed. I think I could have gone even higher."

"Even one is too many!" Leesha said. "Lying about dead children; have you no respect?"

"Respect for what?" Elona asked. "The poor souls of children who don't exist?"

Leesha felt the muscles twinge behind her left eye, and knew a terrible headache was coming on. She massaged her temple. "It was a mistake coming here."

"It's a little late to see that," Rojer said. "Even if they let us go, it would be the same as spitting in their faces if we left now."

The pain behind Leesha's eye flared sharply, bringing on a wave of nausea. "Wonda, fetch my herb pouch." Her mother would be easier to deal with after she had taken a tincture for blood flow to ease the headache.

Jardir arrived soon after the lower rooms were ready and her friends escorted down to them. Leesha wondered if he had purposely waited until she was alone before visiting.

He stood in the doorway and bowed, but did not enter. "I do not wish to give dishonor. Would you prefer to have your mother present to chaperone?"

Leesha snorted. "I'd as soon be chaperoned by a coreling. I think I can handle you if you put a hand where it doesn't belong."

Jardir laughed and bowed again, entering. "Of that, I have no doubt. I must apologize for the meanness of your accommodations. I wish I had a palace worthy of your power and beauty, but alas, this poor hovel is the best Everam's Bounty has to offer at the moment."

Leesha wanted to tell him she had never seen a place so beautiful short of Duke Rhinebeck's keep, but she bit back the compliment, knowing the Krasians had stolen the place and deserved no praise for its splendor.

"Why didn't you tell me you were already married?" she asked bluntly.

Jardir started, and she saw honest surprise on his face. He bowed deeply. "Your pardon, mistress. I assumed you knew. Your mother suggested I not speak of it because your jealousy rivals your beauty, and thus must be terrible indeed."

Leesha felt her temple throb again at the mention of her mother, though she could not deny a flash of pleasure at the compliment, sugared though it might be.

"I was flattered by your proposal," Leesha said. "Creator, I even considered it! But I do not fancy being a part of a crowd, Ahmann. Such things are not done in the North. Marriage is a union of two, not two dozen."

"I cannot change what is," Jardir said, "but I beg you still to not rush to decision. I would make you my First Wife in the Northland, with power of refusal to all who come after. If you wish me to take no other greenland brides, it shall be so. Think carefully on this. If you bear me sons, my people will have no choice but to accept the Hollow tribe."

Leesha frowned, but she knew better than to refuse him flatly. They were in his power and knew it. Again, she found herself regretting her rash decision to come.

"Night will fall soon," Jardir said, changing the subject when she did not reply. "I have come to invite you and your bodyguards to *alagai'sharak*."

Leesha looked at him for a long moment, considering.

"Our war with the *alagai* is the common ground our people stand on," Jardir said. "It will help my warriors to accept you, if they see we are . . . siblings in the night."

Leesha nodded. "All right, though my parents will stay behind."

"Of course," Jardir said. "I swear by Everam's beard that they will be safe here."

"Is there a reason to worry to the contrary?" Leesha asked, remembering the glare of Damaji Ichach.

Jardir bowed. "Of course not. I was simply stating the obvious. Forgive me."

☙

Leesha was impressed with the tight units the Krasian warriors formed for inspection as Jardir led Leesha and the others to *alagai'sharak*. Abban limped at her side, and Leesha was grateful as ever for his presence. Her understanding of the Krasian language was progressing rapidly, but there were hundreds of cultural rules she and the others did not understand. Much like Rojer, Abban could speak without moving his lips, and his whispered hints of when to bow and when to nod, when to placate and when to stand fast, had kept them all from conflict so far.

But more than that, Leesha found she *liked* Abban. Despite an injury that put him in the lowest echelon of his society, the *khaffit* had managed to keep his spirits and his humor, and had risen to new power, of a sort.

"That can't be all of 'em," Rojer murmured, looking at the assembled *Sharum*, over a thousand in number. "No way that many men took a whole duchy. We can field that many fighters in the Hollow."

"No, Rojer," Leesha whispered, shaking her head. "We can field carpenters and bakers. Laundresses and seamstresses who will pick up a weapon at need to defend in the night. These men are professional soldiers."

Rojer grunted and looked out at the assembled men again. "Still ent enough."

"You are correct, of course," Abban said, obviously having heard every word of their whispered conference. "You see but a tiny fraction of the warriors at my master's command." He gestured to the twelve units of men in the courtyard by the great gate. "These are the most elite fighters of each of the twelve tribes of Krasia, chosen as honor guards to their *Damaji* in the city proper. Before you is the most invincible fighting force the world has ever seen, but even they are nothing compared with the million spears the Shar'Dama Ka can muster. The rest of the tribes have dispersed throughout the hundreds of villages in Everam's Bounty."

A million spears. If Jardir could field even a quarter of that, the Free Cities would be best off to surrender quickly, and she should get used to the idea of being Jardir's bed toy. Arlen had seemed convinced the Krasian army was much smaller than that. Leesha looked at Abban, wondering if he was being honest. Dozens of questions popped into her mind, but she wisely kept them to herself, lest they reveal even more of her inner counsel.

Never let anyone know what you're thinking till they've a need to, Bruna had taught her, a philosophy Duchess Araine seemed to agree with.

"And the people living in those villages?" Leesha asked. "What became of *them*?"

"They live there still," Abban said, sounding genuinely hurt. "You must think us monsters, to fear we are slaying the innocent."

"There are such rumors in the North, I'm afraid," Leesha said.

"Well they are untrue," Abban said. "The conquered people are taxed, yes, and the boys and men trained in *alagai'sharak*, but their lives are otherwise unchanged. And in return, they have pride in the night."

Again Leesha studied Abban's face for a hint of where exaggeration might become lie, but she found nothing. Levying boys and men to war was a horror, but at least she could tell the distraught refugees back in the Hollow that their captured husbands, brothers, and sons were likely still alive.

There was a buzz through the ranks of warriors at the sight of Leesha and the others, but their white-veiled leaders barked, and the *Sharum* fell silent and stood for inspection. At their forefront stood two men, one in a white turban above warrior black, the other clad in *dama* white.

"My master's first son, Jayan," Abban said, indicating the warrior, "and his second, Asome." He pointed to the cleric.

Jardir strode out before the men, and the power he radiated was palpable. The warriors looked at him in awe, and even his sons had a fanatical gleam in their eyes. Leesha was surprised to find that after only two weeks of instruction, she understood most of what he said.

"*Sharum* of the Desert Spear!" Jardir called. "Tonight we are honored to be joined in *alagai'sharak* by *Sharum* of the Hollow tribe to the north, our brothers in the night." He gestured to Leesha's group, and a shocked murmur went through the warriors.

"They are to fight?" Jayan demanded.

"Father, the Evejah states clearly that women are barred from *sharak*," Asome protested.

"The Evejah was written by the Deliverer," Jardir said. "I am the Deliverer now, and I will say how *sharak* is fought."

Jayan shook his head. "I will not fight alongside a woman."

Jardir struck like a lion, his hand a blur as he seized his son by the throat. Jayan gasped and pulled at his father's arm, but the grip was like iron, and he could not break it. His feet left the ground, toes barely scraping the dirt, as Jardir flexed his arm to its full length.

Leesha gasped and started forward, but Abban blocked her with his crutch, applying surprising strength.

"Don't be a fool," he whispered harshly. Something in the urgency of his voice checked Leesha, and she eased back, watching helplessly as Jardir choked the life from his son. She drew a relieved breath as the boy was cast to the ground, gasping and thrashing but very much alive.

"What kind of animal attacks his own son?" Leesha asked, aghast.

Abban opened his mouth to speak, but Gared cut him off. "Din't have no choice. Ent no one goin' into the night followin' a pa who can't even keep his own boys in line."

"I don't need advice from the town bully, Gared," Leesha snipped.

"No, he's right," Wonda piped in to Leesha's shock. "I din't understand what they said, but my pa would've smacked my nose off, I took that tone with him. Reckon it'll do 'im good to eat a little dirt."

"It seems our ways are not as different as they first appear, mistress," Abban noted.

Alagai'sharak was a nightly sweep around the perimeter of the city. The *Sharum* exited the north gate and spread out, shoulder-to-shoulder and shield-to-shield, six tribes heading east and six west, killing any *alagai* in their path until they met at the south gate. To avoid further conflict, Jardir deliberately sent Jayan and Asome east while taking Leesha and the others west. Abban was left behind at the gate.

None of the Hollow tribe carried shields, so Jardir put them behind the line, personally escorting Leesha with Hasik and a handful of the Spears of the Deliverer. Demons filtered in quickly after the *dal'Sharum* passed to feed on the corpses of corelings left for the sun, and they did not hesitate to attack the small group.

At first the Krasians had sought to protect them, but as Jardir had hoped, Leesha and the others quickly disabused them of the need. Rojer's fiddle tricked the demons into traps or set them against one another. Leesha hurled her fire magic at the *alagai*, scattering them like sand in the wind. Gared and Wonda strode into packs of demons with impunity, the giant Cutter hacking them to pieces with his axe and machete as Wonda's bow hummed like the strings of Rojer's fiddle, killing every demon she so much as glanced at from afar. She even took several out of the sky before they could swoop down on the shield wall.

She was well away from the others when her arrows ran out. A flame demon hissed and charged at her, and one of the Spears of the Deliverer gave a cry, rushing to defend her.

He needn't have bothered. Wonda slung the bow from her shoulder and grabbed the demon by the horns, pivoting to avoid its firespit and turning it to the ground with a smooth *sharusahk* twist. A warded knife appeared in her hand, slashing the demon's throat.

She looked up, and the ichor lust in her eyes matched that of any *Sharum*

Jardir had ever seen. She smiled to the dumbstruck *dal'Sharum* who had a moment before been rushing to save her, but then her eyes widened, and she pointed to the sky.

"Look out!" she cried, too late, as a wind demon dropped from the sky, tearing through the warrior's armor and laying him open with its deadly talons.

Everyone reacted at once. A warded knife appeared in Rojer's hand, flying to strike the demon at the same time as Wonda's thrown blade and three spears, dropping it before it could take back to the sky. Leesha lifted her skirts and ran to the fallen warrior. The *alagai* was still thrashing, mere inches away, when she knelt at his side. Jardir hurried to join her as Gared and his Spears put an end to the demon and stood watch for others.

The warrior, Restavi, had served Jardir loyally for years. His armor was soaked with blood. He struggled madly as Leesha tried to look at his wound.

"Hold him down," Leesha ordered, her tone no different than that of a *dama'ting*, one used to obedience. "I can't work with him thrashing about."

Jardir complied, taking Restavi's shoulders and pinning him firmly. The warrior met Jardir's eyes, his own wide and wild. "I am ready, Deliverer!" he cried. "Bless me and send me on the lonely road!"

"What's he saying?" Leesha asked as she cut through his thick robe, casting aside the shattered ceramic plates within. She swore as the size of the gaping wound became apparent.

"He is telling me his soul is ready for Heaven," Jardir said. "He asks that I bless him with a quick death."

"You'll do no such thing," Leesha snapped. "You tell him his soul may be ready, but his body isn't."

How like the Par'chin she is, Jardir thought, and found himself missing his old friend deeply. Restavi was obviously dying, but the Northern healer refused to let him go without a fight. There was honor in that, and he knew well the insult she would take if he ignored her wishes and killed the man, even at his request.

Jardir took Restavi's face in his hands, meeting his eyes. "You are a Spear of the Deliverer! You will walk the lonely road when I command it, and not before. Embrace the pain and be still!"

Restavi shuddered, but he nodded, drawing a deep breath as his struggles ceased. Leesha looked at the men in surprise, then pushed Jardir aside and set to work.

"Have the shield wall continue on," Jardir told Hasik. "I will wait with the mistress as she attends Restavi."

"To what end?" Hasik asked. "Even if he survives, he will never lift the spear again."

"You know that no better than I," Jardir said. "It is *inevera*. I will not interfere with my betrothed any more than I would a *dama'ting*."

The Spears of the Deliverer remained behind, forming a circle with Leesha and Restavi at its center, but there was little need. Rojer wove a shield of sound around them, and no *alagai* dared draw near.

"We can move him," Leesha said at last. "I've stopped the bleeding, but he'll need more surgery, and for that I'll need a proper table and better light."

"Will he live to fight another day?" Jardir asked.

"He's alive," Leesha said. "Isn't that enough for now?"

Jardir frowned, choosing his words carefully. "If he cannot fight, he will likely take his own life later."

"Or else he becomes *khaffit*?" Leesha asked, scowling.

Jardir shook his head. "Restavi has killed hundreds of *alagai*. His place in Heaven is assured."

"Then why would he kill himself?" Leesha demanded.

"He is *Sharum*," Jardir said. "He is meant to die on *alagai* talons, not old and shriveled in some bed, a burden to his family and tribe. This is why the *dama'ting* do not see to the wounded until dawn."

"So the ones injured most deeply will be dead?" Leesha asked.

Jardir nodded.

"That's inhuman," Leesha said.

Jardir shrugged. "It is our way."

Leesha looked at him and shook her head. "And there is the difference between us. Your people live to fight, while mine fight to live. What will you do when you win Sharak Ka and have nothing left to fight for?"

"Then Ala and Heaven will be as one," Jardir said, "and all will be paradise."

"So why did you not kill that man when he asked you to?" Leesha asked.

"Because you asked that I not," Jardir said. "I made the mistake once of ignoring such a plea from one of your people, and it almost cost our friendship."

Leesha tilted her head at him curiously. "The one Abban calls the Par'chin?"

Jardir's eyes narrowed. "What did the *khaffit* tell you of him?"

Leesha met him with a stern gaze. "Nothing, other than that they were friends, and that I reminded him of him. Why?"

Jardir's flare of anger at Abban faded as quickly as it came, leaving him feeling empty and sad. "The Par'chin was my friend, too," he said at last, "and you are like he was in some ways, and different in others. The Par'chin had a *Sharum's* heart."

"Meaning?" Leesha asked.

"Meaning he fought for others to live, as you do, but for himself, he lived to fight. When his body was broken and the odds without hope, he clawed his way to his feet and fought to his last breath."

"He's dead?" Leesha asked in surprise.

Jardir nodded. "Many years since."

Leesha worked deep into the night in the surgery of a former Rizonan hospit, cutting and stitching the injured *dal'Sharum* back together again. Her arms were covered in blood and her back ached from bending over the table, but Restavi would live, and likely recover fully.

The *dama'ting* who had taken over the building whispered among themselves as she worked, watching Leesha in something part wonder and part horror. She could sense their anger at her intrusion, especially at night, and their resentment of her barked orders, but her translator was Jardir himself, and none of the white-covered women dared refuse the Shar'Dama Ka. Wonda and Gared had been forced to remain outside, as had Rojer and Jardir's bodyguards.

The *dama'ting*, acting like captives in their own home, breathed an almost palpable sigh of relief when Inevera stormed into the surgery. Her face was livid with rage as she strode right up to Leesha, standing nose-to-nose.

"How dare you?" Inevera growled, her Thesan heavily accented but clear. Perfume hung about her in a cloud, and her wanton dress reminded Leesha of her mother.

"How dare I what?" Leesha demanded, not backing down an inch. "Save the life of a man you would have let bleed until dawn?"

Inevera's only response was to slap Leesha in the face, her sharp nails drawing blood. Leesha was knocked aside, and before she could recover, the woman drew a curved knife and came at her again.

"You are not fit to stand in my husband's presence, much less lie in his bed," Inevera spat.

Leesha's hand darted into one of the many pockets of her apron, and as Inevera drew close, she snapped her fingers in the Damajah's face, scattering blinding powder in a tiny cloud.

Inevera shrieked and fell away, clutching her face, as Leesha righted herself. Inevera splashed a pitcher of water in her face, and when she looked back at Leesha, her face powders were running in horrid streaks. Her red-dened, hate-filled eyes promised death.

"Enough!" Jardir shouted, interposing himself between the two. "I forbid you to fight!"

"*You* forbid *me?*" Inevera demanded, incredulous. Leesha felt much the same—Jardir could no more forbid her anything than Arlen—but Jardir was only focused on Inevera. He raised the Spear of Kaji for all to see.

"I do," he said. "Do you intend to disobey?"

Silence fell over the room, and the other *dama'ting* looked at one another in confusion. Inevera might be their leader, but Jardir was the voice of their god. Leesha could well imagine what might happen if Inevera resisted further.

Indeed, the woman seemed to realize it as well, and deflated. She turned on her heel and stormed from the hospit, snapping her fingers to the other *dama'ting,* who all followed after her.

"I will pay for that," Jardir murmured to himself in Krasian, but Leesha understood. For a moment, his shoulders slumped, and he looked not like the invincible and infallible leader of Krasia, but like her own father after a fight with Elona. She could almost see Jardir imagining all the myriad ways Inevera could make his life miserable, and her heart went out to him.

But then a woman's scream cut the silence, and the tired man vanished in an instant, replaced again by the most powerful man in the world.

CHAPTER 29

A PINCH OF BLACKLEAF

:: 333 AR SUMMER ::

THE GREENLAND GIANT WAS roaring like a lion when Jardir burst from the *dama'ting* sanctuary, Leesha following close behind. Amkaji and Coliv had put lines on his wrists, and three *dal'Sharum* pulled on the rope to either arm, hauling at him like a raging stallion. One warrior, clung tenaciously to his great back, his arms crossed in front of the giant's throat in an attempt to choke him down, but if Gared even noticed, he gave no sign. The warrior's feet swung far from the ground, and even those pulling on the lines stumbled to keep him contained.

Rojer was pinned helplessly, almost casually, against a wall by another *dal'Sharum* who held him in place with one hand as he watched what was transpiring, an amused grin on his face.

"What is going on here?" Jardir demanded. "Where is the woman?"

Before any of the *Sharum* could answer, there was another cry, coming from an alley between the buildings. "Any warrior touching one of the greenlanders when I return will lose the offending hands!" he shouted as he charged to the alley, flying past the others at blinding speed.

Wonda was in the alleyway, held from behind by a warrior who howled as she bit into his arm. Another warrior lay on the ground, clutching between his legs, and a third, Jurim, leaned against the wall, staring in horror at an arm twisted in an impossible direction.

"Release her!" Jardir roared, and everyone looked up at him. Wonda was released instantly, and she drove an elbow into the stomach of the warrior behind her, doubling him over as she reached for the knife at her belt.

Jardir pointed his spear at her. "Do not," he warned. Just then, Leesha made it to the alley, gasping at the sight. She ran to Wonda immediately.

"What happened?" Leesha asked.

"Those sons of the Core tried to rape me!" Wonda said.

"The Northern whore lies, Deliverer," Jurim spat. "She attacked us and broke my arm! I demand her life!"

"You expect us to believe that Wonda lured the three of you here and attacked you?" Leesha demanded.

Jardir ignored them both. It was obvious what had happened. He had hoped Wonda's prowess on the battlefield would impress the warriors enough to dissuade this sort of behavior, but Jurim and the others had apparently felt the need to remind her that off the battlefield, she was still a woman, and an unmarried one at that. By Evejan law, she had no right to refuse a *Sharum* or attack a man for any reason. Jurim and the others had committed no crime, and were within their rights to demand the girl's life.

But the greenlanders did not see it that way, Jardir knew, and he needed their warriors, man and women alike, for Sharak Ka. He glanced at Leesha and knew, too, that not all his reasons were selfless. The *Sharum* would have to be taught to control themselves. An abject lesson like the one he had given Hasik so many years before.

Jardir swept his arm at Jurim and the others, then pointed at the wall. They obediently lined up, backs straight, all of them ignoring wounds the girl had inflicted. She was a born warrior, whatever her gender.

Jardir heard the intake of air in Leesha's mouth and held up his hand before she could speak, pacing before his men.

"I am intended toward Mistress Leesha," he said calmly. "An insult to one of the mistress' servants is an insult to her. An insult to her is an insult to me."

He looked Jurim in the eyes, lightly touching his chest with the point of the Spear of Kaji. "Have you insulted me, Jurim?" he asked softly.

Jurim's eyes widened. He looked frantically at Wonda, and then back at Jardir. He squirmed under the speartip, though its touch was feather-light, and began to shake. He knew his life might depend on his answer, but to lie to the Deliverer would cost him his place in Heaven.

Jurim collapsed, falling to his knees and weeping. He pressed his forehead into the dirt and wailed, clutching at Jardir's feet. "Forgive me, Shar'-Dama Ka!"

Jardir kicked him, taking a step backward and broadening his gaze to take in the warriors on either side of Jurim. Immediately they, too, fell to their knees and ground their foreheads into the dirt, wailing.

"Silence!" Jardir snapped, and the men quieted instantly. He pointed to Wonda. "That woman killed more *alagai* this night than the three of you combined, and so her honor is worth the three of your lives."

The men cowered, but they did not dare to speak in their defense. "Go to the temple and pray through the night and the coming day," Jardir said. "You will take your spears and go into the night tomorrow, shieldless and clad only in black bidos. When you are pulled down, your bones will go to Sharik Hora."

The men shuddered with relief and wept, kissing Jardir's feet, for in those words, he had promised them the only things a *Sharum* truly feared to lose: a warrior's death, and entry into Heaven's paradise. "Thank you, Deliverer," they said over and over.

"Go!" Jardir snapped, and the men ran off instantly.

Jardir looked back at Leesha, whose face was a sandstorm. "You just let them go?" she demanded. Jardir realized that their exchange had been in Krasian, and she had likely understood only a fraction of what was said.

"Of course not," Jardir said, switching back to her tongue. "They will be put to death."

"But they thanked you!" Leesha said.

"For not castrating them and stripping them of the black," Jardir said.

Wonda spat on the ground. "Would serve the coresons right."

"No, it would not!" Leesha said. Jardir could tell she was still upset, but he had no idea why. Should he have killed them personally, in her sight? The greenlanders had different rules for their women, and he had no idea how they handled such matters as this.

"What else do you require?" Jardir asked. "They did not succeed in violating or even harming the girl," he nodded respectfully to Wonda, "so it is not expected that they should compensate her for her virginity."

"Ent a virgin, anyway," Wonda said. Leesha looked at her sharply, but the girl only shrugged.

"But it's required they pay with their lives?" Leesha demanded.

Jardir looked at her curiously. "They will die with honor. They will go naked into the night tomorrow, with only their spears to protect them."

Leesha's eyes bulged. "That's barbaric!"

It was then Jardir understood. The greenland taboo was death. He bowed. "I had thought the punishment would please you, mistress. I can have them whipped, if you prefer."

Leesha looked to Wonda, who shrugged. She turned back to Jardir.

"Very well. But we require to bear witness, and I to treat the men's wounds when the punishment is complete."

Jardir was surprised at the request, but he hid it well, bowing deeply. The customs of the greenlanders were fascinating. "Of course, mistress. It will be done at sunset tomorrow, for all the *Sharum* to see and remember. I will administer the lashes myself."

Leesha nodded. "Thank you. That will suffice."

"This time," Wonda growled, and Jardir smiled to see the fierceness in her eyes. Three Spears of the Deliverer it took just to hold her, and none of them able to do the deed! With further training, even *kai'Sharum* would fall before her. Looking at her, he came to a decision, one that he knew might well tear his army asunder, but Everam had chosen him to lead Sharak Ka, and he would lead as he saw fit.

He gave the woman a warrior's bow. "There will not be another, Wonda vah Flinn am'Cutter am'Hollow. On this, you have my word."

"Thank you," Leesha said, laying a hand on his arm, and Jardir's spirit leapt at the touch.

There was a loud knocking on the door.

"Whozzat?" Rojer cried, starting awake and looking about. His room was dark, though he could see cracks of light at the edges of the velvet curtains.

The bed was a wonder unlike anything Rojer had felt since his time in Duke Rhinebeck's brothel. The mattress and pillows were stuffed with goose feathers, and the sheets smooth and soft beneath a down comforter. It was like sleeping on a warm cloud. Hearing nothing more, Rojer was unable to resist its pull as his head fell back into the pillow's embrace.

The door opened, and Rojer cracked an eye as one of Abban's wives, or perhaps one of his daughters—Rojer could never tell the difference—entered. She was clad as they all were in loose black robes that hid everything save her eyes, which were cast down in his presence.

"You have a visitor, son of Jessum," the woman said.

She moved to throw back the heavy velvet curtains and Rojer groaned, throwing a hand over his eyes as light streamed in through the windows of his richly appointed bedroom. Leesha might have a whole floor of the giant manse, but Rojer had still been given a full wing of the second floor, more rooms than the entire inn his parents had run in Riverbridge. Elona had been furious to learn of the largesse the Krasians had heaped upon him, having only gotten a bedroom and sitting room herself, luxurious though they were.

"What hour is it?" Rojer asked. He felt he couldn't have slept more than an hour or two.

"Just after sunrise," the woman said.

Rojer groaned again. He hadn't slept an hour. "Tell whoever it is to come back later," he said, flopping back into the mattress.

The woman bowed deeply. "I cannot, master. Your visitor is the Damajah. You must see her at once."

Rojer sat bolt upright, all thoughts of sleep forgotten.

The whole palace was astir by the time Rojer felt presentable enough to leave his chambers. His Jongleur's paintbox had taken the circles from beneath his eyes, and his bright red hair was brushed and tied back. He wore his best motley.

The Damajah, he thought. *What in the Core does she want with me?*

Gared was waiting for him in the hall, and fell in behind him. Rojer could not deny that he felt safer with the big Cutter, and by the time he made it to the stairs, Leesha and Wonda were descending from above with Erny and Elona in tow.

"What does she want?" Leesha asked. She had gotten no more sleep than him, but she showed it less, even without paint and powder.

"Search my pockets," Rojer said. "You'll find no answers."

They all followed Rojer down the stairs, making him feel as if he were leading them to a cliff. Rojer was a performer, used to being the center of attention, but this was different. He put his hand to his chest, clutching his medallion through his shirt. The hard shape gave him comfort as he followed the gestures of Abban's women into the main receiving hall.

As before, Rojer felt his face heat at the sight of the Damajah. He had bedded dozens of village girls and more than one cultured Angierian royal, all of them fetching or pretty or even beautiful. While Leesha surpassed them all in beauty, she seemed almost unaware of that fact, making no effort to take advantage of her power.

But the Damajah knew. The perfect curve of her chin and gentle shape of her nose behind her transparent veil. The wide exotic eyes with long sweeping lashes, and the oiled black curls that spilled in rivulets down her shoulders. Her diaphanous robe covered everything and nothing, showcasing the smoothness of her arms and curving thighs, the round fullness of her breasts and the darkness of her areolae, her hairless sex. The air about her was sweet with perfume.

But more, her every gesture, every stance, every expression, brought all these things into a harmony that sang to every man in her presence. What Rojer did to demons with his fiddle, the Damajah did to men with her body. He felt himself stiffen, and was thankful for the looseness of his motley pants.

She stood in the receiving hall, two girls standing behind her, covered in the Krasian fashion Inevera disdained, though their robes were fine silk. One was clad in the white of a *dama'ting,* the other in black. Long black braids fell from the back of their headscarves, bound in gold bands and reaching past their waists. Their eyes danced at him from behind their veils.

"Rojer asu Jessum am'Inn am'Bridge," Inevera said in a thickly accented tongue that made Rojer shiver with pleasure. He tried to remind himself she was his enemy, but it seemed futile. "I am honored to meet you," the Damajah went on, bowing so deeply Rojer feared her breasts would fall free of her robe. He wondered if she would care if they did. The girls behind her bowed even deeper.

Rojer made his best leg in return. "Damajah," he said simply, not knowing the proper form of address. "The honor is mine, that you have come here to meet one as insignificant as I."

"Don't lay it too thick, Rojer," Leesha muttered.

"My husband bade me come," Inevera said, "telling me you accepted his offer to find brides for you, that your magic be passed on to a new generation."

"I did?" Rojer asked. He remembered the exchange back in Deliverer's Hollow, but he had thought it all a jest. They couldn't possibly believe . . .

"Of course," Inevera said. "My husband offers you his eldest daughter, Amanvah, for your *Jiwah Ka.*" The girl in *dama'ting* white stepped forward, kneeling on the thick carpet and pressing her face to the floor. It pulled her silk robe tight, hinting at a womanly figure beneath. Rojer tore his eyes away before he was caught staring, looking back at the Damajah like a terrified rabbit.

"There must be some . . ." *mistake,* he wanted to say, but the word caught in his throat as Inevera beckoned the other girl forward. "This is Amanvah's servant, Sikvah," she said, as the girl followed Amanvah to the floor. "Daughter of Hanya, sister to the Shar'Dama Ka."

"His daughter and his niece?" Rojer asked in surprise.

Inevera bowed. "My husband has made it known that Everam speaks to you. He would not honor you with less than his own blood. Sikvah will make a suitable second wife, if you wish. Amanvah can then take over seeking future brides in accordance with your own taste."

"Creator, how many wives does one man need?" Leesha said.

Jealous? Rojer thought irritably. *Good. Have a taste of it, for once.*

Inevera looked at Leesha with disdain. "If he is worthy and they of him, a man should have as many as he can provide for and keep with child. But some," she sneered at Leesha, "are not worthy."

"Who is Amanvah's mother?" Elona asked before Leesha could respond.

Inevera looked at her and raised a brow. Elona spread her skirts and dipped into a smooth, respectful curtsy that seemed utterly at odds with the woman Rojer knew. "Elona Paper of Deliverer's Hollow. Leesha's mother."

Inevera's eyes widened at this news, and she smiled widely and went over to the woman, embracing her. "Of course, I am honored to meet you. There are a great many matters for us to discuss, but that is for another time. I understand the son of Jessum's mother is with Everam. Will you stand for her in these proceedings?"

"Of course," Elona said, nodding, and Leesha glared at her.

"Stand for her, how?" Rojer asked.

Inevera smiled coyly. "To ensure you behave as they lift their veils, and to verify their virginity." Rojer felt his face heat again, and he swallowed a lump in his throat.

"I . . ." he began, but Inevera ignored him.

"I am Amanvah's mother," she told Elona. "Does that meet with your approval?"

"Of course," Elona said gravely, as if there were any other answer a sane person might dare speak.

Inevera nodded and turned to regard the others. "If you will excuse us, please?"

Everyone stood still for a moment, but Elona clapped her hands, startling them all. "You heard her, shoo! Not you, Rojer." She grabbed his arm as he turned to go with the rest.

Only Leesha stood behind.

"You have no place here, daughter of Erny," Inevera said. "You are not family to the groom or brides."

"Oh, but I am, Damajah," Leesha said. "If my mother stands for Rojer's, then I, as her daughter, may take the place of his sister." She smiled and leaned in close, lowering her voice. "The Evejah is quite clear on the matter," she said smugly.

Inevera scowled and opened her mouth, but Rojer cut her off. "I want her to stay." The words ended in a squeak as Inevera turned to him, but then a wide smile licked across her face, and she bowed. "As you wish."

"Lock the doors, Leesha," Elona ordered. "Can't have Gared stumbling back in saying he forgot his axe." Inevera laughed, and the sight of their joined amusement frightened Rojer more than anything. Elona seemed to know far more than Rojer about what was happening.

Leesha seemed equally disturbed, but whether it was from the laughter or the casual way Elona ordered her around, he couldn't be sure. She turned and strode to the huge gilded doors, throwing the bar with a sound that made Rojer jump. He felt more like they were locking him *in* than Gared and the others *out*.

Inevera snapped her fingers, and the two girls straightened their backs, though they remained on their knees on the floor.

"Amanvah is *dama'ting*," Inevera said, laying a hand on her shoulder. "Healer, midwife, and chosen of Everam. She is young, but she has made her dice and passed every test."

She looked at Leesha and smiled. "Perhaps she can treat those cuts on your face," she said, indicating the red lines on Leesha's cheek from where Inevera had scratched her.

Leesha smiled in return. "You seem to be blinking a great deal, Damajah. Do your eyes sting you? I could prepare a rinse, if you wish."

Rojer looked back to Inevera, expecting a vicious response, but Inevera simply smiled and went on. "I myself have given my husband eight sons and three daughters. The women of my family are similarly fertile, and the bones say Amanvah will breed true."

"Bones?" Leesha asked.

Inevera scowled. "That is no concern of yours, *chin*," she snapped.

In an instant her smile was back in place. "What matters is that Amanvah will give you sons, son of Jessum. Sikvah's mother was similarly fertile. She, too, will breed well for you."

"Yes, but can they sing?" Rojer asked, hoping to deflect the discomfort he was feeling. It was the punch line of a favorite bawdy joke of Arrick's, a tale of a man who could never be satisfied no matter how many women he bedded.

But Inevera only smiled and nodded. "Of course," she said, snapping her fingers and barking an order to the girls in Krasian.

Amanvah cleared her throat and began to sing, her voice rich and pure. Rojer didn't understand the words, and had never had a knack for singing himself, but after years of performing with Arrick, the greatest singer of his time, he knew well how to listen and judge it.

Amanvah's voice put Arrick's to shame. It lifted him like a great wind, stealing the footing from under him and sweeping him away on its notes.

But then a second wind came, wrapping itself around the other as Sikvah smoothly joined in. They found harmony instantly, and Rojer was stunned.

Women or no, if they went to the Jongleurs' Guild in Angiers, their careers would be assured.

Rojer said nothing, standing in silence while the two women sang. When Inevera finally ended their song with a wave, he felt like a puppet with its strings suddenly cut.

"Sikvah is also an accomplished cook," Inevera said, "and both have been trained in the art of lovemaking, though they are unknown to man."

"The . . . ah, art?" Rojer asked, feeling his face heat again.

Inevera laughed and snapped her fingers. Amanvah immediately rose, coming gracefully to her feet as she lifted a hand to unfasten her veil. The thin white silk drifted away like a wisp of smoke, revealing a face stunning in its beauty. Amanvah was her mother's daughter.

Sikvah came up behind her, undoing some hidden fastening at her shoulders, and Amanvah's entire robe seemed to simply dissolve, the silk running off her to whisper to the floor. She stood naked before him, and Rojer gaped.

Inevera circled a finger, and Amanvah obediently turned so Rojer could inspect her from every angle. Like her mother's, Amanvah's body was perfect, and Rojer began to fear even his motley pants were not loose enough. He wondered if he would be expected to undress as well, and have all the women see his arousal.

"Creator, is all this truly necessary?" Leesha asked.

"Be quiet," Elona snapped. "Of course it is."

Amanvah turned and unfastened Sikvah's own silk robe, and it vanished like a shadow in the sun, becoming an inky pool at her feet. She was not as beautiful as Amanvah, perhaps, but apart from the other women in the room with him just then, Rojer had never seen her equal.

"You may verify their purity now," Inevera said.

"I . . . ah." Rojer looked at his hands, and then hid them in his pockets. "That won't be necessary."

Inevera laughed. "Your women," she clarified, her smile mischievous. "Something must be saved for the wedding night, after all." She winked at him, and Rojer felt dizzy.

Inevera turned to Elona. "Would you care to do the honors?"

"Ah . . . well . . ." Elona said, "my daughter is more qualified . . ."

Leesha snorted. "My mother wouldn't know a hymen if she saw one," she whispered to Rojer. "She was rid of hers before she had a good look at it."

Elona caught the words and scowled, but she said nothing, glaring at Leesha.

"Oh, all right," Leesha growled at last, "anything to get this business concluded." She bent to pick up the girls' robes, then took their arms and led them into a small curtained servant alcove to the side of the hall.

Leesha lowered the curtain, blocking them from view, and the girls obediently leaned over a small table, presenting themselves like brood mares. She had examined hundreds of young girls in her years as an Herb Gatherer, even the duchess of Angiers herself, but it was always for their health, not some honor ritual. Bruna had little patience for such nonsense, and her apprentice was no different.

But Leesha knew too how fragile their relationship with the Krasians was. She would win no allies by publicly spitting on their traditions.

Amanvah's hymen was intact, but when Leesha reached for Sikvah, the girl flinched and gave a slight gasp. There was a sheen of sweat on her, and her olive skin seemed paler than before. She clenched tight when Leesha slipped a finger into her, but it was not enough. She wasn't a virgin.

Leesha smirked. As barbaric as this ritual was, it had just given them reason to claim offense and refuse the girls before Rojer said something foolish. But then the girl looked back at her, and the fear in her eyes was a slap in the face. Amanvah caught the look and scowled.

"Get dressed," Leesha told the girls, tossing them their robes. Sikvah quickly dressed and then moved to assist Amanvah, who glared at her as she fastened the *dama'ting*'s silk robe.

Leesha's face was serene as she returned with the girls. Rojer knew the verdict was irrelevant—he was no more going to marry Jardir's daughter than Leesha was the man himself—but for some reason, his heart was thudding in his chest as if his life depended on the answer.

"Both virgins, for what it's worth," Leesha said, and Rojer took a deep breath.

"Of course," Inevera smiled. But Amanvah did not seem to agree. She moved to her mother, whispering in her ear and pointing first at Sikvah, and then at Leesha.

Inevera's face darkened like the sky before a storm, and she strode over to Sikvah, grabbing the girl by her long braid. Rojer started for them, but Elona grabbed his arm so hard it hurt, holding him back with surprising strength.

"Don't be stupid, fiddle boy," she hissed. Sikvah shrieked as she was dragged behind the examination curtain. Amanvah followed, pulling it shut behind them.

"What in the Core just happened?" Rojer asked.

Leesha sighed. "Sikvah's not a virgin."

"But you said she was," Rojer said.

"I know what can happen to a girl when people start questioning her 'purity,' " Leesha said, "and I'll be corespawned before I do it to anyone else."

Elona shook her head. "Can't save people from themselves, Leesha. Your little lie's probably made it worse for her still. You'd just told the truth and let me ask for a bag of gold to make up for her lost value, it would be done with already."

"She's a human being, Mother, not a . . . !"

Rojer ignored them, his eyes on the curtain, and the poor girl with the beautiful voice. There was some muffled shouting, but Rojer could make no sense of it over the shrill cacophony beside him. "Will you both please shut it?!"

Both women glared at him angrily, but they quieted. There was no sound from the curtain now, and that scared Rojer all the more. He was about to rush over when it opened and Inevera strode back to them, Amanvah and a weeping Sikvah in tow. Amanvah had her arm around the other girl, comforting her and offering support. Rojer's heart went to them, and his hand slipped up to touch his medallion through his shirt.

Inevera bowed to Rojer. "I apologize for the insult to you, son of Jessum. Your weed picker has lied to you. Sikvah is impure and will, of course, be punished severely for her lies. I beg you not to doubt my daughter's honor by her association with this harlot." She fingered the jeweled knife at her waist as she spoke, and Rojer was forced to wonder what sort of punishment these hard people considered "severe."

There was a pause as everyone waited for his response. Rojer's eyes flicked around the room, and it seemed as if every woman was holding her breath. Why? They had given no thought to him at all a moment ago.

But then it hit him. *I'm the offended.*

He smiled, slipping into a Jongleur's mask as he straightened his back and met Inevera's eyes fully for the first time. "After hearing them sing, I'll not break the set. Sikvah's voice is more important to me than her purity."

Inevera relaxed slightly. "That is most forgiving of you. More than this harlot deserves."

"I'm not deciding anything yet," Rojer clarified. "But I would prefer she not be subject to . . . undue stress that might affect her voice before I do." Inevera smiled behind her gossamer veil as if he had passed some kind of test.

Elona took Rojer by the arm, yanking him back. "This will affect the dower, of course."

Inevera nodded. "Of course. If you will agree to chaperone, the girls may stay in the son of Jessum's wing, that he might accustom to them and ensure their lack of . . . stress before he makes his decision."

"Oh, my mother is an excellent chaperone," Leesha muttered. Inevera looked at her curiously, as if unsure about the sarcasm in Leesha's tone, but she said nothing.

Rojer shook his head, as if coming out of a dream. *Did I just get promised?*

Abban arrived just before sunset to escort them to the whipping. Leesha made a last check of the herbs and implements in her basket, breathing deeply to quell her churning stomach. For what they did to Wonda, the *dal'Sharum* deserved no less, but that did not mean Leesha wanted to watch their backs torn open. After seeing how lax the Krasians were about healing, though, she worried the wounds might infect and kill the men anyway if she did not treat them herself.

In Fort Angiers, she and Jizell had weekly treated men off the magistrate's whipping post, but she'd never been able to watch the punishment without weeping, and usually turned away. It was a horrid practice, though Leesha seldom had to treat the same man twice. They took the lesson and remembered.

"I hope you understand the honor my master pays you and the daughter of Flinn by administering the whipping personally," Abban said, "rather than leaving it to some *dama* who might be lenient in sympathy to their act."

"The *dama* have sympathy for rapists?" Leesha asked.

Abban shook his head. "You must understand, mistress, that our ways are different from yours. The fact that you and your women walk freely with your faces and your, ah . . ." he waved a hand at Leesha's low neckline, "charms showing offends a great many men, who fear you put illicit ideas into the minds of their own women."

"And so they sought to show Wonda her place," Leesha said. Abban nodded.

Leesha's brow furrowed, but her stomach suddenly calmed. Intentionally hurting another human being went against her Gatherer's oaths, but even Bruna had not hesitated to hand out a few painful lessons to folk who failed to act civilized.

"My master has commanded that the *Damaji* attend as well, with their *kai'Sharum*," Abban said. "He wishes them to see that they must accept some of your ways."

Leesha nodded. "Ahmann said it was much the same when he met the Par'chin."

Abban's face remained carefully neutral, but Leesha saw his coloring change slightly. It wasn't surprising that Arlen had that effect on people even before he began to tattoo his flesh.

"My master mentioned the Par'chin?" Abban asked.

"I did, actually," Leesha said. "I was surprised that Ahmann knew him, too."

"Oh, yes, my master and the Par'chin were great friends," Abban said to Leesha's surprise. "Ahmann was his *ajin'pal*."

"Ajin'pal?" Leesha asked.

"His . . ." Abban's brow furrowed as he searched for the proper term, ". . . blood brother, perhaps you would say. Ahmann showed him the Maze, and they bled for each other. Among my people, this is as binding as having the same blood in your veins." Leesha opened her mouth, but before she could say more, Abban cut her off.

"We must leave now, if we are to arrive in time, mistress," he said. Leesha nodded, and they gathered the rest of her delegation from the Hollow, including Amanvah and Sikvah, who attended closely to Rojer.

They were escorted to the town circle of Fort Rizon, a huge cobbled ring at the center of the city eyed with a great well and surrounded by bustling shops. Leesha saw Rizonan women shopping as well as Krasians, but though they still wore their Northern dresses, the women's faces were wrapped in cloth that draped over their necklines as they went about in public. Many of them stared wide-eyed at Leesha and her mother, walking about uncovered, as if expecting their *dal'Sharum* escorts to turn on them at any moment.

Many of the Krasians had already gathered, including the *Damaji* in their canopied palanquins and many *Sharum* and *dama*. Three wooden posts had been erected in the circle, but there were no shackles or ropes to be seen.

There was a commotion and the crowd turned to see Jardir enter the circle, followed by Inevera on her palanquin and his other wives in tow. Leesha counted fourteen of them, but had no idea if that was all. They came and stood next to Leesha and the Hollowers, close enough for Leesha to smell the Damajah's perfume.

Jardir walked to the posts, waving his hand at the Spears of the Deliverer. The three *dal'Sharum* needed no urging and no escort, walking out into the square and stripping to the waist. They knelt and touched their foreheads to the cobbles before Jardir, then stood and wrapped their arms around the poles with nothing to hold them in place. The one whose arm Wonda had broken had the limb in a white cast.

Jardir reached into his robe, pulling free a three-tailed whip of braided leather, with sharp pieces of metal woven into the last few inches of each tail.

"What is that?" Leesha asked Abban. She was expecting Jardir to use a simple horsewhip. This seemed more brutal by far.

"It is called the alagai tail," Abban said. "A *dama's* whip. They say being struck by it is like the lash of a sand demon's tail."

"How many strokes will they each get?" Leesha asked.

Abban laughed. "As many as they can stand for. *Sharum* are whipped until they lose their grip on the pole and fall."

"But . . . that could kill them!" Leesha said.

Abban shrugged. "*Sharum* are great warriors, but not known for their intelligence or instinct for self-preservation. They think it a test of manhood to endure as many strokes as possible. Their brethren will be betting to see who endures longest."

Leesha scowled. "I will never understand men."

"Nor I," Abban agreed.

It was brutal to watch, each strike of the alagai tail leaving bright lines of blood on the backs of its victim. Jardir gave each man a stroke before returning to the first, but Leesha didn't know if it was a kindness, or an attempt to keep them from growing numb to it. She flinched with every blow, feeling as if it were striking her, too. Tears streaked her face, and she wanted nothing more than to flee the awful scene as the backs of the men became huge open wounds that showed their ribs to the world. None of them even cried out or had the sense to fall.

At one point she looked away and saw Inevera watching the proceeding with utter calm. She saw Leesha looking her way, and sneered at the tears on her face.

Something broke in Leesha then, a flare of anger acting as a ward against the suffering of the men. She straightened her back, dried her eyes, and watched the rest of the whipping with the same cool detachment the Dama-jah showed.

It seemed to go on forever, but at last one of the warriors fell, and then another. Leesha saw warriors exchanging coins over the results, and wanted to spit. When the last man fell, Jardir nodded to her, and Leesha rushed out to the men, pulling out the thread, salves, and bandages she had prepared. She hoped she had enough.

Jardir thumped his spear, making her glance up at him.

"Spread the word to all who would see paradise at the end of the lonely path!" Jardir bellowed, his voice booming through the circle and into the streets. "Any woman who takes a demon in *alagai'sharak* shall be *Sharum'-ting*, and have all the rights of *Sharum* accorded her!"

A shocked murmur ran through the assembled warriors, and Leesha saw horrified faces on *dama* and *Sharum* alike. Angry protests began, but Jardir silenced them with a roar.

"If any oppose this decree tonight," he said, baring his teeth, "let them step forward. I promise a quick death with honor. To any who oppose my word tomorrow, I will not be so lenient." There were many scowling faces in the crowd, but none foolish enough to step forward.

The next day, Abban arrived in the courtyard of the Palace of Mirrors with a *dal'Sharum* at his side. The warrior's red night veil was around his shoulders, and his black beard was shot through with gray. There was nothing else remotely weak about the man, but Leesha was still surprised. Few of the Krasian warriors seemed to live long enough for their beards to be touched with gray at all. He walked proudly, but his hard face was pinched, as if he was biting back a scowl.

"May I present Gavram asu Chenin am'Kaval am'Kaji, Drillmaster of the Kaji'sharaj," Abban said. The warrior bowed at the introduction, and Leesha spread her skirts and dipped a curtsy in response.

The warrior said something in Krasian, too fast for Leesha to follow, but Abban was quick to interpret. "He says, 'I am here at the Deliverer's command to train your warriors for *alagai'sharak*.' Drillmaster Kaval was instructor to the Shar'Dama Ka and myself when we were in *Sharaj*," Abban added. "There is no one better."

Leesha's eyes narrowed, and she looked at Abban, searching for the elusive truth in the practiced smoothness of his face. He was crippled in *sharaj*, after all.

Leesha turned to Gared and Wonda. "Do you wish to train?"

Kaval and Abban had a short exchange, again speaking so fast that Leesha, despite understanding many of the words, could still not follow. Abban seemed to argue a point, but Kaval balled a fist, and the *khaffit* bowed in submission.

"The drillmaster asks that I tell your warriors their wishes are irrelevant. The Shar'Dama Ka has given a command, and it will be followed."

Leesha scowled and opened her mouth, but Gared cut her off. "S'allright, Leesh." He put up a hand. "I want to learn."

"Me, too," Wonda said.

Leesha nodded and stepped aside as Kaval beckoned the two forward for examination. He grunted in approval at giant Gared, but seemed less impressed with Wonda, though she was as big and strong as most *dal'Sharum*. He then came back to Leesha.

"I can make a great warrior of the giant," Abban translated, "if he is disciplined. The woman . . . we shall see." He did not look hopeful.

The drillmaster stepped back into the courtyard, his movements quick and graceful. He looked at Gared and barked a command, thumping his chest.

"The drillmaster would like you to attack him," Abban supplied.

"Din't need you to translate that," Gared said. He stepped forward, towering over the drillmaster, but Kaval seemed unimpressed. Gared roared and attacked, but his punches, careful though they were, met only air. He lunged to grapple and found himself on his back a moment later. Kaval twisted his arm until Gared screamed, and then released him.

"He will be even harder on you," Abban advised Wonda. "Steel yourself."

"Ent afraid," Wonda said, stepping forth.

Wonda lasted longer than Gared, her moves smoother and quicker, but the outcome was never in doubt. Twice, Wonda's blows came close enough that the drillmaster required contact to block them, but he responded once with a backhand to her jaw that sent her reeling and spitting blood, and the next time with a heavy blow to the stomach that doubled the girl over as she vomited the air from her stomach.

Kaval caught her arm before she could recover and twisted her to the cobbles. Wonda kicked him in the face as she went down, connecting solidly, but Kaval was unfazed, his mouth widening to a smile as he twisted her arm. Wonda's face grew pale and she gritted her teeth, but she refused to cry out.

"The drillmaster will break her arm if she does not submit," Abban warned.

"Wonda," Leesha said, and the girl finally had the sense to let out a cry.

Kaval released her and said something to Abban in a grudging tone.

"Perhaps I can make something of her, after all," Abban translated. "Please leave us, so we may train without distraction."

Leesha looked at Gared and Wonda, and nodded. "Why don't you join Rojer and I for tea, Abban."

"I would be honored," Abban said, bowing.

"But first," Leesha said, her voice hardening, "make it clear to Master

Kaval that there will be the Core to pay if I come back to find warriors too injured to fight tonight."

Abban's wives tried to serve them, but Amanvah hissed and they backed off. She clapped her hands, and Sikvah scurried to prepare the tea. Leesha wrinkled her nose. The girl might be Jardir's niece, but even she was little more than a slave.

"They've been doing this since yesterday," Rojer said. Amanvah said something in Krasian, and Abban nodded to her.

"It is our place to service Rojer's needs," he translated. "We will suffer it from no other."

"I could get used this," Rojer said with a grin, stretching back and putting his hands behind his head.

"Just don't get *too* used to it," Leesha said. "It isn't going to last." She saw Amanvah's eyes tighten at that, but the girl said nothing.

Sikvah returned soon after with the tea. She served silently, eyes down, and then retreated to where Amanvah stood by the wall. Leesha took a sip of her tea, swirled it around her mouth for a moment, and then spit it back into the cup.

"You added a pinch of blackleaf powder to the mix," she said to Sikvah, putting the cup back on the table. "Clever. Most people wouldn't have tasted it, and at that dosage, it would take weeks to kill me."

Rojer gasped, and spit his tea all over himself. Leesha caught his cup as it fell, and ran a finger along the porcelain rim, tasting the residue. "Nothing for you to worry over, Rojer. Seems they're not quite so eager to be rid of *you*."

Abban carefully put his cup back on the table. Amanvah looked at him and said something in Krasian.

"Ah . . ." Abban said to Leesha. "You make a serious accusation. Do you wish me to translate?"

"By all means," Leesha laughed, "though I've no doubt she understood every word."

Abban spoke, and Amanvah shrieked, running over to Leesha and shouting at her.

"The *dama'ting* calls you a liar and a fool," Abban supplied.

Leesha smiled and held up her cup. "Tell *her* to drink it, then."

Amanvah's eyes blazed as she snatched the cup from her without waiting for translation. The liquid was still hot, but she lifted her veil and quaffed it in one gulp. She glared at Leesha with a look of smug triumph, but Leesha only smiled.

"Tell her I know she can just take the antidote tonight," she said, "but if it's the same one we use in the North, it will give her bloody shits for a week." The color drained from the tiny patch of skin visible around Amanvah's eyes even before Abban finished translating.

"The next time you try something like this, I'll tell your father," Leesha said, "and if I know him at all, your shared blood won't keep him from stripping that pretty white robe off your back and tanning your hide, if he doesn't kill you outright."

Amanvah glared at her, but Leesha simply waved a dismissal. "Leave us."

Amanvah hissed something. "It is not your place to dismiss us," Abban translated.

Leesha turned to Rojer, who looked like he was going to be sick. "Send your brides to their chambers, Rojer."

"Go!" Rojer barked, waving his hand. He didn't even make eye contact. Amanvah's brows met in a harsh V, and she spat something in Krasian at Leesha before she stormed off with Sikvah on her heels. Leesha memorized the words, filing the curse for future reference.

Abban laughed. "It's no wonder the Damajah fears you."

"She doesn't seem afraid now," Leesha remarked. "Bold as brass, trying to kill me in broad day."

"After Ahmann's last decree, it is little surprise," Abban said. "But take heart, they do you great honor. In Krasia, if no one is trying to kill you, it is because you are not worth killing."

"Maybe it's time to leave," Rojer suggested, when Abban left. "If they'll even let us." He could not deny he had been tempted by Amanvah and Sikvah, but now all he could imagine was knives hidden under the soft silk pillows of their chambers.

"Ahmann would let us go if I asked him to," Leesha said, "but I'm not going anywhere."

"Leesha, they tried to kill you!" Rojer said.

"*Inevera* tried, and failed," Leesha said. "Running off now would be just as good for her as if I'd died. I refuse to be driven off by that . . . that . . ."

"Witch?" Rojer supplied.

"Witch," Leesha agreed. "She's got too much power over Ahmann as it is. I'm not giving up his ear without a fight."

"Are you sure it's his ear you're after?" Rojer asked. Leesha glared at him, but he met her gaze coolly. "I'm not blind, Leesha," he said. "I see how you look at him. Not like a Krasian wife, perhaps, but not like a friend, either."

"How I feel about him is irrelevant," Leesha said. "I have no intention of becoming part of his harem. Did you know Kaji had a thousand wives?"

"Poor bastard," Rojer agreed. "Reckon one is more than enough for most men to handle."

Leesha snorted. "You'd do well to remember that yourself. Besides, Abban and Ahmann both know Arlen, and both claim to be his friend."

"That's not what he told us," Rojer said. "About Jardir, anyway."

"I know," Leesha said. "And I want to learn the truth."

"What about Amanvah and Sikvah?" Rojer asked. "Do we send them away?"

"So they can kill Sikvah for lying about her virginity and failing to kill me?" Leesha asked. "Not a chance. We took responsibility for her."

"That was before she tried to kill you," Rojer said.

"See the light, Rojer," Leesha said. "If I told Wonda to put an arrow in Inevera's eye, I have no doubt she would do it, but the crime would be mine. Better we have them here where we can watch them and perhaps learn something useful."

It was deep in the night when Leesha awoke to the sound of shouting. There was a pounding at her door, and she lit a lamp and she pulled on a robe of Krasian silk that Jardir had sent to her. It was cool and deliciously smooth against her skin.

She opened her door to see Rojer standing there, looking haggard. "It's Amanvah," he said. "I can hear her wailing in her chambers, but Sikvah won't even open the doors."

"I knew it," Leesha muttered, cinching her robe tighter and tying on her pocketed apron. "All right," she said with a sigh. "Let's go see to her."

They went down into Rojer's wing, and Leesha pounded on the door to the chambers the two Krasian girls had claimed. She could hear Amanvah's muffled wails through the door, and Sikvah shouted in Krasian for them to go away.

Leesha frowned. "Rojer," she said loudly, "run and fetch Gared. If this door isn't open by the time you get back, have him break it down." Rojer nodded and ran off.

As expected, the door cracked open a moment later, and a terrified Sikvah peeked out. "Everything sunny," she said, but Leesha shoved past her into the room, following Amanvah's voice toward the privy chamber at the back of the room. Sikvah shrieked and tried to interpose herself, but again Leesha ignored her and tried the door. It was locked.

"Where is the key?" she demanded. Sikvah ignored her, babbling in Krasian, but Leesha had had enough. She slapped the girl hard on the cheek, the crack echoing through the room.

"Stop pretending you don't understand me!" she snapped. "I'm not an idiot. You say one more word in Krasian and the Damajah's anger will be the least of your worries."

Sikvah did not reply, but the terrified look on her face made it clear she had understood.

"Where. Is. The. Key?" Leesha asked again, biting off each word with a show of teeth. Sikvah quickly reached into her robes, producing it.

Leesha was through the door in an instant. The richly appointed privy stank of waste and vomit, only made worse by the jasmine burning in the incense brazier, a sickly combination that would have made most anyone heave. Leesha ignored the stench, going straight to Amanvah, lying on the floor next to the commode, wailing and moaning. Her hood and veils were cast aside, and her olive skin seemed almost white.

"She's dehydrated," Leesha said. "Bring a pitcher of cold water and set a kettle on the fire." Sikvah ran off, and Leesha continued to inspect the girl, as well as the contents of the commode. Finally, she sniffed at the cup on the vanity table, tasting the residue.

"You brewed this poorly," she told Amanvah. "You could have used a third as much fleshroot and still safely counteracted the blackleaf." The young *dama'ting* said nothing, staring blankly as she labored for breath, but Leesha knew she heard and understood every word.

She took a mortar and pestle from her apron, hands darting from pocket to pocket without so much as a glance as she filled it with the proper mixture of herbs. Sikvah brought the hot water, and Leesha brewed a second potion, bidding Sikvah to hold her mistress up as she forced it down the girl's throat.

"Open the windows to blow in some fresh air," Leesha told Sikvah, "and bring pillows. She'll need to stay by the commode for the next few hours as we hydrate her."

Rojer and Gared stuck their heads in, and Leesha promptly sent them to bed. She and Sikvah tended Amanvah until her insides calmed and they could carry her to the bed.

"Sleep's the best thing for you now," Leesha said, putting another potion to Amanvah's lips. "You'll wake in twelve hours and then we'll try to get some rice and bread into you."

"Why are you doing this?" Amanvah whispered, her accent thick like her mother's, but every word clear. "My mother would not be so kind to one who tried to poison her."

"Nor would mine, but we are not our mothers, Amanvah," Leesha said.

Amanvah smiled. "When next I face her, I may wish the poison had killed me."

Leesha shook her head. "You're under my roof now. No one is going to do anything to you, including forcing you to marry Rojer if you don't want to."

"Oh, but we do, mistress," Sikvah said. "The handsome son of Jessum is touched by Everam. First and second wives to such a man, what more could any woman aspire to?"

Leesha opened her mouth to reply, then promptly closed it again, knowing any answer she gave would fall upon uncomprehending ears.

Elona was sitting in the hall when Leesha finally emerged from Amanvah's chambers. Leesha sighed, wanting nothing more than to crawl into her bed herself, but Elona stood and moved to walk with her back to the stairs.

"It true what Rojer says?" Elona asked. "The girls tried to poison you?"

Leesha nodded.

Elona smiled. "Means Inevera thinks you've got a good chance of stealing him from her."

"I'm fine, if you care," Leesha said.

"Course you are," Elona said. "You're my daughter, like or not. Ent no desert witch going to stop you once you've got a shine for a man."

"I don't want to steal another woman's husband, Mother," Leesha said.

Elona laughed. "Then why are you here?"

"To try and stop a war," Leesha said flatly.

"And if the cost of stopping a war is stealing the husband of a woman who tried to murder you?" Elona asked. "Is that too high a price to pay?" She snorted. "Ent stealing, anyways. These women share husbands like hens share roosters."

Leesha rolled her eyes. "Oh, to be so lucky as to be one of Ahmann's laying hens."

"Better than the ones gone to slaughter," Elona shot back.

They reached Leesha's apartments, and Elona followed her in. Leesha fell onto a pillowed divan, putting her head in her hands. "I wish Bruna were here. She'd know what to do."

"She'd marry Jardir and tame him," Elona said. "If she had your body and youth, she'd've bent both Deliverers to her will by now, and gotten her toes curled to sweeten the pot."

"You can't know that, Mother," Leesha said.

"I know better than you," Elona said. "I was apprenticed to that miserable old hag before you were ever born, and there were a scant few alive then old enough to remember Bruna in her prime. Her legs never closed, to hear them say it, until she married late in life, and she ran that town even more surely than she did in her dotage. More surely than you run it now, because she had power, not just here," Elona poked Leesha in the temple, "but here, as well." She stabbed a finger to point at her own crotch. "*That* is a woman's power, as much as gathering herbs, and only a fool chooses not to take advantage of it."

Leesha opened her mouth to protest, but for some reason her mother's words rang true, and no rebuttal came to her. Bruna had been a filthy old woman, full of bawdy remarks and tales of her promiscuous youth. Leesha had dismissed many of the stories, thinking the old woman had simply liked to shock people, but now she wasn't so sure.

"Take advantage how?" she asked.

"Jardir is obsessed with you," Elona said. "Any woman can read it on him at a glance. *That* is why Inevera fears you, and why you have an opportunity to take this desert snake by the throat and turn it aside from your people."

"My people," Leesha said. "The Hollow."

"Of course, the Hollow!" Elona snapped. "Rizon's sun has set, and ent nothing for it."

"What of Angiers?" Leesha asked. "Lakton? Every hamlet between here and there? I might be able to protect the Hollow, but what can I do for them?"

"From Jardir's bed?" Elona asked, incredulous. "Is there a place in the world you could influence the war more? Slake a man's lust, and he will give you anything you ask. Surely that big brain of yours can think of a few simple requests to turn the worst of his tide."

She bent close to Leesha, putting her lips to Leesha's ear. "Or would you rather it be Inevera's voice that whispers advice in his ear as he drifts off to sleep each night?"

It was a terrifying thought, and Leesha shook her head, but she still felt unsure.

"The gates of Heaven don't lie between your legs, Leesha," Elona said.

"I know you wanted to wait for your wedding night, and truth be told, I wanted that for you, too. But it din't happen that way, and life goes on."

Leesha looked at her mother sharply, and saw Elona's defiant visage staring back at her, ready to stand by every word.

"You see the world very clearly, Mother," Leesha said. "I envy you, sometimes."

Elona was taken aback. "You do?" she asked, incredulous.

Leesha smiled. "Not often, mind."

CHAPTER 30

FERAL

:: 333 AR SUMMER ::

RENNA WAITED PATIENTLY AS the rock demon materialized. She had chosen her perch carefully, high in the single tall tree atop a hill where a large facing of bedrock jutted from the ground like a broken bone sticking through flesh.

The pattern of tracks in the soil told her the giant coreling, some dozen feet tall, materialized in this same spot almost every night. Over the last six weeks, Arlen had taught her many things, including the fact that rock demons were creatures of habit, and lesser demons would have learned to stay clear of any rising place claimed by a rock demon.

As the foul gray mist seeped from the bedrock, slowly coalescing into demonic form, she closed her eyes, breathing deeply as she embraced her fear and found her inner center.

It was amazing how well the Krasian technique worked. It had been a challenge at first, but now it took only a moment to shift her perspective, going to a mental place where there was no pain, no fear of foe or failure.

The world looked different as she opened her eyes and stood, bare feet gripping the tree limb in perfect balance. In her left hand, she gripped Harl's knife, running her thumb absently over the wards she had carved into the bone handle. In her right, she held a single chestnut.

A cool breeze rustled the yellowing leaves around her, and she inhaled deeply, letting the air caress her bare skin, feeling as much a part of the night-time world as the unsuspecting demon materializing below her.

Her waist-length brown hair had gotten in her way and was now a short, spiky remnant with only a single braided tail to recall its former length. She had discarded her dress entirely, cutting her shift into two parts: a high vest laced tightly to hold her breasts in place but open below to reveal her warded belly, and a skirt slit high on both sides to free her warded legs.

Arlen still refused to ward her flesh for her, but she had ignored him, grinding her own blackstems. The ink stained her skin a dark brown that lasted many days before fading.

She looked down, seeing the demon solidify at last, and flicked the chestnut. Without waiting to see if it struck its mark, she stepped off the branch into thin air, dropping silently.

The chestnut hit the demon's far shoulder as she fell, the heat ward she had painted onto its smooth surface blazing bright in the darkness as it sucked magic from the powerful coreling. The tough nut became superheated in an instant, and exploded with a bang.

The rock demon was unharmed, but the flash and noise turned its head the other way just as Renna landed on its broad armored shoulder. She grabbed one of its horns with her free hand for balance and drove her knife into its throat. The wards on the blade flared, and she was rewarded with a jolt of magic and a hot gush of black ichor that covered her hand.

She snarled and drew her arm back for another strike, but the demon howled, throwing its head back, and it was all Renna could do to hold on to its horn and keep her perch.

She swung wildly to avoid the talons as the demon clawed and punched at its own head in an effort to dislodge her, stabbing with the knife and kicking her warded feet at whatever targets came in range. Magic bucked through her with each strike, an electric thrill that made her faster, stronger, more resilient with every touch. The wards around her eyes activated, and the night lit up with magic's glow.

Her blows distracted the demon, but they did little more. She could no longer access the more vulnerable eyes and throat, and she did not have the leverage to stab through its thick skull. Sooner or later, one of its wild swings would crush her. She laughed at the thrill of it.

Sheathing her knife, Renna reached into her waistband, pulling free the long string of brook stones Cobie Fisher had given her in what seemed like another life. She whipped the necklace around the demon's throat, letting go its horn to catch the far end as it came around. She crossed her arms and dropped down into the groove between its armored shoulder blades, hanging from the ends of the leather cord just out of the enraged coreling's reach.

She was slammed about but kept her grip, using her full weight to pull the warded beads tight around the demon's throat. Renna had painted the smooth stones with wards of forbidding, and they flared to repel, the magic crushing inward from all sides.

In moments the giant rock demon's thrashing and thunderous footfalls became twitches and staggered steps. The string grew warm as the magic built in intensity, brightening the night.

At last, there was a crack and a final flare before the magic winked out. The giant horned head fell free, and Renna kicked off, leaping out of the way. She landed lightly on her feet as the giant demon came crashing down next to her. She could feel the stolen magic tingling in her skin, healing every scrape and bruise received in the battle. She looked at the black demon ichor on her hands, and laughed again, winding up her beads and running off to continue the hunt.

She had never felt so free.

A flame demon came at her, a lone coreling hunting through the brush by the trees. Renna set her feet as it charged, waiting for the telltale inhalation.

Flame demons always opened their attacks with a blast of firespit as soon as they were in range. The spit could set anything alight, and usually stunned their prey into helplessness while they pressed the attack with tooth and claw. But if the initial blast could be avoided, there was a brief period before they could spit fire again.

Renna crouched, face low to the ground, presenting a clear target as the demon pulled up short right in front of her, inhaling. It squinted its lidless eyes shut as it began to blow, a reflex not unlike when a human sneezed, and Renna dashed to the left in that instant, the bright blast of firespit arcing through empty air.

By the time the coreling opened its eyes and saw she was gone, Renna was behind it, grabbing its horns. She yanked its head back and gutted it like a hare caught in her father's field.

The flame demon's ichor spattered her, burning like embers from a fire, but Renna was in a place beyond pain. She slapped mud where the drops had fallen, cooling her skin, and rose.

A low rumbling told her that in the scant moments the battle with the flame demon had taken, she had been surrounded. She turned to see a wood demon hunched before her, standing six feet at the shoulder, stooped. Farther back and waiting in the trees, her warded eyes caught its two fellows, their rough armor blending into the surrounding woods, but unable to mask their magic. When she engaged the first, the strongest, the others would come at her from the sides.

Renna had killed wood demons many times, but three was two more than she had ever faced at once without Arlen beside her.

Is three more than I can *face?* She pushed the useless thought away. There was no outrunning demons; nowhere to hide once they spotted you. There was only kill or be killed.

"Come on, then," she snarled, pointing her knife at the demon before her.

The Warded Man watched Renna from the trees on the far side of the road, shaking his head. It had taken him some time to track her down. He had gone to gather herbs and firewood, and made her promise to wait at the keep until he returned, so they could hunt together. This wasn't the first time Renna had gotten impatient or simply ignored his wishes and gone off on her own.

Watching her slip around the flame demon's blind spot, laying it open from tooth to tail with her father's knife, he had to admit she was a fast learner. More than even Wonda of the Cutters, Renna Tanner had thrown herself into the art of demon hunting body and soul, and her skill level after just a few short weeks was a testament to that.

He wondered if he had done the right thing, teaching her to embrace her fears. Renna had taken it too far and quickly become reckless; as much a danger to herself as the demons.

He understood what she was going through—more than she would ever know. The night was unforgiving, even to one who embraced its ways, as shown by the copse of wood demons he saw stalking Renna while her attention was focused on the flame demon. Likely she would only see the one that came at her openly, the trunk, and the branches would have her.

The Warded Man nocked an arrow to his great bow, holding it at the ready. He would wait until she saw all three, and knew doom was upon her, before killing them. Perhaps then she would begin to take better care.

The wood demon roared, an act meant to terrify and stun her, much like the flame demon's spit. All along, its fellows crept closer, positioning themselves to strike.

But Renna never gave them a chance, charging forward in a seemingly suicidal attack. The wood demon bared its rows of teeth and hooked claws, throwing out its chest to accept her initial strike. Wood demons were second only to rock demons in strength, and likely the beast had never had its bark-like armor pierced.

Renna pivoted, using her momentum to power a circle kick. Her warded instep and shin exploded into the demon's chest, and it was thrown back in a blast of magic, stunned.

The other demons roared out of the trees, and Renna charged at one, grabbing its wrist and setting her feet, twisting her hips to turn the force of the demon's attack against it. It was almost effortless, the way she made the heavy wood demon sail through the air into the third member of the copse. She ran into the press, Harl's knife stabbing into every opening that presented itself in the tumble as the two corelings tried to untangle and right themselves.

One of the demons swiped at Renna from its prone position as she came within reach of its long, branchlike arms. She threw herself back, feeling the air whistle across her chest as its claws passed. She had been unable to effectively ward the cloth of her vest, and the claws would have cut deeply had they connected. She envied Arlen his ability to fight shirtless.

She righted herself unharmed, but her momentum was lost, and all three wood demons had regained their feet to threaten her again. They carried scorched wounds where she had struck, but even as the magic she'd leeched from the corelings healed her own wounds, so too were they recovering quickly. In moments they would be fully healed.

She reached into the pouch at her waist as they charged, hurling a handful of warded chestnuts their way. The demons shrieked and threw up their arms defensively as the heat wards flared, the chestnuts bursting into intense flames with tiny pops.

The two outermost corelings escaped unharmed, but the one in the center took the brunt of the salvo and its shoulder caught fire. In a moment the whole creature was aflame, shrieking and flailing about madly.

Seeing their fellow ablaze, the demons to either side backpedaled away from it, separating farther and giving Renna the opening she needed. She charged back in at one, stabbing up into the vulnerable gap between the third and fourth ribs on its right side. Her long knife pierced the coreling's black heart.

She ducked under its death throes and grabbed its shoulder with her left hand as it lunged. The ward on her palm flared hot, burning the demon's knobby armored skin, and she felt flush with strength and power as a portion of its magic arced into her. She pivoted and drove her knife in deeper, using it to lift the two-hundred-pound demon clear over her head. She shrieked, sounding like a demon herself, and threw it into its blazing companion.

Harl's knife, still deep in the demon, should have come free then, but the crosspiece caught on its lower rib. She cried out as the blade was torn from her grasp.

Seeing her unarmed, the last demon roared and charged her, tackling her into the scrub and dirt.

Wards flared all over her body, but the demon, mad with rage and pain, bit and clawed wildly until its searching talons found purchase. Its claws dug deep, Renna screamed, and hot blood soaked the ground.

There was a rustle in the trees, and Renna knew more wood demons, drawn to the light and activity, would soon be upon her. Not that it mattered, if she did not end the fight with the demon atop her quickly.

The demon roared again, and she roared right back, shoving hard against it and reversing the pin. It was a basic *sharusahk* move, one any novice could have prevented, but corelings had only instinctive knowledge of leverage. She pumped her knees continually, hitting the demon's thighs to keep it from shifting its legs up to claw at her. She had owned enough cats to know the fight would be over quickly if it gained that advantage.

She managed to free a hand, grabbing at her beads, and whipped them around the coreling's corded neck, tucking in close to minimize the demon's reach and leverage as she crossed the ends and pulled in opposite directions. Its claws continued to tear at her, but she embraced the pain and held on until the wards flared and the great horned head severed with a pop, spraying her with black, smoking ichor.

The Warded Man had unconsciously eased the draw of his bow when Renna threw her chestnuts. He knew the heat ward; it was common enough in Tibbet's Brook, and his parents had used it often in winter, painting large stones around the house and barn to absorb and hold the heat. He had tried making weapons with it in the past, but while it was good for arrowheads, it always either consumed hand weapons or burned through the wrappings of the hilt to scorch his hands. Even the tiny heat wards on his skin burned horribly when activated.

It had never occurred to him to ward chestnuts with them. Barely a few weeks into the night, and Renna was already warding creatively in ways he had never thought of.

He watched the wild look in her eyes as she lifted the demon over her head, and wondered if he had looked the same the first few times he'd felt the rush of coreling magic. He imagined he had. It was a heady feeling, and gave delusions of invincibility.

But Renna wasn't invincible, and that was made clear an instant later as she was disarmed and the wood demon tackled her. The Warded Man cried out, fear making him go cold as he fumbled for his bow. He tried to take aim as they struggled on the ground, but he was unable to get a clear shot, and wouldn't risk hitting Renna. Dropping the bow, he burst from hiding to rescue her.

Only to find his aid unrequired.

He stood there, his heart thudding in his chest at the sight of Renna, beautiful Renna, whose soft childhood kiss he had dreamed of on so many lonely nights in the wild, bloodied and battered atop the demon corpse.

She turned his way snarling, until recognition lit her eyes. Then she smiled at him, looking like a cat that had just laid a dead rat at its owner's feet.

Renna rolled off the corpse, struggling to regain her feet before the other demons were upon her. She was covered in her own blood, though already she felt the flow decreasing as her stolen magic began to knit the wounds. Still, she felt in no state to keep fighting.

She snarled, refusing to give in, but when she raised her eyes there was only Arlen there, glowing brightly with magic like one of the Creator's haloed seraphs. He was clad only in his loincloth, and he was beautiful, pale muscles rippling under the pulsing wards crawling across his skin. He wasn't tall like Harl or bulky like Cobie, but Arlen exuded a strength those other men lacked. She beamed at him, flush with pride in her victory. Three wood demons!

"You all right?" he asked, but there was sternness in his voice, not pride.

"Ay," she said. "Just need a moment to rest."

He nodded. "Sit down and breathe deeply. Let the magic heal you."

Renna did as she was told, feeling the deep cuts all over her body beginning to close. Soon most would be nothing but thin scars, and even those would fade quickly.

Arlen picked up the charred remains of one of her chestnuts. "Clever," he grunted.

"Thanks," Renna said, even the simple compliment sending a thrill through her.

"But clever wards or no, that was stupid of you, Ren," he went on. "You could have set the forest on fire, not to mention the foolishness of taking on three wood demons at once."

Renna felt like he'd punched her in the stomach. "Din't ask them to stalk me."

"But you did ignore me and go huntin' ripping rock demon by yourself," Arlen scolded. "And left your cloak back at the keep."

"Cloak gets in the way when I hunt," Renna said.

"Don't care," Arlen said. "That last demon nearly killed you, Ren. Your ground form against it was terrible. A *nie'Sharum* could have broken that hold."

"What's it matter?" Renna snapped, stung, even though she knew he was right. "I won."

"It matters," Arlen said, "because sooner or later, you won't. Even a wood demon can get lucky and break a hold, Renna. Strong as you feel when the magic is jolting through you, you're still not half as strong as they are. Forget that, cease to respect them even for an instant, and they'll have you. That means you take every advantage you can get, and being invisible to demons is a big one."

"Then why don't *you* use it?" Renna asked.

" " 'Cause I gave it to you," Arlen said.

"Demonshit," Renna spat. "You were huntin' through your bags for it like you hadn't seen it in weeks. Bet you ent never worn it, either."

"This ent about me," Arlen said. "I been at this much longer than you, Ren. You're getting drunk on the magic, and it ent safe. I know."

"If that ent the night callin' it black!" Renna shouted. "You do it, and you're fine."

"Corespawn it, Renna, I ent fine!" he shouted. "Night, I feel it changin' me as we speak. The aggression, the disdain for day folk. It's the magic talkin'. Demon magic. A little makes you strong. Too much makes you . . . feral."

He held up his hand, covered in hundreds of tiny wards. "Ent natural, what I done. Made me crazy a good sight, and I don't reckon I'm even half sane now." He put his hands on her shoulders. "I don't want it to happen to you, too."

Renna took his face in her hands. "Thank you for caring," she said. He smiled and tried to look down, but she held his face and kept eye contact. "But you ent my da or my husband, and even if you were, my body's my own, and I'll do with it as I will. Ent living my life how other people tell me no more. I'll follow my own path from now on."

Arlen scowled. "You following your own path, or have you just latched on to mine?"

Renna's eyes bulged, and every muscle in her body screamed at her to leap upon him, kicking and clawing and biting until he . . . She shook her head, drawing a deep breath.

"Leave me alone," she said.

"Come back with me to the keep," Arlen said.

"Damn your ripping keep!" she shrieked. "Leave me alone, you son of the Core!"

Arlen looked at her a long moment. "All right."

Renna locked her jaw tight, refusing to cry as he walked away. She got to her feet, keeping her back straight despite the pain as she retrieved her knife from the charred remains of the demon. Despite the conflagration, the weapon was undamaged, and still tingled with residual magic as she wiped it off and returned it to its sheath on her hip.

She stood a long time after Arlen left, two sides warring within her. One wanted to scream and charge into the night, looking for demons to vent her rage upon. The other part wondered if Arlen was right, and threatened to drop her weeping to the ground at any moment.

She closed her eyes, embracing both the pain and the rage and stepping away from them. It was amazing how quickly she calmed.

Arlen was simply being overprotective. After all she had done, he still didn't trust her.

In a place beyond feeling, she set her feet and began the first *sharukin*, flowing from one move to the next, trying to force the forms into her muscles so deeply that they would come without her even thinking of them. As she did, she recalled every moment of the night's battles, searching for ways she could improve.

He might be the almighty Warded Man to others, but Renna knew he was just Arlen Bales of Tibbet's Brook, and she'd be corespawned if there was anything he could do that she couldn't.

That went well, the Warded Man thought sarcastically as he walked away. He didn't go far, sitting and putting his back to a tree, closing his eyes. His ears could hear the scraping of caterpillars on leaves. If Renna needed him, he would hear and come.

He cursed the childhood naïveté that had kept him from seeing Harl for what he was. When Ilain had offered herself to his father, he had thought her wicked beyond words, but she was just doing what she needed to survive, as he himself had done out on the Krasian Desert.

And Renna . . . if he'd gone back with his father instead of running off when his mother died, she would have come back to the farm with them, safe from her father and spared a death sentence. Their own children would be promising age by now.

But he had turned his back on Renna; another path to happiness abandoned, and her life had become a horror as a result.

He was wrong to have brought her with him. Selfish. He was thinking only of himself to damn her to this life just to keep himself sane. Renna was choosing his path because she felt she had nothing left to lose, but it wasn't too late for her. She could never go back to the Brook, but if he could get her to Deliverer's Hollow, she could see that there were still good folk in the world, folk willing to fight without giving up the very things that made them human.

But the Hollow, even if they took the straightest route possible, was still more than a week's travel from their keep. He needed to return Renna to civilization immediately, before her new wildness became the only thing she knew.

Riverbridge was less than two days away. From there they could go on to Cricket Run, Angiers, and Farmer's Stump before reaching the Hollow. Every chance that presented itself, he would force her to interact with people and remain alert through the sun instead of sleeping the mornings away and tracking demon patterns in the afternoon as both of them had taken to doing.

He hated the idea of spending so much time amid people himself, but there was nothing for it. Renna was more important. If people saw his wards and began to talk, so be it.

Euchor had kept his word in letting refugees cross the Dividing, but with all of Rizon's harvest lost and summer solstice come and gone, it was hard times for all. Riverbridge was swollen on both sides of the river by a growing tent city of refugees outside the walls of the town proper, poorly warded and rife with filth and poverty. Renna crinkled her nose in disgust as they rode through, and he knew the scene was doing nothing to dissuade her rejection of civilization.

The number of guards at the gate had increased as well, and they looked disparagingly at the Warded Man and Renna as they approached. It wasn't surprising. Covered head-to-toe even in the hot sun, the Warded Man's appearance never failed to draw attention, and Renna, clad in scandalously revealing rags and covered in fading blackstem stains, did little to reassure them.

But the Warded Man had yet to meet a guard in any city or town who didn't turn welcoming at the sight of a gold coin, and he had many in his saddlebags. Soon after, they were inside the walls, stabling their mounts outside a bustling inn. It was early evening, and the Bridgefolk were returning home from a day's toil.

"Don't like it here," Renna said, looking around as people passed them in the hundreds. "Half the folk're starvin', and the other half look as if they expect us to rob them."

"Ent nothin' for it," the Warded Man said. "I need news, and that can't be had out in the wilds. Get used to towns for a while." Renna didn't look pleased with the answer, but she kept her mouth closed and nodded.

The taproom of the inn was crowded at this time of day, but much of the activity was centered at the bar, and the Warded Man spotted a small empty table in the back. He and Renna sat, and a barmaid came to them after a few moments. She was young and pretty, though her eyes had a sad, tired look to them. Her dress was clean for the most part, but it was worn, and he knew at once from the tone of her skin and the shape of her face that she was Rizonan, probably one of the first of the refugees, lucky enough to find work.

There was a raucous table of men seated next to them. "Ay, Milly, another round here!" one of them cried, and slapped the barmaid's rump with an audible crack. She jumped and closed her eyes, taking a deep breath before putting on a false smile and half turning to the men. "Sure as day, boys," she said cheerfully.

Her smile vanished when she turned back to them. "What'll ya have?"

"Two ales and dinner," the Warded Man said. "And a room, if there's one to spare."

"There is," the girl said, "but with all the folk passing through town, price is dear."

The Warded Man nodded, laying a gold coin on the table. The maid's eyes bulged; she had probably never seen real gold in her life. "That should cover our meal and a night's drinking. You can keep the change. Now, who should I speak to about that room?"

The girl snatched up the coin instantly, before any of the surrounding patrons could see it. "Talk to Mich, he owns the place," she said, pointing to a large man with rolled sleeves and a white apron, sweating behind the bar as he tried to keep all the mugs being thrust at him full of ale. As he turned to look, the Warded Man saw her thrust the coin into the front of her dress.

"Thank you," he said.

The girl nodded. "Have your ales right away, Tender." She bowed and scurried off.

"Stay here and keep to yourself while I get us a room," the Warded Man told Renna. "Won't be long." She nodded, and he moved off.

There was a tight press at the bar, men looking for a last few ales before retiring behind their wards for the night. He had to wait at the end for the innkeep's attention, but when the man glanced his way, the Warded Man flashed another of his gold coins, and he came swiftly.

Mich had the look of a once burly man gone fat. Formidable enough to toss an unruly patron, perhaps, but success and middle age seemed to have sapped the strength of his youth.

"A room," the Warded Man said, handing him the coin. He pulled another from his purse and held it up. "And news of the South, if you have it. Been out Tibbet's Brook way."

Mich nodded, but his eyes squinted. "Ent nothin' passing for news out there," he agreed, leaning in a bit to try to see under the Warded Man's hood.

The Warded Man took a step back, and the innkeep immediately backed away, glancing nervously at the coin, afraid it might disappear.

"South's all anyone talks about these days, Tender," Mich said. "Ever since the desert rats stole the Hollow's Herb Gatherer as a bride for their leader, the demon of the desert."

"Jardir," the Warded Man growled, clenching his fist. He should have snuck into the Krasian camp and killed him the moment they came out of the desert. He had once thought Jardir a man of honor, but he saw now it was all a façade to mask his lust for power.

"Word is," Mich went on, "he came there lookin' to kill the Warded Man, but the Deliverer's up and disappeared."

Rage welled up in the Warded Man, burning like bile. If Jardir harmed Leesha in any way, if he so much as touched her, he would kill him and scatter his armies back to the desert.

"You all right, Tender?" Mich asked. The Warded Man flicked him the mangled coin that had been in his clenched fist and turned away without waiting for a room key. He needed to get back to the Hollow with no delay.

Just then he heard Renna shout, and there was a cry of pain.

Renna sucked in her breath as they entered the tavern. She had never seen a place like this, where folk gathered in such a tight, uncomfortable press. The din was overwhelming, and the air was hot and stale, choked with pipe smoke and sweat. She felt her heart pounding, but when she glanced at Arlen, she saw he stood tall, his stride sure, and she remembered who he was.

Who *they* were. She straightened as well, meeting the eyes of those who stared with cool indifference.

There were hoots and catcalls as some of the men caught sight of her, but she glared at them, and most quickly turned their eyes away. As they pushed through the crowd, though, she felt a hand paw at her behind. She whirled, gripping her knife handle tightly, but there was no sign of the offender; it could have been any of a dozen men, all studiously ignoring her. She gritted her teeth and hurried after Arlen, hearing a laugh at her back.

When the man at the table next to them slapped the barmaid's bottom, Renna felt a rage fly through her like nothing she had ever felt. Arlen pretended not to see, but she knew better. Like her, he was probably fighting the urge to break the man's arm.

After Arlen left to speak with the innkeeper, the man turned his chair to face her.

"Thought that Tender would never leave," he said with a wide smile. He was a tall Milnese man, broad-shouldered, with a coarse yellow beard and long golden hair. His companions at the table all turned to look at Renna, pawing at her bare flesh with their eyes.

"Tender?" she asked, confused.

"Yer chaperone in the robes," the man said. "Figure a girl as pretty as you needs a Holy Man to 'scort her about, 'cause no other man could keep his hands off." He reached under the table, his large hand wrapping around her bare thigh and squeezing. Renna stiffened, shocked at his boldness.

"Figure you're woman enough for all three of us," the man husked. "Bet you're already dripping for it." His hand probed higher beneath her skirt.

Renna had had enough. She reached down and gripped his thumb with her left hand while putting the knuckle of her right hard into the pressure point between his thumb and forefinger. The big man's grip weakened to nothing as he gasped in pain, and a *sharusahk* twist bent his wrist back and planted his hand firmly on the table.

Where her knife cut it off.

The man's eyes bulged, and for a moment time seemed frozen as neither he nor his companions reacted. Then suddenly blood began to spurt from the wound, the man started screaming, and his friends all leapt to their feet, knocking back their chairs.

Renna was ready for them. She kicked the screaming man into one of his fellows and leapt onto the table, crouching with her feet set wide and her father's knife in a downward grip beneath her forearm, hidden from most onlookers, but ready to slash out at any who came near.

"Renna?!" Arlen cried, grabbing her from behind. She kicked and twisted as he pulled her down from the table.

"What's going on here?" Mich demanded, shoving through the gathering crowd carrying a heavy cudgel.

"The witch cut off my hand!" the blond man cried.

"Lucky I din't cut off more'n that!" Renna snarled at him over Arlen's shoulder. "You had no right to touch me there! I ent promised to you!"

The innkeep whirled on her, but then caught sight of Arlen and his eyes widened. Arlen's hood had fallen back as he struggled to hold her, revealing his warded flesh to all.

"The Warded Man," the innkeep whispered, and the name was repeated as it spread through the crowd.

"Deliverer!" someone cried.

"Time to go," Arlen murmured, grabbing her arm. She kept pace with him as he shoved past those who did not scurry out of his way. He tugged his hood back in place, but there was still a sizable crowd following them from the inn.

Arlen quickened his pace, dragging her to the stables where he flipped the hand another gold coin and headed for Twilight Dancer.

Moments later they burst from the stables and galloped from the town. The guards at the gate shouted after them as the crowd from the inn came running up behind, but dusk was falling, and no one dared follow them into the gloaming.

❧

"Corespawn it, Ren, you can't just go around cutting people's hands off!" Arlen scolded when they stopped for the night in a clearing not far from town.

"Deserved it," Renna said. "Ent no man gon' touch me there again, 'cept I want him to."

Arlen made a face, but he gave no retort.

"Break his thumb next time," he said at last. "No one'll look twice at you for that. After what you did, there'll be no going back to Riverbridge for some time."

"Hated it there anyway," Renna said. "This," she spread her arms as if to embrace the night, "this is where we belong."

But Arlen shook his head. "Deliverer's Hollow's where I belong, and with what the innkeep told me before you pulled your crazy stunt, ent got no time to waste gettin' there."

Renna shrugged. "So let's go."

"How can we, when you've just cut us off from the only ripping bridge in Thesa?" Arlen cried. "Dividing's too deep to ford and too wide for Dancer to swim."

Renna looked at her feet. "Sorry. Din't know."

Arlen sighed. "Done is done, Ren. We'll figure something out, but you're going to need to cover up a bit in towns. Fine to bare your wards to the night, but that much flesh will put ideas in the head of any man sees you in the light."

"Any head but yours, it seems," Renna muttered.

"All they see is bare legs and cleavage," Arlen said. "I see the blood-drunk girl who thinks with her knife more than her head."

Renna's eyes widened. "Son of the Core!" she shrieked, and launched herself at him, knife leading. Arlen slid to the side effortlessly, grabbing her wrist and twisting the knife from her hand. He put his hand against her elbow and used her own force to throw her onto her back.

She tried to rise, but he fell on her, grabbing her wrists and pinning her. She tried to put her knee hard between his legs, but he was wise to the move, and moments later his knees were pinning her thighs with his full weight. Her magical strength had dissipated with the sun as it did every day, and she could not force him from her. She screamed and thrashed wildly.

"Making my point for me!" he growled. "Stop it!"

"Ent this what you wanted?" Renna cried. "Someone din't slow you down? Someone who wern't 'fraid of the night?" She pulled at his grip, but his arms were iron. Their faces were mere inches apart.

"Din't 'want' anything, Ren," Arlen said, " 'cept to get you out of a bad situation. Din't mean to make you . . . like me."

Renna ceased struggling. "You din't make me do anything 'cept look hard at myself. Everything else, I done 'cause I wanted. You leave me tomorrow, I'll still paint my skin. I ent going back to prison now I've had a taste of bein' free."

She felt his grip weaken and could have pulled her hands free if she'd wanted to, but there was something in Arlen's eyes, a flicker of understanding she hadn't seen before.

"Thought of the night we played kissy in the hayloft a lot when I was a girl," she said. "Meant that kiss as a promise, and I felt it on my lips years after, while I waited for you to come back. Always thought you would. Din't kiss no other till Cobie Fisher, and by then it was the only way not to be alone with Da. Cobie was a good man, but I din't really love him any more than he did me. Barely knew each other."

"You barely knew me, too, when we were kids," Arlen said.

She nodded. "Din't know what promisin' meant, either, or that what Lainie and Da were doin' was wrong. Din't understand a lot of things I do now."

She felt tears welling in her eyes, and had no choice but to let them fall. "Seen what you are and how you live. Ent got any illusions. But I could still be a wife to you. Want to, you'll have me."

He kept looking at her wordlessly, but his eyes said more. He bent even closer. Their noses touched gently, and she felt a shiver go through her.

"Sometimes I can still feel that kiss," she whispered, closing her eyes and parting her lips. For a moment, she was certain he would kiss her, but then he let go her arms and rolled off. She opened her eyes in surprise to see him get to his feet and turn away.

"Don't know as much as you think you do, Ren," he said.

Renna wanted to scream in frustration, but a sadness in his tone softened her. She gasped, coming to her knees. "Creator. You're married already!" She felt like she couldn't breathe.

But Arlen looked back at her, and he laughed. Not the polite barks he might give at a jest, or a cruel sound meant to hurt, but a full laugh that shook his body so much he needed to put a hand on Twilight Dancer to steady himself. She felt her lungs ease as the sound denied her fear. Something in her gave way, and she found herself laughing along as he roared at the joke, hugging her sides and kicking her feet. It went on a good while, and the tension between them had vanished when they finally slowed to sporadic giggles, and then fell silent.

Renna got to her feet and put a hand on Arlen's arm. "If there's something I don't know, then tell me."

Arlen looked at her and nodded. Again he pulled from her grasp, walking a few feet away, his eyes on the ground.

"Here," he said after a moment, kicking the dirt. "There's a path to the Core right here."

She came over, looking with her warded eyes. Indeed, the glowing mist eddying about their feet was flowing from the spot like smoke from a pipe.

"I can feel it," Arlen said, "stretching all the way to the Core. It's calling to me, Ren. Like my mam at suppertime, it's calling me, and if I wanted to . . ." He began to fade away, as if he were a ghost . . . or a coreling.

"No!" Renna shouted, grabbing at him, but her hands passed right through. "You tell it to throw its call down the well!"

Arlen solidified after a moment, and she breathed a sigh of relief, though his eyes were still sad. "The paint ent why I can't live a normal life, Ren.

This is where drawing too much magic leads. I'm more demon than man now, and honest word, each dawn I wonder if today's the day the sun's gonna burn me away for good."

Renna shook her head. "You ent no demon. Demon wouldn't be worried about Deliverer's Hollow, or Tibbet's Brook. Demon wouldn't care if some girl he knew got cored, or put his life aside for months to try'n help her."

"Maybe," Arlen said. "But only a demon'd ask that girl to become one herself."

"You din't ask me nothing," Renna said. "I make my own choices now."

"Then take time and make it with care," Arlen said, " 'cause it ent one you can take back."

CHAPTER 31

JOYOUS BATTLE

:: 333 AR SUMMER ::

ROJER TOLD EVERYONE HE practiced his fiddle by the great stairwell of the manse rather than in his own wing because that precise spot would let the sound echo throughout the building. It was true enough, but the real reason he had chosen the spot was that it afforded a perfect view of the door to Amanvah and Sikvah's chambers. For three days, he'd seen no sign of the girls.

He didn't know why he cared. What had he been thinking, standing up for Sikvah when he had the perfect excuse to refuse them both? Or letting them stay after they had tried to kill Leesha? Was he actually considering becoming son-in-law to the demon of the desert? The thought of marriage had always terrified Rojer. He had left hamlets half a dozen times in the last few years to avoid that noose.

Marriage is professional death, Arrick had always said. *Women are eager to bed Jongleurs, so we oblige them. But once you're promised, suddenly all those things that drew her to you in the first place need sorting. They don't want you traveling anymore. Then they don't want you performing every night. Or at odd hours. Then they want to know why you always choose the sunny girl to throw knives at. Before you know it, you're working as a corespawned carpenter and lucky to sing on Seventhday. Sleep in any woman's bed you like, but keep a packed bag next to it, and leave the first time you hear the word* promise.

Yet he had leapt to Sikvah's rescue without a thought, and even now, the beautiful harmony of their voices resounded in his head. Rojer ached to join that harmony, and when he thought of how their robes had fallen to the floor, it brought another kind of ache, one he hadn't felt for any other woman since he met Leesha.

But Leesha didn't want him, and Arrick had died drunk and friendless.

Abban's women appeared now and again to bring food and remove commode pots, but the door to the girls' chambers never opened more than a crack, and always slammed shut before he could so much as peek inside.

That night at *alagai'sharak*, Rojer kept a nervous eye on Jardir. Kaval had Gared and Wonda fighting with spear and shield alongside the other *dal'-Sharum*, and they acquitted themselves well. Gared might be too clumsy for *sharusahk*, but in a shield-press, there was no one stronger, no one who could reach his spear farther from the warded shield wall.

But Rojer felt his absence acutely as he, Leesha, and Jardir followed the press with several Spears of the Deliverer, even though Rojer kept them bathed in his music and the demons did not approach. Sooner or later, Jardir would ask Rojer's intentions toward his daughter and niece, and if his answer was not satisfactory, violence and death might quickly occur. His.

But thus far, Jardir only had eyes for Leesha, doting on her like a man truly in love. Of course, that made spending time around him no easier, especially when Rojer caught Leesha returning the gazes. He wasn't a fool. He knew what that meant even if she didn't.

Rojer breathed a sigh of relief when the sweep ended and they were dismissed into the city. He was thoroughly miserable, his fingers numb from playing and every muscle in his body aching. He was bathed in sweat and coated in a greasy layer of soot from burning demons.

It didn't help that Gared and Wonda, flushed with demon magic, looked as if they had just hopped out of bed instead of heading back to it. Rojer had never tasted the magic. After seeing the Warded Man dissipate and talk of slipping into the Core, it terrified him. Better to keep the demons at a distance with music and throwing knives.

But after close to a year in Deliverer's Hollow, the effects of the magic on those who regularly partook were obvious. They were stronger. Faster. Never sick, never tired. The young ones aged faster, and the old ones aged slower, or in reverse. Rojer, on the other hand, felt like he was going to collapse.

He stumbled to his bedchamber, thinking to fall into oblivion for a few hours, but the sweet-smelling Krasian oil lamps in his room were lit, which was odd, since it had still been light out when he left. A pitcher of cool water was on his nightstand, along with a loaf of bread that was still warm to the touch.

"I have had Sikvah prepare you a bath as well, intended," a voice said behind Rojer. He shouted in fright and spun around, throwing knives coming into his hands, but it was only Amanvah, with Sikvah kneeling behind her beside a great steaming tub.

"What are you doing in my room?" Rojer asked. He told his hands to put the blades away, but they stubbornly refused.

Amanvah knelt smoothly, ritually, touching her forehead to the floor. "Forgive me, intended. I have been . . . indisposed of late and depended overmuch on Sikvah in my recovery. My heart aches that we have not been able to attend you."

"It's . . . ah, all right," Rojer said, making the knives vanish. "I don't need anything."

Amanvah sniffed the air. "Your pardon, intended, but you do need a bath. Tomorrow begins the Waning, and you must be prepared."

"The Waning?" Rojer asked.

"Dark moon," Amanvah said, "when Alagai Ka the demon prince is said to roam. A man must have bright Waning days to hold him steady in darkest night."

Rojer blinked. "That's beautiful. Someone should write a song about that." Already he was thinking of melodies for it.

"Your pardon, intended," Amanvah said, "but there are many. Shall we sing one while we bathe you?"

Rojer had a sudden vision of being strangled in the bath by the two of them, nude and singing. He laughed nervously. "My master told me to beware things too good to be true."

Amanvah tilted her head. "I don't understand."

Rojer swallowed hard. "Perhaps I should bathe myself."

The girls giggled behind their veils. "You have already seen us unclad, intended," Sikvah said. "Do you fear what we may see?"

Rojer blushed. "It's not that, I . . ."

"Do not trust us," Amanvah said.

"Is there a reason I should?" Rojer snapped. "You pretend to be innocent girls who don't speak a word of Thesan, then you try and kill Leesha, and turn out to have understood every word we've said. How do I know there isn't blackleaf in that tub?"

Both of them put their heads to the floor again. "If that is your feeling, then kill us, intended," Amanvah said.

"What?" Rojer said. "I'm not killing anybody."

"It is your right," Amanvah said, "and no more than we deserve for our betrayal. It is the same fate we will face if you refuse us."

"They'll kill you?" Rojer asked. "The Deliverer's own blood?"

"Either the Damajah will kill us for failing to poison Mistress Leesha, or the Shar'Dama Ka will kill us for attempting it. If we are not safe in your chambers, we are not safe."

"You are safe here, but that doesn't mean you need to bathe me," Rojer said.

"My cousin and I never meant you dishonor, son of Jessum," Amanvah said. "If you do not want us as wives, we will go to our father and confess."

"I . . . don't know if I can accept that," Rojer said.

"You need not accept anything this night," Sikvah said, "save a song of Waning and a bath." As one, the Krasian girls lowered their veils and began to sing, their voices no less beautiful than he remembered. He didn't understand the words, but the haunting tone spoke well of strength in darkest night. They rose to their feet and came to him, gently guiding him to the tub and pulling at his clothes. Soon he was naked and sitting in the steaming water, feeling the delicious heat leach the pain from his muscles. They wove a veil of music around him as mesmerizing as any he had cast over a demon.

Sikvah shrugged, and her black silk robes fell to the floor. Rojer gaped as she turned to unfasten Amanvah's robes as well.

"What are you doing?" he asked as Sikvah stepped into the tub in front of him. Amanvah got in behind.

"Bathing you, of course," Amanvah said. She went right back into her song, scooping bowlfuls of hot water over his head as Sikvah took a brush and a cake of soap.

She was firm and efficient, scrubbing the dirt and blood from him while massaging his sore muscles, but Rojer barely noticed, eyes closed, drunk on their voices and the feeling of their skin, until Sikvah's hands dipped below the water. He jumped.

"Shhhh," Amanvah whispered, her soft lips touching his ear. "Sikvah is already known to man, and trained at pillow dancing. Let her be our Waning gift to you."

Rojer didn't know exactly what *pillow dancing* meant, but he could well imagine. Sikvah's lips met his, and he gasped as she moved onto his lap.

Leesha hadn't realized Rojer's bedroom was directly beneath hers until she heard Sikvah's cries. At first she thought the girl was in pain and sat up, ready to fetch her apron, but then she realized the nature of the sounds.

She tried to go back to sleep, but despite the indiscretion, neither Rojer nor the girl seemed inclined toward quiet. She put a pillow over her ears, but the sounds broke through even that barrier.

She wasn't surprised, really. In some ways, it was more surprising it had taken so long. Sikvah's state, after Inevera had been so encouraging of a virginity test, had never sat well with Leesha. It was too easy a play on Rojer's chivalry, too convenient a way to tempt him into accepting them as brides. Rojer was only a man, after all.

She snorted, knowing it was only half the story. Inevera had played her, as well.

In truth, though she did not approve of a man taking more than one wife, she thought Rojer would have a good influence on the girls, and perhaps the responsibilities of a husband might help mature him, as well. If this was what he wanted . . .

Even if it is, I don't have to listen to it, she thought, giving up on her bed and walking down the hall, choosing one of the many empty bedrooms on her floor. She fell gratefully into the covers and expected to drift off immediately, but the sounds had affected her, bringing unbidden images to mind. Jardir, his shirt stripped off, his muscled skin alive with wards. She wondered if they would tingle to the touch as Arlen's had.

When she finally drifted off, it was to thoughts of passion. In her dreams, she remembered the heat of the fireplace as she and Gared had squirmed together on the floor of her parents' common room. Marick's wolfish eyes. The ardent feeling of Arlen's kisses and embrace.

But Gared and Marick had betrayed her, and Arlen had shunned her. The dream became a nightmare as flashes, more detailed than ever before, came back to her about that afternoon on the road when she was pinned by three men. She heard their jeers and jests again, felt the way they had pulled her hair, relived what they had done atop her. Things she had blocked from her mind, but knew were horrid truth. Through it all, she could see the sneer Inevera had given her at the whipping.

She woke up with her heart pounding in her chest. Her hands shook for something to defend herself with, but of course she was alone.

When she reoriented herself, the fear fled, replaced by harsh anger. *They took something from me on that road, but I'll be corespawned if I let them take everything.*

Leesha felt the paint and powder thick on her face as she tried on what felt like the hundredth dress, all the while being careful of her pinned hair, lest it lose its shape.

Jardir was coming to court. He had sent word that morning that he wished to visit in the afternoon to continue to read to her from the Evejah as he had on the road, but no one had any illusions regarding his intent.

Abban's First Wife, Shamavah, brought dozens of dresses for her to try, Krasian silks smoother than a baby's skin, brightly colored and scandalously cut. She and Elona dressed Leesha like a doll, parading her before the mirrors lining the walls and arguing over which cuts were most flattering. Wonda looked on in amusement, probably feeling vindicated for the similar treatment she had suffered at the hands of Duchess Araine's seamstress.

"This one's too much, even by my standard," Elona said of the latest choice.

"Too little, you mean," Leesha said. The dress was practically transparent, like something Inevera would wear. She'd need one of Bruna's thick knitted shawls to feel half decent in it.

"You don't want to give it all away," Elona agreed. "Let him work a bit to earn more than a peek." She chose a more opaque dress, but the silk still clung to Leesha in a way that made her feel as if she were naked. She shivered, and realized why such fashion was not as popular in the North as the desert.

"Nonsense," Shamavah said. "Mistress Leesha has a body to rival even the Damajah. Let Shar'Dama Ka see well what he cannot have until the contract is signed." She held up a wrap of cloth so diaphanous and scant Leesha wondered if she should bother to dress at all.

"Enough," she snapped, pulling the dress Elona had chosen over her head and throwing it to the floor. She took a cloth and began to wipe away the paints and powders Shamavah had applied to her face while Elona looked over her shoulder and bickered over the colors.

"Wonda, go and fetch my blue dress," Leesha said. Her tone wiped the grin off the girl's face and sent her scurrying.

"That plain old thing?" Elona asked. "You'll look—"

"Like myself," Leesha cut her off. "Not some painted Angierian whore." Both women seemed ready to protest, but she glared at them, and they thought better of it.

"At least leave your hair," Elona said. "I worked all morning on it, and it won't kill you to look nice."

Leesha turned, admiring the job her mother had done with her rich black hair, sending it in curling cascades down her back with a rebellious cut across her forehead. She smiled.

Wonda returned with Leesha's blue dress, but Leesha looked at it and tsked. "On second thought, fetch my festival dress." She threw her mother a wink. "No reason I can't look nice."

Leesha paced back and forth in her chambers, waiting for Jardir to arrive. She had sent the other women away; their talk only made her nerves tighten further.

There was a knock at her door, and Leesha made a quick check of the mirror, sucking in her stomach and giving her breasts a last lift before opening the door.

But it was not Jardir waiting on the other side, only Abban, his eyes down as he held a tiny bottle and a tinier glass.

"A gift for courage," he said holding the items out to her.

"What is it?" Leesha asked, opening the bottle and sniffing. Her nose curled. "Smells like something I'd brew to disinfect a wound."

Abban laughed. "No doubt it has been used for that purpose many times. It is called couzi, a drink my people often use to calm their nerves. Even the *dal'Sharum* use it, to give them heart when the sun sets."

"They get drunk before going off to fight?" Leesha asked, incredulous.

Abban shrugged. "There is a . . . clarity in the haze of couzi, mistress. One cup, and you will be warmed and calm. Two, and you will have a *Sharum's* courage. Three, and you'll feel you can dance on the edge of Nie's abyss without falling in."

Leesha raised an eyebrow at him, but the corner of her mouth curved in a smile. "Perhaps one," she said, filling the tiny cup. "I wouldn't mind a little warmth right now." She put it to her lips and tossed it back, coughing at the burn.

Abban bowed. "Every cup is easier than the last, mistress." He left, and Leesha poured herself a second cup. Indeed, it went down more smoothly.

The third tasted just like cinnamon.

Abban was right about the couzi. Leesha could feel it wrapped around her like her warded cloak, warming and protecting her at the same time. The warring voices in her mind had fallen silent, and in that quiet was a clarity she had never known.

The room felt hot, even in her low-necked festival dress. She fanned her breasts, and noted with amusement the furtive glances Jardir cast while trying to feign disinterest.

The Evejah lay open between them as they lounged on silken pillows, but Jardir had not read a passage to her in some time. They spoke of other things; her improving language skills, his life in the Kaji'sharaj and her apprenticeship to Bruna, how his mother had been outcast for having too many daughters.

"My mother wasn't pleased to only have a daughter, either," Leesha said.

"A daughter like you is worth a dozen sons," Jardir said. "But what of your brothers? That they are with Everam now does not diminish her gift of them."

Leesha sighed. "My mother lied about that, Ahmann. I am her only child, and I have no magic dice by which to promise you sons." As she spoke, she felt a weight lift from her. As with her clothes, let him know the real her.

Jardir surprised her by shrugging. "It will be as Everam wills. Even if you have three girls first, I will cherish them and hold faith that sons will follow."

"I'm not a virgin, either," Leesha blurted, and held her breath.

Jardir looked at her for a long time, and Leesha wondered if she had said too much. What business was it of his anyway, if she was or wasn't?

But in his eyes it was, and her mother's lie weighed on her as if it were her own, for she confirmed it by her silence.

Jardir looked from side to side as if to verify they were alone, and then leaned in close, his lips practically touching hers. "I am not, either," he whispered, and she laughed. He joined her, and it felt honest and true.

"Marry me," he begged.

Leesha snorted. "What need do you have of another wife, when you already have . . ."

"Fourteen," Jardir supplied, waving a hand as if it were nothing. "Kaji had a thousand."

"Does anyone even remember the name of his fifteenth?" Leesha asked.

"Shannah vah Krevakh," Jardir said without hesitation. "It is said her father stole shadows to make her hair, and from her womb came the first Watchers, invisible in the night, yet ever vigilant at their father's side."

Leesha's eyes narrowed. "You're making that up."

"Will you kiss me, if I am not?" Jardir asked.

Leesha pretended to consider. "Only if I may slap you, if you are."

Jardir smiled, pointing to the Evejah. "Every wife Kaji took is listed here, their names honored forever. Some of the entries are quite extensive."

"All thousand are listed?" Leesha asked doubtfully.

Jardir winked at her. "The entries don't begin to shorten until well after a hundred."

Leesha smirked and picked up the book. "Page two hundred thirty-seven," Jardir said, "eighth line." Leesha flipped through the pages until she found the correct one.

"What does it say?" Jardir asked.

Leesha still had difficulty understanding much of the text, but Abban had taught her to sound out the words. "Shannah vah Krevakh," she said. She read the entire passage to him, trying hard to mimic the musical accent of the Krasian tongue.

Jardir smiled. "It gives my heart great joy to hear you speak my language. I am penning my life, as well. The Ahmanjah, written in my own blood as Kaji wrote the Evejah. If you fear to be forgotten, say you will be mine, and I will pen an entire Dune to you."

"I still don't know that I wish to be," Leesha said honestly. Jardir's smile began to fade, but she leaned in, giving him a smile of her own. "But you have earned your kiss." Their mouths met, and a thrill ran through her greater than any magic.

"What if your mother catches us?" Jardir asked, pulling back when she made no effort to break their embrace.

Leesha took his face in her hands, pulling him back to her.

"I barred the door," she said, opening her mouth to his.

Leesha was an Herb Gatherer. A student of old world science, and a conductor of her own experiments. She loved nothing more than to learn a new thing, and whether it was herbs or warding or foreign tongues, there was no skill she could not master and bring new innovation to.

So it was for her in the pillows that day, as they shed their clothes and Leesha, who had spent the last decade and a half learning to heal bodies, finally learned to make them sing.

Jardir seemed to agree as they rolled apart, sweaty and panting. "You put even *jiwah'Sharum* pillow dancers to shame."

"Years of repressed passion," Leesha said, stretching her back deliciously, unashamed at her nudity. She had never felt so free. "You're lucky to be Shar'Dama Ka. A lesser man might not have survived."

Jardir laughed, kissing her. "I am bred for war, and will fight this joyous battle with you a hundred thousand times if need be."

He stood and bowed low. "But I fear the sun is setting, and we must step into battle of another sort. Tonight is the first night of Waning, and the *ala-gai* will be strong." Leesha nodded, and they reluctantly pulled on their clothes. He took up his spear, and she her pocketed apron.

No one said anything to them as Gared, Wonda, and Rojer met them in the courtyard with the waiting Spears of the Deliverer. Leesha felt so different, she was sure it must be obvious to the others, but if it was, they gave no sign.

Even during *alagai'sharak*, Leesha found it hard to keep focus so near to Jardir. He seemed to feel it, too, never straying from her side as she inspected and dealt with the few minor wounds the skilled warriors incurred.

"May I read to you again tomorrow?" Jardir asked when the battle was done. He would be needed for hours more, but the Hollowers were allowed to return to the Palace of Mirrors.

"You may read to me every day, if you wish," she said, and his eyes danced at her.

The coreling prince kept a respectful distance as it watched the heir and his men kill drones. The mind demon had been watching the heir every cycle for several turns now, and as the princes had feared, he was a unifier. It was clear he did not know the extent of the powers of the demon bone spear and crown, but nevertheless his power was growing, and the human drones beginning to organize into more than an inconvenience. Already it would be difficult to kill the heir, and even if the coreling prince succeeded, there were many who could potentially take his place.

But the Northern female was a new variable, a weakness in the heir's armor. Her mind was unprotected, and she knew much about the heir and the one its brother tracked in the North.

When she broke off from the others, the mind demon followed.

Back in the palace, Leesha practically flew up the steps to her chambers.

"What's got into you?" Wonda asked.

"Nothing that hasn't gotten into you, it seems." Wonda looked at her blankly, and Leesha laughed. "Find your bed. Drillmaster Kaval will be here shouting at you before you know it."

"Kaval ent so bad," Wonda said, but did as she was bade.

Leesha walked on tiptoe past the door to her mother's chambers, praying the woman would at least have the decency to wait until morning before interrogating her. She thanked the Creator when she managed to slip past and lock herself in the suite where she and Jardir had made love.

Alone at last, the wide smile she had been resisting all night broke out on Leesha's face.

And a hood was thrown over her head.

Leesha tried to scream, but a cord at the base of the hood pulled tight, cutting off her breath and turning her scream into a muffled gasp. A strong hand yanked her arms behind her, and that same cord was used to bind her wrists. Her assailant kicked her knees out from behind and tied her ankles with the end of the cord. Leesha thrashed about at first, but every movement tightened the cord about her throat, and she quickly calmed lest she strangle herself.

She was hefted over a strong shoulder and carried to the window, shivering in the cool night air as she was taken out and veritably run down a ladder. They made no sound, but Leesha could tell by the way the ladder bounced that she had at least two captors.

If her weight hindered the man who held her, he gave no sign, running swiftly through the night streets with even breath and steady heart. Leesha tried to stay oriented, but it proved impossible. She was taken up a set of steps and into a building, down a series of hallways, and then through a door. The men stopped, and she was unceremoniously dropped to the floor.

The landing knocked the breath from her, but a thick carpet kept her from real harm. The cord at her ankles and wrists was cut, and the hood was yanked from her head. The room was not brightly lit, but after being hooded, the oil lamps stung. Leesha raised a shaking hand to shield her eyes while they adjusted. When they did, she found herself strewn on her belly on the floor before Inevera, lying on a bed of pillows and regarding her as a cat might a cornered mouse.

The Damajah looked to the two warriors behind her. They were clad head-to-toe in black as all *dal'Sharum,* and their night veils were up, but they carried neither spear nor shield, each with a ladder held in perfect balance on one of his shoulders.

"You were never here," Inevera said, and the men bowed and vanished.

She looked down at Leesha and smiled. "Men have their uses. Please, come join me." She gestured to another pile of pillows across from her.

Leesha wobbled slightly as the blood returned to her numb feet, but she stood as quickly as she was able, resisting the urge to rub her throat as she looked around the large room. It was a pillowed love-chamber, dimly lit and scented, every surface coated with velvet or silk. The door was right behind her.

"No one guards the other side," Inevera said with a laugh, waving her hand as if to give Leesha permission to check. She did, reaching for the brass pull-ring, but there was a flash of magic and she was thrown backward, landing with a thump on the soft carpet. She saw wards flare around the lintel, jamb, and sill of the door, but they faded in an instant, gone except for ghostly afterimages that danced before her still-adjusting eyes.

More curious than fearful, Leesha got back to her feet walked up to the door, studying the wards masterfully painted in silver and gold around the frame. Many were new to her, but she noticed wards of silence worked in with the rest. No one outside would hear what went on within.

She flicked a finger against the net, watching the wards around the contact point flare for a moment, illuminating the tightly woven net.

What's powering it? she wondered. There were no corelings about to provide the necessary magic, and without magic, wards were just writing.

Given time, Leesha knew she could disable the wards and escape, but that was time she would have to take her attention away from Inevera, and there was no telling what the woman might do. She turned back to the Damajah, still lounging on her pillows.

"All right," Leesha said, walking over and taking a seat opposite Inevera. "What is it you'd like to discuss?"

"Do you mean to play the fool?" Inevera asked. "Did you think I would not know, the moment you touched him?"

"So what if you do?" Leesha asked. "There was no crime. By your own laws, a man may bed whom he pleases, so long as she is not the wife of another man."

"Perhaps behaving like a harlot is the way a woman gains a husband in the North," Inevera said, "but among my people, such women are kept in line by the wives of their victims."

"Ahmann asked for my hand long before I bedded him," Leesha said, intentionally goading the woman while she worked out her escape. "And I doubt he considers himself a victim." She smiled. "His willingness was quite apparent in his vigor." Inevera hissed and sat upright, and Leesha knew she had gotten to her.

"Renounce my husband's proposal and flee Everam's Bounty tonight," Inevera said. "I give you this one chance to live."

"Your last two attempts on my life failed, Damajah," Leesha said. "What makes you think another would have success?"

"Because I won't leave it up to a fifteen-year-old girl this time," Inevera said, "and because my husband won't find us here in time to save you. I shall tell everyone that you came to murder me the night you seduced my husband. No one will question my right to end you."

Leesha smiled. "*I* question whether you can manage it."

Inevera produced a small object from beneath her pillows, and there was a gout of fire that brightened the room, striking Leesha with an intense flash of heat before it vanished.

"I can incinerate you where you sit," Inevera promised.

It was an impressive trick, but Leesha, who had been brewing flamework for over a decade, found the effect less profound than the means by which it was created. Inevera had struck no spark, mixed no chemics, made no impact. She looked more closely at the object in Inevera's hand, and it all became clear.

It was a flame demon skull.

That's how she's powering the wards, Leesha realized, wondering why she hadn't thought of it herself months ago. *Alagai hora. Demon bones.*

The realization brought endless possibilities, but none that mattered if she could not live through the night. She couldn't draw wards to counter the fire before Inevera incinerated her.

"Is that how you power the doorframe?" Leesha asked, turning to glance at the door. "Are there *alagai hora* hidden in the wood?"

Inevera glanced toward the door, and in that instant Leesha's hand darted to a pocket of her apron, coming out with a handful of toss bangs she threw Inevera's way.

The little twists of paper exploded with cracks and flashes, perfectly harmless, but Inevera shrieked and threw her arms in front of her face. Leesha wasted no time, crossing the space between them in an instant and grabbing the wrist that held the demon skull. She pressed her thumb hard into a nerve cluster, and the skull fell to the floor. Leesha's other hand was not idle, curling into a fist. The weak cartilage of the Damajah's nose crumpled most satisfyingly.

Leesha drew back for a second blow, but Inevera rolled onto the floor and twisted, grabbing Leesha's shoulders and driving a knee between her legs with force that would have done a camel proud.

"Whore!" Inevera shrieked as pain exploded through Leesha. "Did my husband thrust well?" she shouted, kneeing Leesha's crotch again. "Did my husband thrust hard?" She struck a third time.

Leesha had never felt such pain. She grabbed blindly for the Damajah's hair, but Inevera caught her sleeve cuffs in tight fists, guiding Leesha's arms away as a Jongleur might guide a puppet's. In her heavy skirts, Leesha was helpless to resist as Inevera slithered behind her and dropped the sleeves in favor of a choke hold.

"Thank you," Inevera whispered in her ear. "I would have killed you with clean fire and spared the paint on my nails, but this is much more satisfying."

Leesha rolled and thrashed, but it did little good. Inevera locked her legs around Leesha's waist and kept her face covered by her arms. Leesha could reach no vulnerable point with hand or powder, and the world began to blur as the air in her lungs depleted. She reached for the demon skull on the floor, but Inevera kicked it away. Leesha was beginning to black out when she pulled the warded knife from her belt and drove it into Inevera's thigh.

A hot jet of blood struck Leesha's hand, sickening her, but Inevera screamed and lost her grip. Leesha was able to kick away, sucking in a life-giving breath as she rolled to her knees with the knife held out before her. Inevera rolled the other way, reaching into a pouch at her waist and throwing something Leesha's way.

Leesha dove to the side as what seemed and sounded like a swarm of hornets shot past. She cried out as one of the projectiles passed clear through her thigh, and another lodged in her shoulder. She pulled it free and found she held a demon tooth. It was covered in her blood, but she could feel with her thumb the wards etched into its surface. She shoved it into a pocket for later study.

Inevera was back on her feet by then, charging at Leesha, but Leesha put her knife up as she got back to her feet. Inevera checked herself and began to circle. She pulled a curved knife of her own from her belt, the warded blade sharp as any of Leesha's scalpels.

Leesha put a hand into another of her apron's pouches, and Inevera made a similar reach into the black velvet bag at her waist.

The coreling prince watched in amusement as the females postured like high princes when the queen was preparing to mate. It had intended to consume the Northern female's mind and replace her with its mimic to get close and kill the heir, but their own politics were so much more delicious. They could break both the heir's spirit and his dream of unity at once.

All they needed was a nudge.

CHAPTER 32

DEMON'S CHOICE

:: 333 AR SUMMER ::

IT WAS THE DARKEST part of the night when Jardir finally returned to his palace. He was not tired; he had not truly felt tired of body since he had first used the Spear of Kaji, but he longed for his bed nevertheless, if only for a chance to close his eyes and dream of her to while away some of the hours before he could visit again.

Leesha Paper truly was a gift from Everam. Her acceptance of his proposal seemed assured, and with it his foothold in the Northland. But he found that mattered less to him now than the thought of having her at his side. Brilliant, beautiful, and young enough to bear him many sons, she also contained a boundless passion that came out in her anger, and in her loving. A worthy bride for even the Deliverer, and a valuable check against the Damajah's rising power. Inevera would try to stop the marriage, of course, but that was a worry for another day.

Jardir saw the light on in his chambers and frowned. Everam's Bounty had no Undercity for women and children, even on Waning. His wives instead took turns waiting in his private chambers with a bath and a willing body, but Jardir wanted neither water nor woman. His lust could only be sated by one, and beneath his robes, her scent was still on his skin. He wanted to keep it there a little longer.

"I require nothing," he said as he entered. "Leave me."

But the women in his room were not lesser wives, and they made no effort to leave.

"We need to talk," Leesha said, and at her side Inevera nodded.

"For once, I agree with the Northern whore," Inevera said.

There was a moment of silence that seemed to Jardir to last for many minutes, as he struggled to embrace this new development and return to his center.

He looked more closely at the women. Their clothes were ragged and torn. Inevera had a blood-soaked scarf tied around her leg, and Leesha's shoulder was similarly bound. Inevera's nose was twisted and swollen three times its normal size, and Leesha's throat was purple and bruised. She favored one leg.

"What has happened?" Jardir demanded.

"Your First Wife and I have been talking," Leesha said.

"And we have decided we will not share you," Inevera said.

Jardir made to go to them, but Leesha held up a finger that checked him like a child. "You keep your distance. No touching either of us again until you make a choice."

"Choice?" Jardir asked.

"Her or me," Leesha said. "You can't have us both."

"The one you choose can be your *Jiwah Ka*," Inevera said, "and the other shall have a quick death at your hand in the town circle."

Leesha gave Inevera a look of disgust, but did not argue.

"You agree to this?" Jardir asked, surprised. "Even with your Gatherer's vow?"

Leesha smiled. "Strip her naked and cast her into the street for all to see, if you prefer."

"Weak, like all Northerners," Inevera sneered, "leaving enemies to strike another day."

Leesha shrugged. "What you call weakness, I call strength."

Jardir looked from one woman to the other, unable to believe matters had come to this, but their eyes were hard and he knew they meant every word.

The choice was impossible. Kill Leesha? Unthinkable. Even if it wouldn't destroy any potential alliances in the North, Jardir would sooner cut out his own heart than harm her.

But the alternative was equally impossible. The *dama'ting* would not follow Leesha, and if he stripped Inevera of power—and in favor of a Northern woman—they might choose to follow Inevera still, causing a schism through his empire that might never heal.

And she was his First Wife, the mother of his children, who had orchestrated his rise to power and given him the tools to win Sharak Ka. Despite the pain she regularly caused him, he looked at her and found he loved her still.

"I cannot make such a choice," Jardir said.

"You must," Inevera said, pulling her warded knife. "Now, or I will cut the whore's throat myself."

Leesha drew her own knife. "Not if I cut yours first."

"No!" Jardir cried, throwing the Spear of Kaji. It struck the wall and embedded deeply, quivering between the two women. He pounced on them, cat-quick, grabbing their wrists and pulling them away from each other.

But as he did, the wards on his crown flared to life, illuminating the women, and both shook their heads as if waking from a dream.

Leesha was the first to come to her senses. "Behind you!" she shouted, pointing.

"Alagai Ka!" Inevera cried.

Alagai Ka. The name Jardir and his men had laughingly given to the rock demon that followed the Par'chin, but it was an ancient name, one that carried an aura of immense power. Alagai Ka was consort to the Mother of Demons, and he and his sons were said to be the most powerful of the demon lords, generals of Nie's forces.

He spun to meet the demon, but there was nothing to see at first. Then, as he concentrated, the Crown of Kaji warmed once more and he could see that part of the room was clouded by magic. There was a ripple in the cloud, and suddenly a demon more fearsome than any he had ever seen leapt at him.

He reached for the spear, but it held fast in the wall for the split second it took the demon to cross the floor and tackle Jardir. He was knocked over the bed and the two of them landed hard on the far side, the demon clawing madly at him. He felt the ceramic armor plates in his robes shattering under its claws, but they blunted the initial attack. The demon seemed to sense this, and its mouth widened impossibly, growing rows of new teeth right before his eyes as it became a maw large enough to swallow his entire head.

Jardir rolled and pushed out with his arms, gaining enough space to work his leg up between them. He kicked out, knocking the demon away long enough for him to tear off his robes and reveal the scars Inevera had cut into his skin. They flared brightly as he met the demon's next attack head-on.

Leesha hadn't known the demon was in her mind until Jardir touched her and the wards on his crown flared. She heard the demon's whispers then and knew them for what they were. The demon was in the room with them.

Inevera knew it, too. They had just enough time to shout a warning before the demon bodyguard struck Jardir, knocking him across the room and taking the aura of power around his crown with it. She felt the mind demon attempt to reenter her mind.

Leesha resisted, as did Inevera, thrashing wildly against its control, but the outcome was never in doubt. The demon would have them in a moment. Already she felt an enormous weight in her limbs, as the mind demon commanded her to lie down, helpless and weak, while it watched its bodyguard kill Jardir.

Leesha looked around frantically, spotting an incense tray on the nightstand that had not yet been cleaned. She flung herself toward it as she went down, pretending it was an accident as she stuck her hand in the greasy ashes and knocked the tray to the floor in a cloud.

Inevera hit the floor as well, limbs flopping weakly, and Leesha rolled toward her, using the last of her energy to draw a ward on Inevera's forehead. The same ward at the center of Jardir's crown.

Immediately the symbol flared, and even as Leesha fell, her limbs useless, Inevera sat up. The demon seemed not to notice, its attention on Jardir, fighting for his life.

Inevera scowled and grabbed Leesha's hair. "You are still a whore," she growled, and spit in Leesha's face. There were long veils that went from her sleeveless bodice to the golden bracelets at her wrists. She gathered one and used her spit to wipe the soot from Leesha's brow, then dipped her finger in the ashes, drawing a mind ward on Leesha's forehead as well.

Leesha sat up, reaching for her warded knife. Inevera took what looked like a warded lump of coal from the black felt pouch at her waist and held it toward the mind demon. She whispered a word, and lightning arced from the stone to strike the demon. It shrieked as it was thrown across the room, hitting the wall with a crunch before dropping lifeless to the ground.

The demon changed shape continually, but Jardir pressed his attack, wards sizzling as he struck it with elbows and knees, fists and feet. He matched the demon's raw aggression with the fury of a warrior bred for the Maze. His crown flared brightly, and he felt so suffused with power that the wounds the demon inflicted began healing before the full damage was done.

I am fighting Alagai Ka, he thought, *and I am winning.*

That thought carried him forward for a moment, but then the demon picked up a heavy table in one giant claw and smashed it down on him as a hammer strikes a nail.

The wards on his skin offered no protection against the wood, and it was only the magic coursing through him that kept him from being killed. Still, bones splintered on the impact, jutting from his leg and stabbing into his innards. He felt the magic speeding his body's natural healing along at an incredible rate, but it could not set the broken bones, and he felt them healing at odd angles.

It mattered little, though, as the demon lifted the table again to finish the job. Jardir, weaponless, could do nothing but watch.

But before the demon could bring the table down, it shrieked and grabbed its head, dropping the table. Jardir kicked out with his good leg to deflect it as the demon's flesh seemed to melt like wax, and it stumbled about, thrashing madly.

Jardir looked up then and saw why. He hadn't been fighting Alagai Ka at all. Leesha and Inevera stood over the smoking body of a slender demon with a gigantic head. Even from across the room, Jardir could sense the power and evil the creature radiated. The demon he had fought was its Hasik: brainless muscle to clear paths and break skulls that were beneath its master to shatter personally.

The slender demon lifted its head. Inevera shrieked and sent another bolt of lightning at it, but the demon drew a ward in the air, dispersing the energy. It reached out, and the demon bone flew from her hand. The slender demon caught it, and the bone glowed briefly in the demon's grasp before the magic was absorbed and the bone crumbled to dust.

The demon reached out again, and Inevera's *hora* pouch flew to its hands. She shrieked as it upended the bag, dropping her precious dice into its clawed hand.

Leesha and Inevera charged the demon with their warded knives, but it drew another ward in the air that flared to throw them across the room as if picked up by a great wind.

The *alagai hora* glowed as the demon absorbed their power. Jardir felt a strange mix of fear and relief as the dice that had controlled his life for more than twenty years crumbled to dust. Inevera wailed as if the sight caused her physical pain.

The mimic demon regained its senses as soon as its master recovered, but Jardir was already moving, springing across the broken bed on his good leg. He caught the Spear of Kaji in his hands as he rolled off the far side, letting his weight pull it from the wall.

Pain screamed through Jardir's mangled leg as he came to his feet, but he embraced it effortlessly, his movements sharp and decisive as he drew back and threw.

And before either demon could react, the fight was over. The spear blasted through the mind demon's skull, leaving a gaping, blasted hole and continuing on to stick quivering in the far wall. The mind demon fell dead, and without it, the mimic fell to the ground shrieking and thrashing about as if on fire. Finally it lay still, a melted pile of scale and claw.

Leesha came awake at the sound of a sharp crack, opening her eyes to see Jardir, his eyes closed and his face serene as Inevera pulled hard on his foot to give herself play to reinsert the bone jutting from his leg.

Shaking off her own pains, Leesha fumbled to her side, taking the bone in her hand and guiding it back into the incision Inevera had cut. As with Arlen, the wound began to close almost instantly, but Leesha still reached for needle and thread to stitch it evenly.

"There is no need," Inevera said, rising to her feet and going to the mind demon's body. She drew her warded knife and cut off one of its vestigial horns. She returned with the foul, ichorous thing, then removed a thin brush and bottle from her pouch. She drew neat wards along the edges of Jardir's wound, and as she passed the horn over them, the wards flared, closing the incision seamlessly.

She did the same for her own wound, and then wordlessly tended to Leesha, not meeting her eyes. Leesha watched in silence, memorizing the wards Inevera used and the fashion in which she knit them together.

She looked at the horn when she was finished. It was still intact, and Inevera grunted. "I'll make better dice from this one's bones, anyway." Leesha went to the mind demon's body herself, cutting off the other horn and one of its arms. These she rolled in a heavy tapestry for later study. Inevera's eyes narrowed at her, but she said nothing.

"Why has no one come to investigate the sounds of battle?" Jardir asked.

"I expect it was simple for Alagai Ka to draw wards of silence around your chambers," Inevera said. "They will likely remain in power until the sunlight strikes the walls."

Jardir looked at them. "It controlled everything you said and did?"

Inevera nodded. "It . . . ah, even made us fight each other, for its amusement." She touched her swollen nose gingerly.

Leesha felt her face color, and she coughed. "Yes," she agreed, "it made us do that."

"Why play such cruel games?" Jardir asked. "Why not just have one of you cut my throat as we lay in the pillows?"

"Because it didn't want to kill you," Inevera said. "It's more afraid of your power to inspire than to fight, and none inspires more than a martyr."

"Better to discredit you and splinter the unity of your forces," Leesha put in.

"But you are the Shar'Dama Ka," Inevera said. "There can be no further question, with Alagai Ka dead at your hand."

Jardir shook his head. "That was not Alagai Ka. It was too easy. More likely, this was the least of his princelings. There will be more, and greater."

"I think so, too," Leesha said, looking at Jardir. "Which is why I'm holding you to your promise, Ahmann. I have seen Everam's Bounty, and now I wish to return home. I must prepare my people."

"You do not need to go," Inevera said, and Leesha could tell how hard the words came to her. "I will have you as one of my husband's *Jiwah Sen*."

"A 'lesser' wife?" Leesha laughed. "No, I don't think so."

"I will still make you my Northern *Jiwah Ka*, if you wish it," Jardir said. Inevera scowled.

Leesha smiled sadly. "I would still be one of many, Ahmann. The man I wed will be mine, alone." His face fell, but Leesha held firm, and Jardir nodded finally.

"The Hollow tribe will be honored regardless," he said. "I cannot prevent the tribes from trying to steal a few of your wells, but know that they will be subject to my wrath should they war upon you."

Leesha dropped her eyes, afraid she might cry if she saw the sadness in his eyes any longer. "Thank you," she said tightly.

Jardir reached out, touching her shoulder and squeezing gently. "And I . . . apologize, if what happened in the Palace of Mirrors was not your own will."

Leesha laughed out loud, all fear of tears gone. She threw herself at him, hugging him tightly and kissing him on the cheek.

"We did *that* in the light of day, Ahmann," she said with a wink.

"I am saddened to see you leave, mistress," Abban said a few days later, as his wives packed up the last of the endless gifts Jardir had bestowed. "I will miss our conversations."

"And miss having the Palace of Mirrors to hide the comeliest of your wives and daughters from the *dal'Sharum*?" Leesha asked.

Abban looked at her in surprise, then bowed, smiling. "You've learned more of our tongue than you let on."

"Why don't you just tell Ahmann?" Leesha asked. "Let him discipline Hasik and the others. They can't just go around raping whomever they want."

"Your pardon, mistress, but the law says they can," Abban said. Leesha opened her mouth to reply, but he held up a hand. "Ahmann's power is not as absolute as he thinks. Disciplining his own men over a *khaffit's* women would sow discord among the men he trusts to carry spears at his back."

"And that's more important than the safety of your family?" Leesha asked.

Abban's eyes grew hard. "Do not assume you understand all our ways after living among us a few weeks. I will find a way to protect my family that doesn't threaten my master."

Leesha bowed. "I'm sorry."

Abban smiled. "Repay me by letting me build a pavilion in your village. My family has one with every tribe, to trade in goods and livestock. Everam's Bounty has more grain than it needs, and I know there are hungry mouths to the north."

"That's kind of you," Leesha said.

"It is not," Abban replied, "as you will see when my wives haggle with your people for the first time." Leesha smiled.

There was a call from outside, and Abban limped over to the window and looked down into the courtyard. "Your escort is ready. Come, and I will see you down."

"What happened between Ahmann and the Par'chin, Abban?" Leesha asked, unable to contain herself any longer. If she did not learn the answer now, she likely never would. "Why did Ahmann seem angry that you mentioned him to me? Why were you afraid when I told you I mentioned him to Ahmann?"

Abban looked at her, and sighed. "If I will not put my master at risk for the sake of my family, what makes you think I will do it for the Par'chin?"

"Answering my question puts Jardir at no risk, I swear," Leesha said.

"Perhaps it does, and perhaps not," Abban said.

"I don't understand this," Leesha said. "You both claim Arlen was your friend."

Abban bowed. "He was, mistress, and because it is so, I will tell you this much: If you know the son of Jeph, if you can get word to him, tell him to run to the end of the world and beyond, because that is how far Jardir will go to kill him."

"But why?" Leesha asked.

"Because there can only be one Deliverer," Abban said, "and the Par'chin and Ahmann have . . . disagreed before, as to who it should be."

Abban went right to Jardir's throne room from the Palace of Mirrors. The moment Jardir saw the *khaffit,* he dismissed his advisors, leaving the two men alone.

"She has left?" he asked.

Abban nodded. "Mistress Leesha has agreed to allow me to set up a trading post for the Hollow tribe. It will help facilitate their integration, and give us valuable contacts in the North."

Jardir nodded. "Well done."

"I will need men to guard the shipments, and the stores at the post," Abban said. "Before, I had servants for such heavy duty. *Khaffit,* perhaps, but fit men."

"Such men are all *kha'Sharum* now," Jardir said.

Abban bowed. "You see my difficulty. No *dal'Sharum* will take orders from *khaffit* in any event, but if you would allow me to select a few *kha'Sharum* to serve me in this regard, it would be most satisfactory."

"How many?" Jardir asked.

Abban shrugged. "I could make do with a hundred. A pittance."

"No warrior, even a *kha'Sharum,* is a pittance, Abban," Jardir said.

Abban bowed. "I will pay their family stipends from my own coffers, of course."

Jardir considered a moment longer, then shrugged. "Pick your hundred."

Abban bowed as deeply as his crutch allowed. "Will your promises to the mistress of the Hollow tribe alter your plans?"

Jardir shook his head. "My promises affect nothing. It is still my duty to unite the people of the Northland for Sharak Ka. We will march on Lakton in the spring."

CHAPTER 33

A PROMISE KEPT

:: 333 AR SUMMER ::

"WHY ALL THESE RAFTS, if there's a perfectly good bridge?" Renna asked, gesturing toward the nameless collection of huts, too few to even be called a hamlet. Each tiny structure had a raft out by the water, surrounded by wards staked into the bank of the Dividing.

A few demons prowled the area, testing the wards on the huts, but Renna was wrapped in her warded cloak, and Arlen radiated such power that the occasional hiss and eye contact were enough to keep the corelings back from him as they walked along the riverbank.

"Merchants who don't want the bridge guards rooting through their goods sometimes pay raftsmen to take them across the Dividing," Arlen said. "Usually because they're carrying something, or some*one*, they shouldn't."

"So we can hire one?" Renna asked.

"Could," Arlen said, "but that would mean waiting till dawn and dealing with more rumors. Can't swing my arm in these parts without hitting some-one who acts the fool 'cause they think I'm the Deliverer."

"Don't know you like I do," Renna smirked.

"There," Arlen said, pointing to a raft big enough to carry Twilight Dancer comfortably. There was a great groove in the riverbank where it was hauled up and down each day. He handed Renna one of his ancient gold coins. "Go and leave this by the door."

"Why?" Renna asked. "It's new moon. He ent gonna see us take it, and even if he hears, he sure as the sun ent gonna cross his wards to run after us."

"Ent thieves, Ren," Arlen said. "Smuggler or no, someone earns their keep with that raft." Renna nodded and took the coin, leaving it on the hut's doorstep.

Arlen examined the raft. "Not even a ripping water ward!" He spat on the bank.

Renna returned, kicking at one of the stakes. "These ent worth spit, either. Dumb luck much as anything, protectin' these rafts."

Arlen shook his head. "Can't explain it, Ren. Any ten-year-old in the Brook can out-ward most folk in the Free Cities, where they been raised not to trust anyone without a guild license to ward a ripping windowsill."

"Can you ward it now?" Renna asked, nodding at the raft.

Arlen shook his head. "Not so it'll be dry before dawn."

Renna looked out at the wide expanse of water. Even with her warded eyes, she couldn't see the far side. "What happens, we try to cross without wards?"

"There's usually froggies that hide right at the bank," Arlen said. "We kill those first . . ." He shrugged. "It's a new moon. No light to shine on the raft from above and point us out to the river demons, so odds are we'll get across the deep water safe. By the time we reach the far bank, the sky will be lighter and most of the froggies will have gone back to the Core."

"Froggies?" Renna asked.

"Bank demons," Arlen said. "Folk call 'em froggies because they look like big fly frogs, 'cept they're big enough to eat *you* like a fly. They jump up out of the water and catch you with their tongues, swallowing as they drag you in. Put up too much of a fight, and they dive into the river to drown it out of you."

Renna nodded and drew her knife. There were fresh blackstem wards painted on her knuckles. "So what's the best way to kill one?"

"With a spear," Arlen said, taking two and handing her one. "Watch."

He moved slowly toward the water's edge, emitting a shrill whistling noise. For a moment all seemed calm, and then the water by the bank exploded as a giant, wide-mouthed coreling sprang out. It gripped two stubby, webbed feet on the bank and snapped its head, shooting its thick, slimy tongue at him.

But Arlen was ready and stepped easily to the side. The demon croaked and leapt fully onto the bank, covering some ten feet in a single hop. It shot its tongue at him again, but again Arlen sidestepped, this time charging in close before the tongue could retract. With a quick, precise thrust, he put his spear through the folds of tough skin at its chin and up into its brain, twisting sharply. The crackling magic lit the night as he pulled the spear free, and when the demon struck the ground, he stabbed down once more to be certain it was dead.

"Trick is to get 'em up on shore," Arlen said, returning to Renna's side. "Dodge the first tongue, and they hop out of the water to try again. They're good jumpers, but their forelegs ent got the reach of a spear. You can stab from a safe distance."

"Ent much fun in that," Renna said, but she gripped her spear and headed for the water, trying to mimic his whistle.

She expected it to take a few moments to get a response, but almost instantly the water burst and a bank demon was shooting its tongue at her from more than a dozen feet off. She pivoted out of the way, but she wasn't quite fast enough, and the tongue caught her a glancing blow, knocking her down.

Before she could recover, the demon leapt from the water, landing on the bank and trying again. She rolled to the side, but the tongue caught her about the thigh, slowly drawing her in. Renna dropped her spear to claw at the riverbank, but to no avail. The coreling's mouth, wide enough to swallow her whole, was filled with row upon row of short, sharp teeth.

Renna ignored it, turning instead to Arlen, who was already running her way.

"You stay out of this, Arlen Bales!" she growled, stopping him short.

She was almost in range of the bank demon's teeth when she turned back to it. She flicked the sandal off her free foot and kicked it in the jaw with a flash of magic. The demon's tongue slackened slightly, and Renna twisted, cutting right through it with her knife. As the coreling recoiled, she leapt to her feet, stabbing it in the eye. She hopped back to avoid its death thrashes, then moved in quick, putting her knife in its other eye to ensure the kill.

She looked back at Arlen, daring him to criticize. He said nothing, but there was a hint of a smile at the corner of his mouth, and his eyes glittered.

There was shouting from the hut, and lamplight flickered in one of its windows, roused by the commotion.

"Time to go," Arlen said.

The one was on the move. The coreling prince hissed in frustration, but immediately leapt upon its mimic's back and took to the sky, following his trail.

It had been a risk, letting the human live another cycle, but one the mind demon had deemed acceptable in hope that it might learn how the one had come into powers long since stamped away. The one killed drones nightly, but their number was insignificant, as were the weapons he spread. He was not a unifier, like the dangerous one to the south.

But it was in his power to be. If he but called, human drones would flock to him, and if that happened, they could threaten the hive.

And now he was moving with great decision back toward the human breeding grounds. The coreling prince was certain he would call to the human drones then, and a unification would begin. That could not be tolerated.

The mind demon spent the remainder of the first night tracking the one. Just before dawn it reached the river and hissed when its prey came into sight. Nothing could be done now with the sun about to rise, but it would find them quickly the next night.

The mimic dropped lightly to the riverbank, bending low so the coreling prince could dismount. As they began to dematerialize, the mimic growled softly, sensing its master's anticipation for the kill.

Renna and Arlen kept riding when the sun rose, passing a branch in the road with an old signpost a few hours later.

"Ent stopping in the town?" Renna asked.

Arlen looked at her. "You can read?"

"Course not," Renna said. "Don't need to read to know what a sign on the road is for."

"Point," Arlen said, and she could sense him grinning beneath his hood. "Ent got time to waste with other towns right now. I need to get to the Hollow quick."

"Why?" Renna asked.

Arlen looked at her for a long moment, considering. "A friend's got herself into a fix," he said at last, "and I reckon it's more than a little my fault for staying away so long."

Renna felt a cold hand clutch her heart. "What friend? Who is she?"

"Leesha Paper," he said. "Herb Gatherer of Deliverer's Hollow."

Renna swallowed. "Is she pretty?" She cursed herself the moment the words left her lips.

Arlen turned his head back to her with a look that mixed annoyance and amusement. "Why does it still feel like we're ten summers old?"

Renna smiled. "Because I'm not one of these folk sees you as the Deliverer. They din't see the look on your face after you clicked teeth with Beni in the hayloft."

"Your kiss was better," Arlen admitted. She tightened her arms around his waist, but he shifted uncomfortably.

"We'll cut off the road soon," he said. "Too many folk on it these days. There's a path I know will take us to one of my caches for fresh weapons and supplies. From there we can ford the Angiers River and be in the Hollow in a couple of nights."

Renna nodded, swallowing a yawn. She had felt charged with energy after killing the bank demon, but as always, that added strength had faded away with the sun. She dozed in the saddle for a time until Arlen gently shook her awake.

"Best dismount and put your cloak on," he said. "Getting dark, and we have a few hours left to go before we get to my cache."

Renna nodded, and he pulled the horse up. They were in a sparsely wooded area with tall conifer trees spaced widely enough that they could walk on either side of Twilight Dancer. She dropped from the saddle, her sandals crunching on the forest floor.

She reached into her satchel and drew forth the warded cloak. "Hate wearing this thing."

"Don't care what you hate," Arlen said. "Corelings are thicker this side of the Dividing; more towns and ruins to draw them. Treetops around here get rife with woodies, swinging from branch to branch and dropping on you from above."

Renna looked up suddenly, expecting a demon to be hurtling toward her at that very moment, but of course they had not risen yet. The sun was only just setting.

As the shadows grew, Renna watched the mist rise slowly through the detritus of needle and cone carpeting the ground between the trees. It curled around the tree trunks like smoke rising up a chimney.

"What are they doing?" she asked.

"Some like to materialize up in the trees, out of sight so you don't see 'em coming," Arlen said. "They usually wait till you pass, then drop on your back."

Renna thought of the rock demon she had killed in similar fashion, and drew her warded cloak tighter about her, glancing up in every direction.

"There's one up ahead," Arlen said. "Watch close." He let her take Twilight Dancer's lead and walked a few feet ahead of them.

"Ent you gonna take your robe off?" Renna asked, but Arlen shook his head.

"Gonna show you a trick," he said. "Don't even need your skin warded, you do it right."

Renna nodded, watching intently. They walked a bit farther, and then, as predicted, there was a rustle from above and a bark-skinned demon fell from the trees toward Arlen's back.

But Arlen was ready. He twisted and ducked his head under one of the falling demon's armpits, putting his free arm around the coreling's neck from behind, grasping it under the snout. With a sharp pivot, he turned, letting the force of the demon's own fall break its neck.

"Sweet day," Renna gasped.

"There's several ways to do it," Arlen said, putting a warded finger sizzling through the fallen demon's eye to confirm the kill, "but the principle's the same for all. *Sharusahk* is about using their power against them, like wards do. It's how the Krasians survived these last centuries, fighting *alagai'sharak* every night."

"They're so good at killing demons, why do you hate 'em so?" Renna asked.

"Don't hate the Krasians," Arlen said, and then paused. "Not all of them, anyway. But their way of life, making slaves of everyone who ent a man and a warrior . . . it ent right. 'Specially not forced on Thesans at the end of a spear."

"What're Thesans?" Renna asked.

Arlen looked at her in surprise. "We are. All the Free Cities. I mean for 'em to stay free."

The one had traveled far while the coreling prince waited out the day in the Core, but the mimic was swift, and it wasn't long before the mind demon caught sight of its prey, walking his mount through a sparse copse of trees. The mind demon circled above, watching as wood drones attacked the human. The one killed these with quick efficiency, hardly slowing his pace.

The mind demon's cranium throbbed, and the mimic banked to the side and dove into the trees, its wings melting away as it took the form of a giant wood demon. It caught a thick tree branch before they had fallen far, smoothly pulling out of the fall and into forward motion. It swung easily from branch to branch, still carrying its mind.

They came to a stop at a high vantage, watching the one approach. There was no sign of the female, though the mind demon could not recall her trail ending. It sniffed the air, tasting her. She had been about, and recently, but it could not sense her now.

Pity. She would have been a useful tool against the one, and her mind was deliciously empty, yet flavored with powerful rage. A meal worth tracking after the one's mind had been similarly consumed.

ϑ

" 'Nother woodie ahead," the Warded Man sighed as what must have been the eighth wood demon that hour swung into view. It was larger than most, almost too big for the tree branches to support. Closer to a rock demon.

"Can I try this one?" Renna asked.

The Warded Man shook his head. He glanced back at her, but it took him a moment to find her. The warded cloak still made him dizzy, and it was easy for his eyes to slide right off it without seeing, if his mind was not focused.

"You need to sleep when we get to the cache," he said, "and you won't if you're all charged with magic."

"What about you?" Renna asked.

"Got warding to do tonight. I'll sleep when we're back in the Hollow," he said, watching the demon out of the corner of his eye to see where it perched for its ambush.

But the wood demon didn't wait for them to pass, picking up momentum and launching itself at him from the front. It was an unexpected move, but the Warded Man still had plenty of time to duck to the side, reaching out for its lead talon to twist and turn its own force against it.

He must have misjudged the length of the demon's limbs, though, because he somehow missed its clawed foot, which grabbed at his robed leg and pulled him from his feet. They both hit the ground heavily, and the coreling rolled away, rising on equal footing with him.

They faced off, and immediately the Warded Man knew something was different about this demon. It circled him patiently, waiting for opportunity. A few times, the Warded Man lowered his eyes or seemed to turn away, inviting attack, but the coreling didn't take the bait, watching him intently.

"Smart one," he mused.

"Need help?" Renna asked, reaching for her knife.

The Warded Man laughed. "Be a cold day in the Core when I need help killing a lone wood demon." He reached down to open his robe.

The coreling growled and launched itself at him before he could untie the garment, tackling him to the ground. The Warded Man fell on his back and kicked at it, delivering a blow greater than even Twilight Dancer could have done, but the demon's arms became the tentacles of a lake demon, wrapping tightly around him. They dug in with a sharp, horned surface even as suckers latched on to his robe, holding it tight and keeping his wards covered. The demon's maw grew before his eyes, becoming like a bank demon's, large enough to swallow his entire head and shoulders.

The Warded Man snapped his head forward, butting the demon's lower jaw with the impact ward atop his head. There was a flash and the demon howled as a few of its teeth shattered, but there were hundreds more, and it did not let go its grip. The Warded Man had exhaled sharply with the blow, and now found he could not draw a new breath.

With the last bit of air in his lungs, the Warded Man emitted a shrill whistle, and Twilight Dancer tossed his mighty head, yanking the lead away from Renna and charging in, horns lowered. They tore through the demon's shoulder in a blast of ichor and magic, and it shrieked in agony, finally relaxing its grip. The Warded Man rolled away, gasping for breath.

The coreling melted away from Twilight Dancer's horns and grew again, its armor shifting and changing color as it became a rock demon. It swiped a backhand blow at the stallion, never taking its eyes off the Warded Man.

Even without its barding and saddlebags, Twilight Dancer weighed nearly a ton, but the powerful demon still sent the horse flying. He struck a tall tree, and the Warded Man could not tell if the resulting crack was the tree's trunk or his horse's spine.

"Dancer!" the Warded Man screamed, tearing the robe from his body and launching himself at the demon. Renna ran to see to the horse.

The Warded Man's blows rocked the coreling back, and it gave ground freely under the assault, but the wound Twilight Dancer's horns inflicted was already healed, and the Warded Man's punches and kicks seemed to have no lasting effect. Its flesh pulsed around the scorched impact points, healing them instantly.

He knocked the demon down on one arm, but it dug its great talons into the ground, throwing an enormous clump of dirt and wet leaves at him. The Warded Man had no chance to dodge, and was struck full-on. He recovered his feet quickly, brushing the filth from him, but he knew his wards were weakened where it clung to him, if they still worked at all.

But he was no more injured than the coreling, and there was no way he was going to let this powerful demon get away. They circled again, baring their teeth and growling. One of the demon's arms became half a dozen tentacles, each ten feet long and ending in a sharp horn.

"Night, what part of the Core did *you* come from?" the Warded Man asked. The mimic gave no answer, lashing out with the new limbs.

The Warded Man dodged to the side, rolling and coming up at a run to get inside the demon's reach. There was a gap in the armor plates at its armpit, and he drove his stiffened fingers, painted with piercing wards, into the crevice, trying to reach some vital part that might cause lasting damage.

The coreling screamed and twisted, and its flesh dissolved around his hand. It was only then, when he was in contact with the demon as it changed, that he realized what it was doing. It was dematerializing and re-forming, the same way he did, or any coreling for that matter. This demon could simply reform in different ways. A thousand possibilities opened to the Warded Man at the realization, too many to even consider. He brushed the epiphany aside like an irritating fly and focused on his adversary, striking again.

In the split second when the demon was in transition, the Warded Man dematerialized as well, intermingling with it slightly to keep it from solidifying. The demon still felt solid to him, but Renna's scream sounded as if she were a mile away. He knew how it must seem to her, both of them fading away, ghostlike, but there was nothing for it.

He'd fought another demon this way once before, and knew that in this state strength and wards were meaningless. It was *will* that was power here, and the Warded Man knew his will was greater than any demon's.

He locked on to the mimic demon's very molecules, keeping them scattered and immaterial, shepherded by his will. He sensed the creature's sudden fear, and returned it with his anger and rage, dominating its will the way a parent would a disobedient toddler.

But just as he felt the mimic's will breaking, another will touched him, this one a thousand times stronger.

The coreling prince clung to a high treetop above the battle, but its mind rode behind the eyes of the mimic, giving its servant commands through the battle.

Against any other foe, the kill would have been swift, for the mind demon could simply have read its opponent's thoughts, countering attacks before they were even made. But the thoughts of the human mind were warded, so the demon was blind to his plans. The mimic would still have prevailed, but then the human did something even the mind demon could never have expected.

He dematerialized.

The coreling prince had never seen the like, had not even imagined it was possible for a surface creature. For a moment, it felt a touch of fear at the human's power.

But only for a moment, because then, as the human broke the mimic's will, the coreling prince touched his mind. Wards had no power in the between-state. Any hatchling prince knew that. The one had foolishly made himself vulnerable.

The mind demon lashed out before the human could recover from his surprise, and then, at last, it Knew its foe, diving into the river of his memories. The human was horrified at the invasion, but helpless to stop it. His impotent rage was intoxicating.

Then the one surprised him again. A lesser being would have faltered, but the human left his memories behind, unguarded, and threw his will at the mind demon's own river, the essence of its being. He burst through the mind demon's defenses, unprepared for such ferocity, and they Linked for just a moment before the coreling prince managed to gather its will and sever the connection.

The moment his mind was free, the one solidified, forcing the mimic to do the same.

"Renna!" the human called, and the coreling prince looked in shock to see the air ripple and the human female appear as if from nothing, stabbing the mimic with her warded knife.

The mind demon ignored the mimic's howls, studying the distortion in the air about the female, a garment trailing behind her as she struck. Powerful warding, to have hidden her from even a prince's eyes.

The moment the one solidified, his mental wards returned, but he also lost his control over the mimic. The mind demon had its servant shove him back, then throw itself upon the female, rending the warded garment from her and knocking her to the ground in a tumble.

By the time the one came to his feet, two females squared off before him, identical in appearance and action. The mind demon Linked their thoughts so that the mimic could mirror her utterly, then let go the claws that held it to the trunk of the tree. It stepped out into the open air and drifted to the ground as gently as a falling leaf.

The Warded Man blinked, seeing two Renna Tanners before him, identical down to the blackstem stains on her skin in varying degrees of fading. They looked at him with the same eyes, wore the same ragged clothes, carried the same knife. Even the magic they radiated seemed the same.

He ran to Twilight Dancer's side, forcing himself to ignore the horse's labored breaths as he snatched up his great bow and fitted an arrow. He wavered, unsure who to point it at.

"Arlen, she's the demon!" both Rennas shouted in unison, pointing to the other.

They looked at each other in shock, and then turned back to him. "Arlen Bales," they said, both planting their hips in the exact way Renna did when she was angry, "don't you tell me you can't pick me from a coreling!"

The Warded Man looked at both of them and shrugged apologetically. Two sets of identical brown eyes glared at him.

He frowned. "Why'd I have to play kissy, that night?"

Both Rennas seemed to brighten at the question. "You lost at succor," they said in unison, and then again turned to look at each other in horror.

The Warded Man concentrated, watching them both at once. "How'd I lose?"

The Rennas hesitated, then looked at him. "Beni cheated," they admitted. A murderous gleam came into both their eyes, and they turned to each other once more, raising their knives.

"Don't!" the Warded Man said, raising his bow. "Give me a moment."

They both spared him an irritated glance. "Corespawn it, Arlen, just let me kill the ripping thing and have done!"

"You ent a match for it, Ren," the Warded Man said, and both women glared at him again. "Real Renna would mind me," he added.

The women threw back their heads and laughed at that, but they made no move to attack each other. The Warded Man nodded.

"Might as well come out!" he called loudly into the night. "I know you're there! That changing demon ent smart enough for this!"

There was a rustle off to the side, and a demon appeared. It was small and slender, with an oversized head and a high, knobbed cranium. Its eyes were huge black pools, and it bared only a single row of sharp teeth at him. The talons at the end of its delicate fingers were like an Angierian lady's painted nails.

"Been wondering when I'd run into one of you bastards," the Warded Man said. He tapped the large ward tattooed in the center of his forehead. "Warded myself up special for it."

The demon tilted its head, studying him. Beside him, the two Rennas stiffened slightly.

"Your mind may be shielded, but this female's is not," the Rennas said in unison, as the demon continued to regard him. "We can kill her at will."

The Warded Man drew and fired in an instant, but the demon traced a quick ward in the air, and there was a flash of magic that reduced the arrow to ashes before it struck home. He drew another arrow to his ear, but it seemed a useless gesture against this new demon. He lowered his bow, easing the tension in the string.

"What do you want?" he demanded.

"What does your steed want from the insects its tail swats?" the Rennas asked. "You are an annoyance to be crushed, nothing more."

The Warded Man sneered. "Come try."

But the Rennas shook their heads. "In time. You have no drones to defend you, while I have many. Soon I will lay open your skull and consume your mind, but it amuses me to let you bargain for the female first."

"You said I had nothing you want," the Warded Man said.

"You don't," the Rennas agreed. "But giving up something you wish to keep hidden will cause you pain, and that will sweeten the meal we make of your mind."

The Warded Man's eyes narrowed.

"Where did you learn of us?" the Rennas asked.

The Warded Man glanced at them, and then looked back at the mind demon. "Why should I tell you? You can't pull it from my head, and she doesn't know."

The Rennas smiled. "You humans are weak about your females. It is a failing bred carefully into your ancestors. Tell us, or she dies." As they spoke, both women lifted identical warded knives and stepped close, holding them to each other's throats.

The Warded Man raised his bow, wavering it between them. "I could shoot one. Got a half chance of killing your changeling."

The women shrugged. "It is only a drone. The female, however, holds great meaning to you. You will suffer much if she dies."

"Great meaning?" the Rennas asked, and the Warded Man turned to look at them fully. There was fear in their eyes, and despair.

"I'm sorry, Ren," the Warded Man said. "Din't mean for this. Warned you."

Both Rennas nodded. "I know. Ent your fault."

The Warded Man raised his bow at them. "Ent gonna be able to save you this time, Ren," he said, swallowing the lump in his throat. "Not even if I knew which one was you." Renna bit back a sob, and he could almost feel the mind demon's pleasure.

"So you're gonna have to be strong and save yourself," he said. " 'Cause that monster's the face of evil, and I ent gonna let it get away."

The mind demon stiffened as it realized what he meant, but it was a second too late, as the Warded Man dropped his bow and leapt at it, covering the distance between them in an instant. Before it could command Renna and the mimic to kill each other, his warded fist struck the coreling prince's bulbous head with an explosion of magic.

The slender demon was thrown several feet by the force of the blow and landed on its back, hissing in rage. Its cranium throbbed, and the Warded Man could feel the thrum of power it sent out, though it did him no harm.

Behind him, the mimic shrieked, but the Warded Man ignored it, leaping at the mind demon again, pinning it and delivering heavy blows. Each wound healed instantly, but he did not let up, keeping it stunned until he could find a way to kill it. If it dematerialized, he was prepared now to match wills against it.

But the mind demon stayed solid, perhaps fearing just such a thing. With each blow, it grew more dazed, taking a split second longer to recover. The Warded Man slipped around the demon into a *sharusahk* choke hold, the pressure wards on his forearms growing warm as they flared against its throat, building power. It would be over in seconds.

But then a wind demon crashed into him, breaking the hold and knocking them apart. The Warded Man rolled atop the wind demon and struck it hard in the throat, stunning it, but a wood demon swung down at him from the trees before he could finish it off. It was followed quickly by several more.

The mind demon felt its connection to the mimic sever when the shock from one's blow blasted through its skull. It had never known such pain. In the ten thousand years since it was hatched, no creature had ever dared to strike the coreling prince. It was unthinkable.

The demon struck the ground hard, and immediately sent its distress out in a general call. Drones would come from all around to answer it. The mimic answered with a cry, but failed to come. The human leapt atop the mind demon, hammering it about the head with his wards.

Used to fighting through its mimic, the mind demon was unprepared for the pain and confusion of physical combat. The human gave it no time to recover, and it was helpless to prevent the one establishing a primitive dominance hold. His wards activated, sucking the coreling prince's own magic and turning it into pain.

That might have been the end, but at last a wind drone answered its call, knocking into the one and breaking his hold. Other drones followed, flocking to defend the coreling prince. The moment it was knocked away, the mind demon healed its wounds, hissing in outrage at the affront. It sent another call, meaning to bury the one in drones. It could sense dozens of them in the area, running hard to join the melee, but the mimic was strangely absent.

The human flung the wood drones from its path, charging the coreling prince again, but this time it was ready, drawing a ward that sent a blast of air to strike the one like a physical blow, hurling him across the clearing. By the time he rose, he was surrounded again by wood drones. At the mind demon's command, they broke branches from the trees to use as weapons, circumventing even the muddied wards of forbiddance on the human's skin.

The mimicking of her words and actions was horrifying enough, but Renna was truly revulsed when the mind demon rose up to take control of her voice and she realized it had been hiding within her all along, like a stowaway suddenly taking control of the cart.

It was an unspeakable violation, worse than anything Harl had ever done to her. Worse than the outhouse, worse than being staked at night. She could feel the demon burrowing through her thoughts like a field vole, taking her most cherished and private memories to use as weapons against Arlen.

The thought filled her with rage, and she sensed the mind demon's pleasure at the response. *I've taken you before,* it whispered in her thoughts. *Many times.*

Renna looked at Arlen, and despaired at the resignation in his eyes. She had thought she was strong enough to walk his path. That she could do anything he could. But now that lie was proven. All she could do was get him killed.

She choked on a sob and tried to raise her knife to bury it in her own throat, but the mind demon controlled her body like a Jongleur's puppet, and she could not act against its will. Even if Arlen guessed right and somehow managed to kill the mimic, the mind demon could make *her* stab him in the heart just as easily. She wanted to warn him, but the words would not come.

But then the look in Arlen's eyes changed, as if he had come to some decision, and he gazed at her with a trust no one had ever shown her before.

"You're gonna have to be strong and save yourself," he said. " 'Cause that monster's the face of evil, and I ent gonna let it get away."

Her fear fell away at that look, and her eyes hardened. She nodded, and felt the mind demon's sudden start, taking Arlen's meaning the same moment she did. It tried to react, but it was not quick enough as Arlen struck a blow to its head that lit the darkness with magic.

The demon's presence in her mind vanished, leaving Renna stunned and disoriented. She glanced at the mimic, still in her form, and saw it stagger similarly, cut off from its mind.

Tightening her grip on her father's knife, Renna growled and leapt at the creature, putting the blade into its bare midriff. She put her free arm around the demon, pulling it in close as the blackstem wards on her skin activated. Magic shocked through her muscles, filling her with strength as she heaved the knife upward, opening up the creature from navel to collar.

The mimic's body may have looked like her on the outside, but the black, stinking ichor that burst from the wound was nothing from the surface world.

She looked at its face, the same face she had seen a thousand times in the surface of water. Renna was almost brought to tears by the pain and confusion in her own eyes, but then the face snarled like a dog, and its teeth began to elongate as it hissed at her.

Renna twisted as the mimic lunged, turning its own energy against it as Arlen had taught her. She grabbed its thick braid in her free hand as it passed, pulling it up short from its fall and baring its nape. The move gave such power to her pivot and slash that her knife passed through its neck effortlessly.

Just like that, the fight was over. The demon's body fell to the ground lifelessly, and she was left holding her own head by the hair, eyes rolled back and black ichor dripping from the neck. She inhaled, taking what seemed like her first breath in hours.

She looked up, expecting to see the mind demon dead at Arlen's feet, but instead she saw Arlen surrounded by wood demons holding branches in their claws, and the mind demon backing away. The corelings took no notice of her yet, focused solely on Arlen.

Renna looked around, dropping the head to the ground as she snatched up her warded cloak. The mimic had torn the ties at its throat, but the garment was otherwise intact. Sheathing her knife, she flung the cloak around her shoulders, putting up the hood and using both hands to hold it closed from the inside.

She rose carefully, walking toward the battle scene at a slow, even pace to allow the wards their greatest advantage. One of the wood demons struck Arlen across the shoulders as she drew close to him. He cried out and was knocked to the ground, spitting blood. The other demons followed suit, and he rolled desperately to avoid their blows, with only partial success.

She wanted nothing more than to rush to Arlen's aid, but she knew in her heart that he would not want her to. The mind demon stood boldly again, no longer trying to escape. It would be worth more than both their lives, if she could show it the sun.

The Warded Man felt his ribs snap as the branch struck him to the ground. He heaved up a foul mix of bile and blood and spit it into the dirt.

Before he could recover, another branch struck him. He rolled to dodge the third, and the fourth, but he could not regain his footing to rise, and the fifth struck him full in the face, tearing skin and popping one of his eyes from its socket to hang from a string of muscle. The sound of the blow echoed in his head, drowning out all else.

With his one good eye, he looked up, seeing several demons swinging branches at once. For a moment he thought it was his time to die, but then his senses returned for a split second and he cursed himself for a fool.

As the branches came down, they struck only mist. The Warded Man slipped from the center of the copse, reforming behind one of the wood demons, his wounds healed instantly. He kicked out one of the demon's legs, grabbing it by the horns as it fell and using its own weight to flip it over and break its neck. He leapt at the next demon, putting his thumbs through its eyes. A third demon swung its branch at him, but again he dematerialized, and it struck only its blind brother. The Warded Man solidified again, stabbing his stiffened fingers through a crevice in the attacking demon's barklike armor and bursting its heart like a popping chestnut.

He had known no mortal weapon could harm him if he saw its approach, but now he realized it was much more than that. Anything short of death or dismemberment could be healed in an instant. The corelings around him had become nothing but flies to swat from his path. They weren't smart enough to dematerialize offensively on their own, and the mind demon would be wary to do it through them, lest it meet his will on that other plane.

He ignored the remaining wood demons, passing through them like a ghost and only solidifying when the path to the coreling prince was clear. He looked at the demon, and a wave of dizziness overcame him. The confidence that had suffused him a moment earlier vanished as he realized he was only just discovering powers the demon had known for thousands of years. It bared its fangs and lifted a talon to draw a ward in the air.

But then the tip of a blade burst from its chest, flaring bright with magic. The dizziness left him as Renna's cloak fell away and he saw her holding the demon around the throat with her free arm while the contact wards along her blade built in power.

The coreling prince shrieked in surprise and pain, and the Warded Man did not hesitate, leaping forward to strike hard blows to keep it off balance. Renna let go her knife, whipping her brook stone necklace around its throat. The wards flared, and the mind demon opened its mouth as if to scream, but no sound came out. Instead, its cranium pulsed, and the resulting thrum struck the Warded Man like a harsh wind, knocking him back.

Renna seemed not to notice the effect, but all through the trees and seemingly for miles around, demons shrieked in agony. A wind demon dropped from the sky, crashing through the branches of a tree to hit the leaf bed, dead. The wood demons that had attacked him likewise collapsed, killed by the demon's psychic scream.

And in that instant, the mind demon fled.

The coreling prince had never known fear. Never known pain. It was above such things, tasting them only vicariously through the minds of its drones or its prey—delicacies to be savored.

But there was nothing vicarious about the death of its mimic or the blade in its chest. The choking cord around its throat and the blows that scattered its attempts to assert its power. It screamed, and felt the minds of drones all around burn out from the pain.

The one was distracted for an instant, and the coreling prince took the chance, dematerializing and fleeing for the Core. There it would bond a new mimic and grow strong for the next cycle, when it would return with a host of drones the likes of which the surface had not seen in millennia.

Renna shrieked, and the Warded Man whirled back to see the mind demon melt away from her grasp, breaking into mist that fled down a nearby path to the Core.

Instinctively, he followed.

"Arlen, no!" Renna screamed, but it was a distant thing.

The path to the Core was like following a brook upstream in the dark. He could feel the path, but sight had no meaning on the path to the Core. He simply felt the flow of magic stemming from the center of the world and followed back against the current. The Warded Man kept his will focused on the evil taint of the coreling prince ahead of him, and it seemed they raced for miles before he drew close enough to grab at the demon.

He had no hands with which to grab, but he willed his essence to latch on to the demon, and like two men blowing smoke into the same cloud, they mingled and their wills clashed.

The Warded Man had expected the demon's will to have weakened, but it was no less potent now, and they clawed through each other's minds, jabbing fingers into any delicate crevice they could find. The coreling prince laid bare all his life's failures, mocking him with the fate he had abandoned Renna to, or brought upon the Rizonans. Teasing him with images of Jardir forcing himself upon poor innocent Leesha.

It was almost too much, but in his pain he lashed out, cracking through the mind demon's own defenses. He saw in that moment a glimpse of the

Core, a place of eternal darkness, but lit with magic's glow more brightly than the desert wastes.

Instantly the demon's will retreated, ceasing its attack to protect its own thoughts. The Warded Man sensed the advantage and pressed his assault. The coreling prince shrieked in his mind as he learned of the Hive.

The Warded Man might have won then, if not for the horror of the sight. The corelings that came to the surface to hunt were but the barest fraction of what the Core could spew forth. Millions of demons. Billions. For the first time since he had found the wards of old, he despaired that they could ever be defeated.

The mind demon's will roared over him, and their struggle fell to a more basic level, the simple will to survive. But here the Warded Man held the advantage, for he had no fear of death, and did not look over his shoulder as it approached them both.

The demon did, and in that instant its will broke, and the Warded Man absorbed its magic into his own essence, leaving a burnt remain he threw from the path to the Core to scatter away forever.

Alone on the path, the Warded Man could finally hear the true call of the Core, and it was beautiful. There was power there. Power not evil in itself. Like fire, it was beyond good or evil. It was simply power, and it beckoned him like a teat to a hungry infant. He reached for it, ready to taste.

But then another call reached him.

"Arlen!" The voice was a distant echo that reverberated down the path.

"Arlen Bales, you come back to me!"

Arlen Bales. A name he hadn't used in years. Arlen Bales had died out on the Krasian Desert. The voice was calling a ghost. He turned back to the Core, ready to embrace it.

"Don't you leave me again, Arlen Bales!"

Renna. He'd left her in dire straights twice now, but the third would be the deepest cut, damning her to the very life he sought to escape after she had worked so hard to save his.

What could the embrace of the Core offer that hers could not?

Renna's throat was hoarse from screaming when the mist seeped back up from the ground and began to take Arlen's form. She laughed through her tears and nearly choked. It seemed only a moment ago that he was as good as cored and she expecting no better, but now suddenly every demon in the area was dead, the night hauntingly quiet as she and Arlen stared at each other. The mind demon's magic feedback had been intense, and Renna's senses felt more alive than they ever had in her life. She practically crackled with energy, and her heart was pounding like a Jongleur's hand drums. Arlen glowed so intensely he hurt to look at.

"Dancer," Arlen breathed suddenly, breaking the silence. He ran to his horse.

"Broke a lot of bones," Renna said sadly. "Ent never gonna run again, even if he makes it through. Da would say to put him down."

"To the Core with anything your da would have done!" Arlen growled. Renna felt his pain like a slap in the face, and knew in that moment how much he loved the horse. She knew what it was like, when an animal was your only friend in the world. She wished he could love her half so much.

"Wounds've stopped bleeding," she noted. "Must've taken some magic off that changing demon before he was struck."

"Mimic," Arlen said. "They're called mimics."

"How d'you know?" Renna asked.

"Learned a lot, when I touched the coreling prince's mind," Arlen said. He reached out, gripping one of the stallion's broken legs and pulling the bones straight. Holding them in place with one powerful hand, he drew a ward in the air with the other.

He grunted in pain, but the ward flared and the bones knit before her eyes. One by one, Arlen tended the horse's wounds, but as Twilight Dancer began to breathe comfortably, Arlen's own breath began to labor. His magic, so bright a moment ago, was dimming rapidly. Already it was darker than she had ever seen it.

She touched his shoulder, and felt a flash of pain as some of her own magic flowed into him. He gasped and looked up at her.

"Enough," she whispered, and he nodded.

The Warded Man looked at Renna and felt a profound sense of guilt.

"I'm sorry, Ren," he said.

Renna looked at him curiously. "Sorry for what?"

"Turned my back on you once when we were young, leaving you to Harl so I could chase demons," he said. "And then tonight, I did it again."

But Renna shook her head. "Felt that demon in my head. Felt it slither into me worse'n Da ever could. It was pure evil, straight from the Core. Killing that monster was worth more'n a thousand Renna Tanners."

The Warded Man reached out and touched her cheek, his eyes unreadable.

"Thought so before," he said, "but now I ent so sure."

"I ent takin' back my promise," Renna said. "If this is your life, then I aim to support it like a proper wife should. No matter what."

Dawn was approaching, and the Core called to the Warded Man still, but it was a distant thing now, easily ignored. Because of her. Because with Renna he finally remembered who he was. The words came easily to him.

"I, Arlen Bales, promise myself to you, Renna Tanner."

ABOUT THE AUTHOR

Raised on a steady diet of fantasy novels, comic books, and Dungeons & Dragons, PETER V. BRETT ("Peat" to his friends) has been writing fantasy stories for as long as he can remember. He received a bachelor of arts degree in English literature and art history from the University at Buffalo in 1995, and then spent over a decade in pharmaceutical publishing before returning to his bliss. He lives in Brooklyn with his wife, Danielle, their daugher, Cassandra, and an evil cat named Jinx.

Visiter Peter online at www.petervbrett.com.

ABOUT THE TYPE

This book is set in Fournier, a typeface named for Pierre Simon Fournier, the youngest son of a French printing family. He started out engraving woodblocks and large capitals, then moved on to fonts of type. In 1736 he began his own foundry and made several important contributions in the field of type design; he is said to have cut 147 alphabets of his own creation. Fournier is probably best remembered as the designer of St. Augustine Ordinaire, a face that served as the model for Monotype's Fournier, which was released in 1925.